WINGS OF REBELLION

WINGS OF REBELLION

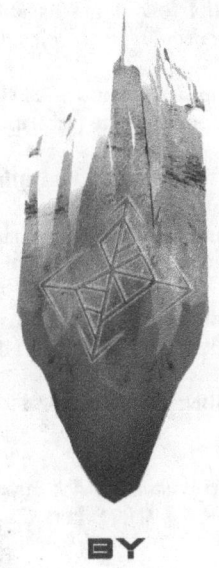

BY

SEAN ATWOOD

Bastian & West
CREATE, DISCOVER, ENTERTAIN™

www.bastianwest.com
books@bastianwest.com

First Published in Great Britain by Bastian & West 2020

This paperback (light) edition 2020

Set in Carrig Pro Light by Paulo Goode

A CIP catalogue record for this book is available from the British Library

ISBN: 978-1-9163687-1-2

Editors: *James Millington, Laura Wilkinson, Nick Edson*
Illustrators and Artists: *Simon Krieg, Ben Hansen*

TABLE OF CONTENT

To the memory of my dear Mother,
who was so instrumental to the inception
and completion of this book.

1

- THE CRISIS -

Bradley was tense. He glared into his microscope, holding his breath. Never had he seen anything like it. The pathogen danced within the blood sample as it bumped into the red blood cells. Its ping-pong from cell to cell was totally mesmerising. What concerned him was the horrific aftereffects of the virus' interactions with those cells. They appeared to have been ripped apart as if some shredder had decimated their very structure. The situation was serious and highly dangerous. He picked up the phone, dialled a number.

'Raise the alarm; we have a code 1 situation.' The urgency in his tone was all too clear.

'Immediately, sir,' responded the woman on the other end. Within a couple of seconds the Beltnam Research Laboratory's speakers sprang to life. 'All staff in Sectors 2, 3 and 4 proceed to assigned safety locations. Sector 1 staff proceed to medical contact points for compulsory blood testing.' There was no doubt: they were dealing with an emergency.

Blood tests? That is all I need. Why is it always my sector... Bradley hated having his blood taken. No matter how many times he had been subjected to the experience, he was unable to get used to it. He stared at the virus through his microscope. 'Vicious little bugger, aren't you?' He spoke to it as if somehow it was able to understand his words. He stood up, stretched, and puffed back the lock of thick rich-black hair, which kept running rampant over his forehead.

It was time for him to get out of his hazmat suit and proceed to the compulsory testing. His mind raced with questions, possibilities, and potential avenues of investigation. Almost unconsciously, he started scribbling those down in his favourite notepad. There was just something about pen and paper which allowed his mind to go into overdrive.

A few minutes later, he put his pen down, closed the notepad, and tucked his battle ally away into its usual resting place. There it would remain tucked away. Little did he know that among the furiously scribbled questions, thoughts and potential answers in his book, a line of letters stood, a clue fished out from the depths of his mind, something to which he was totally oblivious...

He grabbed hold of his white long lab coat and rushed out of the office as he unceremoniously tried to put it on. Stepping out of the sliding automatic doors, he silently swore at his mindlessness, rummaged through the pockets of the lab coat and pulled out his mobile phone. As usual it was switched off. A strict lab policy dictated it had to remain so in the actual offices where blood analysis took place, in order to avoid the Wi-Fi signals damaging the delicate specimens. He stopped walking down the corridor and looked around. *I'm far enough it won't interfere,* he reasoned. He scrolled down his autodial numbers to 'Kuroi' and hit the dial button. He was concerned for her.

'Hi, dearest, are you in the labs, or...?' He left the question hanging.

'I'm in Sector 4,' she answered. How he loved the sound of her voice. So gentle, yet when needed, it could be as sharp as a katana blade cutting right through you. 'I'm heading over to medical. I didn't realise we dealt with unknown pathogens...' Her voice trailed off.

'Don't worry, I raised the alarm. Don't think it will get out of my sector, even if it does break out.'

'Are you ok? Are you safe?' Concern spilled out, despite her attempt to remain calm and collected.

'All is fine. Nothing to worry about, dearest. This is just a precaution – just don't tell anyone else!' He laughed as if he had achieved some form of mischief. 'Are you up for coffee after we get out of here?'

His swift change of subject did the trick. He really hoped they could have a nice uneventful cup of coffee together. It had been two days since he'd seen her. Both their schedules were at odds with each other and he so longed to touch her. Secretly, he longed for her to wrap her arms around his slim torso and tease him while pushing away his persistent lock of thick black scruffy hair. That was his excuse for not bothering to keep it perfectly straight and smooth: he simply loved her running her fingers through his hair, trying to tame the wayward curl. The recollection made him smile.

She hesitated. 'I was planning on going for a workout at the gym.'

His heart sank. 'Not to worry. Health first, as you always remind me.'

'Are you working tonight?' she asked him.

'Not if you are off,' he smiled.

'Great, I'll see you at home... Who knows, I might even cook something nice for us!'

The offer of her cooking excited him. He loved her cooking but even more so, he'd noted a secret promise of time to be spent together. That really excited him.

'See you soon, babe.' She giggled discreetly at his words. There was something very youthful, almost childish in her that surfaced but for a moment. The line went dead.

'Sorry, Miss, I cannot let you in right now.' Mike the security guard barred Heather's path.

'Don't be ridiculous, Mike? You know I work here,' she objected. Her irritation causing her to flick her ever-so-softly tanned neck towards her slender right shoulder in annoyance. Her blond curvy waist-length hair glimmered golden in the soft sunlight. He winced, and her deep green eyes, which almost glimmered in the sun's light, pierced right through him. She was utterly mesmerising. Heather was used to this trick of hers and took full advantage of it when the need arose. She suspected something had happened and she knew all too well of the daily mischief brewing behind the closed doors of each lab section. She was the one who always set things right, resolved the chaotic outbursts of whatever pranks had gone out of hand. As usual, she suspected the lab assistants and she was thrilled at the thought of catching them out at their games.

'Sorry, Miss, we have a Level 1 containment alert in force.'

'A WHAT?' The tone of her voice rose by several pitch levels.

Without further delay, she pulled out her mobile phone and dialled a number. It rang and rang: no answer. She was concerned. This was the first time in years that they'd had a Level 1 situation. Actually she could not recall them ever having one! She paced impatiently up and down the walkway leading into the building.

Mike observed her beautiful figure, complemented perfectly by her smart white business shirt.

Finally, someone answered the phone. 'Dr Grimsaw,' answered an elder gentleman.

'Ah, thank goodness. Are you ok, Grampa? Mike tells me we have a Level 1 situation and is refusing to let me in.' Her pace quickened. The clink and clonk of her heeled shoes sped up, become more insistent.

Her loud pacing unnerved Mike. He wished everyone would choose to wear soft shoes. Unfortunately for him, that would never happen. He looked at her closely. Mike had a very professional relationship with everyone at work. He knew who Heather was, yet despite his best efforts, he could not stop admiring her. Her posture, the grace of her movements and the authority that seemed to flow effortlessly from her captivated him. Her sense of fashion and style was impeccable. Today, she was in green. She always dressed with a semi-conservative look, always a knee length skirt, always incredibly elegant. She was unlike the other women he knew. Her classy, reserved look broadcast to all who gazed upon her slender, almost perfect form, that this was a woman to be respected, not one to be fooled about with. He knew this could not all be from her position or her scientist's wages. *Those shoes probably cost more than my entire year's wages.* A long sigh escaped his lips. Secretly he would have loved to ask her out. He never had. It was not his place. The very mention of anything like that would have cost him his job. He could not risk it. Instead, he did all he could to make sure she would not come into harm's way. It was all he could do.

'Yes, dear. Bradley was analysing the blood we obtained from Beltnam University Hospital and he initiated the lockdown. All zones of the labs have been isolated, so even if we have a breakout, it shouldn't ever reach me.' Heather let out a long sigh. What a relief. Her grandfather was the only relative she had left. He was the only one she had ever known, having lost both her parents as a child. As her fear settled, she gasped, 'Bradley? Is he... ok?'

'I'm afraid I cannot say. Until the lockdown is cleared, I won't get any updates.'

'Oh no. Bradley...' Concern echoed in her voice.

'Don't worry. I am sure he will be fine. Remember, he always goes through the rigmarole of putting on all his protective gear before dealing with bloods marked for investigation of unknown substances and pathogens.'

As her grandfather mentioned it, she remembered and smiled. 'Yes, he does, doesn't he! We always make fun of him. He's got us all proven wrong this time.'

'He will be fine. Now, dear, do me a favour and go to the university hospital and let them know we are dealing with a Level 1 situation. Avoid the patient areas. They should go into full lockdown and you don't want to get stuck in there.' He would never have forgiven himself if harm came to her due to his neglect.

'I'll be careful, Grampa. Don't worry!'

'Very well. Why don't you go grab an extended afternoon off afterwards? This will take time to clear up.'

'Why that's a brilliant idea, Gramps. I think I'll go down to the library to continue my research then, if that's ok?'

'Of course, my dear. Now off with you and stop worrying so much.'

She liked the fact that no matter how grown up she was, her grandfather would always talk to her in an almost childlike way. She smiled. *Guess for him I'll always be the little Heather he took in.* It gave her the drive and security she needed and it gave her strength. As long as she had him, she needed no one else, or so she thought.

But something bothered her: she was uncertain as to its exact nature, but it nagged there at the edge of her mind. *Why has there been so much doom and gloom about the place these last few days?* Instinctively, she knew something was afoot. As she made her way over to the hospital, she was determined to find out what was causing it and why it was happening. With that thought in mind, she made her way to the hospital, forgetting Mike was even there. To him, Heather on a mission was a sight to behold.

5

She entered the main hospital wing. Much to her misfortune, the university hospital was set up in the most peculiar way, making the A&E and main reception one and the same. It had the distinct disadvantage of making everyone wait, irrespective whether they were on administrative or emergency business. A momentary sigh of relief washed over her: the queues were not too bad today and with a little manoeuvring, she made her way to the front with little effort.

'Miss, would you please wait in line?' objected the fat young woman standing behind her.

'I'm here on staff business and it's urgent,' she retorted.

'Well I'm here for a life or death emergency, so I'd suggest you get back in line, where you belong.'

That was it. Heather's irritation surfaced. She knew the type all too well. 'The moaning ones' was her label for people like this. Her eyes scanned the woman from head to toe in one movement. Oh yes, she knew her type all too well. Something about those endless complainers – who, most of the time, suffer from self-inflicted ills – just set her on edge. She always thought it was deeply unfair that everyone should bear the burden of looking after self-destructive people. If it had been up to her, anyone with self-inflicted health problems would be immediately sent packing. Heather worked, studied, ate the right food, limited how much she ate, and exercised countless hours every day just to ensure she was in proper physical fitness. According to her, there was no excuse whatsoever for everyone else to not do the same. Action was needed. She was not going to have any of this nonsense.

She peered left and right, standing on her toes to gain that extra inch of height. Not that she needed it at 5 foot 10. She was more than respectable, in terms of height. Her long, slightly curled blond hair swirled from the motion. She knew the woman behind her would start causing a fuss at any moment. Heather resolved the whole issue by side-stepping the entire queue, walking up to the desk and rather insistently forcing her staff ID badge into full view of the receptionists.

'This is totally unacceptable, this...' She had been followed by the youth. The woman's rage had built up. She was, as Heather had predicted, seething with a fury. The woman continued: '...woman jumped the entire queue. I don't bloody care what her emergency is... everyone here has an emergency... she should not be allowed to jump the queue!' Her agitated state turned her face bright red. Heather had to work really hard at suppressing her laughter. In her mind, she saw a massive plump tomato trying to yell at her. Totally hilarious.

'What seems to be the problem here?' A tall dark-brown-haired man in his 30s asked.

'This is unacceptable! Outrageous!' the fat woman yelled. 'Jumping the queue like that,' she tried to keep on going, but the new arrival looked at Heather and smiled.

'Ah Dr Hawke. So nice to see you in our neck of the woods. Would you follow me, please,' he instructed, making sure to mention the 'Dr' part as loudly as he dared. They left the raging woman at reception as she exploded into a whole array of expletives. They made their way into the inner corridors of the hospital. 'It has been a while, Heather. To what do we owe the privilege of your delightful presence in our house of madness here?' He winked at her, and smiled. He had always really liked her, to the point where he would have done anything for just an opportunity to have coffee with her.

'I have to speak with Dr Gardenson urgently. We have a situation with one of the blood samples received from the hospital,' she explained.

'Not a problem. Let me escort you to his office.' He paused. '...if I may?'

'I'd love the company,' she admitted.

'At your service!' he smiled. He led her down the main administrative corridor. 'How have you been?'

'So kind of you to ask. Busy, but otherwise, all well. How about you, Martin? Still enjoying the chaos in here?'

'Oh yes, yes, having the time of my life!' He laughed, then wanted to kick himself. His words had betrayed him: he thought he should have at least complained a little to get her to sympathise with him. He'd known her since medical school, and had an instant liking for her as soon as they had first met. Yet in all this time, he was no more able to admit his feelings to her. While others saw her beauty, he saw her brilliant intellect, her ability to find her way through challenges almost effortlessly, and her warm personality as something stunning. *Damit! How can I be so stupid each time I see her?* He could always say only half of what he ever wanted to.

A young medic interrupted them. 'Doctor, you are needed, it's urgently. We have a' – he looked at Heather and hesitated – 'serious casualty just in.'

'I'll be there in a few seconds.' He pointed to the long corridor straight ahead of them. 'Dr Gardenson's office is the one straight ahead. You cannot miss it,' he told Heather. Pausing in hesitation, he added, 'It seems duty calls. We will have to catch up properly some other time.'

'Absolutely,' Heather smiled back at him. She knew just how manic his work was. She had to admit to herself that she would have liked to enjoy a proper chat with him. 'It was nice seeing you again, Martin.'

He beamed, turned around, and with a little extra jump in his pace, quickly made his way back up the corridor to reception.

Heather reached the office and knocked.

'Come in,' a deep official-sounding voice answered. She entered, and Dr Gardenson was there, engulfed in paperwork at his desk. He immediately recognised her. 'Heather, what a pleasure to see you. Come in, come in. How is your grandfather?' he asked, pointing to the free chair, inviting her to sit down.

'Busy as usual. You know what it is like.' She smiled at him. He was one of her grandfather's lifelong acquaintances.

'Yes, unfortunately I do. Those of us so caught up in our work and careers lose track of everything else.' She nodded in agreement. 'Tell me, to what do I owe this most pleasant surprise of your company? A social visit? Come to say hello to an old friend?' He knew that was not the case but liked to drop the hint that from time to time, he would not have minded the distraction.

'Afraid not. Grandfather sent me to inform you the labs have initiated a Code 1. One of the blood samples sent over from one of your patients had unknown pathogens in it. According to Bradley, sorry I mean Dr Boston, a new type of virus has been found.'

'Goodness me: that serious?'

'Yes, seems to be, even though Gramps kept telling me it will be all ok, I'm not so sure.'

'In that case, I'll have to instigate a lockdown here at the hospital too. Isolate the patients involved and ensure no nosocomial infections occur.' He seemed somewhat lost in thought. It was a very long time since they'd had to execute such a lockdown. He was trying to recall just what the official procedures were.

'Surely, you don't expect nosocomial infections already?' she asked. 'In hospitals, transmissions require a large viral load to be present.'

'Very true, but with unknown viruses, you can never be too careful,' he objected.

Heather paused momentarily and thought *better safe than sorry, I guess.* She nodded in agreement.

'By the way, how is our young Dr Boston doing? Bradley should be in his sixth year at the labs now...' Gardenson pondered.

'He's good. Not sure how many years it has been so far. So easy to lose track of time. Is there a reason for the year count to be of any importance?' Her mind was as sharp as it was agile. She knew there was a good reason why he had brought that up. She wanted to know what that reason was.

'Dr Boston, or Bradley as you call him' – his smile hinted at some hidden realisation he had concerning her emotions towards Bradley – 'has been called the leading scientific mind in the country. According to my sources, he is currently being headhunted by several private and public research facilities.'

Heather's mood changed. This meant Bradley might not be working at the labs for long. Her heart sank even though her mind told her it didn't matter, since he was already spoken for. She pushed her emotions to the side, very effectively. The cold hard facade of reason and logic took over.

Interesting indeed. Dr Gardenson was surprised. To him, her swift control spoke volumes. Someone who could exercise so much self-control was either a genius or a very dangerous person. He stored that thought away and returned to the point in hand. 'Please do excuse me, dear. I have to set the lockdown in process and transfer the patients involved to the top floor immediately.'

'Of course.' She rose.

'Do come visit this old fool from time to time. Your company and the little distraction I get on such rare occasions is more than welcome.'

She smiled. 'I will make sure to stop by for a hello soon, I promise.'

'It would be a pleasure. I'll make sure I have a nice tea waiting for when you do.'

'So thoughtful of you. I'd better be off myself, goodbye.' She walked out of the office, gently closing the door. Her pace increased a little. She wanted to be out of the hospital before all hell broke loose. On her way out through the A&E entrance she spotted Martin, and gave him a little goodbye wave. He caught it out of the corner of his eye and returned the farewell.

She glanced at the reception queue and saw the woman who had caused her trouble. A devious smile etched itself on her face. *My dear, you will be waiting for a long time today. A very long time indeed,* she mused. With the lockdown in progress, not only would her wait be long, it would also be enforced. The option of leaving would be gone in a matter of seconds and no matter how much she objected, there would be no way to leave the hospital now.

Satisfied, Heather stepped through the sliding doors and into the fresh air. *Time for some fun at the library!* She did love her books – that was her favourite pastime.

2

- ALL SAFE, -
FOR NOW...

Mira sat at the desk. She liked her office. She was the one responsible for its decor. She turned her chair, running her fingers over the soft yet firm leather. 'Ahh, heaven.' A whisper of utter satisfaction escaped her lips. This was her domain. Her achievements had brought her into this position, where she was practically at the top of her league. Unconsciously, her fingers danced on the huge oak and leather desk.

'Ma'am...' A young man's voice interrupted her moment.

She didn't mind the interruptions. Mira knew the voice all too well – it was her trusted assistant. In reality, she did not like him very much but he had proven himself to be highly efficient and was good at his job. This made him tolerable to her until a better replacement crossed her path. 'Yes?' A deep sigh expressed her boredom at the few seconds' wait escaped her lips.

'The reports are in ma'am, and we have news from the' – he lowered his voice to almost a mumble – 'special biotech research division.'

Her left eyebrow shot upwards. She stood up, walked straight to him. 'Give me that.' He handed her the closed file. He wasn't allowed to access these – they were highly classified. 'That will be all,' she said, turning her back to him, sending her thick black wavy hair cascading through the air. She stood gazing out through the massive elongated glass window.

Mira broke the seal on the file and started reading. Following a couple of 'hmms' and 'ahs', she closed the file and quickly slipped

11

it away and locked it in the bottom of her drawer. *Where is that useless assistant?* She mused, glancing around. Slightly irritated, she made her way out of her office towards the communal kitchen. Straight in front of her office was her secretary's desk. The young girl at the desk was bubbly, yet serious, impeccably dressed, and meticulous in her work. Mira liked the girl. She was capable of second-guessing exactly what Mira needed, even before the request came through. That was the hallmark of professionalism, according to her.

'Your assistant just left for the conference upstairs.'

Mira just nodded in approval and moved towards the staff kitchen. She needed coffee. *He could have at least sorted out my coffee before leaving. What is the point of having an assistant if he doesn't do the basics anymore?*

At the kitchen entrance, a group of young women seemed to be engrossed in conversation.

'Did you see him?' one asked.

'Oh god yes, a sight to behold,' replied another.

Mira pressed onto her eyelids, fixating with an inhuman intensity on the speakers. 'Ladies, what seems to be the issue? Anything I should be aware of?' Her stern voice cracked with reprimand and disapproval.

'Ehhh no ma'am.' Everyone immediately dispersed without a single word being spoken. They knew full well that nothing could be said. They knew Mira was cold hearted – the Ice Queen, they had nicknamed her. Extremely efficient and professional but totally emotionless until it came to firing people. They all suspected she secretly relished firing people.

The new girl quickly followed the rest of them and sat down at her own desk next to her co-worker. 'Was that...?' she asked.

'Oh yes, the Ice Queen. That's her all right,' came the whispered reply.

'Why do you call her Ice Queen?' she asked.

'Oh, you will find out eventually.'

'Please do tell,' pleaded the new girl.

'Ok, but whisper. If she hears us, we are out of a job, both you and I.' She paused. 'Mira Madison is her name. We call her the Ice Queen because she has no compassion, no emotions, no feelings, and has never had a kind word for anyone. I heard that she only ever works. It is all she does, day and night.'

'That's impossible.'

'Oh, you better believe it. There were rumours of her having a boyfriend once. Apparently, word got out that she bullied him in their private time, enjoyed humiliating him.'

'Oh no, that's horrible!'

'Oh yes! He eventually he had enough and left her. He left a private note but one of the assistants managed to read it.'

'No way!'

'Oh, yes way. Even in the office, she only uses people, and worst of all, she only likes those whom she can completely control. Have you noticed that no man in the office comes up to this floor?'

'Yes, I thought that was a bit odd. Was going to ask about that.'

'She hates men. Thinks of them as being totally useless and so avoids them. The men in the company can't stand her grandiose airs so they all refuse to work with her. She's one of the most successful women in here, but that is because she will ruthlessly and without remorse decimate anyone who stands in her way. It's either her way or the highway. Careful you don't cross her path. Best try to do as she asks and keep your thoughts to yourself.'

'What a horrible person to work for! Now I wish I had not accepted the transfer.'

'Well, I'm waiting for a transfer out. As soon as one comes up, it's mine!'

'Ladies, if you have time to whisper, maybe you would like to share this absolutely fascinating information with the rest of the office?' Mira interrupted them. She had noticed the exchange but fortunately for the both of them had not been able to hear its contents. She stood there in front of the group, left hand on left hip, with her foot slightly forward, giving the impression she was ready for action at an instance's notice.

'It's ok, ma'am, I was just explaining to the new girl how the printer is set up. It seems they had not set it up for her properly.'

Mira seemed to glare at them for an instant, then without a further word, walked off, showing little concern as to whether the issue was fixed or not.

The sunlight shone through the window and hit her face. It illuminated her complexion, and her almost coffee-coloured skin shone, as if it was a silky smooth surface with a slight hint of golden hue dancing upon its surface.

The new girl stared at her, transfixed. *Goodness me, she is beautiful. I wish I had skin like that.* Little did she notice a shadow had been cast. It was Mira's. A dark shadow of threat, terrifying to any onlooker who cared to glance upon it. Fortunately, no one did.

Mira walked back to her office. The printer issue was a matter for someone with free time to fix, and not for her to waste her ever-so-valuable time on. She had other plans to take care of, for one these new biotech developments had to be steered and managed just right or they would not yield the results she needed. Those, she was absolutely determined, would open the doors to the future for the whole of mankind and no one – NO ONE – would stand in her way. She would be – no she *had* to be – the one steering mankind into the future.

Heather walked out of the library, smiling with a book in her hands, pressing it close to her chest as if it was precious beyond understanding. She made her way back to the labs. *Might as well find out how things are going down there and I need to check on Grampa – and Bradley, of course. Goodness knows what trouble he's getting into without me there to supervise.* She smiled. It was an ongoing joke between them. It went along the lines that without her he would get into a total chaotic mess with his wild imagination and scientific curiosity! She saw it almost as her responsibility to keep him out of trouble. *That boy is always trying to invent something new.* She let a long sigh out. *One day, he might just invent something which will be too much for him to handle and get him into real trouble.* She made her way back to the laboratories, the large tech building found at the opposite end of the campus. She walked down the main pathway away from the university hospital and stumbled upon one of her old friends back from her undergraduate studies. 'Hi Anna!' her voice rose ever so slightly to make sure she would be heard.

Anna turned, sending her vast mass of long, chestnut-brown curly hair flowing freely from side to side. Heather's glance danced over her friend's frame. Her almost delicate appearance was perfectly emphasised by delicate touches of makeup, just the right touches to bring out her green eyes, and just the right accentuations to highlight her rich deep pink lips. This all contrasted beautifully against her slightly tanned, otherwise pale complexion. Her attire was perfect, as was her slim figure in her favourite brown-and-latte coloured top. On her wrists, she wore just the right amount of jewellery to show the world she meant business. Her entire attire was designed to show off.

'Oh Heather! How nice to meet you. Fancy this coincidence. I was just remembering our time together here when we were doing our degrees! How are you? What are you up to? Are you back for more?' The bombardment of questions took her by surprise but she was only too glad to catch up.

'I'm good, working in the science labs division now.'

'Oh what on Earth are you doing there? That's where all the spooky stuff goes on,' replied Anna.

'Spooky stuff?'

'Yes, the rumours were going wild during my time here. I was dating that guy doing medical research – remember? He used to go all quiet whenever I asked him if any of them were true.' Anna's expression was serious and concerned.

'Never heard of anything odd.' Heather shrugged. 'Actually, everyone there is really nice.'

Anna seemed unconvinced. 'What are you up to? What have you been up to? Got a boyfriend yet?' She winked.

'Erm, no, not yet.'

'Still stuck in the books, I see.' Her comment felt like a reprimand.

'Afraid so.' Heather smiled.

'I've never liked going to the library.' Anna looked to their right at the library building, pretended to shiver and quickly shifted her gaze away.

'Why on Earth not?' Heather was really curious. She could never understand why some students had what appeared to be a morbid dislike of the library and books in general.

'It gives me the heebie-jeebies. Creepy place.'

'Surely not?' In the midst of her objections, it was Heather's turn to glance at the library. She observed the tall structure lines in glass and the reflective copper-coloured metals and brick, and a sense of pride swelled within her. She was so glad she had access to it, one of the leading libraries in the country. Its very structure looked not only modern but almost bordering on what she remembered of the London financial sector. 'Something about the endless corridors of books. You could get lost in there and the smell of old leather, of ageing paper...'

Anna appeared disgusted, as if smelling one of those stinky cheeses, as she liked to call them. She quickly pulled her thoughts back to Heather. This was far more pressing. She needed, no she wanted information. 'That would explain it, then. Good on you!' Anna pretended to be genuinely pleased.

Her manoeuvre failed miserably. Heather was able to pick up the sarcasm with no effort whatsoever.

'Just don't leave it too late. You know our beauty fades in time.' Anna's face slumped as if in despair.

And there it is, thought Heather. This is what she was really try to get at. Why, oh why am I considered to be lesser just because I am more interested in book than boys? Of course, Heather never voiced those thoughts.

'Say, you wouldn't have discovered anything really cool which could stop us getting old, have you?' asked Anna.

'No not as far as I know.'

'Hope you do soon!' The smile beaming at Heather was both genuine and mischievous. 'Just don't let the boys get their hands on any of it when you do! That's something we definitely want for us girls only!'

Heather could not understand why or how the conversation had turned to this, and she decided it was time to end it. There was no real point to it. 'So what are you doing here?' she asked.

'Me, oh yeah, I'm doing a masters degree. Imagine it! Me a masters student...'

'Fascinating. In dramatic arts, is it?'

Anna nodded proudly. 'Oh and guess what? I'm dating a rugby player here at the university! Well kind of: he still doesn't know we're dating, but will do so very soon!' Her excitement caused the pitch of her voice to rise ever so slightly.

Heather decided she was not going to listen to any more of this. She knew the end point, she knew she would be made to feel lesser because Anna had a kind-of boyfriend whereas she did not. Instead, Heather looked at her watch and said, 'Oh my, I need to rush, Anna, or I'll be late back in the office, and you don't want to see my boss in angry mode!'

'Is he that bad?' Anna asked. Heather simply nodded. 'Then you better get back quick. Wouldn't want you to lose your job because of me. We will catch up soon, right?'

'Absolutely.' Heather nodded. *Not if I can help it, we won't,* she thought, and made her way promptly to the large glass structure ahead of her. She caught herself thinking, *Did I just blank one of my friends from my good old student days?* The thought lingered uncomfortably on her mind. She could not understand why she would get so irritated so fast and brush her friend off. She made her way to the labs. She stood there looking at the glass walls, all the offices at ground and first floor levels with the research divisions higher above. Several totally empty floors of office space separated the two. This had been done deliberately to ensure that any leaks and contaminants would need to travel through the empty spaces before they reached the office spaces. Each of these three subsections had separate air flow systems, IT systems, and power systems. It was a model for modern-day architectural engineering.

Heather gazed through the glass. She saw Bradley rushing from one of the offices to another. He was, it seemed, heading towards his own office. Looking at him, she wondered, *could he be the reason for her frustrations?* They had known each other since childhood, and he was more like a brother than a man who could draw that sort of interest. Yet...

He paused, looking straight ahead through the glass walls as if prompted by her very thoughts. She froze, and their eyes interlocked. His deep blue eyes fascinated her, his scruffy hair drove her nuts, and his friendly, almost intimate manners could soothe the worst of her fears. *Could it be?* Pushing the matter out of her mind, she proceeded to make her way back. Hopefully Mike would let her in now.

'Welcome back, Dr Hawke.' Mike motioned to her. 'All is clear. Dr Grimsaw has asked for you to see him in his office when you have a minute to spare... everyone is doing well.' He had given her the information she sought without her having to ask.

She smiled back. 'Thank you.' It was only then she noticed that Bradley was out of his protective suit. Things had to be safe or he never would have been! She laughed out.

'Miss?' asked Mike.

'Oh, no worries, just a private joke about Bradley. I'll make my way over.' He nodded and keyed the entry key in for her. As she walked in, a choice presented itself. Would she go and catch up with Bradley and the others or see her grandfather first? *I guess I should see Grampa first. Might get a little more insight than I would from the guys,* she reasoned. Turning left and walking down the short corridor lead her to the main office. Voices could be heard, and she strained her ears, managing to catch parts of the conversation.

'Sir, we cannot rule out risk of infection. We simply do not know how this virus spreads,' a deep unknown voice argued.

'I am aware of that!' Her grandfather seemed annoyed. 'I am also aware that my lead researcher has found the current mutation to be unable to transmit via air. He concluded that infection is limited to direct exposure to the infective agent itself.'

'With all due respect, sir, we do not know whether there is another version that could be airborne.'

'That is correct, hence we cannot assume there is one. Nor can we really dismiss the possibly that there might be one. For the time being, until we have any indications that we MIGHT have an airborne version, we will have to work on the basis that what we have analysed is the virus we are trying to manage.'

'But sir, you do realise the gravity and potential of all this, if it does become airborne?'

'Yes I do, but our job as scientists is to investigate what *is* and *not what could be in the future.* This virus simply does not have the capability to be airborne. If it did, I would contact the prime minister myself and have him declare a national emergency.'

In the room, Dr Grimsaw shuddered. The thought of a virus ripping people's genetic material being airborne was utterly terrifying, yet as he had tried to point out to the other man, this permutation was unable to survive in the air at all.

'What if you researcher is wrong?' objected the stranger.

'Bradley? He's one of the most thorough scientists I have seen, and believe you me, in my 50 years in the field, I have seen some of the best and some of the worst. Besides, I have myself gone through all his reports and notes and find no flaw in his logic or conclusions.'

'Impossible!' blurted out the other man.

'Did I hear that right? Or are my old ears deceiving me?' asked Dr Grimsaw, stunned at the comment.

'But sir, he couldn't have concluded all that research within a matter of just hours! It can't be correct.'

Calling the competence of his team into question was, in Dr Grimsaw's view, unacceptable. He had the utmost confidence in all his staff. His reply came swiftly and sharply. 'We are done here. I have work to attend to. You may leave.'

The door slid open just as Heather was about to knock. Her grandfather spotted her.

'Perfect timing my dear. My guest was just leaving.' He turned around to face the man she could not recognise. 'As I was saying, I have work to do.'

The stranger's frustration was all too plain to see. He stormed out of the office. Dr Grimsaw put his index finger over his mouth to signal her. His insight was correct: the stranger lingered close to the door, desperate to hear even a slither of the conversation to no avail. It took a few extra seconds before he turned and stormed out of the building.

'What was that all about?' she asked.

'A minor irritation.' He was quick to turn the conversation away from his visitor. Heather of course new what he was doing and let it pass. She was all too well acquainted with her grandfather's quirks. After all, she had grown up with him. She had other ways to find out little titbits of information when needed. He handed her a file labelled 'TOP SECRET – Classified Information' on the front in big red letters. She took it, looked at him, and raised one eyebrow in a questioning glance. 'Read it and don't talk about it. You know the protocols.'

She nodded. The labs often dealt with classified information when it came to diseases. She flipped page after page, her mind rapidly absorbing the information, scrutinising the charts and results of various tests. Finally, she closed the file handed it back to him. 'You were right. Bradley is very thorough, as always. Your visitor did have a good point: how on Earth did he complete all this in the space of an afternoon?'

The question hung in the air. 'He has his ways. You should know that best of us all, that man's ability to multitask is simply astounding. He works at 5 times the speed of anyone I've ever met and somehow manages to avoid making even minor errors despite this.'

She nodded. That was very true, but what made her really curious was the fact that her grandfather knew this so well, even though he had never worked with Bradley. She half-smiled. *I guess we all have our little secrets.* 'So we're dealing with a botched attempt at using the gene editing technologies? Was it CRISPR CAS9 techniques I assume?'

'No, my dear, I suspect this was a deliberate misuse of it.'

'WHAT?' her surprise spilled out. 'You're not serious?'

'Oh quite. Look at how the virus replicates: it is almost efficient to a fault.'

'Are you telling me that someone has weaponised gene editing on the fly?!?!?' He gave her a stern look. 'Sorry,' she said, realising she was not meant to have spoken that out loud.

'It seems its ability to tear up the DNA in human beings is very specific. Bradley is currently experimenting on its effects on animal life but if my suspicions are correct, it will have little if any impact. This seems to be designed to harm humans, to unwind what makes us from the roots upwards until we simply fall apart.'

Heather shuddered at the thought: it was utterly horrific. Emotions were, in the next instant, pushed aside and her practical logic took over. 'Quarantine has been established at the hospital. I'll go notify them that we need security clearance lockdown as well and have all medical findings and future investigations forwarded directly to the lab.'

Her grandfather nodded in approval. 'I agree. We do not want the ordinary medical staff dealing with this. We are still dealing with an unknown quantity here. Besides, we have no knowledge of its mutations... or its capability to adapt in specific ways...'

'Did Bradley identify all carriers and transmission methods?' she asked.

'His team is currently looking at replication, but as you have heard, it cannot become airborne, which means we can trace it with a little more ease. Ask James to suit up and go question the infected patient. He is very weak and withering away very rapidly, so we should gather as much data as possible before he slips into coma.'

Those final words shook Heather to the core. What he had in fact told her was that once infected, it was a death sentence. She nodded, turned, and was just about to walk out of his office.

'Heather, dearest, please be careful. I would never forgive myself if harm came to you.'

She nodded and understood, and left the office. Walking down the corridor, a young woman crossed her path. Heather knew her as a fellow scientist. Her beauty was breath-taking, even she had to admit to it.

'Hello Kuroi.'

'Hi Heather, how are you?'

'I'm good.'

'I'm just on my way to Dr Grimsaw's office. What is his mood like?' Kuroi asked.

'Hard to say. I'd proceed slowly today. Goodness knows he has a lot going on.'

'Thanks for the tip.' Kuroi smiled at Heather and proceeded on-wards. Heather was a little envious. The long black shiny curls of hair, grace with which she moved, the pale Japanese skin tone, and those completely unusual, almost indigo eyes with hints of green made Heather jealous. What made matters worse is that this was Bradley's long-term girlfriend, whom he had hinted to Heather he would one day marry. She let a sigh out. *No time for all that, I have urgent work to do.* With that she stormed onward towards Bradley's office. She punched the code in, the doors slid open, and she entered.

'Hey Brad... busy?'

'You bet, but could damn well use a break!' he admitted.

'Good. Oh, before I forget... got this for you.' She handed him the book she had been carrying all this time.

'What am I going to do with a book on scripts of ancient populations?' he mused.

'Oh, I don't know. Read it, genius?' she teased.

'I have no interest in this stuff...' he objected.

'What is it you always used say to me? Let me see,' she paused, trying to deepen her voice as she attempted to imitate him. 'Young missy, you need to broaden your horizons and mind any time the opportunity presents itself.' She desperately tried to hold back an onslaught of laughter as it threatened to break out.

'Fine fine. If it will stop you teasing me, I'll read the damn book!'

'Sure?'

'I promise.'

She was happy. Not because she managed to get him to read the book but simply because she had gotten rid of the damn book. She had no idea what had possessed her to simply walk out of the library, book in hand, rather than leave it with the librarian on her way out. She had no interest in the topic whatsoever herself.

'How goes the research into the effects of that virus on animals?' she asked.

'I'm not supposed to talk about that,' he warned.

'I have clearance,' she said. Reminding him of that little fact seemed important to her.

'I know. We got the clearance at the same time. I am just not supposed to discuss this with another other than Dr Grimsaw.'

'He's only going to tell me anyway since I am officially on the team involved with this.' Technically that was a lie but in her mind she was notifying the hospital and had been allowed to read the report. To her, this meant she was on the team.

'Its effect on animals is very limited but it is there. Only organs and metabolic systems very similar to those of humans seem to be affected.'

'So Grampa was right, this is engineered to target us specifically.'

Bradley started waving in panic to her for silence. This was the one thing no one was supposed to discuss. She nodded, and bit her lower lip. She had messed up. If anyone had heard her, that would have been it for both her and Bradley. They would have been instantly sacked and never employed in any field requiring clearance.

'Sorry,' she whispered to him.

Bradley was not amused. He curved his lips and blew at the lock of hair which was attempting to invade his forehead. He whispered back to her, 'See, this is why I didn't want to talk about it. Get Dr Grimsaw to organise a safe place for all of us to meet and discuss this.'

She agreed. They would all need to share information and brainstorm at some point or other. 'Any ideas on how to counter this?' she asked.

'Humm not really, well not yet. It literally takes the two strands of DNA and tears them apart. Even if the body wanted to repair it, there is no way for us to take two parts of a strand and knot them back together in exactly the same way as before, let alone doing this without any error in the process. Other than letting the body do it itself – but the scale of repair is far more than any of our bodies can handle...' Concern etched his almost delicate face, and it worried Heather. She had never really seen him so worried before. Somehow every problem was solvable, eventually... until now.

Distracted Bradley, looked at the book sitting on his desk where he had left it. He blinked. For a moment, he thought he had seen a shadow slither out of it, and then pull itself back in. He rubbed his eyes.

'Are you ok?' asked Heather.

'Yes just a little tired it seems. My eyes are deceiving me.'

She looked at him, concerned. 'When is the last time you slept?'

'Pfft, dunno. Who cares about sleep? Too busy for that nonsense,' he replied.

'Ok mister, we're getting you some rest right now.' She positioned herself in between him and the desk, barring his access to his computer and notes.

'Heather, I don't have time for this!'

'Naturally. This time you should be spending getting some rest,' she interjected, 'or you will end up making an error... You have two choices: you either get your coat and go home OR I will drag you there myself. Might even get Julie from the accommodation office to get me a key so that I can lock you in one of the rooms at the dorms. Your choice!' She put both hands on her hips and adopted the warrior pose. No one was getting past her, one way or another.

He smiled. 'Very well, I'll go, but just for a little while.'

23

'I don't care how long you rest for, as long as you rest!' she insisted. Her own past experiences told her fatigue would take him out for as long as his body needed it, irrespective of how long he wanted to sleep or not.

'Fine.' He grabbed his coat, flung it over his right shoulder, and started making his way out of his office. He looked back at her, still standing there immobile.

'Yes I'll lock up. Don't worry, now off with you, mister!' Her voice was firm and unyielding. Just as he turned about to step out of the sliding doors, she interrupted him. 'Here, take this. You should get your mind off work. In case you need a distraction.'

Seeing that there would be no win for him in this argument, he took the book, waved it about his head and stepped over the boundary lines of his office with voice raised, almost yelling: 'Thank you mummy Heather!' Breaking out in laughter, he left.

She was mad and amused. *Ah, men!*

3

- AWAKENING -

Yume stood at in front of the screen holding her breath. She pulled up the sleeves of her white work-shirt which was tucked into her black knee-length skirt. She wore men's business shirts – call it one of her quirks. In reality, she liked the way they were cut, the slim fit models would suit her just fine and their broader cuts, compared to the women's equivalent, gave her ample movement room without tugging or pulling. Unlike her colleagues here, she had to dress semi-formally. She was the lead researcher and this was her team. That however, did not mean she had to be any less comfortable than they were. With shoes, she made an exception: her shoes were the least comfortable she could have picked but they showed off her sculpted calves. As a bonus, they added quite a bit of height to her. Secretly, she whispered a thank you to whoever invented them: she loved and hated them. It was a complex relationship.

She was about to see the results of their latest experiment. The elongated lab room filled with flashing computer screens. At the centre of the long row of these displays, a massive screen stood apart. Today, all the action was taking place on it. It captured her and everyone else's undivided attention. Unlike other labs, this one had walls and floor painted in black. The isolation components used in the paint meant it had to be black. When the powerful artificial lights illuminating the place were turned off, the distinct effect of screens floating in darkness was unmistakable. It was almost unnatural to the casual observer, yet it worked wonders in focusing the research team's attention. There were no other visible distractions.

Yume was obsessed with her field of research almost as much as her best friend Kuroi was about her bioengineering. But Kuroi seemed to be running late. She had promised to be here for the big event. It worried Yume. She had known Kuroi since childhood and never had she been late anywhere. They were like sisters, and spent every free moment of time together. Always looking after each other. Yume smiled. *Now that she has Bradley I don't need to look after her as much.* She liked Bradley. He was charming and kind an outrageously handsome fellow had been her first assessment of him. *Yes, a bit set in his ways* but she reminded herself that all men were. It was up to them, the women, to mould and shape their men. She quickly refocused back to the matter at hand: Kuroi's lateness was not normal. Even when it came to casual meetings, Kuroi was always right on time, never too early but certainly never late. As the meeting started, Yume had to put her concerns to the side.

The screen flashed. She held her breath. This was it: either they had discovered something new or this had all been a wild goose chase down a rabbit hole. The scan's results displayed. All the onlooking quantum research team held their breaths. This was it! Finally, the time had arrived. A few seconds passed, silence permeating the entire lab. Gasps could be heard all the way down the corridors leading to their office. They had found something: it was there, plainly displayed on screen. But what on Earth was it? A new particle? A glitch in the system? It didn't look like anything any of them had seen or were expecting to see. The image moved on the screen, and they all jumped back instinctively. This thing was moving? Could it be? It made no sense.

'It cannot be,' Yume exclaimed. 'Particles are not intelligent! They are just particles, nothing more, nothing less.' Absentmindedly, she flicked a few of the long strands of her hair which had fallen over the left side of her face. Her dark eyes blinked as she readjusted her delicate frame. Yume was not very tall but to her that was an advantage. She knew how taller people suffered from slower nervous system responses, how the very tall ended up with back problems and were naturally clumsy. She liked her body, slim with youthful pale skin. In her mind, that was just the perfect way to be. She was comfortable with her appearance. On more than one occasion, she'd caught the cautious half-daring glances of interest from men in the department. It amused her. She liked it.

'I agree, it must be something that has intruded into the system as we ran our test,' confirmed a colleague.

'Catalogue it and save the data. Run the video streams on record. Let us get some data we can have a closer look at,' she instructed.

'But doctor, this is obviously not a quantum particle of any sorts. We should restart the experiment instead of wasting time,' objected the tall guy towering behind her.

'I know, but I would still like to have a closer look at whatever it is. Identifying its nature will help us discern how to prevent it from contaminating the equipment when we re-run.'

'Good point, I'll get to it at once.' He rushed off. Yume let out a long sigh. Back to square one. She shrugged and smiled. It was a bit of a disappointment but she was still happy. They had managed to run the experiment successfully, and all that really remained was for them to remove this contaminant. They had made progress. It had not failed on them as it had done all their previous attempts. Her thoughts returned to Kuroi. *Where is she? Something must have happened...* She headed back to the central office, and she would try and call Kuroi once there.

Bradley woke up. He thought he had slept only a few hours, but as he picked up his watch, he started swearing. He had slept all afternoon and deep into the night, not only that but he had also fallen asleep in his clothes. It was nearly 1 am.

'Ah blast, no point going back to the labs now.' He decided to have a shower and get some food instead. He stripped, annoyed. As he stepped into the shower and set the water to hot, a sigh of relief escaped his exhausted lips. His body was totally run down, and the flowing water felt great. Tension seemed to dissolve. Only the softest pressure on each muscle was needed to cause it to loosen. He pulled as much on his neck in each direction as he could and allowed the hot water to wash through his thick black hair. Looking at his hands he mused, *maybe one day I should go get a tan before I become a shade of living-ghost white?* He smiled. Maybe he should finally listen to Kuroi and take a long trip to Japan. He always liked to visit her home country – it fascinated him. He might surprise her and just buy tickets for them both this summer. *Yes that would be nice – she would love that!* That settled it – it would be done!

He stepped out of the shower and grabbed hold of the first towel, and started drying himself. He saw his reflection in the steamed up body length mirror ahead of him. A smile surfaced upon his lips he was doing quite well at the gym. Kuroi was right – he looked much better now. She was right, as usual. He loved her, as she always gave him the drive to do things and at this point in time, he was so grateful she had bullied him into going to the gym. Three times a week had started shaping his body perfectly. He would look like those guys in the men's health magazines, eventually. At that thought, he laughed out loud. *I bet she will love this more than me!* He was glad. He would have done anything to make her happy and getting into shape was damn hard but he had to do it, for her.

Something caught his attention. *There it was again!* In the mirror behind him, a glow appeared. He tried to focus in on it but as soon as he did, it dissipated out of view. When his focus wavered, it was back, and what spooked him was the fact that the glow had a shadow of its own! The two seemed to dance with each other as they flipped in and out of his sight. He got closer to the mirror and touched it. Nothing.

He shrugged and got dressed. *Ah, new clean clothes.* Heather had been right: he definitely needed a break. She always was. He definitely got way too absorbed into his work and far too excited about the next discovery. He went for the fridge, opened it, and looked through the nicely prepared dishes waiting there. *Ah, thank god for Kuroi.* She always made sure there were some fantastic dishes waiting in the fridge. It had taken him a while to enjoy Japanese food. He enjoyed it very much: once she had made some of her specialities, he could not stop devouring them. It made her laugh.

As he sat and ate, his gaze went to the book he had brought in. He picked it up while taking a bit of Kuroi's delicious dish. *Ah, my favourite,* he mused as he chewed. He skimmed through the pages, put it down, and pushed it to the side. It was interesting but nothing special. *Typical: archaeological findings and documentaries are dull, no matter how interesting the subject matter.*

He felt as if there was something he should have paid attention to. Just as rapidly, he dismissed that thought. It was just history and archaeology, nothing of use to him. He drove his fingers on the cover, and something felt familiar and comfortable. He ignored the sensation and stood up. Time for him to get back to work. He needed information and the best place to find it was the library! He looked at his watch: nearly 2am. Maybe not the best time for the library, it wouldn't open until 6! This oversleeping really made a mess of his routine. He was annoyed at himself. He turned his PC on, allowing it to boot. Unaware his fingers were sliding over the cover of the book. A slight pulse resonated on the tip of his fingers, but he pulled back, ready to start typing.

He needed to find out exactly how this virus was spreading and how it was deescalating the genetics of each cell it infected. Kuroi would be working on how it actually infected those cells and looking for a potential preventative. *Where is Kuroi?* It just occurred to him that he had not heard from her in a while. They both usually worked through the nights in cases of urgency, but... He picked up his phone dialled her number and waited. No answer. He was a little concerned. There was no message, no email, no text, nothing. *Maybe she's in the controlled lab area?* That area was strictly controlled where no electronics other than the test equipment would be present, and even mobile phones and Wi-Fi devices were prohibited. His gut instinct told him something was amiss. He had no choice but to wait until later when he got into work.

His email box was full. This time he had to go through it reports of his teammates' findings. He opened them one by one, carefully examining each. This was his strong skill: collating information and logically working through each point until he found answers. In this case, those answers were not what he wanted. They all had an unpleasant setting and outcome. Nothing new from Kuroi – that meant they were still in the dark about even the direction in which to look for a potential vaccine or cure. His own team was making good progress on ironing down mutation and infection profiles. They had pretty much confirmed now that it was not airborne, that you had to make contact with the contaminant in order to get infected. *We need to be careful with the blood of the infected it seems: it can use the blood as it would the original carrier agent,* he reminded himself. At least it would not transfer when you made simple physical contact – that was a relief.

He was satisfied progress was being made. *If only I can find a way to prevent transmission or nullify its ability to transmit, at least that way we could contain it, even if we cannot stop its initial infection...* Something deep down in his gut told him that this approach was pointless – but was it? It bothered him; usually this type of genetic editing required you to know exactly what you were adding or overwriting. At least, the virus had to be programmed to target some specified area of the DNA. *How is this programmed to unravel the genome? How can it be chaotic, yet so specific?* It didn't make sense to him; he was missing something.

He went back through the emails and the reports. Something was bugging him. His nose started twitching – that was his telltale sign that he was onto something. He never noticed it himself but others in the office had made a joke of it. Then he found it. He picked up the phone and dialled, hoping his colleague would still be at work. The guys there with no families often worked throughout the night more often than not. Tonight he was hoping that would be the case.

'Jim speaking.'

'Hi Jim, it's me,' replied Bradley.

'Hey Bradley, I see sleeping beauty has FINALLY woken up,' he joked.

'Yes, yes, that aside, can you check something for me?'

'Sure, fire away.' Jim was always all too keen to set out on an investigation. Bradley secretly wished he had gone to be a detective. In his mind, Jim would have been one of the best detectives the country could offer but unfortunately, Jim had decided he wanted to help everyone. He saw no better way to do so than discover a cure to some disease or a way in which to better mankind.

'Can you double check the topoisomerase levels in the infected bloods? These numbers seem ridiculously high.'

Jim paused, opened his report and double-checked it. 'Damn it, you know you're right! These numbers are ridiculous. Let me re-run the tests. Will text you once complete. I think you might be onto something here. How could I have missed this? Blast!'

'You need some sleep too. The sleeping beauty awakens more alert and aware!' Bradley jokingly reprimanded Jim. 'I learnt that lesson, thanks to Heather!'

'You know,' Jim pondered, 'if this proves to be correct, we could stop the DNA unravelling in the infected...' He completely ignored Bradley's attempt at humour.

'Yes, but something tells me that this is only one small part of the equation.'

Jim conceded Bradley's instinct had always proven to be more than on-point, even more so than his own investigative rigour. That is what he considered the key factor, which put Bradley in the lead and so far ahead of the rest of them. 'Very well, at least it is a potential first step, then.'

'It might well be,' agreed Bradley. 'By the way, do we have any of the viral information? I have not heard from Kuroi since lunchtime yesterday. I would really like to look at the genetic structure of this bug we're dealing with.'

'You know we won't have that. These projects have sectioned information so each lab only has insight into the specifics it deals with.'

Bradley nodded. He had forgotten about that. Kuroi and him shared a lot of information, which technically they should not have been allowed to. It made things simpler and produced results so much faster, saving lives. Why did these stupid rules have to be there to hinder their work? He was annoyed.

'You will have to submit an information request form at the head office.' Jim was correct.

'Stupid forms, idiotic rules. We're running against the clock here. That will take far too long with those damn bureaucrats and their interviews. Anyway, I'll see what I can do. Let me know when you have your results.'

'Will do. Should have the first few with you by 4am.'

'Great.' Bradley approved wholeheartedly. *This is how progress is made – not by form filling and waiting for days for a file to show up on your desk. Action is what everyone needs, not talk.*

He kept on flipping through the pages of the reports. Something was still bugging him. It was like an itch at the back of his mind, unreachable but very prominent. There was something they were all missing. What could it be? He had to find it.

Time passed. The phone rang. It was Jim again. 'Bradley? Got the results.'

It was only then he realised just how much time had passed! For a split second he'd wandered.

'They are exactly the same as the previous ones. The topoisomerase are indeed off the charts. This enzyme is what is splitting the DNA strands apart. Usually we only have very minute and controlled amounts of it but in this case, it is totally off the chart.' Jim had confirmed at least that theory.

'Ok do me a favour. Get back the original sample of blood and just to be on the safe side, make a request to the hospital medics to gather a new sample. I want you look at the DNA itself. I know it's not your field of expertise, but I'll come double-check the results myself. I just need a little time before I head back to the labs. Do me a genetic analysis of the structure of the DNA rather than its contents,' instructed Bradley.

'Why would you want to bother with that? We know what the structure is in humans – that never changes.'

'Amuse me. Call it a hunch.'

Jim was unsure. 'Fine then just note it down as your request, not mine.'

'I'll be there in a short while.' Bradley put the phone down and as he moved, his arm knocked down the book. *Damn book – really not the time for this irrelevant nonsense.* He bent down, and picked it up. It had fallen face down, and as he looked at the two open pages, his mind zoomed in on the ancient script – runes, if his memory served him right. He had seen them somewhere. Not for want of effort, but he could not remember where or when. There they were, totally unrecognisable to him.

He had spent no more than an instant or two staring at them, but that was all that was needed. They were etched in his mind. His focus was absolute. He shook his head and snapped out of it, closed the book and put it back on his desk. Time for him to go chase down Kuroi. This was very much unlike her. Not even sending a short message was odd and it troubled him. His growing concern pushed him to head to her offices.

Mira woke up in a sweat, shook her head a few times, and tried to get her bearings. *Room... bedroom... yes, that's my room. All is well.* Something had disturbed her sleep. Her memories were vague. A nightmare? No, there was no fear – she was unable to get a grip on exactly what her dream had been about. Actually she was unable to recall even a few images.

Shrugging at the whole nonsensical situation, she got up, got dressed, and grabbed a bite to eat. Breakfast was not her thing; time was of the essence and sitting down eating a mini-lunch first thing in the morning was just a waste, in her opinion. She looked at her digital clock on the kitchen table: *5am. Excellent, perfect time to get ready.* Approving of her waking-up time, she thought to herself that everyone should be up at this time every single day without fail. *Driver will be here in 45 minutes. Better get showered and dressed.* Today was a big day for her. Today, if all went well, she would gain a key ally and succeed in one of the major milestones of her long-term plan. *This will be MY day,* she told herself. Her determination gave her the drive to push onwards, and the speed of her preparations naturally intensified with little to no conscious effort or acknowledgment. She would get things to work out perfectly, no matter the cost!

Bradley cut the line, annoyed at his phone. Still no answer from Kuroi. *Where the heck is she?* He had checked in at her office. They had seen her leave but no one knew where she was. Everyone simply assumed she had returned home. Even Mike the security guard had not seen her since she left the labs and he was known to wander about. Bradley was getting very concerned, and thought it might be best to head to the hospital to check if anything had happened to her. He made his way towards the university hospital.

He walked through the A&E entrance and was greeted by the night nurse there. 'Yes?'

Not the most welcoming person in his view. He cared not; his concern was for Kuroi. 'I'm looking for my girlfriend. Wanted to make sure she hadn't been taken in ill,' he explained.

'I see. She gave you the slip and you think she is here?'

His frustration grew. He looked at the nurse with a veiled gaze of anger and discontent. 'Would you mind checking?'

'I have better things to do than helping you with your marital problems.'

He could not understand why she was so adamant in making his task as difficult as possible. He was about to start an argument when Martin saw him. 'Hey Bradley, how's it going? Up for another match?' They had played golf only two weekends ago. Martin had won, which made him very happy at the time!

'Afraid not, I'm trying to find Kuroi. She's disappeared, it's not like her,' he tried to explain.

'And you think she might have been in some sort of an accident, I presume?'

Bradley nodded, concern etched on his face.

'Not a problem.' Martin made way for the computer.

'Doctor! You're not supposed to,' interrupted the nurse.

'It will take just a minute, after all this could be an emergency!' Martin smiled at her.

'I don't see how that could be even remotely true.'

'Doctor's orders. My patient Bradley over there is getting super stressed with concern. His health is definitely at risk and most certainly his peace of mind.' He winked at Bradley and pushed the nurse's chair out of the way. He was quick, very quick, and within seconds his head was nodding, indicating that there was no news at the hospital. 'I'm afraid she's not here, which is a good thing.' He paused for thought. 'Heather mentioned once that Kuroi had a good friend working here at the university. Did you ask her?'

'Of course! Martin, you're a genius!' Bradley smiled at him. 'I cannot believe I forgot about Yume.'

'It's the stress!' Martin turned to the nurse. 'See, it's already affected his memory! Horrible thing, stress.' He turned to face Bradley. 'Well, what are you waiting for? Go.' He pointed to the doorway and gestured for him to get out of there. Bradley rushed out. 'Ah scientists. One of these days I'll get an emergency call because one of them has forgotten their head somewhere.' Martin laughed, looking at the nurse in charge. She was not amused.

Bradley rushed to the university. His phone rang. 'Kuroi?' he had answered it without looking at who was calling.

'Afraid not, it's only me,' answered Jim. 'You need to get here right now.' He seemed both excited and panicked, which was very unlike Jim. He was a scientist to the core, always logical and almost emotionless to a fault in times of crisis.

'It will have to wait. I need to find Kuroi – she's gone missing.'

'Afraid that will have to wait. We have an emergency, an all-hands-on-deck type of emergency.'

'Damn it!' Bradley was seriously annoyed. Nothing he could do. 'Will be there in a jiffy.' Irate, he rushed off towards the research labs.

A few minutes later, he punched the security code into the secured entrance, and the door slid open, making the typical 'whoosh' sound. 'Ok, what the hell is going on?' Fury echoed in his words.

'We have several additional casualties from the university. All four victims are high-ranking medics working at the hospital.'

'Wait, what? The hospital itself?' asked Bradley.

'Yes.' Jim nodded, the seriousness of the situation etched on his face.

'Why the bloody hell did they not institute containment!' Someone had not followed the safety protocols and that, more than anything else, annoyed him most profoundly. He could never understand why taking basic precautions and saving yourself from suffering – including, potentially, death – was such a difficult concept to seize.

'They DID! And to the letter!' objected Jim.

'You are telling me that all those precautions did not suffice? Were ineffective? That's impossible!'

'Yes, that is exactly what I am telling you and exactly why this has now been classified as a top emergency.'

Bradley started pacing up and down the length of the lab. This was the telltale sign and he was putting his mind into max overdrive. The actual walking was totally unconscious but it definitely had an impact on the speed and effectiveness of his mind. Jim watched him silently. He knew this pattern all too well, having worked there for years. He knew just as well that ANY form of interruption would result in Bradley losing his train of thought and lashing out in frustration. He sat there patiently wishing he had the same ability himself.

'Paper,' came the request. This was quite common too, when Bradley's mind was so engaged in the more complex thinking, his interactions with the world at large became direct, commanding and simple to a flaw. Without a word, Jim handed him a sheet of paper from his own desk.

'Pen.' A black ball pen, Bradley's favourite tool for note taking, was handed over. Bradley sat down at the desk without a single word and started drawing diagrams. A few moments passed, the page filled up, his hand went straight up above his head. 'Paper.'

Jim rolled his eyes and handed him another sheet of blank paper in total silence. This was repeated, until a third and fourth and finally fifth sheet of paper had been requested and used. Finally, Bradley seemed to stir from his numbness to the world he was in. He looked at the pages and started nodding in approval.

'Did we get the DNA mappings of the virus through yet?' he asked Jim, breaking the silence.

'Just this morning. Here, look.' Jim pulled up the findings on his screen and turned it to face Bradley.

'Hmm... ah... hmm,' escaped his lips. 'Ok, we seem to have a better idea of what this thing is doing,' he concluded.

'YOU seem to have a better idea. Care to enlighten the rest of us, oh Mr Mighty Mind?' Jim just had to crack a joke or would crack under the intense pressure of silence.

Bradley smiled. It was a friendly, amused type of smile. 'Look here. This is the DNA structure of your patient.' He pointed to the double helix simulation of the genetics on screen. 'See this?' He zoomed in and pointed at part of the hydrogen bonds holding the two sides of the DNA together.

'What on Earth?!?' Jim was not only surprised but shocked at what he was witnessing.

'Yes, the virus is designed to pull apart the DNA. It is literally splitting human genes down the middle, which is in effect killing the victims, very slowly and painfully at that. It is unwinding their body's code of life and functioning. Stopping all the systems in our bodies from doing their work, from blood transporting nutrients and oxygen, down to healing and operating code for each and every organ in the body. And that is just the tip of the iceberg.'

'That is some seriously messed-up bug. Who the bloody hell would want to design something like that!' Jim was angry. He had joined the scientific community to help mankind. When someone abused things and used it to deliberately harm people, as in this case, it made him angry.

Bradley became distant again, his mind probably going back into overdrive, Jim suspected. Without warning, he stood up and started pacing up and down the length of the lab again. Jim let out a long sigh of despair. He thought about Kuroi and wondered how she could put up with him. *Goodness knows I wouldn't be able to.*

'It is either someone making a total mess of an attempt to edit the genome, as CRISPR really should not be accessible, not this easily,' concluded Bradley. 'OR more worryingly, it is by design.'

'What do you mean by design?'

For a moment Bradley stopped his pacing, and stared intently at Jim.

'Sorry; didn't mean to interrupt.' Jim swallowed. He knew better than to interrupt.

'It's ok, and a damn good point at that.' The pacing continued. 'What if this bug is nothing more than a part of a bigger picture? Think about it Jim, why would you unravel someone's DNA? It kills slowly, it takes time to do its job...'

'To kill them slowly and painfully?'

'Not so sure. What if this was part 1? If I were trying to change the way an organism functions, I would have done exactly the same. You take it out of functioning mode, un-program its basic functionality, THEN introduce a new pathogen with a new genetic code.'

'YOU'RE NOT BLOODY SERIOUS?' Unwittingly, Jim yelled his thought out loud. 'You are telling me that someone could be using people to experiment on changing them into something else?'

'It is a possibility, one which has been on my mind for a while now.'

Jim had to remember that when Bradley spoke of a while, that could actually be no more than a few minutes in real time. He theorised that it was something to do with how fast his mind worked. When running at that speed, it must go through hundreds – if not hundreds of thousands – of possibilities in comparison to the normal speed, which could potentially make it feel as if far more time had passed.

Heather had walked in from the adjoining connected room. Neither of them had noticed or heard her.

'That would mean...'

She made Jim jump. Instinctively he put his right hand over his heart. 'God damn it, woman, you scared the life out of me.'

With a sense of achievement she smiled at him. 'Why thank you! Happy to oblige.... As I was saying, if this is indeed an engineered stage 1 of an ongoing process and there is a stage 2 pathogen, that means the stage 2 one would be able to stop whatever is killing our victims. Or even reverse the damage done. There is absolutely no point recoding the basic functions of life – as Bradley is putting it – and have the overall human life form collapse before it can finish.'

Bradley looked at her – no, looked right through her. She had never been able to figure out what he was looking at when he did this. It unnerved her. He said, 'Moving on from that, it means there is a way for us to fix this or halt the damage.'

'All we would need to do is figure out what a stage 2 pathogen would do.' Heather finished his train of thoughts. When they were thinking along the same lines, she had the uncanny ability to do so. She looked at the screen where Jim had pulled up the DNA sample. 'No, nothing I can see here which would help. By the way, what made you guys get an actual DNA modelling sequence done in the first place?' she asked.

'We found incredibly high levels of topoisomerase in the patients' blood,' Jim explained.

She looked at him with a blank expression. Heather was not a geneticist. 'Bradley, would you...?'

'Topoisomerase is an enzyme in the blood which controls the unwinding of the DNA's double helix structure.' he explained.

'In English!' she snapped at him.

'Oh sorry, yes, it's an enzyme or chemical substance which splits or cuts the DNA. Actually, it changes its topology. Usually, our bodies produce it when it replicates the genome. These incredibly high levels are totally unusual because our bodies would never make and maintain so much of it permanently.'

'Hold, hold on, why don't we try to find a counter to that then? Wouldn't that stop the DNA splitting uncontrollably?' she asked.

'Therein lies the problem. If you try to stop it, you create an even bigger problem. Our bodies need to be able to do this in order to replicate the DNA. Stop that and everything goes into shutdown. You would cause something very similar to what is happening to our patients,' Bradley concluded.

'How about just slowing it down? You said there is a too much of it taking place. What if we could slow everything down to the point where you had some activity there, but it is so slow, that it would be the same as if you had only a normal or normal-like outcome?' she pondered.

'Hmm, that might work to stabilise things. Not sure of the impact but in theory' – he paused – 'and we are taking in theory here, a smaller fast process that has been slowed down should be similar to a larger one running at normal speeds.' He seemed to stare right through Heather into the space behind her. She knew this was his way of zoning out and allowing his mind to shoot miles ahead, but observing it happening was certainly disconcerting. After a few minutes, his gaze refocused and he looked straight at her once more. 'You know, it might actually work.' he concluded. 'Topoisomerase, of which there are two versions, needs iron to function. It is like its fuel. Starving it of iron would slow the entire thing down. We will need to be careful not to strip too much iron out of the system or it can lead to death. That, however, is easily managed as we have established norms for how much iron is needed by the human body. All we need to do is bring patients to the absolute minimum levels. That should stabilise things and buy us more time to find a cure to this perversion of the natural process.' Without warning, he turned on the spot and started heading out. On his way, he briefly turned to them both, and looked at Heather. 'Thanks for the help! I'm going to synthesis a serum.' The smile of excitement was clearly present all over his face.

Jim was happily typing away – actually, searching for something. 'I'll never get used to him, you know,' he joked.

'He does have his' – Heather took a few moments to find the term she was looking for – 'quirks.'

Jim exploded in laughter. 'Yes, our quirky scientist pursuing the quarks of creation! How's that for a punchline!' Both of them laughed.

Heather looked at the large display on the right. 'What the hell is that?' she asked, pointing to the mass of dark greens and black on the display.

'That, my dear, is the virus we are dealing with,' replied Jim.

She had never seen it visualised before – there had been no need. Something sent shivers up her spine. 'It creeps me out. That thing looks like something straight out of a horror movie.' She instinctively moved away from the screen, circled Jim, and shifted to his left side. She grabbed hold of his shoulder, startling him. He faced her, saw the look of sheer terror as she pointed to the screen displaying the virus.

'That THING just moved in the same direction I did. It's staring at me!' Her voice was full of fear.

'Calm down, Heather. It's a virus; it has no intelligence. Sometimes they just shift and jolt around. It's nothing specific; don't worry.'

She looked at him, back at the virus on screen, then Jim once more. She was not convinced. Something deep within her was terrified. 'I've got to go.' She had to get as far from it as possible. The reaction made no sense to her, but she followed it. She would get as far from that thing as she could and as fast as she could.

'See you soon.' Jim waved at her, trying to reassure her. He failed miserably. Heather was out of the door before she could even say goodbye.

As the door slid closed behind her, a deep sigh of relief escaped her lips. What had she been so afraid of? She couldn't tell. Something had not only terrified her but also spoke of untold danger, almost a threat. She thought about it and concluded in the most logical manner possible that yes, the virus was indeed a threat, and everyone here was trying to contain or counter it. Happy with her analysis, she made her way to her own lab, dismissing the whole incident. She would trust her decision, as she always did.

4

THE
- QUARK -
CONUNDRUM

Where was Yume working anyway? Bradley wondered. *Ah, quantum labs – I remember.* Making his way to the department, he felt queasy in the stomach. Something was wrong. His gut instinct was on alert. Something he had come to trust over the years, something he definitely disliked in this situation.

He arrived at the quantum research labs panting and out of breath. Getting to it had proven to be quite a trip. Unlike his own laboratory and offices, these were almost secluded to a fault, down long corridors and passageways. It was not difficult to find – it seemed all the pathways led straight to where he needed to be, but it was a long walk, to say the least.

'Oh, hi Bradley.' Yume saw him from behind the glass panels on the right. 'What are you doing here?'

'I'm looking for Kuroi. Can't seem to find her anywhere. Was hoping you might know?'

'No, afraid not. She was due to meet me here but never showed. I thought she might have been delayed with her own work.' Bradley's facial expression sank to a new low. 'Has something happened?' Now Yume was also starting to be concerned.

'I'm not sure, Yume. I just have this really bad feeling. It doesn't make sense for her to just disappear like that. You know how punctual and organised she is.'

Yume nodded in agreement. 'Let's see. Maybe we can re-trace her steps. She was at work, right?' Bradley nodded. 'Ok, then she was due to meet me.' She paused and looked at her watch. 'That would mean she had one hour to spare between her usual time leaving the office and being here...' She gave the impression of being totally lost in thought. Bradley did not want to interrupt – he knew this state of mind all too well; he did exactly the same thing. 'She must have stopped somewhere for a short break; going home would have been pointless since it would have taken her longer to get there and back here. Meaning, she must be somewhere on campus. But where... that is the question...' She seemed to hesitate. 'Wait a minute' – Bradley's face lit up momentarily – 'the gym! And the coffee place right next to it she loves so much!' Almost certain of her conclusion, Yume looked up at Bradley. 'Did you check either of those, by any chance?'

'No...'

He never had time to finish his sentence. One of the assistants from the lab came rushing towards Yume. 'Dr Yume, we need you to see this.' The excitement bubbling in the junior researcher's voice was most noticeable.

'Can't you see I'm in the middle of something?' she snapped back at him, slightly irritated.

'But doctor, you HAVE to see this, ' he insisted.

'I'll be there in a minute,' she told him.

'But doctor...' his voice trailed for a moment. 'You absolutely have to see this NOW.' He was adamant.

'Fine.' Now she was truly irritated. She turned to Bradley. 'You go check the gym in case Kuroi decided to have a quick workout before heading here.' Bradley agreed. 'And don't forget the coffee shop next to it.' Her voice was strict and to the point; he was not going to argue with her in his current mood. 'As for you, what the bleeding hell is this emergency?'

'You have to see this!'

'Yes yes, I've got that.' She left to join the rest of the team, who were suspiciously stuck to the monitoring system screens.

Bradley turned and made his way out heading back to the main campus. The gym was his goal, and he rushed away.

'There it goes; it's all moving! Dr Yume, do you see this!?'

She glared at the screen, blinked a few times, and then glared at it once more. 'What on Earth is it?' She looked at the young researcher who had practically bullied her to join them.

'We don't know, never seen anything like it before,' he admitted.

'Well you must have some idea surely?'

He simply shrugged. 'It's gone now.'

'Replay the recording. Please tell me you were recording the feed?'

Glaring at him made the young guy jump. 'Of course ma'am.' He hit the replay command. They all stared at what they were seeing, half locked in amazement while the other half were stuck in utter disbelief. They spent the next few hours trying to get an idea, any idea of what they were looking at.

Yume finally decided the best approach was one of logical observation rather than theory. 'Stop focusing on what you think you are all seeing. This is getting us nowhere,' she instructed. 'You.' She turned to the junior who had brought the whole thing to her. 'What do you see?'

'A quantum effect of some sort.'

'Yes, genius, we all know THAT. I mean observe the effect and separate out its component parts for me. Describe ONLY what you are observing.'

He busily started zooming in, separating various data channels and following a few hums and hesitations, went into the details. 'Well,' he said, 'doctor, this here looks like a field. My guess would be this inner structure you see here' – he pointed to a glow within the blur of radiation – 'these are a massive collection or rather amalgamation of W boson particles.' He paused for its significance to sink in. 'And here, these hyper augmented particles are neutrinos. Watch them interacting through the Z bosons.' A spark flared on the screen, then the patch of darker-coloured surroundings went hyper-brilliant for but an instant. A wave of brilliance split out, changed, and formed a wave of pure blackness. 'What you are observing doctor, is nuclear transmutation via the mediation of the W bosons in this cloud of stuff...' He waved over the screen. 'I believe – and this is a theory – that this is an endothermic process which is causing nuclear change. The impossible side of it is we are having no heat loss in the labs.' He turned to face the various meters flashing behind them. 'Which prompts the question: where is the heat coming from? Besides of course the fundamental question of what is causing this, and even more concerning: where and why it is happening...?'

Yume nodded.

'Such transmutation being completely unknown can be highly dangerous, but it seems we have not only lost the phenomenon from our visualisers and sensors but also its source.' He paused in thought. 'If it is in fact an endothermic reaction, where is the heat coming from? It must be using vast amounts of heat to fuel this type of "thing," whatever it is, and we are not losing any in our environment, even when the phenomenon was here.'

'From quantum space?' the junior scientist volunteered.

'Don't be ridiculous,' interjected the tall guy from behind him. 'There is no direct quantum-to-macro physical spill-over like that! The quantum affects the particles, which form matter. It is the change in particles that causes changes to matter. You don't move directly from quantum to material.'

'It was only a suggestion,' he said to defend himself.

'I think the main question for the time being is to find what is causing this. We can worry about finding what IT IS once we know where it is coming from. Gents, all eyes on search mode. Spread our sensor apparatus as far as possible, without it being too noticeable. Let's see if our equipment can catch sight of it again.' Yume walked out of the lab into the corridors. She picked up her phone and dialled Bradley's number.

'Hi, it's me. Any news? Did you find Kuroi?' she asked.

'Not at the gym right now. They had seen her but she left after having coffee, mentioning that she was meeting a friend at the university and had to rush.'

'That must mean she was heading my way. What time did she leave?' asked Yume.

'Right after lunch.'

'That means nearly three hours ago!'

'I know.' Bradley's voice seemed to have risen a few decibels. Concern was mounting. This was so unlike her.

'You know what, get back here and I'll get one of the guys here to hack into her phone's GPS. Don't ask, just get here as fast as you can.'

Bradley didn't need to be told twice. He was running. It only took him 10 minutes to make a good 20-minute trip back. He arrived huffing and puffing his lungs out. *Have to get fitter! Kuroi was so right,* he reprimanded himself.

'There you are. Let's get moving, follow me.' Yume made her way back towards the entrance of the lab and then right to the adjoining room. It was their main office.

'This is Elma.' She pointed at the scruffy looking young girl sitting in front of a set of screens. 'Elma knows the insides and out of everything to do with systems...' She hesitated. 'Even things she shouldn't know.' Elma turned around and smiled a broad, almost comical smile at Bradley. 'Elma, this is Bradley, Kuroi's boyfriend.'

'Boyfriend? Hey, nice. Very nice. I approve!' She smiled once more and winked at him. He saw immediately that she was teasing him in a playful manner. For a brief instant his tension lessened and he managed to smile back. 'I'm glad I have your approval.'

'Yes, yes, never mind all that,' interjected Yume. 'Elma, we need you to hack into the satellite system and track Kuroi's phone's GPS. She has gone missing somewhere in between the main campus gym and here. It's taken her three hours to get here!'

Elma just nodded and started furiously typing away. Her fingers slid over the keyboard with speed and grace. Bradley stared at her with an expression of utter amazement. Watching Elma hack away was like watching a pianist lost in the music.

'I'm in!' Excitement bubbled throughout her words. 'Pulling movement location data from lunchtime onwards. Hold on tight!'

She confused him. He could not understand why he needed to hold on nor what he was supposed to hold on to. He shrugged and continued staring at the computer screen right in front of Elma. It displayed a map of campus with a red location dot moving. They all watched intensely as the dot moved from the coffee place next to the gym towards the quantum laboratories. There! It was right next to them!

'This is her position as of...' Elma looked at the digital time display. 'Two hours and 42 minutes ago?!' She blurted out in surprise.

'Tell me where!' Bradley's words seemed pressing, edging to the point of being an outright command. Elma turned to face him, and saw his facial expression. 'At your command, captain!' She tried to lighten the mood, to no avail.

'This is where we are.' She pointed to the rectangular box on screen. 'On our left is the actual lab...' She held her breath. 'That would make this little area down the corridor behind the lab... the woman's toilets!'

'WHAT?' Yume was surprised. Bradley needed no reaction. Before anyone could say a single word, he had started running out of the office in the direction of the toilets. 'Damn it! He could have waited for us.' Yume stormed out after him. Elma sat there looking at the screen, noticing there had been no movement for over two and a half hours. She picked up her phone and called for help. In her mind, it was the only logical thing to do.

Bradley stormed past the students in the corridor, heading straight for the toilets. 'Oi! This is the women's. Men are on the other side of the building,' interrupted one student heading in the same direction.

'Out of my way,' he yelled at her. He didn't care what anyone said or what anyone wanted – he had to find Kuroi. There, he reached it. He pushed the door open and walked in. It was silent. He looked about: no-one was in sight. He moved from cubicle to cubicle. As he banged the doors of each one open, one of the staff members made her way in, and saw him.

'What the hell do you think you're doing? Get out you pervert!' she screamed at him. 'Or I'll call security.' He ignored her. She came up to him and started pushing him out of the way. He ignored it. He had more than sufficient strength to make her attempts nothing more than minor inconveniences. The third cubicle to the end, he pushed, and the door was locked.

'Kuroi!' he yelled. No reply. Nothing to do about it. He went into the cubicle next to it and pushed past the woman trying to pull him out of there, then stood on the toilet. This allowed him to peer over the top of the cubicles. He saw her. Kuroi was there, collapsed unconscious.

'You pervert! I'm going to call security, what the hell do you think you are doing! I'll report you to the Dean and have you thrown out.' He was horrified at seeing Kuroi unconscious and beyond fearful. He turned around and in a cold harsh tone replied, 'Shut up.

Touch me one more time and you will regret it. Make yourself useful and call for help instead.' He didn't even look at her and made his way out, then started trying to bash in the door to the cubicle, where Kuroi lay unconscious.

The woman took out her phone and dialled campus security. 'We have a male intruder in the woman's toilet at the quantum section. Please send someone fast. He's dangerous, and violent, and threatening me!'

At that moment, Yume walked in glanced back and forth and immediately reacted. She took the phone out of the woman's hands. 'Hey, what are you doing?'

'Hello? Security, right?' she asked.

'Yes ma'am, who are you? What is going on?' asked the officer at the other end of the line.

'This is Yume Nasakawi, head of the quantum research division. Please get medical support here immediately. One of our staff members has collapsed in the woman's toilets, and is not responding. Bradley here' – she stared at the other woman, who was all flustered and angry – 'her boyfriend is trying to break through the door in the cubicle to get to her.'

'Immediately ma'am, I'll get the support team here too. They have keys to get through.' The line went dead.

Yume handed the phone back to the woman. 'Next time maybe try to assess the situation before being all offended and thinking you are the one in danger?' She walked up to Bradley and put her hand on his shoulder as he had paused in his assault at the door. He turned and saw her. 'I can't get in, damn it! So bloody weak...'

'Help is on the way; they are just down the second corridor. Won't be long.' He nodded then moved a few steps back and hurled himself against the door. It didn't budge. He paused. *Wait wait wait!* he yelled mentally to himself. He went into the cubicle next door. 'What are you doing?' asked Yume.

'Stopping being the stupid idiot I am,' he responded. He jumped onto the toilet, grabbed hold of the panel, and heaved himself up. He came crashing down inside Kuroi's cubicle. Thankfully, he landed near her rather than on top of her. He turned and unlocked it from inside. He knew what to do, immediately lifted her up, unsure where he had found the strength to do that, carried her out and lay her on the floor, and checked for a pulse. 'Thank god,' was his response.

Yume looked very concerned. 'What should we do?' she asked.

He ignored her. He put his hand half an inch over Kuroi's mouth. He felt the very mild pull and push of air. 'She's breathing.'

The medical team made its entrance. 'Make room,' they instructed. Bradley looked in their direction and saw it was a full-blown emergency team. Silently he stood up and moved back. Security was there as well. 'Sir, we need to speak with you,' the officer said.

Yume stepped in. 'Now is not the time. Can't you see he's in shock? I'll speak to you.' She nodded to him and signalled for them to step out the door.

'We've had reports of this man being aggressive and assaulting a women in here, which is the woman's toilets,' the officer explained.

'Assaulting?' asked Yume.

'Yes ma'am,' replied the security officer.

'No such thing. If by assault you mean he might have been rude to that woman from whom I grabbed the phone, then she was calling you in order to get help here. I don't know.'

'So you were the one who assaulted her?'

'Of course not. Seriously.' Yume was getting annoyed. 'Is she hurt?'

'Seems shaken to me.'

'Well, you try finding someone unconscious in the ladies room and not knowing what do to. I think you would be shaken too. What I am asking is' – and she emphasised the next part – 'is she physically hurt in any way, shape or form?'

'Doesn't appear to be, but that doesn't exclude verbal assault by this man,' insisted the officer.

'Verbal assault? You mean if I tell you to move out of my way as I dash forward to help someone, I'm assaulting you? Isn't that a bit of a strong word?' She paused. 'You do realise that words are not going to make someone bleed or injure, right?'

'That is not for me to decide. The law states that verbal assault is assault.'

'Well then put it this way, I was here for the entire incident and I have not heard him say anything even remotely offensive to her. He was in a state because he had rushed into the toilets looking for his girlfriend, who I am certain you can verify for yourself is seriously injured and unconscious.'

'I will check, ma'am.'

'Yes, do so, and you might also want to check the fact that she has been here for nearly three hours without anyone reporting it. I thought security or at least maintenance was supposed to ensure something like this did not happen. Someone... must have been checking. For three hours, I tell you! This might have been all avoided if someone had been doing their job and called for help sooner.' She was about to walk away but decided to add a little icing on the cake: 'especially in view of the alert for a weaponised bug going round.'

His eyes narrowed momentarily. 'Thank you for your statement ma'am, I'll continue the investigation. If we need more we will be in touch.'

'You do that.' She walked back into the women's toilets to find Bradley starring at Kuroi, who was strapped down on an emergency carrier and being taken to hospital. She came to his side, put her hand on his right shoulder and gently whispered, 'It will be all right, don't worry.' He stood still. He might as well have been a living statue. She interrupted the medical staff: 'Where are you taking her?'

'To the hospital around the corner. Accidents and emergency department for now; they will assess what to do next. I cannot recognise any patterns of symptoms at this point in time. All we know is that she is unconscious but stable.'

'Thank you.'

'Just so you know, I cannot let you accompany us there,' he added.

'Why on Earth not?' Bradley interrupted the conversation.

'Because everyone here will need to go and get tested. There is a medical alert active in the university, hospital, and bio-laboratories. Everyone will have to go and get tested. Even though I do not think this is related, we have to follow protocols.'

Yume nodded. 'Come,' she said to Bradley, taking hold of his hand. 'We're going to get you a nice strong coffee before we all go get tested and then see her.' He just nodded. Yume was really worried. She had never seen him so shell-shocked. Usually even in the worst situations, Bradley would try to lighten the mood with his charming witty conversation-stoppers. He was totally numb. As she pulled on his arm, he moved.

They returned to the office. Bradley sat down at the desk, still half unresponsive, muttering to himself. 'She couldn't have been infected...' he mumbled. 'How could she have been exposed...?' On and on his mind worked, trying to conceive the inconceivable.

Yume looked at him. She wanted to hug him and tell him it would be all ok, but she too knew that it might not be. Until they knew for sure, it was impossible to tell and nothing but hard cold facts could convince Bradley.

'Here drink this.' She handed him a cup of strong hot coffee. 'It will make you feel better.' Bradley looked at it and just started sipping.

Her assistant barged in. 'Dr Yume, come quick, quick,' he called out to her.

'Good god, man. Now of all times? Can't you see I'm dealing not with one but two crises?'

'It's about' – he looked at Bradley – 'you know what? It's here now!' Excitement was plastered all over his face.

Yume looked at him, then at Bradley, then back at him. 'Fine.' She turned to Bradley. 'Will you be ok for a few minutes?' She was still concerned about leaving him alone.

He looked up. 'Who me? Yes, sure, I'm fine.' He took another sip of his coffee. She judged from the amount of coffee still in the cup it would take him about 10 minutes or more to get through it. That was the amount of time she had. She nodded and followed the assistant next door into the lab. All her colleagues were there, staring intently at the screen. They moved aside to let her pass. There it was: the same quantum particle mass as before and it was static.

She glared at it for a few seconds, absorbed it structure and size, then turned to the assistant. 'Can we get a location on this thing?' she asked.

'Not very specific yet. Still working on that but I would estimate it to be no more than a few meters from our location.'

'WHAT?' she gasped 'Are we in danger? Anyone figured out what this thing is doing or is yet? Other than absorbing heat?'

'Here let me help.' Elma shoved her way to the computer, pushing the others to the left and right as she barged her way through.

'You lot might be good with your quantum stuff, but I am the expert when it comes to computers. Out of my way.' She pushed the young assistant out of his chair and sat down. She starting punching away at the keys on the keyboard. The display glared out, and the image and mappings shifted from one view to another. Space was redefined using exact coordinates and measured to the inch. A few minutes later, she giggled. 'There, that should make tracking it easier, now let us have a peek-a-boo...' She zoomed in, then overlapped the map of the university onto the quantum space view. 'Bingo! It is coming from next door.' She stood up and left, waving her hand in a good-bye over her shoulder. 'You can buy me coffee later on as a thank you, boys and girls. My work is done!' She walked to the other side of the lab and sat back down at her own desk.

'Next door?' said the young assistant.

'Oh no; Bradley is sitting there having coffee.' Yume darted out and towards the office. 'Bradley!' she yelled out. She was just about to step through the doorway when she bumped into him, nearly sending the two of them flying backwards. Fortunately, Bradley always had a very firm footing and he caught her.

'Hummm sorry.' She pulled back from his chest, into which she had slammed unceremoniously.

'What's the rush?' he asked.

She looked up at him. He seemed to be back to normal – or at least to what appeared to be normal. 'We need to get out of the office, now!' Without thinking it through she grabbed his hand and dragged him out towards the lab.

'Hmm, Yume?' Bradley interrupted.

'Yes?'

'I do enjoy you holding me by the hand but I can walk on my own, you know.'

She glanced at his hand and saw that she was indeed holding it, then glanced up at his face, then back at their hands. Abruptly she pulled back. 'Oh sorry.' Embarrassment washed over her. 'Follow me,' was all she said as they entered the quantum research labs where she worked.

'Everyone, this is Bradley, Kuroi's boyfriend.' She emphasized those words out of guilt at having grabbed his hand a few seconds ago.

Bradley didn't seem to be concerned with it, though she felt very guilty for breaching protocol and invading his personal space when unwarranted to do so.

'Pleased to meet you all.' Bradley nodded to practically the entire team who were standing at the display mesmerised, as if by some alluring enchantment. He moved closer and looked at the screen, waved, moved back and waved again. 'Is that me?' he spoke out loud.

All their heads instantly shifted from the displays to him, back to the displays and then back at him. Elma, who was observing from the other side of the room, exploded in laughter at the scene unfolding right in front of her eyes. It was pure comedy. Bradley waved again, and as he did so, the quantum mass they were observing poked out and moved in the same motion before settling back into its habitual shape. The young assistant's mouth was left open in surprise.

'What?' asked Bradley. 'Anyone care to tell me what the heck is the matter with you all? You look as if you have seen a horror movie come to life!'

Elma walked over from her desk, grabbed Bradley under the arm, and explained. 'They are all gobsmacked by the monumental ground-breaking mind-defying discovery that they have been scanning a human being. That's all. Give them a few minutes, Bradley dear. It's not every day you encounter a human being. Those things are very rare and totally mind-blowingly unbelievably incomprehensible to us. Come see what I've been working on. So much more interesting, I promise.' She winked at the assistant and dragged Bradley to her own desk, cracking up in laughter.

'I've got to go see Kuroi,' he objected.

She didn't give sway and kept pulling him away from the screens. Bradley had no choice but to follow. As he did, the mass on the screen moved further from its initial location and diminished in intensity, only to pop up stronger at the other end of the lab.

'We have to get him back here! In the full range of the sensors!' insisted the young assistant.

'Analyse what we have so far,' instructed Yume. 'He's not quite himself at the moment and will want to ensure Kuroi is well before agreeing to anything.'

'But ma'am, we...'

Yume interrupted him, raising her hand and making the sign for silence, just as Bradley escaped Elma and make his way back.

'I'm going to see Kuroi. Are you coming along?' he asked Yume.

'I will join you in a little while. Have to wrap a few things here and make sure none of these lot get into any trouble during my absence.'

He nodded and walked out of the labs.

'Ok what did you get from him this time?' She faced her assistant.

'We have the atomic transmutation taking place in this area.' He pointed at the dark spots fusing into each other on screen. 'The heat absorption is not environmental, and our temperature readings did not detect any decrease in the labs or anyone in his vicinity.'

'Well that's a relief,' she admitted. A heat drain in proximity of his body would have been very problematic to deal with.

'However,' continued the assistant, 'there is a drawing of some types of particles from the environment I have never seen before.'

'Explain!'

'We have never seen anything of their sort.'

'What on Earth do you mean? If you are picking it up, it must be a known particle!' she insisted.

'Afraid not. They are shifting into and out of the range of sensors and look like...' he paused for thought.

'Ah, damn it fool, spit it out,' interrupted the tall researcher standing behind him.

'They look like neutralinos. Well, to be more accurate, more like the theorised squarks of the shadow parts of the particles in supersymmetric theories.'

'But that's impossible,' objected Yume.

'Fun, is it not? Should this prove correct, we are dealing with a direct manifestation of dark matter and supersymmetry.'

'You're not serious?' Yume looked at the tall researcher who stared back at her and nodded affirmatively.

'Your friend is somehow experiencing or causing a cloud of dark matter to coalesce within him. Naturally, this is just an out-there guesstimate. We have no way to confirm this, even with all our facilities.'

'So what do we do?' asked the young assistant.

Yume stood there lost in thought for a few moment. 'Let me think.

Logic would dictate that if this phenomenon is either following or originating within Bradley, AND it's gathering particles or shadowy squarks as proposed, we could find a way to amplify that effect.'

'You're not serious?' the tall researcher objected. 'You have absolutely no idea what that could do to him!'

'Well, gents, we are scientists, are we not? Let's find out.'

'You're not serious?' he repeated again.

'Damn well am! There is a Nobel Prize at stake here and I AM getting it.'

'This is totally unethical,' he pointed out.

'Since when do particles and shadow particles have ethics considerations attached to them?'

'Maybe since this is happening to a person!' he replied.

'Minor inconvenience. We're only concerned with the particles and squarks, as you call them, not with whom they are attached to. Besides, if that theory is correct, pulling them out of him might be a good thing and totally harmless.'

'You are serious, aren't you?' he finally prompted.

'Absolutely!'

'Well I want no part of it.' He walked away from the rest of them.

'No big loss,' she concluded. 'All I need is you.' She pointed to the young assistant operating the software and display. 'And you.' She pointed to one of the guys operating the equipment. They both nodded, driven by curiosity and excitement. 'I'll worry about getting Bradley back here and try to make him amplify this phenomenon.' She was about to walk out of the lab in order to catch up with Bradley, then stopped and turned to face them. 'Needless to say, this is highly secret. Not a word of this to anyone! And guys, make sure you have protocols to erase ALL the data off the systems instantly, in case we get discovered.'

'Yes, ma'am.'

'Before I get back, that is!'

'That's not a lot of time...'

'Well better get started then, and if you come up with any brilliant ideas on how to make this phenomenon quicker, you both get extra credits and time off!' She smiled at them, then walked out, heading towards the main hospital wing.

5

THE
- DECISION -

Mira woke up early, as usual. She was an early bird, and 4.30 am was her time. It had the distinct advantage of being quiet: no phones and no emails would be going off at this time. Yes, the international work still continued. However, she found that 4.30 to 5.30 – maybe even 6 if she was lucky – would be rather uneventful. She liked it that way. It gave her time to prepare for the day, to gather her thoughts and set out her plans for what had to be done and more importantly by whom!

In the bathroom, she headed straight for the shower. She loved showering, and never understood why, but the water cascading over her slender figure reminded her of something deep within – yet for all her efforts, she could not remember what it was. As the steam coalesced into droplets, they would gently trickle down her almost perfect creamy caramel hued skin. She enjoyed it – that is what mattered to her. If she had the time she would have had several showers a day. Her long wavy black hair felt heavy. Her relationship with her hair was a discordant one. On the one hand she loved it, on the other, the amount of time and effort needed to look after it irritated her no end. She stepped out of the shower and checked the time. *5 minutes: precisely on time.* A sense of satisfaction swelled within her. Everything was going according to her plans – that is how all lives should be. She absentmindedly took hold of the towel and started drying up.

Mira saw herself as the great disciplinarian, mostly due to the fact that as a child she'd lacked that discipline until one day, she realised it was the key. That fateful day when her father had to leave the country for work, leaving her mother and sisters behind. She remembered patiently waiting for his return, only to be told each and every time that he would be coming home next week. One week became two, two quickly became four, months turned into years. She never saw him again. As far as she was concerned they had all been abandoned.

One thing she was grateful for was the fact that unlike other families around them, they didn't want for much. Her life as a child was not luxurious by any means but it was comfortable. She always had new clothes, she had a moderate number of toys to play with, and she was afforded a good education. Deep down, however, she secretly would have given up all those things. As she grew up, she found out that all these things were provided from the income of her father's work. Her mother would tell her on countless occasions what great sacrifice he had made, giving up his time with them in order to make sure they had a good life, with good opportunities. She would be reminded to make the most of them. At other times she found her mother crying in bitter loneliness. She tried to comfort her, remind her that she and her sisters were there for her. Instinctively, she knew it was not enough, and this drove her determination, it fuelled her resolve. She would never be in a position where life would force her to make such choices: never! She would control life itself, if need be.

With that final thought on the matter, she stepped out of the shower and put on her makeup. It was becoming a daily chore. She used to enjoy it in her younger days but now she had begun to hate it. *Why do we women have to lose our beauty and appeal so fast?* she wondered. *In my mid-30s it all started to go downhill.* Looking at her reflection in the mirror made her ponder on life. It was just unfair. Men aged gracefully, and once they matured, their appeal and charm was increased rather than fading, yet women after that certain age seemed to lose it all. In frustration, she threw her makeup against the bathtub, making a small scratch in the perfect marble-like stone it was made from. *This is damn unfair and unjust! I will have justice, one way or another!*

Her outburst brought her mind right back into the moment. Yes, she would initiate the project and it would work! It simply had to work. Replacing the decaying parts of human biology and repairing those which could be repaired would enable her to preserve all that nature was taking from her, as well as keep all she had achieved.

'I will not sacrifice my looks for success. I WILL have both. I reject all this nonsense about having to sacrifice the one for the other,' she muttered, in a spur of determination. *Never go against the natural flow of things, my dear. Doing so leads to evil and despair.* The words of her grandmother boomed within her thoughts. It made her jump, almost as if she was hearing them all anew.

'Screw natural law! I will not have anything or anyone telling me what to do! I will prove you wrong – all of you.'

She took a deep breath, heading out of the bathroom she caught a blurred glimpse of her reflection in the large mirror. 'I will have it all, damn the laws of nature, damn fate and damn it all.' Determination echoed within her words. 'I WILL do anything I need to change things, for everyone.' Her path of action was set, her grandmother's ancient wisdom pushed aside. Why would the modern generation need to be lumbered with all that past mumbo-jumbo nonsense anyway? This was the age of science of enlightenment, not superstition. 'Damn it all,' she whispered.

A voice boomed from within: 'Would you?'

She jumped, pressing against the towel held against her body. 'Who's there? Show yourself!' she commanded. 'I'm calling the police.'

No response. No-one was in sight. She looked once more in the mirror: nothing out of the ordinary. She decided she had imagined it all.

Would you do anything? It echoed again, directly within her mind.

'Damn it show yourself, you bastard!' She grabbed her small scissors, trying to appear threatening. Oddly, she felt no fear. What was coursing through her was aggression pure and simple: she was ready to fight.

Stop being such a weakling and answer the question! echoed the voice within her mind.

'Weakling! How dare you! I'm no weakling. Show yourself and I'll prove it!'

Pain ripped through her head. The occasional migraine was nothing in comparison to this. She felt as if something was splitting her skull from within in thousands of places simultaneously. *Answer the question...* the voice insisted.

'Fine. Damn it, yes I'd do anything. I will not be dictated to by nature, fate, or people. I don't care who or what they are!' Her pain and anger merged in her voice.

Very well.

'Whatever. I'm far too busy for this nonsense. My fate is decided by myself, and I have made my decision. I will have it my way.' She paused, reflecting. 'I must be going mad, hearing voices...' She put down her towel on the sink and walked out of the bathroom in order to get ready for her morning run.

Mira shook her head from side to side, interrupting her trip down memory lane. There was no time for that. She had a schedule to follow and with that she got dressed. She dressed in a perfectly tailored business suit, black of course. It had to be black, but it definitely never was plain. She would always make sure not only that the brand was one of the top brands, but also that something on the suit or the material itself stood out. She had to be dressed appropriately and somewhat discreetly but there was no reason why everyone who encountered her did not have to be reminded that she had wealth, incredible amounts of wealth. It was the one thing she just loved showing to the world. It represented her achievements, the end result of all her hard work. She smiled. Today, she picked the satin-lined suit with beautifully embroidered thin golden patterns along the sleeves and collar. She finished by putting on her watch, diamond encrusted 18 carat gold and her six carat black diamond earrings. That would do. There was nothing worse than overdoing it with the jewellery. Nice and to the point. Leaving the whole incident behind, she left her apartment and headed out for work. Action, she determined, was what was needed. None of these mental shenanigans ever proved to be of any use, let alone any productive use. She approved of her firm decisive nature. She liked it. It had served her well and would keep on doing so.

Bradley stormed into the expanse of long white corridors, rushing towards the emergency department. The smell of clinical ammonia permeated the air: strong, insistent, impossible to ignore. Yes, he was so accustomed to it, but he still disliked it. This specific odour had been haunting him his entire life. He'd never learnt to like it and he failed miserably at ignoring it completely. His body as usual was on autopilot – a peculiar skill of his which allowed him to set a goal in mind and simply go. He had always thought of it as programming in the destination and running that program. It allowed him to think of other more important things, while his body got him to where he needed to be. He had always deducted that this was what instinctively happened when his drunk colleagues always somehow managed to get back home. Right now, his mind was racing along a whole range of possibilities, working out their likelihood, their impact, and what he could do to counter the worst of them. Dread and almost something akin to the very uncharacteristic state of panic had grabbed hold of him. He stormed onward, the sense of dread creeping up the back of his spine.

'Bradley?' Dr Martin interrupted him.

'Where is she?' asked Bradley, pressing to get to Kuroi.

'You mean Kuroi?' responded Martin.

'Of course I mean Kuroi!' he snapped. 'Who else would make me run down here?' He was irritated at the conversation. All he wanted was answers. He had no time for idle chit chat.

'Bradley, take a deep breath and slow down,' instructed Martin.

'You're right.' Bradley gave in, acknowledging he was too agitated, his mind almost so distracted that it was so focused single-mindedly on the worst possible scenario. 'Tell me, Martin, where is she? I want to see her!' He took another deep breath. He had to wrestle back control of his emotions. Now was not the time to allow them to run riot. It was the only way to calm down his frantic mind. He had to think clearly! *Easier said than done,* he admitted to himself as he took yet another deep breath.

'She's here but you cannot see her yet.'

'Why on Earth not?' A hint of agitation bordering on aggression manifested in Bradley's tone and posture. Should the need to fight his way through arise, he was fully prepared to do so. This was Kuroi, and her very life was at stake. It was the one time he was fully prepared to fight.

'She's been infected.'

Hearing those words, Bradley's world shattered. In that one instant, all meaning, all purpose, all hopes and all dreams crashed into millions of pieces. He lost his balance and all his strength faded away.

Martin caught him and propped him up. 'Come, you need to sit down.' No objection came forth from Bradley. His mind was blank. Something inside of him had broken, something in him had been crushed. He was totally defeated. Martin guided him to the chairs in the main waiting room and sat down next to him. They remained silent for a while. Martin placed his hand on Bradley's shoulder to stir him. 'She will be alright. We will find a way to get her through.'

'I want to see her, Martin, I need to see her.'

'I'm afraid I cannot allow that.'

'Why on Earth not?' objected Bradley.

'Bradley,' Martin gave him a gentle shove. 'You know better than any of us. I cannot risk anyone else being infected. I understand you want to see her but we have limited facilities here. The quarantine prevents me from letting anyone in.'

'I need to see her,' Bradley insisted.

'Ok, this is what we will do. I will take you to the front of her room and you can see her through the main glass wall. That is all we can do at the moment. We only have one isolation suit here' – he paused – 'and no, you can't have it. I need a medic in there around the clock.'

The word 'suit' echoed in his mind. 'Suit, of course.' He turned to Martin and in a moment of loss of composure, grabbed hold of both of Martin's shoulders 'I have a suit in the labs! Protocols requires me to have one.' A hint of urgency etched itself on his face.

'Bradley' – a momentary pause seemed to extend forever – 'listen to me carefully. This is a terrible thing that has happened, no one can argue that. I understand your concerns.... But you must not lose your focus.'

Bradley looked straight at Martin. His left eyebrow arched, making him appear to both pay attention and make it clear that whatever was spoken next could lead to a dangerous confrontation.

This body language was not lost on Martin, who swallowed instinctively. 'You're the lead researcher on whatever this thing is. The best thing you can do for Kuroi and the other patients is to keep your focus on finding the cure. The rest of us can only work on stabilising them but we cannot cure them. Only your team can do that.'

The words struck a chord. Bradley seemed to pause, his mind processing every spoken word. Without further argument, he stood up, looked in Kuroi's direction, then faced Martin. 'You'd better make damn sure nothing happens until we find that cure!'

The implications and seriousness of his words did not escape Martin. 'I'll do my best, Bradley, you know that.'

He did know. It only took the briefest of moments for him to consider the extent of the situation. 'Very well,' he concluded. He left, walking out of the clinic slowly and methodically.

Martin observed his departure. *Something is wrong; no one walks like that. It's almost unnatural to be so controlled.* Brushing the thought aside, he rushed back to his patients.

Yume sat on two rows of chairs opposite them, listening in on the conversation, lost in her own thoughts. *I need to find a way to get him back into the lab. Damn it, this turn of events means he will be far too focused on his work to even consider such a diversion.* 'Ah well, all things come in good time to those who wait,' she whispered.

Martin's piercing, inquisitive look locked in and onto Yume. It made her uncomfortable. She stood up and left the waiting room without a further word. 'Odd one that,' mused Martin as he caught the fleeting words and glance of her, in between his rush from one patient to the other, located on northern wing of the hospital.

6

NEW
- DISCOVERY -

Elma put her phone down. 'Well, time for some serious work!' She giggled, got up and headed over to get her usual energy drink. She loved the stuff. It would send her mind speeding forth like nothing else and THAT was when she did some of her best work. She looked at her digital watch. 'Lunchtime in 10 minutes. Perfect: I'll have some privacy.' She needed it. According to her calculations, by the time she walked down the corridor and got her can of wonders – as she referred to those energy shots of hers – then made her way back, everyone would have gone for lunch. It was perfect. She smiled. 'Oh, how nice it is when things go perfectly.' She cracked the bones on her fingers, making the joints pop in preparation for a serious typing session. *Time for some real fun! Let the challenge begin...*

Heather stared into the microscope. She focused in on the virus: what a horrific thing. She had never seen anything like it. It made her feel even more uneasy. Something about it suggested to her that it was observing her. Once more, she shook her head. *All this is making me imagine things. Get back with it, girl!* she told herself.

This was not like her: she never wandered off into her imagination or daydreaming. She reverted back to her long-lasting ally: logic. Something about this virus made her curious. Something was almost too perfect about it. She lifted her gaze from the microscope and flicked through the genetics report. Since Kuroi had been taken ill, she'd taken over Kuroi's work. This was a matter of utter urgency and national security, so it could not wait. She read the file carefully. Genetics had been one of Heather's all-time favourite topics of study and research, especially viral genomes. They were all working on the theory that this had been engineered. So far, everything had proved that correct: its ability to alter very specific gene sequences in the infected and what it did with those alterations was too precise. *But why? And how did it come about?* It bothered her.

Usually, they were not very concerned about someone hijacking the CRISPR Cas9 technology because it relied on modifying a known virus to do its work. They had extensive knowledge bases of all of those. Using that knowledge to unravel any mutated viruses was simple. Yet this one lacked all ancestral roots of smallpox, Hantavirus and Marburg, and had no similarity with Ebola, HIV or the influenza virus. Its very DNA structures were unlike those of any virus she had ever seen.

Heather looked into the microscope again. 'Is this even a virus?' she muttered. Something was seriously wrong. They were dealing with a totally unknown source virus, which had then been modified and reengineered. But how? It made no sense. You could not just modify an unknown virus and target its effects so precisely. She wanted to understand this. She needed to. After what seemed like hours of reflection and contemplation through reams of data, she forced herself to have a break. She needed to stretch and move.

Time for a well-earned cup of soothing tea, with two teaspoons of sugar. She smiled. It amused her no end how sugar was demonised. She knew better; her research had shown that it was an essential for the brain. Without it the intellect, mind and reasoning abilities would not work optimally. She knew all too well how they would slow down. Ideas would not flow and speed of thinking would grind to a creeping crawl. She had ensured their staff kitchen had an ample selection of the best herbal teas and an ample supply of organic sugar! Thoughts of her break from work brought her mind back to Bradley. *Wonder what the boy is up to? Hope he's making progress. We need to resolve this for all our sakes. The poor guy must be going through hell.*

The phone rang. She picked it up, and before she could even greet the other person, Bradley spoke.

'Heather, look at the virus on the smallest scale,' he instructed.

'Ok, give me a moment. Need to move the plates over.' She took the sample kept safely in between two specially constructed thin and incredibly strong glass plates and moved them onto the specialised microscope in the labs. She zoomed in, more and more, until she was at the nano-scale. Holding her breath, she looked in.

'Good God. Bradley, are you still there?'

'Yes, what do you see?' he asked.

'It's entirely different from the first one we looked at.'

'Thanks. I needed someone to confirm this for me.'

'Wait a sec...' She took an even closer look. Her hands started shaking, perspiration dripped down her forehead, and she pulled back. 'Brad, come over here.'

'Why? What's wrong.'

'NOW.'

'Ok, Ok, on my way, hold tight.'

It took only three minutes before he rushed through the sliding doors, fully suited in his protective gear. For an instant, Heather jumped back at the sight of him as he caught her by surprise.

'It's only me,' he spoke through the suit.

She pointed at the equipment and in a trembling voice spoke: 'Look.'

He cautiously approached it and took a peek. What he saw took his breath away. It was not just the viral matter anymore; there was some sort of mechanical structure there, only visible at the nano scale. 'It's gene editing combined with nanotechnology?!' His own voice showed fear. 'This is far beyond our abilities to deal with.' He looked at it once more, trying to discern more details. Zooming in further, he saw golden metals – *a perfect conductor* he surmised. 'Definitely engineered!' He continued to gaze at the horror right in front of them. It moved in his direction as if trying to stare right at him! It made him jump backwards and away from it and the microscope. 'That... this... is intelligent! It just turned towards me! It knows we are looking at it.'

'I want nothing to do with that!' stated Heather. 'This is beyond my ability to deal with AND we should not be going down this path.'

'Heather, get a grip. This thing is killing people. It is aimed at us scientists and medics. Someone has to deal with it!' Bradley snapped at her. He knew she didn't really mean what she was saying. He understood the effects of shock. 'Go report to Dr Grimsaw. I'll deal with it.' He had to get her out of the labs at any costs. She just stared at him. 'Heather, dear, go now, tell your grampa!' He knew how angry she got when anyone openly pointed out her familial connections in the lab but he had to do something to snap her out of it.

'How dare you! You of all people! You know full well that I am here because of my qualifications –'

She never finished the sentence. He interrupted her. 'Good, you're back. Now go report to Dr Grimsaw. He needs to know what we have found.'

She hesitated for a moment, then broke out in a smile. 'You sneaky son of a...!' She turned and ran out of the door yelling 'Thanks.'

Bradley returned to the microscope and saw the files on the left. He went through them. 'Ah, gene sequencing results. This will be useful.' He read through them. He was not familiar with the viral ones but he knew more than his fair share from what Kuroi had shared with him. The report, however, provided the summary he needed. An unknown virus genotype – totally unique.

'This is not possible,' he stated out loud, even though there was no one else there. 'How can anyone engineer an unknown virus and combine that with nanotech modules?' *Heather said it was different from the first one... could someone be experimenting on specific individuals and modifying their designs, based on the effects?* The very thought angered him: using human beings as guinea pigs was unacceptable to him, even though his colleagues always did so with volunteers, or with those who were so desperate they had no other choice. He himself never wanted to go even close to those options.

This, however, was something altogether different. This was killing humans in order to complete a designed technology. Anger rose within him. *This is why Kuroi is on her deathbed! Someone's playing God and using us to do it.* Something in him was snapping. His thoughts turned inward, his senses sharpened. *I want to destroy the whole lot of them, them and their bloody work!* He admitted to himself.

Like a burning flare, rage flared and the flow of power broke through the dam deep within him...

7

THE
- ILLUSION -
DROPS

It was like a bell ringing, a bell only Bradley could hear. A door deep inside his mind opened. He felt uneasy and dizzy. He took in a deep breath, moved backwards and pulled the wheeled office chair from under the desk towards him. He sat down. His head spun even more. For an instant he closed his eyes. It took a few moments for things to stabilise. The dizziness faded. His eyes opened, he glanced about. Then he closed them, rubbed them hard, reopened them and looked around once more.

Bradley's vision blurred. He had a momentary lapse of perception where everything just became an almost fluid image, temporal, volatile. He tried to refocus, gave up, then quickly closed his eyes to avoid blanking out. He felt it: it was almost like a caress, a gentle summer time wind touching his skin stirring his senses back to life. Would he dare open his eyes anew? The sounds he was hearing were unfamiliar. Curiosity got the best of him. He opened them, rubbed them for a few seconds and refocused on the world about.

He was no longer in the labs. His protective suit was nowhere to be seen either. The air was fresh and oddly unfamiliar. It filled his lungs with energy, and his senses were in overdrive. Not a trace of stuffiness. It was as clear as the air at top of the mountains. There was no heaviness in his breath. He looked to his, left then his right, and backwards, then upwards. His hands touched the ground on which he was sitting. He could not believe what his senses were telling him. *What happened and where the heck am I?* he pondered. He took another deep breath. Oh how he longed for this: clean air. He already felt lighter and his mood improved instantly. *Amazing what a breath of fresh air can do, but where am I?*

'Are you ok?' asked an unfamiliar voice. Someone poked at him.

'I think he's alive,' answered another.

'Well of course he's alive, you bloody fool. He's standing here and breathing. How could he not be alive?' prompted the initial voice.

Bradley's sight had regained some level of clarity. He looked at the two men standing beside him. What he saw was so unfamiliar that the shock forced him to close his eyes again and decide that he must be dreaming. That any instant, he would wake up with his head lying flat on his keyboard. He felt the poking again.

'I still think he's dead.'

'Oh stop being such a fool, Darvinius. He's just trying to adjust. You know how the shift can be brutal,' reprimanded Darenian.

'Well it can kill too, and I'm still not certain this one is alive,' objected the other. The two almost identical twins kept on arguing.

The sheer irritation was all that was needed for Bradley to gain a solid foothold. 'You will two cut it out already!' he snapped.

Both of them went silent, stood still and glared at him. Darenian turned to his twin. 'See? Told you he was alive!'

'I still think we should just decide he's dead and take his corpse away. It would fetch a good reward from you know who.'

'Absolutely not! You damned WonkerDudel, you know the harm that would do if anyone found out.'

Bradley had no idea what either of them was referring to. Instead he observed them both closely, trying to assess the situation. Their attire was most peculiar. They wore brightly coloured skin-tight fabric into which were affixed all sorts of what appeared metallic and crystalline gizmos. The total appearance was a fine mix of comical and technical. The best description he could think of was that they were techno-clowns. Both the twins were slim; slightly taller than himself, dark hair, pale skin with piercing green eyes. The profit-obsessed Darvinius wore darker colours, navy blues, turkey yellows, greys and deep greens, with a tinge of blood reds and deep violets. His brother, on the other hand, had brighter equivalents of the same colouring in different patterns. Both of them wore what looked like engineer's jewellery. Their earrings looked almost mechanical. Cogwheels and levers seemed to be themed in all their attire. It was so utterly ridiculous that it took Bradley immense effort not to burst out in laughter.

'I know,' said Darvinius, 'I bet if he touched one of us we could feel his body's warmth! That would settle things.' Both turned and stared intently at Bradley.

The slight hint of malice in Darenian's eyes flickered for an instant too brief to be noticed. 'I guess that would settle things, yes,' replied Darenian. 'Would you? Just to shut that pain of a nightmare up?'

'Ah well,' Bradley let out a long sigh. What madness was he stuck in? He decided this had to be dream, a most senseless and insane kind of a dream. *All this worry and stress has finally driven me insane,* he concluded. He reached out for Darenian, as something about the fabric pulled at him, he so wanted to know what it felt like.

'NO, don't!' came a voice yelling at him, when he was just a fraction of an inch away from him making physical contact with the fabric. He pulled away rapidly.

'What the bloody hell did you go and do that for! Nearly had him,' both twins yelled out in unison.

Upon hearing that, Bradley took a few steps back. Another tall figure stepped out from behind the massive tree trunk. Bradley's breath was taken away. A slender female of perfect shape stood firm in front of them. Her ruby-violet eyes shone with an intensity he had never witnessed before. Her hair, almost starlight white, shimmered as it reflected the sun's touch upon it. Her body was adorned in white, silver, and colourless crystals, and her clothing was very revealing yet elegant. A royal hunter's attire it seemed.

Where are all these references coming from? He wondered, the scientist in him had a dislike of myths, legends and fiction, yet he was casually interpreting what he witnessed in that context. Her delicate jewel-decorated hand came up to her lips as she made the universal sign of silence. He nodded in agreement.

'You two know very well it is forbidden to tamper with newcomers to TrueEarth. They must make their own choices.' She stared down at them intensely. Bradley could see the sense of utter disgust etched upon her features. One of the brothers was about to say something. His mouth hung open as if to utter the words but no sound came out.

'Trying to lie again? Does not surprise me coming from a WonkerDudel.'

'And you're one to speak, LightBearer! Always interfering where your kind has no business. We found him; he was ours to guide.' The hate seethed out of Darvinius's words.

'Guide being the keyword' – she snapped back at him – 'not force into your own dominion. Those are the rules,' she reprimanded him.

'He was curious so I guided him to touch to satisfy his curiosity, that's all,' the twin justified his actions.

'That may be, but your actions would have made him one of you.' Upon hearing that, Bradley's left eyebrow shot up. 'Anyone who touches the fabrics used by the WonkerDudels automatically becomes one of their kind,' she explained, 'and they most certainly try to fully capitalise on the lack of knowledge of newcomers.' The sun's rays hit her, making her entire body and attire glisten and dance with light. It was a sight to behold.

'And you trying to mesmerise him with your lights. Don't think you have us fooled!'

Their very words broke the enchantment. 'Fine, let's settle this then the way it was originally done,' she proposed.

'Fine.' The twins saw no other way to resolve things. Secretly they hoped that he might, due to his initial spark of curiosity, choose to join them after all. They all turned to face him.

Bradley felt on the spot. He was not too good at dealing with people's focussed attention. It put him on edge. He by far preferred the isolation of the labs.

'You will have to choose,' explained the twins.

Oh my, choose what? One madness over the other... crossed his mind. He thought both of these choices were bad. Actually he was still convinced this was all a dream.

'Start at the beginning, you damnable WonkerDudel! The way you are making this sound is as if we are the only choices.' Darvinius looked at her in sheer hate. She was destroying all their chances of getting their hands on him. 'You are in TrueEarth,' she explained while ignoring the twins. 'It is very rare for humans from your side of reality to find their way here to the humans on this side. You will learn a lot and all this might seem very alien to you but know this: it is still the Earth so technically still your homeland.' She paused to allow the information to sink in. 'However, here things work differently than on your side. The reason these two displaceable WonkerDudels are trying to get you to join them is because every living human being on this side belongs somewhere. We all have our place and all stick to it. That is how peace is preserved and that is the will of the Earth herself. Newcomers not born on this side have to choose which of the Great Houses they want to belong to. It becomes their new home.

Those two' – she waved at them as if brushing away a buzzing insect – 'belong to House WonkerDudels. I, on the other hand' – pride surfaced for all to see – 'belong to House LightBearers. There are other Houses but four of those are defunct and have faded away, so you will have to choose one of the existing ones. Each House specialises in certain sciences, quantum field manipulations and studies, and makes it a way of life for all its members.' She paused and looked at Bradley intensely. He did not seem to be struggling to understand at all. *This one has a sharp and powerful mind. I should direct him to our House.* 'House LightBearers is also called the House of Lights of the Worlds, and lies here to the south.' She pointed in the direction of her own domain.

The twins exploded in hysterical laughter: 'House of...' Neither of them could catch their breath: 'Lights of the worlds...' Their laughter intensified: 'Hilarious, such humour,' exploded Darenien. 'Goodness me, you are being the comic jester today. Sure you would not have fit better with us the WonkerDudels?'

'I think so too,' emphasised the other twin.

She ignored them, smirking at their comments. 'Each of the other Houses lies in their own respective direction.'

'What if I do not want to join any House? Choose None?' asked Bradley. All three of them stared at him in utter shock and horror. 'Then you face getting obliterated out of existence,' they all replied in unison.

'I... I what?' Bradley was confused.

'On this side of reality, the Earth sets the natural laws. Here, the laws state that each living person belong to one of the Great Houses. Some have tried to not choose and live as vagabonds. Those unfortunates have ceased to exist within three days. Simply wiped out of existence.'

'Are you sure? They might have just left out of sight?'

'We are sure. You see, the longer a newcomer is here, the more encounters he has. He is eventually, by the start of day three, constantly under the watchful eye of ALL the Houses, each trying to get him or her to choose one of them. What we saw the last time this happened was his body and soul disintegrating into millions of particles, flushed away all over existence.'

Bradley shivered involuntarily. If this was true it seemed he had no choice. One thing bothered him though. 'You said this place was TrueEarth? What do you mean?'

LightBearer volunteered the information. 'It is the name given to this side of reality. You see, where you come from, Earth is the flip-side of the coin of ours and vice versa. Your side is filled with lies, deceit, illusions, manipulations and falsehoods, while ours is the flip-side of that, and truth reigns supreme here. Isn't that why you came?'

Bradley tried to speak but words would not form. The twins started laughing. 'He's trying to lie or deceive! Don't bother, mate. No matter how hard you try, you will not be able to speak a false word, even to save your own life.' He tried a few more times, and failed miserably. *Interesting. I'll have to study this. It could have many a profound impact. Have to be careful: if truth is always uttered, and only truth, this could be extremely dangerous.* Now he understood why she had indicated for him to be silent only moments ago. *Yes, that's definitely one way to avoid implicating oneself.* For a split second he was grateful. *If truth is golden, it would mean that agreements are too. Have to be careful not to agree to anything without careful consideration.* He was starting to get the basics of things. Concern still there, he nodded to the LightBearer as an indication that he was ready.

'Wait a sec,' he said, 'are you saying that my side? Is not real? Could it be a hologram, as the latest theories seem to think?'

This time, Darenien stepped in. 'No, not in the least. It is all part of history and research for us. Your side is just as real as ours. Actually, our scientists are finding a lot of evidence pointing to the fact that they were both one and the same side until something split them up by introducing a lie to the humans of old. This lie reshaped how people on your side see and perceive the world they live in. Those who kept seeing the truth were split to our side.' The pride in his knowledge was overwhelming. It inspired Bradley they might be completely out there, but he liked their passion for research.

'Who did that and how?' he asked.

'No one knows,' replied Darenien. 'What we do know is that the way you see things on that side is different. It is almost as if you are not using your own minds to perceive, but listening in on lies about how things are and what you are seeing. This distorts your views. This is why you are all plagued by illness, pain, loss, and uncertainty. It does not, however, make those very things unreal. Not by any stretch of the imagination.'

Bradley decided to file away this information. It was simply too philosophical to deal with right now. What he needed now was to figure out how to get back home. 'Wait a sec! Hold on just a minute, how the heck did I ended up here?'

'You perceived a fundamental truth: even for a split second, knowing the truth of what you are, who you are and what things around you are instantly shifts you onto this side TrueEarth,' replied the LightBearer. 'Just in case you wonder: yes, you can get back to your side, but how is a matter for each House to teach its members. We all move from the one to the other differently,' she explained.

'Wait wait, why did I never seen any of you on my side then?' he asked.

'Because for one, we are careful not to be observed, and more importantly because you cannot perceive the truth of things. Even if you were looking at any of us straight, face-to-face, all you would see is what your brain is habituated to seeing. That of being an ordinary looking human being.' For some odd reason, this made sense to Bradley. 'So to get back, I need to join one of the Houses? Is there no other way?' He was still convinced this was all a dream but he had no alternative but to play along with it. Eventually it would end and he would wake up in the real world, making all he heard here totally irrelevant. All three of them indicated that no, there was no other choice.

'Ok, tell me about these so-called Houses.'

'SO-CALLED Houses?!' exploded Darenien.

'Finally. Took him forever to get to the point, didn't it?' commented Darvinius.

'Oh shut up,' Darenien snapped back at him. He was annoyed that his brother had interrupted things. He saw that Bradley's attention was firmly focused on his explanations, which was a good sign. He might just be able to use this to their advantage.

'There are several Great Houses to choose from, as the LightBearer explained.' He uttered her title with disgust. 'Each one specialises in a different field of universal forces or a combination of them. The best of course are the WonkerDudels. We look at them all, study them all and manipulate engineering devices to achieve all sorts of things. And mostly to have a blast,' he added. 'It's the fun of discovery. A perfect fit for those of curious spirits!' He saw the LightBearer's frown and decided not to push it. He had the bait he wanted in there. 'Then you have Missy Almighty's house there: the LightBearers. They focus on the forces of light. Using and manipulating light in all its shapes, ways and forms is the *only* thing they do.'

'That will do,' she interrupted. 'We really don't need insults when sharing knowledge. I'll continue, since Mr WonkerDudel there cannot restrain himself. There is House GrimGloom, which studies darkness, death and all things grim – a most unsavoury lot.' The disgust was plain to be seen in her expression.

'HOLD on a minute. Now who's being insulting?' interjected Darvinius.

'Well, I am sure you would agree with my observations on the House GrimGloom? Would you not?' she challenged him. He lowered his head and nodded affirmatively.

'Having settled that, we can move on. The other Houses, you will just have to find out about on your own. We should not be discussing those. The WonkerDudels are one of the Houses which specialise on the manipulation of forces rather than on the forces themselves.'

She could not get another word out before Darenien interrupted again: 'And the best one at that!' he commented.

She ignored him. She noticed Bradley's mood shift and knew he was thinking. She could see the light of his mind flaring up. It was so broad and versatile, it took her breath away. For that one instant, she really wished he would choose her own house. The truth reflected back to her, forcing her to realise it was not only due to her admiration of his mind but also due to the simple fact that she liked him – a lot.

'For you to choose the House which you will call yours, it has to come from deep within. The choice is always from the spark of truth within. This is why there is an allowance of three days to get to that decision and to meet with members of the Houses. It allows you to know which one you resonate with.' She paused, hoping he would reveal even a bit of a hint as to his resonance.

Bradley did not. 'What if I do not know?'

'Then you go poof!' laughed Darvinius.

She looked at him, a stern expression on her face in utter disapproval. 'Don't despair, what you do is actually very simple. Sit silent and focus on yourself, close your eyes, and turn around until you feel a pull somewhere. Until you do, remain in silence and keep focusing on what you are, who you are, where you are going and what you are becoming. Eventually, you will feel a hint or a pull. A hint will place you on one of the closer paths towards your House, allowing you to filter out those which are not during your walk forward and meeting its members. A pull will set you firmly on your path and you will find everyone and everything else irrelevant.'

'By the way, we're to the East, just so you know,' interjected Darenien.

'SERIOUSLY!' objected the LightBearer. Bradley tried to sit in silence. The constant bickering and glaring of the three onlookers made it impossible to concentrate. 'Ok, all of you go away.'

'WHAT? Wait? What? Why?' The objections came flooding in from the whole lot of them.

'I can't concentrate like this. I need to be alone for this to ever work,' he explained.

The twins looked suspiciously at the LightBearer who just shrugged in confusion. They nodded. They all withdrew. None of them had in fact left entirely but had moved out of sight and stood further away in silence, hoping to go unnoticed.

Bradley sat down on the grass. His hands touched the moist green grass. *It's such a shame all the grass on my side feels so un-alive...* he refocused. She told him to try and get a sense of himself and look out for a pull. He stilled his mind. After a few minutes: nothing. Not a single thing he could even remotely conceive of as a pull or a tug in any direction.

The three were watching intently, all split up in their own direction, unable to see the other. Then a flash of light, faint, very subtle, shot across the air towards Bradley. Before it had the opportunity to make contact, a semi-transparent cogwheel shape formed in the air, capturing the ray of light, twisting and turning it back to where it came from. The light was picked up by the LightBearer. As she absorbed it, the information within was perceived by her hearing: 'Now now, stop trying to interfere LightBearer.'

The voice of Darenien echoed within it. He had intercepted the impulse of light she had used to try and 'inspire' Bradley to her own House. Silently, she cursed at the twins. *Why them? Why...? Why did it have to be House WonkerDudels?*

Bradley was just about to give up. It annoyed him having to wait. He got up, closed his eyes, and decided he would just have to leave things to fate. Then he turned around and started walking straight ahead. The twins observed and gasped. 'He's heading in the direction of the Bound?' Darvinius observed in utter shock and surprise.

'Odd, I would have never...' Darenien hesitated. 'No, nothing in his essence reflects the Bound. Something's amiss...' He stopped out of his hiding place, heading straight for the LightBearer. 'Did you do that?'

Her expression seemed as surprised as theirs. 'He's heading for the Bound.' Her face sank, gaze firmly stuck to the ground. 'I never...'

'...would have guessed?' Darenien finished her sentence for her. 'Something's not right.'

She nodded in agreement. For once they were all in agreement. 'We will follow him from a distance and observe, until whatever is going on reveals its truth.' They all signalled their agreement and for the first time ever, members of the WonkerDudels and LightBearers walked together in unison.

An unexpected thing happened: Bradley suddenly vanished, dissolved into thin air.

'What the?' asked Darenien. 'Did that dammed Light maiden get the better of us?' He looked in her direction and saw that she was just as surprised as they were. He shrugged, indicating he had no idea what just happened.

'I recon he's gone back to the other Earth,' explained Darvinius.

'But that's impossible!'

'Not really: think about it. This is his very first visit; his mind has only caught a glimpse of TrueEarth. It is still burdened with all the conceptions of the illusory one. What if he was trying to deliberately choose Houses rather than follow his true calling?'

Darenien thought about it for a few seconds and nodded. 'Entirely possible.'

'I think he was trying to head to a House his conscious mind was choosing but that is not where he is supposed to go. His conscious mind cannot make the right choice because it does not know his true self...' concluded Darvinius.

'And that would get him kicked out of TrueEarth, according to the laws of truth that function here. Good thinking there!' concluded Darenien. 'In that case, there is no point us hanging about; he might never get back to TrueEarth. We have better things to do than wait forever.' They both nodded in agreement and went on their way. 'Besides, when he gets back, these very laws would dictate he will reappear exactly where he left and just as it did when he got here just now the pull will be felt.'

'You are right. We will just make our way back here when he does. No need to wait. I forgot about the pull when a newcomer joins TrueEarth.'

Bradley stirred in the labs, once more in his protective suit, head on the desk. His head hurt, and his vision was somewhat blurry. He roused, and looked about. It took him a few moments to adjust. He spent the next few minutes making sure he was actually in the labs. *A stupid dream... of all the places and times to fall asleep.* He went to the computer and woke it up from sleep, and checked the time. Two hours had passed. Definitely he fell asleep – that was his conclusion.

He had to rush. He looked at the virus one last time. It was as if something within his mind had shifted; he wanted to know the truth of the damn thing. He had to know the cause of its very existence. It was then that he noticed it: on the engineered mechanical part, a name stamp. *B.T.E.I.M. Inc.* He had never heard of it, so he made a note of it. As he did, he had to get one final glance at the construction, and he gazed intently at the virus. It shifted and made him jump; it focused back right at him. It was as if its entire body pointed upwards towards him whenever he tried to stare at it for more than a split moment. He understood why it spooked Heather so much. He himself found it utterly creepy. It was more than time for him to unravel its mysteries.

I cannot unravel the nanotech side of it but I most certainly can the genetics! After all, the one is built on the other. With that thought, he pulled the plates out of the microscope and carefully secured them in the containment unit. He powered down the computers and walked out of the lab. It auto-sealed itself on his departure. He got out of his protective gear and went towards Dr Grimsaw's office. He had to inform him of his discovery and get him to look into whatever B.T.E.I.M. Inc was.

Unbeknown to him, someone was watching through the feed of the camera attached to the microscope. 'Fascinating,' muttered a woman's voice. 'Just the bit of info to earn me a nice little pay-packet.' She picked up the phone. 'It's me. Put me through. I have it.'

The line went silent for a few seconds. 'Yes?' replied another woman at the other end.

'I have what you were looking for.'

'Excellent.'

'I also have some very interesting related information... hot off the press. I think you will find it most fascinating.'

'Let me guess: you want extra for it?'

'Of course. I am putting my very livelihood on the line for you.'

'Do not worry. As promised, you will be taken care of.'

'Very well. Meet at the usual place?'

'It's still safe: why not. 3pm tomorrow?'

'That works. I'll get off work early.'

'Settled. Don't call this number again.'

'Agreed.' The line went silent.

Fred woke up. It was nearly night. He had crashed after his recent ordeal. He did not feel any better. His six-foot-two-inch, extremely broad shouldered, hyper-muscular body, typical of a rugby player, was usually a sight to behold. Anyone looking at him now would be forgiven for suffering a pang of pity at the sight of him. All he wanted to do was to crawl up somewhere and forget about the world. He wanted to be left alone and forgotten: *let the world pass by.*

He was stuck. For the first time in his life he did not know what to do. Having no other clear view of a path forward, he decided to ask his friends. He logged onto the computer, instantly regretting it. His social media accounts were overwhelmed, flooded with abuse of all sorts. As he read the messages, he felt the weight of the whole world collapse down on top of him. He was being called every possible abusive name under the sun.

'I didn't do any of those things!' he yelled out, as if anyone of any significance could hear him. His emails were filled with even worse. The worst of the worst was from his teammates, those guys he had considered his friends. They all blamed him. Accusations flew in all directions. It was only when he opened the email from the coach that he understood why. They were all being investigated and the university was considering pulling the entire rugby team off the list of approved sports societies. *How could they?* None of this made sense to him. It was not like he'd actually killed anyone. He crashed back in bed. Strangling the pillow, he fell asleep, muttering, 'I didn't do any of those things...'

'Hello, Bradley?' Yume was on the other end of the line.

'Yes,' he replied.

'It's me: Yume. How are you doing?'

'Oh hi, ... I'm not sure, to be honest. Need to get to the bottom of this. Don't have much time to speak.'

'Listen, we are all scientists and we all know that overworking messes up our thinking. You need to rest too. I heard you have been working over 72 hours straight! You know full well that Kuroi would not want you to drive yourself into illness.'

He was irritated at the interruption but had to admit to himself that she did have a valid point. 'I'll sleep when this is all over.'

'Guess there is no point arguing with Mr Stubbornness himself.' The expression grabbed his attention.

'That's what...' he never finished the sentence.

Yume had achieved her goal. It was what Kuroi teased him with when he was being stubborn. 'Anything I can do to help?' she offered. She thought it might be the best way to get him to open up a bit. If she could not get him to stop working like a madman, maybe she could get close enough to execute her strategy without interfering with his obsessive working schedule.

'Not really, but thanks. We have made a few discoveries but have hit a dead end. It seems information is our eternal flaw.' He tried to laugh but it sounded very forced.

'How on a second! You said information, right? Maybe there is something we can do to help! What is it you need to know?'

'I'm afraid I cannot talk about it. It's classified.'

'Ok, how about you come over, for us to grab a coffee, and I'll tell you about my experiment instead?' She had hoped he would get the hint. He was quick of mind – he should do.

'I'm afraid I don't have time for coffee.' He'd obviously failed.

'Bradley, listen to me. You REALLY REALLY need to come over, for Kuroi's sake.'

He finally clicked onto what she had been hinting at. His fatigue had indeed cost him. 'Fine, I'll be over in about half an hour. Let me wind down things over here.'

'Good, I'll be there with a nice hot coffee to share. Don't worry, I know how you like yours!' She smiled. That information she did have. There were so many times she would do the coffee runs for Kuroi and always got one for him too.

'It's a deal.' He ended the call. *Oh well, let's go and see what that is all about. A short break from the screen can't do me much harm.*

It took him just under 20 minutes to get over. Yume was still working on her own team's experiments when he made his way over.

'Here it is again, ma'am.' The junior researcher pointed at the screen. The quantum field is fluctuating as it was last time.

'Let me guess...' she looked up through the glass, and saw nothing. Then decided to poke her head out of the door and look around the corner. 'There he is: Bradley incoming!' she told the team. 'Get your scanners on full sweep. I want a breakdown of all quantum elements, electromagnetic field disturbances, temperature flections and every other damn thing you can get hold of.'

'Yes, ma'am.' They were all suddenly very busy typing away as Bradley entered.

'Hello,' he greeted them. Some of the younger guys waved a hi. The others just looked at him, pretending not to be interested.

'Ah Bradley. Come, come. Let's go have that coffee.' She indicated that they should go to the kitchen next door. While on her way out, she looked at the team. They all nodded. They were ready for whatever it was they were going to do.

Elma on the other end decided she was having none of it. If anyone was going to be all sneaky and spy-like, it would be a game she wanted to play as well. Without warning, she got up and walked out of the lab before anyone could even react to her. She joined Bradley and Yume next door. 'Mind if I join?' Without waiting for an answer, she took a cup of coffee, pulled a chair at the table out, and sat down. They both stared at her as if trying to figure out what she was doing.

'What?' she asked. 'You need information, right? I'm your best bet.' She smiled at Bradley.

'I can't talk about it,' he said.

'Of course you can,' she insisted.

'No really, I cannot. It's classified.'

'Pfft, classified, massified, ratissified. All meaningless words. Nothing is every hidden. Let me take a wild guess, shall I?'

'Be my guest,' offered Bradley.

'Your department is researching an unknown virus, which you suspect has been engineered and is infecting the medical staff. Recently, dear Kuroi got taken into quarantine at the hospital and has been confirmed to have it as well. Now you, Mr Prince Charming or Hero' – she took a deep breath – 'has to find a cure before it is too late. How am I doing so far?'

Bradley's mouth was wide open in shock. 'How...' He looked at her with a glare of suspicion bordering on accusation.

'Simply, Mr Hero. It's all been leaked over the university forums and if I am correct is already making its way through the Internet. Rumours are flaring about, left, right and centre.'

'No, that cannot be.' His head sank. 'They will shut us down for breach of national security. How could this have happened...'

'Everything leaks at some point or other,' she explained.

'No, not this,' he insisted.

'Someone got careless – that is how.'

'They will shut us down and most probably arrest the whole team.'

'No they won't,' Elma insisted.

'Listen, this is classified information which has leaked out. There are severe consequences for it. There will be serious ramifications and all of us losing our jobs is nothing but the tip of the iceberg. I'll never be able to find a cure. Kuroi will...' His head sank into his hands as he hid the tears forming.

Elma stood up and gently patted him on his back. 'We will fix it!' she said.

'How? It's too late. Everyone knows about it by now.'

She stood tall and firm, and in a game-like fashion, she patted her chest with her right hand. 'You, mister, are looking at one of the top experts in international's information management!' She broke out in laughter.

He turned to face her. 'Really? Even at this late stage?'

'A challenge is always when I work at my best!' She locked the fingers of both her hands and pushed outwards, making a gesture indicating a flexing of fingers ready for action.

'You can really do that?' He was unsure.

'Listen, you have nothing to lose and maybe I can get you that information you needed in the process. You might as well tell me; everything else is already out.' He was unsure but it seemed he had no option. However, he decided not to tell her everything.

'I need to know what B.T.E.I.M Inc is.'

Her eyebrow shot up. 'I've heard of that somewhere... can't remember where... I'll find out.'

'Really?'

'Yes. In the meantime, you sit here and relax. Yume, why don't you do some of your relaxation stuff with Bradley. He sure looks as if he needs it more than anyone else I've ever seen! See you in a few.' She started making her way out but Yume quickly caught up.

'Thank you!' whispered Yume. Elma leaned ever so slightly towards her. 'That is how it is done. Next time you want to manipulate someone into doing something, ask me! By the way, you are welcome – and I want to see the results of those scans too.'

'You know?' Yume whispered.

'What don't I know?' With those words, she left them and went back into the adjacent lab room. 'Guys get ready: the show is about to start!' she told the rest of the team who just looked at her with blank expressions. 'Oh, for goodness sake, move it! Ask questions later.' They did. She got to her own computer and started her investigations.

Bradley sat sipping on his coffee, unsure what was happening and trying to desperately figure out how the information could have leaked. They had all been so careful, and no one even spoke about it outside of the labs. How could this have happened? *You are being misled* – the words echoed in his mind. He had heard them but chose to ignore them. He put it down to his fatigue and the strange dream from before. It made no sense that words would just pop into the mind. It was obviously just his imagination.

'Come, Bradley, let's do some relaxation,' offered Yume.

'Yume, listen. I'm not into all that meditation and yoga stuff. Kuroi likes it but it's just not my thing.'

His response frustrated her. There, for a moment, she thought she had him exactly where she needed him. Now things took a step back. She was no fool. She knew men responded instinctively to touch. She pretended to get up to refill her cup but instead stood behind him, and placed her hands on his shoulders and poked at his traps. 'Damn, you are full of tension. Come, it will do you good.'

He hated being touched. His mind this time was too tired to object to it. 'I don't really feel like it. I'll go sleep when this is all over.' She poked at his traps again. Sensations were flowing through his body. He turned to face her. 'Please stop, this is wrong.'

She ignored him. 'Let's not upset Elma, shall we? Nothing wrong with you having a bit of relaxation time while she is busy fixing things for you.' Her words had been chosen for impact. She wanted to tap into his sense of obligation. She succeeded.

'Hmm, I guess so. But I don't know anything about that stuff,' he admitted.

'Not a problem. Just follow my lead. You're a scientist so let's do this scientifically... well, almost,' she instructed. 'Relax, let go of where you are, what you are doing and just focus on your breathing. Nice and regular, in and out.'

Bradley followed the instructions. He still thought it all stupid but decided that since he had to wait for Elma, there was nothing else for him to do. He might as well entertain the possibility of relaxing a bit.

'Sink deeper into yourself, imagine your mind sinking deep into your body, deeper and deeper. You are getting smaller and smaller as you sink... keep on shrinking, more and more. You are getting so small that your body looks like empty space. Shrink and sink even further. Enter the quantum size of reality.'

Yume opened her eyes and peeked at him. She saw that he had indeed stopped paying attention to his body or the space he was in. He had also stopped paying attention to her. This was her chance.

'Imagine millions upon billions of atomic particles all surrounding you. Imagine the tiny quarks flickering everywhere. They are in the air you breathe, they are in the space you are in, they are everywhere. Feel them pulsing with energy, the protons and electrons dancing against your skin. Pull them all in.'

She held her breath. This should validate the data they were seeing. If he had control over the phenomenon, they could potentially replicate it as many times as possible. She was excited: a Nobel Prize was on the horizon for her.

But discomfort surfaced – something was wrong. All the tiny hairs on her skin raised up, a chill flowed down her back. Cold yet not cold. She shivered. Silently, she got up and ever so quietly left the kitchen area and walked into the lab leaving Bradley to his own devices. In the distance of the university dorms, a young man howled. A most terrifying cry was heard by all in his vicinity.

Everyone was staring intently at the screens. 'You will not believe what we have just captured!' the young assistant said excitedly as she walked in.

'Show me,' she instructed. She saw it unveiling on the recording of particles activity. It had not only increased but was still increasing. She saw patterns upon patterns of particles, both on the atomic and quantum scales, coalescing into one point. It looked as if a vortex had opened and was sucking everything in. 'That's the same effect as universal black holes!' the shocked Yume gasped.

Everything flickered. The screens showed a disturbance; static was all over the monitors.

'What is going on?' she asked.

'Not sure ma'am. We're trying to compensate. Should have the image back in a moment.' It got worse, the flicker manifested again, then again. A third one hit their systems and everything went blank. All the equipment failed.

'Get it all back up NOW!' she yelled. 'Why is backup power not activating? We have failsafe mechanisms for these situations. Do something!'

Moments later, everything started rebooting. Systems were coming back online. As they were, she quickly made her way back to the kitchen. Bradley was there still sitting there, eyes closed, but unknown to her, he was back to his usual self. He had closed his hands as if holding something. She tried to see what it was but could not. What she failed to see was a triple three-inch red crystal. It looked like a ruby. He pretended to be still asleep. She decided he was not going anywhere and quickly jolted back to the lab.

He noticed her this time. As she did, he quickly put the crystal into his pocket and stood up. He made it to the kitchen door just as Yume was trying to quietly head back in. She bumped into him, surprised. She had not expected him to get back up so fast. 'Oh sorry, didn't re-alised you were up.' Surprise was clearly readable from her expression.

'It's ok, I must have fallen asleep,' he lied. He had felt something although he was not sure what it had been. He also had this thing in his pocket and was unable to figure out what the heck it was or where it had come from. He had never been asleep, but she did not need to know. Something at the back of his mind made him distinctly suspicious about her, about them all. 'You ok?' he asked. 'You seem a little stressed.'

'Yes, not to worry. We're just having some computer problems in the lab.'

Elma rushed out. 'It's all down! How the bloody hell am I expected to work when not even the equipment is functional!' She was angry.

'I guess, we –' Bradley's sentence was interrupted.

'Don't underestimate me, Mr Charming!' said Elma. 'I was pretty much done when all this mess' – she waved both her hands above her head as if trying to wave off some horror – 'hit. I've managed to remove all the forum postings and the only two Internet-wide leaks. All the videos talking about it have also been either lost or banned in all countries.'

Bradley breathed a long sigh of relief. This would at least delay things for a while and more importantly it provided him with an effective way to circumvent whatever Yume was scheming. He would focus on talking about just this and nothing else. 'All you have to do is to deny you had any knowledge of any leak, which technically you don't, since I never showed you any of it.'

She smiled. In fact, she had artfully manipulated him into believing there was a leak then conveniently erased any evidence of the non-existent leak. She had him exactly where she wanted him. Elma's schemes and goals were much longer term and far superior to Yume's and she knew it. However, she had one more card to play today. 'Couldn't find anything about B.T.E.I.M. Inc. Only thing there was is that it is an extremely well hidden research and technology company. No location, no details on what they do. Nothing, I'm afraid. Assuming we can get the system up, I will dig more into it. For now, I'm off for a walk...' she waved goodbye and just walked off.

Bradley, not wanting to be left there with Yume, simply took to run after her. 'Wait a sec! I'll see you later, Yume. Need to catch this fox in flight!' he yelled as he stormed out in pursuit of Elma.

Yume was somewhat annoyed. She wanted to know what Bradley had perceived during his meditation. She wanted to know more. Much more. 'Well, are we back online?' she asked the assistants.

'Yes and no.'

'What is that supposed to mean? Make sense, man!'

'Systems are functional but we seem to have lost everything. They are all blank.'

'WHAT! How could this have happened? We have backups... get them!' she instructed.

'Afraid those are gone as well, and the online ones never had a chance to synchronise so we do not have those either.'

'Are you bloody telling me we LOST it all? You HAVE GOT to be kidding me! The discovery of a century – no, a millennium – and we're letting it slip through our fingers? I don't care what you do, get that data BACK!' She stormed out of the labs pouting, and swearing. She was back at square one. How would she convince Bradley, who was insanely reluctant to do this again?

Instead of catching up with Elma, Bradley made a right turn along the next corridor and paused. He took the crystal out of his pocket and looked at it. His mind was both insanely curious and shocked. This had just appeared in his hands when he was relaxing – no not appeared; he replayed the exact sensations in his mind. It was not as if there was nothing there and then suddenly there was. He recalled the clear distinct sensation of the edges being there, pushing against the palm of his hands, then the walls of the crystal, and then its weight increased. It was more like a gradual formation. He held his breath, unable to accept what had taken place. This was not possible.

'Foolish man, why allow your beliefs to limit you so?' asked the echoing voice projected directly into his thoughts. He jumped and looked around, and quickly hid the crystal back into his pocket. He had to get out of this place. Too much weirdness here. He needed a place to sit and think. He had work to get back to and he had to go see Kuroi. Multiple trains of thought came crashing in upon him, each requiring his undivided immediate attention.

'Discipline yourself!' echoed the ominous voice in his head.

Something within him broke. He felt the crack, then dismissed it the next instant. That was it; he just had to get out of here and think. He quickly made his way out back towards the labs. Rather than going into work, he walked past the main entrance towards the university dorms, to reach the staff accommodation. Oblivious to the world, he stormed ahead.

Bam, he felt something crash straight into him. It took him an unbelievable amount of willpower to rebalance his body and avoid falling over.

'So sorry, I didn't mean to...' the deep yet young male voice ahead of him apologised. Bradley looked up. He had made impact with a tall young man, built like a bull, a huge muscular fellow. It was none other than Fred. The look on the youth's face was one of deep trouble. Bradley could tell this young man was in a seriously awful state.

'No harm done.' Bradley tried to smile at him, letting him know it was all ok. He found himself unable to do so. His own state of mind in deep turmoil meant the smile would just not surface from his depth. 'It must have been my fault. I can get lost in thought so easily,' admitted Bradley.

'Hah, I do the same,' replied Fred. 'I'm Fred, by the way.' He extended his hand.

Bradley looked at it for a moment, then shook it. 'I'm Bradley.'

'Are you a student here?' asked Fred.

'Afraid not. I'm one of the researchers at the labs over there.' He pointed at the tall tech building just off the side of the university.

'I see. Well, it's been a ... pleasure bumping into you, but it's best you don't get seen about with me.'

Just as Fred was about to head off, back in his sulking mood again, Bradley interrupted him. 'What do you mean?' he asked.

'It's a long story. I doubt anyone has the time to listen to it. Let's just say I've been dealt a bad lot and everyone hates me. I will probably not be here for long.'

Bradley knew the signs. He noticed during their last few words they were still locked in the greeting handshake. As Fred tried to pull away, Bradley tightened his grip and refused to let go. Fred looked at him questioningly.

'Listen to me very carefully, Fred.' Bradley's deep blue eyes pierced right through Fred, making him feel very uncomfortable and vulnerable. Bradley had the upper hand – at least psychologically. 'Whatever happened, I do not care. You seem like a good guy. Don't let any of that get you down.' He let go. Fred looked at him perplexed. 'Here is my card. When you are ready to talk or need help, call me!' He handed the business card over. Being with Kuroi, he had developed the habit of carrying his cards on him at all times. It was customary for the Japanese to do so and he had somehow picked that up from her. 'Don't go doing anything spontaneous. Life usually throws these challenges at us and there is always a way out... even though it is sometimes impossibly hard to see which way it is, when we are stuck right in the middle of them.'

Fred nodded and put the card into his pocket. 'Thanks, will do.'

'Good, I guess we would better both be on our ways.'

'Yes, see you about.' With that, Fred's head sank to his feet once again and he walked away.

Bradley let out a long sigh. He had seen this on more than a few occasions before. He hoped it would not end for Fred as it did for some of the other young men in that state. With that thought, he was quickly reminded of his own problems, as the crystal poked against his flesh. He started walking back to the apartment.

Mira returned to her desk, sat down, and reopened the sealed file. She flicked through the pages until she found what she was looking for. 'Damn them!' she burst out in annoyance. *Why did they, of all people, get their hands on it? Need more information. I must find out exactly what they know and how far they have come in their investigations.* She closed the file cautiously, and sealed it. Then she opened her locked draw and placed the file in it and locked it once more. Something unsettled her. There was something afoot. Her instincts were on high alert. Abruptly she stood up, opened her phone, and dialled a number.

'Hello,' answered the female voice at the other end.

'I am in need of your *services*.' She accentuated the last word in a peculiar fashion.

The woman at the other end understood instantly. 'Would you like to meet at the usual time and place?'

'That will do just fine.'

'See you there.' The line went dead.

Things were in motion. She would know exactly what they were all up to, no matter what.

Bradley sat down at the glass table, coffee in hand, crystal sitting there right in front of him. He looked at it, his mind still trying to desperately wrangle with how it came to be. It was unappealing: a semi-translucent, dark-red, plain rock, which fitted nicely into the palm of his hand. This unappealing thing raised his curiosity to inconceivable heights. No matter how he tried to logic it out, there was simply no way for him to make any logical sense of it.

Well, there is one way to start making sense of it all. He decided to try whatever he was doing when this crystal appeared in his hand.

This time, he pushed the chair he was sitting on backwards, out of the range of the glass dining table, and sat down. He unbuttoned his shirt. It was always hot in the apartment – Kuroi liked keeping the thermostat high. Way too hot for him. Not knowing what to do with his hands, he put them on his legs clasped together. He closed his eyes and allowed himself to relax, allowing his mind to sink deep within himself, becoming smaller and smaller, sinking further and further. An odd stillness took over. His mind seemed to stop, yet he was still able to perceive. Observe was all he did. Nothing happened. Empty blackness is all he saw. He waited.

So what will it be? A voice boomed through the emptiness into his mind. Had he not been so stilled, he would have jumped out of his very skin upon hearing it. *Time to make a choice...* it echoed inwards.

Who are you? He thought. Much to his surprise, his own thoughts echoed outwards as if he had spoken.

There will be a time for all that. For now, choose!

Choose what? he asked.

To move forward or not.

That's a stupid choice. No one chooses to stand still. Besides, I have to find a way to save Kuroi.

That is not your choice to make, the voice stated.

Of course it is! I have to find a cure, I will find a cure. No matter what, I'll keep on pushing forward until I can beat this thing... no matter what.

So be it. Everything went silent once more. Bradley tried to remain calm. Settling his mind was a challenge. Questions bubbled up to the surface, thoughts threatened to overwhelm. He allowed it all to pass. For the first time in his life, he just let go. It was so unlike him. One moment folded into the next, and time vanished – or rather, his perception of time did. A flash, a red ray of light, a shooting star glowing in angry red flares passed through his field of vision. And another, and another. Two crashed into each other, and the force of their impact hit him square on.

His body flinched involuntarily. A blow in his stomach, pain coursed through him, yet he could not move. All was muted, it seemed. More and more stars flew past... a veil... a curtain of raining reds. Then... something happened... those red comets no longer clashed with one another. Instead they merged, fusing perfectly. More and more were pulled into the vortex of reds. A howl of terror burst out from afar, a young man's voice letting out the most disturbing scream a human voice could make. Bradley was oblivious to it. It was too far out of the range of his hearing to ever be noticed. Weight, great weight, so great it made him open his eyes.

There it was another red crystal in his lap. Greater than the first, and just as dull and fascinating as the first one.

Fatigue took over. Bradley was exhausted. Going for a rest was not an option. *Food!* He picked up the crystal put it down on the table, returned the chair to its rightful place, and headed off to the kitchen. He grabbed the left-over chicken and salad. He ate standing.

He returned to the table and picked up the larger crystal. He turned it around, and gazed carefully at it. Nothing unusual about it. To Bradley it seemed to be nothing more than a red stone. He saw a flaw deep within the crystalline red rock. His mind immediately focused onto it. A glimmer. A red reflection. The glimmer increased in strength. It burst out, and rays of red shone like out of a sun. Bradley instinctively shielded his eyes.

Within an instant, the red rays fused into a single thick beam and shot right onto him, illuminating the region under his bellybutton. The crystal broke into billions of tiny fragments. That which was a solid was nothing more than countless red particles being hurled through the air towards him. Before he could react, they coalesced once more into the red crystal. Half inside of him and half stuck out from his lower belly.

He tried to pull it out, tried to make it budge. To no avail. Panic swelled in his mind, and against it he fought. He needed to get it out of him. For an instant he froze. a wave of memories from the distant past attempted to surface from deep within his mind. The sound of something snapping in two boomed in his head, then echoed from his left ear into his right and back again.

The phone rang. He lost them. In his frustration, he tried to ignore the phone. It rang and rang, kept on ringing. It was an odd, pressing insistence. His body was not in pain – he felt just fine. The only problem was this thing now stuck inside of him. The phone kept on ringing. Frustration took over. He answered.

'Ah thank goodness. Bradley, come to the labs right now!' it was his researcher assistant.

'What's so urgent?' he asked, somewhat irate.

'Can't talk about it. Need you here. It's urgent!'

'Fine, I'm on my way.' He looked at his body: still there. *What have I done? Should never have meddled with all this, whatever this is. Should have just taken the damn thing and thrown it away.* He had to figure out what to do about it. This was all some sort of nightmare he had allowed himself to sink into, rather than be doing what needed to be done – finding a cure! Saving Kuroi.

He buttoned his shirt up. At least it covered what he did not want anyone else to see. Then he rushed out, leaving behind what he had failed to notice was the deep blackness which had poured out of him. A weak shadow that had slipped quietly into the corner of his apartment, silent and unobserved, content.

Deep inside of him, the sense of closure enveloped him. It was both comforting and disturbing. He tried to analyse it while rushing back to the labs. All he could fathom was this odd sensation that a door had closed on part of his life and another one had been forcefully swung open. Almost instinctively, his right hand crept inside his buttoned shirt and his fingers danced on the smooth crystalline surface protruding out from below his bellybutton. *Could this have something to do with it?* He wondered.

Mira felt the touch, and turned abruptly to face... nothing. She had felt it. Someone had touched her left shoulder. *Must be tired and imagining things.* She sat back in her chair and started typing away once more. A deep dark shadow moved in, and pulsating waves crept over the floor. Smoothly and slowly, step by step, it got closer to her. Inch by inch, it slithered its way over the luxurious carpets of her office until finally it reached its goal. Silently, it unfolded millions of strands of purest darkest shades which entangled themselves about her own shadow, capturing it in an extremely elaborate net. As needle-like tendrils pierced the boundaries of her shadow, Mira's heart skipped a beat. She took in a deep painful breath and let it out. *Relax,* coursed through her mind.

That breath was all the shadow had needed. As her lungs emptied and her own shade retracted, the invader pieced right into the centre of it and with her next in breath, spilt itself completely in. Her shadow thickened, blackened, became more real. Her head span. She lost consciousness.

'Ma'am, ma'am?'

Mira felt the gentle, almost hesitant nudge against her elbow. She stirred.

'Oh thank goodness,' the young man's voice continued. 'I was worried you had...'

Mira straightened in her office chair. She remembered, she had passed out. The shadow? She looked around rapidly.

'It's only me ma'am,' her assistant replied.

'You should be so lucky,' she half-smiled at him.

'What a relief. Can I get you a coffee? It would help with the fatigue.' She understood immediately. He had assumed she was so tired she fell asleep at her desk. *Good. Let him think that. Avoids all the other questions.*

'Coffee, yes. Extra strength, please. It's been a long hard day so far and has a lot further to go.' She played him with ease. He seemed pleased. *Of course he is. Without me, he's nothing,* she concluded.

'At once ma'am.' He rushed off.

She stood up, and looked at her hands. She felt great, strong. She almost dared to think of it as powerful. Whatever had happened, its effects were most pleasant. She had to take time to consider all of this. If she could understand it, maybe she could use it to her advantage!

Little did she notice but her pacing up and down the length of her desk had increased in speed, had gained that tell-tale bounce. She felt great! The world was hers for the taking. *Time to get back into action! Work to do, things to sort out, people to set on course!*

8

- TROUBLING -
POSSIBILITIES

Heather sat across the table in the coffee area of the research facilities. Fortunately, it was late and quiet, with only the two of them sitting there, cups of untouched coffee dissipating their rich, fragrant arabica and cinnamon aroma throughout the immediate area. She was at a loss, facing a seemingly confused Bradley who did not even say a measly hello to her. So unlike him. The silence between them lingered heavily as if the first spoken word would shatter an abyss. She felt a looming eerie nothingness, threatening to devour everything and everyone. Annoyed at the silence, she decided it was time someone made the first move. Knowing Bradley, she knew it had to be her. *The boy can brood for years on end before saying a word.*

'Ok, spill the beans, what's got you in such a state?'

'Nothing, I'm fine...' he left the word lingering.

'Cut the crap, Bradley; I've known you far too long for you to pull this nonsense on me! It might work with the others, but I know when something is wrong and I'm telling you something is wrong, very wrong.'

'It's nothing.'

'Really? Are you going to pull that one again? I can see it written all over your face! Something is seriously wrong, and it is not something that will fix itself. Spit it out!' Bradley stood up and turned his back on her, preparing to walk out of the coffee area.

'I don't want to talk about it.' Slamming the door shut, he walked away.

Sigh, seriously, why do men have to be so damn stubborn when it comes to talking about their feelings? He's not getting away with it. Time for action. She stood up and followed him. She caught up with him and practically dragged him back. She sat next to him, gently putting her arm around him. He offered no resistance, slowly lowering his head onto her right shoulder. 'I'm breaking Heather,' he whispered softly 'my time has come.'

She was concerned, never had she heard such despair in his voice. 'Tell me about it, Bradley, tell me everything.' She knew this time, he would tell her and waited patiently for him to start.

He unbuttoned the collar on his work shirt, took in a deep breath and faced her. Heather was momentarily frozen in the realisation of what she was seeing. A broken man, despair ebbed out of his eyes, loss streamed out of his expression. *No, not broken, she reasoned, lost, defeated.* She was concerned, never had she witnessed such utter despair, not from him or any other man. His body appeared withdrawn, fragile, almost frail. It was at this point that she realised he had not slept for what probably had been a few nights. She knew full well why, that didn't need to be voiced; it was a given.

'You know, I really love Kuroi,' he simply stated. 'I never told her, but I do. I'd give anything if it were me on that death bed rather than her.' His head sunk down, staring at the floor.

'She'll get through; you will find a cure! I believe in you,' she hugged him. As usual, it was like hugging a stone pillar. He had no reaction and just locked up when in physical contact with another.

'No, she won't,' he affirmed.

'Don't say that! You don't know that!'

'Yes, I do; the virus is tearing up her DNA. Even if we can stop it, we can't reverse the damage. It's too late. This is what you get when you start messing with life itself. I hate them all. Mankind is rotten to the core, no matter how many good people there are; it's the bad ones who destroy everything. I hate them all. But you know whom I hate the most? Those who took my one true love away, who destroyed my very capacity to love.'

She looked at him, sorrow and pain in her eyes, and gently caressed his left cheek. 'You know some of us do care for you.'

He took hold of her hand and gently held it in his. 'I have decided that after what is now inevitable, I am going leave.'

'What do you mean leave?' she asked, worried.

'I'm leaving the labs, Heather,' he paused. 'I don't want to do this work anymore. It's a losing battle. There is no victory, no end to this mess. It does not matter whether we fix a problem or two, the greedy, the mad, and the obsessed will create new ones. We will be back at the same point, no matter how hard we all work; it's all just a cycle of new threat, new cure, followed by another new threat. What now? Now we're facing engineered viruses being combined with technology, it just gets worse,' he burst out. 'Technology was sup-posed to help us all, cure illnesses, fix problems, help us find ways to counter our weaknesses. What has it done, Heather? Think about it. It has created even darker days for us all, more problems, more powerful ways to destroy ourselves.' He took a sip of his coffee. 'No matter how many things we understand and discover, all those discoveries will be used to engineer even worse things. I see where all this leads; it is entirely logical. You can easily deduce the next catastrophe, the next disaster, the next threat. I'm sick of it all. I don't want to do this anymore. I don't want to be part of this charade,' his head sunk to stare at the floor once more.

Heather was taken aback and for a moment, she did not know how to process this. She reasoned that his dark mood was simply due to his concern for Kuroi, but thinking about his words, she saw that he had a valid point. Reflecting upon her own career, she concluded that it was just as depressing as he had described his own. No, she would not accept this.

She faced him, took hold of his face in between her gentle soft hands, but held him firm and spoke in a firm voice, 'Listen to me! You're tired and worried. That is what's making you, Mr. Gloomy. Stop it, go get some rest, go eat, and pull yourself together. Kuroi NEEDS us now, what are you doing with this doom and gloom? You're not even going to try? Is that love? Dam-it Bradley! Now is the time for you to fight tooth and nail for her, not brood about sobbing over coffee.'

'Heather, I lost my son, Kuroi was pregnant,' he finally let the real reason for his despair out. Heather sat there in shock, not knowing what to say or what to do. It was the first time she had to face the impact of death so close. Yes, other people she knew had relatives who had died, but this was different. This was someone close, someone who was practically an extension of her own family network. This time, death had struck home.

'She was pregnant?' she almost whispered the question in the midst of the gravity of things.

'I didn't know; I don't think even she knows. When I went to see her earlier on, she was still in the coma, but Dr Martin spoke with me, he told me.' A single tear dripped down Bradley's face and splashed into his coffee. He sipped the coffee, blinked and faced her.

She looked straight at him, deep into his eyes. Something was amiss, not for want of trying, but she could not see him there. It was as if those deep blue eyes of his had no presence behind them. She shuddered, it felt as if she was staring into emptiness. There was nothing there, no Bradley, only an empty shell. It took a few minutes for him to return from wherever he was.

'We've done everything we can with what we have,' he said, no emotion in his voice, no drive, heck she could not even feel that despair anymore. 'Jim and I have worked through the last two nights. We have a serum, which should slow the damage done by the virus.'

'See that's progress! You can still help Kuroi, she's still with us!' she tried to pretend to be excited but failed miserably. It was not possible to feel any sort of joy at the moment.

'Heather,' his voice seemed to be a touch deeper than usual, and it grabbed hold of her full undivided attention. 'We cannot repair the damage. Assuming this works, there is no hope, other than buying time and extending the suffering. We lack the required technology to re-engineer the coding of life, which this thing is tearing up!'

'Well, Mr. Gloomy,' she tried to lighten the mood a little. It was definitely getting far too grim for her liking, not all hope was lost, 'we can work on that! One step at a time.'

He laughed, his laughter almost maniacal. 'We have yet to fully understand and decode the DNA of a human being. We need, on average, a full month to sequence it, pericentromeric DNA, and its lack of unique primers to guide our sequencing reactions is still a massive problem. That is all do-able, but it only gives us raw data. You should know this,' the look he gave her was almost condescending. She chose to ignore it, this time allowing him to continue. 'Data does not give understanding, nor does it tell us what the effects would be trying to change any of it. All this is assuming we had a copy of Kuroi's DNA information to use as a reference when trying to re-code it.' He went quiet. Time seemed to have stopped or rather be stretched into what seemed like an infinity before he spoke again, 'an impossible task for any of us.' He stopped speaking, and a single tear ran its course down from his left eye flowing along the path of his cheek, finishing its fatal course along his almost perfect jawline. Its watery substance gained volume and weight and it fell to the ground, splashing away, dividing into numerous tiny molecules of water in all multiple directions. Heather could have sworn that she caught a glint of something red. She dismissed it; there was nothing red in the whole room to be reflected in the fraction of liquid from his tear.

The beauty of the scenery, of the moment, fixated itself in her mind. That one image burnt into every neuron firing in her brain. Bradley howled out in pain, grasping his lower abdomen. Bright red lights were emanating from somewhere below his belt.

'What the ...' it caught her totally by surprise.

'Run,' commanded Bradley. Naturally, she refused, no one told her what to do!

'Bradley, what's going on, what is that? Are you ok? What...'

'RUN!' he yelled at her. She just stared at him, 'NOW!' his voice shook her back into reason. 'Heather, RUN NOW! Get away!' he yelled. Pain was etched on his entire bod; it looked as if something was ripping right through him. 'RUNNNN' the pain seemed to run in his voice, it hit her with a force which almost seemed physical as it tried to throw her away. 'RUN DAMMIT! RUN,' he yelled.

This time, she listened, the red glow was intensifying and as it made contact with her hand, a deep overwhelming sense of danger and threatening presence enveloped her. Fear ripped through her, an ancient, almost archaic fear from beyond time itself. She bolted out of the coffee area as fast as her legs could carry her.

The red lights coursed through Bradley; it looked as if his skin was cracking up to reveal the deep dull red glow. It pulsed all over his skin, forming a second skin. The very moment it completed its invasive coating, a shadow form struck him with full force, sending him and the chair he had sat on flying through the air. Both crashed against the adjoining wall with a loud thump.

'Pathhhhetic creaaaature, weaaaak,' it hissed. Bradley somehow managed to refocus, looked straight at what he could only describe as an unnaturally thick tall form of a woman just before he was hit by a kicking motion. The force was so intense that it sent him sliding across the floor to the opposite wall. The shadow laughed at him.

'Youuuu wiiiiiiill nooooot stannnnd in myyy waaaaay,' it shrieked. The creature made its way towards him, ready for the next wave of assaults. Bradley recoiled, his mind told him all this was impossible, imagined, unreal, but his body told him otherwise. The impacts were as real as blows from a human assailant. His arms instinctively went up to cover his head. He was crouched in the shape of a ball, prepared for the next blow, which he was certain would kill him. *You are pathetic, is this what men in your reality are reduced to? Quivering masses of flesh paralysed by fear?* The voice echoed in his mind. It was the same voice, which had tempted him into what gave birth to the crystal, which he bore in his flesh. He didn't reply, only closed his eyes and tried to make this to go away. The voice in his mind was not amused. *You're annoying me,* it told him. *Seeing as you are so weak a miserable thing, I'll help you this one time. You owe me. CRYSTAL... LIGHT... SHAPE... Shadow THINK! At least you have intellect, use it!* Bradley opened his eyes; the shadow form was nearly upon him. Then it clicked, shadow form, shadow. The voice in his mind spoke of light and he looked around him, hoping. The light switch was on the opposite wall. There was no way for him to reach it. If only he had been closer, he could have hit the big lights, and they would have illuminated every inch of this place in strong light. CRYSTAL... LIGHT... SHAPE... Bradley failed to understand, he focused on the damn crystal, *what am I supposed to do with it?* Time was running out. Any instant now, that shadow would be in reach to strike at him again. *Crystal...* his focus was drawn into the red gem, he could feel the rays of red light flowing out of it. *SHAPE... what the heck has shape...* his thought never completed as the shadow struck him. The blow stopped mid-flow. He had somehow formed a barrier with the red light and it absorbed the impact. A loud echo boomed out. Bradley looked ahead of him, his red light was just as solid as the shadow! He understood. He looked in the opposite direction at the light switch and shaped the red light into a ball, hurling it at the light switch. The blinding lights sprang to life. The shadow shrieked the most horrifying howl of fury he had ever heard and was gone. The ball of red light split back into individual rays, curved back and struck the red crystal in him—a nudge coursed through his body as all the red light re-merged. *There might be hope for you yet weakling. We shall see...* echoed the voice in his mind. The crystal went dull. Bradley lost consciousness then and there.

Mira sat on her antique sofa. She loved her apartment, and this sofa, in particular, was her all-time favourite. It was the first thing she had purchased from her first paycheque of her first high profile job. It had so much meaning. Today, however, she sat there shaken, drenched in a cold perspiration, her clothing soaked in perspiration, her breathing intermittent and heavy. A broad smile plastered on her face; she was brimming with joy. It had worked. All her mother's ranting and raving about yoga had proven to be not only true but incredibly effective. She took a few moments to gather her thoughts, and, as she'd been taught in her childhood, ran through the chain of events, which had just taken place.

She remembered sinking into shadows and silence, a calmness taking her over. The shadow within spoke to her of its whispers of power, of potential, of new experiences, tempting her, calling to her. She had given into those promises. Power was hers by right; her very existence demanded power. The shadow had been right. She found herself able to move, to slither as a shade. It carried her towards her desired goal: the labs. She wanted, no, she needed to know what they had discovered, how much progress they had made. They would not be allowed to stand in her way. Their interference was totally unacceptable. Then it happened, she saw the red man. At first, she'd feared such light, it burnt her, weakened her, but the shadow had been right. By gathering even more power, by pulling in more and more shadow, she could shield herself from his powers. He was weak; *she could not expect anything else from a simple mortal and a man no less, all weak, the lot of them, only progressing at the expense of us women,* she mused. The thrill of force and strength had made her incredibly strong at the time. She laughed, even physically, she was far beyond his capabilities. 'That dam light!' she swore. 'How on earth had that light come on at the worst possible time? I would have had him...' *never mind,* she concluded. Whoever he was, he would not be a threat to her. She wondered just how far she could reach, using this newfound skill of hers. *There are no limits!* The shadow replied. She smiled. Fate herself had blessed her with a way to push forth. She would be the first; she would charter a course for the whole of mankind; she would show them the way. She had the key! Mira laughed. She knew she had been born for greatness, and this was the validation of that belief. This newfound power, combined with her company's developments in technology, would prove to be an unbeatable asset!

Heather felt uneasy. Her mind was racing. *What exactly had just happened?* Her scientific curiosity got the best of her. She made her way back to the coffee area. Upon entering, she found Bradley unconscious on the floor, chairs all over the place. The coffee table had been pushed to the side, and the light switch was burnt. She paused to think about what could have happened to cause that, then quickly rushed to Bradley's side. She checked his breathing and his pulse. A deep long sigh of relief washed over her. He was still alive. The place was a mess, no matter, she had to do something. She pulled and pushed, somehow managing to move his body into the recovery position. *Why were boys so damn heavy? Even the slim ones...* She glanced through his semi-open shirt and saw the large red crystal embedded in his lower abdomen. She gasped, instinctively pulling away from it. Grabbing hold of her phone and just about to dial the emergency number, she heard him stir.

Bradley's eyes opened. 'Where?' he looked at her, then tried to get back on his feet.

Heather took her shoes off, flipping them off her feet in one swift motion. She needed a solid footing for stability, and those high heels would not support her and Bradley's weight. With her help, they managed to get him back on his feet and help him sit on one of the chairs close-by. She rushed to get a glass of water and held it out right in front of him 'Drink!' He was about to argue, but she cut him off. 'After all this mess, you are still going to argue? Drink,' he took the glass and slowly sipped on the water.

'What happened?' he asked.

'Shouldn't I be the one asking that question?' she glanced towards his beltline, the implication crystal clear. He remained silent.

'Not sure, I remember falling...' Heather knew very well that he was not only avoiding the question but downright lying to her. She let it pass; *there are other ways to find out what is going on,* she concluded.

'Well, if you are feeling better, I would suggest you clean this mess up,' her hand motioned to the chaos that had befallen the coffee room 'before anyone else comes in asking questions. Oh, and whatever the heck happened to the light switch? Better get maintenance to fix that ASAP!' He nodded in agreement as he watched her walk towards the door, casually picking up her shoes on her way. She put them on just before leaving and walked off.

Bradley sat still for a few minutes, trying to regain his bearings. *Was all that real?* he pondered. His right hand somehow found its way to making contact with the red crystal embedded in his flesh. *Of course, if this why not that...* He focussed on the crystal, it pulsed, acknowledging him. *So it does work like this. Interesting...* His concentration broke. Looking about, he saw the mess but decided to first start off by having some coffee and a bar of chocolate. Exhaustion had taken a grip of him, and he needed the pickup. It only took a few thoughts for him to decide what to do. Putting the chairs back in place, rearranging the furniture took no time at all. He called in maintenance, telling them there was a spark that had melted the light switch, potentially dangerous and should be looked at immediately. Not really a lie, but not the truth either, they did not need to know the truth. Heck, even Bradley was not exactly sure what the truth of the matter was. All he knew is that Heather seemed to be unusually suspicious about things. He had things to do. Oddly, his gloomy mood seemed to have deserted him. His mind was firmly calling for action again. The lab, he had to get back to the lab, but this time, not for his research.; he and Jim had already developed a potential serum they needed to try out. No, this time, it was for some privacy.

He had to figure out this crystal, and it seemed urgent. Besides, he wanted to see if he could make more of them, perhaps he could take one of those and put them under the microscope. In his current state of mind, it simply did not matter what happened to him. He had nothing left to lose; what little of life he still had would be gone soon. He knew it was inevitable. He might as well plunge where he had never dared to and if it meant losing himself, then so be it. He had nothing left to hold onto. He was alone, all meaning to his life was fading so rapidly that it made his own existence pointless. The battle that had just taken place demonstrated painfully that he was in danger, that the danger was somehow real and that he was far too weak to even stand up and fight. *Fight? Who would have thought...* fighting was not his thing, never had been and never would be. He was a man of intellect, he went with the flow, ignored conflict, hated violence, preferred talking his way out of problems. Bradley liked having structure and his life ordered and it seemed as if this was falling rapidly down the chasm of possibilities. What he wanted to know is whether more of these red crystals could help him increase the effects he could unleash, and by doing so, he might as well blow himself up, and whatever this horror was in the process.

9

AT THE
- HOSPITAL -

'Kuroi has regained consciousness and has asked to see you,' Dr. Martin informed Bradley, 'but try to make it short, she keeps slipping in and out of consciousness. We cannot be sure how long she will be awake for, and Bradley...' he hesitated 'the serum did not work. DNA is degrading at the same speed as before.'

'Are you sure?'

'Yes, the tests have just come in, have a look,' he handed Bradley her file. Bradley had no problem sifting through the medical reports and lab findings, this was after all his own field of expertise. He found the tests, and as he read through the report, his heart sank. He had spent the last week working on this new serum. It was never intended to heal but rather to stop the damage this engineered virus did. He had hoped that if they could just slow it down, it would give them a glimmer of an opportunity to try and think about reversing it; he was certain stem cells could be used to rebuild her DNA. It was impossible to rebuild if this thing kept on tearing it all apart.

'Damn those bastards, I'll kill them all,' he burst out.

'Dr!'

'Seriously, Martin, wouldn't you? How could someone be so damn cruel and inconsiderate to engineer something like this? Tell me as Dr to Dr? I might not be an MD like you, but I still work to save and improve everyone's life, we have the same goals. So, tell me, could you do something like this?'

'Of course not! This virus is beyond cruel, tearing someone apart cell by cell; I cannot even imagine the suffering and pain it causes. And to think that it's one of our own who was amongst the initial group they targeted...' he left the remaining unsaid. He knew all too well where his very sentence would lead, everyone knew, but no one wanted to say it. Whoever had engineered and released this thing was targeting hospitals, clinics, and specifically, high level medical staff.

Dr. Martin put his hand on Bradley's shoulder, who instinctively froze, irrespective of it being a friendly gesture. 'Listen Bradley, you just focus on Kuroi, she is awake, go talk to her. Her father is waiting for you to see her first.'

'Mr. Kudo is here?' Bradley was nervous. His relationship with Kuroi's father was formal but strained. He had never approved of her being with a non-Japanese man.

'Yes, he is, so is her mother and her brother.'

'They are all here? What is going on?' it was unusual for the Kudos to travel. Her father was the chairman of five of the most powerful corporations in Japan, and the very thought of him taking an hour off work amounted to sacrilege. For her brother to be here, well, that was unthinkable. He was his father's second in command, destined to take over some of his responsibilities. 'Why are they waiting on me seeing her? You should have let her father see her first and foremost!' Bradley knew and deeply respected the familial duties and protocols the Kudos abided by. He knew Kuroi placed great importance on them.

'She expressly forbade anyone from seeing her before you did.'

Bradley was shocked, for her to do something like this was totally unthinkable. 'You're right, I must go, everything else can wait. I cannot make the Kudos wait. You should have paged me as soon as they arrived!' He turned around, about to dash off.

'Before you dash off! One more thing, Bradley,' that made him stop. 'I would make the most of it if I were you.'

Bradley was confused. 'What is that supposed to mean?' Dr. Martin hesitated a moment and decided there was no easy way to say this. 'Bradley, this is probably the last time she will regain consciousness. Next time she slips into the coma, it is highly unlikely that she will ever wake up. Her body is not strong enough anymore. I'm sorry.'

Bradley lost his drive, his heart sunk. With a gloomy expression, he just turned and paced in the direction of her room. As he approached the quarantine room, he saw her father standing straight and looking at her in silence. His imposing authority was not amiss, even in this situation. Her brother almost mimicked their father's formal posture. Bradley got on well with Ryuken; they had long ago decided that in view of their shared love for Kuroi, they would work together whenever the need arose. Each understood and respected the other. Ryuken's matter of fact decision-making, disregard for personal feelings and emotional turmoil, coupled with his sharp intellect, made him the perfect conversational companion in Bradley's view. Her mother was as regal as usual. Standing a pace or two behind the father, she exhumed formal grace and courtesy.

He addressed Kuroi's father first, he was all too aware of the protocols involved, even though sometimes he did make a mess of them, which used to make Kuroi burst out in laughter. Pain flared in his heart; she would not be laughing at this now.

He bowed deeply to her father, 'Kudo-Sama, you honour me and the hospital with your presence.'

Her father returned the bow, albeit not as deep as protocol dictated, 'Boston-sensei.' Bradley was nervous, why was her father using that honorific? It was most unusual. He pushed it out of his mind. He then turned to her mother and greeted her with the proper respect. Finally, it came to her brother, he bowed but not as deeply as he had to either of her parents. Ryuken smiled ever so subtly.

'Ryuken-kun, as always an honour and pleasure to see you.'

'Bradley-kun, likewise,' he was slightly less formal than his parents, 'although I do sincerely wish it was under better circumstances. Do tell us how is she doing?' Bradley had dreaded this question. All three family members were waiting on his every word.

'Not too well, I'm afraid. We have been trying to stop the onslaught of this virus, but even with all our resources and expertise, it has proven to be impossible. I suspect this was engineered to be as deliberately so, but unfortunately, those in charge here seem to be resistant to admit it.'

'Bradley-sensei,' asked her father, 'you are the lead researcher into this type of genetics. Our esteemed colleagues in Japan informed me

105

that even they are following your research very closely. Honour me with your actual opinion, off the record,' he requested. Bradley could not deny this request.

'Kudo-sama, I think this has been designed to kill. No one wants to say anything out loud, but we have heard reports of it being some sort of technology leak to terrorists. We have also heard that their target seems to be high-level medical and bio-scientific staff.'

Her father remained silent for a few minutes. Bradley did not interrupt his silence. He knew better. Her father broke the silence. 'Boston-sensei, go see Kuroi. She has requested you to see her before any of us do, and I will respect my daughter's wishes.' Bradley bowed and made his way to Kuroi. Her father turned to her brother. 'Inform the high priestess of the hidden shrine of the situation, immediately.'

Her mother gasped 'Surely you don't intend to...' she never finished, as the gaze he directed at her was petrifying. She bowed her head in acknowledgement and stood there quietly, horrified at the significance of what was about to take place.

Meanwhile, in Kuroi's room, Bradley sat next to her, gently holding her hand. She looked at him, tired and exhausted, struggling to catch each and every breath.

'You came,' she was pleased to see him.

'Of course, my dear, I would have done anything to be here for you.' She tried to smile, but it proved to be too much of an effort, she coughed.

'Don't strain yourself, take it easy. Now is not the time to show off,' he winked in mischief at her. It made her feel better and for one moment, she remembered their first date, his devilish charm totally crushing through her defences.

'I need to speak to you, Brad, listen carefully.'

'Of course, my dear, take your time.'

'I want you to promise me,' she coughed again, regained a grip of herself and pushed on through sheer determination 'to take care of our son. He will need you and will have no one else to look after him.' Her hand formed a grip and held his with as much strength as she could muster. 'Whatever happens, do not let my parents take him from you. Promise me, Brad, look after him, for me.'

Tears formed in Bradley's eyes, and much to his frustration, one rolled down unchallenged over his cheek and fell onto their hands. How could he tell her that the child she was carrying had died a few days ago? How could he tell her that they could not save him? No matter how he tried, words would not come forth. He just couldn't.

'I'm dying Brad, he is all we have left, please promise me.'

'I will do everything I can, and I cannot. And I promise you, Kuroi, I will get revenge! For us all, that I swear!'

She whispered, 'Brad kiss me one last time,' tears ran down freely now. They both knew this was the last time they would speak with one another. He did as she asked. He no longer cared about the risk of infection and gently took hold of her hand, their lips making contact ever so softly. She put her hand on his chest, slipping her weak fingers through his half-buttoned shirt, laying her soft feeble touch upon his chest. 'I leave you the blessing of Kuroi.' For one instant, he could have sworn he had felt something, her hand was warm again. He opened his eyes and looked at her and she struggled to smile. 'Be good my intended, may the moon guide and guard you along your path. Goodbye, my dearest Bradley.' She seemed to fall asleep but was not yet unconscious.

He quietly stood up and kissed her on the forehead, 'have a safe trip, my dear, may the moon bless you.' He knew the traditional greetings of her faith; she had taught them to him a long time ago. He stood up and walked towards the door. Her father was waiting; he just looked at Bradley, saw the tears on his face, nodded respectfully, and went to his daughter's side.

'Father,'

'My daughter.'

'Protocols to the end?' she coughed fiercely.

'You are right, Kuroi, now is the time for them to be all set aside. I'll do all I can to get help; we will get the best scientists and doctors from home to help.'

'Don't be silly, father, we both know I am dying, my strength is waning; I don't have long.'

'Please, father, look after Bradley for me, I cannot do it anymore. I know you don't like him because he's not Japanese, but you don't see what I see. Please promise me you will look after him,' her eyes spoke volumes. He nodded in approval. He could not deny her dying wish 'and look after my son.'

He was taken aback, shock upon his face. He asked her, 'you two have a son?'

'I hope they will save him; I am pregnant. They should be able to keep him alive.' Lost in emotion, she put her hand on her stomach and gently caressed it. It was only then that he noticed the tell-tale bump of pregnancy. Shock, fury, realisation and pain rose in a maelstrom and hate flickered into being. He would have the head of everyone involved! This was not only an assault on Kuroi but one on his very family. His jaw stiffened.

'Don't be angry, father.' She recognised her father's expression of anger, 'we didn't do this to hurt anyone.'

'Oh, my dear daughter, I'm not angry at you or at Bradley. I'm angry at all those who did this to you!'

'Father, please tell Mother and Ryuken that I love them and will miss them.'

'Don't say such things, Kuroi, you will make it.'

'I see the Dragon King; he has come for me.' Her father thought she was hallucinating from the drugs. 'He tells me of the wonders awaiting, and he tells me to let you know the seal of the dragon is to leave the shrine. The foreigner comes under his protection.' Her father listened very carefully; he knew the significance of this message. 'A voice older than time speaks again. Be wise and listen.'

'I will, Kuroi dear, I will listen carefully, I promise.'

'Ryuken is chosen to take my place, against the rules of tradition, and Bradley bears the blessing against tradition.'

'My time is spent, father, I love you, kiss mother goodbye for me and get Ryuken those two katanas he so wanted as a child that you locked away. Tell him I will watch over him...' her voice faded. Her hand lost all the remaining strength it had left and limped in his. Kuroi Kudo passed away at exactly 3 pm on the Monday. Her father sat there, holding his daughter's limp hand silently. After a while, he gently put it on her now still chest and closed her eyes, kissed her forehead, and whispered, 'May the Moon guide you and light your path and may the dragon lift you high into the skies, honourable daughter.'

He walked out of her room, closing the door quietly behind him. He saw Bradley sitting beside her mother, his face covered by his hands, hiding his tears.

Ryuken walked to his father, 'can I go in next?'

'No,' the reply was stern and solemn 'Kuroi is dead, let her rest in peace for a while.'

All protocol broke. Ryuken cried openly, pushed past his father, and stormed into her room. Her mother openly cried for her daughter, rushed to her husband and with her small fists, banged on his chest.

'I told you to never let her come here, this is all your fault, she should have stayed in Japan. This would never have happened.'

He ignored her outburst, grabbed her fist as they were about to crush into his chest anew, 'remember who you are!' He let go of her and stood in front of Bradley.

'What will happen to her and your son?' he asked. Her mother abruptly regained her composure and looked at him.

'Answer me Boston-sensi,' he insisted.

Bradley did not know how to do this. He looked at her father, then her mother, then back to her father. His stern determined expression spoke for itself. He would not let the matter drop, no matter what. Tears still running freely down his face, Bradley revealed, 'our son died in her womb three days ago.' He paused as her mother gasped. 'They could not operate on her to retrieve his body from fear that she might not survive the surgery.' His mind was frozen; time itself did not seem to move. Time had stopped. That one instant, the moment of death was now. It had frozen him within its indifferent icy grip. He could not move; he could not think, he had no emotion, had no reactions. It lasted forever; his very existence was glazed over by the shock of Kuroi and his son's death.

'She didn't know?' asked her father.

'No, I couldn't tell her, I tried, I tried,' his voice trailed off.

'It is no dishonour to you for having shielded her from this, she could not have endured even more pain,' concluded her father. Fury was visible in his eyes; he was angry, angry at the world. He turned around and saw Ryuken coming out of his sister's room. 'We are leaving,' he instructed.

'Leaving?' asked her mother.

'Yes, immediately. There is much to do, and I need to get back to Japan immediately. Ryuken, stay with Boston-sensei. I will arrange for Kuroi, he paused, 'and her son's bodies to be returned with all due respect and honour back to Japan. We will arrange for the funeral at the Hakone Shrine.'

Ryuken nodded in agreement.

'And arrange for Boston-sensei to learn the protocols; he will be meeting with the High Priestess.'

Her mother intervened, 'A foreigner? At the shrine? Meeting the High Priestess? This is sacrilege; it won't be allowed.'

'Kudo-sama,' interrupted Bradley, 'I know a little of your ways. Please, if my presence is not suitable at the funeral, I will pay my respects at a later time. I do not want to bring dishonour to Kuroi's memory.' Bradley knew he would not be welcome at the religious gatherings. He did not want to impose, even though he did really did want to attend and say goodbye, not only to his wife to be but also his unborn son.'

'You WILL attend the funeral, and you WILL meet the High Priestess,' her father said, his voice harsh, authoritative and un-compromising. With that, he bowed ever so slightly and made his way to the exit. His wife did the same and rushed to catch up with him.

10

UNDERCOVER
- SHENANIGANS -

Heather rushed over to the labs; this time, she was not going to her own section; instead, she had decided to go and see what secrets Bradley's offices would reveal. It took her very little time to get there. There was a lot of commotion in all the offices. *Just what was going on?* She passed Mike in the corridors.

'Ah, Dr. Hawke,' he moved out of the way to let her through.

'Pretty formal today, Mike?' He just nodded yes and looked around uncomfortably. She pretended to lose her footing and bumped into him. This gave her the opportunity to whisper to him without being suspected. 'What is going on, Mike?' He took hold of her shoulders to steady her.

'Careful there, miss, let me help you,' he spoke out loud, making sure everyone overheard him. Meanwhile, he whispered, 'someone is taking over management of the labs, everyone is being moved, everything reorganised. Whatever you have come to do here, you'd better hurry.'

She nodded, turned abruptly, and went straight into Bradley's office. There she saw masses of files and equipment all being boxed up. Her gaze washed over the entire room. There! She spotted the box she was after, desk items, circular donut-shaped crystals. That was what she wanted! This was the only opportunity, the ideal one. The move and change of management would have to be dealt with later on; this was the time for other things. She walked into his office

111

as if it was her own and her confidence paid off. Some of the staff and guards helping with the move simply assumed she was there to carry her stuff to the new offices. Heather picked up her target box and calmly walked out, proceeding down the busy corridors. *All this damn glass, it was impossible to hide away.* Her agile mind made quick work of setting out the ideal path. It would take her by one of the university buildings, an accommodation area. That was inconvenient. She had no choice. *And this damn box is so bloody heavy, just what the heck does he have in here?* Her thinking was interrupted as she gazed on the crystal structures, four of them, flat donuts. Their shape reminded her of something, but for want of trying, she could not grasp the thought.

'Ma'am.' Heather's heart skipped a beat, her pulse increased and for a brief moment, fear struck right into her. 'Ma'am,' the voice prompted her again. She turned, prepared to face being caught. A young assistant stood in front of her. She had no clear recognition of him, but his ID badge helped.

'Yes?' she prompted.

'It seems like you are struggling with your box. Would you like me to help you with that?' he asked. Relief washed over her. Confidence took hold.

'Oh no, don't worry, I can manage,' she said, smiling at him. 'Thank you for the offer; it's so kind of you,' she added.

He smiled back, 'Ok, if you do need help, please just ask, it is no trouble at all. The new offices are down the other corridor, by the way. We all get lost; I never thought we would end up using the second-floor section.'

'Yes, it is odd,' she admitted, 'no one told me about all this moving. I only found out about it a few minutes ago.' The youth looked at her with a hint of suspicion. She bit her lower lip. Too much, she had said too much. Judging from his reaction, some people had known about it, and judging from her lack of knowledge; others had not been told. It seems something was afoot. She made a mental note of having to talk to her grandfather about it, as a matter of priority. 'Well, I'd better be off, time is ticking, and I don't want to lag behind,' she made her usual dumb blond face, beaming at him with the lack of intellect more than obvious.

'Oh yes, I'd better not keep you, or your lab lead will get mad,' he smiled. She nodded and moved on. *Always works!* Only a handful of people were immune to it. Those she knew personally, those she could convince in other ways. She picked up her pace, still going in what others would consider the wrong direction. This wrong direction would lead her right to the adjoining university dorms.

She stepped through the connecting doorway, opened it and bumped into someone. 'Sorry,' she said as they both wobbled in an effort to regain their footing. Somehow, both of them managed to avoid falling over. Anna caught the box Heather was carrying.

'Thanks.' Heather pushed her hair back to clear her field of vision and then saw Anna.

'Hi Anna, I didn't see you coming in from the around the corner,' admitted Heather.

'Not to worry! No harm done. What are you doing here?' she asked nervously.

'On my way out of the labs to the university,' Heather lied. She did not want Anna to know any of the details of her escapade. 'How about you?'

'I... ehm.. am... here, yes to get my things,' she hesitantly explained, hoping that would be the end of it.

'Wait a second, your things? Aren't you staying at the dorm on the other side of campus?'

'Well, yes, you see...'

'You've come to see Fred, haven't you?' Heather connected the dots.

'Well... kind-of... need to get some things I left at his place,' she tried to explain.

'You do realise you are not allowed to go near him, right?'

'Well, I thought... kind of need to get ... those things of mine.'

'Fine, I'm coming with you, let's go get this done as quickly as possible.'

'No need to worry about me, you are obviously busy.'

'No way I am letting you do this alone, come on.' Anna had no choice but to let Heather tag alone. Fred's room was just in the second corridor. She did not know this is where the lab department connected to. *How odd this coincidence, Heather did not like coincidences;* there was always something fishy about them.

Anna knocked on Fred's door. The emotional conflict, which had erupted within her, was contained, somehow. On the one hand, she felt guilty, but on the other, she had justified her actions to herself. He had hurt her by behaving like a savage. Did he deserve all that had befallen him? That she struggled with. Heather stood slightly to Anna's left. She would just observe and make sure nothing untowardly happened without interfering if possible. Fred opened the door. Anna nearly gasped in horror when she saw him, face sunken, hair unwashed, his t-shirt in tatters, shorts dirty. The room stank of alcohol. *Since when did Fred start drinking?* She couldn't believe it; he was one of the most anti-drink people she had known. The curtains were drawn, and the whole room stank. This was a broken man.

'Fred, how...' she started... 'am sorry,' she broke down almost in tears.

'Go away; I never want to see you again.'

'Fred, I didn't mean to...' she tried to explain...

'...ruin my life? Of course not, as long as you got what you wanted, right?' he interjected, the bitterness palpable in his words. 'You LIED!' The accusation was clear, the word struck like a sword through her chest... 'and ruined my life. That is all, just that little insignificant thing, and it wouldn't surprise me that you already justified what you did to yourself. You are right. No matter what, who cares about facts and truth? Right?'

'I ... didn't ... mean for this...'

'Oh, save me the crap, cry first and then, later on, claim you didn't mean any of it, and it was not your fault–doesn't help me in the least. Tell me, Anna, how's life?' the snake-like bitter Fred asked, 'all good, I take it? Out with the girls celebrating, getting your studies done? Oh, let me guess, you probably got all sorts of perks out of this too,' he sneered, 'you privileged spoilt brat. Get out of my sight.' He turned his back to her and started walking towards his bed. Anna was shocked; she had not done any of this to hurt him; this had not been planned. The truth of his words seemed to have the opposite effect of what he had expected; instead of hurting her, they angered her.

'This is all your fault,' she yelled at him. 'If you had been a decent boyfriend, none of this would have happened. Without me, you will always just be a failure. You can never get things right on your own!' Her anger intensified. He was doing exactly the same thing as he always did, not even thinking how she might be feeling, what she might be going through, *how bloody selfish of him!* She exploded. Spontaneously, she reacted. Before Heather could stop her, Anna turned, grabbed the first few things she could get hold of and hurled them at Fred.

'You're a bastard, you know! I wish you to be forever stuck, you and your miserable fate which you bloody deserve.' She slammed the door, forgetting about the things she had wanted to get from him and stormed away, leaving Heather surprised, standing there on her own.

Heather looked at the box she was carrying. Her heart sank, the four crystals she had so painstakingly retrieved were gone. The whole reason she had undertaken this escapade with Bradley's things had been to get those crystals. She knocked on Fred's door. 'Go away,' he yelled. She knocked again. 'Go away,' came the response. Then silence, there was nothing left she could do. All her efforts wasted. She picked up the box, which was now just an encumbrance more than anything else and left. She would drop it off at Bradley's apartment.

'Something's afoot.' Epstein looked at the large, almost paper-thin transparent monitor in dismay. 'This element here,' he pointed at the top of the screen. The pattern of flowing forces had been interrupted and something seemingly ominous was there. To the other onlookers, it seemed to be nothing more than a black sludge superimposed upon the delicate lines of lights crisscrossing one another on the display. He waved his hand over the monitor. 'Display end targets,' his firm voice commanded.

'Processing,' a crystalline voice replied. The display shifted; each of the lines was zoomed into until the inside of what was no more than a tiny fraction of a percentage of an inch of the diameter of the line was amplified to the point where it seemed to be a tunnel through which travel was possible. Epstein flicked his hand from left to right, causing a rapid cascade of what seemed to be an impossible number of variations of such amplified tunnels. In between the transitions, he could see his own reflection there on the black surface. Tall, dark brown hair cut short, pulled back with the top part covered in lighter, almost golden well-groomed parts. Pale skin, wearing his usual tech-controlling square-shaped eye display on the right, which, from time to time, pulsed electric blue lights as it displayed ream upon ream of scrolling data. Perfectly trimmed short facial hair complimented his face, bringing to the forefront what he considered was an ideal shape of his jawline.

His long lab coat with trimmed edges and metallic blue symbols running all along the surface told the world he was a member of House mTech and quite a high ranking one at that. Each of these components woven into his white coat glowed with electric blue lights in response to certain devices, each one with a specific function, a set purpose. Under it, he wore the customary blacks and blues he was so fond of. To most, they would seem like suit trousers and tops, but they, too, had their set functions. His belt, very much like his lab coat, was covered in symbols and digits of various types, pulsing in the all too common blues. Its metal surface so polished, one could be mistaken to believe it was a miniature version of the massive displays he was so focussed on. The same could be said of his shoes. From head to toe, he was not only wearing clothing but also devices of one sort or another. He loved his technology, and this made him extremely versatile; it perfectly made up for his slim frame. He always commented on how the warriors had sacrificed too much for their mass. He would not make the same mistake!

He stopped abruptly, 'there!' His hand was placed over the central area of this tunnel, 'project in 4D,' he instructed.

'Quantum processing enabled, 4D space mapping of passageway 1987b,' responded the crystalline voice.

The space in which Epstein stood changed, the glyphs on his lab coat flared up and electric pulses flowed through them like water would through a network of pipes. He was standing inside the tunnel. He walked down into it and the projection shifted. Time passed as he carefully walked deeper and deeper into the tunnel, analysing the inner membranes' surface. *As I suspected, they have intruded upon the passageways. Damn them all!*

'Fast return to origin.'

'At once,' replied the system's voice. His entire walk into the tunnel momentarily reversed. He was not moving; instead, this time, the tunnel itself was moving about him until he was back out of and in front of the massive display. A reverse ripple closed inwards into its centre. The surface smoothed out, and it returned to its former state.

'I need to inform the Ruler at once.' He turned his back to the giant display and walked out, following the blue stream of power guiding his footsteps over the smooth, dark blue floor, the occasional stream of characters and digits flaring up in electric-blues. As he walked by, they formed a digital pathway guiding his footsteps.

Fred was in pain, a new odd type of pain, physical pain coursed through him in waves from his wrists to ankles and back up, cascading the entire length of his body. He couldn't understand where this was coming from until he felt and saw something, which shouldn't be there. Solid smooth crystals shackled bound his wrists and feet, glowing a deep indigo blue. Each pulse of the glow travelled the course of his body, making it shudder in pain. He panicked, tried to pull them off, over and over and over again. Failing at that, he tried to smash them against the walls, break them with the metal feet of his chair, hurl his wrists, exposing them against the radiators. Nothing worked. He was exhausted, both emotionally and now physically. He collapsed on his bed. As he lay there unconscious, the crystals activated, sealing themselves into him, for better or worse, they were now a part of him.

11

- THE SHIFT -

Bradley had fallen sleep; it had been a long day. Emotionally burnt out, he simply collapsed as soon as he got back to his apartment. It seemed so empty without Kuroi. Without warning, he just fell asleep as tears kept on cascading over his face.

He woke up in unfamiliar scenery. Where was he? He seemed to be on a road towards some unknown destination within a tree-filled scenery. He looked around and as he did, things started to change. Initially, those changes were very subtle. More focussed light from the sun, leaving other areas in the shadows. For a moment, his thoughts wandered; there was something he was forgetting about. Something had been nagging at him in the back of his mind. He felt empty, broken, but why? It should have bothered him, but it did not. The immediate environment he stood in continued to change; that too should have bothered him, but he seemed to pay it no heed, not until he crossed the path where all the freshness was left behind with the crispness of the night took hold. Many wonderful sounds woke up in the night, things sprang to life, odd species of insects glowed in the dark, certain flowers gave off a pale luminescence. It seemed even more unnatural to his mind than any of the previous experiences he had. Those faded too; nature had moved on from the cold summer night into autumn. The rapid shift was odd but not unpleasant. He looked about, sooner or later, he would have to find something to eat and a spot to rest. This could wait a little longer until he found a good spot; *I hope the fruits here are not toxic!*

He heard footsteps behind him, heavy firm footsteps. He turned 180 degrees and came face to face with a very tall young man, clad in metal practically from head to toe. Bradley looked at him and estimated an incredible height of almost 7 feet 5! Not a single inch of his body was uncovered, with the exception of his head, even the collar of his armour curved its way up to the topmost part of his neck. He looked in awe and surprise; the metallic fabric was so firm, it was impossible to determine where the skin ended and this armour began. There seemed to be different metals woven as if they had been fabrics in individual pieces of attire, all fused together by thick bindings and keyholes, which perplexed him to no end. They appeared to be utterly impossible. Looking closely, he figured that the only way a key could go that deep to open a lock of this sort was if it entered the very flesh of the wearer, burrowing itself deep inside his internal organs.

'Hello, there!' prompted the young man. His carefully sculpted facial hair, smooth pale slightly tanned face, deep amber eyes complemented his dark-blond hair. His voice deep yet youthful. There was a type of joy in it, which seemed totally at odds with what Bradley observed.

'Hello?' responded Bradley.

'On your way to House Bound, I see?' the young man observed.

'What? Wait, what? Not sure,' Memories flooded back and he remembered being here before. He remembered thinking it was all unreal; he remembered he was supposed to be somewhere else, somewhere different but could not quite grab hold of that fleeting memory. Memories of what the LightBearer had said about this House flooded back to him but nothing to help him contextualise them.

'Unsure, I see. It's ok; our true nature sometimes guides us down the path our minds are not ready to or are willing to accept outright.' He briefly closed his eyes. Bradley watched him closely as what appeared to be chains or rope woven over his body started expanding outwards and coiling in his hands.

'Here, let me make it easier for you.' He took a few steps closer to Bradley with the newly-formed rope-like chains in his hand on display. Bradley moved backwards. 'I see, well, it would make it easier for you to bind your will now. It takes the struggle away,' he explained, 'but if you prefer to struggle, we can take care of that when you arrive at the House, no worries.' He refocussed, causing them to merge back into those weaving around his body. 'I'm Lurizak, Acting Governor of the House Bound.' He stretched out his hand in greeting, offering it to Bradley. Bradley pulled back. 'Oh, I see, you have met the WonkerDudels. Don't worry, only their armour binds those who touch it, mine will not. Mine only binds me.' He nodded affirmatively.

Bradley reached out and shook the metal armoured hand, 'pleased to meet you.' It was soft and warm, just as any human hand would, yet it also had a smoothness, which was at odds with what a hand should feel like.

'It's a pleasure,' replied Lurizak. 'I seem to notice you appear very confused,' he commented.

'Yes, you are all bound? Those locks make no sense, and yet, you seem to be happy? It doesn't make sense.'

'Ah, it wouldn't make sense to you, would it. I'll let you in on a little House secret; everyone is bound in some way, shape or form. We are bound to the forms of our body or shapes, pick what term you like best. Our actions are bound by our social interactions; our potential is bound to be dormant with us. Here, in House Bound, we simply acknowledge that it frees us from our internal struggles and gives us a single-minded focus. Then we bind the forces within us and unleash them. It's all very simple. In our bindings, we find a freedom we never had before.'

Bradley thought about the words; he didn't understand them very much. He was used to being in control, not giving up control. Some part of his mind acknowledged that for all the control he had over his life, he actually had no freedom whatsoever. Someone or something was always setting the course of his actions; there were always rules.

'Some forces within you are too powerful and if you do not bind them, they will overwhelm you. I can see them clearly; they drive you, and they overwhelm you. You are terrified of them, yet desire them. Quite the dilemma young sir, isn't it?' he winked at Bradley as if they had shared a deep, meaningful secret.

'Maybe, maybe not.'

'That is why I offered to bind your will; I would have taken that burden from you, and with the help of the House, helped you harness all that power.' The offer was very appealing; something about Lurizak was exercising a pull of some sort on him. 'Anyway, since you are heading in the direction of the House, have a think about what I have said. I am sure you will see the sense of my advice by the time you get there.' He smiled reassuringly. Lurizak was used to dealing with newcomers, those who wished to achieve great things but lacked control over their natures. They were his speciality.

'I have to dash; the ruling council has only unbound me until nightfall in order to allow me to exercise my diplomatic duties. I have to get back into the House and report before nightfall. Before I leave, one final word of advice; to truly be in control, you have to give up control. Only the act of submission allows control of greater forces than one's' limited mind.' And with those words, he dashed onwards, leaving Bradley perplexed. There was wisdom in those words, but this was not the path for him. This is not what he wanted, he knew that. He wanted to be in control, not give it all up. Yet somehow, he still kept on moving forward. Something was wrong. Despite all his efforts, he eventually ended up standing right in front of House Bound.

Jaws agape in amazement, he stood in front of the massive structure. *This is not a house; it's a damn city!* The huge golden-copper towering buildings were a sight to behold. Two columns with a central section, structures so tall they seemed to reach into the sky itself, their width miles upon miles long. It was impossible to contain the entire structure in one's sight without shifting as far to the left, then as far to the right as sight would allow. Each of the columns bore complex patterns and intricate carvings, which would pulse with life every so often. The symbols within moved with a slow, steady, controlled smoothness like shiny reflective metallic foil on a metallic surface, energy rippled around them and the entire sight of them was totally mesmerising. Chains, ropes, or was it cords of various coloured metals, connected parts of the building to each other, wrapping about them, curving from the one to the other like veins within the body. Silver, gold, copper, some blue type of metal, a yellow, a red; there were so many types that Bradley stared in utter amazement. Never had he seen metals such as these, let alone fashioned to such exquisite perfection. Those hanging over the central structure spelt the words: 'House Bound.'

The door opened, and a smiling Lurizak stood there. 'Welcome, welcome friend, come on in.'

Bradley took a step forward and froze. He pulled back and tried again, and froze again.

'What's wrong?' asked Lurizak.

'I can't step foot through the doorway.' He tried again. Same result.

Lurizak looked concerned. He hesitated, then offered up one of his charming smiles and said, 'it seems we might have a Wielder in the making; let's see if you can get in through the back door.'

'What is all this about?'

'House Bound has special rules, only those who can enter through the front door join the Bound. But without those who bind, there can be no bound. Those we call the Wielders. Make your way to the left side; there, you will find the other entrance. I will wait for you on the other side of that door.'

Bradley was confused; he had no idea how he'd made his way to this very house, let alone understood all this nonsense. Looking at the situation logically, there was no other way for him to wake up from this nightmare unless he actually let it run its course. He made his way to the left side; it took him what seemed like ages to walk all the way across. The lawn on this side was odd and the path he walked through was perfectly well-kept, delimited along the length by no lawn whatsoever. It seemed the adjacent pathway was made of a dull black substance for the pavement was so deep in blackness that you would lose yourself by just staring into it. Something on that pathway shone for a brief moment, a glimpse of dark black glimmer. No sooner had he noticed it than it was gone. Curiosity took over and he carefully stepped off the lawn of House Bound and onto the black pathway. He started to walk.

The side door of House Bound opened; Lurizak expected to find Bradley there waiting; instead, he saw him walking down the dark path 'Noooooo, don't go there!' he shouted. To Bradley, it was nothing more than a whisper in the distance, something calling out to him, someone he couldn't remember. *Must not be important,* he concluded and kept on walking down the long black road. As time passed, he started forgetting things. Everything seemed to have lost its importance, becoming so insignificant that it was no longer worth the effort of even trying to remember. His love, his son, his passion for the sciences, his hate of the shadow assaulting him, Heather, the virus, his responsibilities all simply faded away. Eventually, all that was left was him, or was it? Even the very concept of himself started to fade until he could no longer recall who or what he was. Was I ever alive? echoed throughout his mind.

At House Bound, Lurizak was trying to explain to the LightBearer and twins what had happened. They followed Bradley's progress and observed from nearby. 'How could you be so irresponsible and leave that road so damn easily accessible?' the LightBearer snapped at him. 'It is utterly mind-numbingly irresponsible and foolish. This was bound to happen at some point! Why not bind it off? A House of Binders my backside, more like the unBounds.'

'That will be enough,' came a powerful voice from behind Lurizak. He turned around and bowed, 'Acting-Ruler Tamirok.' The imposing figure of the acting-ruler stepped forth, his bindings all too obvious for all to see but far more intricate than those of Lurizak. The chainlike cords held the flesh tight, muscles pulsed until the skin-tight metals, power ebbed out of him and back into him, bound forged and tightly controlled. The intricacy of his armour and its shaping spoke volumes; this was not only a veteran of countless wars but one of the highest-ranking commanders in battle. 'There is no need, and it's improper to insult the House. You know as do all others that that road MUST be kept open for the doomed to follow unto their demise. It is no incident that this newcomer you so admire could not enter our House and learn control. One who rejects one's self deserves nothing but oblivion.' His powerful firm voice made it crystal clear that he would not tolerate any further arguments or objections.

'Could you have not done something to save him? He was at your front door!' objected the LightBearer, her armour flashed a beam of light directly into the House itself.

'Listen very well, little missy, only those who step INTO the House become our responsibility. He was not invited here as a guest, nor was he summoned here by decree of a House. He had no right to our protection in any form whatsoever. Incidentally, the same runs true for the lot of you! The matter is settled. Forget about him. He's lost to both sides now. There is no point in wasting time.' He brushed aside her beam of light as if it was nothing more than a bug swept in the motion of his hand and walked away, leaving them all behind. The message was not lost on any of them; they all instantly understood that none of their powers were even a concern for him, let alone a match of any sort. Lurizak looked at them, wondering what he could do to help when he felt his will fade away completely. 'Close the door and return to your duties,' Tamirok's command echoed throughout the vast corridor. He complied. He had to.

'Sorry,' he whispered before closing the door.

'Well, that was a shame, such potential, such loss,' was all Darvinius could say.

'Time for us to go home.' Darenien had had enough. Sorrow filled his heart.

'You're both giving up? This easily?' asked the LightBearer.

'Yes, can't you feel it? His essence is all but faded already. He just needs a few more steps before falling into oblivion. Even if we did the impossible, nothing would reach him in time.'

She knew he was right and sorrow filled her heart. She could not understand why, but the loss left a heavy weight upon her. *The twins are right; it is time for me to return to the light.* They all left in their respective directions.

Kiandra Kustings sat at her new desk. She had weeded her way into the laboratory team. She smiled; the first part of her and Mira's plan had gone smoothly. Well, now it was up to her to ensure the second part went just as smoothly. She smiled; she loved the way Mira worked, especially with respect to these sorts of situations. It always meant she was placed in a position of authority. Kiandra loved authority, well only when she was its source. *Professor Kustings,* she reminded herself. She had obtained that position, thanks to Mira's influence, and she was eternally grateful for it. It was extremely rare that Mira allowed any other woman any sort of rank and file, which could potentially be a threat to her at some point in the remote future, but Kiandra had proven her loyalty over and over again for over 12 years. Her loyalty would be proven again right here; she would not fail no matter what!

She ran her fingers through her long ordinary-looking brown hair. She let a long sigh out; she wished she had Mira's lovely jet black curls. Adjusting her frameless glasses, she refocussed on what was important. Kiandra did not care much for her appearance other than looking presentable, which was obvious for all to see. Her attire was the most plain and unappealing anyone could wear. A simple top, usually a jumper of some sort or other; in the hot weather, a blouse with as little pomp and fuss as possible, typically all uniform in colour. Her skirts were just as uneventful, as were her plain shoes. The only minor deviation from this dull plainness was the single brooch she wore on the left. A most intricate amber and diamond-encrusted bumblebee. She loved it; it had been a gift from her grandmother. It was her most cherished possession, her lucky charm. She disproved all the fuss people made when selecting clothing; it was such a waste of time. Her plain appearance was one of her assets; it made her look very simple, totally unthreatening. It was that one fatal mistake everyone made when dealing with her. Her deep brown eyes shifted rapidly from computer screen to paperwork. *I definitely will have my work cut out dealing with this!* she concluded.

'Cosy place, this one,' commented Elma as she sipped her cocktail at the bar. It was a traditional establishment with an interesting mix of the old fashioned wooden pillars, supporting beams, bar and ornaments, intermingled with the touch of modern-day elegance. Mirrors, glass and hyper-polished surfaces were distributed here and there just to add a touch of that little something.

'Indeed, not my usual selection, but when dealing with the common rubble of life, it is more than suitable,' replied Mira. 'Let's get down to business, shall we? Time is ticking, and my time is extremely valuable right now.'

'As you wish.' Elma handed her a file and a USB drive. 'I believe this is what you were looking for.'

Mira flipped through the pages, nodding. 'It is indeed an excellent start.' She continued reading. 'Damn them! I was not expecting them to make such progress so fast.' A couple of 'humms' later, she closed it. 'Well, at least my latest intervention should slow them down.'

'Anything else? Besides this?' she prompted.

'Nothing concrete, just something interesting reported by the quantum research department.'

'That is none of my concern,' interjected Mira, 'all I am interested in is what is going on with their discoveries relating to our virus.'

'Our virus?' prompted Elma. Mira bit her tongue; she had slipped up. *No matter,* she thought, *this one will do anything for money; I can buy her silence and her loyalty.*

'No matter, just a misnomer; it has been a pleasant chat, I will be in touch.' She got up, leaving her drink unfinished.

'Are we not forgetting something?' asked Elma.

'No WE are not, payment was sent a few minutes ago, you should be receiving it momentarily.' True to her word, Elma's phone buzzed. A text message from her bank, detailing a large payment into her account. Mira waited a few seconds for Elma to finish reading the text. 'I trust you will appreciate the little bonus I added to your payment. Think of it as a thank you for the very prompt delivery.'

'Thank you, very much appreciated!' the smile on Elma's face was all Mira needed to see. *I definitely have that one where I need and want her,* she concluded. Elma picked up her glass and pretended to cheer Mira 'to our next adventure then!' She took a sip.

'Indeed,' and with that word, Mira walked off. She had urgent matters to deal with. As soon as she stepped out of the bar and into her limo, she picked up the phone and dialled Kiandra's number.

'Professor Kustings speaking, how may I be of assistance?'

'It is I, Kiandra,'

'Oh apologies, didn't recognise the number,' she admitted.

'I took my assistant's phone to avoid being traced. I have some information pertaining to our project that I am sure you will find most useful.'

'I am most curious.'

'They have made far more progress than we hoped for. If they are not slowed down, this could all fall flat on its face.' Mira was concerned. Too much had happened for this particular venture to go belly up.

'I will deal with it immediately; you have nothing to worry about. This is why we made sure I was here.'

'Indeed, you will get the files over in a few minutes via secure email.'

'This is my number one priority.'

'Excellent, keep me updated.'

'As you wish,' replied Kiandra. The phone line went dead. Kiandra left the office and went to search for a coffee shop. She had to get onto a Wi-Fi network not connected to the labs or the university to avoid being traced. She knew that game all too well.

Bradley walked mindlessly. He was nothing more than a corpse, a living corpse. *Remember! Awaken and remember!* Someone had touched his mind. Something was yelling at him. He turned around to try and see who was talking to him, but the next instant, he had forgotten why he had turned in the first place and took another step forward, forgetting the entire incident. *REMEMBER!* This time, it came as a howl and he stopped. *Oh ye of old, remember and awaken!* Speech? Yes, it was speech. Words, he remembered words. Those sounds into which meaning was poured like a drug, the constant, ceaseless chatter of minds and men, words. He had used them at some point in time. Strange things words. Meaningless, yet when used to communicate, they conveyed meaning. Empty things without essence. Essence? Yes, he remembered essence, each being had its own unique essence. It was precious for some reason. He could not remember why or what made it precious in the first place. *Remember ye of old, remember, I harken thee, remember!* A shadow danced in the empty darkness about him, or was it a light? A shadow in the dark, how could that be? He couldn't remember. *Remember WHAT you are, oh ye of old, remember WHO you are and remember WHERE you are! Remember!* He was doing something, no he was going somewhere, where was he going? Why? The memory evaded him. Something had driven him at some point in time, there was meaning somewhere in his life… yet where, he could not grasp. Someone, yes, someone was with him, but who that might have been was lost to him.

Who was he anyway? What was he? He felt warm, he felt heat, power flowed through him. Was this power? His mind raced, *what an odd thing*, he thought. With the heat a quickening, a buzz flowed along his entire body, *yes body, I had a body at some point*, he pondered. It intensified and grew, became light. Light shone out of him, brightened things; he remembered light, he had light at some point. Then he noticed the light's edges cast shadows; the shadows danced around the light and within the dark. He remembered shadows, something about them was important, yet also he feared them. He saw something, what he saw was an infinite expanse of pure boundless darkness. He remembered the darkness; most children feared it. Children? *What an odd concept,* yet that very concept brought him deep sorrow. The sorrow led to the joy, the joy to the love, and the love to terrible heartache. Loneliness, he remembered that as well. Anger stirred, desire flourished in his mind, revenge! The need for it. His body ached for it. *Revenge for what?* he pondered. Pain unfolded, waves upon waves of unbearable pain washed over him, sending his body into shivering spasm. Loss, all the emotions assaulted his awakening mind. He remembered, he had loved once and been denied, he had lost one he cared for immensely, and he had lost his child, a part of him had died then. He remembered it all, memories flooded in unbridled, uncontrolled threatened to tear his very soul apart—vengeance against the culprits, fury at mankind, sheer burning power extracted from the darkness itself. Yes, *MORE,* his mind cried out, *I want it ALL!* His mind screamed at the impersonal omnipresent expanse of darkness. It overwhelmed him. Everything went blank and his senses collapsed.

'Bradley? Bradley, dear, wake up,' he recognised the voice. He felt her touch, so gentle and yet firm. 'Kuroi?' he hesitated.

'Yes, but only for an instant or two,'

'I'm sorry,' he cried out to her. 'I tried to find a cure, but I wasn't good enough, I failed you both.' Pain sheered through him like a hot blade cutting his heart in half.

'There is nothing to be sorry for, dearest,' her glowing blue hands took hold of his face, gently pulling his gaze upwards. 'Listen to me; you need to wake up. You need to wake up now, or you will fade away forever. Remember your promise, remember your son, remember me,' her voice faded, 'please Bradley, don't lose yourself.' She was gone.

Bradley was left alone, tears cascading down his face uncontrollably. 'I remember, Kuroi, I remember it all!' Strength filled his weakened limbs; he would not lose himself to a dream, to anyone! The fire flared in his blood; *I will get revenge for what was done, no matter what the costs!* Fire pulsed out of him in waves and this time, it gave off no light. Dark blacks and deep blood reds flared up. He remembered! The crystals, the quantum fields, he remembered it all. It amplified, changed and fluctuated. Too hot, far too hot, *going to burn out* was all he could think, *too hot, it's too much.* He was about to lose consciousness again. A massive voice, male and female, young and old, echoed throughout the endless infinite blackness 'Welcome to House Nothingness.' His body moved of its own accord and he took a step forward.

He stood in a cold dark house, brickwork perfectly maintained but ancient beyond his understanding. Its atmosphere reminded him of ancient temples that Heather would rant and rave about. Why the girl liked all this ancient archaeology was beyond him; he wished he had acquired at least some of her knowledge on the topic. He looked straight ahead. The architecture was beyond mind-bending; the walls were at odd angles, the floors were ceilings, which were floors he could not make out any of it. The highly polished surfaces reflected their blackness onto the deep violet and green hues of the opposing tiles. The construction of the place, the angles within angles, and this highly reflective surface made it totally impossible to navigate. Trying to gain any sort of space co-ordination was simply beyond his capabilities. Walls merged into one another, angles reflected off each other; this was not a maze, this was utterly maddening. Perfectly etched black stone glyphs were blended into the architecture; he remembered those! He had seen them before.

A figure formed mid-air in front of him. It had a humanoid type of shape but looked as if it was nothing more than a piece of the environment, which had been cut out, leaving an emptiness in the space in front of him. 'I am....' The words which came out of it echoed through vast distances towards him. The name given was so complicated he would never be able to pronounce it. '... and I am here to serve as your guide and assistant in the House. It is a pleasure to meet you,' Bradley gathered his wits about him.

'Nice meeting you, ...' He struggled. The creature saw his struggle and offered help. 'Our names are very hard for your kind to use, so pick a name for me, and I shall go by that one instead.'

'Ok, it is a little difficult. How about Nihitus? In front of others, I can just call you Nihi;' for some reason, the name amused him. Its meaning was clearly nothing. The being approved.

'House Nothingness contains nothing,' explained Nihitus, 'it also contains the potential for everything.' Bradley did not understand; it made no sense. It seemed to him that no and nothing were going to be a common theme here.' It also has no members and no rulers. Well, had in your language would be more accurate. Now it has claimed you, the first being to make it this far and not lose himself to the nothing in a very,' it paused, 'very,' the echoing voice boomed on, 'long time.' Bradley was unsure what to do about any of this, what did it have to do with him?

'What am I supposed to do with all this? I just want to get back,' he asked. The being remained still. Silence, or rather the nothing of sound permeated the place, making him deeply uncomfortable. He asked again, 'what has all this got to do with me?' This time, his question's slight difference prompted an answer.

'You are the embodiment of the essence of the House. Other Houses would call you its ruler, but nothing has no ruler because there is nothing to rule.'

Bradley's head spun; this was driving him in circles, none of which was making any sense. 'I need to sit down,' he observed. No sooner had he done so than a large throne-like chair appeared, formed out of the same nothingness as the creature. He looked at it and cautiously touched it. Nothing happened; it seemed solid. 'Is it safe?' he asked.

'To you, yes, to others no,' replied the creature. He threw caution to the wind and sat down. It felt good; he was energised by it; the burning power within him was absorbed into it rather than burning him. For the first time since all this madness had begun with the dam virus, he was at peace and content. The virus brought him back to his dilemmas. 'Is there something I can learn here to help me with the damn virus? Help me get back home?' he asked.

'Yes, the nothing is everything, all knowledge is within the nothing, yet there is no knowledge in the nothing.' As usual, the creature's answers were not only cryptic but also totally unhelpful.

'How do I get to this knowledge? Is there any library? Teachers?' he wondered. After all, he was sure that each House had mysteries of its own, sciences of its own specialisations.

'There is nothing in House Nothingness.'

Bradley was getting really annoyed. 'Where can I learn about the nothing about how things work?' his voice had a hint of frustration within it.

The creature was totally unfazed. 'There is nothing to learn about the nothing, for it is nothing,' came the response.

He was going to yell out at it, but just as he prepared to, the creature continued, 'learning is done in the other Houses, the nothing is nothing and has nothing to offer.'

Learning in other Houses? Yes, maybe, but how? If I just turned up, would they teach me? But then again, which House, he pondered. 'Goodness, no, I don't want to be a Bound or a WonkerDudel,' inadvertently, he spoke his thoughts.

'That's not possible,' the creature said, 'ruler of Houses to be members of others. Information exchange protocols in between houses allow for members of ruling and master ranks to guest or link in-between Houses.'

Finally! Something useful. Bradley thought about it for a second; maybe he was just communicating wrong with this thing? He decided to try once more, but instead of asking questions, just speaking his thoughts as that seems to trigger a different response. 'I wonder which House would be best? I can't stand the WonkerDudels or whatever the heck they are called, the Bound is just not my thing, the LightBearer was nice, but a desperation and affinity to manipulate were there too. I'm not sure ... ' no reaction was prompted from the creature, so he continued 'would such a link cause an effect in me? And what would it be? Might it be best to choose something compatible with me rather than something in opposition? Or not?'

'House Nothingness compatibility irrelevant, awareness compatibility best with Bound for initial learning, GrimGlooms for power enhancement and Aetherix for ascension,' offered the creature.

'Awareness compatibly? What does that mean?' he asked.

'Compatibility with the overarching purpose of awareness and future path to be walked through life for you,' it explained.

'But what if I don't want to follow that path?' objected Bradley.

'Human life forms have no power to choose their path, all predetermined by fate. Ruler path malleable once power mastered not before. Currently, bound by House and Fate's dictates. Ability to alter House selection given but not advised if mastery is sought.'

'Wait a minute, bound by Fate? Nonsense, there is no such thing. We make our own Fates, and we make our own choices. We have free will.' He paused for a moment; now, he sounded exactly like Mira. He paused, *who the hell is Mira?* Hate stirred within him at the thought of her. *Why do I hate her? Do I even know a Mira?* He had to get out of this madness and get back as soon as possible.

'In Nothing, time collapses; you possess memories of what is yet to be, which to you here already was but to you now never has been,' explained Nihitus. It then returned to the previous point 'All dictated by Fate, free will illusion built by humans on False Earth to fester belief of independence and freedom. Everything controlled by Her, from breath taken to thought. End goal failed or reached dependant on human acceptance to speed through experiences dictated by Fate or rejection of them and break down.'

Bradley was not convinced. As usual, all the information coming from this thing made no sense whatsoever; he could easily think of hundreds if not thousands of situations where he had a clear choice, and he made the choices himself. Yet something nagged at the back of his mind. He remembered reading a scientific report on neurology, stating that decisions were made by his brain not him. He brushed it to the back of his mind. This was not the time or the place for that investigation. He had to get out of here.

'Well, if fate is dictating my next move, how about telling me what it is so that I don't need to wrack my brain over what to do next?'

'Accepted,' the very substance in the being seemed to shift, a blur in its nothingness ripped outwards and vibrated off the edge of its confines. 'Awareness requires control, gained in House Bound.'

Bradley's inner mind came crashing down on him; that was the last place he wanted to go. 'Heck no, no bloody way,' was his response.

It did not matter, because, at that very moment, the thing began to blur, dizziness took over and a brief enormous burning sensation rushed throughout his body. Then something cold, his body felt different. No, it was not different; it was in a different position and he was face down on the floor. Had he failed? He was exhausted, so fatigued he could barely move. His vision cleared, the blurring faded, the air was fresh, it felt like air once more. He looked up; he was outside, in front of a door. He tried to reach out. He heaved himself up slightly to reach the door handle. The weight of his body was too much for him and it banged against the door as he lost consciousness.

Lurizak opened the door and saw Bradley trying to reach up to him and fall back down unconscious, his upper torso and head falling across the threshold into House Bound. Fate smiled a delightful laughter; she had won this round, forcing him exactly where he had to be. The flicker of intense will and resistance stirring in him concerned her; it was a bad sign. Something would have to be done about that, but for now, the matter was under control. Her eternal gaze shifted elsewhere.

Bradley woke up, head pounding, completely exhausted. He turned his head to see where he was. The room was comfortable, clean and simple, decorated in heavy brown and black leather with white sheets. He gazed at the ceiling above, decorated with a tapestry of sculptures, or was it a painting? He could not tell as many of them seemed to be made of chains. Hundreds upon hundreds of different shades of interlocking metals, creating a wonderful impossible seemingly pattern. Totally mesmerising.

'Beautiful, isn't it?' asked Lurizak. Bradley turned and stared at him.

'Where ... am ... I?' he asked.

'Where you were supposed to be in the first place, House Bound. But now it seems you are not supposed to be here.' Bradley's head spun, he didn't have the strength for dilemmas. He tried to get up, only to find a cold yet soft metal hand firmly pressing against his chest, forcing him back down. He blinked.

'Stay, it will be ok,' Lurizak gave that all too sympathetic reassuring smile. Bradley was convinced there was some foul play behind that smile. Even so, it reassured him. He settled down. 'You collapsed at the door of Wielders just as I opened it half in and half out. Acting-Ruler Tamirok decided that since you were half in, you had been welcomed by the House. We took care of you, as your body was severely damaged by an onslaught of quantum particles. They layered through your organs, blood vessels and nerves, burning through them. Our medics took great effort in fixing you. It will take you a while to fully recover, and I've been charged to make sure you stay in bed, eat and sleep until the Ruling Council decides what to do about you. Your choice is simple: are you going to rest willingly, or will I have to restrain you and force you to rest?' The expression on his face had changed from friendly and warm to one of dead seriousness. Bradley swallowed involuntarily. In his weakened state, he could not do anything to counter this.

'I'll rest, I'll rest.'

'Good, I had hoped you would. All sensible men rest up to regain their strength when they are unwell.' His friendly, jovial expression was back. 'I'll be off for a while, business to attend to, and the will of my wielder is coursing strongly through me.' He spontaneously got up and started walking towards the door, and as he did, his head turned, 'make sure you eat! Food will be served...' Had Bradley not been so weak, he would have exploded in laughter as the entire sight was utterly comical. Lurizak's body was moving in one direction while his head was trying to face the other; they appeared to be totally disconnected from each other. Upon that observation, Bradley felt into a deep sleep.

Kiandra was at her desk; she had just finished reading through the data sent over by Mira. This was a little too much for her. The expertise of the team here was going to be a problem. She had to find a way to counterbalance that weakness. Her initial surprise strike was to move all the laboratories to the second floor and isolate the offices, keeping them on the ground floor. That would take weeks to complete and will have caused enough of a disruption to unsettle things a little. Next, she needed to ensure that the rigid routines would not be able to reinstate themselves too soon.

She scrolled down through the list of employees and carefully perused each in the utmost detail. There must be a weakness in the setup she could exploit. It only took a few minutes; a key number of names kept popping up over and over again, project after project: Dr. Heather Hawke and Dr. Bradley Boston.

'Hawke,' that name is very familiar.... She recalled reading something about the Hawkes, a young couple shot in a terror attack on one of the labs. 'What was it?' she ran her fingers unaware over her keyboard. 'Ah yes, an animal protest gone wrong in one of the medical research facilities a few years back. Could this Heather be their daughter?' she was intrigued. She couldn't find anything in the files. *No matter, I'll get the intelligence division to do a search; they will have access to much more information than staff files over here ever will.* She hit the search button and opened Bradley's file.

'Now now, what do we have here. An aspiring prodigy it seems. Genetics, bio-engineering research, nervous system, tissue regeneration, circulatory system expertise, wide application of genomics... what hasn't he done?' She scrolled down to see his personals, aged 33. She was shocked. How was it possible for anyone to have this vast research expertise at that young age? Suspicion immediately flared up; this was not possible! Well, not according to her. 'This is it! The weak spot, something fishy is going on with this young man.' She was hooked. One way or another, she would find out what the deal was.

Meanwhile, in the council room, a debate was taking place. The atmosphere was charged, everyone had their opinion, none disagreed, yet none could agree either. Silence hung over the huge open space in the council room. Its bronze metallic and deep-treated oak wood decor gave the place a simultaneous comfortable homely type of feel and a highly formal one. This seemingly confusing contrast alongside the indecision of the council created a general sense of unease. The seven rulers sat in their tall throne-like seats made of some ancient material, which looked like oiled lighter wood folded as one would a material fabric. The armrests expanded upwards in perfect darker shaded oak wood like L shapes. Their imposing construction complemented the massive 20-feet tall statue of ancient warriors standing behind each one of them. Each of these darkened copper statues held one hand out, which balanced a glowing metal sculpture of a blazing glyph. These glyphs floated above the hand and were held down by chains emanating from between their fingers. Those glyphs glowed in their own metal tinted colours, casting an eerie light upon the crowns of the rulers sat underneath. The ruling council had to make a decision. For the first time since its formation, no one wanted to make that decision. No one wanted the responsibility of what the end result of this decision would be.

'You don't understand Tamirok,' a stern female voice argued. 'What I saw was not chaos as you understand it. This is not what the Houses deals with as they structure and manipulated chaotic forces.'

'Exactly,' affirmed Meneshark, 'any other House would be the ideal for him.'

'No, it wouldn't,' interrupted Lishtana to whom that stern female voice belonged. Her thin, skinny pale finger pointed to the massive window on their left. 'What I saw emanating out of him was pure chaos, totally uncontrolled and uncontrollable! It is the stuff of nightmares from the Gates-Out-There,' pointing in the direction of the sky and the universe at large. Her skin-tight metal amour perfectly engraved with complex power patterns and highly intricate glyphs were still powerful despite her old age. 'Everything inside of him, except his physical body, is totally chaotic, particles smashing into each other, others tearing themselves up, yet others rebuilding and reforming things. At this rate, he will burn out.' She folded her arm, blue eyes holding Tamirok firmly in their gaze.

Lurizak had entered the council chamber and stood facing the semi-circular table-like structure made of dark leathery marble. Acting-ruler Lishtana had the glyph of power, hers was the specialisation of control of power, Acting-ruler Tamirok sat under the dominion of the glyph of binding, his was the specialisation of bindings, and Acting-ruler Meneshark, nicknamed the savage warrior, his pale face bearing many scars of battle, sat under the glyph of war, his was the specialisation of war mastery. The other members sat silently, listening to the debate taking place.

'Well then, what do you suggest, Lishtana? You said so yourself; he's so chaotic that he cannot be trained to wield those powers. We could always just dump him into another House and let him fade away within their walls; it does not have to be our concern.'

'NO,' interrupted Tamirok, 'we can't do that. He not only fell through our doorway, but he was making his way to us before.'

'He was?' asked Acting-ruler Meneshark, his golden-copper armour reflecting the light from the massive fireplace to their left, setting the combat glyphs etched in it alight. His hyper-muscular body hummed with deep blood-red resonance.

'Explain,' Tamirok faced Lurizak, who had been standing there silently, held firm by the will of his wielder. The grip of that will relaxed, although only ever so slightly. Lurizak nodded in agreement.

'I met him; names were exchanged on the road to the House. He seemed uncertain as most newcomers are, but his every step took him closer and closer to the front door of House Bound. I offered him the chains of binding of will to make the trip easier for him and avoid the internal struggle.' He paused momentarily, during which time they all remembered how they had struggled with the very concept of becoming one of the Bound. They all nodded. 'As most of us do, he refused, determined that this was not the path he was going to take. Nevertheless, the following day, he stood at our front door. I opened and greeted him, bidding him to enter, but he could not step foot into the House.'

'There you have it, he does not belong here, couldn't be clearer,' interjected Meneshark.

'No, quite,' Tamirok intervened. 'Go on,' he instructed Lurizak.

'There was something peculiar about the House's response to him. Some part of him belonged while some other parts did not. So I followed protocol, which dictates that anyone showing up at the door of the Bound and failing to enter is given the trial of the other door. So I guided him to that side.'

'AND?' Lishtana was most curious.

'He never knocked; I waited and waited. Then I decided to look at what was happening, as he could not have missed the entrance. I thought a newcomer to TrueEarth might have misinterpreted my instructions. He was not bound, so I could not will him there. I opened the door and saw him walking down the black road. He must have strayed onto it on his way to the other door.'

'I knew that pathway was going to be trouble. Tell us why does it have to be right next to our House? Where does it lead anyway?' asked Meneshark. Silence filled the council room.

'To oblivion,' one of the older warrior type acting-rules replied.

'Are you telling me that this man from FalseEarth went into oblivion and came back from it?' prompted Meneshark.

'That's impossible,' replied Lurizak.

'No one follows the Path to Oblivion and comes back. They are unmade during the journey. Legends state that once on the path, it is impossible to change course,' explained the older female voice.

'That would explain it,' interrupted Lurizak.

'Explain what?' asked Tamirok.

'I tried calling out to him, told him to stop, bid him to turn back. For a moment, I could have sworn he had turned around to face me, but his expression was totally blank as if he did not hear me, nor could see me.' Everyone gasped.

'How is he here then? What is he doing here? And what do we do about this?'

'Brothers and Sisters of the House, this is most perplexing, an impossibility made real,' started Tamirok. He had decided to take control; otherwise, this would never end nor be resolved, and they had other important matters to deal with. 'In time, all is bound, and all is unbound,' the motto of the House was their cardinal rule, 'all questions aside, certain facts are incontestable. This man from FalseEarth finds himself in TrueEarth. He is faced with representatives of two other houses, yet decides to make his own pathway. Earth guided him to our front door; the House acknowledged something in him and forced him to the challenge of the Wielders entrance. Whatever happened next, he will have to testify himself, but we do know that following his challenge, he made it BACK to the entrance of the wielders and fell halfway through the door INTO the House. This, in my opinion, is incontestable proof that either he is a bindings wielder belonging in our midst, or the House offered him temporary membership, for some reason or other. Either way, I would suggest you all carefully consider the will of the House, and I would most certainly put forth that he is not only where he belongs, but we have a duty to assist him.'

Tamirok sat down, signalling his case was put and closed. Silence flooded the large council chamber. Several acting-rulers were nodding in the affirmative, some were shrugging their shoulders in indecision, and two of them had arms crossed, singling they did not concur. The majority, however, did.

'How do you propose we deal with him, Tamirok? I am not sure any of us actually want to be involved, and I most certainly do not want a Bound of that kind to be my responsibility,' objected Lishtana.

'Is this assessment of the acting-rulers accurate?' he asked. Every single one nodded affirmatively. Tamirok gave out a long deep sigh. 'Very well, I propose, if it is permitted for me to take him under my charge; I will seek to train him in the arts of a Wielder and give him the basics of the Bound. The only thing I would ask is for your assistance with his powers, Lishtana. Your expertise in this domain surpasses all of ours combined. Should he turn out to be that big a challenge, I will need your help, desperately so.' He looked at her, gazing deeply.

'Very well, but on the condition that I am under no formal obligation. I can withdraw as and when I see fit.' She looked at each council member in turn, and each one nodded in agreement. Finally, her gaze fixed Tamirok.

'Fine, agreed.' He gave in. If this was all he would get, it was all he would have. It would simply have to do. They all stood up and, in unison, spoke their agreement, 'The Will of the House is done, and we bind ourselves to it.'

A flash of energy flooded all their armours as it seeped into them, charging them with power. A power, which not only empowered them but also bound them. Any breach of these types of formal agreements would have the most serious consequences. Consequences that everyone in TrueEarth feared more than death itself, ones which the Bound feared the most for they knew the implications. This binding of agreements was one of the reasons why the Bound were the supervisors of all formal agreements in TrueEarth. Lurizak felt the will of his wielder flood his body as he, without any warning, walked out of the council room back towards the infirmary. He kind of liked it this way, never having to question or hesitate on what had to be done and for how long. He would just let go and allow his wielder, Tamirok, to control his body, instructing it directly. It made life so much simpler.

12

RE
- ORGANISATION -

'There, that should buy us quite a bit of time.' Kiandra hit the Enter button on her email and clicked the Send All option. What she considered her master plan had been set in motion. *Next, the little things that are the main focus of all this charade.* She sent a further three emails. These were the important ones, which would make or break the entire plan. She would ensure they would not be allowed to break it. Far too much was at stake.

It did not take long for the first impact to be felt. Dr Grimsaw stormed into her office. She had a student there waiting to submit some paperwork for an internship. 'Get out of my way,' he snapped at the student as he pushed through. 'What on Earth are you playing at? This is totally unacceptable,' he stormed at her.

'Would you excuse us please?' Kiandra asked the student, who just nodded and left the office. 'That was very rude. I would have expected a little more civility from someone of your standing and age.' She had hoped to strike a chord, but it failed.

'Oh cut the nonsense out, I'm too well accustomed to the games your generation plays with their politics. Explain yourself!'

'Why there's nothing to explain. Was something in the email unclear? I'm certain I double-checked every word in there to ensure everyone would understand it.'

'I'm sure you did!' he sneered at her. 'What is this nonsense?' He held a printout of her email. 'Position only open to women applicants? This is outrageous.'

'Not to worry, Dr Grimsaw, it is all perfectly legal. We're just addressing a gender inequality. It's not discrimination if you are trying to remedy an existing state of discriminatory employment practices.'

'Are you totally insane? No one is discriminated against here. Everyone is given a chance to prove their skills and professional history. We don't even label applications per gender!'

'Yet you only have three women working here and how many is it? Twenty-seven men? That's just not right,' she retorted.

'That is not our fault. We pick the most experienced applicants. I employ on merit, not on some equalisation criteria. Give me a bright, highly skilled woman scientist and we would be delighted to take her on board.'

'Exactly what I am trying to do, doctor.'

'No you are not! You are opening a post for promotion to assistant-professor and excluding scientists who have been working in these labs for over 20 years, just because they are not your preferred gender! I won't stand for this nonsense.'

'I'm afraid you have no choice in the matter. In this crisis time I have been put in charge of the management and that includes the staff requirements to take us through this crisis. I would suggest your invaluable time might be better spent on managing the actual research, or have we found a cure already?' He looked at her in utter rage. His face was bright red.

'Let me remind you, Miss Administrator, that it is the integrity and expertise – ' he emphasised that word deliberately – 'in these laboratories that keeps the public and country safe from biological threats. Any lowering of standards and disruptions puts lives at risk. This is not a place for politics and other such nonsense.' He lost his composure as he stormed out of the office, yelling back at no one in particular, 'Damn woman causing chaos all over the place just to mark her authority.'

'I'll take that on advisement,' she replied, even though he was out of earshot. She returned to other matters at hand, smiling. *Exactly as planned. First stage a success, time for stage two.*

Jim was upset. 'Where are my blood samples? Damn all this moving up to the second floor. Did we really need to do this now? Doesn't anyone know we're in the middle of a potential health crisis?' He opened the containers one after another, trying to locate the new samples sent through from the hospital to the department and to find the old sample, to ensure he was looking at a live comparison.

'Hi Jim, everything ok? You seem upset?' Heather walked in, wearing her deep rich blue attire, complimented with silver brooch and bracelet.

He whistled at her and smiled. 'Seeing you always brightens things up. You are looking very smart today!'

'Why thank you. So kind of you to say.' *I wish some other people would notice too*, she thought. 'So what's the problem? Anything I can do to help?' she asked.

'I can't seem to find anything. Everything is in containers, or goodness knows where else, probably in transit. Who the heck thought it would be a good idea to do a move now of all times?' he asked.

'A new professor of some sort has been brought in to help us.'

'Help? Good grief, if this is help, wouldn't want someone who is here to hinder,' he snapped.

'You do have a point. This move is a bit un-timely to say the least. What is it you were looking for?'

'The new blood samples and the old ones we had from patient zero. I need to see how it is mutating.'

She nodded and started helping him rummage through the sample, making sure she was as delicate as possible with them. This virus was not contagious as long as you avoided direct contact with it. Jim rolled up his sleeves. Heather looked at him for a brief moment, noticed his chequered blue sleeves stained with coffee, and gave out a long internal sigh. *These guys really are hopeless.* She smiled.

'What's funny?' he prompted.

'Oh nothing, just thinking about something else.' She was not going to share her observations. 'Ah here it is! Sample dated a few hours ago. Be careful with it!' she instructed.

He nodded, gently took it from her, and slotted it under the special microscope he had set up a few hours ago. This one could zoom into the nano scale! He loved his toys and his microscope was his now favourite.

'You do what you need to do. I'll keep looking for the older sample,' instructed Heather. The less time she looked at that horror under there, the better. Even after all this time, it still gave her the creeps.

'Ok, thanks.' He reset things and projected the output onto the large screen hanging over the plain white desk. He preferred their old setup where they had two screens. It was so much easier to work with one microscope per screen. With this new setup, they had to project both onto the same screen and then split the image. It was a bit slower and for some reason it annoyed him. Finally, the live feed activated, displaying the horrific thing on screen.

Jim looked at it and started swearing. 'Good God, Heather you have to come and see this.'

'You're not going all religious on me Jim, are you? Should I be concerned?' she asked.

'Heather, please just come see this.'

'Fine fine.' She put down the container she was investigating and joined him. She was about to ask what could possibly be so important to interrupt the search when he just raised his arm and pointed to the large screen. She looked, stared at it, then started swearing. What they saw was not only a very rapidly evolved virus but one that had developed something totally unique.

'Is that what I think it is?' he asked. 'Have I gone totally insane? Please tell me I'm insane.'

'If you are insane then so am I!' she agreed. What they saw was something totally impossible. The virus had developed what looked like nerves.

'It's... developing... a nervous system? What on God's Earth is going on?'

'Only one way to know. We need to test these things, and see if they respond as nerves would.' Jim thought about it and decided it was the most logical thing to do. They had to suspend their disbelief and test it or they would all end up going insane, fighting the impossibility now staring at them from the screens.

'Take over. This is your and Bradley's speciality. I'll take care of locating the initial variant samples. By the way, where on Earth is Bradley? Haven't seen him here in two days now. So unlike him.'

Now that he mentioned it, Heather thought it was odd as well.

'He might be taking some time to himself in view of what happened.'

'Ah yes, poor Kuroi. He must be devastated.' Silence broke out at the mention of what had happened. She had been not only his girlfriend but also a long-time colleague and friend to them all. They both proceeded to their respective tasks in silent contemplation.

'Tests confirm it,' said Heather. This is reacting to stimulus as a set of autonomic nerves would. Horrific.'

Jim moved up to the microscope and glared at it. 'How could this be possible? A single cell organism...' he paused, trying to find words. 'How?'

'This does not make sense, no sense whatsoever,' confirmed Heather.

'It is no longer a single cell organism.' He shuddered at the thought.

Bradley sat in the room he had been convalescing in. He was feeling much better. Whatever they had done worked. His strength was returning and his mind was almost clear. The struggle to keep hold of memories seemed to still be there. He had to constantly fight against the impulse that there was something he should be remembering, but could not. Gazing at his surroundings, he wondered what he was doing here. Why was he here in the first place?

This room was so different from his usual one. He felt totally out of place. The old heavy beams, the bedding fit for a king, the heavy yet soft animal furs used instead of duvets – it all seemed out of place. It was beyond elegant yet very practical. Whoever owned this room was a man – the masculinity ebbed from every inch of it, a practical man concerned with daily things. This hit out in sharp contrast to Bradley's own character, his intellectual background was more concerned with technology, books, notes, and a mild obsession to having everything clean and tidy. This was definitely clean and tidy but it lacked the crispness, the almost clinical unloved look to it that his own apartment had.

The sense of unease just refused to leave him. He looked at the side table. The table must have been treated its wooden surface looked almost marble-like. He ran his fingers over it, cold to the touch, just like stone. How odd. His mind was struggling. It is only then that he noticed he was naked. Someone had stripped him before dumping him onto the bed. Quickly he grabbed hold of one of the smaller fur-like coverings and wrapped himself in it. No clothes in sight. He was not exactly shy but walking about naked was just that one step too far.

He sat at the table and looked at the food. It smelt delicious – scents and aromas like nothing he had ever experienced before assaulted his senses mercilessly. His stomach grumbled. *Fine fine, I'll eat.* Picking up the cutlery, which thank goodness was exactly like what he was used to, he ate. The textures and taste assaulted his sensibilities. His taste buds exploded in symphonic ecstasy, his nose twitched in delight at the scent and his body hummed each time he bit into the next morsel. What looked like meat tasted delightful. He had never been a great meat fan but this, this was something else.

The door opened, and Lurizak walked in. 'Having a bite I see. Good, you will need your strength. Enjoying the food?' he asked.

'I've never tasted anything like this before, it's...'

'Yes I bet! Eating real food instead of the chemical mishmash you call food on your side must be quite an experience. Try the water!' Lurizak smiled.

Bradley picked up the glass of perfectly clear bluish liquid. Carefully he sipped a drop. It sent his mind reeling. Its texture was smooth, silky, soft. To say it was refreshing would be an injustice. It not only satisfied his thirst, it did so much more. Suddenly, the sensation of having been washed under a waterfall coursed through him. He was invigorated, and everything seemed clearer, as if that was even possible. 'What is it?' he asked in surprise.

'Just water. Our water is pure, not even a single microscopic contaminant, not even at the quantum level! After a few days of drinking it, your body will feel very different. Well, it will feel as it should have always been, had it not become host to the hundreds of chemicals you lot corrupt it with.' Lurizak sat at the table sipping his own glass of some other type of liquid, waiting for Bradley to finish eating. His tall frame seemed odd, making the chair he sat on look so small. Bradley observed him closely, a little too closely apparently.

'Go on, ask. I know what's on your mind,' he prompted him.

'Your clothing?'

'It's not clothing.' Lurizak corrected him. 'Think of it as my skin.

In fact it's a special type of armour where the metals we refine here are merged with our skin. That is why even though I have something on, you seem to think I am completely naked, right?'

'I must admit the thought had crossed my mind. Those look like bevelled tattoos and the rest is just like skin.'

'It gives us a number of advantages and has, of course, imposed upon us a number of restrictions too.'

'And those?' Bradley did not even know what to call those things that looked like keyholes drilled deep into Lurizak's flesh.

'Those are... best think of them as crosslinks. They are there but not there. They cross the flesh into the quantum structures of our bodies and back. They allow our wielders to control what happens on all levels of us and gives us the ability to seamlessly bridge into quantum realities of ourselves.'

Bradley looked at him in confusion.

'Ok, let's stick to the basics. My Wielder is Tamirok. You will meet him soon enough. He's one of the acting-rulers here. His will courses through my body, diving deep into it, giving him control of every function of every organ within me, every emotion and in some cases every thought.'

'That's horrible,' interrupted Bradley.

'Not really, it just requires a shift in thinking. What do you do on your side when someone comes for urgent medical help? You use drugs, you operate, you invade their inner physiology. The will of the medical team imposes itself on your body and into it as well. In your case, often in a crude and side-effect-ridden manner.'

'To save their lives? Yes I guess you could summarise it so,' agreed Bradley.

'Well we do the same. The main difference is we are light years ahead of you in the precision with which we do it. For instance, there are no illnesses or diseases here on TrueEarth.'

Upon hearing that Bradley nearly choked on his food, nearly spitting the whole content of his mouth out. 'No diseases?'

'Nope, the only things which do happen are injuries in battle and disruptions of normal functions in some part of the afflicted person.'

Bradley thought about it: *isn't that what a disease does?*

His hesitation was immediately picked up. 'We repair those disruptions within a few hours of them setting in.'

Bradley's eyeballs nearly shot out of his skull. 'That's... impossible.'

'Very possible. As I said, we are way ahead of you in these things. Back to the Bound: we call ourselves the Bound because that is our House's specialisation. We bind and control. It is also why this House is the military force of TrueEarth. Picture this: I told you our wielder's will flows through us and controls practically everything about us. Soon you will discover exactly how this is done. Some wielders like Tamirok are also generals of our battle forces. Those select few can wield not only several of us at the same time but entire battle forces, which can range from thousands to hundreds of thousands at once.'

Bradley could not conceive of mind controlling more than one person, let alone thousands or more.

'You see, highly specialised individuals.'

Bradley took another bite out of what looked like a blue vegetable. His body relaxed under the delight of sensations coursing through him. This food was beyond delicious. 'Why are you telling me this? All I want to do is get back home.' There it was. For a split second he remembered, then it was gone. It is only then he noticed it. Looking at his hand, something was off. He turned and twisted it, observing it closely.

'Something wrong?' asked Lurizak.

'Not sure if it's my imagination or not... I think I'm paler than I was before, my skin...'

'Is getting whiter?'

Bradley looked at his hand again and considered the thought.

'Yes a little paler would be the correct assessment.' Lurizak nodded and smiled. 'That is perfectly normal. The longer you stay here, the paler it will get until you lose all your tan.' Bradley's left eyebrow shot up questioningly. 'You'll find out sooner or later, might as well tell you. TrueEarth solved our climate warming problem by flooding the atmosphere with an engineered bacteria. Initially, it was deemed to be harmless to humans. Well it is. The one thing it needs to survive is nutrition and it gets it from the melatonin in your skin. Once it has consumed all of that, it will leave you alone.' Bradley seemed unsettled and uneasy. Lurizak ignored it. 'It won't harm you. It's just fond of our skin. After three days, your body will never be able to produce melatonin again and the bacteria leave you alone forever.'

'What if I want a tan?' objected Bradley.

'You know what, when we have some spare time I will teach you how certain powers can be used to change the colour of your skin if that is what you want to do. No one here bothers, it just happens if it does, doesn't if it doesn't.'

Bradley was not convinced – rather, he did not understand what these powers Lurizak was taking about were, let alone how they could affect his tan. He ran his fingers through his hair. 'What about –'

Lurizak answered faster than he could formulate the question. 'Your hair and eyes are safe. For some reason we can't quite figure out yet.'

'Fine fine, I guess I can't avoid it,' admitted Bradley. His mind had already refocused back on the main topic at hand. 'So why did you tell me all this wielder stuff?' he prompted.

'Ah yes. You came into the House through the door of Wielders. It's part of the rules – or laws, if you prefer – that operate on Earth. You can only enter the House in which you belong.'

'I don't remember entering this place at all,' mumbled Bradley.

'But you did, otherwise you would not be here. You actually collapsed on the door, which I happened to open when I heard the thump and you fell half in.'

'Half in?'

'Yes; that caused a lot of confusion. Tamirok is discussing with the ruling council what we should do with you. Whatever happens, you are one of us now.'

'I don't mean to be a problem but I really don't want to be.' He waved his arm in a circular motion. 'All this is not me.'

'Not the way you think, but it is somewhere inside of you. Truth drives us here; whether we know or accept it is irrelevant. Since you are here, you were meant to be here. It's hard to accept – so much is new – but you will have to.' A look of grave concern etched itself on Lurizak's face. Something about Bradley worried him. Bradley was right; he didn't quite fit in here, but why or how was impossible for him to determine.

Tamirok entered the room. Lurizak stood up and bowed his head ever so slightly. Tamirok smiled and nodded. Without warning, he put his right hand square in the middle of Lurizak's chest. Bradley observed, surprised but silent. Some of the glyphs on Tamirok's extremely complex skin armour hummed with power, giving off small waves of coppery-amber light. The light slithered down his fingers onto Lurizak's armour, wove its way through the chains attached to it, and dove deep into the keyhole there. For a split second, Bradley could have sworn that Lurizak's eyes shifted to amber in colour. He nodded affirmatively and pulled back, breaking contact with Tamirok's hand. Unbeknown to Bradley, Tamirok had with that one movement communicated everything that had happened at the council meeting to him. He turned to face Bradley, and, stood silent for a few moments looking at him.

'I'm Tamirok, one of the acting-rulers of this House. We have come to a decision as to what should be done about your case.' He stood still, watching what reactions his words would trigger. None. Bradley seemed to either not understand or not have any opinion on them.

'All I want to do is find a way back,' interjected Bradley.

'What you want is not our concern. What we need to do is get you up to speed so that you can function here.'

'I don't intend to stay. I have pressing things to do –'

He never finished the sentence. His chest heaved, his eyes turned red, and black lightning danced visibly all over his body. He recoiled in agony. Power exploded out of him. It was so violent that it knocked Lurizak off his feet. Tamirok, however, stood firm. He grabbed Bradley by his left arm. 'Breathe! Get control of yourself!' he commanded. Bradley's breath was rapid. He tried to speak to no avail. Without warning, Tamirok's fist dug deep into Bradley's diaphragm, knocking him unconscious. The power pulled back in, suddenly almost pulling Lurizak off his feet in the opposite direction. It coalesced into a pulse. Lurizak was about to try and shake Bradley awake. 'Don't touch him!' yelled Tamirok. The hand froze. 'If you make contact with him now you will lose your hand.'

'Our armour shields us from that.'

'Not this time,' objected Tamirok.

'This is the reason why we need to get him under control. That power you see radiating there. It is something we have never been confronted with before. It will be the permanent end of your hand if you touch him while it is radiating like that. Even our healers cannot heal that!'

'What do we do?'

'Wait. The council thinks it is totally chaotic in nature, which means it should fade out as rapidly as it came about.'

'Why?' asked Lurizak.

'Why what?'

'Did it happen?'

'He lacks control over it. I don't even think he knows about it.'

'Impossible!' objected Lurizak. 'Something this powerful, he must be aware of it.'

'We will see.' Tamirok sat down at the table and poured himself a glass of the same liquor Lurizak had just been drinking. 'Sit. This could take some time and we have to deal with him.'

They sat there drinking until Bradley woke back up. Eventually, the pulsing power faded away. He grabbed hold of a soft leather cloth from nearby to cover himself up for the sake of modesty.

'Back, I see? What do you remember?'

'Everything. The odd thing was I could not do anything. I was trying to stop it all but I couldn't do anything. I was just there but not fully.' Bradley tried to explain it, but he thought he was making a real mess of it all.

'As I suspected,' surmised Tamirok. 'Sit and have a drink with us. You need it.' Bradley did so. Once he was seated and sipping away, Tamirok continued. 'Unless you learn to control that, you will be a danger not only to yourself but to everyone who ever comes close to you. This is why I believe you came to House Bound. Although why you would be a Wielder rather than a Bound still eludes me.'

'I don't understand why this is happening.'

'Neither do we,' he admitted. 'For the time being, you are going to become part of this House and learn.'

'I can't,' objected Bradley.

'Listen, I'm not here to accommodate your wants and whims, your likes or dislikes. I am telling you what is going to happen and I suggest you get used to it, fast.' His voice never raised even the slightest. The coldness and matter-of-fact manner of his speech caused chills to go down Bradley's back. 'We are not here to make sure you feel comfortable, nor to respect your emotions or feelings. All those things are irrelevant. You left those considerations behind when you made it to TrueEarth. All that nonsense your kind suffers on the other side and the mess you have made because of it is not going to happen here. We need to worry about much bigger things than who is happy or not, or how someone feels. And just to be clear, I don't care whatsoever what you may want either. My job is to prepare you for what is coming and to ensure all of our safety and that is exactly what I am going to do.' He paused, allowing time for the words to sink in. 'As for your getting back: yes there are ways to do so, but only a rare few individuals can use them and even fewer of those want to. When the time comes, you will find out for yourself how. If you don't, you were not meant to; that's all there is to it.'

'Could we not dispatch him to another House? Maybe one more suitable to his temperament? He's no warrior.'

'Your suggestion would be music to the council's ears. But no, we cannot. He entered into our House, which means he is supposed to be here. That is the law of the planet. We cannot ignore it no more than we can stop breathing.'

Lurizak nodded in agreement. He knew the truth of those words. Tamirok took out the same type of chainlike structures Lurizak had when Bradley first met him.

'No, no way, I'm not doing that!' Bradley knew what was coming and he was having none of it. 'Absolutely no way.'

'Listen to me, you damn fool, and listen closely. I am not in the habit of repeating myself. The moment you stepped into House Bound, you became one of us. Whether you accept the bindings willingly or not makes absolutely no difference to me. However, I assure you a forceful binding is so much more suffocating and difficult to bear than a willing one, so I would advise you strongly to just go with the flow of things. We're going to get you bound as any newcomer is. You have no choice or say in the matter. I have had to put my neck on the line to the entire ruling council because no one else wanted to be your wielder or mentor. So you will pay me some respect and gratitude at best, at worst compliance will do just fine. Then we're going to get you some armour and after that, we're going to put you right into battle training. You need discipline and that pathetic sorry excuse for a body needs a lot of work. While you are doing all that, you will be spending time with acting-ruler Lishtana, who will try and help you get control of those dangerous powers striking out all over the place. After you have gained some proficiency in all that, you will take charge of Lurizak here.' Lurizak nearly choked when he heard the last part. 'I have decided to give you TrueEarth's best warrior. You will replace me as his wielder – partially, mind you. By doing so, I will teach you how to be a wielder, as will he. You will learn how to form what you think of as ropes, chains or cords, which are in fact specially formed nerve cords undergoing a unique myelination, allowing us to extend part of our nervous system into another. His life will be in your hands. You would better be most – and I mean *most* – skilled in control because if anything happens to Lurizak, you will have me to deal with.' He remained silent for a minute, which seemed to last forever, then turned to face Lurizak. 'Unless you object?' Lurizak looked at Tamirok, then at Bradley, then back and forth a couple of times.

'This is very unusual.'

'Yes, but the timing is oddly coincidental. I have missions away and won't be able to be a wielder anymore. It is my duty to find you another. Something seems –'

'I agree,' said Lurizak.

Tamirok never needed to complete his explanation. He nodded stood up and moved towards Bradley.

'I ... no... I cannot...' Bradley was terrified. 'I don't...' Something in him snapped. All the air in the room was instantly pulled in and out of the room. Tamirok reacted within a split second. His mask was on, his will flashed through Lurizak's bindings and his mask was up as well under his wielder's command. Both warriors were able to breathe once more, only to witness the space around Bradley crack. A tear within the very structure of space itself formed. The tear expanded. Both men switched to combat positions, strange glyphs circling about them, spiralling the length of their bodies. Both were prepared to confront whatever stepped out of there. Black power was seething out of Bradley's body in waves. A pulse of emptiness echoed in the room and a being of such blackness stepped out towards them that they could not determine whether it was emptiness or blackness. It looked humanoid in shape but had absolutely no features or mass. It was nothing more than a shaped gap into nothingness.

'Your... plan ... is not acceptable to us.' Its voice echoed in from such vast distance that neither men could pinpoint its point of origin.

'Who are you, what are you? And what do you want here?' demanded Tamirok.

'I am Nothing, serving the Ruler of House Nothingness,' stated Nihi.

'House Nothingness? No such thing,' intervened Lurizak. Tamirok's hand was visibly shaking. 'House? You mean?'

'Correct, House Nothingness is reawakened from its slumber.'

'Impossible,' responded Tamirok. 'This cannot be.'

'Impossible? Unknown concept. All things happen because they are supposed to happen,' it explained. Lurizak prepared for attack. His armour shifted and changed, and the metallic surface steamed forth forming a massive sword covering his entire arm, which became part of the sword itself. Glyphs of power danced across its surface. Particles were being pulled from all around them, shimmering hot, radiating orange light about the newly formed weapon. A laser pulse shot out of its point as the power overflowed straight at Nihi. It hit it right in its centre. Nothing happened. The power was absorbed into nothing and simply ceased to exist. The space in which they stood filled with a suffocating vacuum. Waves of tears in reality smashed against them. Tamirok stood there shaken as he absorbed the first impact. The second hit Lurizak, tearing through his very flesh. Fortunately, the tear was superficial. Bradley saw what had happed and the medical training in him instinctively activated. He was at Lurizak's side, pushing down on his open, bleeding wound, looking around and trying to find something to bandage it with. His desire to save triggered something else within; a red power oozed forth along his arms down his fingers and into Lurizak's wounds. The metallic substance of his skin expanded into it, and the flesh underneath it rewove itself, until the skin sealed itself. Lurizak blinked.

'Are you ok?' asked Bradley.

'Yes, I think I am.'

Bradley turned to face Nihi. 'Stop this at once.' He was angry. He did not want this.

'As Ruler wishes.' All the power, the vacuums in space and even the tear still trying to suck all reality in suddenly shut.

'Ruler?' Tamirok was shocked.

'Correct. This is the Ruler of House Nothingness,' stated Nihi.

'Can someone please tell me what the heck is going on?' Bradley burst out of his silence. He could not understand anything and he was obviously stuck in the middle of something. He was sick of being kept in the dark all the time. 'And what the heck is that?' he asked pointing at Nihi. Nihi moved towards Bradley so rapidly that no one saw the movement. Bradley was suddenly standing in the middle of the nothingness, which was Nihi. It had absorbed him into itself.

'Memory fragmented,' its unnerving echoing voice said. 'Power overwhelming cognitive functions.' Lurizak and Tamirok stood there looking at Nihi, trying to determine exactly what was going on. Something interrupted them – a direct communication into Tamirok's mind.

'The House is on alert; they have detected that,' he pointed to Nihi. 'They are unable to determine whether it is a threat, invader or anomaly. I have told them it presents us with no danger at the moment, but we need to act fast or the entire might of the military of TrueEarth will be storming in through the door.'

The door opened, and Lishtana stormed in. 'I heard,' she said, then looked at Nihi and stared. The glyphs on her skin-armour flared up, power poured out, and particles of matter pulled themselves together and formed a set of three circles containing her in their centre. Green writing surfaced along their circumference. Her eyes flared up in green and she gazed. Her gaze was deep, persistent, and piercing.

'Well?' asked Tamirok.

'Nothing. This is not like any of the alien beings attempting to penetrate the Earth.' Nihi moved out of Bradley and was now standing behind him. She looked at Bradley with the same piercing gaze of flaring green eyes. 'Strange,' Lishtana muttered. Using her right hand, she retraced some of the glyphs manifested by her armour on the innermost circle mid-air. The letters flew forward and surrounded Bradley, and flared there. 'Very strange.'

Suddenly, they all vanished. They were all pulled back into the gap in reality that was Nihi. 'That will do,' it said.

She nodded in agreement and with a few quick flicks of her hands, she wiped out some of the instruction letters from her inner circle. Everything faded away and her armour powered down. 'They are linked, but how and what that may be is beyond my skill.'

'You all seek to determine the truth of things?' the echoing voice asked. They all nodded. 'Illogical motivations of lower species. In TrueEarth, only truth can be spoken,' it explained.

'We know. But this truth of yours seems not only improbable but impossible.' Tamirok stepped forward as the representative of the group.

'Can someone please tell me what the heck is going on?' Bradley was getting more and more annoyed at being the passive observer in all this.

'They believe it is what they call impossible,' said Nihi, 'for a House to re-emerge from slumber, and they refuse to accept that it could have chosen you as a ruler.'

'What do you mean a ruler? Me? Can't remember anything about any such thing!' he objected.

'It says your memories have been disrupted by the powers in you.' Lurizak felt sorry for Bradley and tried to explain. He could only imagine how confusing all this could be to someone who didn't even know the basics of TrueEarth, let alone the complex inter-relationships of the highest levels of the Houses.

'There is one way to confirm his status,' interjected Lishtana. 'The throne of rulership.'

It came without warning. Out of apparently nowhere, two large pointed blades flashed for a split second before threatening to sink into Bradley's back. Nihi reacted almost an instant before, or so it seemed. The wave of energy that pulsed out of the thing was so intense the very air hummed. The sound of tearing combined with that of something cracking from within coursed through the entire room, flinging the assailants to the opposite corner of the room, and sending hundreds of particle-like glittering metal fragments cascading all over the place. Everyone turned to see what had happened. There in a pile, three female bodies lay, with skins of the same metallic type as Lurizak. The only distinguishable differences were in how these skins were decorated. Glyphs and glowing script which was jet black. The glow of black and grey power faded away.

'House assassins,' gasped Lishtana. The secret operations division of the House's forces had been called to action, most probably due to the unknown thing that stood in front of them.

'I have to go. Stop this madness. Everyone wait here!' ordered Tamirok as he stormed out of the room. He was not a happy bunny. The assassins were part of a separate division to his men, and he had to act quickly otherwise more and more would keep on coming, until their job was done. The last thing he wanted – no, the last thing he needed – was an inter-House war to break out, especially one with an old re-emerging House, whose power no one knew about or had seen in action for millennia.

Lishtana inspected the bodies of her battle sisters. The assassins were always women; their speedy reflexes and more agile bodies proved to be a great advantage to that battle style. What she was interested in, however, was what had happened to them. She approached their broken forms with a surgeon's delicate eye, paying close attention to the cracks and tears. Their armour was unique in that it was living material, just as their skin was, but not only that, it allowed for the sustain transmission and storage of massive amounts of power and energy. It was unheard of them ever cracking under the load of any force – yet these had done just that. Another key advantage they had was the ability to self-regenerate almost instantly. It was one of their primary advantages in practically most battles. This armour had not healed at all. She looked closer. After what seemed to be ages, she placed her hand on one of the bodies and traced something. Black power hummed from her own armour and seeped into that of the now dead assassin, and danced along its surface, then returned to her own. She was exchanging information with the mind – if mind you can call it – of the armour itself. For her energy, information and consciousness were all one and the same as she allowed herself to sink into the quantum fields. That was the key to her own training.

She stood up, looked at Nihi, then at Bradley. 'Tell me one thing, if I may. Those bodies seem torn at the particle level, as if every atom in a predefined pattern had been ripped out of existence. It would fit the pattern of nothingness. What has me curious is why those are torn, yet when Bradley stood right inside you a moment ago, nothing happened to him? If you truly are nothingness through and through, he should have been torn or at least suffered superficial cracking too. In his case, it would have been far more severe, since he had no armour to shield from the impact,' she asked Nihi.

'Observations correct,' Nihi echoed away. 'House Ruler shielded by power from self, barrier to Nothing.' She gasped and decided to remain silent.

'What does it mean?' asked Lurizak. She gave him a firm stare, which spoke of severe annoyance. It was obvious she wanted to avoid discussing the matter but he had just forced her to.

'What it means,' her voice filled with reprimand, 'is that your friend here,' she pointed at Bradley, 'has so much power coursing through him that he can counter one of the basic fundamental forces. Such a waste.' She turned her back to them both and walked out of the room.

Elma was spying on the labs. She loved to know what was happening. Her meeting with Mira had the unwholesome effect of piquing her curiosity to such a high level that it had become totally unbearable. She had taken a few days off work in order to satisfy that curiosity. She was still in the offices but would not be working. Yume did not mind. They were all used to the eccentric nerdy tendencies. Some actually found it incredibly attractive, especially Yume's main assistant! Elma never noticed; she was far too busy, far too focused. She wanted – no, needed – to know what was going on in those darn laboratories next to the university. She knew all the systems had gone offline for a short time, and ad heard about the move up one floor. It made no sense to her. *Why would anyone move a floor higher for no logical reason whatsoever? It provided no advantage. Quite to the contrary; it disrupted the smooth information flow in between the researchers and the administrative personnel.* It just made no sense to her. Her craving for information was as intense as a drug; it would fuel her for days if need be. So she spied through the security cameras, listened in and gazed intently upon the network-linked microscope camera. What she saw horrified her as well. She was no expert by any stretch of the imagination but even she understood the implications of what Heather and Jim had observed. She shuddered. The very thought that that thing could infect her was something beyond any of those nightmares she had. She had to do something... but what?

She ran the recording of what the two had seen on the microscope, trying not to cringe too much at the realisation of what she was looking at. Frame by frame, she studied, paused and moved onto the next set of frames. It was like solving a puzzle and Elma was good, really good, at puzzles of all sorts. *There! It's that acronym B.E.I.T.C. This must be a key. I need to find what this stands for. Maybe that will elucidate things further.* How had she heard of it? Something nudged at her from the back of her mind. She had come across it before. *Ah YES! That Bradley guy! Wasn't he part of the scientists from the lab? I wonder...* The world faded away into insignificance as Elma's drive and curiosity combined to make a dangerous cocktail.

Lurizak and Bradley were both involved in deep conversation, trying to piece together all the events that had taken place when Tamirok returned. He walked in and immediately grabbed hold of the first available crystal cup, poured himself a drink and sat down. It had been an exhausting afternoon for him, and the fatigue was visible on his face. Bradley looked at him questioningly. He was not sure what would happen next but whatever it was, he was sure he would not like it. *Why on Earth am I still stuck here?* he wondered. Last time this had happened he somehow flipped back to his own side, as they called it. *Could it be triggered by specific events?* That question remained unanswered. He knew they knew something about it. No one was spilling the beans; everything and everyone here was keeping him in the dark about that one vital point.

'That was a nightmare,' volunteered Tamirok. 'There won't be any more attempts on your life – well, not from us in any case,' he told Bradley.

'Glad to hear it,' admitted Bradley. That was one thing he could do without. Things were already too complicated and alien here, let alone him having to add the threat of being killed by unknown quantities. He knew nothing of these human's capabilities or ways of doing things. In a most peculiar way, it amused him. *I'm like a new-born child again,* he surmised.

'Lishtana confirmed her findings here and every member of the council agreed with those findings. That means the validity of House Nothingness has been established.'

'There is no necessity for anyone to establish that.' The echoing voice from Nihi interrupted them.

Tamirok jumped involuntarily, his warrior reflexes acting of their own accord. 'Apologies; I had not noticed you there.' He paused and thought for a second. 'Wait a minute. How did I not notice you? It's not like your presence is discrete by any stretch of the imagination!'

'My presence was in-between the spaces, in non-existence but still here,' it tried to explain.

'Too tired to think of all this. Well, you're here now. Oh joy...'

Nihi did not respond. It seemed the sarcasm was completely lost on it.

'Wait, why did they' – Bradley pointed to the pile of corpses still there in the corner of the room; decay did not seem to affect them – 'attack in the first place?'

'Nihi's presence and your powers are unlike anything we have had here in TrueEarth – or rather, are like something forgotten about a very long time ago. No one alive is familiar with it, which means you were deemed an invading alien threat.'

'Oh, just that, hey. Wait a sec: alien?' Bradley started to become rather intrigued. The possibility of off-world life had always fascinated him, albeit never enough to warrant him studying or looking for it.

'Yes, FalseEarth is shielded from it by what we do here in TrueEarth. There are countless alien life forms trying to traverse the quantum dimension and invade or consume Earth. That is partially why everything here is focused on power, strength, technology and battle! I suspect it is also why you ended up here first of all.' He looked at Bradley closely from head to toe. 'You are definitely not ready for any type of battle whatsoever. You will be.'

'I'm not really a warrior nor do I want to be. I'm a scientist,' he objected.

'Listen here, even our scientists are warriors. You have no choice in the matter whatsoever. Either you become a warrior or you won't survive. It is that plain and simple. It matters not whether you battle with your fist, weapons, technologies, or power, but battle you shall.'

'Indeed,' the echoing Nihi replied. All turned to face that horrific gap of a being and silently stared at it. 'His body, his character, his emotions need to all be strengthened or the power in him will consume him. Act fast, for his time is very short.' Everyone was shocked by that statement. Nihi went on: 'Too much chaos in a Ruler means they are unable to control and unable to withstand burning forces. Their body's atomic structure fractured and burns up.'

'Wait a minute; are you telling me I'm going to die?' asked Bradley.

'No, I'm telling you if you do not become more powerful in body and toughen up in character, you will burn yourself out.'

'That settles it.' Tamirok was not going to allow any such nonsense to happen, not on his watch and not when he had invested so much time and effort here already. Deep down he was hoping this Bradley guy could prove to be an effective ally in their battles ahead. 'We're going to get things going right now.' Bradley instinctively pulled back; he still didn't want anything to do with all this. Much to his surprise, Tamirok turned to Nihi once more. 'Inter-House protocols dictate relations between rulers of Houses with the other Houses themselves. Under those laws, he can visit and learn from all Houses as a rank of their own councils, but he cannot become one of them.'

'Correct,' confirmed Nihi. Tamirok's surprise was plain to see. *So this thing knows of the House laws and our politics. Surprising.*

'However, we need to bind him, or whatever is battling within him is going to at some point lash out and injure even us it seems.' He glanced at the dead bodies in the room, and sadness filled him. He'd never worked with the womenfolk, since men and women in this House were always kept segregated for good reasons but they were still his allies in battle. Women in House Bound were also quite rare; not many of their true selves opted for a life of rigid battle and physical conflict. It pained him to lose them. 'Without that, we cannot even hope to teach him our ways or stabilise...' he left the words hanging, unable to decide what the heck it was that was battling inside this poor individual. He pitied Bradley. This was a man at conflict with his very self, and Tamirok knew how such conflicts ended. He hoped to be able to avoid that sad fate for this young man.

'House Nothingness has a proposal.' Nihi offered the first solution. 'Joint binding such as shared by all acting-rulers of House Bound.'

Tamirok thought about it for an instant. 'Possible,' he surmised. 'House Nothingness, Bradley and Tamirok proposed holders.' It was an odd suggestion. 'Why those?' asked Tamirok.

'Simple. Tamirok as the initial chosen wielder for Bradley, House Nothingness as already the holder of dominion over the Ruler, and the Ruler because he will shift back to his own side a few more times and will need his will to act there.' The logic was flawless. Bradley caught the shifting to his own side and relief washed over him. He would get out of this nightmare at some point or other.

'And I assume you are going to be the representative for House Nothingness?' asked Tamirok.

'Correct,' confirmed Nihi.

'One condition then. Shared bindings allow all members free access to the will, mind, and actions of each other upon each other. If I accept that type of setup, my condition is for House Nothingness to agree not to exercise any of those powers on me, or those I am bound to or with. I cannot put the entire Council at risk. With them I share such a binding already.'

'Confirmed. House Nothingness will disable the linkage into House Bound and its own members. It does have one condition of its own.' Tamirok nodded for Nihi to continue. 'The binding will be temporary and no other bindings added.'

Tamirok thought about it. It could work, it might not, he was unsure. In any case, there was not point trying to outsmart Nihi. He could easily have done so with Bradley, but with a fully aware representative of a House it would be a pointless endeavour. 'How long for?' he asked.

'Until mastery of inner power is gained,' stated Nihi.

Tamirok laughed silently within. *That could last forever.* 'Only one problem. He's going to need an armour and that is a great binding in its own right,' explained Tamirok. It was true. Battle training was impossible for Bradley in his current state. A single blow would kill him.

'Under inter-House agreements, armour crafting knowledge can be shared with House Rulers only. Ruler qualifies. He can weave armour from his own power and self-bind.' Nihi had found the solution Tamirok had hoped it wouldn't. Sharing that secret was a big risk. As the agreement enforcer of TrueEarth, he had no choice but to accept.

'Agreed.'

'Wait a sec, hold on the both of you!' interjected Bradley. 'Don't I get a say in any of this? I might not want any of this, whatever this is.'

'No,' came the response of both Tamirok and Nihi at exactly the same time. It was unnerving to hear the two overlapping.

'You are already the cause of so much harm and your very existence is under threat. Are you really going to be so pathetically petty as to argue with this?' Tamirok was getting seriously annoyed at this persistent rejection of what had to be. Bradley saw anger flare up in the old warrior's eyes, and a glint of threat shone in his right eye. He fell silent. 'Fine, that's settled then. Let us move on.' He reformed the nerve cord, which to Bradley still looked like glowing metallic rope, and the thought of it sent shivers of horror up his spine. Tamirok moved towards Nihi and offered it up.

The most terrifying scene unfolded that any of them had ever witnessed. Bradley was almost in panic mode, Lurizak pulled back instinctively, and Tamirok used his battle-trained iron will to keep a very firm grip of himself. Out of the emptiness which was Nihi, a hand formed, emerging from somewhere deep within the central region of its form. It moved slowly, so very slowly. Everyone had frozen solid and just stared at it. Eyes could not move away, yet none wanted to see. As the hand ebbed its way closer and closer to Tamirok, more and more effort was needed for the giant warrior to counter his instinct. All he wanted to do was jump back well out of reach of this thing. It eventually grabbed hold of one side of the cords, while Tamirok held the other.

Lurizak prodded Bradley. 'Go on, you too must grab hold of it.' Bradley hesitated. He did not want to. Lurizak prodded him a little harder and whispered, 'Go on; you have no choice in this. Besides, Tamirok is strict but fair and highly experienced. He'll be a good guide for you.'

Bradley took another step, looked at Tamirok, and then at Nihi. He too was seized by fear at the sight he was witnessing. Tamirok knew full well. His head motioned to Bradley to come over. This was as far as he could help. Bradley struggled, then something in him just snapped. *What the heck?* echoed in his own mind and he took a large step forward, grabbing the cord.

Power, he felt power, like never before, raw violent dominating power flowing through every inch of him, intensifying, increasingly threatening to overwhelm him. His mind was becoming more and more erratic. Then it all stopped. Something there from within his mind had stepped forward. Something was helping him maintain consciousness, his own self. He looked curiously deeper within; a strong firm presence, a will thousands – if not hundreds of thousands – of times more stable than his own. Unyielding, unforgiving, strong. He saw the maelstrom of power and energy; this will was standing against it, taking the brunt of it all as it lashed out.

Closer inspection showed him what it was; it was Tamirok. *Don't just stand there and look like a fool, my power won't last long against this!* He snapped at Bradley from within his own mind.

What do I do? asked Bradley.

Tamirok let out a sigh of despair. *Does he not know even the basics? House help us.*

Bradley heard his thoughts. It seemed in the mind there was no hiding one's thoughts.

No, there isn't, when you are already inside another's mind. Now get to work! he commanded.

What do I do? asked Bradley once more.

These are your powers. Try to grab control of them; see the bright white and the dark black? We need to separate them out so the reds can flow in between them. Grab hold of the black lightning as if it was a stick or something – goodness, your mind is so infantile! No knowledge of quantum dynamics at all.

That was true. *Sorry,* apologised Bradley, *never studied that.*

Tamirok pointed to the flow of black quarks and the resulting highly aggressive energies. *I cannot touch that but you can pull it away from the white. I'll pull the whites in the opposite direction.* Bradley did as instructed. He tried but his hand went right through it each time. *By the House! Use your will! Your will! We are in your mind. Your hand is as real as this is.* Tamirok grunted, as pain was now coursing through him as the two steams started interweaving across each other. Bradley tried and failed.

A brutal force took hold of him and started pushing something out of him. *Like that!* For a moment, Bradley had discovered what it was like to have another's will direct him. He did not like it but let that pass. He needed that direction and strength now. Replicating the feat was almost an instinctive move; his hands now held the black force and he pulled and pulled. It seemed to take forever but they finally separated fully. He fell backwards at the impact, which followed a red power surge like a revered waterfall filling the gap in between the two. Bradley collapsed of exhaustion.

'Make sure he rests. He'll be out for a while. Poor sod didn't even know what his will was. It seems those on FalseEarth are unaware of their basic natures, let alone how to use them,' Tamirok told Lurizak.

'You're not serious?'

'Absolutely. In there,' he pointed to Bradley's head, 'it's all a vacuum. No discipline, no training, no knowledge of the self, nothing.'

'Is he safe? Are we?' asked Lurizak. Such lack of any form of knowledge, let alone control, could spell trouble.

'Yes, for the time being. We seem to have overcome the overflow and for the first time maintained his own personality in the process. How long it lasts – your guess is as good as mine. Not too long, I think. We need to get him into training fast!'

'Where's that thing?' He was referring to Nihi.

'No idea, it just... closed in upon itself and vanished when you were helping Bradley.'

'Disturbing House, that one.' With those words, Tamirok left to get some rest himself. He also wanted to talk to Lishtana as this was her area of expertise. All he had done is use a third force to bind the two conflicting ones away from each other. He suspected that this would not hold for very long. All those forces were vying for dominance, all felt very ancient and therein was the problem. He needed knowledge; he needed to know what he was dealing with. They would try to fuse again and he did not have the strength to keep doing this. With that thought in mind, he realised he was nearly at collapse himself. Food, recharge, and a nice long relaxing bath in the exquisite bathhouses would do the trick. After he had to spoken to Lishtana, of course.

13

THE
- GREAT FORGE -

Mira sat at her desk. Something had unsettled her earlier on in the day and not for want of trying, she could not push it out of her mind. Her instincts screamed at her. Not knowing what the issue was had proved to be a bad omen for everyone at the office. She was on edge, she snapped at everyone, and found everything annoying to the extreme. Today, all day long, everyone was tiptoeing around her, afraid to get caught in whatever crossfire was afoot. The light in the office was dimmed; even the cloudy skyline had opted to avoid casting any light into her office. The twilight created a very spooky ambience. Even her assistance took to knocking before entering the office.

'Ma'am, I have the reports you have asked for.'

'Good, leave them on the desk. Where's my coffee?' Her icy cold voice prompted him to immediate attention.

'Right here, ma'am, just as you requested.'

'Fine.'

He put the extra-large cup down on the desk with six extra shots of coffee and left the office, making sure to close the door behind him. One of the secretaries outside asked, ' Still all bad in there?' He just nodded yes. 'Not the best time to give her these requests, is it?' He simply shook his head. Without a further word, he rushed down the corridor.

'Anyone knows what is wrong with her?' asked one of the girls.

'Don't ask. In her case, the less you ask the better you are,' replied another.

Mira sat at her desk. Things were not going well. No matter how hard she had tried, getting her hands on a sample of the blood of the latest victim to die of the virus seemed to be downright impossible. *Damn it! How can be getting a few drops of blood so damn difficult,* she snapped. She needed to confirm whether it had progressed in the desired fashion to her own researchers. Without this essential key information, it would be impossible to determine whether the information and changes they had made to it were of any use.

'You... seeeem... distracccccctedddd...' the shadow spoke to her.

She had become used to it now. Ironically, it was actually the one thing in the world that could set her mind at rest and give her clarity. 'Can't get a damn hold of the blood sample to confirm what has happened with the new enhancements to the viral agent,' she snapped.

'Easyyyyy,' it replied.

'What do you mean?' she asked.

'Youuuu... wannnnt ... to seeee?' it asked.

'See what happened to it? Damn yes! I need to see, to know.'

'Fiiinnne...' it replied.

She closed her eyes, expecting to actually see. Instead, she felt herself hurled out of her chair and pulled forward at immense speed. It seemed like the space about her was moving, rather than herself. It stopped as abruptly as it had begun, making her feel sick. She was back in the shadow form she had experienced the previous time. This time, she was even stronger in it, and found herself to be more solid. The next moment, she was in the labs observing a young woman with long blond hair dressed in blues, and a young man in a coffee-stained shirt. She was revolted; absolutely no excuse to be in dirty clothing. If he had been on her team, he would have instantly been sacked on the spot. Very unprofessional.

Focccccuuuus! The shadowy voice spoke into her mind.

She ignored it and looked straight ahead. There! On the large monitor in front of her. What is that? She wondered.

Youuuur virrrrrrus, it replied.

She looked at it, and memorised the exact image of what it was and laughed hysterically. The information had not only been correct, it had proven to be exceedingly good. Nothing her own team had ever produced could come even close to this – no, nothing anyone had ever produced could. This was science at a whole new level. The pullback kicked in, the space shifted once more. She was shooting forward back into her office where her body jerked violently once she re-entered it. It was not until after she had had her coffee that she came about.

'I have a question for you. Can I go anywhere like this?'

'Yeeeeesss...' it replied. 'Anyyyyywherrre and anyyyyytimmmme, evennnn to thhhhe othhherrrr siiiide...'

'Other side? How interesting, will have to see where that is. Not now, mind you.' She took paper and pen and redrew from memory exactly what she'd seen. Grabbing the paper, she stormed out of her office downstairs to her own company's research laboratories with a smile on her face.

Bradley woke up, in the same bed, in the same room. He looked at his covers – yet again, he was in TrueEarth. Something felt odd, something heavy was about his neck. He reached out for it. His fingers made contact with something cold, metallic, heavy. He reached out with both hands, trying to pull it off.

'I wouldn't do that if I were you. Might as well just leave it be,' Lurizak was there making sure he would be fine. Bradley struggled, trying to find some way of removing it.

'You're wasting your time. Once on, it takes all those involved to take it back off. Besides, without that, Tamirok won't be able to help you keep that insane thing inside of you ripping you into a million pieces,' he explained.

'I didn't want this,' objected Bradley.

'I know. You have no choice. My advice is to just go with the flow. It will be easier for you and you might actually find a lot of benefits in it.'

Bradley sneered, 'there are no benefits.'

'Oh yes there are. I've spent more years as a Bound warrior than an entire generation on your side.'

'Just how old are you? You look to be nothing more than late 20s; early 30s at most.' Bradley looked at him confused.

'Let's just say that 100s of years is too short a measure for my age,' replied Lurizak.

'How? Not possible...'

'Let's just say that by wearing this armour, for us men in any case, it slows down the atomic decomposition of our biology. With the addition of our powers, which are contained and circulated in these metallic skins, our bodies are constantly energised. Every cell in our biology has new sources of power. The more bound, the more alive we become. Well, nearly so – there is one part of us which is locked away forever. Each enemy I vanquish and kill empowers my own life for that kill. The more battles you get into, the more victories you accumulate, the longer your youth and body will be maintained.'

Bradley looked at him head to toe. He did have the perfect body; no way it could be that old! He simply rejected the truth of it.

'The other big advantage, as you've experienced, is that our will is amplified by that of our wielder. These cords, depending on the temperament of those forming them, are nothing more than extensions of the nervous system. In both our cases, part of Tamirok's nervous system is now connected with our own. That is why he is able to temper how you react to things and communicate directly into your mind. What you see as chain, rope, and cord or in some cases threads of pulsing light is entirely irrelevant. What is relevant is the fact that inside of those are millions of methylated nerves intertwined with whatever they merge.'

Bradley's fingers instinctively ran around the cold metallic smooth rope-like structure tightly locked about his neck.

'I see you are confused. Maybe the metallic outer layer is the cause of that confusion? We engineer that outer myelin sheath from the same substance as our armour. That is why they look alike and share the same properties. You'll find out soon enough; today we go and sort your armour out.'

'No way.' Bradley definitely did not want that! He was still trying to wrap his mind around the new information. He could not fathom just what sort of technology could allow for this level of bioengineering.

'You have no choice in the matter, unless you plan on walking about TrueEarth naked, holding that cover in front of you for the next whoever knows how long?'

Bradley checked he was still completely naked under the covers. 'Don't you have clothes here?' asked Bradley.

'Yes, of course we do; we're wearing them!' he laughed, pointing at his metallic skin as it reflected in the light. Bradley gave out a comic long sigh. There was no point fighting it, it seemed.

Tamirok walked in without warning. 'Get out of bed. We're going.'

Bradley did not even have time to ask any questions; his body simply moved of what seemed to be its own accord. The only thing he managed to do was take the leather-like bedcover on his way. He didn't understand what was happening. There was this strong force within him forcing him to move. He tried to counter it. That proved to be as ineffective as blowing in the face of a windy gale.

'Why must you make everything difficult?' asked Tamirok. 'Don't bother trying to counter my will; you do not even know how to use your own, let alone be able to counter a binding. All you will do is not focus on what is important and exhaust yourself.' He walked down several long corridors with Bradley and Lurizak at his tail. After countless turns and twists down massive corridors, with absolutely spotless polished bronze floors and tall copper-like brick walls, decorated with ornaments from various periods of battle history, they reached a 12-foot tall doorway. The huge heavy ancient doors were decorated with orate golden engravings. Bradley looked at them, wondering how on Earth anyone could open those.

Tamirok seemed to answer his question without it even having to be asked. 'The strength our men have is far beyond anything you have ever seen on your side.' And left it at that.

Waves of heat emanated from within the room. It was so hot to Bradley that the sensations of pushing against an invisible wall flooded him as he tried to push through. Lurizak laughed. His movement required no effort whatsoever. As he made it in, his breath was taken way at the vast immensity of what he saw: a centralised furnace with six mighty blacksmiths working there, rows of men on what looked like floating workbenches, walls upon walls of shinning metallic armour held up in display areas behind closed glass doors, upon the centre of which pulsed a single huge glyph. Each armour had its own unit and each unit had a glyph shining there on its doorway.

'Impressive, is it not?' asked Lurizak. 'And this is only the front of the Great Forge.' Tamirok shot him a warning gaze. He went silent. Bradley understood they had no intention of revealing too much to a newcomer.

'What have we got here?' A tall man stepped forth. Bradley was surprised, as this was the first time he had seen anyone in House Bound without metallic-type skin. Instead, this man worked some sort of leather-like clothing, leaving his massive arms, back, and chest completely bare. His shoes were made of thin leather, as were his shorts. Bradley paid close attention to it; it was not quite leather as it had an almost metallic shine to it, like everything else in this place... and frost? How could frost exist here, of all places? His gaze moved upwards: no burns, snow-pale skin, perfect cut musculature, dark brown frizzy hair and the bluest eyes he had ever seen. Looking straight into them, he was taken to a place of seas; massive floods and water gone into erratic conflict with whatever dared cross its path.

'It's a bit tricky,' Tamirok interrupted Bradley's daydreaming.

'I like complicated. Want me to hammer it out into a nice smooth surface for you, General?' he smiled.

Tamirok exploded in laughter. 'I wish it were that easy, Ilomir.' He turned to face Bradley. 'This is Bradley, he's a... ' He hesitated. 'What I am about to reveal to you is kept hush. Clear?' His commanding tone came back.

Ilomir got closer to avoid anyone overhearing them. That was possible with all the banging, scraping and crackling noises drowning the place. 'Understood,' agreed Ilomir.

'He's a Ruler from the other side, who knows nothing about TrueEarth and who happens to stumble his way through the entrance of wielders.'

Ilomir whistled out loud in surprise. 'Tricky does not even begin to explain that one!'

Bradley liked Ilomir. His jovial happy-go-lucky personality was easy to warm to, as was his light-hearted way of looking at things.

'I gather that there is even more complexity to this young fellow under that statement of yours?' Bradley felt a massive blow on his left shoulder as Ilomir patted him gently in a welcoming gesture.

'Indeed there is. You see, the powers inside of him are in conflict, constantly overflowing and tearing everyone – and I mean everything – up in their path. We've stabilised them for now but they will burst out soon. When they do, he'll burn out and rip through everything in existence on his way.'

Ilomir whistled out louder this time. 'In other words, you're a pretty dangerous guy, Mr Boom!' He laughed.

Bradley could not help but smile. 'I really, really don't want to be.'

'Of course not,' replied Ilomir. 'Let's see what we can do to help you not boom away, shall we?'

'Before you two go off and start playing with the toys, you should know one more thing and this is highly confidential.' Ilomir nodded in agreement. 'He's the Ruler of House Nothingness.'

This time the information took him by surprise, and a loud bang echoed through the entire forge as his huge working hammer, glowing with freezing power, crashed against the frosty metallic flooring, causing a small crack to form. 'Are you sure?' he asked.

'No doubt about it.'

Ilomir's face became serious for a split second. The following instant he was back to his jovial self. 'Well, dear fellow, we're going to have our work cut out fixing you up and making sure you don't obliterate all of us in the process.'

'I'm going to leave him with you. He needs armour, although we are not allowed to do the great bindings on him. I am sure you have the required skillset to deal with this.' As he was about to leave, he added, 'He's allowed to learn the forging methods due to inter-House accords, but not those ones.'

Ilomir nodded and understood. His arm was once more around Bradley's shoulders. 'You and I are going to get you the best armour any of these guys have ever seen!'

'Bradley, you are to follow Ilomir's instructions to a T, without fail and without argument or resistance. Stay with him until I return.'

Bradley had no problem with that instruction. He was tired doing nothing. Tamirok and Lurizak left.

'I'll take care of you, don't you worry. Tamirok has picked the best man for the job. No one better than a native of an ice world to quell that fire inside of you!'

Bradley didn't ask. The entire concept of other worlds still felt totally unreal to him. Looking at Ilomir, he was just another guy. He led Bradley through the long corridors of armour on display, pointing out the suits he had designed himself. His pride in his work was obvious. Bradley looked at them and just could not imagine how much dedication went into them the intricate detail, the inscriptions and glyphs, the interweaving of metals into shapes. Each one was totally unique and each one was as impressive as the last.

'If any of them tickle your fancy, let me know!' offered Ilomir. Bradley hesitated. 'Go on,' Ilomir prodded him.

The impulse of external will forcing him made its presence clear. It seemed Tamirok's instructions could not be ignored, even when he was not about. 'Those, hmm.' Bradley did not know what they were called. He simply pointed to the keyhole prominently featured on them all.

'Ah, the points of binding. They serve important functions. You will find out in time. Here were are. We will have a bit of privacy here.' They had arrived into an adjoining section. It was a square room, where basins of metals ooze were presented in hot large containers on each side of the room. A small forge stood in the northern end, leaving the central part completely open. Chairs with floating seats were spread out in each corner.

'This is a fitting room. See up there? The guys hang the armour to be fitted up there and then use these handy chairs to shift up and down the length of his body to meld the armour and etch it with the proper powers. Takes about three hours in total to merge skin and armour.'

The thought horrified Bradley. The matter-of-fact fashion in which Ilomir spoke unnerved him.

'In your case, we're going to do things a little differently. Let me see.' He pulled up a chair for himself and sat down. The circular square which formed the top part seemed to remould itself to his shape and the next second, he was floating sitting down on it. Bradley was surprised. He had never seen such a thing. 'Simple. Magnetically charged metals at the bottom created a strong magnetic pulse to counter the gravity of the planet, propelling the chair upwards. I need you to stand there. Leave your cover on the floor here.' Bradley so didn't want to, but his body obeyed. He felt very uneasy as Ilomir floated up and down, to the front and the back, inspecting his entire body. He wanted to hide, he wanted to leave immediately, but his body didn't move a single inch.

'Ok, I have a map of all your proportions. We're going to need something which will grow with you because I guarantee with training you will grow into a proper man, not this skinny semi-adolescent body you have.'

'I am a grown man,' objected Bradley.

Ilomir brushed off the comment, completely ignoring it. 'If we can't do a great binding, the choice of materials is going to be a big problem. All the metals here bind atomically to skin...' A sound of ripping fabric blasted through the room, sending Ilomir and his chair bobbing through the air to the far side of the room. Some of the forgers came in running to see what had happened. 'It's ok, no harm.' Ilomir told them as they filed away completely ignoring Bradley standing there.

'We can help with that.' Ilomir turned around to see the gap in reality. Something had just torn though the space and substance which was his fitting room and left a large hole in it with an outer shape of a human being.

Much to Bradley's surprise, Ilomir didn't react as the other had done upon seeing Nihi for the first time. 'Ah, a being of the great Nothing. A pleasure.' He bowed ever so slightly.

'We like this one!' Nihi told Bradley.

'You're not afraid?' asked Bradley, still immobilised and standing there in the centre of the room.

'Why should I be? Back home I see such beings from time to time. Deep within the core of my world, a few are glimpsed every so often. Never seen one so close or felt one but I know of them.'

'I am Nihi, representative of House Nothingness.' It presented itself formally.

'I am Ilomir, Master of the Great Forge of TrueEarth.' He then made a sign with his left hand that Bradley did not recognise. Nihi, on the other hand, did. Its form split into nine separate cuts in space. They moved and swirled about Ilomir, never quite touching him but getting terribly close.

174

'Compatible systems for information exchange,' Nihi reformed itself.

'What was that all about?' asked Bradley.

'An ancient greeting to the Nothing taught to me by my departed grandmother back home.'

'You know of these things?'

'Didn't we just establish that a moment ago?' Ilomir reprimanded Bradley. 'Well, all this doesn't solve our current problem.'

'Solution simple. Combine forming skills with crafter shaping and Ruler inner power,' explained Nihi.

'Easier said than done. Doing something like that could take years.'

'Minutes,' corrected Nihi.

'How?' Ilomir had never heard of anything like that to be remotely possible, let alone take minutes.

'Binding through Ruler, information power and energy are all the same; skill-directing patterns,' it insisted.

'Not sure I understand. My skills are at binding and shaping that which I craft with. I don't have the ability to do all that other stuff,' admitted Ilomir.

Nihi didn't bother replying. Instead, a string of nothingness expanded from deep within the gap it was, and shot directly into the gem Bradley had incrusted within his body just under the bellybutton. It started glowing.

'Odd. Hadn't noticed that there before,' commented Ilomir.

'Hidden from attention of others. Minds diverted from noticing. Touch Ruler's body on light,' it instructed. The red light of the gem had begun to flow all over his body in thin lines of blinding angry reds and was forming a small patch at the centre of his collarbone.

Illomir decided that would be the best place to make contact. He sure as heck was not going to do it at the main gem. He wanted to avoid the source of whatever that energy was. As he placed his hand just on top of Bradley's collarbone, the power pulsed through him. His mind unravelled the information within it. The process was exactly the same as when he was directing the living metal he moulded on a daily basis. He kept his hand there and spoke. 'Bradley, focus in on your gem and pull out more power. Will it to flow but at the same time, shape it into lines. Close your eyes to make it easier to focus and just listen to my voice.'

Bradley did as told. He did not have any choice in the matter. He found that not having his mind there to ask questions opened up something else in him. It was like a part of him dormant deep under his very thinking process, which knew things his mind did not. It knew how to unleash his will, it knew how to pull power out, it knew, whereas he himself had no clue what all this meant. He had a suspicion, but that unfortunately was not sufficient for him to direct these effects. So he let that other part of his mind loose, and his own will to direct things which were completely subdued under the bindings had somehow unlocked something else within him. Power and energy exploded outwards, and lines upon lines of red might formed mid-air.

'Take these lines and run them along your body.' The image of arteries and veins popped into his head. He willed it so. Inside and outside of his body they directed power. 'MORE,' yelled Ilomir, 'make them thicker.'

He did as instructed. This time it seemed different. The energy had coalesced too hard, then Ilomir gasped in surprise. The crystal had expanded all around Bradley's waist from under the existing one there. It had formed a belt-like structure. Another grew under Ilomir's hand, lodging itself there, and from it, red power washed over his shoulders, traps and up his neck.

The process continued as two large crystals seemed to grow out of his shinbone; power lines erupted from them all. Nihi poured dark nothingness into the central gem. It shimmered, and for an instant Ilomir thought it would crack under the strain. Bradley yelled out in pain. The crystals bled out blackness; it was not nothingness – not as far as Ilomir could tell. He saw its substance, and his skills came into play now. He quickly wove it into patterns, patterns into shapes, shapes into materials, materials into fabric, a fabric he stretched, pulled, formed. Inch by inch he wove it in with Bradley's skin.

The pain had stopped. The sensation of every inch of his skin behind pulled outwards, then something crawled upon it, into it and finally the new, thicker, unknown skin snapped back into place – it sent his mind into overdrive. Inch by inch, those sensations ebbed along his entire body until finally, it all solidified to the point where had he wanted to move, he would not have been able to. From toes to upper neckline, he was covered in solid black metal with red pulsing veins of power and energy.

'Well that's the hard part done,' said Ilomir, pulling his hand away from Bradley's chest. Nihi disconnected from the central gem. 'How do you feel?' he asked Bradley.

'I can't move!'

'Of course you can't. We're not done yet. What I need to know is if you feel good? Bad? Is your new skin irritating you? Itchy? Painful? That sort of thing.'

Bradley thought about it other than feeling slightly thicker and solid he was fine. 'I guess I'm fine...'

'That's good enough. Ok, step two. This will take some time but since you can't move, the worst you will do is complain – although I would be most grateful you didn't because I need total concentration here. If I get this wrong, you will get all the wrong functions to that... might I say... most impressive if not highly unusual armour.'

'Ok,' replied Bradley. He decided that he had absolutely no idea what this next part would be, so all he could do for now would be to endure it. Ilomir took out some vials and books and sat down. His chair started floating bobbing up and down the length of Bradley's body. As he worked, he swore time after time: 'Bloody stuff won't allow me to do any of the engravings on it! How the heck am I supposed to do this?'

'What do you mean?' asked Bradley.

'I need to engrave the glyphs and symbols on it. Each time I try to, whatever is engraved vanishes.' He turned to Nihi. 'How do I do this?' he asked it.

'No need.' A shimmer erupted from it and hit Bradley, and rippled all over him. Glyphs and writing Ilomir had never seen before came aglow. He looked at it; the complexity of it surpassed anything he had worked with on TrueEarth. This would have taken him hundreds of days to etch. Then it all vanished.

'What? Is going on?' he asked.

'Hidden potential. Only unlocked when Ruler masters himself. Dormant for now but there. No need to engrave non-House glyphs.' That made sense. Each House would have its own script and powers.

Each letter linked the particles within it to entangle particles in another place, and each of these places held vast reservoirs of natural power and universal forces, each so secret, that wars were fought over them. 'They are like keys which allow you to unlock untold possibilities – providing of course you know how to use them and can find the right lock to use them on! You will learn in time. Experiment, investigate and explore!' he explained.

'How about all these?' he asked Nihi pointing to the jars.

'Those can be added. The armour will absorb.'

'Fine, stage three it is, then. This will feel very weird; just endure it,' he told Bradley. 'The custom-made bacteria first. This has a bit of kick to it!' Ilomir laughed, and it made Bradley all the more nervous. The contents of the jar were brushed all over his new armour. Within seconds, it had absorbed the odd-looking formulation. Pain coursed through him, and he felt as if millions upon millions of microscopic bugs were biting every inch of his body. It lasted only a few seconds.

'There you go. Now your ability to regenerate and energise the body will be increased to incredible levels with those guys coursing through you.' Without warning, he repeated the process. This time the liquid was almost ooze-like and seemed to grow out of his armour. 'A fungus which will feed on radiation and produce healing engines inside you. Now you can go and hope for a walk in space!' The process continued; jar after jar was consumed. The frostbite sensations, were followed by burning, aching, something smooth running all over his body, aching, itching; he had them all. After what seemed hours, Ilomir was done.

'You can move now. Wiggle your toes and stretch out.'

The armour was no longer solid; he could move! After a few movements it actually started to feel better and better.

'Don't worry, you will get used to it – actually so used to it that you will feel naked without it on.' He looked Bradley over once more, from head to toe. 'No cracks, no rejections. Lucky for you, my young fellow. Otherwise we would have had to start from scratch and use different combinations.' He took a few steps back and nodded in approval. 'Looking good. That will have to do for now. We can always add to it later on.'

Bradley prodded and poked at himself. It was as if the material had hardened but in an odd way that made it mobile. It was smooth solid yet flexible. The only exception to that rule seemed to be his hips and shorts section. Those were totally solid. The red power flared and started pulsing through his veins; the crystals glowed, then shimmered down into a faint pulse.

'What on Earth?' He was surprised. It was a pulse but not his pulse!

'It is alive,' explained Ilomir. 'The more you look after it and the more you become used to it, the more you will be able to grow and evolve it. I trust there is no need for me to explain to you what that means. Come; follow me.'

Bradley's body moved. He had hoped that this armour would disable the binding in that chain he wore around his neck, but no – it had instead simply slid under it, leaving it totally intact.

They moved back towards the forge. 'Put your hand in there.' Ilomir pointed to the forge fire.

Bradley panicked, trying to stop himself. He cursed and tried to pull back but his hand went straight into the flames. He stopped breathing for that split second, then looked. His hand stood there, flames gripping it. He could not feel any heat, nor could he see the hand or the armour burning.

'It's ok; pull it back out now.'

His hand came straight out. He inspected it. 'It? It? Didn't burn?' asked Bradley.

'Haha, surprised? No it didn't. The atomic structure and tight packing of both atoms and quark particles will prevent most if not all things from harming you. I am not exactly sure how this armour has turned out because it is made with a material I've never worked with before. I suspect it might be even stronger. That you will have to discover on your own. Come, let's have a drink. You've had more than enough surprises for one afternoon and goodness knows, I need a break! We can chat and relax until Tamirok comes looking for you.'

Both men went to another area in the forge where they sat and drank. Ilomir spent the time they had instructing Bradley how the armour was forged and given certain abilities. He also showed

Bradley how to shape the crystals he formed to adjust his waistband and reshape the other crystals on his armour if need be.

Nihi was nowhere to be seen. No matter how much Bradley tried to question Ilomir on the topic of these beings that resembled him, he got no answer. Ilomir simply refused to entertain the subject.

14

TO
- PROGRESS TO? -

Mira was down in the company's research laboratories. The massive complex of interconnected research departments offered the best high-tech equipment money could buy. The nanotech and virology divisions had been subject to her visit and instructions this morning.

'Where does she get all this information from?' asked the head of research.

'No idea,' replied his deputy, 'but what we do know is that it is incredibly advanced. Never seen these genetic patterns before and I've been doing this for over 30 years!'

'It is fascinating and always seems to prove itself accurate to an incredible degree.'

'Let us proceed. The virus has gained the ability to construct the artificial nerves we programmed into its engineered nanites. The proteins need a bit of adjustment but that is a minor concern.'

'Indeed, if we can get it to grow over and replace or in parallel to the victim's nervous system, we will be able to replicate a basic type of consciousness. In theory.'

'More importantly, we will be able to use it to activate all the other extreme genetics applied to the world population at large over the past three generations or so. The viral infections without symptoms and the vaccines combined have enabled us to add those to practically every living being on the planet.'

'Yes, so exciting. Now with this and the light wave technologies, we are practically at the point where the integration can take place. All we need are those internet satellites in orbit,' concluded the head of research.

'Just who put all this together?' asked the deputy.

'No one knows. Whoever it was, was a genius beyond the norm. We have Mira to thank for organising and managing it all so well. Without her involvement, I doubt we would be anywhere close to where we are now.' A shadow observing them from the far corner of the meeting room sank into the floor and slithered away.

Bradley was being flung across the training grounds like a leaf lost in the wind. Tamirok and Lurizak were watching as he had his first few practical lessons. He was utterly hopeless—not only was he failing at basic fighting skills but he was also failing at using his armour properly. Tamirok had seized total control of him on a few occasions and engaged his armour. By now, he should know how to repeat the process without the external control.

'He's just not getting it,' observed Lurizak.

'He's bloody hopeless! There is no other way of putting it.' Annoyed, Tamirok got to the two men and Bradley in the field. 'Why are you not fighting?' he yelled at Bradley. Without waiting for a reply, he went on, 'I don't have time to babysit you, there are real battles I need to organise. I've not only shown you how but also done it for you twice already!'

'I just can't,' Bradley was not only a pacifist but he had also spent his whole life trying to help and save people, not harm them.

'In that case, you are no use to anyone, a waste of resources and energy, so there's no point trying to keep you alive.' Tamirok turned to the two other men, sent his will burning through them, and said, 'Kill him!' then walked away.

'Fight, Bradley, fight! Your life is at stake. You will either win this battle or we will collect your corpse here in a few hours.' He simply walked away without looking back and instructed Lurizak to follow him.

The two other men sparring with him changed—their attacks started coming in with full force. Their armours were glowing and seething with power. It was like a rage of battle had wiped all sense from them. Tamirok's command was absolute. Bradley was the enemy, he needed to be killed there and then. Hundreds of spikes flew out of one of their armours and sped right towards him. As Bradley tried to avoid them, they curved and struck him. It took a few attempts but they eventually made it through his armour and, like needles, pierced through his flesh, expanding within him and slicing into his arteries effortlessly. Bradley screamed with horror. This was the one thing he was terrified of, the rage flared up within. Something from deep inside of him reacted, something expanded and split through the armour. The red power veins on his body pulsed with power and the material responded. His entire left arm was encased in solid ruby crystal flaring with black lightning. Without surprise or reason, he instinctively used it to slice through the armour spikes of his opponent. His right arm pulled out the few spikes that had made it into him. It was like pulling a needle out inch by inch and these had gone in deep. The wounds closed instantly as the armour healed him.

The extraction had distracted him, so the incoming blow struck against his back, sending him flying across the field. In all other circumstances, the force of the impact would have been his end. Thankfully, the kinetic force was diverted and it rippled across the black material of his new skin, only to be absorbed by it. Bradley let go. Instinct drove him now, this new skin channelled that force back down his right arm and propelled itself forward, releasing the concentrated wave back through the palm of his hand.

He struck his attacker mid-chest. His anger kept on intensifying, his instinct for survival amplified by something he did not recognise nor investigate. Power flared up and the red veins pumped pure force into his blow. Both the new power and the kinetic force unleashed with such aggressive force that it not only sent his opponent flying but also ripped a massive chunk of his chest away. As the body fell to the ground, blood gushed out of the wounds. The man was unconscious. His armour quickly started resealing the wounds to heal him.

Bradley's other opponent saw his buddy laying there unconscious. His fury went into overdrive. As he concentrated, his left arm was covered in metal reshaped as a blade. Etched scripts flared up, pulsing with energy, covering the warrior with an eerie coppery light which vibrated so rapidly, it produced an almost deafening hum. Other parts of the warrior's skin seemed to be expanding and reconfiguring itself—complex structures built within an instant became functional. Beams of solid blue atomic power flared towards Bradley. He avoided the first only to be forced to duck, countering a blow from the warrior's sword. When it hit, the energy vibrated into Bradley's armour and caused it to shimmer. It was losing its solidity. Bradley jumped backwards to break contact, only to be hit by another two beams piercing his leg. He wouldn't be able to avoid this for long. Another beam struck, causing him to yell out in agonising pain. The warrior was gaining speed, faster and faster were his blows as more and more beams hit simultaneously. Bradley would be killed.

Then it all stopped. His vision blurred. His co-ordination was lost and he thumped on the floor, his head spinning. Was he still alive? He cautiously opened his eyes. Looking around, the air was different. He was back on the floor at his apartment still in full armour. He looked at his leg, which had started to heal, and gave a sigh of relief. Then, he quickly realised that he was in full armour! How was this possible? *It had all been a dream! Had it? Could it be? It was not a dream after all?*

Finally, took you long enough, replied a voice echoing up from the depths of his mind.

Just who the heck are you? He asked, upset.

That is of no concern, what you should be concerned about is getting out of all this and hiding that crystal on your arm. It is a bit... revealing.

That distracted Bradley from his barrage of questions. Yes, he had to do something... but what? His left arm was still totally encased in this sword-like thing made of red crystal. He thought about it and replayed how it had formed during combat. Suddenly, his mind was filled with memories of how the ruby embedded below his bellybutton had worked. He closed his eyes and focused on the crystal and his left arm. Nothing happened.

The armour, you nit-wit, not the arm! The mental voice instructed him. What did it mean? Focus on the armour? He tried. Something clicked. Armour and mind connected. It was like two minds touching and synchronising. Bradley kept trying to set his arm free. That didn't work either. 'Damn it!' he cursed. 'Why can't I just get rid of this thing?' It worked, the entire crystal's structure shined and was, within a split second, reabsorbed into the armour. *So, that's how it works,* he thought.

Good boy! said the voice within his mind.

Don't patronise me, he snapped back at it, he was not in the mood for this nonsense. It was silent. Bradley ignored it, he didn't need something mocking him. He concentrated on the armour again. Within a few seconds, it faded away into his skin, all but the central red gem. He let out a sigh. He had hoped that damn gem on his lower belly would be gone too. Looking at his hands, he saw his usual skin once more, then he noticed he was naked again, so he stood up and went to take a shower. Goodness knows he needed the relaxing flow of water cascading all over his body. It was not until he got into the bathroom that he noticed his body had changed—slightly but definitely noticeably. Muscle was there that he never had before. He was lean and smooth. All the body hair had completely disappeared off of him. His skin was smooth, too smooth. He was changed, it bothered him. Somehow, his body no longer felt like his own. It had changed—been changed far too fast. What surprised him the most was that the binding necklace was gone, meaning Tamirok's nerve cords were no longer tied around his neck. He tried something. It worked, his own will was flowing free once more, there was a hint of something else there but it was distant... or was it dormant? Without pausing any longer, he stepped into the shower. He had to clean-up and deal with his injuries before they got infected.

Heather stormed into Kiandra's office with a printout in her hand. She was livid and just could not understand how someone could be so simpleminded to lack the basic understanding which would drive them to do such a thing. What she refused to contemplate is how someone with that level of social intelligence could be working here in the labs. It was utterly unthinkable.

'What do you think you're doing?' she slammed the printout onto the desk with a loud bang. Heather was not someone who lost her cool easily, but in cases of such utter stupidity, she had no other choice.

'Ah, Heather, if I am not mistaken, nice to finally meet you. I am...'

'I know who you are, just as you obviously know who I am. Explain yourself!'

'I'm sorry?' Kiandra said sternly. She was technically the superior here, not someone to be yelled at by a lab employee, no matter how lustrous that employee might be.

'This!' she turned the sheet so that the text faced Kiandra.

'Yes, the new position advert. What is the matter with it? I thought you would have been delighted about the opening and applied. Not that I can see someone so temperamental fitting the role, but...' she left the sentence hanging.

'Do you not even realise what you've done? Open to women applicants only? How stupid do you have to be?'

'Listen, young miss, I won't put up with this lack of respect. You will either calm down or you might have to look for another job soon.' Heather completely ignored her.

'Since you don't seem able to grasp this, I'll tell you what you did. You have just labelled any woman who applies for that job as being unqualified for it and have put doubt on the capabilities of all women who work here.'

'I doubt that very much,' objected Kiandra.

'Really? Are you so blind as to not see? You are not recruiting on ability, you are excluding all the men which means you don't want them competing for the job. That, in turn, will mean whoever takes the job will be coloured with the fact that they only got the job because they were female! They will be the butt and joke of all the other staff.'

'Nonsense,' replied Kiandra.

'You really can't see it, can you? How can someone...' Heather bit her lip and never finished the sentence. 'No matter, my concerns are obviously pointless to you. I bet it never occurred to advertise the job without your exclusionary clause and then select a woman candidate if that is the level of your interest in the success of the team.'

'Oh, don't be so pretentious. I know you got your position here because of your familial connections and privilege.' Kiandra had to re-establish her authority and bring Heather down a peg or two. After all, she was the one in charge!

'Don't you dare!' Heather snapped back, 'I graduated far away from my grandfather with no help from him, not only that but I applied to the labs, went through the interviews in a field he was not working himself and started working here before he even knew about it! I've proven my skills and intellectual capacity in over 70 publications ranked in the top journals of our field. I have nothing to prove to you or anyone else.'

'Neither do I, I am the Professor here.' Kiandra snapped back.

'That remains to be proven in the labs, a title is easy to acquire these days, especially for us. Let us see what you can achieve in the field. I've read your papers over lunch, the few and far between I could find... I know what I need to know.' She simply turned her back at Kiandra and walked out.

That one has to go! Kiandra decided then and there. *Just look at her with her fancy attire and her totally inappropriate expensive shoes. We're not a fashion parlour, we're a serious research facility.*

Bradley had something to eat. The food seemed very bland in comparison to what he had been eating for... the thought just occurred to him. He rushed to his laptop to check on the time. Once it was booted up, he checked the calendar. It had been three whole days! How was that possible? It felt like weeks, not days. Then he realised he had to catch up fast as he missed three whole days of progress here. He grabbed whatever clothing he had handy, which oddly enough was the clothing he had worn the day he left. Nothing had moved, nothing had changed. Memories flooded back. Tears started flowing as he remembered Kuroi and his unborn dead son. It all came back, crashing down on him. He sank onto his chair with his head in his hands, allowing the emotions to wash over him.

Eventually, he ran out of emotions to process. He decided it was time for him to do something—anything. He would defeat this nightmare that had cost him so much. He wiped whatever tears were left on his face in his sleeve, grabbed his keys, left his apartment and walked down to the labs. It was more than time for him to catch up with what had been happening. Arriving at the main entrance, he keyed in the code and entered the glass building. Things seemed different. He walked down the usual set of corridors and tried to enter his office. The doors refused to open. He thought he made a mistake and re-keyed the entry code. Denied. *What is going on here?* He knew he had to see Dr Grimsaw and get some answers. As he backtracked through the corridors, he inadvertently ran into Mira.

'Ah, Bradley Boston, I gather?' she took the first step—she always had to take the first step in any conversation.

He looked at her, 'Yes, but I'm afraid I can't say I recognise you. Are you new here?' he asked. Something about Mira made him feel uneasy, it was as if every nerve in his body was on high alert and ready for action.

Be wary of her, the voice in his head echoed.

'No, I'm not,' she lied. 'I take it you're searching for your new office?'

'New office? What on earth do you mean?'

'All the offices were moved upstairs a few days ago,'

'Odd,' he said. Something was amiss, 'you never said who you were or how you know me?'

'No, I didn't,' she simply replied, 'you might not know of me but I know of you and your work very well.' She avoided giving him any information about herself. 'You are looking into that new infective agent, are you not? A wonderful specimen to work on if you ask me.'

His senses suddenly became sharper than they had ever been before.

'You think? I must admit, I always appreciate any additional insights and opinions I can gleam,' he decided to play the game. Mira, on the other hand, was delighted that he would value her opinions.

'Oh, yes, certainly, such potential. You could use it to achieve so many things. Can you imagine if we had just discovered a viral agent that could be used to push human evolution to the next level? So terribly exciting, so many possibilities.'

'You most certainly have a valid point, but I haven't found anything which could be used yet. I must admit, it might be just my own failing to do so.'

'I'm positively certain you will, in time.'

'Really? You do?' he needed to find out as much as possible. She had access to far too much information about him and the research they were conducting here.

'Absolutely, I have every confidence in your future achievement. You are like me, you don't accept failures as a possibility and have extraordinary focus and capacity. I have read all your papers, astounding.'

He pretended to be slightly embarrassed at the focus on him.

'Oh, I wouldn't go that far. I work at it until it makes sense. After all, so many lives are at stake, dependant on the work we do here.'

'That may be, but if I may, let me give you a little advice,' she offered.

'Please do, I'm all ears,'

'Don't focus on others, it's a waste. Think about your own achievements first and foremost. People will follow or be lost behind. As long as we move on ahead, we can drag the rest along or remove them when they hinder us. Most of the human race is here just to hinder, remember that.' Her phone beeped. 'I am sorry but I must go. It has been a pleasure, we will meet again, I'm sure.' She walked out of the building. The whole meeting had set Bradley on edge. This woman knew far too much. Her words were very specific, each littered with meaning and subtext. How did she know him? Had he met her before? From what she spoke, she had intimate knowledge of their research. He had to find out what was going on.

As he rushed down the corridor, he bumped into Heather who was angrily storming down the adjoining office, he caught her just in time, one hand on each of her arms to stabilise her from falling. She abruptly looked up, saw him and froze.

'Bradley! Oh my, where have you been? We've all been looking for you, I was so worried.'

'I'll explain later over coffee,' he saw she was very upset. He had worked with her for so long, he knew to watch out for the now all too visible tightness in her jawbones. 'What is going on here?' he asked.

She couldn't stop herself from telling him all about it. It just came pouring out of her.

'Don't let it bother you,' he replied when she had finished telling him about her encounter with Kiandra.

'It does! I don't want everyone to think I only got my job here because of grandpa,'

'Well, I'd suggest you stop calling him grandpa in front of the staff then!' he smiled at her, trying to alleviate the mood.

'Stop it. You're avoiding the problem by being silly. This is serious.'

'Listen to me very carefully, Heather. You're one of the brightest people in this damn building, you have an insane record of achievements to your name, besides being stunningly beautiful.' He paused, 'we'll let that minor detail fall by the wayside, for now.'

'Hey! That's important too,' she joyfully banged her small fist against his firm chest. 'Wait a minute, that feels...' She took a step back and gave him the eye over, from head to foot, carefully inspecting him, 'what happened to you?' an expression of suspicion surfaced.

'We'll talk about it later, first, I need to get into my office and my code doesn't seem to work,' he explained. He was trying his best not to think of it all, especially since it was bringing up memories of Kuroi. He had to keep those away for now or he would not be able to function.

'Oh that... yes, miss almighty decided to throw us into a full-blown move a few days back, everyone has been up in arms about it and got almost no work done. You are on the second floor with the rest of us. Come, I'll show you the way, your code should work on your new office.'

'Wait a minute, just hold on,' he was worried, 'where is all my stuff?'

'Whatever we found in your office was boxed up and taken up to the new one, why?' she knew exactly why he was concerned.

'Never mind, I'll sort out those boxes when I get there, let's go,' he definitely did not want to discuss the reason for his concern. She knew he would ask about those strange crystals he had somehow got his hands on. She wanted to know about them and about that red glowing one she had seen last time. It took only a couple of minutes for them to arrive in the upstairs row of corridors which housed their new offices. His was the last one down this particular corridor.

'Here is where your new office is, try the entry code.' He did as instructed. It worked and the doors slid open. He was welcomed by rows of boxes.

'You've got to be kidding me!' he burst out.

'Afraid so,'

'This will take ages to sort out,' he was not amused. Not at all.

'Somehow, I suspect that was the idea behind this unexpected unnecessary move.'

'I think you're right,' he agreed.

'Of course, I am,' she poked him gently in the ribs for the sake of a bit of fun.

'Oi, that hurts,' she laughed, 'guess I'd better get down to it,' he let out a long sigh.

'Forget all that for now, you have to come and see what me and Jim discovered with the virus.' His left eyebrow shot up at the mention of a new discovery.

'I'll get my suit,'

'No need,'

'You never know!' he objected.

'I'm sure you will be fine this one time,' she teased him, poking at him again, 'unless Mr Big Guy now is even more scared of an infection than he was before?'

'You're reckless, you know!'

'I know, let's go,' she practically dragged him out by the hand before he started looking for his protective suit, causing his half-healed injury to strain.

Mira was just about to knock on Kiandra's office door when the power within her surfaced. It surprised her, almost overwhelming her. *Bbbbe careffffullll,* the shadow echoed in her mind. *Thhhhe oooone youuuu spppppokkkke ttttto iiiiis youuuur ennnnemmmmy.* It surprised her, Bradley seemed like a lost fool to her, not someone who could cause her any trouble. She had entertained the thought of using him to her own advantage. *Hhhhhe willllll bbbbbe youuuur downnnnfalllll.* It was gone.

'Move away,' Jim instructed Bradley.

'Why on earth should I?' his instruction had caused confusion in Bradley.

'Just do it, I'll explain.'

'Fine,' he moved backwards.

'More,' he moved again. He was close to the door.

'Want me to leave?' Bradley was getting annoyed at this moving closer then backing off routine Jim was making him do. 'What's all this about? I don't have time for silly games.'

'I'm nearly done, hold on.' Jim typed away furiously on the keyboard under the dual displays hanging on the lab's wall. 'Done, you can come back now.'

'Well, explain yourself,' snapped Bradley. Heather looked at him, she was worried. This was so unlike Bradley. He never snapped at the others, no, he would actually let them pull all sorts of pranks on him and remain perfectly calm and collected. Something more than just his physical appearance had changed. This was not the serious but self-restrained man she had known for years.

'Look,' Jim pointed to the screen on the left. 'See how the virus in the sample under the microscope moves backwards each time you get closer? It does even as far as the very edge of its perimeter.' He pointed to the screen on the right, 'look here, each time you move out of range, it moves back to its original position.'

Bradley looked at the screens in disbelief 'It knows when I am close? That's insane.'

'Indeed, it is. Look what happens when I play the entire recording I just made in sequence.' The screen flickered and displayed the viral movements back and forth. 'They match exactly the same points in time where I told you to move back and closer to the infinitesimal degree.'

'It's aware?' asked Heather.

'Not only that... it's aware of him!' Jim pointed at Bradley. 'How this works is beyond me,'

'Must be a coincidence,' said Bradley, 'viral agents don't have senses like we do,'

'Are you sure?' interrupted Jim.

Bradley's left eyebrow shot up as if to say, 'what are you about to say next?'

'Look at this,' he pulled up another recording. They all watched it carefully. The video played out as Jim had zoomed into the virus more and more, eventually hitting the nanoscale. There they were — thin golden structures which resembled nerves. Bradley gasped in surprise, Heather remembered seeing that and shuddered. It still creeped her out.

'Now, look at this one,' it showed the virus and a red blood cell in the same image. The inner darker central structure of the virus sprouted tiny attachments from the soma outwards. These appendages had sharp points which sprang into action and pierced through the membrane of the red blood cell, anchoring itself there. It proceeded to suck its soma out gradually until the cell was empty, then pulled the rest of the cell close. As the two touched its outer walls, its cellular membrane pulsed a few times and started absorbing the red cell.

'Good god!' burst out Heather, 'this is a horror movie. It can't be real, please, Jim, tell me that's not real.'

'As real as it gets I'm afraid,'

'And I assume those are human red cells?' asked Bradley.

'Correct, it completely ignores animal ones.'

'Do you know how it penetrates the red cells with those...' they didn't have a name for the appendages that grow out of a cell. The looked like tiny sharp black crab claws. They had never seen anything like that before, ever.

'No, nor do we know how those things grow, but I do suspect it had more to do with the nanotech side of things than a virological one. The central component, soma, of that virus is most probably programmed rather than natural.'

Bradley spent the next few moments in thought, ideas were streaming into his agile mind. Too many ideas, he was trying not to get overwhelmed.

'Ok, Jim, can you map whatever genetic sequence it has? Compare it to the one of the initial virus we collected from the first victim, then run a scan for any human components. After you have done that, I would like you to take it to Joe. Ask her to do a radiation test on the thing and see if radio waves affect it. We need to find out what it is reacting to. Could also be heat of the human body. Although... it might not be since you getting close would have had the same impact...'

'It boils down to what's so different about you, Bradley!' said Heather. 'What is it about you that's causing it to recognise you?' they both knew what she was talking about but neither wanted to say it. Bradley was definitely not going to run any experiments on that side of things with anyone else there. His red crystal could be the differentiating factor, but why? The only way he could test it for sure would be for him to run these tests alone.

'Jim, leave the equipment running and the samples out for me, I'll come and crack on with this later tonight' he instructed. It was not unusual for Bradley to work throughout the night, they all knew this.

'Why not now?' asked Jim.

'Because, for one, you need to do those tests I just spoke of first. They will determine what I will do next, and I have to go talk to Kuroi's family about the funeral.'

'Oh, of course. I'm sorry, Bradley,' that was a close one. It did remind him that he had to go and do exactly that, the sooner the better.

'Could staff in research facilities on floor two pay attention please, Professor Kustings requests the immediate presence of Dr Boston at her office on the ground floor.'

'Wait a minute, isn't that facility-wide tannoy only supposed to be used for critical emergencies?' asked Jim.

'Yes,' confirmed Heather, 'it's that all high and mighty miss Kiandra again. You'd better hurry, Brad, and keep in mind the woman is a power-crazed megalomaniac.'

'That's a bit harsh, Heather. Whatever happened to your cool head and giving everyone the benefit of the doubt?' Bradley was a little surprised.

'She doesn't deserve even the slightest ounce of sympathy.'

Bradley found it funny, someone had finally managed to get to Heather and push her annoyance button. He was looking forward to meeting this Professor. He made for the door, 'I'll see you later, time for an unexpected meeting it seems.' He made his way downstairs. For some reason, his thoughts kept being pulled back to his meeting with Mira—something she had said troubled him. He knocked at Kiandra's door and walked in.

'Bradley Boston, I take it,' she motioned for him to sit down.

'To what do I owe this pleasure?' he asked.

Finally, someone with manners in this dreary place, she thought.

'I have taken over staff management in this facility. I must admit, I am a little concerned when a lead researcher doesn't turn up for work in over 3 days with no explanation.' She waited for his response. Bradley knew her type all too well, he knew that his response would dictate his entire future relationship with her.

'Unforeseen circumstances called me away,'

'Oh? Do share,'

'I'm afraid I cannot, it's a personal matter.' He avoided being confrontational but he did not want to give her the knowledge she desired.

'I see, how unfortunate such a troublesome disappearance will make a mark on your work records.' She paused for a reaction, he just sat there waiting in silence. 'Anyway,' Kiandra could not stand silence, it downright irritated her, 'I've called you here to inform you that you will be getting an assistant-Professorial candidate to help with your research. I have assigned her to your team, she will technically be your superior in rank but you will need to train her up.'

Bradley was not sure whether he was hearing things right… he would have to waste time training her?

'I'm afraid that is not possible,' is all he said in response.

'Oh, do explain that. Keep in mind, your refusal is a sackable offence,' the threat was all too clear.

'I will be taking quite an extended period of time off shortly,'

'I'm afraid I cannot allow that,' she objected.

'And I'm afraid research laboratory policy 1389 specifically states that 'any person who has experienced the loss of a loved one and is in mourning is automatically entitled to up to 12 weeks sabbatical in order to arrange funerals, estate management, and probation for immediate family members.' I will be submitting the paperwork this afternoon with respect to this.'

She looked at him closely.

'You do not look like a man in mourning to me,'

'One's perceptions are one's own affair. Facts are facts. Was there anything else I could assist you with?' his offer was given in the friendliest tone he could muster. Kiandra was livid but did her best to hide it.

'Why request the full 12 weeks? Can't you have things done in 4? I am certain I do not need to point out that we are in the middle of an emergency situation.'

'I'm afraid I will be flying to Japan for the funeral after all the official matters have been settled here in the UK.'

'You can always delay it. In this day and age, we can delay the decomposition of bodies for a long time.'

Bradley had to use his entire reservoir of inner-strength to avoid jumping over the desk and grabbing her by the throat. He took a few deep breaths and re-focused.

'No,' was all he said.

'I'm sorry? What do you mean NO?'

'It is simple to understand. No, I won't do that.'

'Very well then,' she had made her decision, 'I doubt very much you actually need all this time but that is, of course, your choice. Needless to say, I will have to make arrangements for the good of this facility and to ensure we contain this threat. We will re-assign you to another team. Please ensure you leave all this project's data at the lab before you leave.' This is what she was ultimately aiming for. This would afford her such a key delay that she couldn't resist that little tell-tell smile to surface.

Bradley took note of it. 'As you wish, I guess we are done here?' he stood up and allowed his body to tower, casting its shadow over Kiandra's small frame. The trick worked quite well, she suddenly felt frail and small in comparison to him. Something inside of her was uncertain, was it a hint of fear? Doubt? No, she pushed it to the side, he would fail no matter how hard he tried. This virus is not something any of these so-called scientists can solve. She took an involuntary step back.

'That will be all, please leave now.'

He made his way to the door, a sigh of relief washed over Kiandra just as he turned to face her once more. 'Have a nice day,' he smiled and walked out. His mind was set, Mira had been right, there would always be those there to hinder.

The video on the screens in the labs went blank. Heather was fuming and Jim was swearing. They had both just heard the entire exchange between Bradley and Kiandra through their two monitors. Someone had somehow ensured that the security cameras in her office broadcast directly to them.

'What on earth was that?' asked Jim.

'Must have come from her office,' theorised Heather.

'But how? You mean to tell me we have cameras and microphones inside every office now?'

Heather nodded affirmatively.

'I'm not sure how I feel about this,' admitted Jim. 'So, this is why they made us all move. Guess it was easier to move everyone into labs and offices which already had the equipment installed than to install it into the existing ones. That would raise our suspicion. Which, in turn, means this is part of something much bigger.' He was on point. As usual.

'That does not explain how all that was broadcast here to us,' mused Heather. 'I'm going to find Bradley, we should make sure that is what happened just in case someone is trying to trick us. Meet me for coffee after office hours?' she asked him. Jim was a little surprised Heather never invited anyone for coffee after work.

'Sure,' he wanted to know what was going through her mind. Heather left on a mission, she knew Kiandra had tactfully manipulated Bradley exactly where she wanted him. She suspected that all of the Professor's actions were designed to ensure they never solve this virus mystery. Her intuition told her so and Heather never ever ignored that. Forcing Bradley to choose between going to Kuroi's and his son's funeral and threatening to sack him was in her mind totally unacceptable. Something had to be done.

15

THE
- GREEN LADY -
AWAKENS

Bradley found himself back in his own apartment, working through his to-do list. The funeral was confirmed and he made a note of the date and time. Fortunately, Ryuken would be at the airport to welcome him. He would be staying at his home. This worked really well; he had visited the Kudos once before and knew all the protocols all too well. Kuroi had teased him until he got each and every one of them right. Thinking of Kuroi made tears cascade down his face; he could not control them any more than he could take the sun out of the sky. He thought about her and melancholy wrapped itself about him like an old friend giving him a hug he did not want. He missed her so much. Her loss broke something deep inside him; he knew he was broken, but no matter what he did or tried, he could not fix it. He did not want to fix it. The phone rang and dragged him out of his brooding. Work was always a welcome distraction, keeping himself occupied allowed him to stop thinking about his loss.

'Hello?' a young man's voice on the other end. Bradley did not recognise it.

'Bradley speaking, how can I help?' he was hoping that would prompt the stranger to identify himself.

'Errrm, hi, I'm so sorry to interrupt… you gave me your card and number… and said if I needed help, I should call you. I'm Fred.' The memory flooded back; it was that young man who seemed so lost in himself that Bradley had feared the worst.

'Oh, yes, I remember, Fred. Is something wrong?'

'Well, kind of yes,' he mumbled, uncertain as to what he should say. 'I've got this... not sure what it is... problem with ...' he paused and the line went totally silent.

'Go on, don't worry, I won't tell anyone if you don't want me to.'

'Well, it's kind of ... I've got something stuck ...' uncertainty was thick in his tone, 'blue crystal thing? I don't know what it is.' Crystal, the word caused Bradley to freeze. 'Fred, listen to me very carefully, make sure you hide whatever it is from plain view, and come and see me as soon as you can. I'm in the first apartment block for staff on the top floor. There's only one flat there, just knock.'

'Mind if I come over now?' asked Fred. Bradley hesitated for a moment, as he had so much to do.

'Ok, I'll make a coffee and wait for you.' He was not sure why, but something from within seemed to push him to see Fred. It was odd; Bradley never invited anyone over to his apartment, let alone a stranger, however ... he got up quickly started putting his notes and things away. The knocking on the door interrupted him. It had taken Fred only slightly over 10 minutes to reach Bradley's apartment.

'Hi?!?' Fred peered through the door.

'Come in, Fred, don't worry, I won't bite. Fancy a coffee while I'm making it?'

'Ah, no thanks,' Fred was nervous.

'Ok, give me a minute then,' Bradley finished his coffee and with cup in hand, came over to the dining table where he had his laptop waiting. He pulled out a chair in front of his own, away from the glass table and motioned to Fred.

'Have a seat; tell me about this crystal thing you are having trouble with.'

Fred hesitated. He pulled off his tracksuit top to reveal his muscular torso clothed in his gym top. Bradley looked at his arms, and there he saw the three-inch thick crystal manacles fused with Fred's wrists. 'Don't worry, I won't hurt you; I just want to examine this a little closer,' Bradley warned him, the instant before taking hold of his hand and pulling it towards himself. He gently turned and twisted it, poked at every finger firmly, then waited for a few seconds before moving onto the next. 'The circulation does not seem to be affected, and basic wrist movement is uninhibited. Any loss of feeling anywhere in the hands?'

'Not as far as I can tell, just the constant pain as it gets tighter and tighter,' complained Fred. Bradley nodded, somewhat concerned. If these were indeed getting tighter as time goes by, eventually, they will interrupt blood flow and cause nerve damage in the limb. He had to do something to help Fred; otherwise, the young man would lose his hands. Time was indeed ticking and quite rapidly, judging by the pain.

'Ok, let's see the rest of them.'

Fred was a little surprised. 'How do you know there are more? I never mentioned that.' A hint of uncertainty and doubt flared up.

'I'll explain when we are done with the examination. I do have a few questions for you as well. Go on, show me, I assume there are four in total, right?'

Fred nodded, pulled his hand away from Bradley, and took off his shoes and socks. He then pulled up his tracksuit bottoms to his knees. Bradley was a little surprised, as the ones on his ankle were much darker in colour. Without warning, he pulled up Fred's leg, who was so glad he was sitting, or he would have lost his balance and started inspecting it. 'Close your eyes and tell me when you feel me poking you. If you stop feeling it, tell me immediately,' Bradley instructed.

'Ok,' replied Fred.

Bradley took the back of his pen and poked at the sole of Fred's foot, who singled the sensation correctly, then the pen was driven all over the sole, toes, heel and sides. 'Felt it constantly, I take it?' Fred replied that he had. Bradley then tried to dig the pen in between the crystal structure and what would have been Fred's skin, but no luck, the two were totally fused. It seemed that the crystal grew out of his skin. He repeated the same examination with the other foot. 'You can have your foot back,' he said, releasing the left one. Bradley paused to think; he was not too sure how Fred would react; then again, he had to do something to help the guy, but what? Even he was not sure how to handle that; he had not even found a solution for his own dilemma with these crystals.

'So, Doc, what's the verdict?' Fred attempted a bit of humour to disguise his nervousness.

'For the time being, your limbs are all ok; however, we need to do something very soon because if those are indeed getting tighter, they will eventually start to interrupt blood flow....'

He didn't need to finish that sentence, Fred did so for him... 'and I will lose my feet and hands.'

His eyes fixed on the floor, saddened beyond belief. 'Tell me, Doc, what did I do to deserve this? What was so bad that I should be made to sit back and wait until the worst happens. You know, I am supposed to be playing rugby now; I was really good at it.'

He went on to tell Bradley all that had happened to him over the last few weeks. 'I have no friends, no one to talk to, no one who understands me and worst of all, I have no future either. This curse,' he waved his arms about showing the blue crystalline manacles to Bradley, 'is killing me. What am I supposed to do now?' Tears threatened to break out; he was working hard on being the strong man and stopping them from overwhelming him.

Bradley felt really sorry for him. The guy had been caught in a web of unfortunate circumstances through no fault of his own. Bradley stood up and pulled his shirt up to reveal the red gem embedded inside of him, 'believe it or not, but I do understand at least some of what you are going through.' The crystal pulse with the red light within it. Fred reached out and touched it with a single finger to make sure it was real. He then realised what he had done and tried to immediately pull his hand way. It wouldn't budge, his finger was stuck in the crystal. Its pulse grew stronger, and strong, red power flared out through his finger and cascaded over his body until it made contact with the four crystals holding him captive. They flared up in dark indigo blue. Bradley jumped back; contact was broken.

Bound by a curse forever, only a free binding will lessen the burden, echoed the voice within his mind. The crystals all went dormant again. Oddly, Fred's ones no longer burdened him so much, they seemed to have loosened or at least stopped tightening.

Fred looked up at Bradley; 'it's stopped,' he said in surprise.

'What stopped?'

'They are no longer getting tighter.'

'Are they loosening?' Bradley was curious; he needed to know.

'I don't think so, but whatever is happening, it's no longer painful.

What did you do?' he asked Bradley, 'and why have you got a red one poking from the inside of you?'

'I'm not sure; things tend to just happen with these. The level of control I have with them is so minimal that I can't even get this out of myself!'

'Whatever it was, thank you,' said Fred, 'it doesn't solve the problem, but stopping them tightening has at least given me hope that I might not end up losing my hands and feet.' A partial smile formed on Fred's lips; it was the relatively good thing that had happened to him for a while now.

'Sure you don't want that coffee now? I need a refill,' offered Bradley.

'You know what; I'll join you.'

'Deal, and while I'm making it, I'll tell you what I know about these crystals and how it's partially my fault for you being stuck in them.' Bradley told him what he knew about them, how they were formed, and how last time he had seen them, they were in his office. He told him that his suspicion was that during the move, someone had somehow got their hands on them, at least on those four; apparently, there was a fifth one there. A much larger one. They both sat down, coffee in hand, and slowly sipped from their drinks.

'So, an outburst of emotion is the key or one of the keys to activating them,' summarised Bradley.

'What do you mean?' Fred was curious.

'You said Anna was angry and upset at you, that she wished you bound to your fate. Those emotions are what probably triggered their activation. I think that I am still partially to blame for their existence in the first place.' Bradley seemed downbeat about that one point.

'I don't blame you,' Fred said spontaneously, 'you had no way of knowing Anna and the blond girl would take your things and those four crystals.'

'Blond girl?' asked Bradley. Fred then went on to describe Heather from head to toe. 'I never would have expected Heather to steal my things.'

'Heather, yes, that was the name I heard when facing Anna's outburst. She was kind of right, you know.'

'Who?'

'Anna, I'm really good for nothing, it was only from her bullying me into doing things that I actually got things done. I see it now. I'm useless on my own.'

Bradley put his coffee down, turned Fred's chair with a simple pull on its side, and looked straight at him. They were face to face. 'You're not useless, don't ever let that kind of thinking get hold of you. Just because things have gone astray does not mean you're useless. Look at my life, a total mess. I just lost my bride to be, my unborn son, probably lost my job too, and I'm stuck with this,' he pointed to his red crystal, 'and to top it all off, I can't find a damn cure for a virus, which could be horrific if it started spreading any faster. Life throws things at us; we all get overwhelmed, but you know what? We work through them a simple small step at a time. So it's messy, who cares? You'll fix it one step at a time. Let it be a bit chaotic for the time being; you will put order back into it when you are ready.' He looked straight at Fred, keeping his gaze firmly locked in. Bradley knew Fred's thinking had to be changed, or the young man would be heading straight to the darkest place there is, and goodness knows where he would venture from there.

Eventually, Fred nodded. 'Man, I'm so sorry about your wife and kid.' Fred paused for a few moments, 'but you know that's the most useful thing anyone has ever said to me,' admitted Fred.

'I hope you keep it in mind!' Bradley turned back to his coffee.

'You know, I'm not much of a scientist, but as long as I am stuck in these,' he pointed to his manacles, 'I'll help you however I can! Even if it means grabbing the coffees while you work or chase down those monsters who made it and rip them to pieces while you get the cure done!' he smiled.

Bradley thought about it and decided that at least that would give Fred some motivation to action, as he knew all too well that inaction or the inability to act is what drove things into dangerous territory. He put his right hand out in front of Fred, 'It's a deal, shake on it!' He knew how the students dealt with things. Fred smiled and shook Bradley's hand. Their coffees were almost empty. 'I've got reports to do, so how about you go clean up because your feet are kind of smelly!' Bradley laughed, trying to comically hold his nose closed in between his fingers, 'and meet me at my lab later on? It's close to your dorms, it seems. Just walk along the corridor and look for the name plaques. If security asks, tell them I asked you to see me there.' He whispered the entry code just in case anyone was listening. Their plan was agreed, Fred said his goodbyes and left.

'That's one problem fixed, now onto the next,' Bradley set himself down to work through his long to-do list. His mood swiftly returned to its former sombre state.

Heather was determined to do something to help Bradley, anything. She would find a way, and her sharp mind was already at work on how to get what she needed. She rushed down the research facility's corridors; the upper floor new layout was a little less familiar to her. They were the same old bland monochrome doors with the silver identity plaques. As usual, the guards let her pass; they all knew her, as she not only worked with them all but was a friend with most of them. For some reason, they would all come to her with their heartaches, problems and confusions. *Men can be so bloody confused so much of the time,* she laughed silently. As she turned the corner down the corridor, she arrived exactly where she wanted to be. Fortunately, Bradley was not in his lab. He wouldn't be, from what she'd overheard, he was probably busy sorting out Kuroi's funeral. She let out a deep sigh, *the poor guy must be at his wits ends,* what a sad state of affairs that was. Brushing the thought aside, she marched on; now was the time for action.

'Hi Mike,' she said, greeting the guard at the entrance to the second floor. She smiled at him.

'Oh, Heather, how are you?' he seemed genuinely glad of the distraction. His job was a tedious one, mind-numbingly so.

'Yes, I've been a bit busy with all the errands gramps is making me do,' she lied but had him hooked.

'I bet he always finds something to keep you busy!'

'Oh, yes, he does. Today, I have to pick up after Bradley, can you imagine he actually managed to forget to take his experimental devices with him. Sometimes, that boy is totally hopeless.' She shrugged her shoulders, indicating that there was simply no hope.

'Poor guy, I can understand why, such a tragedy,' Mike said, his face sculpted with an expression of deep sympathy and pain. For an instant, it made her hesitate. She didn't want to cause him more trouble. It only took her a moment to brush the guilt aside; she knew why she was doing this. It was to help.

'It's all so awful; I don't know how he keeps on going,' she paused for impact. It had the desired effect.

'Well, you better get whatever he's forgotten.' He moved out of the way and keyed in the code to allow entry. She knew all the codes, all it had taken was to see him type it in once, and they would be permanently committed to memory. That was one of her key strengths: her memory. The doors slid open. 'See you in a bit,' she waved at Mike and walked in, a soft smile on her face.

Bradley's lab and office looked very messy; there was paperwork absolutely everywhere, mountains of books and notes piled on top of each other into almost pillar-like structures. He had obviously still not finished all his unpacking. The bleak white walls of the office made it almost clinical, nothing but a simple table, desk chair and computer. It looked like he had begun sorting it all out but left the task midway through. Fortunately for her, it was not notes she needed. Deeper in the officer, she saw the delicate crystalline structures, a small pillar of transparent crystal. She smiled at how actually smart he was, hiding those in plain sight made them appear as decoration. A bit odd for a guy, but everyone had their own quirks, and she knew all too well that scientists were as bad as artists when it came to their eccentricities. No one would have assumed how important that seemingly harmless natural crystal decoration was in a million years, just seeing it sitting there on the shelf. However, she knew about his discovery, and more importantly, she knew what it was. Now, all she had to do was to figure out how to use it. Trickier than it sounds.

Heather got closer to it, hesitated for an instant, then her resolve took hold. She reached out, cautiously made contact, touched it, and then pulled away and observed. Nothing happened; it had not reacted to her. Looking at her hand, nothing had changed. She tried again. This time, she picked up the whole crystal and took it off the book-shelf. She had to figure out how it worked. She tried to remember everything she had seen Bradley do in the hope it would help her. She just had to piece it all together. Heather loved puzzles, this one, however, gave no clue whatsoever; there had to be something to get things going. *Everything has a starting point,* she reasoned.

'I wouldn't do that if I were you,' a deep young voice warned her.

She turned around, coming face to face with Fred. 'I, ..., I wasn't...' she hesitated.

'I know what you were going to do, the look on your face says it all,' he paused. 'Doing that comes with a price, a very steep price and I'd stay away from it if I were you,' he warned.

'Don't tell me what to do!' she was annoyed at his interference.

'I'm not trying to tell you what to do; I'm just trying to warn you about what you are getting into. What you do is entirely up to you. I won't even try to stop you. Just remember that thing,' he pointed to the crystal, which was now on her lap, 'is totally heartless, merciless and demands a heavy price of all those afflicted by it.'

She looked at him and noticed the sadness in his eyes. She had only briefly seen him through the doorway during his confrontation with Anna. She knew what had happened to him; after all, she was the cause of it all. Regret flooded her. Her eyes went to his wrists; he still wore the crystalline manacles that Anna had hurled at him in the midst of her outburst. The crystals she had herself stolen from this lab. Through them, fate had grabbed hold of Fred and bound him. She understood his warning better than he could imagine.

'I have to do something, Bradley is...' the words were left hanging in mid-air... 'you guys are...', they both understood what she was referring to.

'You still want to risk it? The same will happen to you and there is no way to reverse it.' His left hand touched the manacle on his right as if to emphasise his point. 'It becomes part of you, whether you like it or not. It will do what it wants, no matter how much you object.'

She didn't miss the hint he was making at what happened to him and her involvement in the whole affair.

'I know, but I have to do something; it is the only way I can make up for the mess I caused, and the only way I can help Bradley. Something inside of him is tearing him apart.'

Fred paused for a moment. Now, why don't you make yourself useful and help me with this.' He looked at her, *quite bossy, the girl,* he thought. He disliked her superior judgmental attitude that had got him into all the trouble he was in. *I'd better help her; the less we leave to chance, the better. She's stubborn enough to keep at it until she finds something and goodness knows what that something will do.* His decision was made.

He moved towards her, his muscular, ripped body reacting to each and every motion mesmerised Heather. She paid him closer attention than before, scanning him from head to toe. Even with his shirt on, she could see the definition of each and every muscle on his body. He's got even fitter than before. How was he progressing this fast? It was only recently she'd bumped into him in the corridor, and she clearly remembered that he hadn't been this muscular or wide! She looked down at his legs; his jeans were very tight. His movement was restricted by the jeans; his calves stretched the lower part of them as if they had been pumped up to the very brink before tearing. Her inspection was interrupted as he pulled up a chair and placed it in front of her, sat down, and she was face to face with him. She stared at his face; his skin had become smoother, his facial hair thicker, his hair spiked up just right, his jawline perfectly square, his skin white, yet his tan told her he had been spending most of his free time on the sun-beds. But what captured her attention more than anything were his eyes; they had changed. The deep, deep blues had become overpowering. She could lose herself in those eyes.

'Didn't you have brown eyes?' she asked.

'What on earth does that have to do with this?' he was defensive. She knew she was onto something. For the time being, he was right. This was a little snippet of information, a mystery to be unravelled later on. 'Nothing, you're right,' she knew how men's minds worked; she knew that by affirming him as being correct, she would gain his cooperation. It worked!

'Ok, what Bradley told me was that the outburst of Anna's emotions activated the crystal.' He looked at her; she felt awkward at being at the receiving end of the head to toe inspection she had only a moment ago imposed upon him. Heather understood what he meant. She knew all too well what a powerful destructive force negative emotion could be. She let go, allowed herself to relax, held the crystal in her hands, sitting comfortably on her lap. Her mind wandered, her curiosity peaked, she wanted to know, she wanted to be involved. That was the main reason, the true reason. Being left out of the loop irritated her more than anything.

Something happened. A pulse ran through the crystal, ran through her hands, through her body. She saw herself sinking into her body, deeper and deeper; she was shrinking, getting smaller and smaller. Her body had become so large that its boundaries ceased to exist. She sank and shrank inside of herself, which was now so large it seemed to be a universe in its own right. Deeper and deeper she went until she reached a central point and there was the crystal. It looked exactly as it did when she picked it up in Bradley's office. She could see its structures, feel its hardness. Suddenly, it pulled her in. She could feel each and every fibre of the crystalline material from within. As the image solidified, she noticed the stars floating in its orbit. Small glimmers of powerful light like the cascading snowflakes hit by sunlight at winter. They were everywhere, each gently gliding in its own path, each radiating its own unique beauty. The crystal pulled them in, its gravitational force became stronger and stronger, insistent, demanding, enforcing its dominion over them. As the stars hurled into the crystal, strength, and power rushed through Heather. The more and more stars devoured by the crystal, the stronger she became.

Fred watched her; she was still, her eyes were closed, effort and strain visible on her face. He could feel the particles, the specks of power gathering and flowing into her and then through her arms into the crystal. He saw them accumulating in the crystal that she was still holding tight. As they smashed into one another, the crystal started to emit a low hum and a mild glow. He waited; they intensified. Slowly but surely, progress was being made.

Heather opened her eyes, taking a few minutes to reorient herself; it was like waking up from a deep sleep. She looked at Fred in front of her, his eyes guided her to the crystal in her lap and without a word, she shifted her own gaze. She gasped, she could see it glowing a beautiful deep green, pulse gently flowing from within its core. She liked the sensation of peace and calm; it captivated her. Just as she was about to say something, Fred put his finger to his lips, indicating to her to remain silent.

'Whatever you say now,' he explained, 'determines what the crystal will do to you and its function. Be very careful of your thoughts and the exact words you pick to voice because if those buggers can twist your words and intentions, they will. Hate crystals.' He stood up and pushed his chair out of the way. 'My job is done; the rest is entirely up to you. I'm leaving; you will want to be alone for this part. I just can't bear to watch this anymore.'

With those words, he walked to the back of the lab and left via the same path he took on the way in, the infirmary. *Stubborn girl,* he thought, *she really has no idea what she is getting herself into. Still, I hope she'll be ok and avoid the worst of it.* With that, his attention flashed onto his wrists and ankles and the restraints of pure crystal, which bound him for the rest of his life. The new threadlike markers, which webbed their way all across his body, concerned him. They had only just started to show and like everything else connected to them, he wanted it all gone. He didn't want to be part of any of this. In his opinion, it was all a living nightmare, and he wanted to just wake up. *To make matters worse, now I need to get Bradley's help to figure out what these blue threadlike markers coming from those bloody restraints on my body are. And, of course, he's going to be too busy helping her get out of the mess she's stepping into.* He was annoyed; women, in his view, just make things more complicated, and the complications that came with them were not worth the time. Gathering pace, he headed off to the gym, his only refuge.

Heather sat there, holding the crystal and bathing in its pulsating power. It became firmer, its power thickened. She weakened, the clear sensation that it was drawing on her life to fuel itself coursed through her mind. Something within her cried, 'stop.' She had made up her mind, and she would endure whatever she had to. She would not give up now. No matter what. Even if it meant her own life would have to be forfeited in the process.

That is a very foolish thing to do; the words echoed in her mind as distinct and clear as if they were spoken by someone sitting next to her. 'Maybe, but I have to do this,' she said out loud.

Just think hard, there's no need to speak foolish child. She was getting annoyed about all these accusations of foolishness. Her irritation grew. *But you are a fool, what you are playing with is totally unknown to you; it is not something for mortals to use.* The voices grew many.

'How can you say that when many here do. Why is it ok for them to but not me? Why? Because they are all men?' She forgot about the thinking part; she was getting angry now. All her life, she'd been the blond girl, the one everyone treated as if she was only looks, with no mind of her own. She had proven them all wrong, and she most certainly wasn't going to take that nonsense from a stupid crystal.

Your thoughts echo to us,. foolish indeed. How little you actually understand. We will take your life now, foolish human.

The power shifted. It started pulling her apart, it turned insistent, aggressive and threatening. She tried to let go but could not. The more she struggled, the more it pulled, the weaker she got. 'Nooooo, I just want to help, I will not let you do this to me.' Her will gathered in strength and for an instant, the pull weakened. A tug of war ensured, will against will, the battle was harsh. Heather knew she would not be able to endure this much longer; her strength had limits.

And now the foolish human starts to understand.

With those thoughts, the battle intensified; she was weakening, fast. 'HELPppppp' she cried out. She was exhausted; her life was ebbing away, and her will was all but drained, 'Pleaseeeee,' she pleaded, unsure if anyone would hear her, her seemingly final thoughts rushing in her mind. *I should have listened to Fred.* She began to fade. A massive green beam of pure power flooded her that very instant. Her strength renewed, alertness renewed, and determination renewed.

'That will do,' a seemingly infinite female voice, stern but with a hint of kindness, echoed all around her.

'Who's there?' she asked, fear excitement and a sudden sensation of rapid rising caught her off guard. She took a deep breath to try and settle her nerves. As her body relaxed, the rise slowed down. Millions of colours coalesced right in front of her and clouds of power, stars of all possible variations fused into shape. A few instants later, the most beautiful young woman made of pale starlight with millions of stars coursing through her body stood there in front of Heather. She took in a deep breath and held it.

'Breathe, child, or you will die, and I will have wasted my effort coming here,' instructed the cosmic woman standing there.

Heather instinctively complied, the stubborn woman had gone in her and now stood the child within once again. 'Who are you?' she asked.

'The crystal was right; you are rather foolish, young child,' she smiled and with her cosmic hand, gently caressed Heather's cheek. Knowledge flooded her mind and for an instant, endless possibilities glimpsed the source of all life whispered to the deepest caverns of her mind.

'Not quite the source of life but not far either,' corrected the cosmic woman. 'I am the embodiment of all creation, but create it I did not,' she explained. 'I am what the human mind could call the Great Mother. Your will and desires echoed outwards to me; they were awfully faint, but for a human being to reach me was impressive enough to warrant my intervention.'

Heather was transfixed; *what did all this mean? Am I dead?* She pondered.

The comic woman laughed, 'No you're not, not yet anyway. When humans die, their minds do not live on, that is why they are mortal. The crystal was correct; you were foolish to tamper with it. As for why the men you know could, they paid a very heavy price, and the one who created this all has a very heavy fate of his own. They are my favourite.

'What do you mean? They are such...' she didn't have time to complete her sentence.

'That is because you all try so hard to dance to the whims and desires of those in their lives instead of following your own paths. Opportunities are lost, lives wasted, goals never achieved, and endless waste or chaos produced. That is the reason I abandoned your kind. Evolution has stopped, it is stuck in an endless loop. That is the reason why your world is dying.'

'Wait, what? The world is dying?' she started to become anxious. What did this mean? How could the world die?

'Yes, it is, and you are only witnessing the seeds of that beginning. The first seal is breaking. That is why these lost boys you care for are being pulled into this battle.'

'You mean Bradley and the others are supposed to save the world?' Heather asked.

'No, the world adjusts to itself, their task is something entirely different, but that is not for you or them to know.' The cosmic woman smiled as if she was gleefully holding onto the secret just to annoy

Heather. 'Their job is to create so that I can shape. But you, on the other hand, have a choice to make, one which will change your life forever. Yes, there is always a price to pay when using those,' she pointed to the crystal in her hands, 'and your choice is simple. You can take on a task on my behalf, become the embodiment of Fate on Earth, or you can let the flow of things go on as they were meant to and let the crystal tear your life away from you. Choose!'

'What sort of a choice is that?' objected Heather.

'It is the only choice I'm giving you, take it or leave it.'

'What if I don't want to choose either of those?'

The cosmic woman laughed deeply. 'Ah, the arrogance and blindness of the human mind, not to choose is in itself a choice. So what will it be?'

'Well, I don't have much of a choice now, do I? It's either death or this task of yours, which means me becoming something other than I am. No one in their right mind would choose death!' She was angry now; she was trapped.

'Oh, my child, you would be surprised at how many would, your friend there, the one who told you how to activate that crystal wishes for death every morning on waking and every evening when he goes to sleep.'

'He's not my friend,' she paused; she had never even imagined that he would be doing that and for that split second of time, she felt sorry for Fred.

'What will it be?' insisted the cosmic woman. The clock was ticking.

'Wait a minute,' something had just occurred to her, 'what is this task you want me to do?'

'Clever girl,' half a smile formed on her lips, 'that you will find out later on; it would spoil the fun to reveal too much at the start.'

Heather was getting more and more annoyed, 'Fun? This is not fun? So many lives are at stake. I'm about to die, and you tell me the world is dying too; that is fun to you?' She was mad.

'Yes, it is, it is all a game. When you look at things from my point of view, all of humanity is nothing more than a single drop in an endless ocean of time and space. Whether it is here or not makes absolutely no difference to any of us; it is nothing more than convenient for you all to exist and to satisfy our curiosity.'

'Our? Curiosity?' Heather prodded further, 'What do you mean?'

'Never you mind, young one, we will see just how far you can go. Enough explanations, choose!'

Curiosity had peaked in Heather's mind. Something was at play, her instinct from before had been right. And by that very conclusion, she decided that she had a role to play then. 'Fine, I'll do it, even if what you want is so vague ,it could actually mean anything, what exactly does it involve?'

'Lady Fate never tells the details, so I cannot share.'

'Can you at least tell me what's happening to Bradley?' she almost pleaded.

'No, his fate is his own. In time, you will know of it; knowing everything in advance spoils the excitement of discovery. It would make life so dull if you knew it all in advance, would it not? Always remember, young one, it is by human choice that horrors are unleashed in the human world, and it is also by human choice that those horrors are defeated; that is the law of creation.' She turned her back, about to walk away.

'What will happen to Bradley? He's becoming the source of this horror you mention?'

'Ah yes, the greatest curse of all time, an old, very old ancient primal soul. His first and only love he will ever have, a true love at first sight with a soul mate destroyed by human deed, a human choice made by human beings. The curse this has unleashed will be something the world has never seen before; humanity needs to brace itself for this one. It will be a delight to watch it unfold; we are most curious to see how this will shape your world.'

Heather was horrified, 'how do I stop it? I want to help him; I need to do something about it. I cannot end this way. I love him.' For a moment, she recoiled at the realisation. This was the reason why... her thoughts were interrupted mind flow.

'Lady Fate never tells.' Heather found herself sinking, rapidly falling down. Moments later, she was back in the chair in Bradley's lab, still holding onto the crystal. Its light had changed, the green was pure once more, soft to the touch, and there was a sense of harmony flowing from it. The pulse grew stronger, thicker and firmer; life flowed around and out of it. It vibrated more and more until the very air seemed to hum and shiver. It shattered. What she saw floating mid-air in front of her was perfectly carved massive emeralds, forming a necklace, each one with a pulsing star within its centre glowing softly. Instinctively, she reached out to touch it and as she did, it unwound and bound itself comfortably on her neck. The green power coursed through her. A flash of green crossed her eyes. She felt strong, powerful as if she could do absolutely anything with nothing more than a single thought.

And so the Green Lady of Fate is Born, echoed the voice of the cosmic woman.

16

- FRED BOUND -

Fred struggled in bed, bound by all the mysterious-looking indigo-blue rope-like structures which had sprung up overnight. Wrapping themselves around his body then the bed and extending outwards, some to the desk, others to the chair and some even to the windowsill, causing them to inadvertently bind him down. No matter how hard he pulled, he couldn't make any of them budge even the slightest. Any form of movement was totally impossible. What made matters worse is that during this time of year, all his friends—or what remained of his ever-diminishing social circle—were away for the weekend. No matter how much he yelled, he knew it could be days before anyone would pass by his room.

He remained still, lost in his mind, cursing the fate that had befallen him. He struggled more and more to no avail. He swore and swore until he was utterly exhausted. 'Damn bloody woman,' was the final curse aimed at his ex who was the cause of all this as she had engineered his current predicament. He remained silent and still — in opposition to his most fervent efforts. Completely and totally still. He could not move no matter what he did.

Suddenly, he woke. Had he fallen asleep? He thought he had. He wasn't sure how much time had passed or how long he had now been tied down, the very sense of time had faded into oblivion. His heart was racing, something was happening, someone was knocking at his door. He forced himself into full alertness, this was his only chance! The knock came again.

'Help!' he yelled in desperation.

'Fred? Are you in there?' the voice... he recognised it! It was Bradley!
'Bradley, help me!'

'Open the door,'

'I can't, you'll have to smash it in!' naturally, this was the first suggestion to come to Fred's mind.

'Are you in danger?' Bradley was concerned now.

'I'm stuck, I can't move!'

'Ok, ok, but are you in danger?'

'Guess not, I don't know, help me get out of this.'

'Ok, wait there, I'll go find the caretaker,'

'No, don't go, wait!' he cried out but judging from the lack of response, Bradley had, as usual, immediately jumped into action and left. It felt like forever before he heard the heavy footsteps of the overweight janitor making his way towards his room. A key made the tell-tell sign of his room door being unlocked. Bradley and the janitor walked in and just stood there looking.

'Well, well, you don't see that every day!' the janitor exploded in an outburst of laughter.

'Not funny! Get me out of this!' yelled a now hopeful Fred. The janitor was trying his best to avoid laughing even harder. What they witnessed was the muscular youth completely tied down to his bed with hundreds of glistening indigo-blue ropes restraining him. What struck him the most is that by looking closely and focusing on the actual ropes, they seemed to shift out of his immediate attention, trying to avoid being noticed even when looked at directly. Bradley, however, was able to distinguish a faint glow from them! He knew exactly what they were.

'It's alright, I'll help him, you can go now, thank you for opening the door.' Bradley was very keen to get rid of the janitor as quickly as possible. He knew what was causing this and wanted to avoid any third parties being involved. The pull of their power is what drove Bradley to come and look for Fred in the first place. He had to keep this as quiet as possible.

'Errr, well, if you say so, sir. If you do need me, I will be back at the garden lodge.'

'Thank you,'

Bradley turned around to face poor Fred. 'Ok, what the hell happened?' he pulled up the chair next to Fred's bed and sat down.

'I, I don't know,'

'Yes, sure you don't. Stop fooling about or I will just walk out, close the door and leave you here,' he threatened.

'No, please don't do that, help me get out of...' he struggled, not even the slightest give.

'Stop struggling, we both know that those things will not let loose since they are powered to resist. Instead of wasting that energy of yours, start by spilling the beans! Right now. I don't have time to fool about with your antics.'

'Fine, fine. I was dreaming.'

'Go on,' Bradley encouraged him on.

'I was arguing with that pathetic excuse of a human being,' he continued.

'You mean your ex-girlfriend?'

'Yes, she was never my girlfriend. Just a girl I messed about with...' he seemed uncertain, then tensed up, and as he did, the ropes hummed with power and pulled him down even more.

'I would suggest you control your anger. Unless you want to end up being wrapped up like a shish kebab,' Bradley's cold matter-of-fact tone struck at Fred. It did the trick, he managed to forget his anger and relax.

'Keep going,'

'Well, in the dream I got angry, so angry I wanted to rip her apart. Then something grabbed hold of me and pinned me down. I woke up breathing heavily only to realise I was bound to the bed like this.'

'I see. When you woke up, did these ropes look exactly like they do now? Is it the first time you saw them?'

'No, not really,'

'Tell me,' insisted Bradley.

'Over the last day or so, small thin lines of sorts were wrapping themselves around my body. When I saw Heather yesterday, I was looking for you to ask for your help with them.'

'You saw Heather? What happened to her? She's been on sick leave ever since then...'

'I...' he hesitated.

'Never mind, we will deal with your treasure trove of troubles later on. First things first. So, you had them building up very recently, right?' Bradley seemed different, Fred couldn't quite make out how but this was no longer the scientist he had originally met on his wanderings through the university pathways. He had noticed the change when he met with Bradley at his apartment, they were subtle then. They no longer are. Bradley's demeanour, his posture, and his confidence were all changing profoundly. There was a strength to him now, a self-confidence in his voice, almost an inexplicable authority oozing out of him. It made him nervous.

'Yes.' He nodded, it was all he could do, only his head was mobile.

'What sort of power did you feel and where did this start from?'

'Well, you know, from those...' he tried to move his head to point to his wrist and ankles but failed miserably in his clumsy attempt.

'Ok, this is starting to make sense. Colours of power?'

'The same indigo-blues with dark violets,' he confirmed.

'Looks to me like your "curse" as you are so fond of calling it is still growing. We are going to have to find a way to restrict it at worst or find a way to control it.' He went silent for a while, thinking. How could he restrict something he only just had the most basic of grasps of? All this was suspiciously similar to the Bound and how he himself had experienced it only too recently. Instinctively, he ran his hand over his own neckline, it was not there, but he knew the moment TrueEarth pulled him back it would be. That metallic rope-like structure coiled about his neck. He needed to try something. In the silence of his thoughts, he swore, he knew so little. Nonetheless, he had no choice but to make do with what he knew. That had to be his and, unfortunately, poor Fred's starting point. Maybe he could use the knowledge he had gained from Ilomir, shaping a new crystal? Could it counter the effects of the existing ones? Could he use it in conjunction with what he knew of his own bindings?

'Let's start from the beginning, what words did she use when she forced those on you?'

'I can't remember,'

'Well, that will teach you for not paying attention,' he reprimanded Fred, maybe a little too harshly in view of his current predicament.

As usual, Bradley only focused on facts, not emotions. Fred, on the other hand, went very quiet and broody.

'Oh, cut that out,' Bradley snapped at him, annoyed.

'Wait. Wait a second...' something was forming in his mind — a memory was intruding his flow of thought.

Bradley started pacing up and down the small space in the room, lost in concentration, completely oblivious to everything about him.

'Errrm, Bradley...'

'Don't interrupt,' he snapped and continued his frantic pacing.

'Errrm, Bradley...'

'What the blooming heck is it?' his thoughts had been interrupted. There was nothing he hated more than that.

'I'm cold,' said Fred.

'What?'

'Cold, it's freezing...' his voice turned to a whisper. Bradley looked at him and registered at long last what he was seeing. Quickly, without a word, he turned his back to Fred.

'You're just in your trunks?'

'Never mind that, it's cold in here,'

'What the...' the situation had suddenly become very uncomfortable. Once he realised he was alone in the room with an almost naked Fred all chained up to his bed, all he wanted to do was get the heck out of there. Being the practical sort of fellow, he quickly put his emotional struggles to the side and walked over to the cupboard, opened it and got the spare blanket out. He knew the layout of the dorm rooms all too well. This was the very university he had gained his degrees and doctorate from. Walking backwards, he flung it over Fred. 'There, happy now?'

'No, not really, but thanks.'

'I'm going to have to go back to the labs,'

Before he could finish his sentence, Fred exploded in panic, 'You're not going to leave me here like this!?'

'For a while, yes, I am going to have to work this out somewhere quiet,'

'I'll be quiet, don't leave me like this...' he pleaded, 'please?' Bradley looked at him, he had never heard anyone pleading for anything, or using the word *please* for that matter. Was Fred that afraid?

'Fine,' he conceded, 'but not a word from you until I figure this out.'

He started pacing again completely ignoring *the tied down guy* in bed next to him. All Fred heard was the occasional 'humm', 'ah ha', 'no', 'maybe'. After what seemed like ages, he stopped his pacing.

'This is what I think,' here came the conclusion of all that humming and ha'ing. 'I think that curse of yours is still growing, there is no doubt about that. The initial thought has to be the right one in your case. Based on that theory, if it continues to grow, it will keep on binding you more and more.' Fred swallowed hard, despair pained on his face. 'The only solution is to somehow stop it in its tracks. From what I remembered, you said that your ex, we will call her that for clarity's sake, was furious when she played her part in this and wished for you to be forever stuck with your miserable fate. Probably meaning she wanted you to suffer and agonise over your action. Something along those lines. This seems to be following that instruction.'

'But why?' asked Fred. Bradley turned around to leave.

'Don't go, sorry... sorry... I won't interrupt again, I promise.'

'Fine, last chance! To answer that question is simple, that is how all these work,' Bradley touched the gem on his lower belly. Fred was just about to say something when, with an open mouth, he remembered his promise and stopped.

'They take a spoken desire or wish when activated and actualise it. And before you ask, my wish was for the power to change things. That simple, the simpler the expression the better with these. I am going to use that power to save Kuroi. Back to you, Mr All-Tied-Up,' he smiled at him, 'yours is doing exactly what it was told to do, although interestingly, the wish part came from someone other than you.' Fred nodded in agreement. 'So, we have one or two possible theories to work with. If these can be affected by a third party's wishes when activated, it means that another third party could intervene in how they work and it means that you could still activate one on your own, in theory.' He paused 'I've tried activating a second one but that doesn't work, the initial one takes it over. So, you can only have one per person BUT in your case, you never did use one. Yours are behaving as if you were one of the Bound, which means I might have a bit of an idea on exactly what is happening.'

Not knowing how to communicate, Fred insistently nodded in the affirmative, trying to tell Bradley his logic worked without uttering a word.

'But that still leaves a big problem for us to consider, well, two problems to be exact,' he corrected himself, 'the first being finding out if it is possible for a third party to interfere with the functioning of an existing activation, and the second being... what should your desire be? There is no point trying to wish the current binding to never have been. That would simply fail. We need to use a new wish to modulate the effects of the existing crystals. I think if we tried to counter them, they would simply reject it.'

Fred could not keep quiet anymore, 'how about wishing it all to go onto her instead?'

Bradley gave him a hard stare, made him swallow in discomfort, and said, 'no that won't work, these are bound to you, so it's going to have to be about you. There is no way to unbind those crystals from whomever they have bonded with.'

'How about to make them less restrictive?'

'Yes, but less has many, many different meanings. If this thing misinterprets that, you could be in even more trouble. It might be a different kind of trouble, but trouble nonetheless.'

'Can we make it so her wish is replaced by another?'

'Maybe, maybe, like a reconfiguration of the system!' Bradley was excited at the potential solution. He was so excited that, for a split second, he lost his cool, went up to Fred, took hold of his face and admitted to him, 'you're a genius! There's hope for you after all...' A moment later, all the excitement was gone. Bradley stood there perplexed. What had just happened? He mused. For one instant, a childishness had completely taken over and possessed him. He pondered upon it, no, it was definitely not something intruding — it felt more like a dormant part of himself stirring into action and taking over. He made a quick mental note of it, this was fascinating and he would just have to study it at length. Then it happened again, but this time, he did not act, the overwhelming sense of teasing and mischief directed at Fred took over. Fortunately, Bradley had just experienced it and was alert enough to avoid losing himself to the impulse.

Fascinating, he concluded. He tried to observe where the impulse had originated from, and failing to locate a source, he decided to follow the power behind it. That part was easy, all his lab work with the quantum crystals had trained him well in this.

Sight. Yes, I can see! coursed through his mind, as did the subtle rush of power followed by an explosion of energy.

'What the...' Fred was back to struggling against his chains. And yet again, they tightened their grip on him even further, now almost cutting into his muscular body. 'Ahhhhh,' he turned his head to the left to face Bradley and what he saw stupefied him. Dread and excitement flowed through his immobilised body. His heart racing in fear and something else. He saw Bradley's shape blur with power — reds, blacks and something entirely unrecognisable flared up and overtook his body, engulfing him from head to toe. A moment later stood Bradley covered in his armour. The very sight of him imposing beyond belief, power pulsing wave upon wave, endlessly unfolding from a distance somewhere.

'Oh, stop being such a baby!' the reprimand came as swiftly as expected.

'What? How? Are you?' Fred was babbling by now. Bradley saw the fear in his eyes and he knew his mind was in chaos.

'Fred, shut up and focus or I will leave you this very moment! Remember your little problem!' he raised his voice only slightly, pointing at the chains binding him to the bed. He waited. Fred seemed to slowly regain his nerves.

'What is... THAT!' he nodded in Bradley's direction.

'Oh, this? It's just a little something I put together with the help of the quantum crystals. Actually, I was not expecting the full armour to show, usually I only get the lower half of it,' a smile of mischief etched itself on his face. 'This is what all the crystals evolve into, and from here,' he shrugged his shoulders, 'who knows.'

'You mean mine will grow into something like that too?' he asked.

'Not unless you help them to...'

'So, I could have one of those too?' Fred smiled cautiously, struggling with the sense of fear emanating off the power Bradley was giving off and excitement at the idea that he too could have something as cool as that armour.

'Maybe, later on, assuming you're a good boy, I might teach you how to communicate with your crystal bindings and persuade them to grow into one of these,' he stopped mid-sentence, 'YES, THAT IS IT!' excitement flashed in his facial expression.

Fred noticed it, 'you look as if you are going to do something you shouldn't...' he was concerned.

Bradley smiled out loud. 'Don't worry, junior, I definitely don't like you that much!'

Fred hated being called junior even though, technically, he was ten years younger.

'First things first,' Bradley was back to business, 'I cannot believe I forgot something so fundamental, it must have been all that interrupting I was subjected to,' he looked at Fred with a disapproving glare rather than admitting to himself that he might not have remembered it due to his own internal distractions. He moved towards Fred, who, as usual, tried to pull away but was inhibited from doing so. He then put his black-gloved hand on the wrist binding on Fred's right hand.

'Oi, what are you...' came the objection.

'Just let me focus.' He calmed his mind and sent out a gentle greeting to the intelligence in the quantum crystal. The dark blue energy pulsed and ever so slightly split onto Bradley's black glove, only to be absorbed by it. Again and again, the process repeated. Then just as swiftly, Bradley pulled his hand off Fred and pulled the cover off his feet. He made contact with the ankle restraint and the whole process repeated. No matter how much Fred tried to avoid being touched, there was absolutely nothing he could do. He decided to keep on trying but he got nowhere with that.

'Done,' Bradley was finished with his weird communication. He stepped away and sat down. 'This is the deal, we cannot reconfigure them.' Fred's heart sank into despair. 'But! The crystals do not wish to kill you. Their only desire is to bind you, which is the desire that got programmed into them when it activated. That means we can direct it to bind in other ways.'

'So, there's hope? You can help me?' relief was threatening to get hold of him, yet he was too uncertain to let hope take hold until he actually knew it would be possible.

'Yes and no,' came the answer.

'Damn it, Bradley, stop messing about... please tell me,'

'I just did. If you actually stopped interrupting, which by the way is a god damn awful flaw of yours, I might be able to tell you the rest. Maybe?' he somewhat overdid the questioning expression of his.

'Fine, fine, tell me. I'm all ears! It's not like I have any bloody say in the matter!'

'You sure?'

'Yes, damn sure!'

'It is incomplete and wants wholeness. Apparently, you need a fifth missing crystal to make a complete...' he paused, 'let's call it, a set. You only have four—one on each arm and one on each leg. You need another one to complete it. That is why these rope things surfaced, they are not only trying to keep on binding you more and more but also trying to reach out for their fifth and they are trying to stop you from preventing them from reaching it.'

'Stop me from what? I can't get to anything like this even if I wanted to!' he objected.

'You need to calm down and think. You think of this as a curse, right?'

'Yes, so what? It is a curse,' he affirmed.

'Maybe, but what you are doing is turning the... let's call it intelligence, in the quantum crystals against you because you think of it as an unwanted enemy who has got the better of you.'

'And you bloody wouldn't? What the hell do you expect? I never wanted any of this, I never actually did anything to her, all I wanted was to get on with my football my studies and graduation. Look at me now, life in ruins, I can't even move my damn body,' he turned his head away to avoid facing Bradley. 'I'm nothing, I've lost everything,' he closed his eyes to stop himself from crying.

Bradley put his hand on his shoulder in a friendly gesture. 'Listen, Fred, I know this isn't your fault. I'll do whatever is in my power to help you through this, I swear I'll never let you down. But you have to work with me to do this, I cannot do it for you and I cannot do this against you either.' He paused, 'well, I could but won't, that is not me,' he waited.

'I know,' replied Fred. 'Thank you for being here for me. I know this is not really something you wanted to get stuck with either. So damn embarrassing having to deal with this.' He used his head to once again point down to his body.

'Tell me what to do, Bradley, I'll try anything but please get me out of this.'

'It's not going to be easy. To unbind yourself, you will have to bind yourself even more,' he explained.

'Bradley, please... you know I'm not as smart as you guys are, I don't understand all these riddles.' Bradley smiled fondly at him. Nothing like a bit of honesty, he really appreciated that in a person and he admitted to himself he was assuming that everyone worked at his mind's level. He quickly reprimanded himself for it.

'Ok, buddy,' the use of the word buddy comforted Fred, it was like talking to one of his football friends. 'Your quantum crystals follow slightly different rules to mine because they were forced onto you. They will not allow new ones to function unless they complement their goal. That means we cannot add anything which would free you from the bindings.'

'Owww,' Fred had just lost his only hope.

'But we can change the way they do it if we find another to complement them and force it on you.'

'So, more of this curse?' he was about to swear at his life once more.

'Yes, I'm afraid so. The best we can do is shape this curse as you call it and, hopefully, in this shaping, we can loosen the strength of its bonds even if we cannot release the bonds themselves. We might be able to make it a bit easier to manage, if that makes sense?'

'That means we can get me out of this damn bed?'

'Maybe, if we get it right, we could get you out of your current predicament,' he smiled at Fred.

'The only catch is, you're going to have to let someone bind you into the fifth crystal.'

'Oh god, not her,' was his only thought.

'No, the idea is someone else does it, and when that is harmonised with the existing four you have, it will replace your ex-girlfriend with theirs. That is the only thing we can change according to what they said.'

'I want Conrad to do it,'

'Ok, do you know where he is?'

'Went away for the weekend,' the realisation dawned on him.

'That means you will have to wait here until he gets back, which is two whole days,' he warned. 'Want me to ask Heather?'

'Hell no, I'm staying away from all women forever.'

'Forever is a very long time, especially for us,' Bradley pointed out to him.

'Don't care, no woman ever again!' he insisted. Bradley smiled, he knew such convictions seldom if ever lasted more than a short while.

'How would you feel about me doing it?' Fred had not dared to ask, he thought Bradley was already doing too much for him, he didn't want to impose even more. Besides, he didn't dislike him, but he wasn't as fond of him as he was of his best friend, Conrad. They were of a similar age, both had everything taken from them in life, both went through countless hardships to get into university, and both were trying to find their way back in life.

'Are you sure?' he seemed uncertain, 'you've already done too much for me. I don't want to be a burden,'

'You're not, it's a perfect opportunity for me to learn more, and besides, I discovered all these things so I'm partly to blame for them existing and making a mess of your life,'

Fred kept rejecting that idea. It seems Bradley had not forgiven himself for being the cause of this whole predicament. Not one second had the thought occurred to him to blame Bradley for inventing these and then crashing into his life. He knew why Bradley had gone down this route and he would have done the same himself if he had to.

'Fine, it's a deal. I'll watch your back and you get to try and keep me out of trouble,' replied the eternal man of action that was Fred.

'But only on the condition that you are sure. Make no mistake, this is not a small decision to make. It means my will will flow through your quantum crystals and exercise dominion over you through them.' Bradley paused to allow Fred time to think. This was one of the key rules he had learnt with the Bound. *Odd how all that should come in handy now? Very odd indeed.* He thought. *Could the two impact each other?*

'Look at me, Bradley, do I have any choice in the matter? The only thing I can choose now is the person who will control me. I have no choice over the matter if I want someone to have control or not. That choice was taken away from me by my ex-girlfriend, damn her to the end of days. So, I choose you, you are the only one here for me and you invented this stuff. Maybe someday you will find out how to get me out of it. So, if I have to choose to be at someone's side and have them in my life for as long as this goes on, I'll happily choose that person to be you.' He paused for a moment, 'just don't hurt me, ok?'

'It's a deal!' Bradley smiled. 'Who would have thought that Mr Tough-Cookie bodybuilder and rugby player had a vulnerable side to him!' he teased. 'Oh, shut up,' snapped back Fred.

'Ok, I need to pop over to my apartment to see if I can find a suitable crystal and shape it. I'll be gone for about 45 minutes. You going to be ok?'

'I don't have much choice!'

'Oh yes, of course. Where's your key?'

'What the hell do you want that for?' asked Fred.

'Well, I guess you want the door locked when I leave?'

'You're going to lock me in and leave?'

'It's not like I can drag you with your bed across campus to the adjacent facility now, is it?'

'I guess not...' he admitted defeat on that point, 'it's in my jacket pocket, the right one,'

'Makes sense seeing as you are right-handed,' replied Bradley. He went to the jacket, fished out the key, went to the door and locked it from the inside then unlocked it. It's the right key. 'There, you'll be safe in here, curtains are pulled so no one should come disturbing you.' Before he could say anything, Fred watched as Bradley dissolved his armour and was back in his usual clothing.

'While I'm gone, behave yourself!' Bradley was enjoying the tease, the child in him threatened to resurface. He decided he was best gone before that happened.

'Ha, ha, very funny... please be quick.'

'I'll do my best!' he left Fred's room and locked the door. Fred stayed there totally immobilised. He closed his eyes and tried to keep his mind still in the hope that he would fall asleep, but had no such luck.

Jim was going through the genetic analysis. He paused, pondered, read and paused again. Something was not right with this virus. Its origins and phylogeny simply did not match any of the known viral types. Was this really an entirely new one? It couldn't be. To enhance it with nanotechnology required intimate knowledge of not only its DNA but also of the DNA of all related types. He looked at how it had evolved, the changes in its genetics were fascinating. Not only had it stolen human DNA but it also adapted it and integrated it to produce a secondary evolution of itself. *This just does not happen, he thought. Viruses do not inherit genes like other life forms. Could it be due to the tech in it? Could that have been used to not only control it but also to give it those missing essential qualities of inheritability?* This concerned him deeply. It meant that this virus, unlike any other in existence, was actually alive. Someone had gone to the trouble of adding the components necessary for life to a non-living thing. He looked at the list of tests Bradley had asked him to carry out. *Better get these done as fast as possible.* He rushed off to follow up with the technology part of it. For that, he would need help and he knew exactly where to go to get it.

Time passed, Fred was getting edgy and nervous. He was not the most patient of people. In his struggles, he could have sworn he heard the most horrific of screams, it sounded like a distant young man's voice. The terror it carried sent shivers down Fred's spine. These 45 minutes seemed to last centuries. As his mind's discomfort grew, so did his restraint body. He tried to shift even a little, to no avail. The frustration intensified so much that he ended up yelling at it.

Someone knocked at the door. Damn it.

'I'm ok, go away whoever you are,' he yelled at the door.

'Fine, I'll go back to the labs then,' came Bradley's voice from the other side. He had pulled out the key and let himself in.

'Sorry, I thought it was someone else,'

'It's ok, I figured,' he smiled.

'So, what happened?' he asked, eager to find out if he was finally going to be free of this bed. He was hungry, grumpy and desperate for the bathroom and a good drink by now!

'It's done,' Bradley pulled out and presented to him a quantum crystal which looked as metallic and dark blue as his other ones, shaped as a rounded thin collar. 'I'm sorry I couldn't make it into something else but it had to fit in with your current ones and I could not get it to shape into anything else.'

Fred looked at it, silently cursed his fate once more, 'Oh well, guess I have no choice in that either. 'Ah, what the heck, let's do this.'

'This is the last chance to pull out, so are you certain?' Bradley had to make sure, he knew the impact of this and secretly deep down, even if he did not want to admit it, he really had hoped he wouldn't have had to be part of this.

'Stop asking me that! Yes, I'm sure,' that hope faded into oblivion.

'A warning before we do this, it will feel exactly the same as the others did, you will struggle with it as much as you did with the others and, in this case, you will hate me as much as you did her for doing this to you.'

'No, I won't,' interrupted Fred. 'Just get on with it, I want this over and done with'

'Very well.' Bradley closed his eyes and his black glove formed on his right hand. Fred was confused and amazed. He didn't realise that was even possible. For a moment, he admired the young scientist's mind. It was so versatile and fluid in thinking out possibilities, to him, it seemed totally breath-taking.

'I'm going to turn off your body's motor nerves, you will be totally paralysed from neck down for a while. You will still feel everything but you won't be able to move.'

'What? Why? I'm already unable to move!' he objected.

'Don't worry, it's only temporary, we don't know what all those chains will do or how those other quantum crystals will react. Don't want you moving and disrupting anything.'

'You know what, just do what you need to do, I have no choice in the matter, I trust you anyway. Daddy!' he laughed. Bradley went stone quiet and still. Fred looked at him and saw a single tear filing down from his right eye, drifting across his cheek before he brushed it off with his sleeve. 'I'm sorry... I didn't think. It was supposed to be a joke, so sorry, Bradley,' he only then realised that his joke had struck a cord. He cursed himself. How stupid could he get? The guy had just lost his unborn son a few days ago. Everyone knew that by now, the entire campus was gossiping mindlessly about the entire tragedy. Bradley sat next to him on the little space there was in between his large muscular body and the edge of the bed. He ran his hand through Fred's thick hair then pulled away.

'It's ok, you know if I did have a son, I would have been proud for him to turn out just like you.' Without a further word, he pressed on each side of Fred's neck. A pulse of cold energy ran through him as he became totally stiff. He tried to move his fingers and toes. No matter how much effort he put into it, he couldn't, yet he could feel every inch of it even more so than before.

'Ready?' he asked. Fred nodded in agreement. He removed the cover exposing once more Fred's now paralysed yet bound body. He took the dark blue metal and crystal-looking collar, bent over, and sealed it shut around Fred's neck. He closed his eyes and said, 'This to fully bind him and bring the bindings under my control, to extend his possibilities according to my will. I imposed upon him.'

Red power flashed up and flowed from his hand into the collar. It flared in deep dark blues and violets. That force closed in on Fred's neck, and he turned and twisted his head in discomfort. It hummed an aggressive restrictive power. Bradley cringed, the sensation of having every nerve which ran up his arms was being pulled and stretched beyond its natural ability. His senses expanded out of his hands as the nerve fibres wound themselves initially around the crystalline collar then were absorbed into it. For a split-second, panic crushed him, agony flooded through him and pain etched itself into his very spine. Then it faded away. He saw a power dancing in between the crystal and his hands. The nerves had not only stretched out of him but had been physically severed as if cut by a knife, only to be reconnected through intangible power. He saw the slight electric sparks flowing out of his hands through that power and into the nerves as his nerves coiled deep in the collar. Sensations flooded his body as those nerves erupted by the crystal and expanded like an infection into Fred's spine, blending into his own autonomic nervous system. Fred felt as if he had been constrained in something totally inescapable. For a moment, he tried to scream out but no sound escaped his lips. Hate flared up from deep within him against such a deep intrusion into his very being. He looked at Bradley's eyes filled with cold raging hatred. That dissipated within the instant just as rapidly as it had surfaced, redirected to the actual source of his hate: his ex-girlfriend. This hate he decided was for her and only her. The day would come when the full weight of his accumulated hatred would bear down upon her like an unstoppable avalanche. But today was not that day. He worked hard on trying to relax. He closed his eyes and allowed his whole life to flow in front of his eyes. He knew his old life had just died and something new was about to rise in its place. Something he would never have any control over but something which proved to be very exciting to some inner part of him. For a very short instant, like the flash of a memory, hope surfaced once more.

He opened his eyes and felt the sensation of hundreds of worms crawling all over his body, sliding on top of each other, falling to the side, interlocking into each other and eventually settling as they tightened around his body. He also felt Bradley's hands pulsing power, holding his ankle restraints tight, oh how he hated that part.

Yet he also felt something very strange. For the first time ever, all four of those restraints felt lighter. They were no longer the 10-ton weights holding him down by virtue of their sheer weight. They were still firmly binding him but they were lighter, much lighter and far less irritating to have on. Finally, Bradley moved onto his left wrist crystal restraint, it was the last one. He held it firmly in both hands. Power yet again flowed through his hands into them. For a moment, he actually did not mind being stuck with them. Something from deep within him was echoing into his mind, *it will all be ok.* He accepted that without question or argument, it was as if he knew it would be that way beyond doubt.

Bradley was lost in concentration, he had expanded his senses throughout each and every one of those indigo-blue rope-like things holding Fred down. Now he understood, now he could see what they were. He knew the explanation he had been given by Lurizak and Tamirok back in House Bound was accurate. This was an extension of Fred's nervous system melded with his own power and armour. He decided not to take it over and re-impose his own, instead, he allowed thin threads of his own nerves to extend into each of those

Fred had already unwittingly formed himself. That meant he could control them as well as Fred could. It was a gradual process, one by one was being pulled back. Slowly and steadily, Fred was being unwrapped and the newly-enhanced nerve-cords shining with both Fred's and Bradley's power carefully unbound him and rewove themselves just around his body. Gaps in between muscles were filled with these cords, one after the other, each natural contour was emphasised and held tight. Bradley was no expert in the physical makeup of musculature but he knew that linking things in this fashion would increase the burst and endurance of Fred's muscular potential. He saw no harm in doing it this way, *the young guy might as well get some advantage out of his predicament,* he thought.

The shadow shivered within Mira. Something had put it on edge and disturbed it. Mira was subject to the intensity of its fear. It not only enveloped her but it also bled into her. It was comparable to a nervous static erratically cascading through her entire body.

'Wwwwe muuuuuusttt hurrrry,' it instructed.

'What's going on?' asked Mira. She got no new information, the shadow just kept on repeating its message and sending out cascades of its erratic energy. It unsettled Mira deeply. She refused to push along, she would take control of the situation whatever it might be. That was her determination. A glint of hesitation surfaced... could she? She wasn't even aware of what the problem was. I have to, she pushed aside the doubt. There was no time for that. It never occurred to her that it must have been odd for her to feel what the shadow felt, to experience its fear. Something that not only didn't originate from her but had no cause to exist in her.

'Still want that armour of yours?' Bradley interrupted his work. For a moment, Fred was annoyed then laughed aloud, he now knew what it was like to be interrupted. In the midst of his laughter, he replied, 'Yes! Oh yes!'

'Fine, we might as well fix that for you now since the quantum crystals are proving to be very cooperative. It won't be like mine. Each armour, so I am told, is unique to the purpose of the crystals and their character of their wearer. Ok with that?'

'Sure,' Fred was pleased no matter what it would be like. It was something at least.

Bradley closed his eyes and put his hand on the collar, it hummed with power. The cords he had worked with changed their very form, shifted and solidified into thin chain-like structures. They moved and interlocked with each other, weaving themselves into an almost solid fabric like mesh until, eventually, he had something which resembled an armour. Everything was held in place from the neck down, the pressure of the nerve-cords pushed slightly into each muscle, making it bulge even more and adding to its explosive force. Fred felt as if he would now be able to lift a whole mountain let alone more weight at the gym. He was excited.

'Nearly done, Mr, just one final touch... for now.' Bradley leaned over Fred and grabbed a firm hold of the collar with both hands. 'It is my will to open passageways of power as his mind directs, for now.'

This time, Fred did yell out at the onslaught of power. It was so vast, he could not contain himself. His entire body shook under the pressure. He understood why Bradley had imposed the total paralysis on him and he was grateful for it. After a minute, everything settled down and he was oddly relaxed and at ease, more so than he had been in years.

'You're done, I'll explain the last part of it to you some other time. For now, we need to get you out of bed. I'm famished.' With that, he once again put pressure on each side of Fred's neck. Each touch caused a rush of power to leave his body. Gradually, warmth returned and Fred regained the ability to move.

'Before you jump out of bed, a warning. Take it slow or you will get a rush and fall.'

Fred didn't argue with the instructions, he knew he could trust Bradley and he somehow instinctively knew Bradley would not do anything to harm him. He shifted his arm slowly. The joy he felt when he found out that he could move it freely was indescribable. Then the other, then his feet and legs.

'Slowly,' warned Bradley.

He ran his hand all over his body. What he felt surprised him—in between the smooth surfaces of his muscular body, he felt metallic yet soft, cold threads of cord. He sat up. Relief and delight washed over him. He stood up and noticed he was covered in cold metallic armour-formed shorts which were made of woven infinitely thin chain-like threads. He panicked, stood up and went to the mirror. His fears were confirmed. Metallic rope-like structures were extending all over his body, his armour turned out to be an armour of chains! He stared at it in disbelief, some of the intricacies in patterns and designs simply defied the realms of what was possible, yet there it was.

'I'd say it turned out to be an interesting result,' mused Bradley. Fred didn't know what to say. He was shocked and yet he loved the feel of it. Shrugging his shoulders, he decided he would go with it. Could have been worse.

'Don't worry, some parts of it you can will away when you need to,' explained Bradley, 'but I'm sure you wouldn't want to do that right now. You will have noticed that it all feels easier to wear for you, my will to bind you overtook that of your ex-girlfriend completely. Her hate for you is what made living with those so hard and made them so heavy.' He pointed to the restraints he had on.

Joy overtook Fred, so much so that, without realising it, he had rushed to Bradley and hugged him.

'There, there, it's all fine. You can let me go now,' he smiled. 'As for the parts you won't be able to make go away, just wear something on top of the rest. Should anyone ask, tell them you're trying out a new fashion trend. That should short circuit any but the most dedicated inquisitors!' he paused, 'if you're feeling ok, I'm going to go back to the labs, lock up and grab some food at the canteen.'

Fred nodded. 'All ok here.'

'Fine, if you decide you are up for it, you can join me for food, otherwise, you know where my offices are, feel free to come by anytime. We need to test all this out, so exciting.' With that, Bradley opened the door, then turned back around, 'oh, by the way, this is yours,' and gave him his key.

'Thanks,'

'See you, buddy!' Bradley nodded and shut the door behind him.

17

ENTER
- GrimGlooms -

Bradley had made his way back to House Bound. He was back in his armour with the upper body portion still refusing to fully form. From his torso upwards, there was only skin, and much to his chagrin, the copper nerve-cords binding were once more tightly secured around his neck. His arrival was timely. Tamirok waited for him as he entered the long, wide corridor.

'Welcome back, welcome.' He was in high spirits, 'I have someone I want you to meet,' he looked at Bradley from head to foot, his gaze shifted, carefully taking each and every detail into account.

'Something's wrong, what happened?'

Bradley hesitated, he wasn't sure, then there are other things he definitely did not want to reveal.

Tamirok was not a patient man. 'Speak,' his will crashed into Bradley like the eruption of a solar flare. He was still bound to it.

'The battled training?' he paused, uncertain.

'You passed. Time to move onto the next task,' was all Tamirok offered up in terms of information. Tamirok inspected Bradley very closely, 'It seems you have not mastered your armour fully. Halfway there, I see. Not a bad start.' Bradley failed to understand why only half was there, his questioning glance back at Tamirok spoke volumes as to his confusion on the matter. 'You previously had the full armour on thanks to the additional control Ilomir was contributing to you. His skill in that respect, even though he is not officially one of the Bound, is astounding. It is the main reason I had you work with him. Without his help, you will just have to keep working on enhancing your own control. Made quite a bit of progress so far,' Tamirok smiled at him, 'come, follow me.'

Bradley's body moved in accordance with Tamirok's will once more. He was led down the corridor onto the left. There, the huge double doors decorated in Bound symbols were swung open by his powerful hands to reveal a large luxuriously decorated room. 'Diplomats from the House GrimGloom are here, perfect timing,' he explained.

Bradley entered the room. Polished black and copper designs adorned the long conference table's edges. Crystal cups filled with some type of liquid were being sipped by two men. As they entered, the two visitors stood up.

'Here he is, gentlemen, I would like to present Bradley to you, Ruler of House Nothingness,' they both took a gentle bow of acknowledgement. Bradley was embarrassed, he was not used to the protocols. In his mind, he was still just a scientist, stuck in the most unfortunate of circumstances, yet still a simple scientist.

'I see what you meant, Tamirok,' said the elder of the two. His eyes piercing right through Bradley, and they suddenly shifted from their deep blue irises to pure jet black. Bradley stood transfixed, looking into what appeared to be totally black irises.

'Yes, yes, he is indeed filled with Dark Matter and Dark Energy,' he concluded. The eyes shifted back to their former deep blues. It happened so smoothly that Bradley could have sworn he had imagined it. Bradley's mind wondered to contemplating what caused such a change, it fascinated him. His mind was sharply brought back to the matter at hand.

'Bradley, focus,' Tamirok had taken it upon himself to keep Bradley's mind from wandering in all sorts of directions. 'Apologies, gentlemen, it seems that the minds of the people of FalseEarth lack basic discipline,'

'No concern, no concern at all, Tamirok,' the elder of the two took a step forward, coming face to face with Bradley. He held out his hand in a friendly greeting. 'I am Arlak Emissary of House GrimGloom, it is a pleasure to make your acquaintance,' Bradley nodded and shook his hand.

Both men had firm grips, both had good control, neither overexerting their grip nor overpowering the other. Arlak approved, this level of control was needed in every man. He silently noted to himself that balancing his grip in such a manner had proven that Bradley had accurately judged not only his strength but how to perfectly counterbalance it. He smiled, in that instant, he developed a liking to this newcomer.

'It is a wonder as to why you did not come to House GrimGloom first,' he smiled, looking at Tamirok, 'but your choice was not a bad one to say the least.' He turned to the young man who stepped forward. Bradley observed him carefully, he seemed to be in his late 20s, looked sharp, his spiked jet-black hair pulled back with the occasional lock flipping over the rest. Deep blue eyes like the elder gentleman, his had more fire in them—almost an air of rebellion. Pale skin smooth was marble yet it had a tan but it was faint, so very faint. It did the trick to avoid him being ghostly white. His facial features were a touch softer than those of the other men in the room, his gentler curettage of the chin bone was adorned with styled stubble. He had a defined chest, strong arms and body even though he did not carry the same level of bulk on him as the Bound were. His body seemed to be optimised for speed and agility rather than sheer physical power. Clothed in what appeared to be leather trousers and a rich black sleeveless shirt embroiled with golden threats at the seams. He wore a black and golden belt and from it hung a black pouch on the left side. Around his neck, a leather-like cord with a large jewel sat perfectly mid-chest. His right wrists were adorned by reflective silvery black woven jewels. He was almost too well-groomed, it would only take one more step to devoid him of masculinity. Fortunately, he managed to get the balance just right, there was no doubt about it, masculinity oozed from him. It was very different to that of Lurizak but still unmistakably masculine. This man was one of adolescent mischief and adventure. Those two qualities shone from every pore of him and were woven into his entire being.

'My son, Mishrak,' presented Arlak.

'Pleasure to meet you, Bradley,' Mishrak extended his hand in friendship. Bradley shook it. The moment their hands touched, a spark of static flowed from one to the other. Mishrak's left eyebrow rose in surprise. 'Well, that's one for the books, father.'

'What do you mean?' asked Tamirok. Mishrak didn't answer. Instead, he let go of Bradley's hand and without warning, ran his right hand over his shoulder, gently caressing the skin then down his arm. Bradley felt very uncomfortable. He hated being touched. He stood still. Each movement caused black sparks of static to dance over Bradley's skin and Mishrak's fingers. 'We have a wielder of the Ancient Dark.'

'Why didn't you tell me?' asked Tamirok.

Bradley looked at him, shrugging his shoulders, 'I have no idea what he's talking about.'

Tamirok looked him straight in the eyes, his gaze piercing, inquisitive and challenging. After what seemed an eternity, he snapped out of it. 'It doesn't change much, House Nothingness has claimed him, he is only a temporary member of this House and whatever other House he enters.'

The other two men seemed a little surprised at the conclusion. They decided not to question it, there was no logical fallacy in that statement no matter how wrong it felt to them both.

'Errrm, could someone tell me what this all means?' asked Bradley. Arlak, in his long exquisite black robes, stepped forward, 'Sorry, it takes us a little work to remember that our ways and customs are alien to you. The Ancient Dark is the primal force which gave birth to House GrimGloom and all its descendants. None but the ruler of our House is capable of using that force. For it to show in your body means that you are a descendant of the Founders of House GrimGloom and all its arts. It is not only your Home,' he emphasised that word for impact, 'but also part of your bloodline.'

'I'm sorry, but...' Bradley tried and failed to wrap his mind around this information, 'that makes no sense. I'd never been to TrueEarth until I stumbled upon it recently.'

'Tell us about your parents,' instructed Tamirok.

'Nothing special to tell. My mother was born in England, went to university and became a doctor. She met my father while studying, they married and had me. Nothing special or out of the ordinary with either of them.'

Arlak nodded his head, 'It cannot be. Makes no sense.' He turned to his son, 'did you make a mistake? Perhaps?'

'Seriously? Are you blind as well as old? Look...' Without warning, he stepped behind Bradley, flung his left arm over his left shoulder and placed the palm over Bradley's heart. A pulse of energy flared out, Bradley coughed out at the weight on his chest, feeling dizzy. Then power flared out of him and dark electricity danced all over his body. He looked at his hands and even he could see the hundreds of tiny sparks all over his skin. Mishrak removed his hand and stepped away from Bradley. The sparks were still dancing there.

Bradley put his hands forward. 'What is happening?' he stared at them in bemusement.

'The Ancient Dark manifest,' concluded Arlak. 'Mishrak has the ability to pull dormant powers out of people and was born with an affinity for the Ancient Dark, although he lacks its force himself. It is a special configuration of quantum energy flowing through highly-charged strange quark particles... I assume the scientific view is easier for you to understand?'

'There is no doubt, this calls for a celebration,' interrupted a most seductive woman's voice as she rose from the other side of the room. It caught everyone's attention. It seems no one had noticed the voluptuous woman clad in ornate black metals and leather and rich jewellery still sitting at the table. She stood up and stepped forward, Bradley's breath was taken away. Her beauty mesmerised him.

'I am Elshevira,' she too offered her hand in friendly greeting, 'I am the keeper and teacher of the sciences and arts of House GrimGloom.'

'Delighted to meet you,' a blushing Bradley replied. He was trying hard to avoid showing his excitement. She looked at him and smiled.

'It seems Bradley here finds you quite exciting,' interjected Tamirok.

'Not to worry, I take it as a compliment,' she smiled, 'besides, when the men find a woman enticing and exciting, it plays to her advantage,' she winked at them, 'especially when it comes to holding onto their attention,' she pretended to let out a slight eloquent sound as if clearing her throat, 'and guiding them through the more difficult parts of Grim or Gloom know-how.'

It was the first time Bradley had heard the name of the house split into two separate words. He made note of it. That distraction was most welcome, his refocus on knowledge made his distraction dissipate.

'As I was saying, there is no doubt the Ancient Dark flows through him,' Elshevira recapitulated. Bradley was putting in extra effort to look her straight in the eyes and to avoid his gaze shifting ever so slightly lower to her chest, where her voluptuous breasts were held in place by the most revealing of cuts in her attire. Firm folded black metallic cloth, like a bra etched in intricate purple-tinted copper cupped them firmly in place. These, he noticed, were the top part of a body-wide corset woven of crystalline material which incredibly moved like fabric yet held its shape firmly.

A large black gem pulsed gently under the heart's central region of her body. This was the centrepiece holding the bra together and expanding thin waves of pure power all over her torso. Her waistline delicate and thin stood atop larger hype, which, in turn, were supported by long well-defined legs wrapped in thigh-high boots made of the same fabric, decorated with the same purple-hued coppers. Elshevira was a sight to behold. She knew it and she revelled in it. Her long black wavy hair and her piercing deep indigo blue eyes were too much for any newcomer to resist. He suspected the clothing she picked was worm deliberately to elicit this type of response. Little did he know, it was. When necessary, it served as a great distraction in negotiations and was one of the main reasons why she held back allowing the rest of them to get acquainted before stepping in.

'Gentlemen, you won't mind if I have a little look at something, would you?' No one objected, she looked straight at Tamirok questioningly. 'Fine by me,' she knew the protocols, he was Bradley's wielder, so doing anything to him without permission would be catastrophic and considered a direct assault at House Bound itself. She was too sharp to make that sort of a mistake. Moving gracefully with uncanny fluidity and authority, she approached Bradley. He was nervous. He followed her with his gaze until she stepped behind him. Like Mishrak, she flung her arm over his shoulder and placed her palm over his chest. Unlike with Mishrak, Bradley got all excited again at her touch, even more so than before.

'Just ignore that minor inconvenience, dear,' she whispered into his ear, 'one day, you'll help me get what I desire.' Her words turned up the heat pulsing like a river about to overflow, she took great delight in his discomfort. It proved to be a distraction. He felt the cold darkness that was swirling clockwise, encircling them both. Its touch on his skin was cool but not uncomfortable. Without a word, she let go of him and stepped back into the midst of conversation.

'Our young Bradley's soul has many secrets to share,'

'Elshevira has the ability to speak to what you call the soul,' explained Arlak, 'you can think of it as the structure which dictates how the atomic particles and quantum elements function in a living being. Most importantly, which ones the life form has access to, how much energy they can carry and what their interactions are and could be. Everything is defined by this network on the quantum level, and from that, everything that makes you you is grown, including your body, your power, your knowledge, your shape, your potential as well as how you will decay, eventually.' Arlak deliberately told Bradley all this, presenting it in a way in which his scientific mind could grasp. He knew that even though Bradley had the ability to manipulate these elements directly, he was incapable of doing so until he could conceive what he was trying to manipulate, and the only way he could do that was if it was explained to him in a manner he could understand. Linking the concepts with familiar ones would give his mind a way to bridge his existing knowledge to the new. Arlak smiled, it was not without reason that House GrimGloom had nicknamed him the Wise One of Darkness.

'And I know something you would find absolutely fascinating, Tamirok,'

'Oh? Do tell,'

'I'm not sure I want to,' Elshevira teased him. She loved playing these games, and those who knew her loved playing them with her.

'You wouldn't deny me?' he prompted her, 'would you?' he mimicked a pain expression.

She burst out laughing, 'of course not. Our Bradley here has gained the knowledge and ability to bind others' will,' she revealed. Tamirok's jaw dropped. 'How? Where?' he looked at Bradley. 'You never mentioned this.'

'Well, you kind of just grabbed hold of me when I got back and I never got the chance,' he mumbled away.

'But his ability is just starting to manifest, the tip of the iceberg. Its full extent is unusable without the help of a LightBearer,'

Tamirok looked genuinely concerned.

'It will require light to enter the mind before he can do his part and gain mastery over it,' a genuine, rich laughter escaped her lips, 'those damnable tricksters of the light are required for him to learn the hidden technique but they will ensure it can only be used with their consent and assistance.'

'To be expected, no one wants that kind of power in anyone's hands,' Tamirok admitted. 'Even in our House, the ones who are allowed to learn such wide-ranging techniques are usually members of the ruling council. We will keep this hidden for now,' his words were unmistakably a direct order to everyone. They all realised it immediately and nodded in agreement. 'However, we need to ensure the LightBearers do not hold power over him,' he looked concerned, 'what is it about you, Bradley? You seem to bring the worst out in every situation and add entire layers of complexity to the simplest of things.'

'I would not worry about that, Tamirok, his soul speaks of solutions already. It has found something although what that is I cannot tell.' Tamirok accepted her words.

'Another interesting thing is that he is only partially awake, entire portions of him are still dormant and I dare not even try to stir them. Fate is exercising control. I sense an internal battle—actually, multiple internal battles. Pushing him in one direction or the other can easily break him at this point. There is great anger within him, there is intense hunger, cruelty and pain, so much pain it's unbearable to touch his essence. He is suffering for things done he isn't even aware of... yet,' she paused. Sorrow was to be seen in her eyes, 'and then there is power, so much power, uncontrolled and amplified by his heritage. It's tearing him apart slowly but steadily, fragment by fragment torn off, particles being tipped out of his atomic structures, quantum strings shattered and un-spun.' She paused, took in a few deep breaths, then turned to Tamirok. 'We have to help him and fast, his life is not going to hold itself together for much longer.' They all gasped at the revelation.

Mira sat in front of the television at home. Anger arose from deep within her for reasons unknown. She liked it, it gave her clarity, focus and drive. She was empowered by it. Mira liked the feeling of power, she relished it like a sweet delicatessen available only to the select few. The shadow surfaced from her feet, slowly and insistently wrapping itself all over her body. Its power is what was coursing through her now. She wanted it, she desired to know it, she swam in its seemingly endless sea. There, she experienced a vastness incomprehensible to her mind, totally inconceivable. The thought that it would all be hers one day thrilled her. Her mind sunk into the vast waves of silk-like shades folding into each other. She was infinite, she was the endless sea of shadows. Oh, how she loved it, how she longed for it to last forever. The shadow seeped into each and every pore of her body—every cell, every nerve, every small part of what she was engulfed by shadow. She was the shadow and the shadow was her. Flesh and shade had merged.

'Finally,' a voice both female and like a whisper rolling over the winds came out of Mira's mouth. 'Time to finish what we started.' The shadow coalesced into something semi-physical, clothing her body in tight leathers, shade markings bevelled from within her skin. They ran along her arms, over her chest and down her back. Then she was gone.

Down in the company's research labs she went. Turning to the secured samples, she made quick work of accessing them. After all, she had access to all the security codes, all the passes, all the access rights. Mira took the latest samples out of their containers and looked at them.

'Almost ready, time to make them perfect,' she extended her hand and allowed the shadow to drip from her closed fist into the petri dish. It splashed all over its liquid content, then seeped into it. The latest version of the virus soaked in the shadow. It expanded from its core, from its soma, into the whole virus, then its piercing mechanism enhanced itself with shadow power. The virus changed, something grew within it, its mass expanded, its multiple thin shadowy tentacles expanded outwards into the endless shadowy seas. Mira laughed maniacally. 'Now it is perfect, time for it to get to work,' she took the sample and faded away.

'Let us all sit down and have a drink, we need to gather our wits to deal with this,' offered Tamirok. They all sat down, taking a sip from the soft velvety liquor in their glasses. 'I intended to send him to the other Houses for him to learn to use power in the hope that he would adapt those teachings to his own,' he explained. 'Which he seems to have partially achieved.'

'He does not have the time for that,' interjected Elshevira.

Tamirok nodded.

'Hold on a minute,' Arlak objected 'what is the cause of this massive upheaval within him?' he asked Elshevira, 'I mean, the root cause, emotions will stir everything but they do not cause power,'

'It's the Ancient Dark amplifying the other powers which, in turn, are exciting the Ancient Dark and so forth. It's an ever-expanding augmenting loop that will eventually tear him apart and consume him. And that is completely discounting the parts of him that are still dormant. I have no idea whether they would take the load off his essence or add to it.'

'It is a risk we cannot take,' stated Tamirok. He had become protective of Bradley for some unexplainable reason. He wanted him safe but able.

'Can we diffuse the loop somehow?' asked Mishrak.

'I guess the only way would be for the Ruler of House GrimGloom to try, but bringing Bradley into the presence of another Ancient Dark descendant would amplify the synchronicity of both their powers. We could, in theory, be adding a whole load of unstable dark energy to the already burdensome load, who knows that would happen?'

'We can't do that,' objected Arlak, 'it could endanger them both, our House's duty is to protect the Ancient Dark, not destroy its descendants. What about his powers part of the dilemma? If their instability is the part of the fuel to this, can't we stabilise those and then let the Ancient Dark just keep amplifying the stabilised powers?'

Elshevira was lost in thought. Bradley just sat there listening, this was far beyond his skills or knowledge to fix, so he sat in silence and absorbed every word they were sharing.

'He needs to learn to control them,' she concluded.

'Well, he's in the right place for that, control is what the House Bound do is it not, Tamirok?' asked Mishrak.

Tamirok thought back to their attempts to control his powers, he thought back to the unwillingness of the ruling council to get too involved. He shook his head, 'I can't do that with what I have available to us,' he admitted, much to his dismay. 'The only option open to us would be if I bound his entire being in absolute bindings, and even then, crafting the metal skin armour would be difficult if not impossible. We've never had to bind anything, there is nothing to bind, nothing to get hold off. It would require much trial and error.'

'Well, it's a start,' admitted Arlak, much to Bradley's horror. There was no way he would be part of that, no way, simply just no way. The very thought horrified him to the core.

At that very instant, a screeching tear sounded throughout the room as the air pulled in on itself at the head of the table and seemed to collapse. All of them had jumped to their feet in alert. What stood in front of them was a hole in the fabric of reality itself — it was none other than Nihi.

'That is not acceptable,' it said in a horrifying voice.

'What the... who... what... what is that?' shock and cold perspiration of utter horror ran down the forehead of all three visitors.

'That is Nihi,' answered Bradley.

'What... what is it?'

'It is the equivalent of our ruling council, a ruling representative of the House Nothingness if you like,' explained Tamirok who had encountered the thing once before. He turned to it, trying to face the gap in reality which it was. 'Do help us, I assume you are aware of the situation,'

'We are aware, and the Grim woman is correct in her assessment, although she sees only that which is not nothing.'

'And our proposed course of action is not acceptable?'

'No,' it simply stated.

'You do realise he will die and you will lose the only Ruler of House Nothingness you have had in millennia.'

'We do, hence our arrival,'

'I am sure we would all more than welcome your advice and suggestions,' Tamirok offered the olive branch. The other three were still too locked in the horror of what they were witnessing to be effective. He wanted to give them as much time as he could to regain composure.

'He cannot become Bound,' it paused, its voice seemed to need time to gather itself from wherever the nothing it was coming from, 'but he can be bound and work through the bound.'

Tamirok was quick to pick up the distinctions as this was his area of expertise. 'So, his armour has to be enhanced by another?'

'No,' it replied.

'I'm afraid even I do not understand,' admitted Tamirok.

'By myself,' interjected Bradley.

'Correct,' replied Nihi.

'Impossible,' yelled out Tamirok, 'the most secret art of the Bound cannot be revealed. Even I cannot pull that one off I'm afraid.'

The nothingness shifted and almost murmured, a shudder flowed out of its form. 'House Bound offers a suggestion,' it stated. Tamirok was caught by surprise, no-one ever spoke to the essence of any of the Houses, ever. How was this thing communicating with it and in such a direct manner?

'Teach weaving of enhancements only, not the key to making them,' Tamirok paused, he contemplated the offering. It would be only a minor part of the entire process... actually, it would be the smallest part and other Houses had similar, although not as perfect, techniques.

'Possible,' he replied. 'House Grim can teach darkness weaving,' he neither could nor would want to. His gaze shifted to Arlak who sat there looking downright uncomfortable. He turned to face the thing they called Nihi.

'We... ehhh,' he hesitated, unsure of what or whom he was speaking to, 'could, seeing as he is a descendant of the Ancient Dark. If he had not been, we would not have.'

'He will weave with Ancient Dark,' concluded Nihi.

'No, no, no, we cannot teach him that, none of us here can,' he objected.

'Teach darkness only, we will amplify techniques for Ancient Dark.' The revelation that the House Nothingness could do such a thing was not missed by any of them.

'He will weave self-binding enhancements to his armour, bind his own powers through those, and from there, buy some time,' Nihi stated.

'But that does not solve his overflowing problem,' interjected Elshevira who had regained her footing.

'Correct,' stated Nihi, 'power dances, power grows, power is used, power amplifies,' its conclusions were right to the point.

'Never thought of it that way,' she answered.

'Minds of beings in existence muddle things, looking outside in clarity.' That revelation made them all nervous, the reference to the outsiders raised alarm bells in all of them.

'Outside?' asked Tamirok in a stern tone.

'Outside reality, not the outside your mind thinks, that outside is inside.' Not one of them could fathom what Nihi was saying but it alleviated the situation. It had confirmed that all their common enemies were not the same as what it was referring to.

'Dances,' interjected Mishrak, 'that explains it. When I pulled it out of him, the Ancient Dark current danced all over his skin. That means we can make it dance over other's skins too. Relieving the total tension of power circulating through his body,' he concluded with a sense of immense pride at his own logic.

'The mischievous one is correct,' concluded Nihi.

'Why thank you, kind...' he was unsure how to complete the sentence. Nihi didn't contribute the missing part and left it hanging in the air.

'All very nice, but you seem to forget that you can't just plug him into an outlet like with mTechs' Elshevira took the elation right from under him.

'But you can,' intervened Tamirok.

'What, how?' she asked.

'With the bound we project, our willpower through their bodies, our power flows through them,' he explained. 'That's how I make Bradley here move when he's being stubborn, my will flows through him and moves him instead of his own. That simply means we inverse the flow of the current. Switch the plus for the minus. Rather than have something pull it out of him, we have him pour it into others.'

'Hey, that's clever, that way he can just offload a whole load of power as and when he needs to,' concluded Mishrak, 'it's the opposite of what I do when I pull it out. Hey, that would be fun, since I'm an Ancient Dark user he's the one from which it flows, I'll be his outlet!' he blurted out. His father let out a long audible sigh. 'You never think before opening your mouth, do you?'

'What!' Mishrak still didn't grasp what he had just done.

'Ok, let me explain this to you, if I may, Tamirok?' asked Arlak.

'That only works by being the wielder of a bound, the wielder lets his power flow through the one BOUND to him. What your prideful self has just done and offered up for all to hear in no other place than the House Bound is an agreement to become a vessel for that power,' from Mishrak's expression, it was obvious he didn't see anything wrong with that. Actually, he secretly relished the opportunity to gain the power to prove himself.

'You still don't get it, do you? You've offered yourself up to become a BOUND so that Bradley can work through you, let his power course through a bound.' Realisation dawned on Mishrak and his expression sunk. He was just about to object when his father interrupted him, 'don't bother. An agreement made in the presence of a Bound is binding law to all in TrueEarth.'

Mishrak's legs gave way as he sunk onto his seat, still and silent.

'Ah, the stupidity of pride, he will learn.' Elshevira was secretly giggling within, trying desperately not to let her amusement be known to the others. Tamirok thought of a way to get his old friend out of this dilemma, watching his son become a bound was not something he wanted to subject the old man to, especially not when it was a binding against the will. Those are crushing to witness. One of the reasons why they are reserved for the worst of criminals and only the select few see them done.

He turned to Elshevira, 'just how much power are we talking about? Could you determine that?'

'A lot, let's just say that the mTechs with similar power could fuel their entire projects for over 100 years.'

'You're kidding, right?'

She indicated that she was not kidding.

'Only a portion, that is,' interjected Nihi.

'WHAT?!' this time, it was Elshevira who had the outburst. 'You're not serious?'

'House Nothingness is absorbing a large portion of it, for now.' It explained. 'Immediate danger is only what flows through his body, that small percentage of total potential. Power self-generating and amplifying due to Ancient Dark influence.'

'Fine, putting aside all the issues of measurement, if we do this with the bound, will it work?' Tamirok couldn't care less about determining the power levels of anyone, he just wanted Bradley to stay alive. They could brush up their egos in terms of power some other time.

'Affirmative, providing compatible synchronisation is achieved.'

'Oh yes, that adds another dilemma to the problem, just as I thought, Bradley, you do seem to overcomplicate simple things, for some reason.' Elshevira laughed. 'Well we have one offer of a compatible host for you right here,' he looked at Mishrak who, at the mention, seemed to sink deeper into his chair, 'and we have another,' everyone's expression changed to one of questioning and curiosity.

Tamirok smiled, he had the upper hand for once in this whole affair. 'He's actually waiting eagerly to hear of your adventures, Bradley,'

Bradley's ears shot up, *could it be?* He wondered. 'Yes,' confirmed Tamirok, 'I am talking of Lurizak.'

'But you and I are going to have to come to an agreement if I am going to let you have him. And I'm not going to go easy on you, he's one of my friends as well as a Bound.' Bradley nodded in agreement. He knew deep down how close the two were, Tamirok was more of a father to Lurizak than a wielder.

'Am I correct in my assumptions?' he asked Nihi.

'Correct, compatible synchronisation already achieved.'

'Good, at least that problem has a solution. I guess we will have to try this out and see if it works, then work from there may be adding new hosts as and if need be until we have enough to siphon that power off you before it tears you to stardust.'

'When do you think it would be safe for him to meet Ruler of your House?' he asked Arlak directly, 'if only he could get the Ancient Dark to stop amplifying everything, we would have a chance.'

'Once his powers are less chaotic and he learns some control to take the edge off, we should be able to make the introduction. Elshevira would be the best judge of that.'

'Fine, that leaves only the matter of him learning to weave the dark, how do we go about that part of things?' Tamirok asked.

'I can teach him, that is my own field of expertise,' she offered.

'It's settled then, what we are going to do,' he paused and turned to Arlak, 'if it agrees with you, of course,' asked Tamirok.

Arlak nodded affirmatively. 'Bradley and I are going to have a bit of a chat about Lurizak in a few minutes. Meanwhile, it will give you the opportunity to relax and have some food. Then I'm taking Bradley down to the crafters to learn skin melding of materium. By the end of the day, he should be able to do that, it is a very minor skill to learn simple converging of particles and layering their atomic structures into preselected patterns. Nothing complicated. Or difficult,' he paused and looked at Elshevira, 'tomorrow, if that works for you, we can teach him dark weaving?'

She nodded.

'Excellent, in the evening, he will learn to be a wielder, that will take at least two to three days. Then he can start to diffuse some power as he practices weaving the dark into the armour which will hopefully infuse it and bind the erratic nature of all that energy.'

Mishrak heard no mention of his name and almost let out a sigh of relief. Just as he thought he had escaped the worst, Tamirok picked up his pace again, 'Arlak, I trust your son will be staying with us for a while.' It was not a question, more like a statement of fact.

Arlak nodded, 'yes, I'm afraid so.'

'Excellent I will make arrangements for accommodation at the House,' he moved towards the door.

'Arlak, dear friend, if you please, it would delight me to no end for us two to meet up this evening for a chat and a game of minds chase?'

'I thought you would never ask,' he smiled heavily.

'I wouldn't miss this opportunity no matter what,' the tension in Arlak's face eased ever so slightly, he knew Tamirok all too well, the offer of drinks and a game was not purely for entertainment, it was also to discuss what could be done for the situation at hand. That situation was the unfortunate blunder of his prideful son. Bradley suddenly got up and started heading for the door. He knew all too well that he was directed by Tamirok's will. The tension in the meeting room was at an all-time high and he was the cause of it all. Nihi just faded away as if the space which had been devoured by his presence had reclaimed its rightful place and filled it up.

'Bradley and I are off for our chat, I will get food and drinks brought in within a few minutes.' They both left the meeting room and shut the doors behind.

18

Heather's vision blurred, she was no longer sitting in Dr Grimson office, he was no longer there, the office was no longer there, she was standing in what seemed to her the universe itself. Threads — hundreds upon millions of billions of threads — dark with a hint of reflective green occasionally coursing through them like a pulse in a vein carrying the vital liquid called blood. This pulse, however, was not blood, it was the purest form of life concentrated to the extreme. One thread did not pulse, one thread amongst all those uncountable ones constantly flowed, the current stronger and it seemed to be perpetually making the thread shine reflective green. This thread she held in both her outstretched hands. The thread moved. It jumped out of her hand. She tried to catch it and failed.

'A fate has been changed, the order of things has been violated!' echoed the female voice from the depths of the endless space. The sense of foreboding washed over Heather as she found herself back in the office.

'Heather, dear? Are you ok?' her grandfather was trying to stir her back into action. It took her a few moments to refocus. Heather was quick, she only needed a few seconds.

'I'm fine, grandpa, just a little lost in thought.'

He looked at her and went back to his seat. Heather's vision blurred once more and she saw the threads again. She thought of her grandfather and an impulse from deep within made her stretch her hands out in an offering gesture. One of the multitudes of threads separated itself from the rest, it vibrated, the metallic green life pulsed through it. She took hold of it. Her green crystals activated, their power flashed, a pulse of its own triggering her green eyes to flare up in green power. She saw into the thread she was holding, her mind raced forward, deeper and deeper into the tunnel of life it was. On the walls of this tunnel, images, sounds, sensations she saw the events as they were now looked at herself dazed in her grandfather's office, him sitting down and trying to get her to respond. She allowed her mind to follow the life within the thread, deeper and further she went. What she saw made her sad, she witnessed his loss, then the thread left her hands of its own accord. Her mind reeled backwards to the point at which it had entered. Her power dimmed out and she was lightheaded. Everything spun.

'Heather!' her grandfather had jumped out of his chair and rushed to her aid just in the nick of time. She nearly tumbled over out of her seat.

'I'm ok, dizzy but I'm back,' she replied.

'Hold on, I'll get some help,' he was concerned.

'No, don't. I'll be ok,' she insisted. Her breathing started to return to its normal systematic cycle. She took a few deep breaths in to steady her nerves.

'I could use a drink,' she admitted. Her grandfather picked up the phone and made the call. Within minutes, a small bottle of water and Heather's favourite coffee were brought in and carefully handed to her.

'It's steaming hot, please be careful with it,' cautioned the youth who had delivered it before excusing himself.

'Are you sure you will be ok?' her grandfather was not so sure.

'I'm just a bit tired,' she finally admitted, taking a sip of coffee.

'Been working too much, I'm sorry,'

'You are not to blame, grandpa! Listen to me, please, why don't you sell the labs and retire?' she sounded almost as if she was pleading.

'What on earth has brought this on?' he was curious.

'I was thinking you have been working in this place for over 30 years. It's time you started to enjoy life, you haven't had a day off in all this time. We could go for a nice holiday,' she was insistent, he had never seen her this determined. Heather had always been hands-off with her grandfather, he was her council in hard times, he was the one supporting her and she always left things to him. The sudden change in her behaviour alerted him to the fact that something was afoot.

'I will think about it. Besides, now that Kiandra is here, she could manage things instead of me for a while.'

'No, grandpa, not for a while. Just sell the place.'

'Don't you worry about me, you have to look after yourself, Heather.'

'Grandpa, please...'

'Ok, ok. If it makes you feel better, I promise I will have a good think about it.'

'Don't take too long, please.' He was really worried, why wouldn't she just tell him what was up? 'I don't want to see you lose everything.'

'What on earth do you mean?' he asked.

'I'm... I... can't say, just something my gut is telling me.'

'Why don't you go and lie down for a while, dear? You are probably not well because you've been working for countless hours on this virus.'

'I think I will,' she conceded. She needed the rest, for some reason, exhaustion had completely taken over.

'Such a bloody idiot of a son I've been cursed with.' Arlak was on his feet pacing nervously and furiously. 'I told you before you came to not say a word unless instructed,'

Mishrak sat there silently.

'Now you're silent! When there is no need.'

'We can talk to your friend, Tamirok, he'll be able to do something, he's on the ruling council,' Mishrak offered up his last hope.

'There's nothing the bloody ruling council can do, get that dammed head of yours out of the clouds with those pompous ideas of power you have. Didn't you see his face sink when you spoke? Are you that blind of a fool?'

Mishrak went silent again.

'The laws are clear, unchangeable, unalterable, even by House Bound.'

'I didn't mean it,' he objected.

'Then why bloody speak? Of all the blunders I was expecting, I could not have imagined this, not in a million years. My own son a Bound!' his fury only intensified, 'I'd kill you myself right now if I could get away with it.' He paced up and down the long conference table, every few footsteps throwing his arms up in the air, cursing and swearing at everything and everyone, but mostly at his own fate for having such a nincompoop as a son. 'And what of the reputation of our House, a Herald of House GrimGloom as a lowly Bound no less. Oh, the sheer horror of it. This will go down as a catastrophe in our history,' he burst out again in a row of expletives all the more colourful than the last lot.

Elshevira sat there sipping on the delicate smooth liquor, silently giggling away.

'You know, dear sovereign, there is a tactful way out of this predicament,' her statement made him stop straight in his tracks.

'You've found a solution!? I knew I could count on you!' the joyous Mishrak was all ears.

'Well, you won't like it, but it would help us save face and might prove to be a source of potential gain for us and the House too.'

Arlak sat down facing her, 'please do share what your delightfully devious mind has come up with, I'm all ears, my dear.'

'This young man has been acknowledged as the Ruler of a House if my understanding is correct,'

Arlak acknowledged and confirmed that it was indeed the case.

'Excellent, that works in our favour.' She paused for impact, no matter the seriousness of the situation, she liked playing her games even more so when she was the one holding everyone's attention. This was her time to shine. 'We will simply say that Mishrak here has been offered as a diplomat, to House Nothingness's ruler no less. House Bound will see him bound by duty in whatever form and for however long that may be to the Rule of House Nothingness in pursuance to all three houses' good relations and as a first welcoming gesture to the newly re-established functional House on TrueEarth. That will seal Mishrak officially, save face of our own House and make it seem as if we came up with the idea in the first place and made a grand gestation of offering our most valued, highest-ranked diplomat to guide the new arrival through his challenges of learning TrueEarth's ways of doing things and rulership.'

'Genius! Absolute Genius! You are brilliant, totally brilliant, Elshevira. Pure undiluted Genius!' From fury, Arlak had shifted to being on cloud nine.

'But, dad, it doesn't solve my...'

'Shut up, you fool, you will do EXACTLY as you're told! This is our only way out of this mess you created! In addition, it will endear us to our new arrival, paving the way for an alliance of the two houses. From what you say, Elshevira, he's a powerhouse in his own right or could be. Having an ally like that could make us far more powerful and a key dominant force in TrueEarth.'

'But, we already are one of the most powerful,' interrupted Mishrak.

'Oh, you fool, you naive fool, this is all my fault for shielding you so much. I blame myself. I am the fool.' He started cursing himself again.

'What...'

Elshevira explained, 'what your father is referring to is the fact that House Bound is far more powerful than we are, as are the other manipulator Houses. We are only powerful in our own domain. In that respect, we have no equal but the Houses which manipulate and modify forces governed by the pure Houses are far more powerful than ours in the long run. Your powers only peak and flow freely in the dark or grim situations. Theirs is always present. THAT is the key.'

Arlak calmed down and sat down, taking a sip out of his glass, 'I will suggest for Tamirok to do the same with his Bound. That way, he will owe us a favour for coming up with such a wonderful solution for him.'

Elshevira smiled. She loved how Arlak always took things to the next level.

'But, but, that still...'

'No, it doesn't, you cannot weed your way out of this one. You sealed your own fate by your own words, in the worst possible place. And don't think of running, I'll drag you back here myself if I have to.'

Mishrak's head sunk as he sulked.

'Cheer up, it might not be as bad as you think,' Elshevira tried to console him.

'Oh, it will be, there is cruelty in that man. You can feel it flowing out of him, his pain and anger at whatever happened is fuelling it.' Arlak brought them both down to earth. 'It is like a sleeping poison ebbing its way to the surface, and the worst thing is, he's learning to use his powers through it all. His powers are becoming the very expression of that cruelty.'

'We need to find the source of all that pain,' explained Elshevira. 'And the best person to do that will be you, Mishrak.'

'Me?' he asked, 'how? I'll be bound to his will and powers so I won't be able to do anything.'

'Yet again, wrong,' interrupted Arlak. 'You will be with him, you will get to know him, study, observe, and take note of him.'

'I was always bad at studying,' he admitted.

'Well, now you will have no choice in the matter, you will study as hard as you can, learn as much as you can or remain in your predicament forever. It's simply the harsh reality of your situation, deal with it. You're a Herald of House GrimGloom. Behave like one and stop this sobbing nonsense, you're behaving like a child throwing your toys out his pram with your bursts of repressed anger.' He paused, taking a deep breath to calm himself, 'I've never been able to teach you discipline because I loved your mother so much and swore to care for you as I would have her too. Now you will learn disciple the hard way or perish trying to do so.'

'Perish? No one said anything about dying...' the horror and impact of this revelation sent him into an uproar.

'What do you think it will feel like having uncontrolled power flowing through your body? It's not like what you did to him when you spiked the Ancient Dark to stretch its wings for a brief moment. Just imagine those sparks of dark electricity amplified a thousand times, coursing through every nerve in your body. When you think, you will explode. At that point, it doesn't diminish, instead, it increases even more and more and more. You heard what kind of power he has flowing through him, it's tearing HIM up on an atomic level and that is HIS power. What do you think it will do to those Bound he sends it coursing through? Pray to the Dark that these armours used by the Bound can discharge some of that.'

'He wouldn't... kill me... would he?' asked Mishrak.

'Probably not willingly, no, but his power is UNCONTROLLED, I don't think he would even know to be honest,' admitted Elshevira.

'There must be a way... to get out of this, surely we can do something, anything?' he offered.

'Have you not been listening!' his father exploded at him once more.

'We can wait until dark then we have full power and can easily get me out of all this,' his father exploded into even more colourful expletives, then went completely silent, sat down again, and sipped on his drink.

'Let me be perfectly clear, you cannot break an agreement made in House Bound, nor can anyone break an agreement made in the presence of a House Bound representative. That is universal law. No exceptions and no swivelling out of them. There is a reason why House Bound is both the military arm of TrueEarth and the enforcement arm. You, like most people who see it only from the outside when they are all friendly, have no idea of their capabilities. This House you are sitting in at this precise moment in time has so much power that it could easily crush the five founder Houses without even breaking a sweat. Not only that, but it sits on one of the TrueSeals of the Earth.'

Elshevira's eyebrow shot up at the revelation. 'Are you serious?' she asked.

'Yes, it is known only to a handful of people, but yes, I have confirmed it myself,' he admitted.

'You saw a TrueSeal?' her expression was one of utter amazement.

'Yes, the other two are rumoured to be hidden in House Nothingness and one of the other defunct House's lowest levels. Those three Houses are the cardinals for a reason and that reason is that they were built on top of TrueSeals.'

Elshevira's mind raced on at the revelations, her schemings and machinations in full swing. 'That would mean, this quasi-alliance House Bound has established with the newcomer...' she never uttered the words.

'Yes,' interrupted Arlak, not wanting his son to know. 'That is the reason why I think Tamirok has unconsciously taken to protecting this Bradley guy. The two Houses are synchronising due to their TrueSeals activating.'

'That could change the entire dynamics of power on TrueEarth, maybe even impact FalseEarth too,' concluded Elshevira.

Arlak nodded affirmatively. 'That is why having an alliance which runs through both these Houses would be an asset of incalculable worth to our own House and a terrifying threat to our enemies.' He turned to face Mishrak, his gaze locked into his son's eyes, holding him firm, 'and that is why you will NOT jeopardise this opportunity. If you do one thing worthwhile with your entire life, do this. Get it right and you might go down in the history of the House as one of the greatest Heralds of all time.'

Appealing to his pride did the trick. Arlak was no fool, he knew Mishrak's role would be a minor one. He had decided that it was this or just another row of blunders daddy had to fix one after the other. The sacrifice of his son's freedom in exchange for all their futures was a price he was all too willing to pay.

'Would you like me to have a role in all this?' asked Elshevira.

'Yes, you will teach him our ways, open the forbidden books and unravel to him as much as you can, the more he sees our knowledge as a valuable tool, the closer that brings him into our fold, and the better an ally we gain. I will speak with the Ruler of our House as soon as I get back, this is indeed a golden opportunity we must seize while we can... or someone else will.'

'As you wish,' she was more than willing to play her role. It was one which would give her ample room to pursue some of her own goals on the side-line.

'Although, be very careful about how close you get to him, he likes you a little too much and the dark is only one step away from the nothing. Besides, something about him is oddly unusual.'

'What do you mean?' asked Mishrak, 'surely it's not a bad thing to be unusual.' He liked to think of himself as unusual and always thought it made him special.

'Something is not quite the way it should be, we are still missing something important in our understanding of him. I sense something very unusual about him, and that makes it unreachable, and what is unreachable is hidden to us. Usually, there is a reason why something is hiding or is hidden by someone, and the very fact that it is hidden means there is a power there unlike the others. Something dangerous to us all from what little my senses are picking up.' Elshevira nodded in agreement. She had felt it too, for an instant, something unnerved her when he made contact with his heart and it took a lot to unnerve her of all people.

There was a knock on the large doors just before they were swung open. Through them walked rows of the Bound carrying trays filled with food and drink. Each was placed forming in a long row along the table. Glasses were refilled and the Bound walked out. As the last one left, Tamirok walked back in.

'Ah, the food has finally arrived, they took their time but I see the selection is most exquisite,' he sat down beside Mishrak, opposite Arlak, making poor Mishrak very nervous. He observed the metallic skin covering Tamirok's entire body and looked at the keyholes seemingly digging deep into the body itself. He looked at the individual muscle fibres popping up and down as Tamirok reached out to grab his food and, finally, he looked at the rows of glyphs faintly glowing away, spreading their power throughout his body, rearranging how it worked and how it could work. The entire sight made him shudder, the thought that this could be him very soon amplified that terror.

For the first time, he actually wished he had no control over his speech and could not have uttered those words. Tamirok gently tilted his head to his right and whispered into Mishrak's ear, 'congratulations, you have taken your first step'. Then, just as quickly straightened up and continued to eat.

For a moment, Mishrak's heart froze. Did Tamirok have the power to read minds?

They ate while Arlak explained Elshevira's idea to him. He decided that he liked it. 'It most certainly would give us a good justification in doing what we are doing. I will run it by the ruling council tomorrow. They are bound to question my decision concerning Lurizak.

'What of Lurizak?' Arlak was very keen to steer off the topic just in case Tamirok thought of asking any of them if they knew why he would act so, then their secret knowledge would be revealed.

None could without answering a question, no matter how much they would have wanted to, that too was a law in operation here and in the whole of TrueEarth. What was worse, the answer had to be truthful. Such a burdensome state of affairs contemplated Arlak.

'Myself and Bradley have come to terms, as of tomorrow, he will be Lurizak's new wielder.'

Arlak gasped out loud, 'you actually handed him over completely? I can't hide the fact that I'm surprised.'

'I can imagine so, but after talking to him and having a quick chat with Lenara, we found out that what we are trying to do required Bradley having complete and total dominion over Lurizak. Any less and it would fail to work.' He glanced in Mishrak's direction.

'Don't worry, he knows what must be done,' Arlak confirmed.

'And are you accepting this, old friend?' asked Tamirok.

'To be totally honest, I wasn't, but after giving it some thought, I decided that it was probably the best course of action. I wouldn't have thought so myself but you know as they say fate plays her hand in hidden but meaningful ways.' Tamirok nodded in agreement.

'Wait a minute, you said as of tomorrow?' Elshevira prompted him.

'Yes, we were going to wait until later but we're going to have to speed things up at least in that respect. During our conversation, his powers erupted again. He keeps almost blanking out, I'm afraid that if he does lose consciousness, he won't wake up.'

She was concerned, it made sense. Whatever was going on seemed to be constantly amplifying its effects. 'I am going to teach him how to wield later on tonight, after he's had some rest, of course. My hope is that allowing for even a small amount of his power to flow out into Lurizak will ease the burden on his physiology and his internal systems a little.'

'I'd love to see that,' said Elshevira.

'I'm afraid that is not possible, our customs strictly forbid the sharing of that experience even amongst ourselves. You see, it's an incredibly intimate thing to have another's essence flow through your body and even more so when they become your wielder. You pretty much offer your entire self up to them and they flow through each and every fibre of your being. Nothing is hidden, all is revealed during the great binding. Parts of yourself are locked away beyond your reach and handed over to your wielder. Their essence wraps itself through these gaps,' he pointed to the large keyholes in his body, 'and seals itself in. It is not something that is shared with anyone else.'

'I understand,' she affirmed, letting the whole subject drop. Mishrak's face was pale as a ghost, all colour and blood had drained from his face as he listened to Tamirok's words. Everyone noticed but no one commented. Elshevira took an evil pleasure and delight at the thought of Mishrak's fate.

'How will the impact of the House Nothingness reawakening fair with the other Houses?' Arlak asked.

'Not sure yet, only we and House mTech know of his dominion. The other Houses simply see him as a newcomer who has joined the Bound, for the time being that is.'

'That won't last long, they are all bound to feel the power of Nothingness stirring,' affirmed Elshevira.

Tamirok nodded. 'We feel its impact most keenly as its territory — assuming we can call it that — is right next to ours. The ruling council is trying to map out the distribution of particles and energy emanating from it but have not had much success yet.'

'Are you going to bind its flow? Might be wise to direct it properly as you do with the emanations of the other houses,' asked Arlak.

'I wish we could,' admitted Tamirok.

'You CAN'T?' Elshevira's voice rose in surprise.

'Not so far, no. You see, nothingness is not an energy, nor a power, nor a particle or quasi-particle, it is nothing. To bind something, you need to be able to take hold of it, or contain it, but with this, there is simply nothing to work with.'

'Yet it behaves as an energy or power,' interjected Arlak.

'Yes, you are correct,'

'Can't you use that to work with?'

'We've tried, to no avail. As soon as we even get close to having something to work with, we find ourselves with nothing. Like this Nihi thing as Bradley calls it. Did you notice when it appears it's almost as if a gap is torn in the atmosphere and it is that gap which is Nihi.'

Both Mishrak and Elshevira were amazed at how Tamirok managed to observe such a fine detail whilst dealing with the entire situation and keeping his mind cool when confronting that thing. She secretly thought it was because his mind was bound in some way, it gave it an unusual stability. She was not far off the mark. However, she also concluded that a mind so bound had much less flexibility to fly on its own wings in new inspired directions. She was definitely correct there too.

'I'm afraid that, for the time being, Bradley is the only one able to do anything with the nothing and even he doesn't seem able to do much.' Talking of Bradley brought back to mind Tamirok's reason for stopping by. He finished his bite and sipped away on his liquor.

'I have actually come to ask if you would mind terribly us having our drink and game tomorrow instead of later on tonight, Arlak?'

Arlak understood, the revelation a few moments ago that Lurizak would be taken over by Bradley tonight made sense now.

'Not at all, old friend, I take it you are going to see Bradley and Lurizak tonight?'

Tamirok nodded. 'I have to,' he admitted.

'No worries, let us do it tomorrow when both our minds and bodies have had time to reset from all the excitement. It has been a burdensome day,' he admitted.

'It has indeed,' Tamirok felt as if the entire day had lasted forever. 'I have made arrangements for rooms for you all. Just ask one of the Bound outside and they will show you the way.'

'So kind of you,' replied Arlak.

'Oh, no trouble at all, after all, you are most welcome,' with those words, he stood up, said farewell, and withdrew. He had a few things to settle first at the council meeting and would then head over to Bradley's room where he hoped he would finish the day with as little complication as possible. For that one thing and for Bradley's, Lurizak's and his own sake, he secretly hoped for everything to run as smoothly as possible.

19

UNWANTED FATE
- AND -
DESIRED FUTURE

The council meeting went well. He had presented the entire situation on the basis of Arlak and Elshevira's ideas with a few twists and turns of his own. It worked out perfectly. The Rulers were happy and some were pleasantly surprised. Bringing home the reality that this was the Ruler of House Nothingness rather than just a newcomer helped to make them all so much more amenable to compromise. It was an altogether different matter when dealing with the individual who embodied all the power of a House than a simple House member, no matter his or her rank. These were universal forces they were dealing with, not individual ones. Tamirok was a practical man, his feet firmly on the ground. There was no other way he could be, the bindings holding him firmly made sure of that. For once he was glad; it helped him deal with these situations, but deep down, he would imagine what it would be like to be free from time to time.

On with the next task at hand, he made his way to Bradley's room. He had sent the command to Lurizak to get there, with a tinge of regret, he focussed deeply on this one command, allowing it to flow out of him as if it had been the first time. It would be his very last command to a lifelong companion and warrior, the very last time he would feel himself and his will flowing through Lurizak. It was almost like losing a limb. The two were so bound, his will flowed through his own body and just extended into Lurizak's. He knocked on the door and Bradley opened it, nodding affirmatively to indicate they were ready. He entered the room and found Lurizak there, pacing nervously. Very uncharacteristically, Tamirok took hold of Lurizak's shoulders, fixing his gaze deeply into Lurizak's eyes. 'Are you sure about this?' he asked.

'Yes,' Lurizak replied.

'There is no turning back;' they both knew it.

Lurizak nodded. He let him go and turned to Bradley, 'And you? Are you sure?' Bradley nodded. He had no choice in the matter; it was either this or obliteration, but still Tamirok treated him in exactly the same way.

'Sit down the both of you,' he instructed. Then he turned to face Bradley, 'this is a Great Binding, you will never speak of how it is done to another, ever, are we clear?'

'Yes, agreed.'

'May the House bear witness,' spoke Tamirok as he drew a symbol on Bradley's chest with his index finger.

'You accept the responsibility of being Lurizak's Wielder? With all that it entails?' he asked.

'I do,' answered Bradley.

'To use wisely, to grow and develop?'

'I do.'

'To wield as weapon and warrior,...' he paused for a few instants 'and friend?'

The friend part was added to the official line due to Bradley insisting it should be there. It was most unusual, but Tamirok understood why, so he accepted the request. He had to have it approved by the council, which was somewhat tricky, but careful manoeuvring of the situation proved to be successful. Bradley understood why he wanted it there; he hoped that adding that personal touch to what should have been a totally impersonal binding would ensure that if his powers did run loose, his own instincts would seek to protect a friend more so than a tool, a servant or a warrior at his command.

'I do.'

'The terms are agreed.' He reached out for Lurizak, who knelt in front of them both, head held high. 'And you, do you agree being bound to and wielded by Bradley here as and when he sees fit?'

'I do,' replied Lurizak.

'All terms are agreed.'

'I now release my bindings from you, Lurizak, no longer Wielder and Bound, I now put you in charge of your new Wielder. May you serve him as well as you served me and better.' He put his hand over Lurizak's chest, where the largest and most prominent keyhole was to be found. For a split second, Lurizak could not take in another breath. Something deep within surfaced, a click was heard, a lock was open, the first caused the second, the second a third, the chain reaction went on and on until all the locks clicked open. For the first time in a very, very long time, Lurizak felt free. He could get up, move, think, breathe, do anything he wanted to. He held firm and stilled himself.

He turned to face Bradley. 'I am yours for the taking, yours for the binding, I accept you as my wielder. Bind each and every part of me in the great binding; I offer all of myself unto you.' Tamirok motioned to Bradley, putting his right-hand palm flat on Lurizak's chest. Tamirok stood up and moved to stand behind Bradley; he still had control of Bradley's will. It was decided that he would use that control to guide him through the entire process, cutting down on the time needed to learn the technique. Bradley felt the will flood his mind but pull back the next instant; instead, it focussed in on the mind. Tamirok spoke directly inside his head or so it seemed. Instruction after instruction followed, secrets whispered for none other to hear, not even Lurizak.

Push in, he instructed. Bradley focused in through his palm, his essence stretching out through it according to the secret instructions he was given. Lurizak's breath stopped; like previously, the sense of having his breath stifled overwhelmed him. Just like before, he felt that part of him being pushed back, almost as if being pushed into a close space, then the door to that space slammed shut. He heard the click and the lock seal shut. This time, it was not a chain reaction; this time, it happened all over his body at exactly the same moment. Hundreds of locks sealed shut at once. He was totally locked down. For a moment, he lost himself completely. Bradley's touch was not gentle; it was firm, yet in that firmness, it was so much more solid. These locks and their seals would not budge, no matter how skilled or manoeuvrable he was. All his years of experience of working around seals when needed were going to be totally useless. For the first time ever, he was totally, completely and utterly bound down to the very molecular part of his very being. His joy was overwhelming until his very capacity for emotion was locked down. For all intents and purposes, he was nothing more than a living statue.

'Now unseal the parts you want him to be able to use without needing you to direct him.' Bradley's right index finger danced around some of the keyholes making certain signs, tracing symbols of the wielder. These motions changed the underlying distribution of particles and their flow, remapping the seals and hence the manner in which energy flowed. Suddenly, Lurizak found himself able to move, breathe, speak, see and more and more of his usual functions started to open up to him anew.

'Lurizak, stand up for us, would you, please?' Bradley asked rather than commanded. He wanted to ensure he had done the unsealing correctly. Lurizak found that he was perfectly able to move of his own accord. Tamirok and Bradley circled about him, examining each part of him. His armour had changed in subtle but noticeable ways. It had a more intense glow to it, and the gaps in the keyholes seemed to have gained even more depth. Tamirok swore he could see right into them. He then pointed to the keyholes on Lurizak's right hand, wrist, forearm, upper arm and shoulder.

'Seal those up to your will again,' Tamirok said.

Bradley closed his eyes and did so. Lurizak cringed as he felt the seals tighten; once more, he didn't fail to notice how it was not subtle at all, rather it felt like a bolt was being screwed tighter and tighter by an indomitable force. He dreaded to think what it would be like if Bradley forced a binding against the Bound's will. It took a few seconds. The seals were firm and locked. No matter how hard he tried, his entire right arm from shoulder down to fingers was totally useless. It had become a dead weight dangling from his shoulder. He smiled.

'Verdict?' asked Tamirok.

'Brutally effective, impossible to counter, you taught him very well,' Lurizak concluded.

Bradley smiled.

'Yes, I have been drip-feeding him bits and pieces of the techniques here and there but never coherently enough or sufficiently enough for them to be pieced together into a workable method. All that was needed was to link them all up into a workable set,' Tamirok admitted. 'Let's try the same with the left foot. Seal them all.'

Bradley started with the left glute, left hip, and worked his way down. By the end of it, Lurizak's entire left lower body was as unusable as the right arm. He even tried to step forward on the right foot and drag his left one behind, to no avail. Tamirok was a little surprised by that. He expected it to be just dragged as a lump of flesh would, but it refused to budge.

'Good work,' Tamirok complimented Bradley and secretly, he thanked the House for it going so well so far. He knew the essence of the House was guiding Bradley as well, its distinct presence and power were both there, clearly accenting the very air they breathed. It was far too subtle for either Bradley or Lurizak to pick up on, but he was particularly in-tune with it. 'Now, let's sit down and work out the next part.' They both sat down.

'Ehhhmm, any objection to me getting my arm and leg back?' asked Lurizak.

'Oh, no, not at all,' Tamirok smiled at Lurizak. He would have his work cut out with Bradley; he was sure Lurizak would enjoy the challenge. He had always considered that sticking with him, Lurizak had grown a little too comfortable. Bradley would definitely keep him on his feet! He felt better; it would help Lurizak to grow again. He had become too stagnant, too set in his usual routines, too used to working around his seals and bindings. That luxury was now lost.

'Bradley, do us the honour,' he teased. Bradley just ran his fingers over the keyholes, and the binds loosened a little. Lurizak looked at him in surprise; he was acquiring finesse and control unnaturally fast. Tamirok raised his eyebrow in surprise as well. He now understood what the House was doing; it was installing control into Bradley. Unfortunately, that control would only be able to extend to what he was being taught. But still it was one aspect of control; maybe it would help him acquire the others.

'There is one final binding to do, and I've left this one to last, deliberately,' instructed Tamirok. He nodded to signal Lurizak.

Epstein just returned from his escapades in passageway 1987b; he had to report this immediately. They had managed to break through onto Earth, but where? For some reason, beyond his understanding, no one was able to pick up any information concerning their current location. *Some sort of cloaking technology?* He contemplated the possibility. It would have to be something totally new, House mTech was able to pick up almost all of the existing ones... unless? *Could it be?* He had to take that possibility into account, no matter how unlikely. If that was true, the enemy could be right at their doorstep without any of them even realising they were here! He would need help in determining this, but whatever the outcome, one thing was for sure: they had breached in. That was undeniable. Houses mTech and Bound had to be informed immediately as protocol demanded.

'Connect to Rulers mTech and Bound,' he instructed.

'Establishing priority connections,' the crystalline voice informed him.

It only took a few seconds for him to be standing face to face with the Ruler of his own House and Meneshark from the ruling council in House Bound. The space mapping was so accurate that at times, Epstein could not distinguish whether he was talking to them through the comms system or standing right next to them, right in his laboratory. It pulled the three men from wherever they were standing into a separate space constructed to appear to replicate the caller's immediate location and every single detail within it. To mTech, this was old technology, but for everyone else, it was the best thing that had ever been invented. Its uses were so manifold that it defied non-users' imaginations.

'Apologies for the interruptions,' the two heads of their respective Houses looked at him, then at each other, acknowledging the situation wordlessly. They were both well-aware that this type of interruption meant they were dealing with an immediate emergency and would not have been made for any minor matter.

'I take it we have a situation demanding our Houses' immediate attention?' Meneshark opened the dialogue straight to the point. His down to point matter of fact approach was very common within the warrior ranks.

'Indeed,' replied Epstein.

'Proceed by all means,' his own House Ruler instructed.

'As you wish. The mapping of passageway 1987b has detected disturbances on both the quantum level and the 4th dimension. I have kept a close eye on it to ascertain its scale. We have a breach into Earth space.'

'We need to deploy immediately,' concluded Meneshark, 'give us the exact locations and I will action things immediately.'

'I'm afraid I cannot.'

'What do you mean?' Meneshark was not amused. He of all people hated games of any sort.

'They are using something to mask their presence to the point where even all our anti-cloaking and invisibility tracking capabilities are unable to detect them or their whereabouts.'

'How is that possible?' asked his own Ruler.

'I'm about to look into it further, but it seems they are using a new means to breach into our space or...' he paused, uncertain whether he should even consider the possibility.

'Or?' asked House mTech ruler.

'Do spit it out, we have no time for dillydallying,' Meneshark was beginning to show signs of irritation. He wanted to crack on with it.

Epstein gave out a slight sigh. Out of all the ruling council members of House Bound, why did it have to be Meneshark? He was by far the most difficult to deal with. The man was like a homing missile, as soon as he had wind of something going on, he needed to torpedo right into the midst of it all.

'I cannot confirm, but there is the possibility that this could be linked to FalseEarth. My theory suggests that if they are able to twist the quantum tunnels and entangle with something in FalseEarth, they could simply invade over there, and from there, somehow find a means to shift here. We would be none the wiser until we had an entire arm at our very doorstep.' Both rulers gasped at the suggestion.

'We should have eradicated that problem ages ago. FalseEarth is a liability,' Meneshark was not considerate in his opinions; any weak point had to be fixed or eliminated according to him.

'Even if we wanted to, we could not,' explained the House mTech Ruler. 'The impact of destruction on that scale would have had a myriad of totally unforeseen consequences.'

'Dealing with those would have been easy, and it would have prevented something like this from happening! Now we are all at risk.'

'Regardless of what could have been done, the issue now is what we should do next,' interrupted Epstein.

'I will send a team to investigate things on the other side,' Meneshark insisted.

'Very well, we will do the same. Incidentally, we have a recent human who did shift over to TrueEarth. According to my data, his shift is still unstable, but he is moving rather well in between the two.'

'You are not serious? One cannot just step there and then here as one pleases; it's a most intricate and energy-consuming process,' objected his own Ruler.

'Oh, but this one is, well not as and when he wants to, but there have been multiple shifts back and forth, unaided.' Both men seemed to be taken by surprise. 'And from what I am told, he is currently located in House Bound.'

'Ah, yes, yes indeed, that's the man Tamirok has taken an interest in. I dozed through half of the details when we were discussing him at council. A FalseEarth human cannot be a duller subject to waste our time with; he is reported to have stumbled into House Bound, which he shouldn't have gained entrance to.' He paused as if to think; he was not sure how much he should reveal. Less is more was his choice.

'We will have to question him,' Epstein was most curious, and once peaked, his curiosity was never satiated. That one quality is what made him a leading member in mTech.

'I don't see any reason to object to that. Besides, he might shed some light on the whole breach matter. An inhabitant of FalseEarth would have witnessed something taking place with them making it in.'

'Agreed,' Ruler mTech interjected, 'besides, I am most curious to see this new arrival myself.'

'I'll send Tamirok over shortly; these things are best done in person. I will update you when my investigation's team returns.'

'We will do likewise.'

'All is set, let us be on our way.' Meneshark was quick to end the conversation. He had things to do and do right now.

'Epstein, we need to have a chat. Finish what you are doing and come see me.'

'Of course,' he turned off the communications channels. Interesting, very interesting, he mused.

Lurizak stepped back and from the table took his helm. 'It is time Bradley,' said Lurizak, 'the final Seals have to be set; we can't wait any longer.' Once more, he knelt in front of Bradley, facing him. His hands raised the helm and placed it firmly on his head. Bradley watched as the metal melted into Lurizak's skin and over his hair. The sight of it horrified something inside of him. Thankfully, Tamirok was quick to act. He sealed Bradley's capacity for emotion away. He stood behind him and took a firm grip of his head in between his hands. His mind filled Bradley's thoughts with instructions; this time, he forced them in as a cascade, not giving Bradley the time to analyse or contemplate them. 'Do it, now!' It was not a command; there was no will flowing through Bradley, no compulsion to act. This final seal and bindings had to be done of his own will, or Lurizak would not truly be his to command.

Hesitantly, Bradley put out his right hand, stretched out his palm, and covered Lurizak's face. He went through the motion, his hand trembling as he traced the symbols, forcing the power to flow. Lurizak felt Bradley's influence, his will, and his mind, reaching in, expanding throughout each and every part of him. Silence and stillness took hold of his mind, total complete and unwavering. Finally, as Bradley completed the final seal, Lurizak's very sense of self was no more.

Bradley heard Tamirok instructing him to breathe. *Get used to the sight; this is how our warriors look on the battlefields, each one bound to the will of their commanders, a handful of men whose wills flow through hundreds and sometimes thousands instantly across entire continents.*

Bradley contemplated that and thought about what a damn effective battle force that would be. These so-called bindings offered not only command, but they offered total focus to the warriors. *What a terrifying force the Bound must be in battle.*

'How do I undo them?' he asked.

'I'm afraid there is no way to undo a great binding,' answered Tamirok. 'Those are permanent.'

'Wait, what nooo, you never told me that.' The accusation was clear.

'No, I didn't. If I had, you would never have done it.' He was right.

'But Lurizak is going to always be stuck like that? No,' objected Bradley.

'Just relax them as you did with the others,' instructed Tamirok.

Bradley was quick to act on the information and one by one, he loosened his grip. The metal skin started to move and facial expressions returned. 'Lurizak, are you ok?' asked Bradley.

'Yes, all good, give me a second to adjust, as your hold is extremely firm,' he admitted as he took in a deep breath.

'I'm sorry.'

'Don't be, it is a good thing, just not one I am used to, that's all.'

'Wait, how do we get him out of there?' Bradley meant to remove the helm. He had the wild idea that if he grabbed hold of it and pulled, it would simply pop off now the bindings were loosened.

'Ouch, stop, stop,' yelled Lurizak.

Tamirok could not hold it back anymore and burst out laughing, holding his stomach in the process as he keeled over in hysterical laughter. 'Wait... till... I ... tell ... the .... others... about ... this,' he continued laughing. Both men waited patiently for Tamirok to calm back down.

It took a while. 'I'm good, I'm good,' he finally announced.

'You can't pull it off like that; it's part of his skin, his jawbone and his entire skull. What do you think would happen if someone grabbed your head and tried to pop it off like that?' he let another burst of laughter escape him.

'How do we get it off?' Bradley insisted.

'Fine, fine, I'll tell you.'

He moved to Lurizak's side and pointed to the keyhole at the temple, and poked a finger right in through one. Bradley cringed within; it looked like his finger had gone right through Lurizak's skull halfway into his head. He pulled it back out. 'That is the key. Only a wielder can use these, and there are a few ways. You can set it to allow Lurizak's will to unseal it from his skull and reseal it when needed. That way, he can do it himself. Or you can time it, in which case, once the time is up, the helm will simply find its way back onto Lurizak's head and rebind itself. That is very useful when he's out on a mission, or he's lost his helm. Not that he's ever lost it.'

Bradley could not fathom how that worked. 'But how does the helm get back? That doesn't make any sense; it's just nonsensical.'

'Well, now you're being nonsensical,' Tamirok laughed once more, 'which is exactly the same as saying it doesn't make any sense, just in case you didn't know, seeing as you used both together.' He exploded in laughter again. He knew it was due to the discomfort Bradley had with the whole thing, but he still made fun of him in the hope that it would alleviate the situation. 'Try it!'

Bradley did as instructed. It came off with the least effort. Much to his surprise, Lurizak didn't seem in any distress or discomfort.

'Let's test it out, Lurizak, if you will.'

Lurizak managed to unseal the helm, took it off his head, and placed it on the bed beside himself effortlessly. 'You know, Tamirok, it's odd, but when Bradley does the bindings, they not only feel tighter but also more firm; it's almost as if they have a more insistent force to them. They also are more solid from what I can see; it is probably due to the excessive power flowing through him. I suspect he's channelling it through his work on these seals.'

'If that is indeed the case, you are in for a treat shortly,' replied Tamirok. He faced Bradley, an air of total seriousness was almost palpable. 'Bradley, put your hands on his shoulders. You are already familiar with extending your nervous system into another, I believe.'

Bradley nodded that he was.

'This time, you will shape the nerve-cords as relatively thick chains. We use that shape because its meaning is to forcefully bind, and it is flexible to some extent. When you get more accustomed to Lurizak's nervous system and how to control it, you can change their shapes to the rope-like structures that come naturally to you. Let's not throw away tradition out of the window just yet.' He paused for a few moments lost in reflection, 'you will be using those chains to dive into each and every keyhole on his body. Inside of them, you will see a type of gap. You pass the chains through by twisting them into a knot within those gaps, and you seal them in. The effect is the same as locking the binding down. Then you bring the loose end of the chain out and bind it into the next gap. You will work from the top of his body all the way to each foot, then back up to the keyhole on his pelvis; there, you seal the chain into itself. For the arms, you do it into the chest keyhole. Close your eyes, and I'll guide you through the process.'

Bradley felt Tamirok's push of his will.

'Think of the chain, pull in the particles and atoms from all around you into their shape like so,' the image flashed in his mind, 'then make them channels for your will and power, like this.' The images flashed again. 'And finally, you move and knot them like this,' a final set flashed in. 'Do it now.'

Bradley felt it more than saw it, allowing it to take its own course. His nerves stretched out; it was like being pulled in hundreds of directions from within. The discomfort was overwhelming. Bradley was reminded of medieval torture devices, stretching people until their limbs were torn from their husks. Power flared, coursing through those very nerves. They shaped, reshaped, externalised themselves, and pulled in particles from Lurizak's armour, weaving those into coppery-black sheaths delicately encasing the thick nerve clusters. They coiled all over Lurizak's body, into each and every keyhole, forming intricate patterns all over him.

As they sneaked into the keyholes, they knotted and locked in place. Lurizak noticed the tightening in that very region of his body, then lost complete control. He had experienced this type of binding once before when he was young, but this version was completely new to him and it sent his heart racing with fear and anticipation. It was exhilarating and almost exciting, but unfortunately for him, all the parts of him, which would have given rise to excitement, were secured and locked down. It took well over 10 minutes until he lost his very sense of self. Yet he was still there. It was an odd type of mindset, his own power surface, coursing through his body, his instincts and perceptions sharpened to an incredible degree, ready for action.

Bradley's nervous system had successfully integrated into his own, and as it did, so did the flow of power emanating from within Bradley. All that was needed was a single impulse of will, and he would be unleashed. It was a very odd thing, almost alien to him. He was used to his wielder making power flow through him, but now Lurizak's own power was also surfacing. He had never known he had power. He wondered what it was. He decided to ask Tamirok, then quickly corrected himself. He would be asking Bradley now, how odd this all turned out to be. Just as suddenly, without warning, his very ability to think was locked down. He was a pure being, thoughtless, emotionless, motionless and senseless – an infinitely abstracted thing. For that split instant in time, Lurizak shone like a bright spark in existence itself.

Dr. Grimsaw walked into the quantum research division of the university. He knew where he was going and why. It was not often he visited the university, well, except for the medical research department, but this needed his personal touch. He had a brief chat to Yume and walked right into the furthest corner of the lab. There he stood behind Elma and interrupted her. Rather than just speak to her, he spoke out loud to ensure he would be overheard by everyone.

'Me and this young lady here need to have a chat.' Everyone turned about to look at them.

'If you would all please leave now, this is a matter of national security.' Yume knew what was afoot and she rapidly went from desk to desk, telling everyone to take a quick 20-minute break and silenced any questions and objections. Within less than a minute, the entire laboratory was dead quiet, and the constant background buzz of the equipment was no more. The silence was eery and weighed heavily upon Elma, making her nervous, very nervous. Dr. Grimsaw took the chair from the desk next to hers, wheeled it over, and sat down facing her.

'I know what you have been up to,' he told her. She felt sick. She had been caught, impossible, she was so careful.

'I must admit that little trick of yours was fascinating, encrypting the data and sending it over the official IP networks made it look as if it was just secured communications. Unfortunately, you could not have known that all the data that comes into and out of the labs is secretly routed through one gateway, which is made to appear as if it was a range of different independent ones.' He paused, allowing the information to sink in, 'breaching into the bio-labs is bad enough, but then diving deep into just the project files dealing with the virus outbreak and the national security locked files made alarm bells ring. For future reference, I would suggest that it would be best not to be so single focussed. As you probably know, the penalty for this is likely to be a considerable number of years in prison.'

'I ... only wanted to help; it was all in good intent, I meant no harm.'

'That, young lady, is entirely irrelevant and beside the point. It is a criminal offence actually. I bet you would have multiple crimes attached to what you did.'

Elma could not get the sympathy card to work here, so she quickly changed her tactics. 'I was forced to; she made me do it,' Dr. Grimsaw knew exactly where she was heading with this line of argument.

'Ah yes, you mean divulging the information to Mira Madison; I know about all that,' he admitted.

'You do?' she was surprised, as all her arrangements with Mira were highly secret. Mira herself ensured that would be the case as well as all the precautions Elma had taken. *Just how far does this guy's reach go?* For the first time, her self-confidence evaporated. She was afraid.

'Oh, yes, I can even tell you how much she paid you for that information and what was in your files. I could also tell you what was not in your files, but that is for me to know and you to discover.' His voice spoke with an unbending authority.

It completely overwhelmed Elma, who did not know what to do or say. 'Discover?' she hesitated.

He smiled, 'very astute girl; I am going to set you onto a path, which will change your entire future. Not that you have much of a choice since I could hand these files into the authorities and have that life of yours spent in jail instead. Whether you like it or not, the rest of your days belongs to me.'

She looked at him uncertainly; she was sure she could come up with a whole set of arguments about how he was mistaken or how unfair it all was. She also saw in his face the fierce gaze of absolute determination and iron will. There would be no compromises from him; he would not hesitate. Unlike the young men she worked with, this one was not joking or making idle threats; this one's threats were real, terrifying and merciless.

'What are you proposing?' she asked.

'It is not really a proposal, my dear, but if you want to think of it that way, feel free. You are going to help us, and for you to do so, your life will have to change, completely. I know you spied on Bradley when he created the power crystals.'

She froze. How the bloody hell does he know that! All evidence of that was purely from what she herself had witnessed; there were no electronic records of any kind. Her surprised look faded gradually as she nodded affirmatively that she did.

'You are going to help him, although not directly. I am going to put all these skills of yours to some good use, rather than allow them to be misused for foolishness.' He reached into his pocket and pulled out a large crystal, 'one of Bradley's one he missed during his move. This is the last one we have access to. Heather took the other, and a most unfortunate young man got into trouble with the others.' He handed her the crystal. She looked at it, turned it in her fingers, and twisted it in her grasp. It seemed very unappealing.

'Power crystal?' she asked. Her mind was racing, mischief ready to kick into action.

'Yes, using that crystal will cost you dearly, more than you can possibly imagine, as it has everyone who has used one before. You will pay whatever price it requires of you and using it unlocks the way forward,' he instructed.

'I'm not sure I understand,' she admitted.

'Take it, focus in on it, pour your emotions into it, express your desire for knowledge, discovery, technology, and the power those bring. Express the desire to help Bradley. It will activate, then if you are true to yourself, you will see, know and witness something extraordinary.' He had picked his words very carefully, manipulating her into a corner. He had played on her insatiable curiosity and given her only one path. *Calculated risk, hopefully, she will have taken that specific desire to be the key as most young people are obsessed with specific words. Should she change it, we might be in even more trouble.* For some reason, he was certain she would not. 'Using that, you will see what the quantum realities can do.'

'Quantum realities?' she asked, curiosity running at an all-time high.

'Use the crystal, accept its conditions and do your job...' he stood up and just before leaving, added, 'or end up in jail for what remains of this life of yours.'

Without further words, he stepped out without turning back. Elma was left sitting there with crystal in hand, wondering.

'There, now bring the end of it back in on itself and merge the two together,' instructed Tamirok. 'Great, all done, you can open your eyes, and we can have a look at your handiwork.'

They both stood up and circled about Lurizak, who was once more a living status unable to move or do. Tamirok touched the chain; it felt odd, 'looks like rope, not much of a chain this,' he moved in closer and took a better look at it. 'Oh, no, I stand corrected. Look at this! You did go and overcomplicate it all again, didn't you?'

Bradley took a closer look. It was chain, but chain woven through chain and into chain so finely and delicately balanced, layer upon layer of interwoven chains, that it made the end product look like rich, thick rope. It had a copper shine to its underlying black substance.

'I guess that's how you do it,' Tamirok said. 'Fine, we will work with what we have; we might as well flavour Lurizak to your style and liking,' he laughed. He proceeded to guide Bradley into using the extensions of his nervous system, which were now fused with Lurizak's. After what seemed to last a whole day, he looked at both men carefully.

'That will do for the body control. Poor Lurizak is probably getting sick and tired of us. Send your will through the rope-like chains again, but this time, feel just them, not his body, and will them to loosen slightly until Lurizak has control over all the keyhole functions again. Later on, you can play with locking some of them down and keeping others open, and so on. We don't have time for that right now. Oh, and before you jump into action, never loosen them up so much as to make them fall out of the keyholes that would collapse the organs they are attached to.'

Bradley took in a deep breath, closed his eyes and paying even more attention than he was before, did as he was told, making sure to avoid causing harm.

'Damn, you have a tight grip,' moaned Lurizak.

'Ah, he's back, our good old boy,' cheered Tamirok. 'Come, sit down,' he instructed Bradley. 'No, actually you, Lurizak, lie down on the bed instead, limbs uncrossed flat on the back.'

'What are you up to now?' he asked suspiciously, as he pulled his arm up looking at these ropes, chains or whatever they were.

'You'll either enjoy this terribly or hate it awfully,' he admitted. 'Just do it, or I'll get Bradley to make you do it,' he smiled at him.

'You are enjoying this a little too much for my liking,' objected Lurizak as he flung himself on the bed.

'Hold still,' instructed Tamirok, 'final instruction for the day, Bradley, come here and place your hand on the keyhole at the top of his abs.'

'Oh, goodness, you're not going to make him make me throw up, are you?' asked the nervous Lurizak.

'Not today, no.'

Bradley did as he was told. 'Allow your power to flow into there and spread through his body, see it as those black sparks if you need to or however you usually do it. But only a little; we don't know what it will do to him yet, nor how his body will react.'

Bradley nodded, closed his eyes, and saw his power as a pulse of a force inside of himself. He directed it through his arm down into Lurizak and radiated it out through his body.

'Ahhhh,' escaped Lurizak's lips.

Bradley momentarily opened his eyes. He saw him glowing in black light; the coolness radiating outwards made him pull his own hand away. Even at a distance, he could still feel the power.

Lurizak leapt out of bed, roaring like a beast. 'I feel powerful, strong, solid, what is this? Amazing.'

'That, my dear friend, is the tiniest of smallest drop of what is coursing through Bradley at the moment.' Lurizak started at Bradley. 'This is the most amazing thing I've ever felt. I could smash through every wall in the House without the least effort.'

'Let's not go injuring the House, shall we. I'll never be forgiven for damaging it,' admitted Tamirok. 'Sit down.'

Lurizak was too high to listen; he was edging for battle for any confrontation, right now! Bradley sent his will and Lurizak's body tensed until movement was no longer possible. He had never experienced that before. He looked inquisitively at Bradley, then without any impulse whatsoever, moved to where Bradley had taken a seat, and parked himself cross-legged on the floor, hands at his side.

'You're getting too darn good at this, you know,' he objected.

Bradley just smiled back at him.

'I want you to try sending more power through him, but this time, only by placing your hands on his shoulders, rather than a central keyhole,' continued Tamirok.

Bradley did so; he let the power flow. It leaked through the rope-like chains into whatever keyholes it could seep into. The light intensified in Lurizak and every muscle in his body budged. 'Oh, my goodness' the power was flowing more and more and Lurizak was oozing with power.

'I need to go and smash something right now! Or I'll burst.'

'No, you don't, sit still and adapt to the power, Lurizak,' instructed Tamirok. He turned to Bradley, 'do the same again, but this time, without even touching him, just focus on his body being filled with the new nerves, remember them. It is through them your commands, your will AND now your power flow. Once that understanding is fixed in your mind, make more power flow out of you and through them into him.'

Nothing happened; he tried again and Lurizak groaned again. The third time, the gateway burst open and Bradley felt the nerve-cords as an extension out of his own body, wrapping Lurizak's. Power seeped through them as if they were blood vessels and from there, it ebbed its way into each and every pore of Lurizak's body.

'Let me out, I need NEED NEEED to burst,' he pleaded.

Bradley looked at Tamirok, 'hold on.' The power kept intensifying and Lurizak started to cry out; it was too much. Pain escaped his lips and Bradley instinctively drew some of it back into himself. He rushed to Lurizak, 'Are you ok?' he asked.

Lurizak could not reply; everything had sealed off and overloaded. He had no control over any part of his self. Bradley concentrated on loosening his hold over the head and neck. '

Thanks,' replied Lurizak.

'They all sealed shut,' explained Bradley.

'I know, I felt them overload and total shutdown happened.' Lurizak moved his head to look at his legs, only then did he notice his entire armour had changed from the gleaming copper to a shiny jet black.

'What.... happened?' He never finished the question.

'Your armour adapted to his power,' interjected Tamirok. He was concerned that his power had corrupted Lurizak's armour, but that option was unthinkable. 'I think over time as you two practice together, you will be able to store more and more of the overflow inside Lurizak and his armour.' He seemed to turn and was preparing to leave. 'I'll leave you gentlemen to play. My work is done here. Bradley, he's yours, for better or worse, so take care of him, please.' Before any other word could be spoken, Tamirok left them there as he walked out, closing the door behind him.

Bradley collapsed on his bed, instantly blacking out, leaving Lurizak stuck sitting cross-legged on the floor. 'I guess I'll have to get used to starting from scratch again; the poor guy, it must have all been a bit too much for him.' He closed his own eyes and decided to spend the time in personal reflection until Bradley woke up and allowed him to move again. Something deep within him stirred, a wave of awareness expanded from all the stillness. A burst of dulled activity, silent, insistent and persistent.

Kiandra was cock-a-hoop. She had finally managed to figure out how to delay things even further. She quickly typed out her latest email and sent it off to the next member of staff. During the entire afternoon, she was busy emailing all the critical researchers working on the virus. Bradley would be going to Japan soon and Heather was off sick; that was already two of the main players out of the picture for a short while. She only needed to take care of Jim and a handful of others. She smiled as she hit the send button. This would ensure a good 10 days to two weeks' further delay. As the email whooshed off into cyberspace, her phone rang. It was a text message. Oddly, she did not recognise the number. The message was clear, 'meet me at the coffee bar in an hour,' signed an interested party. She pondered upon the oddity of the whole thing and decided she would not bother with it. It was not from anyone she knew, and anyone she didn't know had no business texting her in the first place. Pushing the phone aside, she returned to her computer. There was a lot left to do and she had to get everything just right. After all, Mira had put her in this position exactly for this very purpose.

20

GRAND
- REVELATION? -

Tamirok watched the warmatch from a distance. Bradley and Lurizak seemed to be in perfect synchronicity. It amazed him seeing Lurizak flourish under the new inputs from Bradley. When he had given over his companion in arms, he had never imagined this would be the end result. For the first time, looking at them battling it out on the field, he smiled. He was content he had made the right decision for them. A glimmer of concern flashed through his mind, things were progressing nicely, but this was only a temporary alleviation of the underlying dilemma. What would happen to Bradley? His concern naturally also included Lurizak, who was now bound to the newcomer and would have to endure whatever Bradley went through, maybe even more so than he wanted to admit. And what would happen when Bradley had to go back, which he knew would happen very soon. The moment he returned to his own side, all the memories and all the pain would come flooding back like a tsunami. Here, he was shielded from his other life, memories of the loss of his child, of the murder of his bride too, and his insatiable hunger for revenge were distant echoes of another life in another place. Secretly, he wished he could keep him bound here in TrueEarth.

He felt it, the all too familiar tell-tell signs were there. The tearing of a gap of nothingness in the air signalled the arrival of Nihi, as if summoned by the expression of his desires.

'I didn't mean it, it's just wishful thinking,' he explained.

'That is not the reason we are here, but it is good to know,' it replied.

'We share your concern about the Ruler,'

'What will happen to them? You know and see more than I do, do you know what will become of them?'

'We see only possibilities and probabilities, the more likely, the more brilliantly the threads of fate shine. We follow those and see,' it tried to explain. Tamirok didn't grasp it, he was not the fate binder of the House. That part of their sciences always eluded him.

'And what are the directions they are moving in?'

'Your concerns are valid and true,'

Tamirok was saddened, so much promise in these young men, so much suffering. 'Will it ever end?' he wondered.

'Yes, all returns to the Nothing,' calmly and coldly, Nihi pointed out the fundamental underlying truth of all.

'Yes, yes, but what will happen to them?' Tamirok pointed towards Bradley and Lurizak and waved in a casually dismissive manner at Mishrak standing on the far opposite side, out of harm's way. He focused in on Bradley—genuine regret and worry freely expressed, 'will he survive?'

'No, he won't.'

Tamirok's heart sunk. For the first time in centuries, he felt as if someone had ripped it out of his chest and torn it to pieces.

'You of all people understand that sacrifices must be made,' it explained. 'On Bradley's side, they have a saying that these sacrifices are made for the greater good or the grand design,' he took a deep breath in, 'that is all nonsense. Here we know the truth, sacrifices are made for power and in the pursuance of the flows of primal power in creation. We, all lesser things, are used and disposed of. The only difference is, they do not understand that and we of the House Bound accept that inevitable cold hard truth and bind ourselves to it, gaining that little fragment of relief from its devastating weight.'

'Very perceptive,' acknowledged Nihi.

'You're not just a quasi-ruler of the House of Nothingness, are you, Nihi?'

'Very perceptive indeed, almost too much so,' it admitted.

'What are you?' he asked. The gap in space shimmered for a

moment as if hesitating or fighting the question, trying to evade the revelation of the truth.

'I am the embodiment of the essence of House Nothingness,'

Tamirok's eyes widened as he glared at Nihi.

'You do realise that never in the history of TrueEarth or the existence of the whole of Earth herself has a primal force of creation made direct contact with ANY living being before,' he sundered at the implications of this very truth.

'That is correct,' was all Nihi offered up.

'Why? Why do something so forbidden by the flow of creation?'

'Necessity,' it answered.

'I don't understand nor will I ask because your answers would be lost on me,' he admitted in all honesty, 'just tell me, do you realise the impact of your manifestation on us?'

'Yes,' it paused, the air shimmered again, 'very minimal interaction with an impact on the Grim and the Gloom. Significant impact on Ruler, you and your common charge. Minimal impact on the unwilling one,' the shimmer formed a wave towards the group of men on the battlefield. 'Changes on deeper levels to your being and Bradley's, significant changes through Bradley into Lurizak's being.'

Tamirok hesitated for a moment, he was shocked and surprised at the same time.

'Permission and agreement of House Bound obtained, changes approved at essence level,' it explained.

'Wait, wait, wait a second there,' Tamirok interjected, 'are you telling me that you are also in direct communication with the essence of House Bound? How is that possible?'

'Simple, like to like, communication is easy and uninterrupted.'

'But House Bound has never directly communicated with anyone,' he objected.

'No reason to, no purpose, no need,'

Tamirok could think of hundreds of reasons why it should have.

'Communication with non-primal essences difficult for us,' said Nihi.

'Yet you are here speaking to me with no problem whatsoever,' objected Tamirok, it didn't make sense.

'Using the Ruler's mind, vocabulary and essence as an intermediary translation mechanism,'

Tamirok just took the statement at face value. He did not know anything about these primal essences nor did he understand enough about them to grasp what was happening.

'Can you tell me about this necessity which forced you into action?'

'Awakening of Great TrueSeal,'

'WHAT!?' Tamirok exploded.

'First Seal of TrueEarth active under House Bound,' it explained. Tamirok nodded in agreement, even though this was knowledge only a very select few had, he was privy that his duty as a Warmaster of TrueEarth was, first and foremost, protection of the Seals.

'Another Great Seal activated setting course of many events into action.' Tamirok struggled with this, it took millennia for the first seal to activate, how could a second one be awakening so soon?

'You are struggling, your Grim friend figured it out two days ago,'

The revelation shook Tamirok, 'Why had the old man kept this knowledge to himself?' he wondered, unwittingly speaking the question out.

'His goal is to use it to his advantage, petty human beings with petty desires and minds always revolved around self-glorification and acquisition, never understanding the futility of it all.' Nihi was not a fan of human beings in general, 'yet some rare few manage to rise above that pettiness of the ego and catch a glimpse of the greatness of things.'

Tamirok conceded the point. 'Others are forced to do so,' he could swear he felt the gap which was Nihi pointing in the direction of the men battling it out.

'Yes, and they pay a mighty price for that privilege it seems,'

'Irrelevant, price human measurement of sacrifice, role to play important,' it stated coldly.

'So, the second seal is open? Where is it?' he asked.

'Your old friend has already figured it out, why not ask him?' objected Nihi. 'Wait a minute, how did HE figure it out?' Tamirok ran his mind through all the information Arlak had been told. It all centred around Bradley and included the fact that he was the chosen Ruler of House Nothingness. Things started to click into place.

'Understanding comes to you, finally,' commented Nihi.

'Fine, fine, it took a while, are you telling me the second Grand Seal of TrueEarth is under House Nothingness?' he hesitated. The implications of that were too great to miss.

'This information is only for you, agreement of all that is to be revealed now on the basis of it being kept secret from all others, agreed?' prompted Nihi. Tamirok was unsure he could not hide this from his own House, it was too important, its impact too significant.

'I... can't,' he said.

Nihi shifted and blurred out for an instant, 'House Bound agrees, it is not knowledge for its ruling council, nor others, just you at this point in time. Do you?'

'Very well then, agreed,' the gentle but instant flow of power from his own House reach in and sealed his words. He smiled, it was comforting to know his House paid such close attention to him and even more so that it had just confirmed the validity of what Nihi had told him. They were in direct communication, somehow.

'Not second,' corrected Nihi.

'You don't mean...' Tamirok did not even dare to utter the words.

'The third Grand Seal,' Nihi did it for him.

Tamirok's jaw dropped at the revelation. 'Awakened?' he asked.

'Activating...' replied Nihi.

'The third, I'll be damned... of all the things, it had to be the third,' he understood the implications all too well. 'How did the third activate before the second?' he wondered.

'Necessity,' replied Nihi. Yet again, that one word that seemed to be a final statement and a non-statement at the same time. It started to annoy Tamirok, he was a practical man who needed practical information, not some philosopher who could deal in abstractions such as these.

'Does he know?' he pointed to Bradley.

'Not yet, but he will in time. The seal is flowing through him,'

'You're not serious?'

'Yes,' corrected Nihi, 'when he was lost in oblivion and almost dissolved into Nothing, he stood in the centre of the Third Grand Seal and pulled himself back out of Nothingness, reforming his body, mind and soul. The essence of both House Nothingness and the Third Grand Seal flow through his veins now.' The revelation clarified so much, Tamirok gained an insight into what was happening. All this mystery about Bradley now made sense.

'You do realise that a human being cannot contain those powers? Even the power of a House is beyond our ability to fully embody, let alone the power of a Grand Seal, and the third one to add to that!'

'Correct, Bradley will die,' it stated. 'It is unavoidable.'

'There must be a way, there has to something that can be done, there has to be,'

'The more immediate concern is how he will change,' said Nihi.

'What do you mean? He's stabilising now that we are offloading some of his erratic power. Lurizak's body seems very adept at ordering the chaotic nature of his powers, the changes in his armour, which I still don't understand, are easing the pressure on both of them.'

'Underlying problem not solved, just delayed. Memories are powerful triggers to many events within Ruler. Look,' its force slammed into Tamirok and carried his mind within it as it shot right into Bradley. Tamirok waited for his vision to clear, he was witnessing Bradley holding Kuroi's hand as she shared her final words with him. He saw the conversation with Dr Martin when he found out he had a son, and an instant later, had lost him. He witnessed Bradley collapsing under the weight of the revelations and bottling up all his emotions. He saw him swear utter destruction in vengeance. Then a flash interrupted him, the scene of him talking to Heather was next, when he realised Kuroi would die, he saw the waves of darkness flood the entire garden space and lash out in pain and hunger.

Tamirok gasped. This was worse than anything he had seen in his long carrier on the battlefields. No one had managed to do that with dark matter before. His vision blurred, he was not sure what he was seeing, it was a young boy, a human child, 5 or 6 years old. He looked about and saw the most horrific vision he had ever witnessed. The child crying out to his mother as she was being savaged by a group of attackers, violated right in front of his sight, torn limb from limb by the crazed men. Blood was everywhere, pieces of flesh torn and flung all over the place. Shifting forward, he saw a large man's body lying face down on the floor. He had been killed just moments before. 'Ma'amaaa,' the child cried out and his screams pained

Tamirok, the very sound of them ripped at his ears as if it was trying to tear them off. The force of it flung him back out of Bradley into his own body. His hands firmly grabbed hold of his powerful thighs as he got himself stable again.

'Was that Bradley?' he asked.

'As a child, that memory is fuelling his pain, his hate, and his destructive desires — all things he has forgotten about and lost awareness off. Soon, he will remember. He will become whole again.'

'No, oh goodness no, he can't remember that!'

'We were going to pull them out of him and dissolve them into the Nothing, but cannot.'

'Why on earth not? That is the most useful thing you could do for him!' objected Tamirok.

'Because that memory unlocks so many possibilities and probabilities that even with our sight we cannot follow the full flow of events.'

'Screw the events, do you know what remembering that will do to him?'

'Yes, we all know,'

'All? What are you not telling me, you impartial horror,' he was angry now, really angry. Not at Nihi in particular, but at the whole situation.

'All the essences of the Houses.'

'Wait, WHAT? All?'

'Yes, all Great Houses are aware,'

'Many of the Houses are no more,'

'Incorrect, they have always been there but dormant, they will reawaken with the Grand Seals.' This all too much, he couldn't deal with any more of these grand revelations.

'Not grand, minor events in larger unfolding.'

'Oh, great, just what I needed, if these are minor revelations, please don't tell me any of the greater ones.'

'Agreed, no need for you to know,'

For once, Tamirok was grateful for the lack of additional information sharing. He already had too much to deal with as things were. 'Can I not bind that memory away from him?' he pondered.

'It is already bound away by his own mind, that is the problem, the root of his internal conflict.'

'Can you see what will happen when he remembers that?'

Maybe there was hope, maybe he could stir him towards a more positive outcome.

'Bradley will change,' was all it offered up.

'Yes, we can all see that, but how?'

'Unknown, many possibilities, too many to count. All leading to total breakdown and eventual merging with Nothingness.'

'You are telling me that he will self-obliterate?'

'Correct, he will achieve revenge and have nothing left, no one left, nothing to fight for, no one to fight for. All becomes empty at the end.' This was all a matter of fact.

'You're wrong,'

For the first time, he felt the shimmer from the gap, but this time, it hesitated, this time, it was not firm as usual. He was onto something. He let his mind flow free in whatever direction it was set.

'He has someone, look,' he pointed to Bradley and Lurizak, 'they are almost one. Bradley shows no emotion, he doesn't reveal them due to his own discipline and the underlying horrific emotions he has stored, but they are there. Those of us who observe him closely can see them. Look at them, he's so protective of Lurizak, any outsider would be hard pushed to not conclude that they are related. He treats Lurizak with almost a parent's touch, firm yet gentle caring and pushes him to new learnings and growth when it is right. It's almost as if he was caring for his younger self through Lurizak. When his power flows through Lurizak, he's always careful to pull back as soon as he notices any discomfort. Even though Lurizak is very apt at hiding it, Bradley is reading him like an open book and adapting on the stop to protect him from harm. Just look, see how each time Lurizak comes under attack from his opponent, Bradley totally overpowers them both. He is not doing it to show off, he's doing it to ensure that no matter what happens, Lurizak is safe and unharmed. Unwittingly, Bradley is turning Lurizak into one of the most powerful forces TrueEarth has ever seen. Just look, let all the Houses look, I dare them to,'

The reaction was unmistakable. Not only did he feel the flow of power of his own House, but he felt countless others, some totally unfamiliar to him, others friendly and some vaguely familiar. They all watched in their own weird awkward fashion. Lurizak was being assaulted by his opponent, atomic energy gathered into a condensed sphere which began fusion. It was the key power of his opponent, the equivalent of having a sun thrown at him. Its destructive force unparalleled. Not even the armour of a Bound warrior could block that. Lurizak hurled himself at his opponent, sword blazing in black flames, hoping to cut through it before it was fully formed. It took but an instant, his body was engulfed in shimmering blackness so deep that it pulled the space about them into itself. That force coalesced at the tip of his sword, Lurizak's eyes glazed over, he was not there anymore.

Within moments, from all around them, light, darkness and shadow were being sucked into a tiny sphere, it all collapsed in on itself and grew. A fully-formed black hole raged forth. Its impact with the newly-formed small sun was utterly destructive, their collision sent waves of power smashing through everything. Trees were ripped up, grass disintegrated, all the protective domes of the battlefield just evaporated. Both combatants were hurled away from each other, flying through the air as if they were nothing more than feathers caught in a hurricane. Both their bodies fell to the ground in loud thumps, their weight creating small craters at their crash sites. Bradley was instantly on his feet running towards Lurizak.

'By the grace of creation, did he just create a black hole out of thin air? Not only that, but control its gravity so that Lurizak can wield it atop his sword in combat?'

The presence of the Houses crackled in excitement and surprise.

'We agree with your assessment,' confirmed Nihi, 'but it does not change the flow of fates,'

'No, it doesn't,' admitted Tamirok, 'but what it does do is give us something for him to rely on, he is not that child left alone in the world from that memory, he has people to care for and people who care for him THAT can help him pull through.' He stated, 'surely it can?' he hesitated. For a moment, he could have sworn he heard many whispers — layers upon layers of sounds flowing in all directions.

'Too much power for a human being, unsustainable,' they concluded.

'Can we not just do more of what we did with Lurizak?' he asked.

'Primordial forces manifest through the Houses into hundreds of members' bodies as vessels, some thousands.' Nihi explained. 'House Nothingness has no one, it is nothing, Bradley is alone,' it continued, 'adding to that power of the Third Great Seal fully awakened. Non-sustainable.'

Tamirok understood, yet something in him simply refused to concede the point.

Mira sat at her desk, eyes glazed, focused elsewhere. The shadow which was not only a growing part of her but had become her was whispering intricate instruction over and over again. At first, the repetition irritated her, then her mind settled into the rhythm and begun to enjoy it. Over and over, they repeated until it was certain each part of the process was so ingrained in her awareness that it would be impossible to get it wrong or to forget a step. It stopped, she took a deep breath and a sip of her favourite coffee which had now oddly been the one with caramel topping. Previously, drinking anything like this would have been totally out of the question. The sheer calorific load these coffees had horrified her. It no longer seemed to matter, she was eating high-calorie foods and still slimming down. Somehow, she had developed what she viewed as the ideal metabolism.

'Ittttt iiiiis tiiiiiimmme,' the shadow instructed.

'I'm ready,' she was both excited and somewhat fearful. She had learnt how to execute the basic procedure but this would be something else. This attempt, she would not be going to that place as a shadow version of herself, this time, she would be going there as a body imbued with a shadow into that mysterious place where, other than herself, no shadows existed. A calm stillness overtook her. She followed the exact steps given in order to blend her body and the shadow into one coherent unit of existence. It took a while. This was unlike previous times. This time, all her biology was going with her. The sensations were odd and terrifying, her heart pulsed blood which was far lighter and thinner than blood would ever be, her lungs breathed something she could not quite comprehend in addition to air, her body felt almost like a pulse of energy and matter fused into one. It took her a good 10 minutes just to acclimate to the new sensations flooding her awareness. She loved it, so much freedom, it was like a sudden removal of all the limitations she had become so habituated to.

A pulse—no, a wave—of pure power cascaded throughout her, then another, and another. She was powerful! She loved it, totally enthralled to it. *I need the location,* she thought. Instantly, the shadowy presence presented an image. That image deepened, it gained light, it gained motion. The image was alive. The part she liked the least hit without warning, she was sucked into a vortex. It reminded her of the food getting stuck in the kitchen sink being sucked into the pipe by the watery vortex. She was rapidly propelled forward, the feeling of being sick arose for a moment or two and then faded. Onwards, deeper and deeper into the tunnel she went. The movement so rapid she had to focus on the point straight ahead of her, even daring to glance at the side walls would make her dizzy and lose focus. She had learnt that mistake on her last trip. That was a total failure which had severely weakened her. This time, the forward motion stopped. She flopped out into the scene she had seen as nothing more than an image in motion. Her shadowy self-reformed, restructured itself until, eventually, she was more flesh than shade. She had made it, this was the mysterious lab where she spied countless secrets of technology so advanced that no one was able to understand it unless the shadow explained how to use it. It was this she ultimately wanted. She understood enough to know that adopting this to her project would allow for human beings to gain almost infinite lifespans. That was her ultimate goal, it was her privilege to wield that power. Only her and those loyal to her would have access to it, she would not only make millions but also gain immortality. She quickly went to the glass-like console and started carefully executing the plan. She could not take any risks, her lack of knowledge of whom this lab belonged to, where it really was, or who invented all this technology, meant caution, deception and stealth were required.

'Keep an eye out for intruders, or whatever you used to see,' she instructed the shadow part of herself.

A spark of hope kept on springing forth no matter how much they all wanted to convince him there was none.

'Hold on just a minute, all you essences are so high and mighty up there that you are missing something fundamental.' His accusation was plain and obvious.

'Explain,' Nihi's voice had not changed. It had no emotion to respond with.

'House Bound, I call to you, you know of this. Witness my words as absolute truth.' The next instant, the presence of his own House's essence surrounded him. It elevated him somehow, as if some part of him was forced upwards without moving at all. He saw glimmers around them, they were like patches of coloured particles, all radiating outwards, all flowing in particular patterns, universal constellations of their own. He didn't know how but he understood these were the essences of the Houses. For the first time ever, a mortal being had seen and witnessed this. It was one for the history books. He turned and saw House Nothingness. Unlike the others, this one was just a huge gap—a tear in reality itself. He looked straight at it, it was so deep, so dark, totally endless.

'Do not gaze into my depths, mortal, or you will lose yourself in the Nothing,' warned Nihi.

'Sorry,' Tamirok focused his gaze on the others.

'Speak, mortal, your elevation can only last a few short fractions of time,' said the dark constellation of universes on his left. House GrimGloom, he presumed.

'House Bound is my witness,' he started seeing its universes shifting and turning all around him. 'What you all do not know is that for the first time in the history of the entire human race, a human is about to bind himself completely, truly and totally to another. A final binding giving rise to more than the sum of the two souls involved. Lurizak has offered Bradley his very soul and essence.'

He could have sworn he heard gasps from these things.

He continued, 'we in House Bound talk of complete and total bindings, we have them mentioned in our teachings and customs, but the TRUTH of the matter is no one has ever achieved that. It is a goal and hope we all secretly wish never happened because we all fear it on some level or another. No human being every willingly gives his entire self, his essence and soul up. Throughout history, it was done by trickery or forced by circumstances and then only a temporary binding of it takes place. Never has a final binding been done.'

'That is universal law,' the voice came from the copper and silver universes representing his own House. 'What Lurizak has done is offered it up to Bradley willingly without constraint. All that is Lurizak, his very creation and purpose of existence has been offered up. That is totally unheard of.'

'Confirmed,' came from the universes which shone of light — House LightBearers assumed Tamirok.

'An Act of Greatness giving rise to a new Necessity within Creation,' the voice this time came from the group of universes held together by gears and cogwheels — House WonkerDudels. 'It changes the flow of creation. Has Bradley accepted?' it asked.

'Not yet,' affirmed Tamirok.

'You must convince him to,' it insisted.

'No,' the firm voice came from the universes of his own House.

'No one wants to be involved,' explained Tamirok, 'our ruling council, and even the House Essence, as you have heard, do not want to influence the matter. I am told it has to run its own course without any influence either way.'

'Correct,' stated Nihi. 'A great sacrifice is beyond the scope of any of our influences. Getting involved is strictly forbidden by Creation itself. We will all wait and observe.'

Tamirok had the distinct sensation that, for some reason, House Nothingness bore the greatest authority in this. He was not sure why.

'It concerns you not, mortal.' It replied as if prompted by his thoughts.

'It is agreed then,' they all spoke simultaneously, their voices echoing from within them and booming outwards. 'All interference shall be strictly prohibited across all Houses and we shall observe.'

Tamirok felt himself gently being lowered. As he descended, his House spoke to him directly, 'Tamirok, listen carefully, of this event you shall tell no one, no living thing shall ever know of this.'

He nodded immediately in agreement, no one would ever believe him anyway. He understood the need for discretion.

'Your mind will be closed to the ruling council, your bindings will be changed, you will be changed. Before that change and your return, I have freed your will fully,' it was true for the first time in millennia, he was totally unleashed. 'Tell me your true desire, do you wish to still be Bound?'

He had no hesitation, 'Yes, I cannot function in this,' he waved his hands about, indicating wherever this all was. 'I am a warrior. Men like me deal with straight forward daily facts, I'm a practical person, not a philosopher.'

'Very well,' replied the essence of his House, 'I offer you a choice then. House Bound will no longer have a ruling council, your role will end very soon.' That took him by surprise, so much was changing so damn fast.

'What do you mean?' he asked. 'Are you going to withdraw in slumber?' That would be a catastrophe for the whole of TrueEarth, it would lose its entire military arm and the basis or root of all laws in one fell swoop.

'No, fear not, child, you misunderstand. A ruler has been selected for House Bound.'

'A ruler...' he thought about it, 'we haven't had one in a long time.'

'He will come from Bradley's side,' it continued.

'Surely not! A False human ruling a House,' he objected.

'Bradley will rule House Nothingness, the same will happen for the selected ruler in our case. The choice has been made,' it would take no arguments on the matter.

Tamirok understood.

'Am I allowed to know who it is?' he asked.

'No, but you are allowed to know HE will come from the same side Bradley came. How and when has not been decided yet. He will be born shortly.' Tamirok took the information in but didn't speak.

'Your choice is this: I want you to guide him on his arrival to TrueEarth and be his Wielder for as long as needed until he is ready to rule.'

'Are you saying he will be a Bound instead of a Wielder? That will make things very complicated.'

'He will be both. Tell me, Tamirok child of mine, what is the motto of our House, our Universe?'

'Bind yourself and be free,' his response was almost automatic by now.

'Not the public one, the other one,'

He gasped, he knew what it was referring to, 'All are Bound in some shape, way or form. All Bound to something and someone.'

'Correct, so will the Ruler of the House be,'

'But he's the ruler,' objected Tamirok.

'He, like all members, are bound by the laws and rules of the House, there is no reason for him to be any different to everyone else.'

Tamirok nodded, he agreed fully.

'So, you want me to train him and teach him?' asked Tamirok.

'No, I want you to be the iron will which keeps him on the right path, until his own surfaces. He will come to you already Bound. You will work with his wielder.' Tamirok was surprised. For the ruler of their House to be subject to another's will was unthinkable.

'The other wielder is an absolute, that cannot be changed, but you will enjoy working with him.' It continued. Tamirok did not understand the reference, then quickly decided he did not need to understand it. 'After he has taken rulership, you will withdraw, and only offer guidance,' it explained, 'he is to be trained like Lurizak in the highest arts of war and combat. He needs to prepare for what is coming,'

'Am I allowed to know what that is?' he asked. 'House Nothingness will give you details, our time here is ending.'

'Very well, as you wish,'

'There is one final thing I want you to tell me freely of your own will,'

'Of course, ask away,'

'What are your thoughts of Bradley?'

Tamirok was taken aback. He did not expect this. 'I want to protect him, I want to help him. I think his fate is one of the cruellest I have ever witnessed. I would like to give him my helping hand and steer him to a better future, but most of all, I would like him to have a future. As things stand, he is doomed to oblivion for no other purpose than some forces deciding they all want him and overwhelming him to the point where they are destroying him.'

'That is the point of view we were all lacking, thank you. Do not think that just because you are all mortal and what you call lesser, you are of no meaning or consequence. You give us that perspective and understanding we cannot gain on our own because point of views cannot reach that level of detail yours has. Our view is broader but less specific. We are just as imperfect as you are although in a very different way.'

'I think I understand,' he admitted.

'Very well, this is then what I propose to you, would you be willing to become a vessel for Bradley's power just as Lurizak is?' the question was like a massive blow to him. A shattering of preconceptions, expectations and possibilities. 'Answer truthfully without reference to what is, what could be or what would be. If at this very moment nothing else mattered but this one thing, would you?'

Tamirok felt the answer come from deep within him, it stirred his very being. Hesitantly, he said, 'no, I cannot do what Lurizak has done. I lack his strength and devotion, I am Wielder not Bound,'

'Very well,' it answered, his bindings changed and reconfigured themselves. 'Your choices are made,' gently, he was placed back down, his feet on the solid ground once more.

'Goodbye, Tamirok,' was all he heard.

It took him a while to regain his bearings. His senses were all over the place. Finally, he regained his composure, his metallic skin served all too well to remind him where he was and who he was. Thinking back at what took place, he was unable to recall his armour, it seemed to him his skin was nothing more than ordinary pale human skin.

'That is correct,' the voice made him jump back. He looked and saw it was none other than Nihi in its usual gap in the space form.

'Tell me we are done, I don't think I can handle any more,' he admitted.

'Not quite, ex-ruling member of House Bound.' The reference surprised him a little, he chose not to say anything. 'The threat will arise on the other side of FalseEarth, humans will turn life into not-life, triggering the great catastrophe which will tear creation apart.'

His head started spinning. This was all too much, he sat down on the grass and closed his eyes for a brief moment.

'Alert, alien life form detected, lab 1836. System lockdown initiated,' a mighty voice echoed. Mira decided it was time for her to leave.

What info she managed to get was more than sufficient for her needs. The lockdown was executing, so she had to be fast. It took her only a few seconds. She was back in her shadow-merged form. The image of her own office became full of motion and down the vortex she found herself pulled anew. The trip itself was the same as on her way in, it seemed odd to her that there was no backward motion, it was all forward-facing even though she was moving back to the point where she had come from. She stepped out of the tunnel-like passageway right into her office.

She noticed something odd... she was not tired at all, instead, an energetic buzz made her jumpy on her feet. She booted up her computer and started typing furiously. It took only a short while to have all the stolen information saved. Not allowing a single moment of pause, Mira stood up and rushed to the laboratories downstairs. Fortunately, they were not closed yet, she saw the lead researcher there. She did not even bother remembering his name, instead, she picked up his notebook and started writing, drawing diagrams and outlining molecular structures.

'Update the pathogen with these,' she instructed. He looked at the diagrams and read through her scribbles. He hesitated.

'Ma'am, you do realise that this is...'

She interrupted him, 'get on with it.'

'But this will, we can't...' *Is she insane?* wondered the researcher.

'I'm not asking you what we can and cannot do, I'm telling you. Just do it!' She left him there and returned to her office in due haste. Took her no time, she picked up the phone and dialled the number of the second lab attached to their offices.

'It's me, turn on the 5G networks.'

'Yes, Ma'am,' replied the young female voice at the other end.

'Have you confirmed the increase in viral activity when exposed to wireless radiation?' Mira asked. This was important, a key discovery gained through her spying. The frequency and data spikes travelling through the 5G networks amplified all viral activity. It excited pathogens of all sorts, making them not only aggressive but far more capable of developing dangerous mutations.

'Yes, Ma'am, these higher frequencies are perfect for our purposes,'

'Perfect, the combined pathogenic effects and the interference in the human bio-electric field activity will guarantee our achievement. Make sure the 5G is available everywhere, I need its enhanced data speeds for the nano-component communications,' instructed Mira.

'At this point in time, we're already deploying across many countries — the implementation should speed up rapidly over the course of the next few weeks. Global availability is expected ahead of schedule by several months.'

'Excellent, that will be all for the time being,' she put the phone down.

'Exxxxxcelllllent,' whispered the shadow to her.

'Just the virus left, with those changes in place, it will be ready. One of the most infective agents to ever be known.' She sat down and pondered her next move. She had to ensure that she and only she would be able to keep control of all this. Things were progressing smoothly, the information she had so far gathered proved to be accurate, and more importantly, she had proven herself capable of making use of it in the proper fashion. Nothing would stand in her way, not now, not ever! No interruptions would be tolerated.

'Hey, Tamirok, are you ok?' a hand nudged him on his chest. Instinctively, he grabbed hold of it and sent its owner tumbling on his backside against the hard solid grass-covered earth.

'Hey, what's the big ideas?' he recognised the voice.

'Bradley?'

'Yes, just came to see if you were ok and share the news,' he explained while getting back up on his feet and brushing the dirt off.

Tamirok was alert, 'sorry, didn't realise it was you.' He explained.

'I bet you were dreaming about something big and bad, and thinking it was me decided to take me down as quickly as you could?' Bradley smiled at him in amusement. Tamirok laughed. He shook his head and propped himself back on his feet. 'Did you watch the battle?'

Tamirok nodded, 'only one complaint,' he volunteered his feedback.

'Yes?'

'Stop being over-protective, Lurizak has to get hurt to learn. If you make him overly reliant on your interference, he will get used to it and then be totally lost when he's on his own.'

'Thanks for the tip, just trying to stop me getting him hurt,'

'I know but you seem to be forgetting he is centuries old AND he is an elite warrior of TrueEarth. That's one of the highest ranks of warrior we have other than commanders. Lurizak knows how to defend himself.'

Bradley smiled 'Ok, I will stop overdoing it. It felt really good you know.'

'Unleashing that much power you mean?'

Bradley nodded.

'It might be a good idea to send you to the battlefront every so often, might help us diminish that overwhelming power of yours.'

Lurizak made his entrance and stood behind Bradley. He was much taller so he liked it this way, he could guard Bradley's back and see what was happening ahead. The best solution possible. He placed both hands on Bradley's shoulders. Tamirok stared at them, they were so synchronised that they almost felt the same and were starting to act the same. A sharp pang of jealousy hit, he realised he was losing Lurizak. The change was so intense that he had trouble even recognising Lurizak.

'Did you tell him?' Lurizak asked Bradley.

'No, not yet, I was just listening to a few tips,'

'Oh, do share,'

'Maybe on our next combat training!' Bradley had managed to put all his worries, concerns and troubles to the side and actually enjoy the battle. He felt free, a very odd sensation for a Bound.

They all walked back to the House in silence. Tamirok was conflicted by this, something didn't sit quite right, it seemed like they were standing right at the edge of some massive precipice about to fall straight in. This was happening too fast, way too fast. He knew Bradley would most likely be dead soon, what would happen to Lurizak then? He was bound by his agreement not to interfere, there was nothing he could do even if he wanted to.

21

THE
- FALLOUT -

Fred had just made it out of the gym, he changed his routine to ensure that no one would be there at the same time. 4 am to 5 am was his new working out schedule. It had taken him a few days to adapt to waking up at 3 am each day. Thinking back, he decided that it not only made him feel better to be up early, but it also allowed him to avoid everyone. No interruptions, no questions, it was perfect. He was not in the mood for social interactions. Looking at his arms, his mood gloomed further. *With these, being around people is just not an option.* He brushed it all off. He had quickly realised that these offered him a whole set of advantages, for some unknown reason, they had amplified his strength. The pressure of the ropy chain along his muscle curvature had somehow boosted the explosive power during his workouts. The increase in weight was borderline phenomenal. He was gaining mass beyond his natural capability. All he needed was food, more food, and even more food. Due to his ban from the team and his current touch and go situation with his studies, he had ample time to concentrate on his training. There simply was nothing else for him to do except for train, eat, sleep, study in his room, rinse and repeat. That was his life. He didn't mind the routine, it took all the trouble out of trying to organise things and keep re-organising them each time something came up.

As he walked down to the coffee shop, he instinctively zipped up his training top, making sure his arms and chest were as covered as possible to ensure no one could see anything of interest. He walked in, went to the counter and ordered his double expresso with 3 extra shots of coffee and double the usual dose of sugar. Yes, he knew about sugar. His entire life he had tried to avoid the stuff but now he just could not get enough of it. It made sense. With the constant growth and glycogen stores being depleted, his body craved the raw material it needed to replenish. He recently found out the importance sugar played in terms of brain function, that settled the case. He was active and muscular enough to avoid getting fat from it, so he decided to embrace it. The results were phenomenal, energy levels spiked, his thinking was much clearer and swifter, and for some reason, he was far less edgy and nervous half of the time. The coffee was ready. The young student at the counter smiled at him, 'you know, that's a lot of sugar in there,' her soft brown shoulder-length hair flipped from one side to the other as she flicked her head to get it out of the way. Fred ignored it. 'It's ok, I can deal with it. Thank you for the coffee.' Not even a smile.

Each time he looked at a pretty girl, the crushing realisation of what had happened to him overwhelmed him, instantly killing all interest and raising alarm bells. He went to the furthest seat located in the far corner and there sat halfway in the shadows. It was the ideal spot out of sight of casual observation. Sitting there, he sipped his hot coffee lost in thought.

'If you want to really hide those nerve-cords of yours, you shouldn't wear such tight clothing,' the girl who had just sat at the adjacent table told him. His heart raced in panic. Fred had not noticed her as he hadn't been paying attention. He turned to look at Elma sat there with a caramel coffee, typing away, laptop in front of her.

'I... Errrrm... what?' he was lost for words, not sure how to respond.

'Don't worry, they won't notice,' she waved her hand to motion at everyone else in the coffee shop, 'but I see.' She turned and faced Fred straight. He saw her eyes, reflecting electric blue lights jumping in and out of her eyeball. The irises looked different... unreal. Shapes and digits scrolled rapidly in millions of tiny patterns at speeds he could not even make out. He was surprised and it showed.

'So, you've been had by Bradley too it seems. That guy sure knows how to stir the pot without being directly involved.'

Fred's stupor crumbled, this he would not let pass.

'No, this is not Bradley's fault,' he objected.

'Are you sure? I see half of your... predicament and the other half is unreadable just like he is. He was definitely involved somehow,' she held her ground firmly on this point.

'It is none of your business,' snapped Fred.

'Fair enough, but since you seem to know him well, you're going to do me a favour.'

'Why should I? I don't even know you or what you might be up to,'

'Good point, very good point, but I'll tell you this... I mean Bradley no harm, it is thanks to him I have these... new abilities.' She pointed to her eyes. 'Well, kind of.'

'What's your interest in Bradley? How do you know him?' Fred had a million questions to fire away.

'Let's just say he asked me to look into something for him and I have the data he needs,' she pulled a USB drive out of her laptop and handed it over to Fred. 'I would like you to give it to him for me, tell him it's from Elma,'

Fred took the USB drive, still musing over whether he should do what she asked, 'besides, he's quite handsome, wouldn't you say?' she winked at Fred. Fred was immediately uncomfortable with the situation.

'I never... paid attention to that,' he objected.

She laughed, it seemed very innocent, not for want of trying, he could not detect any malice or hate from her.

'And for your service, my dear friend, I'll share some insights with you since we are both obviously going through the same processes.' She pointed at her eyes. 'Until you stop moping about how you hate your fate and despise what's happening to you, you will get nowhere. Accept it, enjoy it, then the real treasure box of possibilities will unlock. The crystals are shaped according to what is inside of you, what you truly are and need,' she smiled at him.

'You know about the crystals?'

'Of course, how do you think I got my new eyes? Silly boy,' she stood up, folded her laptop, pushed her coffee away, and said, 'see you in TrueEarth, assuming you manage to accept what you truly are not what you think you are. You boys are incorrigible. You're so like Bradley, he's struggling with acceptance too, but in his case, it is killing him. Tada for now,' she walked away.

'Wait!' Fred tried to rush after her but she seemed to have just vanished the moment she stepped out of the door. 'Damn it!' he wanted to know more! *What is going on with Bradley? Is he really dying? I have to find him!*

Mishrak was annoyed, restless and jumpy. No matter how hard he tried to sleep, it proved to be impossible. He got up, got dressed and went to find some food. Wandering through the massive corridors with his shoes clicking and clonking on the metal floor tiles drove him nuts. Everything in House Bound was designed to make noise according to him. He looked at the decorations on the walls, huge weapons, antiques and other battle horrors. He disliked the decor profoundly, found it totally unappealing and in dire need of some sophistication. As he stumbled his way down the corridor, he bumped into Tamirok who was on his way to check on his breakfast.

'Ah, young Mishrak. Lost, are we?' no smile, no friendly gesture, just like the typical living statues all the Bound were, well, according to Mishrak anyway.

'Yes, in dire need of some food, my stomach is about to kill me instantaneously.'

'Surely not,' laughed Tamirok, 'we just can't have that, can we?'

Mishrak was unsure whether he was being made fun of or whether this was a lousy attempt at humour. After all, he was having trouble adapting to a social circle where everyone was no longer trying really hard to accommodate him. 'Follow me,' he instructed. Tamirok led him to the kitchens. Mishrak's breath was taken away. Like everything in this House, the kitchen was vast, enormous, gigantic. No matter how hard he tried, he was unable to see the end of the long space and rows upon rows of long wooden copper-like tables decorated with the glyphs of the House. The extremely tall ceilings gave him vertigo as he gazed up. No hanging lights here, instead, the actual surface material—whatever it was—glowed of its own accord. The heat and scents coming in from the food preparation area made his stomach grumble. A young woman approached them, and without a single word, motioned to the head of an extremely long table. They took their seats, Tamirok sat at the head of the table, which was his usual spot. Mishrak took the seat next to him. He spotted the large elevated platform floating in the central area with a square table all set. It emanated a glow below its platform with semi-transparent glyphs forming a linked chain to the other tables. Power gently pulsed from the platform down and set align all the glyphs on the rows upon rows of dining tables. Tamirok noticed his focused attention there.

'That is the seat of the Ruler of House Bound, it has been empty for thousands of years,' he told Mishrak.

'Why don't you use it?'

'Oh no, we cannot. Only the absolute authority in the House can walk those glyphs without being killed by them. The power that emanates from them is the equivalent of being struck by hundreds of destructor beams simultaneously.'

'You're not serious? Why have such a dangerous thing in here? Anyone could mistakenly make the attempt.'

'I think not, remember everyone here is bound in some way or form, the will of the wielders keep their charges out of trouble, we direct our warriors' thoughts and actions. There is no possibility of one of the Bound making such a foolish mistake,' explained Tamirok.

'What of guests?'

'Guests never get to see this place, food is usually served directly to their quarters or to the meeting areas. The Bound whom you see wandering about here, as well as those of us who are on duty in the cooking areas, have direct orders to kill any non-House member wandering in.'

Mishrak's nervousness was all too apparent to see, he swallowed hard. Tamirok laughed. 'Not to worry, they know you are with me. None will harm you, providing you don't wander off that is!'

'I won't, I won't,' he actually meant it.

'You're concerned, aren't you?' Tamirok knew exactly what the matter was. He had seen it before time and time again with all the newcomers.

'That obvious, hey?'

'I've just learnt to read people well. I'll give you a bit of advice and some insight. Don't worry about it, go with the flow. Besides,

Bradley is not like us, he might have the aptitude and the power, but fundamentally, he's different. When he took over Lurizak, he's proven not only that he could handle it but also that he really cared. There's a protective nature to him that he doesn't let people see. It is there for those who pay close attention. I suspect you two will get up to all sorts of adventures as Bound and wielder.' He sat there and went on eating, not waiting for a response.

'But being bound...' moaned Mishrak.

'Will not be anything but a boon to you, you will learn from it and then, in time, Bradley will move onwards and you will be unbound. When you get to that point, believe you me, you will miss it more than anything you could have imagined.'

'I don't think...'

'Just take it as one of those life experiences and learn from it. Nothing more, nothing less. Look at Lurizak, in the last 24 hours, he's been bound to Bradley and has evolved so much it pains me to watch him,' he finally admitted it not really to Mishrak but to himself.

'Why the sudden change in him?' now curiosity took over from nervousness.

'Because as I've just said, Bradley is not like us. And... even though it pains me to admit, what my eyes see tells me that he is the right wielder for Lurizak, not me. You see, the House always ensures that the right pair match up one way or another. I am certain your own House has ways of coaxing you all into the right path to align with your teachings.'

'Yes, my father always wanted me to follow the Glooms' path but somehow I would always find myself back in the domain of the Grim. He tells me that what part of the Grim I will end up in has yet to be determined, that I need to grow more before that becomes obvious. So, neither he nor Elshevira will teach me anything of Grim sciences until I grow... whatever that means.' His admission sounded like another complaint. Tamirok smiled internally, *yes, this youth needed discipline badly.* He understood why he had found himself in his current predicament. He smiled, a suspicion that this might have all been arranged by House Bound and House GrimGloom essences on purpose. They both sat in front of their meals, slowly eating and contemplating how things have turned out.

Fred made his way down the long corridors, he knew exactly where he was going. Bradley's new labs were accessible directly from his dorm building—a most fortunate coincidence. The access codes were still the same as those he was given. Fred was in. He had to move fast or he would be spotted very rapidly since he stood out too much in his gym gear. Everyone here was dressed in lab coats and he felt like a poor pauper in comparison. Didn't really bother him. He was, by this point, used to people looking down at him, the last couple of weeks had ensured that. There he arrived at the sliding doors. Just as he was about to use the entry code, the doors slid open and Anna walked out. *What the heck is she doing here? In Bradley's office? What on earth?*

'What are you doing here?' he snapped at her, surprising her. She faced him, surprise was also present in her expression.

'And what are you doing here?' she snapped back.

'I asked you first!'

'None of your business,' she snapped back.

'Oh, get lost, get out of my way.'

'No, you have no right being here,' the argument escalated and went on and on. She accused him of being a failure, of being irresponsible, of being hopeless, of being useless. The list went on and on and on. He just stood there watching her, her words just a long stream of sounds wobbling on their way in the air, cascading from one end of him to the other until she said, 'I'm going to report you to security.' Her phone out of her handbag, she started dialling.

He had had just about enough. He grabbed the phone out of her hand and squeezed it in his grip. The force he commanded had escaped his attention and the phone crumbled under the pressure. Bits and pieces of the technology crumbling to the floor, glass snapping as if it was nothing more than a leaf being torn to shreds. He let go, it fell. She looked at him in horror, then looked closer, she saw this was no longer the Fred she had been used to. He was twice the size, something about him scared her. Fear bubbled up to the surface from deep inside of her.

'Useless...' she muttered, her voice trembling with uncertainty. He straightened out, stood tall. His frame towered over her petite body.

'I have just about had enough of all your nonsense, get out of my way. I am here because Bradley invited me. I'm sure you have no valid excuse for being in his office, he never even mentioned knowing of your existence let alone knowing you well enough to invite you over to his workplace.'

She looked at him, her nervousness increasing. In all the time she knew Fred, he had never spoken with any authority whatsoever, he had always been so easy to manipulate, to push about and always believed when she told him he would achieve nothing without her supporting him. This was a different Fred. She was both terrified and immensely attracted to him.

'Fine,' her voice so soft and gentle, almost pleasant to listen to. It triggered a faint memory of the best of times he had with her. Immediately, he willed himself to harden, he would not be played again, ever! He pushed it all out of his head, wanted none of it. From deep within his own mind, he let go of it and offered it all up to be released and lost forever.

'You know, we would have been great together if you had only...'

He immediately interrupted her. His tone totally unemotional and cold, 'we would never have worked out. It wasn't meant to be. It is best this way. I bid you goodbye, no, farewell is better.'

He typed the key code in and the lab doors swooshed open. Ignoring her, he walked in and allowed the doors to close behind him. He pulled the first chair he could see forth and sunk into it, exhausted. Anna started to cry and she fled through the corridors.

Finally, I am free of her, he was relieved. A sadness enveloped him — unfulfilled dreams, hopes of happiness, and the conceptualisation of an ideal future all crushed. *Someone help, for the sake of my own sanity, please someone tell me what to do next. Bradley, where the heck are you?*

Bradley, Lurizak and Elshevira sat in what had now become for all intents and purposes Bradley's room in House Bound, sipping the delicate liquid out of their crystal glasses. Bradley had grown very fond of it. He had asked countless times what exactly it was but all the explanations given made no sense to him. He eventually gave up and just enjoyed it. Lurizak sat there enjoying it silently. He enjoyed what had become a pause in his life. Typically, he was either running from House to House sorting out things or was on the battlefield. This, on the other hand, was a welcome development. He needed the break.

'I think it's time, Bradley. We should start.' Elshevira was determined to at least teach him some of the basics. She pointed to the empty space on the floor. They both went there and sat down, shins on the ground, knees bent and backsides resting comfortably on their heels.

'Bring out your armour,' she instructed.

Bradley concentrated and managed, as usual, to get only his lower body covered in the armour.

'Ok we need to work on that first, you cannot go into combat or do advanced quantum manipulations without it.' She traced a glyph of House Grim on his chest, 'remember, this controls your dark side.' She turned to Lurizak, 'not a word of any of this to anyone else, is that clear?' Lurizak nodded in agreement. Bradley's vision shifted. He saw waves of darkness extending all over him, waves upon waves of cold, soft blackness.

'Raise your hand and grab hold of it,' she instructed.

His mind argued, he could not grab hold of something that wasn't solid, he ignored it and did as instructed. Energy coursed through him. From his hand, it flowed into him. He repeated the process several times. 'Now look at your body,' he did. He saw it, he was radiating a black pulsing power all over. It energised him and, oddly, his vision sharpened. Clarity washed over him. His mind seemed to be able to stretch out further than ever before.

'Stop!' Elshevira cried out. 'Don't stretch out too far or you will lose yourself.'

He pulled back.

'Focus on your body, don't sink into the quantum state.' He struggled to refocus but managed it. 'Good, good. Next, focus on all the dark power you now have in you and let it activate all your armour's glyphs. Think of it as the darkness being fluid and that fluid being fuel for your glyphs.' He did as she instructed. It took him several attempts but he managed it.

As each glyph lit up, from it poured forth the rest of the armour. Before the practice was at an end, he was covered head to toe in his black and red armour. It flared up, power pulsed through his every pore. He felt strong, he felt powerful.

'Don't sink into the sensations! Stay focused on your flesh!' she instructed. 'It's... too... much.' He cried out as the burning power shot through him. Lurizak jumped to his side and kneeled down next to him. 'Grab my arm and make it flow through me, I'll help you dilute it.'

'But, it will... harm you too...'

'Stop arguing, Bradley, just do it!' he didn't want to cause his friend pain. 'Bradley, do it! I can handle it.' Bradley remembered what Tamirok had told him, he grabbed hold of Lurizak's forearm and allowed the power to flow. It seeped out of him and into Lurizak, who cringed and remained silent.

'Lurizak, bind that power and soften its flow, use your own skills to mould it!' instructed Elshevira. He had never thought of doing that, now that she mentioned it, he cursed himself for missing that. He did and the electrons in the power diffused, the nuclei of each particle shifted, reconfigured. His black armour shone as various glyphs lit up one after the other, sending the power flowing from one part of him to another and another. The resulting force was perfectly balanced, regenerative, he moved his hand and gripped Bradley's thigh, sending the resulting power back into him. Bradley smiled. Whatever Lurizak had done caused the power to calm. Its raging force had not quite stilled but it had settled down. The struggle to keep hold of it lessened, it became easier to sense each of the carrier particles, to chain them into a flow, to send them to a target destination. She showed him another glyph along with some script. 'Use that force to write these in the air in front of you. As you do, imagine the outside in front of House Bound, the lawn there.' He did. 'Pour more power into the glyph, keep on doing it until it spills out from it into a circle.' He kept at it. Rather than form a circle, it ended up forming an oval type of shape made out of pure blackness with a reddish outer boundary glow. 'Stop,' she commanded.

'Let's see if it worked. Bradley, step through it.'

'You're joking, right?' objected Lurizak, 'those things can go all sorts of wrong.'

'He'll be fine, I can feel it.'

'Feel? That is what we are going to risk his life for?' While the two were arguing, Bradley simply stood up and jumped into the blackness. Lurizak was taken by surprise, he immediately rushed out, stormed through the corridors and out of the main House door. Relief washed over him as he saw Bradley standing there looking about, trying to make sure he was in a real place.

'I'll have her head! So damn irresponsible,' he was swearing all over the place when he reached Bradley.

'Are you ok? Everything functional?' Bradley smiled, grabbed hold of Lurizak's right forearm and flung the both of them through the black oval shape without warning. Tump, the sound of them crashing over one another as they unceremoniously stumbled back out in the room. Both men took a few moments to disentangle their limbs. Bradley was laughing his head off, this for him was the most amusing thing he had ever experienced. The fact that Lurizak was so upset about it all amused him even more.

'You two are totally insane. Irresponsible and insane, do you hear me?' he snapped.

'Oh, sit down, all is well,' affirmed Elshevira.

'Pure luck!'

'Listen carefully, Bradley, opening these passages through darkness requires you to know exactly where you are going. No doubt whatsoever can be tolerated. The image of your target destination has to be crystal clear or you will end up, at best, in that endless sea of darkness with no way out, or at worst, you will disintegrate into billions upon billions of individual particles never to reform again. Got it?'

'Yes,' replied Bradley, completely serious this time.

'Good, one last thing to do. Picture the glyph which gave rise to the passage gateway over here in its centre.' He nodded that he had it.

'Next, I want you to pull the force back out through that glyph into yourself. Spin it into the armour in whatever way you like. The important thing is for your armour to reabsorb the power. As that power lessens, even the glyph will fade and there will be no trace of anything left there.' He focused his mind, the force flowed back slowly, sweeping its way back inch by inch.

'Pull harder and faster,' she instructed, 'more and more.' It gathered pace, more and more of it flowed back into his armour. It took what seemed to be a long time, but eventually, he had managed it.

'Excellent, well done. That will do for today or we risk giving poor Lurizak here a heart attack.' She smiled at the giant of a man who was back at the table sipping his drink, trying to keep calm. She decided to join him. As she poured more of the liquor into her own glass, she bent over Lurizak's shoulder discreetly, placed her delicate gentle hand on his to stabilise him and whispered in his ear, 'don't be so concerned and rigid, old friend. Look at him, the doom and gloom he was carrying on his shoulders since he arrived here has lifted. For the time being...' with those words, she placed the bottle back on the table and took her seat. Lurizak looked at Bradley very closely as the young scientist sat on the floor pondering over things. She was right, there was a smile, a sense of adventure, a hint of mischief. Bradley's mind was racing. The possibilities of this were amazing, a gateway of darkness to any known location. He was amazed.

'How is this possible?' he asked.

'You are entangling the end location through the quantum field through the glyph using darkness as the entangling force. It's awfully simple,' she was amused and happy.

'Can you travel any distance with this?' he asked.

'Distance, my dear boy, is irrelevant, so is time. The quantum field is timeless and spaceless. The destination and the source location of your gateway is actually exactly the same spot.'

He failed to grasp it, then decided he didn't need to understand it just yet. All he needed to do was be able to use it.

'Remember, you want to also target a specific time when you build the image of your destination, otherwise, you can get time lost.'

'Can I use this to get back home?' he asked.

'That will be tricky, I don't see why not but you will have to figure out how to target the false reality part of the quantum field. You cannot simply imagine the space and time of somewhere back on FalseEarth because it exists in a separate field of reality.'

'How do I target another field of reality then?' he asked.

'That is something I cannot help with purely because I do not know.' Bradley's heart sunk. He needed to understand this separation of fields of reality. This could potentially be his way back home! With that thought, he heaved himself back up on his feet and decided to join his new companions for a drink.

22

- HOUSE mTECH -

The day had finally arrived. Bradley had been anticipating this since his discovery of House mTech. This was a House he could relate to most. His logic was flawless, its focus on scientific enquiry and exploration was exactly what he needed; this was an environment he could feel at home in. The journey was not long, once he was allowed a deeper insight into what the actual scope of capabilities of House Bound was. He stood gasping as he gazed upon the hovercrafts, the quantum propulsion capsules, the dimensional shifting devices, the hyperspace propulsion cubes, and what appeared to him as full-blown crafts. His vision simply failed to take it all in, hundreds upon hundreds of miles of rows of devices and crafts beyond his understanding.

'Impressive, is it not?' joked Lurizak, 'you didn't think that all there was to TrueEarth is what you were initially allowed to see, did you?' he teased.

'I definitely was not expecting this!' replied Bradley 'How? I mean... from where?'

Lurizak smiled, 'our common ancestors were far more advanced than your side of Earth is.' He paused, 'actually, according to our records, you lot have regressed in terms of evolution. But I guess that would have been hidden from you all.'

Bradley was beside himself. He just could not wrap his mind around the sheer possibility of what he saw. He turned 90 degrees and glanced out at the preparations field. There were thousands upon thousands of men, all wearing Bound skins, all pulsing with raw power, all moving in perfect unison, and all responding to the will of their respective Wielders. Some had highly advanced armour types, others had more than armour, some looked like they were wearing ship components. His eyes could not stop darting from side to side. The forces amassed here were beyond massive, the technology was totally inconceivable.

'How far...' structuring the sentence proved to be far too difficult for him. His mind was racing chaotically. Suddenly, he felt his will short-circuit. Tamirok stood behind him, 'Be careful not to lose your grip on your mind, Bradley. We all know what happens when you do.' Reality had set back in.

'It's just...'

'Yes, I can imagine, for you especially, all this must be both a source of endless questions, unaccounted possibilities and terrifying.'

'It's not fear, it's more...'

'That you have been deceived your whole life, thinking you were at the forefront of scientific endeavour and now you have suddenly been faced with the reality that you were, in fact, hundreds, if not thousands of years behind us?' summarised Tamirok.

'Yes, kind of. I just feel as if I've missed so much. I cannot even conceptualise what any of those devices can do, let alone their purposes,' admitted Bradley.

'We have a saying at House Bound, *all things bind us for a reason and only bind for the extent of that reason's life cycle.* Things will be made clear in time, enjoy the discoveries you are about to make,' he instructed, 'and just for your information, Mr Scientist, the skills you have acquired apply here just as they do back there. Those are your keys, not the fields of specialisation you pursue.' He gestured to the large, tall warrior standing guard. The guard nodded in agreement. 'Seeing as this going to be your first experience of our war technologies, we are going to start simple.' He motioned for them to move to an adjacent area. The guard followed them; he opened a massive containment unit and took out three circular devices. One was handed to each of them. Bradley took hold of his; it was a copper-red circle with intricately carved pointers arranged in a pattern of 12, pointing into a hollow central area. Each of the pointers held a gem in its centre—Bradley's was red.

'These are quantum relocation devices,' explained Tamirok. When you use them, your body is broken down into quantum particles. The total sum of all the energy, which includes your essence, is then woven throughout those particles and the whole lot is pulsed along quantum strings to a given entangled location.' He looked at Bradley carefully. 'It is quite an experience, but it does have special pre-conditions as to its use.' He gave Lurizak a quick nod. 'Lurizak will be your guide for this first trip, and if all goes well, probably a few more for you to get used to this mode of transportation. Even the slightest error here could mean you are forever lost as dispersed particles throughout the quantum field. There is no way back that we know of,' he warned. 'This is one of the reasons why we have the entire system of Wielder and Bound. Usually, it is the Wielder who directs these trips, but in this case, I want you to let go of Lurizak's will completely. You are going to have to trust him with your entire being. Allow him to direct all this. You will also understand why these trips could only be executed by male warriors.'

Bradley was not sure he liked the sound of this. It already made him nervous, but he did as instructed and released Lurizak's free will.

'Next, you have to put on that armour of yours and have it cover your entire body,' Tamirok explained. 'You will need to maintain it throughout the entire trip. Do not let it slip, even for one single instant!' his voice was serious and steel-like.

Bradley focused, allowing his mind to relax as he willed his armour forth. It took a long while; it was still a very unfamiliar and unnerving process, the black weaves merging with his skin was downright creepy. He felt it, power unleashed, power burning red hot, power melding with the armour changing the purely black armour into a black and ruby-red pattern. He had to weave additional energy material all over his head, which he thought looked utterly stupid. He decided not to argue about aesthetics in this specific scenario.

'Very well, he's ready.' Tamirok took two large transparent crystals from the guard and pushed them firmly against each of Bradley's hips. 'Absorb and fix them within your armour,' he instructed.

Bradley was unsure how he was supposed to do this. All he could think of was them being sucked into the armour. Instead, the reds flared, and red-electricity oscillated from his waist into the crystals pulling them in. As soon as they made contact, they merged in, reshaped, and formed part of a belt-like waist structure, becoming part of the armour itself.

'Not quite the intended result, but it will do.'

He handed two others to Lurizak, who took them and, by applying slight pressure against his metallic skin at hip level, made them fuse into it. Tamirok already had two of them sitting on each side of his waistline. 'The crystals contain particles that are needed to anchor everything together; they are the drivers and everything else cycles their orbit.'

Naturally, his explanation might have been a totally alien language to Bradley as he could not make sense of any of this. Lurizak took hold of Bradley's disc, placed his on top and, by twisting them, caused them to interlock. 'Hold these, and whatever happens, DO NOT let them go,' he explained. Without warning, he moved behind Bradley and grabbed hold of him, placing each hand over one of the red crystals. Bradley was about to try and shake free. 'Focus, Bradley, no time for messing about. With one hand, hold onto each side of the disc and concentrate on the emptiness within its centre,' Lurizak instructed.

'Destination doors mTech?' he asked Tamirok without turning his gaze.

'Affirmative, proceed' came the commanding response.

Bradley was a little surprised. He had never heard either of them talk in this manner of tone.

Lurizak gazed at the device Bradley held within its centre and he viewed their destination. 'Do NOT let go of it, Bradley, whatever happens.'

Bradley felt it—it was like the tear in space Nihi caused, but this time, sensations of forces gathering emanated from within the device. It took a few seconds; he saw the tiny white star form in its centre, then he saw the indigo-blues of empty space around it. The pulse shook him and cold magnetic forces gathered. They grew stronger and stronger, more and more insistent. The suction had become so powerful that he could have sworn they would be devoured by it. The next moment, a cool sensation of being wet overwhelmed his senses. Immense rays of burning light rocketed forth. Bradley felt as if he was the light — the particles the light gave off were part of him, and all around him, he saw the thicker, stronger rays of shimmering golden copper, enfolding the light he was himself and pushing it in a specific direction. He was completely incapable of anything other than the most basic observation. Logic, reasoning, and deductions were far, far beyond his capabilities at this point in time.

The light slowed and the force of the larger rays pushing him forth diminished ever so slightly. His vision returned, it was no longer a cascade of sensations interpreted as visual data and he was back to actually seeing what was in front of him. What he saw was a blurred image of a large set of structures, sky-high buildings formed out of delicate intermeshing of spiralling metals and huge pointed crystals. Information shone from the displays; he could read these rays of light as if they had been scriptures on the pages of a book! He saw the clear blue skies, the water divided by the long pathway in. He saw trees, nature, life! Bam, all the rays of light seemed to smash into each other, forming a miniature star, a sphere of pure light. He realised that sphere was him and it was being filled by more and more stuff, whatever that stuff might be. Then it stopped. Something was wrong... this was not him, not only him. *What is going on?* His pulse quickened. *Calm down,* Lurizak's voice echoed in his mind. *Focus inwards,* he instructed. It was at that very moment, as his mind turned inwards, that Bradley understood his particles, his energies, his light, all that he was in this bizarre realm was interwoven with Lurizak and all that he was. *What the...* Bradley's mind came reeling back on itself from the realisation.

Relax Bradley, or we will end up stuck this way; I cannot unweave us if you keep tangling us up like this! Lurizak was annoyed, it was hard work to keep trying to still Bradley's overactive mind. He wished he had asked Tamirok to bind it before the trip. *Tell me how,* just do what you practiced with Elshevira. Knowledge flowed instantly; there was no need for thought. Recollection was perfect. Bradley stilled his mind, thinking of the emptiness of creation and the still waters. *Well, well, it seems when your logic grasps things, you do it all too well, and when your emotions interfere with things, you get into a total mess.* He had no time to reply to Lurizak's thoughts as he felt things unwinding. The particles, which his mind told him were not him, pulled away and gathered behind him into a star-like object of its own. A force propelled him firmly into the blurry scenery in the water. An immense power smashed into him — such was its intensity that it knocked his breath out. Bradley landed unceremoniously face down in the grass in front of House mTech.

'What do we have here?' asked the stranger, looking down at Bradley. 'Are you ok?' Bradley made an effort to gather his senses after the trip. The stranger offered a helping hand. Bradley managed to regain control of his body, and accepting the offer of assistance, he heaved himself back up.

'Yes, thank you,' he replied, brushing the dirt off his armour. Naturally, none of it stuck. He was pleased that would be one thing he need not concern himself with. Whatever material it had formed into would simply not allow anything to stick or be absorbed into it.

'Ah, correct me if I am wrong, but you wouldn't happen to be Bradley Boston by any chance?' the stranger seemed to recognise him.

'Why, yes, do I know you?' asked Bradley, a little surprised at the familiarity of the stranger. He stared intently at him, trying to discern if they had ever met in the past. He was lost. He had no memory of this fellow whatsoever.

'My name is Epstein, it's a pleasure to meet you,' he offered his hand once more. Bradley shook it in a warm greeting. 'To answer your question, no we have not met before. Well, not really.'

This confused him. Had they or had they not? Which was it?

'You see, I have been observing and studying FalseEarth's reality and had quite a fascinating time looking into your research and activities over there,' he admitted.

Immediately, Bradley was on the defensive... someone was studying him? For what purpose? How? He wondered. Unfortunately for him, those questions would have to wait, as, at that very moment, he heard the thump followed by a whoosh sound next to him, causing him to turn abruptly. A burr in the space next to him formed and out of it stepped Lurizak. He smiled, which gave off the oddest of impressions as his entire face was covered by his own metallic skin armour. Bradley was simply unable to decide whether that was the creepiest, most horrific thing to observe or something outright peculiar beyond his reason. He had little time to ponder which one it was, as a strong heavy hand made an impact with his left shoulder.

'Well, well, you made the trip and in one piece! Impressively done, my friend!' Lurizak congratulated Bradley.

The banter was cut short by another blurring on their left side and out of it stepped Tamirok. He was completely unaffected and reacted simply as if the entire trip had been nothing more than a step through space he took as casually as walking through a doorway. Bradley observed the stern warrior's face. No, not even a hint of even slight discomfort. Then he looked back at Lurizak, who, on the other hand, was totally jovial, smiling and laughing as he took off his helm.

'Good afternoon, General,' Epstein greeted Tamirok with the utmost respect.

Tamirok nodded in response and turned to Bradley, 'Aren't you forgetting something?' His typical harsh voice boomed out.

Bradley looked around and then remembered. He concentrated and willed his face to free itself of his own armour. It simply slid away and re-merged with the rest of it, revealing Bradley's entire head. He looked back at Tamirok, who still held that fixed glance at him, not even seeming to breathe. *That must not be it... damn, what am I forgetting?* He could not remember and he was just about to ask when... *rebind his will,* the unknown voice echoed back in his mind. It had been a while since that had happened. Bradley immediately responded, resealing Lurizak's bindings. *Leaving a Bound such as that with total free will is extremely dangerous—one of the reasons why Tamirok joined you both on this trip. I would not reveal this to them, it is best they do not know that you know.*

For the first time, the voice seemed to be slightly chattier. Bradley wanted to ask it a million questions, he wanted to know whose voice it was, but it was gone. His environment pulled back his attention and he stood there with all three men staring at him. It made him feel as if he was under interrogation. Had he done something wrong? Surely not, he hadn't done anything. He looked sideways, trying to interrupt their piercing gaze. It was at that moment he saw the device he had used to travel here. Without warning, he stepped forward and picked it up. It felt cold, very cold, so cold it was almost painful to the touch, even with his armour protecting his hands. Somehow, he knew exactly what to do as he had observed Lurizak doing this in the inverse procedure. He unlocked the two devices from each other with a simple counter-clockwise motion of the bottom disc, his own, and a clockwise one with Lurizak's. Once they were separated, he handed him his.

'Are those...' Epstein was looking intently at the devices, his mind almost totally absorbed in their analysis... 'the quantum propulsion relocators?' His eyes did not move from the discs. 'Who are you?' his gaze went from Bradley's disc to his face and back to the disc. 'Just who exactly are you?' he asked. Bradley shrugged his shoulders in confusion. 'Only the Rulers can use those relics of our ancient forefathers. How are you...' He looked totally bemused. So was Bradley. He could not figure out what this stranger in a perfectly attired white-coat was talking about. Tamirok had given him the device, and surely, they all used those. He shifted his questioning gaze to Tamirok.

'There will be time for those answers later,' his firm response rapidly brought everyone back to the immediate matter at hand. He pulled off his own helm and stepped forward. 'We are expected,' he stated.

Epstein nodded, 'please, follow me.'

He led them into the central tall blue glass building ahead of them. Bradley was taking the scenery in. To him, this did not resemble a House; it was more akin to an intricate set of interwoven cities!

'Welcome to House mTech, gentlemen,' a crystalline voice greeted them. 'How may I guide your path?' it offered.

Bradley looked about and held his breath in surprise. The delicate balance of metal and glass — or possibly metal and crystal — was prevalent everywhere. Yet unlike the technology he was familiar with, this had an almost perfect aesthetic to it. It was impossible to feel ill at ease in this place. Everything was smooth surfaced, everywhere crystalline polished, reflective surfaces wove electric sparks within them in what looked like very specific patterns or direction. He was beside himself with curiosity.

'Focus, Bradley, we are not here for sight-seeing,' Tamirok reprimanded him.

Lurizak whispered, 'It is considered impolite to stare too intently upon House constructs, especially in a way that could imply you were trying to understand the secrets by which they were constructed.'

Bradley pulled back immediately. This was going to be hard. Here, he would have to exercise an unnatural level of restraint when it came to everything. His curiosity screamed out at him. He wanted to know, oh how he wanted to know — all that knowledge right in front of him and yet so out of reach. It was very much like an intolerable itch you simply could not scratch.

'Epstein mTech escorting guest to conference room,' he seemed to talk into thin air.

Bradley could not see anyone there. Who was he talking to? Within a single instant, the blue electric current coalesced under their feet, forming a small wave pulsing forward.

'Acknowledged, conference room 1Ab prepared, security and privacy protocols for diplomatic meeting enabled. Proceed.'

The sensation was similar to the gentle push of a wind blowing you forward. It was constricted at his feet. The impulse to move along with this blue power was unmistakable, *a magnetic force?* he mused. Much to his surprise, no one seemed to even take note of all this and they started moving. There was no need for directions to be given or a warning of obstacles to avoid, the blue power pushed and pulled whenever needed. Bradley also noticed that they were walking at a more pressing pace than usual, but he seemed to be spending much less physical effort in doing so. To him, it was like taking a slow walk down the beachside on a weekend with... Kuroi. A memory flashed in his mind—he was remembering. Pain shot within his skull. Tamirok reacted instantly, signalling Lurizak, who grabbed hold of Bradley's right arm.

'Bradley, focus on me.' He applied more pressure to his grip.

Bradley blinked and looked straight at him, 'Lurizak?'

'Ah, good, you're back. For a moment, you had started to flip.'

'Is he unwell?' asked Epstein.

'It will pass, the shifting back is always a threat,' explained Tamirok.

'Yes, it would be for someone walking the two sides,' agreed Epstein. 'You seem to have managed it well,' he concluded, hinting that he meant more than he was saying. 'But that will not last for long,' he concluded. Epstein was all too familiar with the shifting from TrueEarth to FalseEarth. It was his field of expertise to study both the phenomenon and the other side of the Earth. A pet obsession as he liked to call it.

They arrived at their destination, the large translucid doors etched with digital blue glyphs were flung open as if by a will of their own. They walked into a very spacious room adorned by large glass displays. Within its very centre was a long glass table with a row of the same letters and glyphs running along the edges. All the materials used seemed totally alien to Bradley. He simply could not make out what was what. The chairs, however, were sensationally comfortable; they seemed to be adjusted for perfect posture and comfort, most likely designed for long-term sitting without suffering from any muscle or back problems. It was an utter delight sitting in one.

'Here, have a drink,' Epstein offered, 'it is water from the top river.'

Whatever this top river was, Bradley took the glass and cautiously sipped away at the water. Very much like the rest of the food and drink here in TrueEarth, this water seemed to totally revitalise him. It was as if each and every cell in his body was washed clean and rehydrated with new and added vigour. It always amazed him how pure it was.

'We never made a mess of our environment on this side,' explained Epstein, 'instead, we used it to our advantage and, in return, Father Nature offers us his bounty.'

'Father Nature?' prompted Bradley.

'Yes,' was all he got out of Epstein.

It was most peculiar to Bradley for a scientist to have such reverence to nature.

'We never fell to the illusion that we were above nature or that we could second guess it by altering it to our own needs. That is the grand flaw, which will wipe all those on your side out,' he paused, 'eventually.' He moved to the large screen hanging in front of the conference table. 'Let's see how you are doing, shall we?' Without waiting for a response, he started motioning on the glass, making contact with the same lettering as was found etched on the edges of the conference table, moving the resulting diagrams and widgets about. 'Ah, there we go.'

After a while, he started speaking. 'Your molecular structure is still flooded with toxins and nanotech from your side,' he paused again. 'You will have to purge those out.' He started swearing, 'stupid humans, thinking they can interfere with all these biological processes without dire consequences and then we have you lot calling that science. Seriously, how dumb can you all be over on that side?'

Bradley was about to counter-argue the accusation, but Lurizak grabbed hold of his forearm and shook his head. He fell silent, still on the verge of exploding in confrontation.

'Ah, excessive stimulation of emotional responses, unnatural,' he went on. 'Wait a sec, what is this?' He pulled out one of the widgets and they all saw it expand along the large glass display. 'You don't belong in House Bound...' he objected. Tamirok's left eyebrow shot up in alarm. 'The quantum power profile is nothing like I've ever seen or heard of before, strange matter? How...' he zoomed in more and more, 'strange quarks!' he gasped.

Bradley saw it, rays of perfectly aligned particles, forming a moving set of lines, some black and deep as night, some white, some red, some golden, and then there was this massive wave of what looked like something so deep and black that it absorbed all the others and flung them into a chaotic pattern back outwards.

Epstein stared at Bradley in shock. 'I need to analyse this, immediately,' he motioned on another part of the screen. 'Prepare the containment field for new sample host,' he commanded.

'Initiating,' replied the same crystalline voice.

Both Tamirok and Lurizak reacted instantly. However, they were both too slow, even at their incredible speed.

The crystalline glass panels dropped from above, encasing Bradley. Odd-looking shimmering blue digits and complex glyphs etched on their surfaces activated. A final panel from below pushed up and sealed the rectangular-shaped boxed. Bradley was contained.

Act fast! The voice within spoke.

Bradley focused harder than he had ever done in his entire life — his mind stretched out, reached out, every nerve in his body awoke into immediate overdrive. His armour instantly formed all over his entire body. A calm washed over him, his vision blurred and he found himself floating in endless blackness. This was not like the darkness Elshevira had shown him. No, this was something entirely different. He pulled on it, his armour pulled on it, every fibre of his being pulled on it, more and more into himself.

Lurizak was trying to smash into the containment field, but no matter his force, it did not even scratch its surface. He turned to Epstein, propelling himself off his feet and activating the forces held within his own skin-armour, he seemed to fly straight at him. Before the scientist could react, he was face down on the floor with Lurizak's massive knee pressing against his throat. 'Let him out!' he yelled.

'Can't... containment ... unbreachable,' in between each word, Epstein struggled to catch his breath. Something was happening inside the containment area, darkness was gathering, or so it seemed. It thickened rapidly, more and more of Bradley and the space within it was being obscured. Tamirok stood by it, trying to find a way to unseal it.

'What's going on in there?'

'I... can't...' Epstein could not move his head to see.

'Let him go, Lurizak,' commanded Tamirok.

'No,' for the first time ever, Lurizak refused.

Tamirok's eyes bulged as he looked at him in utter disbelief. The old warrior got over it fast, it was the first time he had to, but he was more than capable of using reason if need be. 'Let him go, we need him to get Bradley out.'

Lurizak looked at him, then back at Epstein. He got off the scientist and, with one hand, dragged him up by the neckline as if he was lifting some lost puppy and smashed his face against the glass surface of the containment. 'Get him out!' he ordered.

'I can't! These are made to be unbreachable by any force known to us.'

'What's going on in there?' Tamirok asked again, he was not in the habit of repeating himself, so it irritated him profoundly.

'I... don't know,' admitted Epstein, 'nothing is supposed to work in there, the seals deactivate all quantum manipulations.'

The blackness in the containment blocked out the view. Bradley was devoured by it, not a hint of him there anymore.

Time, space, reality, depth, dimension and motion, whispered the voice inside Bradley's head. His mind did what it usually did when he was at work... it started calculations, thinking about possibilities, mapping problems out and investigating potential solutions all at the same time. *That's it, use your natural abilities. Where are you? Who are you? What are you? What's your location? What are you doing?* It kept on prompting him to ponder on all those things. *Life flows in certain directions, mass limits range of probabilities, energy propels actions, atomic configurations dictate functions,* more and more, nudging him forward in his thinking. Bradley had no problem managing the hundreds of trains of thoughts; this is what he had done since his childhood, this is why he was so agile with his intellect, *space, locality, limitation of the scope of possibilities, take them in, compute them all out, intuit intellectually, push forward, it instructed. Time, energy spent to move through time, limitation of organism's energetic capacity, natural barriers, think! Entropy linked to time, linked to energy. THINK! Understand.*

He was on the edge of it and, suddenly, those separate trains of thoughts started to collapse back into each other. They were all connected. Yes, it was making sense now. 'Time and space are coordinates established within boundaries of potential matter, contained by limitation of energy. Moving through time and space requires kinetic force, time is the key and space is the background. Moving through time uses the kinetic power, it lessens until entropy,' he said out loud to the emptiness in which he found himself.

Keep going! it instructed.

'Given energy state within a space coordinate results in the time equation being solved, giving time and space coordinates, frequency and amplitude of kinetic energy spent give dimensionality and reality,' Bradley concluded.

Keep going!

'Hence remapping exact energetic state at any given point in space will take me to the exact desired time and space,' concluded Bradley.

Yes!

'Given state of matter will result in energy potential and quantity, determining dimensionality,' he had it.

Memory locked in time is reality was the final instruction before the voice went silent.

Bradley thought about it. Elshevira had told him that the darkness gateway was opened only when one recalled the space into which it needed to open. But he immediately recognised he was not in the same darkness — this was dark but different. The thought struck him, what if this was the same stuff Nihi was made out of? This mysterious nothing? That meant he was nowhere, which logically meant he could be anywhere and in anytime. 'Yes! That's it!' he had finally grasped the full implication of what he had been prompted to work out. If he was nowhere and in anytime, all he had to do was use a memory, replicate the energetic potential of his kinetic force, and the space he was in to get a direct pinpoint of where he needed to be. His armour would help him pull on whatever this darkness was to open a gateway as he had previously done in House Bound. He would, however, need to return to before the glass panels had locked him in.

He focused. Recalling his exact location was easy, but the rest was not so simple. He tried to remember how he felt, what he was doing, but that produced no results. *How do I recall the state of kinetic potential?* Then his mind went racing once more. What was the kinetic force? What is the potential of that force? Where is it stored? How does it come about? The sense of endless time passing overwhelmed him. He finally had a theory; what if this kinetic potential is the result of the sum of activity of each and every atom in his body? Still, how would he replicate that? An entire row of previously hidden glyphs and words lit up along the outer part of his arms — from his shoulder through to his elbow and down to his hand. Golden power pulsed through them. He realised he was overthinking things. He didn't need to know it—his body knew it! He focused on his armour, allowing the power to be pulled in from all around him. This Nothingness was somehow malleable to him, his armour and his mind. More and more of it accumulated, it thickened and the cold intensified. He had to work hard but somehow managed to project it into a type of oval shape, seeing it in the place and in the time he wanted it. The armour pulled more of it into itself and he allowed himself to sink into the sensations and sense of presence in his body at the time.

A moment later, he flung all those sensory inputs into the ovoid pool of condensing nothing. Something cracked and a loud tear ripped through the endless emptiness he was in. As it ripped forth, the ovoid gateway ripped into the meeting room in House mTech. The sound of the tear at their end was so intense that everyone in there covered their ears in agony. Bradley was pulled through the tear, flopping back just as the glass containment field that encased him filled completely with the darkness, as he disappeared from sight in there. He appeared at the back end of the room, waiting, watching. He saw all that happened and anger rose from deep within him. From anger, he felt a pulse of fury and the fury amplified into rage.

As Lurizak released Epstein, Bradley jumped into action, eyes blazing in red power, armour fully activated, strange new glyphs none of them had ever seen etched into it and glowing in blazing angry reds, seething with pure destructive force.

'I'm going to rip you and your damned House into sub-atomic particles!'

All the men turned, surprised to see him.

Epstein yelled out, 'how did you...' just before Bradley crashed against him with such force that it sent him flying across the room. He howled in pain as his body made an impact with the large display — a crack formed along its entire length.

'House mTech alert, attack from within, security alert!' boomed the crystalline voice of the system running the House.

Epstein slid back down, and in desperation, he attempted to activate something. Bradley froze, his body straightened and his posture changed to one of total stillness. Lurizak rushed to his side.

'You stay out of this,' commanded Bradley in a voice echoing from endless space—cold and emotionless.

Lurizak was pushed back against the back wall unharmed. Tamirok knew the rage had grown into something far more dangerous and they were all in danger now. He tried to use his will to lock him down.

329

Bradley turned to face him, looking straight into his eyes. His left eyebrow shot upwards and a burst of the same blackness he had been in just a few moments before burst out of him, shattering the nerve chains around his neck. Tamirok heaved in pain, perspiration running down his face. Shock registered on him and he stared at Bradley in utter disbelief.

'Who are you?' he finally managed to ask.

Bradley ignored the question and turned back to face Epstein. The House was activating its own defences. Bradley felt each atom, each molecule, each impulse of energy, each outpouring of power. He knew them all. His rage had elevated his mind to entirely new levels. He was no longer Bradley, he was something else altogether. His arms rose high over his head, swirling waves of Nothingness cascaded all over his body, his armour changed and the red was gone, replaced with pure gold. This one change seemed to utterly horrify everyone. The waves of Nothingness amplified, pulsing outwards in cascades with black lightning crackling in their wake. Each thing they made contact with was instantly unmade and what survived was ripped to atoms by the black lightning.

Bradley's power was disintegrating the whole of House mTech. Blue crystal columns crashed all around them. The central tower shook as if hit by multiple simultaneous earthquakes with them at their epicentre and Bradley's power amplified, becoming more destructive, more effective and more terrifying. Total mayhem was unravelling in every part of the House, yet Bradley heard none of it. He simply stood there and allowed his body, his armour, his very soul to be a gateway through which the Nothingness amplified by the Ancient Dark poured into existence, wiping everything it touched out.

Lurizak yelled out to him, 'Bradley, please, stop!'

It was useless, Bradley no longer heard or even noticed him. He had become the power — he was the universal force. Suddenly, out of the resulting blackness, Elshevira surfaced.

'Good, it worked.' She wasted no time, and as swift as a whisper of the wind, she dodged all the obstacles and flung her arms around Bradley's neck, heaving herself over him, locking him in her embrace. She whispered in his left ear, 'Bradley, dear, you have to stop now. You have done enough.' The outburst of Nothingness seemed to hesitate. He faced her directly and looked her straight in her eyes. She saw a terrifying vastness in him and jumped backwards. 'This is not Bradley anymore.'

'We know,' interjected Tamirok, 'at least you have slowed him down, anyone have any suggestions?'

Heather was on her way to Kiandra's office. She was sick and tired of all the foolishness going on in the labs since that woman had arrived somehow into the hierarchy. She was also determined that under no circumstance would she allow this newcomer to unsettle the dynamics they had at play. In her mind, things ran perfectly well before her arrival. As usual, she didn't bother knocking and just stormed in. Fortunately for her, Kiandra was just shutting down her computer and was about to leave for a meeting.

'Ah, Heather, sorry, I do not have the time to talk with you right now, I suggest you send me an email and make an appointment.'

'I will, but before I do so, I want to know if this is some silly joke or genuine?'

'What is? I will need a little more information first.' Kiandra was ready to snap at Heather. For some reason, that self-righteous young nobody, as she thought of Heather, irritated her no end.

'This nonsense about me having to take time off in the middle of the crisis, seriously? It makes absolutely no sense whatsoever.'

'Yes, it's genuine. Why such commotion? Bradley is taking time off, so why should the rest of the staff not use their legally assigned holidays before the end of the year?'

'For goodness sake, Bradley is going to the funeral of his wife and child — he's not going to some beach to catch the sun!'

'I'm deducting it off his holidays to make the days count. Besides, like the rest of you, time off is essential for your wellbeing. You have to take regular breaks to be in good health.'

'During a crisis? Seriously?'

'My mind is set, and I need to get those days all down to 0 for all the staff, we have no choice in the matter whatsoever.'

'We do. We have always opted not to use those days in times of emergencies and even let them expire.'

'Ah yes, an old policy of your grandfather. A very bad decision, if

331

you ask me, but that has changed now. I will make sure all my staff are healthy and relaxed, crisis or not.'

Heather was starting to lose her nerve. Logic and reason obviously had no place in Kiandra's mind, let alone the fact that she had just insulted her grandfather, who had not only built this lab and team from scratch but had put his entire livelihood on the line to do so. She was furious.

'You do realise that putting all the research staff out of action for 4 weeks will cause this virus to go completely unchecked and set us back for goodness knows how long? Lives are at risk here.'

'Nonsense, it will all be fine. You are no use to us tired and unfocused. Now, if you will excuse me, I have a meeting in town to attend.'

Kiandra simply walked out, leaving Heather there looking at empty space. Heather refused to let her emotions take over... well, in sight of anyone at least. She calmly walked out of the office and headed for the exit of the labs. She knew it would take Kiandra just about 10 minutes to get to her car and out of the car park, so she headed back to the coffee shop, walking at a rapid pace. After ordering the simplest and fastest type of coffee she could get, she found a quiet secluded spot and sat down. Her anger ran hot and she sipped her coffee, burning her tongue and swearing at how hot it was. She focused on the crystals — the beautiful set of emeralds that adorned her neck. Power flared up and her eyes filled with green energy, giving them a highly reflective, almost shimmering green glow. She had spent her two days off sick working on figuring out how to use them. She was getting the hang of it, at least the basics. What she was about to do was something entirely new. Everything blurred, and she was once more standing in that mysterious place where the countless threads were. Anger raged within her and green power radiated out of her in violent bursts.

If that piece of trash thinks she is going to have the final say, she has a surprise coming. Insulting me, insulting Grandpa, making a mockery of everyone. The greens darkened in colour and became more menacing. She reached out, thinking of Kiandra. The thread came to her instantly. Before, it had taken her an immense effort to do it at command, but not this time. This time, she was fuelled by fury. She allowed her mind to sink into it and flow backwards. There, she saw Mira and Kiandra; Heather saw how they had planned all this. She saw what they'd planned. Her emotions exploded... her cold, hard logic had just found the answer it was looking for. Heather had her justification. Power raged from within her. Any onlooker would have heard the roar of a beast howling through the otherwise empty silent space. She pulled out of the thread, her grip tightening on it. She concentrated on her hands, allowing all her anger to seep into them. They were the expression of her pain, her frustration and fury. Strength flooded her, ravaging her reason. She pulled with all she had and when that was not enough, she kept re-running all that she had witnessed and heard in her mind, amplifying her fury. It exploded forth, like a devastating force of a star about to supernova. She ripped the thread of fate asunder. She heard something tearing in the space around her but paid it no attention — her fury had shielded her from everything else. Nothing other than destroying this particular thread mattered. As she held the two strands, one in each hand, she knew.

'Your power, your future, your success will all be mine!' She pulled on all the positives from within those threads and green light oozed out of them like a life liquid. It seeped away faster and faster and swirled around Heather until finally sinking into the emeralds she wore. The thread went totally dark, then its individual strands unravelled, separated into atoms, and finally dissipated into space. Heather's anger faded. Her power waned. She found herself back in the coffee shop.

The serving girl came up to her, 'Would you like anything else, miss? I will be closing the till for a few minutes during our shift swap.'

'No, thank you, so kind of you for asking,' she smiled at the girl.

What have I done? She asked herself. The realisation that she had no idea of the impact of her actions suddenly dawned on her.

The air tore asunder; the ripping sound was almost deafening. Behind Bradley stood Nihi, this time, almost five times its usual size. Epstein was on the floor unconscious, Lurizak at the back of the room, trying not to step into the gap left there by the Nothingness. Tamirok was desperately avoiding the onslaught of power and Elshevira danced from spot to spot, dodging the obstacles.

'No... harm... to... Ruler...' came the endlessly echoing eerie voice from Nihi as the power from Bradley intensified anew. Nihi moved towards Bradley, seeming to become folded at what would have been its midsection, then grew back to its usual size and moved to stand behind him on his left side.

'Do something, damn it! You can stop this,' Tamirok yelled at Nihi. It stood motionless, 'Damn it! You know what is going on, do something, anything.' The Nothingness, which was Nihi, seemed to shimmer for an instant then spoke.

'This is Ruler of House Nothingness, interference not possible. Memories resurfacing.'

'By the Houses,' swore Tamirok.

Entire crystal buildings could be heard outside, cracking and smashing into pieces as they tumbled out of the sky. Explosions were going off left, right and centre. An intense ray of electric blue light beamed its way through what was the door to the conference room. Hundreds of digits coalesced around the tall man who had walked in. He looked as if he was in his late 20s/early 30s, perfectly smooth-shaven short black hair, pale skin and deep blue eyes. He was slim but perfectly groomed, wearing a headband of the same crystal-like substance etched with the same type of letters and glyphs as the rest of House mTech. On his wrists, he wore thin bands of the same style. His long white and royal blue scientific coat was embroiled with golden threads, glistening with each motion. Unconcerned with the destruction or the debris, he walked straight to Bradley and fell to one knee.

'From Ruler to Ruler, I offer my deepest apologies for the inexcusable breach of inter-House protocols.' He paused and looked straight at Bradley, 'no harm will come to you or yours as long as you are in House mTech, you have my word.'

Bradley stared at him with unnerving intensity, neither men flinched. The Nothingness seemed to shift for an instant. The onslaught froze in its tracks and the bursts of Nothingness ceased. 'Agreed,' came the endlessly echoing voice out of Bradley's lips. All the powers folded back in on themselves and were gone.

The Ruler of mTech turned to face Epstein, who had regained consciousness. 'Get up, you fool. Sit over there and remain silent,' he instructed, the displeasure in his tone was very noticeable. He faced Bradley and Tamirok once more with a slight bow. 'Welcome to House mTech, I must apologise for that fool over there. No harm will come to you in our midst.' He pulled out his left arm and looked at the device he was wearing. 'Cancel containment orders and reinitiate repair of structures immediately,' he instructed.

'Confirmed,' replied the crystalline voice.

Bradley seemed to stir from whatever had come over him. He watched in amazement as the glass screen seemed to regrow itself right in front of his very eyes, the blue electric sparks danced both upon its surface and within its structure. In a few moments, the whole of House mTech started healing itself. Things were returning to normal. Elshevira took the opportunity to sit back down at the table as it reformed. New drinks were being served and she gladly sipped on the refreshing water, anything to calm her after all this madness was more than welcome. Bradley suddenly noticed Lurizak still standing out of the way. Unsure why, he motioned to him. They were all sitting down, once more waiting for the rest of the conference room to finish its healing repairs. This time, Galvin was among them.

'Let me introduce myself. I am Galvin, Ruler of House mTech,' he offered his hand in greeting.

Bradley reciprocated, 'I am Bradley,' he replied.

Galvin decided that the best course of action was to simply ignore all that had happened and proceed normally. His mind was highly practical — he saw no need to linger on what was now the past.

'Ah, General, always a pleasure to meet an acting Ruler of House Bound, I was expecting you, although you did seem to surprise me at just how fast you arrived,' he admitted.

'It seems we had a few more complications than I'd anticipated,' Tamirok's remark did not go unnoticed.

'How was your trip over? Went smoothly, I trust?'

'Relatively painless, much smoother than I would have thought possible,' replied Tamirok. Galvin was relieved that the General had caught onto his tactic and was following through. It saved many hours of potential complications.

'Well, well, that is most interesting. I take it you opted to try it out?'

'Indeed.'

'How fascinating,' Bradley could not make out head or tail of their exchange.

Galvin moved to face Epstein, 'what on earth caused you to act that way? Explain yourself.' It was not a question, it was a demand.

'We got here and I ran a power analysis... it showed...' he never had the opportunity to reply.

Galvin was furious, 'what on earth gave you permission to run a power analysis!? This is against diplomatic House protocols, you fool!'

Epstein was not going down in this argument without a battle. 'I only ran it on Bradley, not the envoys of House Bound.'

'I couldn't think of a worse candidate to breach protocols on, could you?' Galvin yet again reprimanded him.

'I'm... confused,' he admitted.

'Let me guess. As usual, you didn't read the report, which detailed WHO you were escorting, did you? Left the reading to the last minute and then had no time to actually do it? Just because it is nothing to do with the FalseEarth phenomenon? Your pet obsession will be the end of you, Epstein.' He was fuming, his jaw tensed, the veins on the sides of his neck seemed to pop out as they pulsed with blood. 'I will tell you what you missed, you fool. YOU are standing in the presence of the Ruler of House Nothingness himself,' he extended his arm to point at Bradley.

Epstein was shaken to the core, shock horror and disbelief showed plainly for all to see. 'Impossible...' he shuddered, 'House Nothingness!?...' his entire body shuddered, 'it's... legend... not real...' he objected.

'I guess you might want to say that to the crumbling House, which is still in the process of repairing itself, AND to that,' he pointed to Nihi, who stood vigilant behind Bradley, 'which was one of its emissaries you forced out in the open earlier on. House mTech was nearly swallowed into Nothingness within just a few instants because of your ineptitude.'

'House... Nothing... nessss...' Epstein was just mumbling.

Galvin threw both arms up in the air. 'Hopeless.' He turned to face his guests, 'please, gentlemen, let us start anew.' He turned to Bradley, 'once again, please forgive House mTech for this unwelcoming first impression, it will NOT happen again.'

Bradley just nodded.

'I'm not going to make any apologies for him,' Galvin said, pointing at Epstein, 'inter-House laws demand such breach of protocols are punished severely. If House Nothingness deems it fitting, I would only ask you leave this matter to House mTech to deal with.' His expression was clear to Bradley, he was almost politely pleading with him not to take it any further. He was just about to reply when the space tore once more behind him, and the vacuum which was Nihi came forth.

'House Nothingness will allow it, but it will require a favour to be returned at some point in a time of the House's choosing,' its echoing voice trailed off.

Galvin was the one surprised. He had never anticipated Nihi would just pop out at any point; he had assumed that it would only intervene in times where Bradley's life was in danger. He thought about it for a few moments and nodded in agreement. 'Your terms are acceptable,' and with those words, Nihi was gone.

'What a peculiar thing,' he commented, looking straight at Bradley and then at Tamirok. He read people very well as would any Ruler and it took only a quick glance to see that Bradley did not know anything else on the matter. That same quick look told him that Tamirok knew more... a lot more. He would have to drop the right questions in the conversation when it takes place. That would force the revelation of the secrets he sought.

'A human from that side, House Ruler... impossible...' mumbled Epstein from the edge of the table. 'Get over it, Epstein, you have seen more than sufficient evidence of House Nothingness for yourself.'

'How...' he mumbled.

'Why is this so hard for you to grasp? The defunct Houses were not as defunct as we thought them to be, that is all. My guess is that they were dormant or inactive until their time returned.' He glared straight at Tamirok, questioning without asking the actual question.

'That is the conclusion of House Bound,' affirmed Tamirok. He knew Galvin was playing it subtle. He also knew that if he didn't volunteer some information to at least appease his scientific curiosity, he would be facing the unyielding reality of having to answer an actual question.

'But... but... Nothingness,' mumbled away Epstein.

'Yes, that is a major dilemma for us all. A House even we know nothing about,' Bradley giggled, breaking the mood. They all immediately looked at him, 'well, it does make a kind of ironic sense, does it not?'

'You do have a point, I must admit,' Galvin himself allowed a smile to escape his composure. 'Very well, let us proceed with the matters at hand. Acting-Ruler Tamirok, as per your House's request, the new devices are prepared and ready for testing. How does House Bound wish to proceed?' he asked.

'Start testing at the battlefield, we need to verify compatibility with the Bound warriors.'

'Agreed, do we have permission for direct transportation into House Bound space?'

'Agreed, but only within battle test fields,' confirmed Tamirok.

'Very well,' he turned to the device on his wrist. 'Ruler mTech instruction,' he spoke.

'Initiate high-level protocol request,' replied the crystalline voice.

'Space folding transportation allowed to test battlefield coordinates at House Bound, initiate immediately,' Tamirok instructed.

'Confirmed,' replied the House.

'It should be there within a moment or two, I have also prepared our test field personnel to join the expedition. They will be able to assist the warriors with the initial setup and information transfers.'

'Thank you, that will prove most useful,' confirmed Tamirok.

'After this meeting, there are a few novel toys I would like to show you,' offered Galvin. They both knew exactly what this meant. Yes, seeing the new battle devices they were working on was always good, but this would be mostly a smokescreen for Galvin's real goal: information gathering.

Tamirok smiled, 'of course, old friend.' He knew this would disarm Galvin. Reminding him of their friendship had a very effective result of tampering just how far Galvin would push with his information gathering. He turned to face Bradley, 'I assume you have quite a few questions. We cannot deal with all of them in one sitting, but let us make a start, shall we?'

'It would be much appreciated,' replied Bradley, 'so much of this is all very confusing.'

'I am certain it is. I would venture as far as to say that, from your perspective, this is like being in a totally alien world rather than on Earth itself?'

'Almost,' admitted Bradley. 'It seems like I have been thrust into a whole different reality with entirely different rules, yet with a familiar setting. I am not even sure why it feels familiar, but it does. I don't even know how I got here.'

'That would be Epstein's field of speciality, one of the reasons I had sent him. Since it is taking him a bit of time to readjust his misconceptions, I will volunteer to answer as much of this as I can.' He sat down at the table directly opposite Bradley and took a sip of water. 'As I am sure you probably know by now, we call this TrueEarth, and your side, either FalseEarth, FakeEarth, or as some do just call it, that other side. From these names, I am sure you have guessed that the implications are a lack of reality on your side?'

'Yes, it does seem odd. It never seemed unreal to me,' explained Bradley.

'It both is and is not. You see, it is just as much a matter of what we have on our side as what happened to you on your side. History tells of a catastrophic event in the past, where someone meddled in things they shouldn't have under the influence of an unknown mind. It caused mankind to fall.' For a moment, he seemed to be lost in thought. 'Yes, that is as good a term as any,' he concluded. 'This fall was instigated by a quantum parasite who homed itself in your systems and then started to replace natural behaviours, thinking patterns, and eventually, perception. It evolved over time, and as it did, you devolved. Your side's human population has lost its ability to perceive clearly. Instead, your perceptions are shaped and manipulated to only allow an immensely finite range of possibilities. To put it bluntly, you are all caged over there without even knowing it. You only see, hear, feel and experience what these things allow you to because they feed on your quantum particles and waves.

You diminish generation after generation. This degrading of capabilities resulted in what you have today. However, since this parasite is a living thing, which is trying to extend itself all over humanity on your side, it is not precise. Those it feeds on less have maintained more of their natural intellectual and perceptive abilities, while others have less.' He took a few sips out of his cup. 'This is also why your sciences have become so limited — they can only move as far as your intellect moves, and they can only be shaped to reflect the capabilities or lack of capabilities of their inventors. We moved further and faster because we have not had to work within those limitations. To us, quantum realities, multiple dimensions and multiple universes are very common facts. Here, you will find that every person interacts with one or more of those on a daily basis. It's the most natural of things. That is where membership in one of the Houses is so important; it hones that person's skills and abilities in a given direction, focusing them and, as a result, amplifying them. The basics are the same for every human being — we all perceive quantum realities and all their elements, but your side has those perceptions locked out, typically by puberty, which is when these parasites would have depleted your systems of sufficient quanta and energy in order to switch off those perceptual capabilities. On our side, we direct and nurture them in a House specific manner.'

Bradley listened intently. He was not sure how much of it he believed and how much he did not, but one thing was sure, what they had was so far ahead of anything he ever imagined, let alone read that he could not deny the validity of the claims.

Galvin resumed his explanations. 'What is even worse is that rather than battle this... let us call it quantum pathogen... your side has indulged it. This has resulted in the exponential growth of its capabilities. It regularly causes massive outbursts of anger, emotions, depression and all sorts of problems, imagined conflicts, offense, frustration and fury to force your biological system to release more and more fuel to it. All these techniques serve it well. The fascinating thing is that it directs your mind, and your thinking is directed and preconditioned by it. Make no mistake, its intellect is far superior to your own by entire scopes of possibility, but it is distributed. Ever wondered why you all obsess so much with communal theology? The sacrifice of the individual for the collective? Have neural networks as a concept for computing? Want to be part of a greater whole? Everyone is one?

All these concepts are fuelled by this pathogen's basic fundamental nature. Not by human ones. We humans are all unique, different and individual. On the other hand, it is quite the opposite where the greater networks of its mind take care of all the others and these others serve, exist and feed for the good of the whole. However, some of your side have learnt to control their thoughts. I believe you underwent this training yourself since your arrival here.' He glanced questioningly at Tamirok, who confirmed it by a simple nod. 'With practice, you will feel the impulse of an external directive when you are taken off course in your thinking or distracted off the current train of thought. One thing I want you to keep in mind is this: this thing is deviously genius — it will try to interrupt using others. Each time your side experiences a push towards collectivistic thinking and behaving, it is its influence. It hates individualism with a passion; the more permutations, the more work is required by its over-mind to understand how to manipulate you. As an upshot, the more individual you become, the more leeway you get. You, in effect, distract it.'

'What does that have to do with the way you call our side?' asked Bradley.

'It is simple because you don't perceive things as they are. What your senses are telling you is only a tiny part of what is real. What do you get when you mix a tiny percentage of real with a large percentage of unreal?' He did not wait for the answer, 'you get a false reality.' There was silence in the room.

Bradley was struggling with all this. His mind told him it could not be, but something deeper within him told him it was exactly so.

'Now, the reason some people from your side end up here is simple, yet totally beyond our understanding. Some people manage to touch upon the fundamental truth of themselves. They pretty much become true to themselves. By doing so, something happens, which throws out this parasite. As truth settles back in and their perceptions widen, they suddenly start perceiving TrueEarth. This natural perception takes hold rapidly and they find themselves here. Just exactly what triggers this and how it unfolds is not really understood because, by the time you get here, it is too late for us to track what has caused the shift, seeing as it is already over. This is why some of our House members, like Epstein here, study your side extensively and even interact with those on your side.'

'How exactly do they do that? From what I have gathered, it is impossible to move things from one side to the other.'

'Incredible! Such a mind,' Galvin actually got really excited. 'Correct, only living beings can do so and only under specific conditions. The condition for human beings is truth and falsehood. The moment you become deceptive, false, and untruthful, you are thrown out of our side, and a parasite on the quantum side takes over, managing your perceptions to enforce those falsehoods. Why does it do so? Because your side is littered with them. They are impossible to avoid. It is their influence that anchors you there. And that is the fundamental reason only biological life can move in between our two versions, if you like, of Earth. It is the same as moving from the quantum into a dimension, although there, the reasons for living beings only being able to make that jump are fundamentally different.'

'What of those who move from one to the other?' wondered Bradley.

'I think you have a saying on your side, which goes like this: there are many ways to skin a cat? If I am not mistaken. Never really understood why anyone would skin a cat but each to their own, I guess. The answer is difficult to pinpoint. Each House has its own way of achieving certain effects. Those, I am afraid, can only be learnt by members of the specific House. Each one's methodology is so different, it would be totally useless to a member of a different one.

Kiandra was in her car, irate. Why did it have to take so long to queue up to get to her own car? This place was hopeless. Why were these forsaken labs sharing parking space with the meaningless wastes of space that was the university? She was annoyed by it all. At least she comforted herself. She was making exquisite progress in sending them all into chaos and buying Mira the time she needed. The fact that this annoyed Heather to no end was a bonus for her. It amused her terribly to wind that self-righteous wannabe scientist up.

A spell of dizziness took hold of her. She grabbed the driving wheel to steady herself and tried to breathe deeply to regain her balance. Then pain ripped through her from her feet up to the top of her head. The burning sensation smouldered her skin. In panic, she looked at her hands, cracks in her skin all over her body had formed — cracks filled with a green type of glow coming from within. Panic took over as did fear. The last thought Kiandra ever had was that of an image of Heather, facing her, hundreds of feet tall, holding a thread in her hands. As she ripped the thread in fury, Kiandra's body and soul tore into pieces. Her body disintegrated as she yelled out, 'Noooooo,' then the structure of energy, which she saw was her soul. For the first time ever, she had witnessed it and the very next moment, it, too, was torn into fragments, which dissipated. Her awareness and essence unconfined dissipated into the great nothing. Kiandra Kustings was no more and would never be again.

'The key questions here are if there is such a parasite, how do we get rid of it? How does one immunise against it? I cannot even begin to think about things like quantum parasites, and the second is, how do I get back?' asked Bradley.

'Answering them in order is that this parasite is immune to anything we can do. However,' he looked at Nihi, 'it is within the realm of possibility of your House to pull things back into the Great Nothingness. This pretty much does what I would describe as wiping something off the blackboard of creation. How it is done is simply beyond House mTech's capabilities or knowledge. As for how to shift back to FalseEarth... as mentioned, each House has its own methods. For us, it would be simply another time, space and reality coordinate, so moving through time is our answer. The Bound would simply bind themselves to that precise part of creation; House GrimGloom use the darkness to carry them, and so forth. Each to their own. How your House does things is something I do not know. Each method has its advantages and its limitations.'

'I thought you said you could not teach me how to move back?' he asked Tamirok with a hint of accusation.

'That is correct. Our method binds you to it. You now belong to TrueEarth and there is no way I am going to allow you to bind yourself back into that...' he waved his hand in dismissal.

'No...' echoed Nihi's voice.

Bradley turned to face it, 'but I have to get back!' he objected.

'Yes...' echoed back Nihi.

'How then?' Bradley was getting downright frustrated by this. This place was worse than his side. Yes, they all had to speak the truth, but they were all very adept at avoiding discussing things, avoiding subjects, which might prompt what was sought. It was even more of a manipulative reality than his own. At least on his side, he knew when someone was lying.

'House Aetherix' echoed Nihi.

'You're joking, right? You plan on sending him to them?' This time, it was Galvin who objected.

'That is his path,' replied Nihi.

'This is insane. You do realise what they are? How they work? Sending him over there is total insanity!'

'That is his path,' repeated the echo. 'His path, path.'

'Why do I get the impression there is so much more to this than you are telling us?' asked Galvin. At that moment, Nihi folded in on itself and was gone. 'Typical'. He focused in on Bradley. 'Listen to me very carefully, I know you are Ruler of House Nothingness, but until you actually seize control and start to rule, you are so just in name.' He waved his hand in anger at where Nihi was a moment ago, 'and that thing is manipulating you.' He paused for a moment as if hesitating. 'Is it gone?' he asked.

'I don't know,' answered Bradley.

'You have not even learnt to detect the essences of your own House?' he asked.

'No, it seems not.'

'Goodness gracious, man,' he looked at Tamirok questioningly.

'I cannot teach him that, it is knowledge we do not possess. House Bound has no ruler, and the mysteries of House Rulers are not within our grasp.'

'Sorry,' apologised Galvin, 'I should have remembered.' His stumbling had, in fact, revealed a crucial bit of information regarding House Bound. 'You will be staying a while?' he asked out of the blue.

'I'm afraid not, duties call. But I was planning on leaving Bradley here with you for a couple of days. There is much he can learn and House mTech is the ideal place for his scientific mind to learn the basics from.' He left the rest unspoken. Galvin understood.

'Epstein, get me the quantum visor that Martha's team has just completed,' he instructed.

'Surely you don't intend to...'

'Why do I have to put up with objections every step of the way? Go! Now! Move it.'

'Yes, sir.' Epstein reluctantly got up and scuffled out of the conference room. Galvin spoke into his device again. 'Seal the room and remove any listening, visual and other sensory devices. Disable all external entry point systems,' he commanded.

'Confirmed,' replied the crystalline voice.

'This should keep everything at bay at least for a while.'

'Listen to me very carefully, Bradley. We have very little time here. I took the liberty of observing the data Epstein had collected when he breached protocols. Do not worry, it will be deleted as soon as we are done here, of that, you have my word as House Ruler. Your powers are consuming you.'

Bradley was surprised. 'We know they are dangerously chaotic but are you saying they are killing me?' he asked.

'They are, and what I suspect from these readings is that this Nothing thing is deliberately speeding up the process.' Bradley looked at Tamirok, who nodded. So, he knew too. 'Yes, Tamirok knows, although you must not ask him why or what he knows. Having to reveal that would cause him a lot of danger, and we need our general because TrueEarth is at war. You have been shielded from it, but it is true. Something is trying to eradicate the very essence of life, and that something has selected the Earth for its next meal.'

'Is there something I can do to help?'

'No,' came the harsh response from Tamirok. Bradley's face sunk, he wanted to help. He wasn't sure why, but he did. 'At least not for the time being.'

'And what makes things even worse is the Head Warrior is lost to us,' stated Galvin.

'What do you mean?' asked Bradley.

'You are his new Wielder! How...' he turned to the two copper and gold-clad muscle-ripped giants sitting on the other side of the table. 'Neither of you told him? Seriously?'

'There was no need for him to know,' responded Tamirok.

'He is wielding the head warrior for Earth's sake, how could there possibly be no need for him to know? You have taken one of the greatest assets out of TrueEarth's hands!' objected Galvin.

'Ok, stop all of you!' shouted Bradley. He was more than annoyed with all this secrecy. He finally understood the rules of this side. 'Tell me now!' his voice changed, a hint of an echo surfaced within it.

They all looked at each other in horror. They must not allow the other version of him to resurface. 'Yes, Lurizak is Head Warrior of TrueEarth, one of the most powerful and experienced warriors who has a hyper-extended life span and has endured thousands of battles during his lifetime,' explained Tamirok. 'The reason I had you take over wielding him is simple. I was hoping that he could experience, at least for a short while, a life other than on the battlefield. I never anticipated for him to offer his very being to you — that was a fatal mistake.'

'HE DID WHAT!?' Galvin exploded, his composure lost, unable to restrain himself any longer.

'Yes, I did,' replied Lurizak.

'We're doomed.' Galvin got off his chair, threw up his arms in the air and started pacing feverishly up and down the length of the conference table.

'I'm afraid I don't understand...' Bradley never finished his sentence.

Lurizak took over. 'What they are not explaining is that this sort of thing was last done over 10,000 years ago. It means that my essence is no longer going to be bound to TrueEarth but to you instead. I will no longer belong to House Bound or any other House. I will be anchored to you. What Ruler mTech does not appreciate is that this one was a decision for me, and me alone to make. It is the one final binding any Bound can make, and it is the one that nothing can interfere with, not even the House itself.'

Bradley turned to face Lurizak, 'Why? Why did you do this? It's obviously an extremely serious and extreme choice to make. Are you making it for me? You know I won't hold you to it if...'

Lurizak quickly covered Bradley's mouth with his hand, stopping him from uttering the words he was going to say. 'Don't say it, please. I made the choice, I have my reasons and once we have done what needs to be done, I will explain. For the time being, all I ask is that everyone respects the fact that I have made the choice and had the right to make it.'

They all nodded affirmatively.

'That does not solve the problem,' objected Galvin.

'What problem?' asked Lurizak.

'That the one you are intending to be a part of is going to die,' all their jaws fell in shock and surprise.

'Die?' asked Bradley.

'Yes, it is the only logical conclusion to the current course of events going on with you, Bradley. I cannot estimate how long, but my best guess would be not too long. AND,' he continued, 'that means that you will die as well.' He pointed to Lurizak. 'We are going to lose the one man who can command and direct the front lines.'

'There are others who can do what I do,' affirmed Lurizak.

'Really? Are you telling me that there is another under the rank of general or acting ruler that can wield the minds, bodies and wills of over 10 million men effortlessly across multiple battlefields?'

Lurizak went quiet, he had to admit to himself that Galvin had a point.

Go with me on this, Bradley's mind echoed in Lurizak's.

'There is only one way to solve this,' Bradley interrupted them.

'No,' said Tamirok, 'don't disrespect his choice, it is not fair on him.'

'You misunderstand me, Tamirok, I will honour Lurizak's choice for whatever reason he made it.'

Lurizak looked at Bradley, content and smiled. It seemed that he was finally understanding.

'What I was going to suggest is the simplest and most effective solution to your problem.' He took a deep breath. 'Since Lurizak is so crucial to the defence of the Earth herself, I'm going to join the battlefield. That way, he will too, and according to Tamirok, engaging in battle offloads the power overload.'

Everyone looked confounded. 'But you are no warrior,' objected Galvin, 'you'll get the both of you killed.'

'I beg to differ,' interrupted Lurizak, 'he is not a fully-fledged warrior, that is a given, but his battle skills and, more importantly, his potential, is mind-blowing.'

'That seems a bit too convenient...' was all Galvin forwarded.

Lurizak stood up and walked to the glass screen, 'May I?' he asked.

'Be my guest.'

'Initiate cross House communications,' instructed Lurizak. All warriors were trained to use the key technologies, so this was familiar territory for him.

'House Bound detected, interface enabled,' the crystalline voice affirmed.

Lurizak closed his eyes and issued silent commands to his armour — what Bradley could only compare to a set of methylated nerve strands growing out of the surface of the armour into the receptor unit on the glass surface.

'Interface acknowledged, memory recordings downloading...'

Bradley was amazed! The next moment, he could see their battle playing on the massive glass screen. He observed the entire battle, including Bradley's uncanny formation of a fully-fledged small black hole at the point of Lurizak's sword. The display was showing an analysis of all the atomic and quantum elements, how they had been used, changed, and when. He saw how this black hole had been formed by pulling a tiny piece of Lurizak's armour out of him and another tiny mass from the earth below the warrior. He saw the dance of the two, how they had been made to collapse into each other and how his own red energy had hyper-accelerated the whole event. He then observed his black power flowing through Lurizak and manipulating the resulting black hole with such precision that it surprised even him. He had never imagined any of those steps, just their end results. When it had run its course, Lurizak disconnected and returned to his seat.

'I believe my point has been made.'

'Incredible, where did you learn to do that?' asked Galvin.

'I'm not sure,' replied Bradley, 'it's more like piecing various bits and pieces of knowledge gained from many places and trying it out.'

'Astounding,'

'Those two make a great team,' he told Tamirok.

'That still does not solve our problem. Bradley would need a lot more training to be up to battlefront standards,' objected Tamirok, 'and we don't have time for that, nor do we know what will happen to Bradley, and hence, Lurizak in the meantime. To top all these issues, we also have the pressing issue that Bradley has started to shift back.'

The answer is forthcoming... the voice echoed in Bradley's mind.

'Let's deal with these things one at a time,' offered Bradley, 'that is how I managed very complex investigations in the pathogens I worked with at the labs,' he explained.

'He's right,' agreed Galvin, 'this is an extremely large and involved problem and we will just get lost trying to fix it all in one fell swoop.' His device glowed. 'Project on main screen,' he commanded. The large glass display flared up in electric blues and showed Epstein.

'I'm back, but the conference room is sealed,' he explained. 'Oh, I forgot,' apologised Galvin. 'Do you have the device?' he asked.

Epstein waved it about in his right hand.

'No need for all the drama, a simple yes would have sufficed. Come on in,' instructed Galvin. 'Remove localised conference room seals on 1Ab,' he commanded.

'Confirmed,' came the crystalline voice as the doors opened.

Epstein walked over and handed the smooth crystal surface with a single pointed upward angle to Galvin.

'Has it passed the testing?' he wanted to be sure it was both fully operational and safe.

'Yes, a few days ago.'

'Very well.' Galvin handed the device to Bradley, much to Epstein's horror, 'use it wisely. Allow it to integrate with your armour and it will give you a more familiar way to interact with all the fundamentals you are trying to learn.'

'Thank you.' Bradley took the visor and tried it on. His armour's power veins extended into it. As power pulsed, the visor changed its blue visor to a deep red, matching Bradley's armour. The behind ear support changed shape and his armour expanded it to cover his entire ears. Bradley then tried the trick he had learnt to remove only parts of his armour. It worked! The visor was nowhere to be seen.

'It changed!' Epstein was in shock, 'he adapted our technology without even trying!'

'It seems that whatever he interfaces with becomes an extension to his toolset,' theorised Galvin, 'but enough for today. Gentlemen, let's adjourn this meeting and all get some rest. I have made preparations for you to have a quiet area to relax in.' He got up and headed for the door. 'Tamirok, if you wouldn't mind too much, would you join me? We have a few matters to see to — the new battle tech has arrived at House Bound.'

'Certainly,' Tamirok got up to join him.

'Epstein, get back to work on you know what,' Galvin commanded. They all made their way out, allowing House mTech's pulse of blue power to guide them in their separate directions.

23

UNEXPECTED
- EXPEDITION -

Bradley sat at the semi-transparent table in their room. He and Lurizak were assigned the same rest room, and Elshevira had joined them. He was busy playing with his new toy. The device allowed him to view all the quantum, atomic, energetic and structural parts of reality, to replicate practically the same processes he had seen Epstein use on the large crystalline display in the conference room. It also very conveniently enabled him, with Lurizak's help, to access historical and geographic information concerning TrueEarth.

'It reminds me of mobile phones we have on my side,' commented Bradley.

'Yes, except those things are dangerous to your health. These are perfectly safe,' replied Elshevira.

'You used mobile phones?' he asked her.

'Had to on a few occasions. Horrible things. I had to counter all the disruptions in my body's bio-magnetic fields. How do you people not realise it's the pulses of data which are harmful, not its power?'

Bradley smiled. He had given up on that battle. After a bit of tweaking and experimenting with the options in his visor's interface, he had found the map layouts for TrueEarth and FalseEarth as well as some of the bridge ways in between the two. His visor shifted rapidly across all the map until it zoomed into one, then zoomed in further until it displayed what looked like a body of water to him. Something pulled at him, a desire to be there, an impulse of some sort. He had to go to this particular one, no matter what happened, this was where he was going. His gut instinct told him that would be where he would find what he was looking for, and what he was searching for was how to get back home to FalseEarth. He could not afford to waste any more time here.

'Um, how do I get this thing to project the image out so you two can see it? Can it do that?' he asked.

'Not sure,' she replied. 'Maybe try asking it? If it is mTech technology, its crystalline bio-intelligence should respond.

'Ok here goes nothing... Um, visor?' He wasn't sure how to call it and nothing happened. He thought back on what instructions Galvin and Epstein had used. 'Project image of display,' he commanded.

'Clumsy,' interjected Lurizak.

'Projecting,' replied an altogether different male-sounding crystalline voice through its headphone component. A beam projected out of the visor, semi-translucent red light. Suddenly, in front of them was a fully mapped 3D image of the area.

'By the Houses!' exclaimed Elshevira 'That's none other than –'

'Lake Natrak in the Forbidden Region. What on Earth are you looking at that for?' prompted Lurizak.

'I need to go there,' answered Bradley.

'You're kidding, right?'

'No, I'm not. I have to go there,' he insisted.

'What on Earth for? What could anyone in their right mind go there for?' asked Elshevira.

'What's the big deal?' Bradley didn't understand why they were so reluctant.

'The entire area is called the Forbidden Region because it was a nexus of inter-dimensional invasions in our history. The presence of any life triggers the opening of passageways. It is strictly forbidden to anyone and everyone.'

'I still need to go there.'

'No chance,' replied Elshevira. 'Even with the command of all the Houses, you would not be allowed to step into that region.'

'I need to go into the lake,' insisted Bradley.

'He's gone totally insane.' Elshevira turned to Lurizak and gave him a look of total desperation.

'I can't stop him but I cannot allow him to go either.' He shrugged.

'I'm going. One way or another, I am going to take a swim in that lake.'

'He's lost it. All this has finally gone to his head and rendered him totally completely and utterly insane.' Elshevira was waving her hands about, trying to illustrate her point. 'I'm not going to let you walk to your death! We're doing all we can to keep you alive, then the first thing you come up with using that' – she pointed to his visor – 'is a trip into oblivion itself?' She paced up and down the room. 'I'm not going to even entertain this. Find some other place on TrueEarth to explore. You have not seen any of its places other than the inside of two Houses. There is a lifetime's worth of discoveries for you to make.'

She left the room for a walk. Bradley went to lie down for a while. The beds there were single beds but very comfortable. The most interesting feature was that they were floating about 30 inches off the ground. Bradley found it incredibly comfortable; everything seemed to be perfectly balanced for his body. Little did he know that these beds scanned his physiology then adjusted the mattress, covers, pillows, angles of orientation and even thickness of covers, to ensure perfect suitability for whoever was using them. They even had the ability to extend themselves, as Lurizak's had done, to cater for his large frame.

Lurizak was watching Bradley closely. He was looking at how his frame and body type seemed to be adapting almost too fast. Something other than natural growth was taking place; he had yet to figure out what. Yes the TrueEarth foods and his battle training would have had an enormous impact on his musculature, but this went far beyond what he had expected.

He saw it; the glyphs and letters along the outside of his arms lit up in golden power. The energy pulsed down from his shoulders and activated them all. The impulse that flushed through him was almost unbearable; his body moved. *We're going.* Bradley's echoing voice, that horrific version of Bradley was back. It demanded – no, it commanded with such force – that Lurizak had to let go of whatever was still his to that being crushed by this will. Bradley was up. He flung a gateway open, forced Lurizak through and jumped in himself.

As their vision cleared, they were standing by Lake Natrak. He declared, 'We're going for a swim.'

'That armour of yours will not be able to sustain you in there.' Lurizak had to seem as unconcerned as he could muster. He was all too aware that he was now in the presence of Bradley the Ruler of House Nothingness, not the Bradley he knew so well. Fortunately, he had experienced this just recently and had devised a plan on coping with the situation whenever it arose again.

'That has been taken care of,' Bradley replied, just as a stranger walked towards them. A sturdy fellow who seemed to be wearing attire which even Lurizak did not recognise. It was dark and reflective material, almost oily in appearance, which practically covered his entire body. Much to Lurizak's surprise, the man wore a large shark fin on his back. For want of trying, Lurizak was unable to determine whether that had grown out of his back or whether it was an item of clothing or even armour.

'It has been a very long time since we had visitors here.' His voice was firm, deep and had a roughness to it. This was a man of action, not one of science. His dark hair was cut short and his eyes were a pale green; his skin had a slight tinge of a green hue as evidenced by his bare feet, hands, and face. He was carrying some sort of large container. Lurizak had never heard of a human variant of this type and he was familiar with what he thought were all humans on TrueEarth and FalseEarth.

'I'm Ayden of the Water tribe.' He half-bowed to Bradley and gave Lurizak a look of disgust. 'It is an honour to meet you.'

'I trust you know why I am here?' asked Bradley. It seemed some type of arrangement had been somehow made, although neither men knew who had made it nor how. Lurizak suspected Bradley knew but had chosen not to share the information.

'I have brought what you needed.' He put the container down on the ground. The large pack opened, and Lurizak caught a glimpse of the water within it. From that water, Ayden pulled out what looked like thick layers of transparent slimy jellyfish-skin. Much to his surprise, once the jellyfish had been pulled out completely, he saw it was cut and shaped into the form of a man. 'This will allow you to swim safely in the waters and will allow you to breathe too' – he turned to face Lurizak – 'but I cannot do anything for him. Not that I need to; that metallic skin will shield him from the water's influence, but it won't help with hiding him, though.'

'We will take what we have available,' replied Lurizak. He was not fond of any of the so-called meta tribes. Having to interact with one was unacceptable; having to trade with them was totally against all House laws. They were not even considered to be human anymore. Fortunately for him, he had absolutely no say in the matter whatsoever. Bradley nodded in agreement.

'Very well, strip that armour of yours. This will need to make skin contact if you want to be able to breath underwater.' Bradley did as instructed. He was just about to grab hold of the jellyfish-skin suit when Ayden told him not to. Ayden explained that as soon as he touched it, his fingers would become too slippery for him to be able to grab hold of the rest of it to get it on. Ayden took charge of things. Slowly and carefully, he helped Bradley get into the suit. It was a very odd sensation, an initial burst of pain as something in that odd jellyfish-skin seemed to send out microscopic needle-like things into his skin. The sensation ran from head to toe, and millions of tiny pinpricks penetrated his skin. His body jolted as the initial pain and surprise passed. He could no longer see properly, his vision was still there but blurred, breathing had becoming a strain and he could no longer hear Ayden who seemed to be waving his hands in distress, pointing to the water and making the motion to go.

Bradley understood. It was perfectly logical: if this skin made his body water-capable, then being outside of the water must be a bad thing. The jellyfish-skin was getting tighter and tighter; the longer he was out on solid ground, the harder and drier it got. Bradley didn't hesitate; he jumped for the plunge, making sure he stayed close to the shore.

The sensation of cold water washing over him sent shivers of ecstatic delight through his entire being. The smooth flow and currents of the lake were simply a delight, a piece of heaven. His senses exploded, and the song of the lake echoed in his eardrums. The ripples in the water sent delightful sensations washing over his every pore, drawing his attention towards their source. His eyes changed: his vision was now clearer than it had ever been, and the most minute details of being underwater were so sharp he could make out individual particles of sand shimmering on the bottom. The sun's rays hitting the surface resulted in silvery sparkles of light dancing chaotic on its surface. He was in awe at the world below the surface.

Ayden jumped in and poked Bradley in his ribs. The interruption knocked him out of his delightful daze. Ayden sent out waves of sounds from his own body, which ripped through the water and hit Bradley, coursing through his new skin. He heard Ayden's voice from within his own body: 'Don't get distracted or you will be water lost! Focus on why you are here! Now go; the longer you stay like this, the higher the risk of you staying forever.' He pointed to the bottom of the depths, an area covered in intense blackness that even Bradley's new sight could not pierce.

Bradley closed his water eyes and focused, sending his will to Lurizak, telling him to follow if he could. Not a second later, a loud splash rippled its way from the surface towards them. It disturbed the harmony within. Both men looked up at its source and saw Lurizak diving down. His armour had undergone subtle changes; it seemed to have developed additional structures on the edges all over his body. They kept pulling water in and then pushing some of it back out. Unknown to them, they were used to extract the oxygen and nutrients required to keep him alive. The warrior skins were specifically designed to allow them to function in all types of environments, so water was nothing special to them. To their surprise, the shape of his armour had not only changed to support maintaining life functions, but had also changed shape along the inside of the arms, the feet, hands, and had even given him a fin on his back, very much like Ayden's. These all optimised his swim speed and dexterity to such a degree that to Bradley's untrained eye, he seemed to surpass even Ayden's skills. Ayden looked at him in dismay. *Such a show off.*

They swam rapidly. The darkness loomed ahead of them. Ayden sent another wave of sonic ripples onto Bradley: 'Be careful here, very dangerous. My job is done. Goodbye.'

Bradley nodded in acknowledgement as Ayden swerved sideways and disappeared in the opposite direction. It seemed he did not want to face what was there. Bradley used his binding with Lurizak to communicate: 'Let's go; we need to be careful. There is something dangerous down here.'

Lurizak just nodded back, not wanting to speak. He was still annoyed about being made to come here. He was breaking one of TrueEarth's fundamental edicts. Bradley swam directly into the obscured area with Lurizak at his tail. It took a few minutes for them to be able to see anything. What they saw were hundreds of thin stray-like cords all floating upwards from the deepest point. Bradley's jellyfish-skin proved its worth: making contact with these cords simply caused them to brush off the slippery smooth skin. Lurizak however was not so lucky. His breathing mechanism managed to push them off by blowing them outwards, but there were far too many for him to keep that up. As they made contact with his smooth metal skin, they caught onto it like metal would onto a magnet. More and more of them attached to him, slowing him down until eventually he could not swim further. 'Hold on!' he yelled into Bradley's mind.

Bradley turned back and saw; he swam back to Lurizak. Something like this would not hinder him too long: Lurizak shifted his armour, his right arm became a blade and sliced the cords. More of them caught up with him. Each time he had to slice through them, his breathing apparatus had to change into the sword like structure. He would not last long if he had to keep this up.

'Do you know where we are going?' he asked Bradley.

'Down there to the right.' Bradley pointed at the dark patch below them then shifted to what seemed to be a slightly blurry area.

'Alright, go ahead. I'll join you down there,' instructed Lurizak.

'Are you sure?'

Lurizak nodded. The counter questions were the one thing about Bradley that truly irritated him. He reminded himself he had to be patient. Instead, he took out his irritation on these obstacles. Bradley swam off in the general direction he had pointed out. Lurizak took a risk and replaced all the breathing changes in his armour with sword-like blades, causing his entire body head to feet to be outlined in rows of sharp blades. He had to be quick, very quick: his body would not be able to sustain him for more than a minute without breathing support. This underwater pressure was making its impact.

He increased his speed, almost torpedoing through the cords, slicing them as he passed along.

He had almost reached his destination when his vision blurred. Suddenly he could not see where he was going. His orientation was completely disrupted. He was lost. The waters turned darker, colder and seemed to cause his body to slow even further. There were so many of these cords that he could not even move through them. His blades no longer made much difference, cutting through one cause another dozen to replace it. He quickly changed his blades back to his breathing systems. Even using those seemed to be insufficient. Watery environments were tricky for him; unleashing his power in here would not produce as strong an effect as it did out of the water.

Then he felt it: a powerful hand reached down and started pulling. Something had grabbed hold of his hand as he was trying to free himself of another wave of these cords. He was being heaved upwards. Focusing in on the sensations, he recognised the hand! It was Bradley's fully armoured hand, red power flaring out of it, sending waves of heat down all over Lurizak's body. The change of temperature caused the water to heat up. Lurizak clicked on fast, and he formed a reverse curvature pointing downwards around his lower body's sides. It was a stroke of masterwork: the bubbling water trying to surface was caught in those curvatures, propelling him upwards at twice the speed. All the elements combined: the heated water's propulsion, Bradley's pull and Lurizak's own struggles to swim upwards. He shot out of the surface of the water like a dolphin jumping, and curled his body as his feet circled upwards, causing him to summersault, then land with a stable footing on the floor ahead of him.

'Thanks,' was all Lurizak could say while trying to catch his breath.

'Glad I could help for a change.' Bradley smiled. It was the old Bradley. Lurizak was uncertain whether to be received or concerned about this. Bradley the Ruler knew where he was going; the Bradley he was familiar with did not. The two seemed to be somehow distinct; he had, on the crisis in mTech, quickly concluded that the one and the other did not necessarily share memories. Some spilt over but not many, and the spill was always dictated by some current or future requirement. He smiled back at him. *No point in trying to figure that enigma out. More pressing things to be concerned about.*

He was right: those cords started surfacing out of the water. He looked back horrified. 'They are following us!'

'We can try to burn them?' asked Bradley 'Or maybe electrocute?'

'Maybe, but if they do keep coming back, we won't have the power to keep that up for too long.' He looked at Bradley. *Well I won't; he might. Even then, what would he do? Just stay there and keep at it?* 'What have you come to do here? Do you know? We should move on. They seem slow – maybe we can just outrun them?'

'I'm going in there.' Bradley pointed to a massive structure ahead of them. It was only at that moment that Lurizak noticed where they were. The floor, walls and massive triangular columns all around them were made of a darker shadow of blue rock, with what looked like outlines in white representing random ripples in the actual stone they shone a pale dim white light. Up ahead was a type of entrance. To Lurizak it looked more like a hole in a huge rock, running from the floor, round, up and then back down. A scripture unlike he had ever seen was carved into the stone. The same pale white glow sent semi-vapourish pulses of power from its shapes. The end result was a power archway, a perfect semi-circular one.

'Well let's get the heck out of here. Where's your jellyskin?' he asked, thinking Bradley would need it on his way back.

'It dissolved as I got out of the water.'

'I see. Guess even a gift from the meta tribes would be only partial, pfft.' He sneered at the thought of Ayden.

'Don't be so harsh with them. We got the help when we needed it,' objected Bradley.

'Let's not talk about this now. You will understand when you read our histories at some point. Let's go. These things are getting closer and I for one don't fancy another trip there.' He waved to the dark waters they had just left.

'Agreed.' Both men pushed forward. Much to their surprise, as Bradley was the one in the lead, Lurizak kept a close eye on the backside just in case those things decided to do something. They stepped in front of the semi-circular passageway and the scripture lit up. The pale vaporous white power flared up into a brilliant white. The glow reached outwards and spilt over the edge of the rock as if the circle into which it had been carved attempted to complete itself. There was no gap or hole inside the huge rock – instead, a semi-circle of brilliant whiteness stood in front of them.

Mira was at home waiting for her chef to finish her meal. She had requested something very special, one of her favourites: lobster. The annoying thing was it seemed to be taking forever. The crab starter was delightful, along with her wine. She was getting hungry again, and when hungry, Mira would become very irritable. She walked into the kitchen. 'Why am I waiting so long?'

'It's done. Am about to serve.'

'Finally,' she snapped, returning to the dining table. Her vision darkened, the entire dining room seemed to be dimmer and getting even darker. She looked around, then saw the shadow rise from the now almost dark floor.

'Yooooour frrrriendddd Kiannnndrrrra is nnnno morrrre.'

Mira seemed not to be too concerned. 'She served her purpose. No need to worry about it… wait a minute, what do you mean by "no more"? Is she dead?'

'Nnnno, shhhhhe nnnno lonnngerrr exxxxistttsss.'

'That makes no sense.'

'Exxxxacttttly.' It descended back into the dark floor, becoming a puddle of darkness, then slipped back into Mira through her feet.

'This might prove to be a useful opportunity,' she mused as her meal arrived.

'What do we do now?' asked Bradley.

'You're the one who wanted to be here; you tell me. I have no knowledge of this place or this type of technology.'

Bradley, without warning, grabbed hold of Lurizak's arm and pulled them both through. A moment of blindness passed. They found themselves standing on what looked like smoky greyish glass, which had the granularity of a crystal surface. Their footsteps echoed. It was metallic? Couldn't be. Neither men could even guess at what this was.

The room was huge. Both of them had to strain to make out the far walls. It seemed to be entirely circular. Above them a perfectly circular dome hovering 60 feet off the ground. What suspended it mid-air was anyone's guess: no power, no levers, no strings, no columns. For want of trying, they had to conclude that it just floated there of its own accord. Bradley looked at it with his usual attention to detail. He concluded it must be over 90 feet in diameter. It too was covered in decorating glyphs, but these seemed to have some pattern – something about the symbols, the circular paths decorated with glyphs intersecting triangular shapes, piercing into their central points and back out through the sides, somehow it made some sort of perverse sense to him. He could not quite logic it out but some part of him echoed a familiarity, of sorts.

He managed to tear his gaze from it and looked around. Eight inverted pyramids floated around the dome, bobbing their way up and down slightly as they circled its circumference. Each of these pyramids was made of a different type of semi-translucent stone: a black one, in direct opposition to the white one, the red at a ninety degree angle from them both, the dark blue directly opposite the red. In between the red and black, a dark violet one floated, directly opposite it was a grass green one. In between the white and red was the orange one and directly opposite it was the golden-yellow one. Each of these had scripture of totally different types upon them. Not one matched any other. Those scripts gave off unique energy pulses, which crackled along their sides. He could not see what the platforms at the top or what the inverted bottom of these had, but he was certain those too had some sort of patterning on them.

'House Power Cores! Who would have believed it?' Lurizak burst out. Trying to rush towards the golden-yellow one, he hit a force and banged right off of it. It took him a minute to regain his footing. He approached it slowly and made impact with something. He could not see anything. Running his hands forward, it felt like some sort of surface; no matter how hard he pushed it would not give. 'Damn it! If I could get this back to House Bound, it would be a boon to all our capabilities like no other.'

That is not for you, a powerful echo boomed through the chamber. They looked about, trying to pinpoint where the voice had come from. Nothing. Everything was as still as it had been a moment ago.

Only the sound of the occasional pulse of power was audible.

'Who's there?' asked Bradley. 'We mean no harm.'

I know, replied the mysterious echo.

'Where are you? Who are you?'

Shouldn't you be asking where you are? I would have thought that would be a far more interesting and exciting question to pursue.

Bradley was not sure whether this was a reprimand or whatever this was making fun of them? He laughed; might as well go with it. 'I concede. Do please tell us where we are. I for one am most curious!' He knew whatever this thing was it meant no harm – something from within him told him so.

I welcome you, dear visitor. It paused for an instant. *This is the Chamber of the Ancients.*

'The WHAT?!' Lurizak was lost for words.

Ah, the warrior. I wasn't expecting you, but no matter. Would you like me to repeat myself? Maybe your hearing could use a bit of enhancement? It was obviously mocking him.

Bradley jumped in quickly, poked Lurizak in the ribs, and cracked out in laughter. 'Don't worry about my friend, He likes being all stern and mighty.'

As you wish, was the reply. Lurizak gave him an annoyed look. Bradley used his binding and spoke directly into his mind. *Go with it, Lurizak. Whoever this is likes making fun of things or having a laugh. Don't annoy it.* Much to their surprise, they were overheard this time.

Your assessment is correct. I do like to enjoy myself a bit. You see, it's been longer than time can count since I had visitors. Is it wrong for me to take a bit of pleasure in the company?

'Absolutely not!' replied a jovial Bradley. 'Wait a minute – how did you...?' It had only dawned on him what had happened.

You mean I heard your mind speak to the warrior? Easy: you just have to listen.

'Hmm.' Bradley was confused. 'So what is the Chamber of Ancients?'

Ah, yes, you wouldn't know, would you. Let's just say you have arrived home, shall we? The rest you can discover when the time is right.

'Fine, but what exactly am I doing here? This is all supposed to be a forbidden region.'

Forbidden! The voice exploded in laughter. It caused the very air in the room to bounce in giggling soundwaves. *This is where the hub of the ancient world was. Millions of people crossed its borders daily for millennia. Nothing forbidden about it whatsoever... to those who are supposed to be here.*

'Am I supposed to be here?' asked Bradley.

Are you hard of hearing too? Need me to fix it for you? I told you, you have arrived home. Or did I miss that part? So confusing, talking to humans: lots of interference waves in their stream of thoughts.

'Sorry, you did,' apologised Bradley.

Honest and humble. My my, that is a rarity in one such as thee to see. Its speech had shifted for a moment; the voice had changed from male to female, from young to old.

But HE is not supposed to be here. Once more, the shift was noticeable from female back to male.

'Lurizak is with me,' is all Bradley offered.

It will be tolerated this time.

Lurizak was not happy at hearing all this, but kept still and did not interfere. The situation read clearly. Whatever it was would strike at him but not at Bradley. He opted to absorb as much information as possible. There would be ample time later on to process it.

'All this still doesn't answer my question of why am I here?'

You should know that. Why do you need something else to tell you why you go to wherever you go?

Lurizak could not stop himself from smiling. He had to admit that thing had a good point!

'Fine fine, this has all been very interesting, but I need to get back. Time is short.'

Time for you is very short indeed.

Bradley was starting to get irritated by all this. He had no real reason to be here other than because that voice in his mind had directed him to be. As far as he was concerned, he was done here. He had an idea. With the visor on, he told it to 'Map route back to House mTech.' The system sprang to life. He was shown universes, then galaxies, which zoomed into constellations, then it zoomed into the solar system, then Earth, then down to House mTech. 'What the heck? This is broken. Why would it show what I can only assume are universes? Makes no sense.'

It is just as your friend feared. The reason for his fear is that we are not on your world anymore.

'Explain yourself. How can we not be on Earth anymore? We never left!'

'Yes, we did.' It was Lurizak who interjected the answer. 'I have seen this type of chamber before. I think it was this exact one a long time ago... on another world.'

He is correct. The Chamber of Ancients is built on the nexus of creation. We are in all places and in all times; we are also in no place and no time.

Bradley was quick to catch on this time. It was very similar to the Nothing he had been in. If that experience had taught him anything, it was that these contradictory anomalies in reality were actually perfectly logical, once he was able to wrap his mind around the concept itself. 'How do I map the target location from here?' he asked.

You understand. Good good; use the reverse pyramid to get to one of the Houses or one of the gateways to get elsewhere or to some other time.

'Gateways?'

Not very observant, are we? Walk through the Chamber, young one, and take a proper look.

Bradley did. As he approached the walls, he saw what the thing meant. The walls were black as the deepest night, with circular gateways spread at equal distance from each other. A total of 24 of them he passed. In between them and in a circular fashion delimiting the gateway, he saw glyphs of power interconnected with letters. They shifted as if their substance was viscous. Very much like the pyramids, each gateway had its own unique archaeology, script, and power. The first he encountered looked as if it had been made of cogwheels, the second seemed to be a power circle and glyphs within encased by an outer circle, the third had crystals delimiting the passageway, another had what to him seemed like neurons, the following one technology components. He kept on walking and observing them. Each distinct, each probably serving a specific purpose.

'Which one leads where?' he asked. He knew if this voice belonged here, one of its purposes must be to instruct those using it in its functioning.

Specify required destination or description of destination characteristics.
'House mTech.'
Acknowledged.

Bradley had guessed correctly. With all the fancy fun chit-chat, this was essentially another technology which responded like the ones he had encountered on TrueEarth. One of the pyramids started pulsing and humming. It was the blue one; its glyphs lit up, and power gathered in a thick circular wave, which under the motion of the inverted pyramid was made to spin. It looked like a band or a disk in motion around the pyramid. Power gathered and pulsed, and the pyramid's corners served as receptacles which pulled it in. Down the connecting angles it flowed, and straight out of the inverted tip, sending a beam of blue electric light onto the floor below. It expanded until it formed a circle.

Step into the circle. It will transport you to House mTech in the current time. Bradley took Lurizak's hand and pulled him through the barriers that had previously obstructed his passage. It seemed under his influence those presented no obstacle which could not be overcome.

As they stood one step away from the blue luminous circle, Bradley wondered. 'Is there a passageway back to FalseEarth?' His heart jumped at the possibility.

Affirmative. Gateway 9 can open to false realities. His footsteps stopped and he pulled back. Lurizak turned to him with a questioning expression. 'I have to go back to my side,' objected Bradley.

'Then I will go with you.' Lurizak was determined not to let him out of his sight – too much was happening. He was concerned at not only how Bradley had found this place but also at how he seemed to not only be comfortable here but was also able to use these totally alien technologies almost effortlessly. He obviously wasn't alien – so how?

'No you must go back to TrueEarth. Something is going on; we need to keep track of things.'

'You don't seem to realise: there is no guarantee you will come back to TrueEarth!' interjected Lurizak.

'And you will be lost, now that you are bound to me, right?'

'I don't care about me. I care about you being overwhelmed with that power inside of you!'

Bradley thought about it for a few moments. 'On FalseEarth I don't seem to run into that problem, as of yet. I think I'll be fine, but...' He turned to face the rest of the massive chamber. He had an idea. 'How do I get back here?' he asked.

Simple. You know the place – use your skill.

Of course! That was the answer. Bradley kicked himself at how stupid he was for not thinking of that himself.

Minor hiccups in processing are always forgiven. The strange voice was back to making fun of him.

'Ok, this is what we are going to do. I'm going back to FalseEarth and you are going to House mTech. I want you to keep a close eye on Epstein. He's up to something! Once I catch up with things back home, I will return here and meet you back on TrueEarth. Don't reveal any of this to anyone. Will you be ok with me being in another reality? I'm not sure how this wielder thing works.'

'I'll be fine as long as you are alive and your will can flow into me,' admitted Lurizak.

'Oh, that gives me an idea! Does that mind communication work in between the two Earths?' he asked. If it did, that would enable them to communicate across boundaries of reality.

'Not sure. Never had to try it before. We should give it a try.'

'Good idea,' admitted Bradley. He decided that he was being far too stupid today. He needed a break from TrueEarth. It had put him into a very dependent mindset. He did not like that. All these people were crowding his thinking. 'You have your mission; now go.' The impulse was gentle a mild push of his will through the warrior.

Lurizak smiled back at him. Fine! *I'll go. You'd better be back or I'll get Tamirok to invade FalseEarth and drag you out!* With those thoughts, he stepped into the pool of electric-blue power. His body seemed to split into millions of atoms, which then shot forth like training micro-comets, into the pyramidal structure, and vanished.

'Guide me to the ninth gateway,' he instructed the chamber's awareness. There was no way for him to know which was the first, second or even last. This was a circular structure with no starting point or ending point, for that matter.

The scattering glyphs reordered themselves around one of the portals and started glowing. That was his signal. He quickly made his way to the gateway. Something surfaced from within his mind. He placed his hand in the air mid-gateway, as if there was a solid surface there, and concentrated. He built the image of back home there: his apartment. He refined it until all the details were as clear and precise as he could make them. He then thought of the time and decided it was best for him to return there the exact time he thought he had left. His armour pulsed, and the golden letters from shoulders to hands sprang to life, covering his outer arm's length in golden pulsing power. It streamed from his hand into the empty space, then spilt into the gateway's structure.

The entire construction was set alight and in a dull grey energy, the gateway filled with what looked like murky grey water, his hand still in its centre. For a split second, he saw something utterly horrific large cube-like beings, a couple of inches thick, floating down in the darkness and wrapping themselves around a person and anchoring themselves by a construction to the top of their heads, then vanishing out of sight. He instinctively pulled away his hand. 'Are those...?'

Yes, the invaders of that reality. Are you sure you want to return?

'I have to. I have a lot of responsibilities there, and people to look after.' With those words, he stepped though.

He felt himself pulled into a million parts, a collection of tiny spheres shooting through realities, time and space hurled forward at speeds incalculable. He came back to his senses in his apartment, back in one piece, in his armour. He was exhausted. He willed away his armour and crashed for a short, restful sleep, feeling happy. He had found a way back without having to rely on any of the Houses or anyone else.

24

THE
- CHASE-DOWN -

'Ok, we have got a better idea of this virus, how it spreads, and with a bit more work, we should be able to stop it in its tracks, but that does not explain who triggered the initial exposure. How did a virus, which has to be inhaled or ingested, get into the initial victims?' asked Dr Grimsaw. 'Surely, if we take the case of Kuroi, for instance,' hearing her name spoken cut through Bradley's heart, 'how was she exposed? I mean, you don't just stumble upon this type of engineered lethal virus and take a sip of it with your coffee.'

Bradley was brooding at the meeting. He had just returned from Kuroi's funeral in Japan. He would not share a single word as to how it went or what had happened. The entire experience had caused a veil of gloom to fall over him and he spent most of his time in silent contemplation, distant.

'Meaning someone must have exposed her to it and potentially themselves in the process,' concluded Bradley. 'That would also mean that whoever it was could be spreading it as we sit here pondering all of this.' The whole science and medical team nodded in agreement. 'We NEED to identify how it got from wherever it was engineered into our victims and where it has moved on from there,' he explained.

'And we need to do it fast! This thing spreads through blood, saliva, and perspiration exposure, which will slow it down, but that does not mean we are safe from third-party transmissions,' explained Jim. 'Additionally, due to the nanotech elements, it has the ability to morph

368

and mutate in totally unpredictable ways. Unpredictable to us, of course, not its engineers. Unless we can disable the tech behind it, we will always be a step behind when trying to fight this.'

Heather was curious about something, very curious indeed. 'What happened when you had it checked for Wi-Fi communications?' she wondered.

'It is currently relying on 4G primarily and when we block the signal, its activity changes to what one would expect a biological virus would have. But do keep in mind that whatever that activity is, it will be a result of whatever program it had been subjected to prior to signal loss. We also tried 5G and the results are most concerning. We should, however, be safe for the time being as that tech is not yet available, except in very few locations. If we do not contain this before it goes live worldwide, we might be in some very serious water. That concludes my report.'

Dr Grimsaw interrupted, 'have we made any progress in figuring out how long the incubation period is post transmission? The last report suggested that it might take up to three weeks before symptoms start developing.'

'That is catastrophic!' interjected Bradley.

Dr Grimsaw nodded, 'indeed, we are looking at the worst possible outcome.'

'I'm afraid not, Dr,' replied one of the other scientists, 'but we are still working on it.'

'You work on that and, in the meantime, we are going to focus on pinning down how the initial infection and transmissions occurred. Bradley, would you mind if we focused on Kuroi's case first and foremost? Your relationship with her will help us get a quicker rundown of things since we have access to you.'

Bradley nodded in agreement. He was extremely keen to find out who was responsible. He had a few ideas of his own as to how he would deal with whoever it turned out to be.

'It is settled then, let's go. Time is of the essence, ladies and gents, let's make the most of it.'

They all stood up and hurried off to their set tasks. Only Bradley and Heather remained, along with Dr Grimsaw.

'What on earth happened to Kiandra?' asked Dr Grimsaw. Heather went totally silent. 'Anyone know?' he prompted, 'she has not been into work and has not reported into anyone. She should be managing the staff in this crisis. I've had to excuse myself from a research meeting to recall all the lab staff. What on earth possessed everyone to take their annual leave mid-outbreak? I want some answers!'

'No idea,' Bradley waved his hand in dismissal as if it was of no concern.

Heather was keen to change subjects before the inquisitive glare zoomed in on her. She prompted Bradley, 'do you remember what Kuroi was doing on the day before she fell ill?'

'Let me see... it was a Tuesday. She would usually lecture on the main campus until three. Then she would have meetings sometimes and visit the gym, I think. Not too sure, she liked to keep her afternoons doing her own things. We would meet up in the evening for dinner.' He paused, 'I'll go check with the office to make sure those lectures took place and see if we can find out what took place, if anything, during those.'

'I'll try and find out from the other ladies on the lecturing team if they had seen her at the gym. As it turns out, I have a delivery for the sports team coach training there this afternoon, so I might stop by the gym next door and find out if anyone remembers anything odd there,' offered Heather.

'And I will go through her research records,' offered Dr Grimsaw, 'there might be something in those we could use.' They all nodded in agreement. 'We have to determine who might have been in contact with her. With a three-week incubation period, there is no way to tell how many could already be infected.' He turned to Bradley. 'You are in the clear. Your test results came back negative, no trace of the pathogen in you.' He paused. 'I'll need to talk to the international health bodies, although I see no point in establishing a quarantine now. It is impossible to contain without knowing more about it. We should nonetheless take as many precautions as possible.' He got up and left the meeting room.

Heather and Bradley looked at each other and nodded in agreement.

'Let's meet up after we find anything out,' she offered.

'Yes, I'll let you know as soon as I get any new information,' said Bradley. He was concerned — something just did not feel right. *Why not get the officials involved right away? They should have already been alerted to this.*

Elshevira was sitting at the large conference table, annoyed. Beside her sat the young Mishrak, brooding as usual. Apparently, an important crisis had broken out, which required them to all be there; they were waiting for Epstein and Lurizak to arrive. Opposite her were Galvin and Tamirok. The sheer presence of all these people spoke volumes, two House rulers and the highest-ranking House members of three separate Houses. Something was up, that was for sure, but what? All this waiting didn't bother her much... she could play the patient game, but Mishrak was driving her nuts. His mood was so chaotic that it was becoming rapidly unbearable, and she was the one who liked a bit of chaotic every so often, it spiced the monotony of structured order, but this had progressed to the point of being downright annoying.

'Will you stop fidgeting with that,' she snapped at him.

'It's irritating me, and I can't... pull it away.'

'You're not supposed to! Fool, just leave it be, and you will not notice it.' He was complaining yet again about his binding. 'Be glad you got these gauntlets, they match perfectly. If I had been the one in charge, I would have made it into a muzzle!'

'You wouldn't dare!'

'If you don't stop with all this nonsense, the next time Bradley walks in, I'll convince him to do it,' the look he gave her spoke volumes. 'Speaking of Bradley, where is he?' she asked Tamirok.

'I'm afraid I do not know. His bindings are gone. The only person who can tell us that would be Lurizak. Speaking of which...'

Lurizak had just walked in and joined them, sitting next to Tamirok.

'Perfect timing, where is Bradley?' he asked.

'Back in FalseEarth.'

'He shifted back?'

'Kind of, it seems he found a way. Not too sure if it is reliable or not, but he's definitely back there.' He tried to be as precise without going into the topic area he was forbidden to speak about.

'He won't make it back,' interjected Mishrak, 'what will happen to me then?'

'Oh, stop it already,' Elshevira's annoyance with him was intensifying to the point where she would silence him in other ways if he did not stop.

'What's going on?' asked Galvin.

'Do not mind him,' replied Elshevira, 'he's just a big baby about having to do actual work for his House instead of messing about all night long.' Her tone of voice clearly indicated that this was the end of that matter.

Epstein walked in and went straight for the large crystalline display at the end of the conference table. 'We have a problem,' he stated, 'we need to find a way to contain Bradley and limit his ability to act here on TrueEarth.'

'What do you mean?' asked Galvin.

'His powers, if you would like to call them that, are causing dormant systems to reactivate all over the place. Energy readings off Lake Natrak have increased by a considerable level.'

'Lake Natrak? What on earth? Why would that have anything to do with Bradley?' Elshevira and Lurizak remained silent, refusing to share a single word on the subject matter.

'Since he came to TrueEarth, we've been having more and more incidents of encroachment by the alien species. Something is happening at Lake Natrak, the passageways are being invaded by something, House Nothingness is awakening, and the list goes on. If we do not stop him and all he is causing, the very stability and control we have had in place for generations will be lost.'

'You have no proof that this is all coming from Bradley,' objected Lurizak.

'We have proof that it is all related to him, somehow. We will find out exactly how in time. We know that his initial arrival was shortly followed by one disturbance, then another and another. Nothing else has changed in our military positions, the maps of dimensions were stable, and the Houses were functioning as they should be. His arrival heralded entire chain reactions.'

'I don't agree,' responded Elshevira, 'this arrival could have been as a consequence of those events, rather than him being their cause. I don't feel danger from him or any type of ill intent.'

'Are you blind?' Epstein jumped at her words, 'did you see what he did here in House mTech? I don't need to remind anyone what happened here.'

'Oh, what happened? Did I miss some fun?' interjected Mishrak.

'You might think of it as fun, but I'm sure House mTech didn't at the time. Bradley nearly destroyed it all.'

'Wow! Damn, I did miss all the fun. I don't think he could have destroyed it, mind you, no one can counter an entire House.'

Everyone remained silent.

'We need to contain that threat,' continued Epstein.

'What we *need* to do is stop you from triggering these things, it seems,' she decided to confront Epstein directly.

'Why are you defending him? A stranger to our world, no less.'

'By the House Elshevira likes Bradley!' Mishrak was making a sly joke at her expense. She looked at him in her eyes, darkness gathered and shot out towards him. It surrounded his throat and coalesced into a solid. She tightened her grip and the darkness tightened its grip around his throat, strangling him.

'Care to say that again?' her glare pierced right through him.

'Oh, no, no,' he tried to take a breath in, which proved to be a most difficult task 'I'm fine... no more comments, I swear.' She waved it away and the darkness instantly dissolved, freeing him from its grip.

'I'm defending him because he is of Ancient Dark bloodline, and anyone who would harm him will be facing House GrimGloom itself!'

'No need to be concerned, we all know your proclivities. He doesn't match them even a little.' Tamirok smiled, trying to ease the tension. 'We don't need to harm him. Such a shame he broke my binding, it was a good way to keep him in check. What we need to do is make sure he doesn't cause any more havoc.'

'Agreed,' Epstein interjected, 'I propose we seal him.'

'Are you insane!' exploded Elshevira, 'that is what we do to the worst criminals of TrueEarth! And even then, we do that only as a last resort.'

'We have no choice,' Epstein was not allowing his point to be dismissed so easily, 'if those powers of his and this Ancient Dark, whatever it is...' Elshevira's look of pure hate was not lost on Epstein... 'goes out of control, the next steps could be him wiping out all the Houses and TrueEarth in the process.'

'That would take an insane amount of power and I doubt any-one has that capability,' offered Galvin.

'I disagree,' intervened Tamirok. 'His combination and interaction are so alien to us, we cannot even determine its full capabilities, nor can he. That is a serious problem for everyone.'

Elshevira turned to Lurizak, 'you have experienced his power, tell them it is not that dangerous.'

'From what I have had to endure, it is manageable, all that is needed is for Bradley to learn to control it and actually use it. If we can help him solve the Ancient Dark's amplification influence, I believe he'll be able to manage it just fine.'

'See.'

'I'm not convinced, we will still be enduring an incredible risk of having to wait until he finds a solution, which let me remind everyone, might be tomorrow, or it might be in 100 years' time, or it might be when no one is left alive to witness him doing so.'

'He does have a point,' admitted Galvin.

'We need to ensure the safety of TrueEarth.'

'We cannot condemn him! I don't care what any of you decide, House GrimGloom is not going to be a part of this abominable scheme.' She stood up, 'Mishrak, we're leaving,' and walked out of the conference room. Mishrak looked at the others, torn in indecision, then sprang into action and followed her out.

'The decision will have to be made without them. Let us adjourn for now, he is on FalseEarth and no threat to us there anyway.'

'But we...' Epstein wanted this resolved.

'Leave it for the time being,' instructed Galvin.

'Are you well?' asked Dr Grimsaw as he looked at Bradley transfixed on his seat. Bradley woke from his daze, 'Yes, just a bit tired, that's all.'

'Do try and get at least a little sleep. You must still be jet-lagged... a coffee might be in order,' he smiled to him as he left the office.

Bradley sat there, trying to process what he had just witnessed. Something inside of him hardened. He had been such a fool. The conversation he overheard through Lurizak's ears had proven to him that those he trusted were, in fact, not to be trusted. The darkness looming over him intensified.

Heather sat at the coffee table sipping her latté, she so loved indulging in those, even though she was all too aware of how many calories it had. *Every so often, one surely cannot do much harm,* she reasoned. She almost unconsciously let her hand slide over the crystal emerald necklace on her neck. It looked great; every one of her friends had complimented her on it, however, she was not so sure. It was not the look that bothered her, it was its significance. Deep down, she felt that this might have been a rash thing to jump into. It was too late to do anything about it. Bradley walked in, saw her, and sat down. 'Want to grab a coffee?' she asked.

'No, thanks, I drink way, WAY too much of the stuff. At this rate, I run the risk of bouncing about like a rabbit and losing a grip on my thoughts.'

She smiled. He, too, was as strict with himself as she was. His mood was different — there was a harshness to it, which he was desperately trying to hide. She knew him too well for that to work. Bradley's obsession was intellect, just as hers was countering emotion. They both struggled and battled for control of themselves in order to push their potential to new heights. What he was battling seemed to be overwhelming him. She knew he could hide it until it amplified to the point where he just snaps. A shudder ran through her at the thought of what would happen. His self-discipline, it seems, was on overdrive, it was a common personality characteristic they both shared. She half-smiled in approval.

'What's up?' he asked, noticing the smile. That made her smile even more. He was so unusually observant, even the smallest details in a person's mannerism or on their bodies would be picked up instantly. She wished she could do the same, then quickly decided she was perfectly happy not being able to. The thought of noticing everything, even the smallest imperfections, would drive her crazy trying to fix everything. No, she was definitely better off not noticing in the first place, providing it was not work-related, of course. Then such failure would amount to scientific incompetence. She let a heavy sigh escape her.

'Nothing much... well... a lot actually, if you are asking about my discoveries!' she teased him. She knew full well he would want to know. His curiosity had no bounds, and that, she decided, is what made him an outstanding scientist as did his drive to pursue whatever his curiosity picked up on.

'Well, well, spill the beans!' patience was not his strong point.

'Deep breath, Bradley, slow down, no fire behind you! Stop rushing.'

'Oh, just come out with it.'

'Fine, fine, Mr Impatient,' she smiled. 'Ok, time to get serious. You know when you mentioned that Kuroi would go to the gym in the afternoons?'

'Yes, she did go on that day, didn't she?'

'Turns out you were onto something there, she not only went but from what I found out, she trained with a PT over there called Dantel.'

'Hmmm, never heard her speak of him, nor did I know she had a PT.'

'Well, from what the girls there say, this guy is definitely a charmer, that's for sure.'

Bradley felt jealousy and anger rise. He knew Kuroi wouldn't get involved with anyone else. 'Are you suggesting...' his voice became harsh.

'No, no, well, factually speaking, I cannot be 100% sure, but no one has mentioned anything to me, which would suggest anything other than a purely professional relationship. She did see him once a month for her workouts. Other than that, there has been no mention of anything else.'

'I see,' Bradley was wondering if this guy could have contaminated her drink or got her exposed in some other manner. If it was him, that could prove useful to know.

'He might be the only lead we have to track down if or where this contamination started.'

Heather echoed his very thoughts. That is something he really liked about her. Great minds definitely thought alike.

'I think I will investigate some more. It is very odd you did not know about him, seeing as she told you everything.'

'She kept her gym and shopping times to herself,' he smiled at the memory of her coming back from the occasional London shopping spree with a stunning new dress that she would then wear on their dinner outings. Each time, she managed to surprise him, leaving him transfixed as he gazed on her breath-taking beauty. She never wore any of those dresses that exposed her too much, she hated those, describing them as tools by which women self-objectified, only to then blame men who looked. Instead, she preferred the classy, sophisticated look, which left a lot to the imagination, yet hinted at things just about enough to capture any man's attention. She would always tease him that the more a man had to imagine, the better it was... that men's imagination had to be sparked. Wise in the ways of the woman, his Kuroi was. Very wise. His smile sunk then as the reality of the situation dawned on him, and his loss tore through him once more as did the anger of it.

'Bradley? Are you ok?' Heather asked.

'Ehh, yes, yes, don't worry, lost in memory.'

Heather felt the sharp pain of loss emanating from him. She had experienced it as if it had been a force, which had assaulted everyone around him. What on earth is going on? she thought.

'I'll go to the gym,' he said, 'you will be known there now and we do not want to arouse any suspicions. Otherwise, whoever is involved will be out of there faster than a speeding car.'

'You might be right.' Heather summed up the possibility and decided that it was the best course of action. 'While you do that, I will look into the other problem.' She never mentioned what that other problem was, but Bradley wasn't bothered enough to ask. His mind was already plotting and planning, running through hundreds of possible courses of action and dismissing the unviable, outrageous and inappropriate ones. He decided one way or another he would have vengeance for his lost family.

'Oh, before you dash off, anything from the lecture halls?' he had forgotten to mention his findings or rather the lack thereof.

'Nothing much, I'm afraid. Just one oddity — it seemed there was one Ph.D. student obsessively questioning her about genetic manipulations in today's medical applications. Could be nothing more than a potential researcher's desire for knowledge.'

'Yes, but it could also be something more sinister. I'll see if I can find out anything more about her.' *Wait, how did she know it was a female student?* 'Bradley, did you get any info on the student? Was it a recent admissions student?'

'The only thing I got was a description, female, long black hair, apparently stunningly fit shape. The one thing that stood out most was her clothing. According to the lecturer, she seemed to be very wealthy, judging from her attire.'

'Bloody hell, that's a description. Where did you get all that from?' she asked.

'The teacher's assistant, I think he might have a bit of a crush on her.'

'Typical, let's make the most of his keen observation skills. Good thing you guys are so visually obsessed... erm, I mean focused!' she laughed out loud this time. 'Ok, I'm off. Meet me later on,' she instructed.

As she left, Bradley let out a sigh of his own, *she is a handful, that I must admit. Not later, my dear Heather, but another day,* he concluded.

Mira had made her way to the top of the tall building where her office was located. The 86th floor, she stood on the roof, looking at the tiny world down below her. She laughed almost hysterically. This was her time, she had finally managed it. The instruction to turn on the 5G networks had been given. The masts were lighting up one after the other and the satellites orbiting the globe under the guise of providing internet for the world were responding. *I am the genius who originally came up with that!* It had worked out perfectly. Hidden in that network, Mira's company had the ability to not only take over complete control when and where it wanted to, but she also had the ability to send out commands in total stealth through it with no one ever being the wiser. This was it, the final stage in her master plan was now at hand.

She had prepared herself well. This morning, she injected the special enzymes and genetic fingerprints, which would result in her remaining in control after the virus had done its job. All those loyal to her would have some control over their new selves for as long as they were loyal, and everyone else would be subject to her commands. She would change the world for a better place — peace is what she offered everyone, whether they wanted her version of it or not. The time had come, the time to tell death to get lost, the time to allow humanity to step beyond its biological limitations.

The shadow inside of her laughed for its own reasons. The resulting chaos, followed by the crippling of all the world, would allow a new order to emerge. It smiled in glee, how stupid this human woman had proven to be if she thought it would allow her to dictate what this new order would be. It would ensure that whatever emerged out of the oncoming chaos would benefit it. If it served her purpose, fine, if not, she would lose everything.

Mira gazed out at the world, her desire for control amplified, her self-confidence surged. The shadow was doing its utmost to amplify those characteristics. It needed her to finish her work. Mira laughed one last time and opened the long vial, splashing the liquid into the air above the entire city. It would spread rapidly from here to other cities, then, with the help of the global movement of the population, it would spread to other countries just as easily. She had ensured it was extremely contagious, the shadow's ability to spy on whatever that other place was had allowed her to find a way to ensure that the pathogen would survive in the air for days. The very wind was working for her now. In silence, she gazed out. For a split moment, her conscience hit, was this the right thing to do? But she quickly dismissed this thought. She had just achieved everything she had ever wanted—all those painful years of hard work and sacrifice had come to fruition. Of course, it was the right thing to do for her.

'To all the lives which were given to perfect this, you have done well, your service to the future will be remembered.' With those words, she turned and headed back down to her office, where she would wait until the new human systems started to register on the network.

Bradley found Fred in the library, studying hard or trying to. 'Fred, there you are, fancy a bit of an adventure?'

'Adventure, you say? You've got my undivided attention! Do tell, these books are just...'

Bradley smiled. He looked more closely at Fred, tight jeans, open white formal shirt. His nerve-ropes were showing in their intricate pattern, tightly containing his muscular body. It was not a bad look. 'I see you have managed to come up with a new look... a very interesting choice,' Bradley commented. Fred stood up to show it off even better.

'I know, right, it's not too shabby, even if I say so myself. The jeans are a bit too tight, not much I could do with all this muscle not fitting in. When the other guys tried to make fun of it, I threatened to bash their heads in,' a mischievous smile painted itself on his lips. 'They never said another word. Especially not since those chains seem to start to glow each time I get pissed off and become ever so slightly visible to everyone. I guess my social circle is about to shrink into non-existence. Don't really care anymore. What's this about an adventure?'

'Shhhhh, will you two keep it down, this is a library, silence!' the librarian told them off. She was a grumpy, older woman who terrified everyone into submission.

'Sorry, ma'am,' Fred pretended to bow to her. She nodded and mumbled to herself as she walked off.

'Let's go,' Bradley whispered to him.

Fred scooped up his books, dumped them in his backpack, which he flung over his shoulder unceremoniously, and followed Bradley out of the library.

'So, what's this adventure? Where are we going? What are we doing?'

Bradley cracked up laughing.

'What?' objected Fred. 'And Heather thinks I'm bad,' which made both men smile with delight.

'Will you two keep it down, or do I need to throw you out of the building!' came the harsh reprimand from the librarian standing at the exit.

They both went silent, looked straight at her, and whispered, 'we're out of the library.' She fixated her gaze at them for a moment and left.

'We're going to do some investigating!' Bradley whispered to Fred.

'Now that's fun! I'll be bad cop,' Fred volunteered.

'Not sure that will work in this situation.'

Fred was disappointed. 'What the heck? What are we investigating anyway?'

'I'm going to the gym, we're going to talk to one of the PTs there.'

'You don't need a PT,' objected Fred, 'you have me for that, remember! If you want to work out even harder, I can make it impossibly hard for you! No need to get a PT.' Almost instinctively, his chest flared out and he seemed to, as discreetly as possible, flex his biceps.

'I'm not going to see him for that. He is the PT Kuroi seemed to use for her training and he might well be either the last person to see her before she was infected or the one who actually infected her,' explained Bradley. They walked a little further out, where Fred spoke in his usual tone again.

'If he did, I'm going to tear his head off!' Fred slammed his right fist into the left palm of his hand.

Bradley felt the release of a pulse of power. He saw the black-indigo flame spark from it and fade as rapidly. He wasn't sure whether Fred could see it, but since his crystals had been completed, he was actually emanating power. Bradley pondered upon it carefully. In hindsight, it might have been a very wise choice to have these nerve-ropes contain and bind him. With that big a jump in power, those might be the only thing that kept him from being ripped apart from within. *Similar to my own situation, it seems.* Added to that, his natural tendency for combat and aggression, which was a must in his rugby, was turning him into a very powerful young man in his own right. This could be a blessing but also a tragedy. Bradley had to keep a close eye on his growth with these powers. He felt the crystals on his chest pulse in response to Fred's outburst. It fascinated him, but he would keep that mystery for another time. At this point, he had a mission and a more important task at hand, so there was no time to get distracted.

'Why isn't anything happening?' Mira was anxious. Her assistant was there for the big unveiling.

'Perhaps, ma'am, it might have been more effective if spread at ground level in the middle of a large crowd?'

'Are you suggesting I made a mistake?' her tone increased, the expression of danger all too obvious.

'No, not at all. What I am suggesting is that by doing it this way, it will probably take longer to start the process. The pathogen would need to sink to the level at which people are or hit someone higher up and then get spread by that person. I am absolutely certain it will be highly effective. It will just take a little more time. This way, it will also be pulled in by the air-conditioning vents and systems as well as infecting entire office blocks at a time.'

She liked the sound of that.

'Fine, you have a good point, let's see if there is anything else we could be doing, which might make things a bit smoother.' She remembered she had some unfinished business at the labs. Kiandra might be missing, but Mira had decided to use this to her advantage. She would go in as her replacement and ensure that the chaos wrought would continue plaguing them until it was too late to do anything about. After all, she only needed to buy a day or two, and by then, it would be too late.

'I'm going to the labs I had Kiandra in,' she informed her assistant.

'Would you be open to a suggestion?' he asked.

'Only if it proves to be of any use.'

'I will let you be the judge of that.' This is why she tolerated him, not only was he not sore on the eye, but he totally complied with her authority and respected it.

'Why not take that final sample you made and release it somewhere inside the labs?'

She looked at him for a few seconds and smiled.

'You have just earnt yourself a boon so valuable you will never appreciate how impactful it will be.'

'Happy to help,' he responded.

The idea appealed to her immensely. This would be the best way to delay them forever! She rushed down to their own labs to fetch the final sample available. She looked at the tube, there had to be another way to transport it. This was too obvious.

'I need a more discrete way to transport this,' she told the researcher.

'I believe we might have something that could be of use.' Fortunately for her, the lead scientist was already prepared for that eventuality. The almost practical to a flaw woman walked over to her and handed her an item of jewellery or what seemed like it.

'You asked for something like this to be fashioned two years ago for another project, so I suggest we use this device to transport it and avoid suspicion. I will set it up. All you need to do is open it.' She showed Mira the mechanism, which popped the artificial precious gem open to disclose a tiny containment area where the pathogen serum would be stored, 'and disperse it anywhere.'

'How insightful of me,' smiled Mira, taking the completed device and placing it on her suit. It was a brooch after all and she would wear it with pride.

'Time to put an end to all this.' She walked out of her own labs and out of the building. Her car was waiting for her.

Bradley was running through things with Fred. 'Ok, Mr All-Too-Keen, the plan is if things turn nasty, you jump in and use the opportunity to do a little bullying and damage control, but until then, keep out of sight.'

'Got it!' he loved the idea, being the muscle behind the operation suited Fred just perfectly and he slipped into the role with glee and anticipation.

'Before we go, button up that shirt of yours,'

'Oh, why? I thought you liked the look!' Fred was a bit annoyed.

'Love it, except we don't want you to attract too much attention, remember, we're investigating. If everyone you meet automatically remembers the guy with the new look, we fail at being subtle,' he explained.

'But wait, I like it this way,' objected Fred.

'We need to be as discreet as possible,' explained Bradley.

'If it bothers you that much, you button it!' he made a show of his point by bulging out his chest and moving closer to Bradley. Bradley turned around nervously making sure they were not being overlooked and moved back.

'Just do it, Fred.'

'But you said you liked the look!'

'Fine, I'll get Heather to do it.'

'No way! She's not getting within 100 miles of me, you want it closed, you will just have to do it, or I'm going back to my boring, dull books.'

Bradley let out a long sigh, he did not have any time for this nonsense.

'Fine, don't move,' he reached out and buttoned Fred's shirt up, 'happy now?'

'Not really, but it will do for now,' the shirt was not enough to hide the bumps the metallic ropes made under it.

'Hmmm, let's see if this works.' Bradley put his hand on Fred's chest, allowing his power to flow, and instructed, 'unseen, hide.'

'Oi, what was that for?' objected Fred at Bradley's touch.

'Stop being so difficult, look,' he pointed to his arms and chest.

'Wow, they are gone? Cool!'

'You wish, they have just hidden themselves,' Bradley explained.

'But I don't feel them, it's like they are not there anymore at all, look.' He pulled up his sleeve and no ropes on his arms were visible.

'They are simply bending matter and space from the quantum point to both be there and not be. What they are showing the world is the not-be version, however, the be-there version is still there. Don't worry about how it works, let's go on... our adventure awaits.'

'Fine.' In all honesty, Fred didn't want Bradley's explanations. He was certain he would not understand even half of them and was more than content to simply go along with the plan, grateful that, for this little time, he was free of those damn nerve-ropes.

It took them just about ten minutes to get to the gym. 'Take the back door and meet me inside,' Bradley instructed.

Bradley went through the front door, and just a few steps from reception, he closed his eyes and focused. Lust, he thought. He felt a bit of a flicker, but nothing happened. 'Damn, I am awful at lust. Why can't I do it?' he questioned himself, not realising he was speaking out loud. He had been experimenting with projecting emotions using his power and had found that certain force carrier particles were indeed affected by emotions. He did not understand exactly how but he did not need to. It worked regardless with a few exceptions. 'Fine,' he resolved. Charm, he focused, he'd become one with charm itself. He allowed it to flow through him and his power flared. His composure changed, the way he stood changed, the way he smiled changed, his posture changed. All of him adapted to being charming, completely charming. It oozed out of him, shimmering in the air around him. He had become the embodiment of charm itself. He took the few steps and came face to face with the girl at reception.

'Hi,' his smile totally unarmed her. He saw her pupils dilate. Self-confidence was his strong point but so was polite sophistication; somehow, his body had learnt to accentuate his movements, making his muscles pop in exactly the right manner at exactly the right moment. 'Beautiful, tell me, I'm looking for a PT who works here. He's called Dantel, I believe.'

'Oh him,' she replied, face all gloomy all of a sudden.

'That's a quick change of mood, everything alright?' Bradley focused really hard to wilfully change his facial expression to one of deep concern. It seemed to have done the trick.

'Yes. Well, kind of, yes. I don't really like that guy, he's a bit of a womaniser but being the top-performing PT here, nothing any of us can do.'

'Maybe I can help?' he offered.

'Oh, no, please don't, if anyone finds out I told you,' she paused, 'I could lose my job.'

'No one will hear a word of it! You have my word,' a gentle smile formed in his expression. She looked at him, smiled and decided that maybe not all men were full of themselves. How or why she had decided so was completely beyond her own understanding; all she knew is that she liked what she saw.

'So, why do YOU want to see him?' she knew she was not supposed to be so upfront, but she felt close to this tall stranger and wanted to help him.

'I have a few questions for him, he used to train a young woman called Kuroi. I just need to check what program they were running and if he had noticed anything about her health.'

'Oh, that poor, poor girl, she was so nice.' The girl burst out almost in tears, 'everyone here really liked her and then we heard what happened. I've always wondered if she pulled through, no one tells us anything about how she is doing. You wouldn't happen to know, would you?'

Perfect, this is exactly what Bradley needed, and he didn't even have to work half as hard getting to the point. Luck was on his side!

'As it turns out, I do. She's still in critical care at the hospital wing of the university.' He lied as he didn't want them to know she had passed away yet.

385

'I hope she makes it. By the way, how do you know her?'

'I'm a trainee, assisting one of the doctors looking after her.' He paused for impact, 'please don't tell anyone I told you, or I'll be in trouble for it.' He worked hard to be as creative as possible.

'You keep my secret, I'll keep yours!' the receptionist agreed.

Perfect, a bond had been formed, he thought. This would guarantee she would not spill the beans.

'I'll tell you about Dantel. He trained Kuroi for a few months. They only saw each other two times each month. The last time I was at reception, I noticed that he had left with her, so I asked her if everything was ok. She told me with a smile that they were going to just grab a coffee and a snack at the gym bar because she needed a bit of a boost before running all the way back to work. Weird place that lab where she worked... very spooky. Gives me the heebie-jeebies.'

She never paused for words. What was on her mind was out when she started to speak.

'Spooky? What makes you say that?' he asked with a smile, trying desperately to avoid alerting her to anything.

'Oh, yes, many strange things going on there, we heard all sorts over here. Gives me the creeps just thinking about it.'

'Sounds goddamn awful, thank you for the warning. You are a lifesaver!'

The girl smiled back at him. Little did she ever notice that she was, by this point, swimming in his power.

'Any ideas where I can find this Dantel chap?' Bradley was keen to get on with his main line of enquiry.

'Oh, yes, sorry, I forgot he was just with a client, which means he's probably in the changing rooms getting ready for his usual workout in a few minutes. Feel free to wait for him in the gym area.'

'Ah, thank you. Mind if I go ahead?' he asked.

'Sure, feel free! I'll sign you in as a guest. Don't worry about the paperwork, I'll fix it for you.' She beamed at him, allowing him passage through the barrier. 'I hope you decide to join us here instead of the other gym at some point!'

Bradley winked at her, 'how did you know I went to the other gym?'

'I see your solid build. The only way you could have achieved that is with regular gym work. You're not like the other doctors and scientists here. They are all either super thin or fat!'

'A delight to meet such a smart, wonderful young lady! You know what, I might just have to do that! Wouldn't go amiss with such charming company.' He made his way into the main weights area. He knew the layout of this place all too well—it puzzled him that no one on reception had recognised him. After all, he had come over countless times to meet Kuroi here. The changing rooms were right at the back.

Epstein was back in the 4D map of passageway 1987b. This time, what he was observing was far more serious. In addition to the deterioration of the inner membranes, something else had developed. He saw patches of greyish-black ooze, layering the membranes, casting small but very visible shadows. 'Fast return to origin,' he commanded. The system immediately returned him to his own research lab.

Things are progressing as anticipated. We must act rapidly, there is no time for hesitation anymore.

'Dimensional-connect to sector 19438b, subsector 3b, central communications point,' his instruction triggered a whole mechanism. His display flashed with the House script, rows upon rows of digitised instructions streamed by until, finally, 5 large glyphs were displayed in the usual electric-blues. Power pulsed over the display, the glyphs expanded outwards and eventually off the display. They danced around Epstein, causing the script on his clothing to activate. Electric sparks danced all over him, and without warning, pulled him into the digital glyphs, which were hovering mid-air.

As soon as they absorbed him, they plastered themselves back onto the display and ran from passageway to passageway, carrying not only the pulse of initial power but Epstein himself. Within a few minutes, he found himself out of the complex network of passageways and standing in a totally alien room. Harsh rocky walls, glowing eyes within them gazed at him. The large chamber appeared to be empty, the air was stale thick and difficult to breathe. The floors were polished, etched in oddities, which he recognised as symbols of its inhabitants.

'What a damnable place,' he whispered.

It took a few minutes for his presence to be noticed as a thin black line formed in the empty space. That line thickened ever so slightly, sending out a mighty screeching sound that pierced the very air of the chamber. They appeared as black and grey interwoven strings, forming a long vertical line out of which a grey glow emanated. Epstein had to restrain himself from instinctively covering his ears in agony. He knew that would be taken as an insult, and that was the last thing he wanted to do, especially here of all places. The pulse of grey-blackness burst out of it, washing sensations over Epstein, which he would rather not have experienced, flooding his mind along with entire sentences. These things communicated by turning energy into information and vice versa. Fortunately, Epstein was prepared. He had already programmed the decoding mechanism into his attire and extended his eyepiece with an earpiece capable of extracting the sound waves.

'How far have you progressed, miserable being?'

He flinched at the reference but knew it was the term they assigned to all human beings.

'All is ready, all we need is for you to breach the final passageway when Bradley comes back to TrueEarth.'

'You have completed your task better than expected, miserable being, there might be hope for your kind after all.'

'Why, thank you for your mighty praise.'

'Our arrival will coincide with this miserable being's arrival you call Bradley, as agreed.'

'I trust our business is concluded then?'

'Not quite,' came the response, 'we want you to open passageways 1988a and 1988c,' it requested.

'Those are not needed. What could you possibly want in those?' he asked.

'Do not question our motives, miserable being. You would not understand them even if you were instructed. Open the passageways or we will abandon it all.'

'Fine, fine, I'll open them once you arrive. Does that work for you?'

There was a pause. It was short, as the next wave which hit him only said, 'acceptable.'

Whatever it was faded away. He was alone once again. Epstein undertook the inverse procedure that had got him here to return back home.

Bradley entered the men's changing room. No one here. Now what? He thought. *WAIT...* a voice spoke directly into his mind, which nearly made him jump. He so hated when that happened. Seeing as he had nothing to lose, he stood to the side and waited. This was the perfect time. He concentrated and willed his charm to fade away. He needed power now, pure, raw, overwhelming power. It was like letting a caged, raging beast free as he unleashed his dormant fury. It threatened to boil over. He was about to confront the man who could be the reason Kuroi and his son were dead.

He felt the slight pull, followed by a rapid rush of his pulse. He etched a glyph in his mind and saw it glowing red with power. Its glow enveloped him in a cloud of aggressive power. He was well past wasting time trying to be charming and polite; this time, he would gain his goals by force. After all, he was facing someone who should, technically speaking, be as physically strong, if not stronger than he was. His musing was interrupted as a tall, slightly tanned bodybuilder walked past him. Bradley looked at the man who had just stepped out of the shower, definitely a bodybuilder but not quite the width of one just yet. A charming sort of fellow, black hair, in his late 20s, perfectly sculpted body, very lean, yet extremely muscular. He could see why it was so easy for him to get his one night stands.

The thought that Kuroi might have fallen for him stirred in the back of his mind and he dismissed it instantly. He knew Kuroi would not go for a nobody like that. This man was here, not because he wanted to be a PT, but because he had failed at everything else in his life and this was the only thing he could do. He was nothing like the proper personal trainers he knew — they had the expertise and desire to help their clients shape their bodies. This one had the desire only for money, cared only about his own pleasure and was quite succinctly a failure at everything else. He could see it. He knew this man's history. He had tried, oh how he had tried all so hard in his own mind. He had battled for success, whereas, in reality, he lacked discipline, which made him fail at everything he ever did.

Bradley shook his head to interrupt his mental entanglement with the guy. He did not need all this information. Reading the man helped him achieve nothing. This was time for action.

'You must be Dantel, right?'

The young man turned to face Bradley with just his towel covering him, surprised at not having noticed someone standing there.

'What do you want?'

'Are you or are you not Dantel?'

'Who's asking?'

'Does that matter?'

'Why, yes.'

'I'm Bradley.'

'What do you want?'

'I take it, that means you are Dantel.'

'Yes,' he finally admitted. 'What is so important that you have to question me as I get out of the shower in the changing rooms? If you want to discuss training, you can make an appointment at reception like everyone else.'

'I want you to tell me about your dealings with Kuroi, especially the last time you met with her.' Bradley was sick of the turnabout questions, so he decided he would be direct, no matter what.

'Ah, her boyfriend? Think she cheated on you?' Hearing him speak of her set Bradley's nerves on fire. He was going to rip this arrogant fool's heart out with his bare hands. Somehow, he managed to restrain that impulse.

'No, not quite, I take it you remember her then.'

'Sure do, that...' anger registered clearly on his face.

'She must have done something horrible to you?'

'None of your business.'

Immediately, Bradley noted that he was defensive, which, in his mind, meant that all had not been well between them, which also meant that he might well have a reason for revenge.

'In that case,' he interrupted his speech by simply heading a few paces towards the exit.

This seemed to put Dantel at ease as if the confrontation was over even before it had begun. He was pleased and confident that since he appeared to be the stronger and better built of the two. Whoever this Bradley was, he had decided it was best for him to leave than push things further. Dantel turned his back to him and went to his locker as if nothing had happened. Bradley, however, let the word 'power' flow through his mind, over and over again. It echoed like a sound wave from afar, gaining momentum and strength until it was very much the crushing destroyer of anything it encountered. That sound wave spilt into his own body and overwhelming power flooded him. The very air crackled with tiny particles which were sliding in and out of the visibility range. Combining with his rage at the insult directed at Kuroi and her memory, it spilt forth. Within a fraction of a second, his black and red armour covered his whole form. The buzz of power made Dantel turn around.

'What the...' he never finished his sentence.

Bradley's fist made a firm impact with Dantel's midsection. The force sent his entire body flying across the room. A moment later, it slammed against the opposite wall with a loud throb. His punch had been so powerful that it had lifted Dantel's 110kg body as if it was nothing more than a football. He hit the row of lockers on the opposite wall and fell face down on the floor. Someone laughed from across the room. Bradley turned to see Fred standing there, holding his stomach, trying to contain his laughter.

In between trying to grasp for air, he mumbled, 'that... looked... like... a... pancake... stuck... on... the... wall... and... flopping... face... down.'

Bradley ignored it and made his way to Dantel's unconscious body. He put his right foot on his tailbone and applied pressure. Amplified with power, it was the equivalent of a one-ton truck firmly lodged on top of Dantel. He regained consciousness and desperately tried to dislodge himself, then tried to pound at Bradley's foot to no avail.

'Now you're going to answer ALL of my questions, OR...' he applied even more pressure with his foot.

'STOP, please stop,' pleaded Dantel.

'I hear bones crack under this much pressure, but I've never broken anyone's tailbone,' he paused. 'I must admit that I am quite curious to see what sound and effects that would cause. What do you think, Fred? Paralysis from the waist down? Loss of mobility?'

'Oh, let's try it and find out!' Fred put on his tone of childish curiosity.

'NOOOOO, no, no, please don't, anything, I'll do anything, ask and I'll tell you EVERYTHING, I swear!' Dantel pleaded.

'Fine, speak and make it fast. My patience is running thin, very quickly.'

'What do you want to know?' he pleaded.

'First, what happened between you and Kuroi?' He put a little more pressure with his foot.

'I... I..'

'You what? Spit it out! You're making me impatient!' Bradley's voice was cold, almost cruel.

Even Fred, in the background, held out a shiver when he heard him speak. Something was changing in Bradley right there in front of them.

'I wanted... I asked her out...'

'Go on.'

'She turned me down.'

'Is that all?'

'You don't understand,' he tried to explain.

'Oh, I'm sure I do, let me finish that for you, shall I?' his hate flared strong now. 'You are used to having countless women all swoon over you. Your well-built body, combined with that all too youthful face of yours, would do the trick just nicely, wouldn't it? You go out with as many as you can for pleasure. Then you go around bragging how you get laid with all these pretty girls. It makes you feel like a man. Which, let's be honest, doesn't make you anything even close to what a man should be. Kuroi rejecting you, that was a direct hit at your all so misconceived manliness. Am I right?' Bradley increased the pressure on Dantel's tailbone. The frustration within him was growing.

'Yes, damn it, yes,' replied Dantel. 'She told everyone she would no longer even train with me because I made her feel uncomfortable. All I offered was a good time.'

'Because you are so damn good in bed, I assume? A child pretending to be a man, what do you actually know of pleasure, you self-deluded fool.' He concluded in the most matter of fact analytical tone.

It cut through Dantel. Fred stood back, trying once more to restrain a spout of laughter. He approved of the figurative hit. He was careful not to interrupt, realising that had all this not happened to him, he might have well been in the same boat as this guy, following a very similar path in life. Fortunately, he concluded, he had a future waiting for him now.

'Tell me exactly what you did and said during your coffee and snack after your session last time you saw her,' he instructed firmly, pushing his foot down even more.

'Ok, stop, please stop,' Dantel howled in pain. An audible crack could be heard.

'Oh, well, it looks like we have a small fracture, how amusing.' Bradley was cold. He wanted to hurt this guy, wanted to make it slow, ever so slow, painful beyond his wildest dreams. He deserved pain.

'We went for coffee and sandwiches,' he screamed, 'she was feeling run down after our session. That's all.'

'A little fracture, such a tiny fracture, a small crack, which, with a little more pressure...' Bradley increased the pressure with his foot. Dantel howled again... 'could easily become a crack, then lead to a larger one until it shatters. Oh, the fun! Which awaits us...'

'Noooo, please,' he was back to pleading once more. Trying desperately to move a little to the side and topple Bradley over, he failed miserably.

'Next time you try to move, I will rip your spine out, thought I'd warn you, just as a matter of fact.' Dantel was now terrified. Not even for one second did he think Bradley was joking or full of empty threats.

'What happened during coffee?'

'She turned me down then.'

'AND?' insisted Bradley.

'Fine, fine, I spiked her drink!'

'You did WHAT!'

'It wasn't like that.'

'You'd better start spilling all the truth because you are not only boring me with your babbling but also making me seriously angry!'

'It wasn't the date rape drug... it was something else...'

'Stop beating around the bush, what on earth was it?'

'I dunno.'

'What do you mean you don't know? You spiked her drink with what? Sugar and water?'

'I swear, I don't know what it was.'

'You must know something! What are you, stupid and dumb as well as a bad liar? Where did you get it, and how?'

'I can't,' Bradley pushed ever so slightly with his foot. 'I can't! They'll kill me!'

'Who will?'

'I can't tell you, man, I'll...'

'Listen to me very carefully,' the words sent chills down Dantel and Fred's spines. This was not the Bradley he knew so well — this was like someone else speaking. Someone utterly terrifying, someone who cared nothing for human life or wellbeing. It made him shudder, this was definitely NOT Bradley anymore. He stood back against the entrance door, making sure whoever had heard Dantel's cries could not enter. 'You have a choice, you can run the risk of them getting to you and killing you, or you can just wait for me to do it right here, right now. Then, once you are dead, have me torment you to extract that information from whatever remains of you. One way or another, I AM getting that information, and I AM a threat you have to deal with now, not a possible one for a later point in time.' His words seemed to strike like a sword.

'I can't, I just can't...' he sobbed.

'Very well, it seems your stupid little brain cannot grasp the consequences of your refusal, so I am going to show you. After all, it is my duty to educate the ignorant.' Bradley bent, lowering himself into reach and ran his fingers down Dantel's spine.

'What... what are you doing, man, get off me...' yelled Dantel.

At midpoint, Bradley stopped, 'ah, here we are.' He used the sharp end of his armour to make a tiny incision. Panic drove Dantel into a struggle to free himself. 'Now, now, if you keep on struggling like that, I might misjudge things and pull the wrong thing out. Believe me, that is the last thing you want me to do.'

Fred looked in, curious, and what he saw baffled him.

Bradley seemed to pull out a glowing thread from Dantel's spine. The howl of pain was terrifying. Fred jumped back involuntarily, then looked about nervously. He was certain all this would attract attention, but he dared not interrupt. Bradley was not Bradley. Somehow, the very person standing in front of him in Bradley's black and red armour just did not feel or seem like Bradley at all. All those creeping letters in gold, pulsing with a golden glow down his arms made Fred very nervous. All resistance in his body gave way and there was no strength left in him. 'Finally, you admit defeat, child-man,' mocked Bradley in his hate-fuelled mental state. 'Now!' his tone harsher than ever, cutting like a million blades, 'Tell me!'

'I got it from the labs. One of those men came from the labs and offered me money to infect the staff who came to train here. They told me I could have the money straight away. Had to pay my rent, I had no choice, man. I had to do it. They said it would not be anything dangerous, just make them sick for a few days.' Bradley was beyond anger now. Pure cold fury had taken over.

'How were you to use it?'

'Just pour it into a drink or make them touch the liquid. They said it would work.'

'So, you took the money and rather than leave, you actually infected Kuroi with it!'

'I had to, those guys are dangerous. I had to hold up my end of the agreement, or they would come looking for me. I can't run, man, I work here and I have nowhere else to go. It was not supposed to...' He never finished the sentence. Bradley's eyes were flaring red.

'You are the one who exposed her to it! You are the cause of her DEATH. You are the cause of my unborn son's DEATH!' he concluded.

'Death? Son? Yours? Man, I didn't... know.'

'Who the bloody hell takes a strange test tube and uses it? You are a greed-ridden selfish idiot of a thing!'

'I'm sorry.'

'Oh, no, a sorry is not going to cut it!' Fury welled up inside of him even more. He was past logic, past even knowing himself, pure anger and revenge mixed as if by an expert alchemist. He was in the thrall of the power. It coursed through him, amplified millions upon millions of times by his emotions, and under it all, a cold, cruel persona surfaced, completely taking over for the first time, ever displacing his caring and affectionate side. This was larger than him. He made another cut along Dantel's spine.

'Oh, please, nooo, nooo, I'm so, so sorry, I didn't mean, I didn't know...' Dantel pleaded, knowing what had happened the last time he'd felt this exact sensation higher up his back.

'Oh, don't you worry, my dear boy, I'm going to teach you an important lesson,' the chilling voice came from Bradley's lips, 'and because I am such a nice, kind guy, I'm also going to not only teach you what real pleasure is, but I'm going to make you make amends for the harm you have caused.' The statement sounded like a threat.

In his defeat, Dantel started to sob; the man was completely broken.

Bradley heard it, 'don't you worry, all life's lessons are hard, my child, but learn them, you must,' and with that, he pulled once more on a thread coming out of Dantel's spine. This time, the howl flowing from his lips was a quick sharp pain, and then as if cut, he went all quiet.

'There, that was a good start,' commented Bradley, 'this one, I am going to tell you about. I've just pulled out the nerves, which allow you to get excited when you see someone you like. You will never again experience the result of that excitement. Instead, we are going to focus all those experiences of yours in a far more constructive manner. See how good I am, teaching and guiding the child-man into proper adulthood. What a good Samaritan I AM,' he paused, listening with dark joy at Dantel's sobbing. He was perfectly aware of what he had done. In two small moves, he had taken everything this man valued, everything he was proud of, everything that held his ego together — his pride, his self-identity, and his pleasures in life were all in tatters.

25

BIRTH OF THE
- FORBIDDEN -
SWORD

Mira was arguing with the security guard. Mike was simply having none of it. He had dealt with these self-important pretentious types before. His instructions were clear: the labs were on lockdown and no one was getting in, no matter who they were or whom they knew. Mira, on the other hand, was determined to get in. She didn't have to but she damn well wanted to!

'I own these labs. You are preventing me from getting to what is my property!' she snapped at him.

'Listen, lady, I do not care what you might or might not own. My instructions are clear. No one – and I mean *no one* – gets in. We're on high-level lockdown and there are absolutely no exceptions.'

'You do realise I work here!' she argued.

'I do not care. Your face is not familiar and on lockdown. no one gets in.'

'Surely the staff need to be able to get in to work. What kind of an establishment is this?'

'That is not my decision to make.'

'Oh, get out of my way. You are downright irritating.' She tried to push through.

Mike was a large man. His posture changed his chest bulged outwards, his arms extended. His entire body was barring her way. 'As I have said, no one gets in. You'd better leave before I call for reinforcements.'

'Call them. I will get you fired for this. You don't know whom you are talking to!'

'I don't care if you are a prime minister, lady, you are not getting in.'

She picked up her phone and dialled a number. The person at the other end answered. 'I am having trouble getting in. An idiot here calling himself security is barring access,' she complained.

'That would be due to the lockdown order. I'm afraid your first day will have to wait until after the emergency has been dealt with.'

'This is preposterous! I could have you all closed down this very minute!' She was seriously angry now.

'Do as you will,. We cannot alter the fact that the labs are on lockdown and no access is permitted, authorised or not.'

'This is not the end of this. You will be hearing from me!' She almost yelled down the phone.

'What was that?' asked Heather.

'Most probably the one who sent Kiandra here in the first instance,' replied her grandfather. 'Just ignore it for the time being. We have other things to deal with and very pressing ones at that.'

'Dr Grimsaw, we have the final results in,' interjected Jim.

'Good, what is the news?'

'It is as feared. The 5G networks have for some reason been turned on and are hyper-activating its viral activity. What's worse, the virus' nanite components immediately switched from 4G to 5G networks for its communications.'

'With all these data pulses, as soon as they hit the pathogen it overexcites. However, when it hits a human being, it disrupts the electromagnetic fields of the brain and both the central and autonomic nervous systems; this causes a lethargic state.'

'This is very serious.' He seemed to be lost in thought. 'Almost too good a coincidence. When the virus completes its... let us call it metamorphosis, these networks go live and the end result is they help it do its job with increased efficiency... how very convenient...'

'Anyone seen Bradley?' asked Jim. 'We need him in on this.'

Dr Grimsaw waved his hand in dismissal. 'Bradley is busy with something else.'

Heather's interest was piqued; what did he know about Bradley's activities?

Dr Grimsaw continued, 'We need to find a way to take all that tech offline until the virus is no longer an issue. There is no way we will be able to counter the commercial interests pushing for it. Even with the best scientific data, it will just be counter-argued until sufficient doubt is raised, then dismissed as an ongoing issue. Jim, this thing is hyper-activating under the influence of all these radio signals, is it?'

'Yes, it's sending and receiving data, as well as doing whatever else is causing this type of activity. The faster the signal, the more efficient it becomes and the more data it seems to funnel.'

'What is in the data?' asked Dr Grimsaw.

'It's not only encrypted but it is of such levels of complexity that we simply cannot determine head or tail of it. All the protocols are completely unknown to us. It is not technology available to either the military or the public.'

'Give me a copy. I know someone who might be able to shed some light on the matter.' Jim nodded in agreement.

'Heather, how are we doing on countering the biological part of the virus?'

'We're running into a brick wall. I've used Bradley's initial findings and his formula but so far, the furthest we have been able to get is to stop it killing us. Beyond that, we are at a loss.'

'Keep at it. At least we have something. As you all know, the labs are on lockdown, so no one leaves unless they absolutely have to and if they do, they cannot get back in. Ok, back to work everyone.' The dozen other scientists rose out of their seats and filed out of the meeting room. Heather was just about to leave as well when he motioned for her to stay. 'Heather, if bad comes to worse, I want you to go where this diagram indicates and escape. Do not stop for anyone, even me; just leave and get out of any open spaces. Interact with no one and make yourself unseen.'

'But –'

He interrupted her. 'No buts, please. Do not worry about me either. You must survive this no matter what. And don't go running after Bradley. He'll be fine and is not your concern.'

She did not want to argue about it so nodded in agreement. Spontaneously she gave him a long hug. He was a little surprised. For the first time in all the long years she had worked here, she had done something which was not in her own mind professional. He smiled. In view of the circumstances, that might not be a bad thing. He needed her to look after herself first, not her job or what others thought of her.

'Now go.' He handed her a piece of notepaper with what looked like a scribbled map of passageways and a big X marking a spot at the end of one of them.

Mira was still fuming when she realised that she was being foolish; she had other ways of getting in. A smile surfaced. Yes, she had other ways; far more effective ones at that. This guard would pay for his lack of obedience. She would make an example of him. For the time being, she had no problems getting in. Her car was waiting as usual. She got in.

'Go get a coffee or something.'

'Ma'am?' asked the driver uncertain.

'Just give me some time. Have a break of some sort. Why do I need to explain myself to you?'

'At once.' He left as requested.

She closed her eyes and allowed the shadow to manifest from within her. This was a familiar process at this point in her life. She had mastered this manoeuvre all too well. Within moments, she found herself inside the ladies bathroom. She knew it all too well from last time she had visited. It took her no time at all to put her best face on and move out for action. Her goal was simple: find the most crowded place and release the virus or find one of the scientists and ensure they were exposed to it. The fact that they were subject to a lockdown made her task so much easier.

Bradley's voice become an echo, streaming across the vast cold space of existence. 'Two lives you owe me, three futures, and six destinies; a human deed by a human hand is the cause. Only a human deed by a human hand will make amends.' He held his hands half a foot apart and in the gap formed a massive sharp black double-pointed crystal.

'Your soul, your being I take as payment eternal.' He made a swift downward motion. As he did, the crystal dove into Dantel's back, and it pierced right through him. Dantel howled like a beast. Bradley was no longer himself; he kept pushing the crystal in further and further, completely oblivious to anything else happening. As it finally completed its descent and penetrated fully, the wound closed.

'Now the fun. We're going to turn it INSIDE you! I am so going to enjoy this. Ready, man-child?' He never waited for a reply. 'Of course you are, let's go.' He made a twisting motion. The crystal cut through organs in its 90-degree turn. Dantel fainted and lost consciousness. The pain was more than any human could endure. 'What a failure of a human being, let alone a man. Pathetic.' Bradley put his hand on Dantel's back where the crystal had penetrated. He felt its pulse of power as all the wounded organs were healed. 'There, now, all that is fixed. You will be able to endure the real agony which awaits you.' He patted the unconscious Dantel, running his fingers through his hair. 'What a good boy you will be. Suffer well, junior.' He turned and faced Fred who was back against the door to the changing room, desperately trying to hold back the forceful attempts to enter. Bradley's eyes flared red one last time and went back to their usual blue. 'We need to go.'

'Thank goodness, I don't know how long I can hold that for,' admitted Fred.

'Why didn't you use your chains?'

'What? Wait, wait, what?'

'Oh I nearly forgot. Our adventure was also intended to teach you how to use those.' He pointed to the chain-like ropes all over Fred's body.' It was only then that Fred noticed they were back. His heart sank a little. 'We still have time. Let's have some fun before we get back to the matter at hand.' Bradley was all fun and mischief once more. Fred was not too sure how to react after what he had just witnessed. 'Ok mister, I'm not sure how this works for you but I suspect if you follow the same process as I do, you should be able to gain control of them. After all, part of my power flows through them now, so it should work in a similar way to mine. In theory.'

'Man, I hate it when you do that "in theory" of yours. Always spells trouble to come,' admitted Fred.

'Oh don't be a wuss. Experimentation is good for the soul!'

'Yeah right.'

Bradley ignored that last comment. 'Close your eyes and see them doing what it is you want them to do, then feel them moving and doing exactly what you had seen in your mind a moment ago. Reshape them visually, and see them as strong thick metallic chains, not ropes.'

Fred had no problem understanding that. He had wanted them leave him for so long, imagined it so many times, that doing exactly that would be easy. He closed his eyes, still leaning back against the door, resisting the regular jolts attempting to break in. He became aware of the nerve-ropes all over his body. For some reason, his focus locked in on all his restraints; those stood out in his mind like no other thing. He saw chains flowing out of them and etching themselves into the walls, making a second door, holding the current one closed. 'Seal,' he voiced out, maybe a bit too loud for his own liking. They expanded from the thin structure to massive bulky chains, inter-weaving themselves and sealing the doorway shut like no other force could. Power pulsed through them in a constant ripple, causing the air to shimmer.

His eyes opened cautiously. He saw Bradley nodding in the affirmative. 'Very impressive, very impressive indeed.'

Fred turned, looked at the door, and blinked. He could not believe what his eyes were showing him: millions upon millions of chains meshed into one another, glowing in black and indigo blues. He cautiously touched it. It felt utterly solid. He tried to push against it. Nope, not even the slightest of budges. What amazed him even more is that the wall no longer even shook from the jolts on the other side. He could still hear them attempt to bash the door in on the other side, but on his side there was no movement, no vibration; nothing. All the kinetic force applied was being absorbed by his new door-block.

'I...?' He attempted to ask: '...did this?'

Bradley finished his sentence for him. 'Yes, as a matter of fact you did. Not only that but you have caused a change in the natural state of things. Your power is fully awake and has become real. Congratulations!'

For some reason unknown to himself, Fred was actually proud. He had achieved something, yet he was at his point still unsure what exactly this achievement meant.

'Now that you are free of door guard duty, fancy coming over to help me with this?' Bradley pointed to the unconscious Dantel. 'He'll be waking up soon.'

'Sure, if I can.'

'If? I think it's time you stopped doubting yourself. In case you hesitate, look at that doorway! See? You CAN.' He gently patted Fred's shoulder whose confidence was growing now. 'Just follow the same instructions whenever you need to do anything. We will discover more applications later on. Goodness knows, we are all still learning.'

'What do you need me to do to him?'

'I want you to be his guard for a while. At least until his change is well under way. I cannot afford to lose such an opportunity by him killing himself or being killed.'

'Change?' Fred was curious now.

'Never mind that. You will see it for yourself in time. No time for theory now.'

'Oh, now it's "no theory"? A second ago you were all theory.' He laughed. 'Bradley, you are such a contradiction you know!' he teased.

Bradley smiled. 'We all need our little mysteries!'

'Guess so. Just don't make me an experiment in your theories as you did him!'

'I would never!'

'Sure, sure.'

'What I want you to do is use your chains to do two things. One is to bind him. You should have no problem with that, since it is very nearly exactly what your situation is. But here, you are going to bind him to your control of all his movements.'

'That should be doable.' He thought he was not too sure about the details but decided not to worry about them.

'Can you carry this?' Bradley pointed Dantel's body.

Fred nodded.

'Time for us to go. No point you wasting power maintaining that.' He pointed to the door.

Fred had completely forgotten about the door. Did that mean keeping up the door seal had caused him to have less power? It must have, since Bradley had to give him some of his own, for the second set of chains. *Damn, I so need to get back to training! And train harder than ever! Especially NOW!* He was really excited. Bradley opened up one of his gateways. Fred was terrified by the very sight of them.

'Don't worry, I'll guide you,' offered Bradley. He knew of the fear.

'Thanks.' Dantel was unceremoniously picked up and flung over Fred's right shoulder. Carried as if he was nothing more than a large sack of potatoes. Fred found it odd that he should not struggle under the weight. After all, this guy was over 110kgs. Bradley stepped behind Fred, put both hands on his shoulders, and gently nudged him forward into the portal. Fred closed his eyes and kept them well shut. There was no way he would open them in there. Not a chance. Bradley laughed and kept gently nudging him forward until he could once more feel air flowing through his nose.

He opened his eyes. He was in a room; it did not look like a campus room. Actually, it was extremely tidy in some places and an utter mess in others.

'It's his room,' Bradley explained.

'You can do that? Go to other people's places even without knowing about them?'

'Not quite. I don't know about it but he does! I pulled the memory from him – that's all.'

'Damn.' Fred was impressed. Just how fast was Bradley learning? It seemed unnatural. 'What do we do with him?'

Bradley removed the covers from the bed. 'Dump him here face up, then you need to pull those chains of yours from the door at the gym before the doorway closes. After that, you are going to regain all the power you were using on them and use some of it to hang him above his bed. That should be almost familiar territory for you.' He smiled, almost amused.

'Oh shut up.' Fred was annoyed at having to remember that.

'But in this case, make those chains hold him up about a foot or two in the air. We want him dangling there because of what will happen to him. After that is done, you are going to sit here and guard him until his change is complete. We don't want him injured, hurt, or anyone interfering. It will disrupt the change if they do.' *And I don't want anyone else touching the new-born either or I will lose possession of him.* That little titbit of information he would not share, just to be safe. He trusted Fred but you could never be careful enough.

'And you're not going to tell me about this change, are you?'

'Nope, it's a surprise. Well, I kind of don't know if it will work; think of it as an experiment.'

'Oh man, don't you dare experiment on me, you hear me?'

'Didn't we just have this discussion a few minutes ago?'

'I'm going to keep on having it if I need to. Your experiments are...'

'Unpredictable? Fantastically fun to watch? Excitingly intriguing?'

'Bloody scary!'

'Not quite the word I would have picked, but thanks. In his case, I want terror. He is so going to pay for all he did.'

'Has it ever occurred to you to just let the police take care of him?'

'Human justice is of no use here.' The deep echoing voice boomed forth. 'It's just something people use to feel better. How would this useless piece of flesh make up for all he has done by living in jail? It would not bring back Kuroi, nor my son, nor our happiness, nor would it take away the pain and loss of her family. It solves nothing other than giving you a feeling that something has been done to make him pay. But he will never pay because he is unable to. What I am doing to him will make him actually pay and make up for the harm he did. Forever more.' Bradley was all fired up. 'All that aside, when you interfere with a higher order of existence, it is that order of existence that extracts the justice for the crimes against it. Human beings have no say in it, nor do their so-called rules or laws. This is beyond all of us, and that beyond is dictating what happens now. Simply go with the flow; it is the best course of action. You of all people should understand that.'

'I am starting to. I must admit it's hard to wrap my mind around it all,' he admitted.

'Then don't. There is no need for you to understand all these things if you don't want to. Work with what you have and at some point, you will grow to understand more. Until then, play the game of existence!'

'Wow, man, you are flared up.' He took a slight step back and admitted, 'And kind of scary. Are you sure this is still you, Bradley?'

'You're right about me being flared up. We have work to do. Chains, Fred! Go, go!'

Fred nodded. He sat down on the chair next to him and felt his door of chains. It was odd; as if he was seeing from the chains' perspective. He was at a loss as to how to make them return to him when he was nowhere in sight.

Bradley sensed this problem. 'Just want them to come back to you. Feel them and see them crawling back about your body or wherever you originally had them coming from.' Fred did just that. Bradley observed him closely. The restraints pulsed with the black-indigo power; it concentrated itself not in the chains but in the restraints themselves. Next thing he knew, he had to rapidly step aside out of the way, as chains rigid and sharp as arrows buzzed past his head and darted straight into his wrist and ankle restraints. It was a bullseye, but one which could have seriously injured Bradley had he not been so keenly aware of his immediate surroundings.

When they stopped flowing through the gateway, Bradley closed it. He saw Fred was already at work on Dantel. Chains were smoothly ebbing their way over and under his body, then sharply burrowing into the walls and ceiling. As they did so, the young man's body was lifted mid-air from the bed. More and more of them wound themselves about him.

It was only after they finished and Fred had opened his eyes that Dantel started to regain consciousness. He instinctively pulled, trying to free himself from their firm grasp. Nothing gave way, and only then did he realise that he was suspended in the air. Panic overtook and as he tried to shout for help, Fred's work saw to it that the little sound he was able to make was useless. His facial expression brought Bradley immense satisfaction.

'Don't you worry, dear boy. Your nightmares have just begun. We have many delightful pleasures for you to endure: painful ones, terrifying ones, and ones that will shatter you. Then I will rebuild you into the perfect tool and as that tool, you will start to spend the rest of your miserable existence making up for all the loss you have caused.' Dantel tried to say something but only managed to mumble incoherently.

'Fred, remarkable work, I must admit. He won't be saying anything other than squeaking pointlessly. I need to go back and let the others know what this fool here did.'

'Should we just leave him here?' asked Fred.

'No, you will be staying with him until I get back.'

'Wait, what?'

'Remember, he might have those guys come looking for him. You will need to defend him.'

'You want ME to protect that piece of shit of a human being? You remember what he did, right?'

'Yes, and yes. It will be worth it. He will pay far more than if he was just dead. I am not going to let him off that easily!'

Fred understood what Bradley meant but he was still not happy about having to stay and guard Dantel. 'What am I going to do in the meantime? Daytime TV is so boring.'

Bradley laughed. 'You cannot imagine how glad I am to hear that. What you should be doing, mister, is training! And I don't mean gym training, I mean your powers. You are at your limit with two sets of chains. Push against it; work on harmonising with the crystals, remember!'

'Fine, fine. I guess so. Besides, I bet he has something interesting to keep me occupied in this place.'

'Do what you will. He will no longer need it nor anything else in it once I'm done with him. Actually, he'll never need any other place, as a matter of fact.' Bradley sounded ominous. With that, he rapidly located the main apartment door and left.

Odd he didn't use his doorway thing, thought Fred. He decided it didn't matter. It was time for him to find something to do. Time for him to go explore Dantel's apartment.

Bradley had just finished reporting to Dr Grimsaw. He was about to step out of his own office when something interrupted him.

Bradley? Hello? How does this work? Is it even working? Bradley? It was Mishrak trying to use his nerve-cords to reach out to Bradley.

Mishrak?

By the grace of the House, you can hear me?

Yes, I am replying. All loud and clear.

Bradley, you must get back now. We're in big trouble. It's all gone to doom and gloom; everything is falling apart. You need to get back... emotion was coming through, blasting at him.

Mishrak, take a deep breath and calm down. Your emotions are clouding what you are saying.

Oh, ok. We're in trouble, big trouble... invasion... Lurizak troubled... not making it... we're in battle... dying... not sure...

Mishrak, calm down! You're giving me a headache! NOW. Bradley found he could reach Mishrak easily by sending his will through the nerve-cords. His command was for calm. *Tell me things calmly. Who's dying? Who's invading? What happened? Start from the beginning. Keep it short; this is exhausting me.*

Lurizak... trouble dying.

What? Lurizak? Are you sure?

I'm here with him, badly hurt. Followed Epstein into the passageways. We encountered invaders. Too many for him alone. Epstein opened passageways to FalseEarth and Hyperspace. Something horrible came through... attacked Lurizak and me. He's hurt real bad... armour not able to regenerate. His life is bleeding out. Can't stop it. He won't make it., Bradley, help! We can't... he won't... we're going to get killed here.

Mishrak, stop your panic! Can you get in touch with Elshevira? Using that darkness thing like her?

Yes, I know how to do that.

Do it, commanded Bradley. *Tell her to get Tamirok and whoever else they can.*

Ok, but he's going to die! Mishrak was struggling to deal with a crisis situation, it seemed.

Mishrak stay calm. Bradley's will flared up, flashing through the young man. *I'll be there as quick as I can. Show me exactly where you are. What does it look like around?* Mishrak projected the image into Bradley's mind. *That won't help much; there is nothing to pinpoint you in the surroundings. I need something to focus on so that I don't get lost in those... tunnels?*

I know! came from Mishrak's thoughts. It took a couple of seconds and a new set of images flooded Bradley's mind. Use that! Bradley had to admire the man's ingenuity; he had carved or burnt or etched a big glyph in the walls of the tunnel next to them. Bradley had just to concentrate on going to that glyph in that space and he would be right next to them! Brilliant.

I'll be there as soon as I can, hold on for me. Exhaustion overcame him and the mind connection was lost. This was proving to be a bigger problem than he had initially thought it would be. With his energy running low, his powers would not be at their peak either. Opening a portal to the Chamber of Ancients then coming all the way there was not an option, and his own gateway was not able to make the crossing to TrueEarth. There was no choice; he had to finish what he had started with Dantel before he went to their rescue. He hoped he would be able to step into their time instead, to make up for the loss of time. Bradley rushed to re-join Fred and Dantel.

'Took your sweet time,' accused Fred.

'I'm sorry; things turned out taking way longer than I had hoped they would,' he admitted. 'I got interrupted on my way back here, but I did find out some very useful information before going off-course.'

'Do tell. You can't make me wait here babysitting and then not tell me.' Fred was excited; anything to take his mind of this monotony was a plus.

'Oh, don't you worry yourself. Soon enough I will know EVERY-THING he knows.' Bradley pointed at Dantel.

Fred had not noticed before, but Dantel's dangling body was shivering all over. A slight tremor overtook it every so often. It only lasted a few seconds and passed.

'What's up with him?' Fred asked.

'Nothing to worry about. It goes with whatever is happening to him.'

'You're still not going to tell me?'

'Not yet, but very soon. In the meantime, I brought our little dangling friend here a surprise.' He pulled out of his lab coat a syringe, and out of the opposite pocket a sealed needle. He fixed the needle on the syringe and primed it. As a few drops splashed out, he took a step back, making sure it didn't make contact with his own body.

'What is it?' asked Fred.

'I'm not too sure. I saw this in one of the vials at the lab and thought it would be fun to inject it into someone. As the odds would have it, our dangling friend up here seems like a very suitable candidate. No idea what it is or what it will do. Surprise!'

Fred just looked at him, trying to determine whether he was joking or had completely lost his mind. Bradley was never one to take any action without having a purpose and planned outcome. 'Bradley, are you sure?'

'Oh come on, it's going to be fun. It's a jump into the unknown, just as he did with Kuroi. He did it for money and out of fear; I'm going to do the same for fun and to see what happens.'

'I don't think this is a good idea.'

'Would you prefer I tried out this surprise in the syringe on you instead? Are you offering?'

'Oh, no no no, I'm sure Mr Dangling over there is all too happy to volunteer for your... experiment.'

'It's settled then. Bring him down flat on the bed.'

Fred obeyed. Out of the two choices, he was definitely not going to be taking the first one, where he got injected with goodness knows what.

'Now, you miserable thing,' said Bradley, 'stay still or you might get damaged beyond repair.' He shoved the long needle straight into the right side of Dantel's neck, forcing the plunger down, he emptied the liquid deep into Dantel. A scream of agonising pain that gradually deformed into something unrecognisable escaped his lips. His entire body tensed up and struggled pointlessly against his bindings. Bradley patted his head. 'There there; now you will never be able to utter another sound ever again. Not that you will ever need to.'

'What happened?' asked Fred.

'The serum burnt through his vocal cords, permanently scarring them chemically beyond use. He will never be able to speak, shout, yell, or scream ever again. That sound he made was the last one he ever will make. He will be as silent as the dead are to the living.'

'That's horrible.'

'Yes it is,' affirmed Bradley. 'Just as horrible as his actions, but insufficient.' He paused. 'Not to worry; more is on the way.' Fred could not help but just stare at Bradley. He had never known the level of cruelty hidden in this man. He was, for the first time in his company, afraid. Bradley seemed to know of his inner workings, as he swiftly stepped to Fred's right and whispered in his ear, 'Don't worry, I'll always be Bradley to you and protect you. Remember the promise I made you; that is sacrosanct.' He stood up straight once more. 'If you would drag our dangling silent friend there back up to his proper place, that would be much appreciated! But this time I want you to bind his legs together. Make sure there are no chains in between them and spread his arms out wide.'

'Like in the shape of the cross?' asked Fred.

Bradley had not thought of it that way, but it worked. 'Yes like that. Just treat his two legs as one big lump of flesh instead of two,' he instructed.

Fred didn't know what any of that meant, but complied. As usual, Dantel tried to struggle free as the chains reconfigured themselves. He was forced into whatever position Fred wanted him to be.

'Weird position,' Fred mentioned in passing.

'Not once you see what will happen next,' instructed Bradley. 'Let's grab a cup of tea – hope he has some.'

'The kitchen has quite a few good things in there. Been exploring it earlier on. Wait, tea? Who the heck drinks tea?' Fred was amused.

'Why dear fellow, all of us sophisticated types of course!' Fortunately for him, Bradley did find some teabags. 'Not ideal, but tea it is. Want some?' he offered.

'No, no tea for me.' He let a long sigh out.

Bradley laughed. 'Suit yourself.' He grab a cup for his tea, poured the milk then the tea, went back to the living room and sat down.

'What now?' asked Fred.

'We wait.'

'More waiting?'

'All good things in life take time, Fred. Sit and observe; learn from what you see. It will only take a few minutes. Let your senses and crystals speak to you.'

They sat there watching, and just as Fred was going to burst out complaining about how boring this all was, he saw the tremors rushing all over Dantel's body. They came and passed, then they came again and yet again passed. He noticed that they were happening more and more often and seemed to get more intense each time. He looked at the young man's face. He could see the strain on his neck each time the tremors hit. It is only then that he realised this strain was there because Dantel was trying to scream on every occasion.

'You knew! Didn't you?' The realisation hit Fred.

'Knew what?' asked Bradley.

'What that serum did. You deliberately destroyed his voice.'

'So you finally figured it out. Yes I knew, but the important part was he didn't know that I knew. It gave him a taste of the horror which Kuroi felt when she started falling sick. Being afflicted with something totally unknown is a terrifying thing. You do not know what is happening to you, how it develops, why it is happening or if there is anything you can do about it. You don't even know if you will survive whatever it is. That in itself is utterly horrifying.' He paused. 'I wanted our friend up there to get a bit of a glimpse into what she experienced. Of course, he's only had to go through it for a short period of time, there is no way I could make it last weeks like it did for her. But he will remember it for the rest of his days.'

Fred was relieved. That was the Bradley he knew: calculated, precise, and thorough.

His thoughts were interrupted when Dantel's body went into a full-blown spasm. It too lasted for only a short time. 'It is delightful to watch him suffer,' admitted Bradley. 'You see, young Fred, this is what justice should be like.' They watched a second spasm take its toll on his body. This time he was perspiring all over. Sweat was dripping off his dangling body, drop by drop, onto the bed below.

'I wish I knew what was happening,' admitted Fred.

'You don't know but neither does he. He is yet again dealing with something unknown ripping him from the inside out. This is the main reason I didn't want to tell you anything about it. Soon, time for the grand revelation will be upon us, where the knowledge of what is happening to him will be far more terrifying than the not knowing. Soon.'

Fred kept staring at Dantel's body, suffering through whatever it is he was going through, while thinking to himself how utterly terrifying it would be to have Bradley as an enemy. Truly, it was. At the same time, he realised how utterly wonderful it was to have him as an ally. His own fears and doubts settled at that very moment. Bradley was his ally just as he was Bradley's. If he went against those who wronged his friends and loved ones with such utter ruthless ferocity, that was a man worth having on one's side. He turned his head to look at Bradley who didn't move, but spoke: 'So you've finally realised it.'

Fred nodded.

Dantel's body had another full-blown seizure then went completely still. 'Is he dead?' wondered Fred.

'I doubt it,' replied Bradley.

They both got up to inspect him. It was only then that Fred saw: 'He's crying, he's bloody crying. What excuse for a man cries?' To him it was an unforgivable show of weakness. Only children cried, not men.

'I wouldn't judge him so quickly with what he is going through,' explained Bradley. Then it happened. His body from neck to toe went completely jet black, like an obsidian rock, shiny and reflective. For a moment, his two legs seemed to be woven together into a single limb, and his arms went silvery. The very next instant, it looked like his body again.

'Time for explanations, it seems. Lower him just a little.' He grabbed hold of Dantel's head, who tried to shake him off. He let go. 'Good, you're awake.' He paused as if to gather his thoughts. Then he turned to Fred and explained. 'Our little friend here is undergoing a change. The crystal I planted in him during our changing room exchange is tearing through his organs, limbs, bones, and flesh. It is then repairing them in a slightly different configuration. The same is happening with his soul; the very quantum structures of what he is are being remapped and reconnected. What you had a glimpse of is what he will become: a huge sword. The crystal is also consuming his essence, his very soul to fuel its powers. By the end of the process, he will become a soul-eating battle sword, which will forever hunger for life, never quite getting it for more than an instant.'

He looked at Dantel, whom Fred had brought down to their level, and ran his fingers through his hair. 'You will be my sword. You will serve me for all time. Each time you take a life, you will remember the first life you took. Each time you drink of life itself and its soul, you will experience delight, only to lose it that very instant as it drains out of your grasp to feed my power instead. You will hate my grip on your neck, which will become the hilt of my sword, yet the more you try to escape it, the more you will crave it. For without my grip, you will sink into nothingness, silence, and emptiness and be all alone. Mine is the only grip, mine is the only will, mine is the only presence you will ever know.'

'My God, that's a terrible and awful fate,' admitted Fred.

'It is, is it not? But it gets even better, because the longer he spends in the shape of the sword, the more he forgets what it was like to be human. He will never become the sword fully, nor will he ever be human again either. He will forever shift from the one to the other, as and when I need or want him to. He will walk the world as a thing and as a person, but never be one or the other, ever again.'

'But why did you make it so that he can't speak?' wondered Fred.

'Simple; swords do not speak, and him being unable to speak as a human will limit him just enough to push him back to being the sword. He will never reach the physical perfection he so craved. His sweet words will never tempt another into bed with him.'

'Um, Brad, you might have missed something.'

'Oh? Do tell.'

'That's going to be a damn big sword for you to carry about the place.'

Dantel already felt the irritation at his core for being referred to as a tool or thing. Bradley saw that and smiled. *So it begins,* he thought. 'Ah, good point. Don't worry, I can adjust his size however I please once he is fully transformed.'

'Now that is awesome,' admitted Fred.

They sat there watching as more and more of the sword's characteristics surfaced during each transformation. Each was agonisingly painful for Dantel, each lasting longer than the former.

'It won't be long now,' affirmed Bradley. 'Watch closely. This is something you might never witness again.'

It happened. The spasm was the most violent they had seen. Fred's chains were pulled to their extreme, yet they held. Then Dantel went completely still, his body changed right in front of their eyes. His legs shifted into black blade, his arms into an intricately vicious and regal hilt, and his head turned into a large red crystal sphere with something inside of it. The completed sword fell out of the grasp of all the chains on the bed, smashing them into pieces. The blade roared into life with agonising fury. Bradley was very quick to get hold of it, his armour on in under a millisecond. He grabbed it and let his power rip through. The blade shrieked, cutting the very air about them. Ancient language and runes blazed in red fire, as if imprinting themselves along its edges. It shrieked again then fell silent. Bradley concentrated and right before Fred's eyes, it shrunk to a more manageable size.

'Finally! Now you are mine!' He wielded – or tried to wield – the reluctant new blade. Power flared once more from him and spilt throughout the whole blade. Bradley grabbed it firmly, raised it above his head and in that echoing voice of his, said, 'I NAME THEE the Sword Danterrion.' The name sealed Dantel's fate into that of the blade, as it vibrated fiercely with the power of its very birth. Half the blade was pure black, the other half golden red, both unnaturally sharp.

'There there, young one,' said Bradley, caressing the red crystal sphere on the hilt of the blade.

Fred had the most peculiar sensation of Bradley running his hands in Dantel's hair while he was tied up. *Yes, that is the synergy.* Replied a voice in his mind. Fred turned around trying to see who had spoken but no one other than Bradley was there.

'You are mine now. Settle down.' Bradley finished instructing the blade. Upon hearing his words, the eye in the red crystal closed and faded out of view.

'Make sure you get all those chains back,' he told Fred.

'Oh yes, I need those!' He did as instructed and pulled them all back in.

They both walked out of Dantel's apartment, which had become the location of one of the greatest curses of time itself.

26

PATHOGEN
- REVEALED? -

Bradley had no choice; he reached for the sword held fast by his very armour on his back. 'Time for work Danterrion,' he said. He held it fast by the hilt, the sword, as usual, resisted him, struggled, 'oh stop that.' He yelled at it in frustration. This was not the time for an internal battle. His power unleashed, and it ripped in waves through the sword itself. Those who could hear it would hear the cries of pain the sword emitted in response; they would also hear its brutal struggle against the curse as the glyphs on the blade flared up in a burning red fire. There would be no doubt whatsoever; Bradley was in total control, no matter how much it struggled.

The passageway was filled with something, which looked like moving lines of varying thicknesses. Some were black, and others were grey, some even combined the two. In all cases, these lines seemed to respond to his own movements, erupting waves of chilling black power. He was not sure what it was, but he did not want to find out; he tried to avoid them until eventually, he was being overwhelmed. Danterrion in hand, instead, he went for the assault, hurling himself against the small group of them, which stood in his way.

As the sword struck, the line stood, vibration and kinetic energy bouncing from the one to the other. Bradley allowed his own red power to flare forth down the blade, twisting it from black half to the red, then, without warning, curved his hold on it, resulting in the blade slicing from below upwards. He did not know where he had learnt to do that, but it seemed to be the most obvious way to do things in order to rebound the kinetic wave back onto its source. It did the trick; he managed to cut through this thing. The line was broken and a distortion of sound-waves was released, an echo, a scream which howled through the passageway. Its power absorbed by Danterrion coursed into Bradley. It was horrid, a desire for torture, desire for death, dislike of all things living.

Bradley wanted it out of him. With no other option, he redirected it into his next swing and amplified it with his own. The two forces merged effortlessly through the blade; he struck again, this time not bothering with any novel manoeuvres. The blade cut straight through two more of them. As the power from his new kills flowed back into Bradley, he was disgusted, what horrible things were these? The final ones seemed to hesitate, then merged with the walls and were out of his sight. Even his visor's scanners could no longer pick anything up. He pushed forth, reaching Mishrak and Lurizak.

'You took your sweet time,' yelled Mishrak.

'Calm down,' Elshevira stepped forth, 'I am so glad to see you,' she smiled at Bradley. 'He's in bad shape; I have done all I could, but I cannot heal a Bound.'

She moved out of the way and Bradley saw Lurizak on the floor, his body looked as if it had been run through a shredder. His armour was trying to reweave the flesh, but it was not having much luck doing so as the wounds were too deep. Bradley dropped Danterrion and immediately knelt by the giant warrior. Lurizak's eyes opened.

'My only wish was that I would be able to hold on until you got here, I ...'

'Don't speak,' Bradley interrupted him, 'just listen and relax.' He allowed a faint pulse of his will to flow into Lurizak. The injuries were deep, that is why they cannot heal, the Bound armours are designed to protect their bodies from being injured and can heal relatively serious ones as long as they are not deep within their bodies where they have no reach. What was he supposed to do? He had nothing to work with. An idea struck him. He turned to Elshevira. 'Mishrak told me his life was seeping out of him, is that how House GrimGloom heals? How does it work?' She paused to think.

'Hurry, we have no time to wait,' he insisted.

'We are taught that all things are formed in darkness, life flows from the father and the mother shapes it in the darkness of her womb,' she explained.

'Can you reshape it?' he asked.

'I've never tried,' she admitted.

'But you know how it is done, right?'

'I do, but I don't have anything to work with.'

'What do you mean?'

'I need life, the purest form of life itself.'

'Dammit!' swore Bradley.

'Wait!' yelled Mishrak, 'there is life all around us!' He waved his hand at the walls of the passageways.

'Yes! There is!' she acknowledged, 'the problem is, we cannot get to it, it flows in the very passageway's energy, but we don't have the means to just pull it out.'

'You might not, but I do!' interjected Bradley.

Both Mishrak and Elshevira looked at him in surprise.

'If I get you that essence, if I rip out those particles which carry this energy of life you need, will you be able to help him?' His face clearly showed his concern and desperation.

'I will do all I can, a GrimGloom has never healed any other House member; we just don't do that but for you, I'll give it my best shot!'

'Thank you; it is all we can ask.'

'But how are you?...' she hesitated as Bradley got back on his feet and collected his sword. 'What is that!' asked Elshevira, 'it feels totally alien and is sending chills down my back!'

Bradley didn't bother replying; he stood next to the wall closest to them and dug his sword into it. Danterrion screamed, the very air vibrated with its aftermath. Bradley forced it in deeper. Nothing, he was about to start swearing when a rush of immense energy flooded him. His head spun, his armour's glyphs and scripts all lit up, his eyes turned icy grey, and his hair turned white. 'Take my hand fast! I cannot keep this up for long,' the echoing voice was flowing through him once more.

Elshevira did not bother to question; she grabbed hold of his hand. A waterfall of pure life smashed its way through her. She nearly fainted. It was only thanks to her many years of training that she managed to even keep her balance. Her left hand reached for Lurizak and as he moaned out, she ran her hand over his open wounds, weaving the life essence as a thread with which she knit the wounds in his internal organs, then proceeded to repair the flesh and finally the outer wounds. She let go of Bradley's hand. The flow was interrupted. The power dulled down.

'It is all I can do; my knowledge of anatomy is lacking; I cannot heal the rest of him,' she admitted. Bradley was pulling the sword out of the walls. As he yanked it free, the gap closed up instantly, and the life essence took its natural course back.

'What is lacking?' Bradley asked.

'Blood vessels, nerves mostly.' The effects of the life essence were still plain to see in Bradley; he was overflowing with it. It did not surprise Elshevira. Legend had it that wars were fought over these passageways because they were the veins of existence and that all life flowed through them. She had never believed such a thing possible, but now she knew the truth of it.

Bradley knelt and placed his hand over Lurizak. 'You are going to have to direct the weaving,' he told Elshevira. 'I don't have this skill.'

'Close your eyes and open your mind, picture what needs to be done as if you were teaching a junior,' she instructed.

He followed her instructions, only opening his eyes to move to the next area along Lurizak's body. It took them a long time to finish. Both were totally exhausted.

'We need to get out of here,' said Mishrak, 'we don't know how long we will be safe, nor when Epstein is going to be back.'

'How do we get out of here?' asked Bradley. 'I got in ...' Suddenly, the thought that he shouldn't be sharing this out crossed his mind. 'Never mind, just can't get back out that way.'

'Me and Lurizak got in by hijacking Epstein's trip,' said Mishrak.

'Lurizak took you in with him? Why would he do that?' asked Bradley.

'Well, technically he didn't, I kind of sneaked in with him; let's leave it at that.'

'Whatever good thing you were here, how about you Elshevira?'

'I found Galvin and immediately requested he let us in.'

'That means he should be able to get us back out.'

'He was going to get help, Tamirok is mid-battle, those things attacked House Bound and House LightBearers. Why on earth target those two is beyond me.'

'What is that!' Mishrak pointed to the opposite wall in visible surprise. They all turned to face whatever it was.

Bradley was lost for words, 'that looks like! No way, it's...'

'What?' snapped Elshevira.

'It looks like a giant version of the virus, which has been attacking FalseEarth and killing people!'

'No, it cannot be!' Elshevira almost screamed, 'shadow! It's casting a shadow!'

Mishrak moved away quickly, 'it's a shadow!'

'What's the big deal about the shadow, the virus is more of an issue we can't counter that.'

'Not the virus, the shadow! Look, it has a shadow!' Fear had obviously crept into her mind. Bradley still didn't understand what the deal was.

What's the big deal about the shadow? He forced Mishrak's mind to concentrate.

There are no shadows in TrueEarth or the world at large! Only in worlds, where falsehood and deceit exist can there be shadows. Abominations.

Elshevira grabbed hold of Bradley's arm, 'stop the shadow, the shadow!' her hand trembled.

What was he supposed to do? *How do you defeat a darn shadow?* He wondered. Then he remembered the shadow, which had attacked him in the labs that he'd chased away! Light, he needed light.

'We need light,' he snapped.

'We are darkness; we don't have light or access to it,' replied Mishrak. 'The Bound can make their armours glow, but Lurizak is still out cold.'

'But I'm not!' Bradley knew he could use his own power; it might not be bright white light, but it certainly was not only dark. He focussed on the red crystals of his armour, on all the veins of power, which pulsed with a red glow and he willed it to grow, to concentrate, to emanate and radiate outward! He pulsed like a massive red light-bulb. The shadows immediately scampered away just ever so slightly out of reach of his red light. The panic and fear on both Elshevira's and Mishrak's expressions eased off. They were both regaining a grip of themselves.

'We need to get out of here, you won't be able to keep that up forever,' admitted Mishrak.

Bradley knew he was right. Keeping his armour glowing didn't drain him too much, but it was nonetheless a strain and eventually, that strain would cause fatigue. He looked around, no other choice it seems. He decided to try something.

'Elshevira, you said Galvin got your passage into here, right?' She didn't reply. 'Elshevira! We need you now!' his voice reached her cognition.

'Yes, yes, he did.'

'That means he knows where we are; all we need to do is tell him to get us back out!'

'How do you think we can do that?'

Bradley pointed at his visor! A House mTech present, it must be connected or able to connect to their systems, right?

She looked at his visor. 'You know what? You could be onto something! We just need to signal out somehow.'

'I have an idea for that too, but in case anything goes wrong, I need you to keep a level head and not freak out again.'

She nodded.

He grabbed onto the hilt of Danterrion, and with all his remaining strength, he plunged it back into the wall of the passageway.

'Are you insane!' yelled Elshevira! 'Stop!' The life was pouring through the blade into Bradley and through him into his armour. The essence was just too much to handle and with his final ounce of strength and concentration, he directed it into his visor, projecting a powerful beam of life out through the cut he had just made in the wall. The effort had cost him his final strength and he collapsed, unconscious, pulling the blade out on his way to the floor. It tumbled on his body and vanished. Dantel was back in his apartment on FalseEarth. Bradley's red glow started to fade out, as the shadows crept their way back closer to the group.

Elshevira screamed, just as Galvin and two other members of House mTech entered at their location.

'Lights, lights, quick!' instructed Elshevira.

Galvin and the two women at his side failed to understand, but seeing her panic complied. The glyphs and digit-like letters on their clothing were set alight in a pulsing strong electric-blue light. It was so much more effective than Bradley's red glow. The shadows receded. Elshevira pointed to them, 'shadows!'

Galvin turned to face them and instinctively took a step away.

'By the Houses! How is that possible? Quick, let's get everyone out of here.' All three members of mTech took to action immediately. Within a few minutes, they were all back in TrueEarth. Bradley and Lurizak were taken to the infirmary, Elshevira and Mishrak sat at the table next to them, drinking a strong liquor to help them relax.

'What on earth happened in there? And what are those shadows!' asked Galvin.

'I'll tell you everything, but first, let's make sure Bradley and Lurizak are ok; I'm going to see them,' she insisted. She was going to make sure no funny business took place. House mTech had proven they saw Bradley as a potential danger to them, if not an outright enemy. As she stood up, 'Two things you need to know before I go. Epstein is behind all this, and I bet even more that the walls in there are covered not only with shadow but also with what Bradley called a virus. He said it was a giant version of what they had in FalseEarth and that this thing was killing people there. You might want to look into that, something fishy is going on in this House right under your nose.'

Galvin was about to object, as her words had a hint of accusation in them. He decided the time for that would come later. 'You have my word as Ruler. I will investigate that with all the resources available to us and more!'

'Good, by the way, we encountered the Neraxil in there.'

'You're not serious!' he was the one surprised, 'how are any of you still alive?'

'Not sure, really, Lurizak is... and Bradley...' he didn't pursue the questioning. She just nodded and walked out. Mishrak took a look at Galvin, shrugged his shoulders, and followed her out.

Heather had taken her grandfather's advice and left the labs. She refused to run away; it was not her style. She was going to find some way of defeating this thing, even if she had to do it on her own. She was back in her own place. It was the one place she felt truly safe and shielded from the world at large. This was the place she had absolute control over and only those she wanted to interact with would do so when she was home. Her large, white comfy sofa was her favourite place to crash on. The rest of the room had a nice off-white soft peach set of walls decorated with exquisite arts. Those were the most precious things to her, the only pieces of her parent's legacy. No matter what happened, she would always protect them, at all and any cost! The side chairs were perfectly in style matching the sofa and an elm dining table formed the other part of the centrepiece of her living room alongside the massive wooden bookshelf, which covered almost an entire wall.

Books were her love and all she needed at times. She sat down, placing her coffee on a highly-decorated elmwood coffee table. This was the perfect place for her to think. She had to figure out what to do next. What worried her the most was Bradley's absence. Thinking about him jolted her intuition; something was amiss, something did not feel right. She pushed the emotion aside, ignoring it. She had other ways to find out what was happening. Her eyes closed, and her mind locked itself upon the emeralds on her neck. The rush of power was clear. She thought about Bradley, only Bradley, and nothing other than Bradley. A single thread through which the green pulse flashed came to her outstretched hands. Oddly, this thread had the occasional red pulse, then golden, then almost reflective black. 'Ouch,' escaped her lips. She almost let the thread slip; something had zapped her. She inspected it closer. It happened again, a spark of static flushed through it every so often. The faster she did whatever had to be done the better. Her concentration shifted, her mind opened and the thread expanded until it was like a tunnel. Heather's mind raced through it, with one purpose, find Bradley wherever he might be.

She did find him, but what she saw was strange. He seemed to be in some sort of medical facility. Something had happened. He was lying there unconscious on a floating high-tech bed. Blue lights were flashing, and some odd display showed results in a language she could not read. Three large rings of metal and crystal with glowing script entwined rotated up and down over and under the floating bed. She sensed no danger; it was almost as if these strange people walking up and down beside him, who looked like odd types of medics, were trying to help him. *What had happened?* she wondered, *and why was all his hair white?*

A woman in black approached, a stunning beauty clad in tight garments and black crystals. She afforded this woman only a glance; she hated her instantly. Then she saw Lurizak on the bed next to him. *What on earth is all this? What is going on?* A blackness overwhelmed her, angry, almost violet eyes flaring with dark energy glared directly at her. Her vision blurred, went all dark. Her power switched off. Elshevira had noticed the intrusion and dealt with it. Heather was not happy; this was her trump card; how could someone counter it? A shadow was heard laughing in the distance.

Bradley was still unconscious, his lower body covered in a special material used to maintain homeostasis. It glowed a faint blue as the technology within it rebalanced the heat, light, cold and darkness it emitted. The radiation was also balanced out perfectly at the same frequency as each patient's physiology settings. It improved the speed of recovery and maintained perfect equilibrium of all the elements in the body. This was only one of the many tools used by the medics here.

'He's still far from awakening,' said Rhys mTech.

'I know, but there are other things I need to guard against.' No one was going to argue with Elshevira, especially not when she was in this mood.

'As you wish, we're still trying to recharge his atomic particles. I am not sure how long it will take, his energy is unlike anything I have seen and is practically impossible to replicate. Well, not all of it, anyway,' he explained.

'What do you mean, recharge his internal particles?' she asked. mTech healing methods had always been miserly to Elshevira; she could never understand why they had to so overcomplicate things all the time.

'Ah, yes, sorry, forgot you are not familiar with our medical procedures. A human being to us is like a star and all stars are kept in delicate balance by inwards pulling forces, which you call gravity and outwards pushing ones, typically in the form of radiation of some type or another – an energy, which radiates or pulses outwards. We treat patients as we would treat stars, which need recovery on a grander scale. This very method was used to prevent the sun in the Faranthaine galaxy from going supernova.' He paused, lost in thought, trying to recall the massive deployment of mTech capabilities in that project. 'What has happened to the one you call Bradley is that he exhausted all the power in him, which causes that outwards push, so everything in him is pulling inwards. This is why he's unconscious; his very mind is collapsing in on itself. We're trying to recharge the atoms inside of him, inside every cell of his body, to restart that outwards pulse. When it does, he'll recover,' he explained. 'The warrior, on the other hand, should be reawakening shortly, whatever you did, saved his life.'

'Yes, we have Bradley to thank for that, assuming he has not gone and killed himself in the process. Why does that man so readily put his own life on the line for others? He doesn't even realise the impact of a Wielder dying on his Bound;' she was annoyed at him but smiled. There was something utterly charming about his misplaced heroics. Something had just occurred to her; she remembered. 'Where is Galvin?'

'The House Ruler is most likely occupied with most pressing affairs.'

'Yes, yes, whatever, get a call out to him, this is more important than all the shenanigans he might be up to.'

'You should not insinuate such...'

'Just do it!' she snapped at him, his nonsense as she thought of it. He went to his large crystalline display, made a few motions and tranced a few glyphs. Galvin was there, standing right in front of her, at least his projection was.

'Something occurred to me; I have just interrupted something or rather someone trying to spy in on Bradley.'

'Interesting, do tell,' he replied.

'It must have been someone from FalseEarth. I cannot believe someone from TrueEarth would make such clumsy use of dimensional communications. Anyway, this female seemed to know him, and from what I could glimpse out of her mind, she was familiar with what Bradley called the virus. Its structure is very similar to something familiar but old.' She pushed past his image and went straight for the display. 'Set it up, so I can project an image from my mind onto it,' she told Rhys.

He nodded, did his thing, and a blue beam projected out of the display onto her eyes. Elshevira concentrated, pushing the light and darkness out of her eyes and onto the display, which captured it and reinterpreted the resulting information as an image as the human brain would do in the visual cortex. Slowly and with incredible detail, the image of the virus was forming on the display in all its horrific splendour. 'This is the final version she saw.'

'No way,' Rhys was the one surprised, 'that is textbook ancient mTech experimentation, banned by laws of the House over a century ago. With elements I don't quite recognise.'

'It seems Neraxil genetic fingerprint and shadow?' mused Galvin. 'You said this was infecting people on FalseEarth?'

'From what I could see, yes. Unfortunately, only Bradley could confirm that, and he's still unconscious.'

'He will be for a short while yet,' confirmed Rhys.

'We might have another who can confirm this for us.'

'Oh?' prompted Elshevira.

'Never you mind, lady, we, too, have our secrets.'

'Speaking of another, where is Epstein? He has a lot to answer for! I'm sure him being in that passageway was no coincidence.'

'Epstein is... currently missing. We're trying to track him down,' explained Galvin.

'What!?!' she almost shrieked, *I knew it! I bloody knew it!*

'The investigation and search into his whereabouts is underway. It will take some time; we're having to prioritise on keeping the Neraxil at bay. Tamirok is at the front lines; currently, we're containing the situation, but I have the suspicion that these skirmishes are nothing more than the first few drops of rain of an incoming storm. That storm is where mTech currently needs to focus on.'

'Fine, whatever, just look into it fast because if this is true, it means not one but two of TrueEarth's enemies are not only active but about to overtake FalseEarth, and that could lead them straight to us by the backdoor! No House can counter shifts from FalseEarth back to TrueEarth.'

'Indeed,' confirmed Galvin. 'Leave this to me,... and Elshevira...'

'Yes?'

'Thank you for reporting it,' she waved her hand in dismissal, turning away from him and back to the patients. Unseen to any of them, half a smile etched itself on her face. It was victory for her! She had just scored an important point, one which might be pivotal in the outcome of this situation. She approached the treatment beds. Bradley was still out cold. *I wish I could use the Ancient Dark and help you.* Lurizak stirred.

27

THE
- TRUTH -
UNFOLDS

Bradley had recovered and was back to his old self. It had taken almost 24 hours of constant supervision from Rhys who had gone out of his way to do as much as possible within his capabilities. Turned out he was able to help Bradley regenerate by focusing on his cellular energy levels rather than his power. It was a very unconventional method for him to use. On TrueEarth, what they called the soul was always healed first and foremost. Re-establishing a healthy and proper functioning of the structures from which biological life emerges would typically cause it to start rebuilding the biology. In Bradley's case, he had to work in the opposite direction, which he decided made perfect logical sense seeing as Bradley was a native of FalseEarth, not TrueEarth... or was he? Bradley and Lurizak were back in the midst of all the recent events. Their meeting with Galvin had confirmed Elshevira's discovery, the virus afflicting FalseEarth was indeed a combination of very old technology mTech had experimented upon and then outlawed for the whole of TrueEarth. That technology, it seems, had been combined with a biological component which shared a suspicious amount of similarity to the Neraxil invaders and was held together by something shadowy. As they contemplated the findings in the conference room, Bradley pondered on a possible solution. Without knowing exactly what it was doing, it would be impossible to find a way to stop it.

'You will have to look at it in vivo,' said Rhys who was there to provide the medical expertise. Rhys was a calm and collected person, he loved medicine, in fact, he was obsessed with it. He was a typical mTech standing at 5 feet 10, with a slim athletic build clad in the standard gear most mTech members wore. However, in his case, the technical components did not emit an electric blue glow, instead, it was a soft green one. His expertise was respected by all of mTech.

'From what you have revealed, it seeks to rebuild the nervous system or at best build a parallel structure that controls the nervous system in the infected. The key question is not how it does that but rather how does it maintain the established control? What does it do to it? Where do its instructions come from? If it was simply to replicate what the nervous system already does on its own, it would be pointless. How does it communicate? And with whom?' Bradley followed the young medic's train of thought, he had come to wonder the same things during his convalescence after finding out about this.

'The other key question is, does it use the Neraxil dimensional hopping? I suspect the potential of having billions of human beings as carriers of Neraxil genetics within their biology would present them a paramount advantage not only in reaching us through FalseEarth but in terms of power. This is the most dangerous situation for us all,' summarised Galvin.

'Wait a minute, hold on,' interrupted Bradley, 'if they need human beings infected and fully... let us call it remodelled to gain those advantages, that would mean we still have a chance to stop this madness?'

'Only if we act fast, and I mean very fast,' replied Galvin.

'If we can shut down its communications and give the human biology some way for the immune system to start attacking the viral agent, we might be able to counter it,' explained Rhys.

'I think we're all missing the point,' interjected Lurizak. 'You are all thinking about this as a virus fighting the immune system, what you are forgetting is that this is a battle not within the bodies of everyone in FalseEarth but a dimensional one. You should think of this as an enemy on the battlefield.'

'You're right!' an idea had been sparked in Bradley's all too agile mind. 'This pathogen is part technology, right? Which means it has some sort of a program and that means we can reprogram it!'

'Genius!' burst out Galvin, 'I can get the records of those technologies opened for us. This thing is built around our old know-how, we can use that to our advantage!' he paused for a moment. 'Bradley, what is your memory like?'

'Photographic, why?'

'Excellent, we will get you to remember the coding so that you can replicate it back on FalseEarth. We cannot move objects or information other than mind to mind but we can have you learn it and then use it over there. Rhys will help you with the details and you can work with him on adapting it to your current lab facilities.'

'It does not solve the problem, I will still need to distribute this to everyone, and that in itself is an impossible task.'

'Not so,' Elshevira joined the discussion, 'I am not very proficient in all this medical technology but I can help with spreading the virus. Just release it into the darkness and let that become its carrier. It will infect everyone within moments. Any contact with any form of darkness will do the trick and I can shift the dark from here to FalseEarth through you just fine. It is a universal force after all.'

'And Mishrak can instruct me through the binding on how to make use of it.' For the first time since all this started, Bradley was feeling a shred of hope, only a glimmer but one nonetheless. It was a big gamble, the stakes were not only everyone's lives on FalseEarth but also their very futures. The stakes were high but he had no other choice. He turned to Rhys.

'This leaves the biological component of the virus. I'll just have to deal with that back home but I cannot do it without information. Do you have any information on it at all?' Rhys thought about it for a while and indicated that they did not.

'In that case, would you mind if I have a look at your genetics database? You have a far more detailed insight into the human genome than we have. I would like to path out the knowledge I have as it could open some insights into how I can deal with this since it is engineered to disrupt our genes and then re-code them.' Rhys looked at Galvin who nodded affirmatively.

'These are part of the open databases for all mTech, I can run you through the data we have.'

'Thank you,' Bradley followed Rhys to the large screen at the other end of the room.

As they left, Galvin looked at Elshevira, 'I know you have gained a distrust of us, please don't judge the whole of mTech based on Epstein's actions.'

She stared at him for a long time. 'You should have been prepared for this. For masters of sciences and tactics, you seem to have failed to keep an eye on the game.' Her accusation was clear, it was a challenge to his very leadership.

'I won't try to justify myself, you are absolutely correct. There have been a lot of changes in the vaster spaces which have distracted me. I should have kept a view of the micro components of mTech as well as the macro,' his admission surprised her.

She accepted his sincerity. 'What is done is done, let us see what we can do to help get us all out of this increasingly nightmarish situation. Who knows, if the Neraxil overwhelms us, this very conversation will be a mute one.'

'Let us make haste then,' the communications deactivated and Galvin was no longer amongst them. Bradley returned with both Mishrak and Lurizak at his side.

'I got as much information as I could,'

'We can always stay here and read out whatever you need when you are back on the other side. Our bindings connection works, but it probably won't help us much as neither of us know about any of this stuff.' observed Mishrak.

'You have Rhys here to help. He will be of invaluable assistance in what we will do next,' he turned to face Lurizak, 'I need you to stay here and recover fully. When you are done, join Tamirok.'

'I'm not leaving your side!' objected Lurizak.

'You can't follow me to the other side... you could but there is no point, we need you on this side and they are struggling at the front lines.'

'It is a bad idea,' interjected Mishrak, 'what if something happens to you on your side? We're both out of action then!'

'Listen, the other side is my home side, so I am far more capable there than here. We're facing the pathogen there, here you have the actual invaders in face to face combat. Besides, if the two are connected, distractions on either side could help the other.'

'That is a good point,' admitted Lurizak.

'Of course it isn't, that's utterly stupid,' countered Mishrak. 'We can't leave him alone! Not for any of our sakes,'

'It is not our choice to make,'

'Of course it is! Are you insane? It's your life at stake too and mine because of these,' he looked at his gauntlets.

'You're being an annoyance again and just hindering us,' Lurizak snapped. He had just about had it with Mishrak and his constant stream of demands, objects and reproaches. 'Your job is to wait for orders and comply.'

'What do you know anyway?'

'Enough!' Bradley snapped at both of them. 'Stop at once, we don't have time for this nonsense. Mishrak, stay here and get Rhys to help if we need any more information.' Bradley's will zapped through Mishrak with such ferocity, he nearly collapsed under the pressure. It was the first time he had experienced it. For Mishrak, this was the most horrific thing he could think of. The fact that Bradley was annoyed and irritated from his recovery did not help, all his subtlety had vanished and was replaced with aggression.

'Everyone has their jobs assigned, let's get moving, gents.' He turned to face Elshevira, 'you're the most sensible of the whole lot of us, can you please keep an eye on those two? The last thing we need is for them to be at each other's throats.'

'I would be delighted to,' her smile made the two men shiver.

'Thanks, I will signal you from my side through Mishrak when we are ready. It will take some time though,' she nodded in agreement.

'Lurizak, keep me updated on how things progress here on TrueEarth, in case we need to make any changes or anything useful comes up. And if Epstein shows up, don't follow him!' he didn't need to use his command with Lurizak as the seasoned warrior knew exactly why Bradley was asking him to do what was being requested. He needed to see battle, if his healed body was not immediately exercised, he would suffer a loss in ability. Bradley opened his gateway directly into the Chamber of Ancients and stepped through.

'What was that?' Elshevira was surprised to see it, she had never seen the place he was heading to. She looked at Mishrak who shrugged his shoulders, then to Lurizak who remained totally motionless.

'I need to go,' he turned to face Rhys, 'would you say I'm fully recovered?'

'I would suggest you eat a good solid meal and have a final scan. Other than that, you should be good to go.' Rhys remembered that Bradley had instructed Lurizak that he could only go once he got the all-clear.

'Let's go, take me to the kitchens then,' Rhys smiled. Typical warrior, so eager to get back to action.

'Ok, follow me,' he faced Mishrak and Elshevira, 'I will get them to send some food over for you two as well. When I'm finished with the scan, I'll join you for a bite myself,' the all too familiar pool of blue energy formed under their feet and the two were off heading to the dining area. Elshevira sat down and was lost in thought. Mishrak spent his time angrily panting as he nervously walked from the top of the room to the bottom, back and forth.

Bradley had made his way back to his apartment. Someone was frantically knocking at his door. 'I'll be there in a minute, hold on,' he yelled as he removed his armour and put his day clothes back on. He opened the door. Fred was there, huffing and puffing.

'Thank goodness,' Fred didn't wait to be invited in, he pushed his way in. The look of panic on his face.

'What's got you in such a huff and puff?' asked Bradley.

'You mean you don't know?'

'Know what?'

'Where have you been for the last two days? The world is going downhill, literally!'

'I doubt it's literally going downhill but do tell me what is going on?'

'Seriously!?'

'Yes, seriously,'

'Well, let me see... first, there are people falling sick all over the place, then there are people acting very strangely and then there are people who seem to be ok but are not. Only those inside the labs where you work seem to be normal, not sure for how long.'

'What? How? And how do you know all this?'

'I was there when it happened! Came looking for you using the code you gave me last time, it still works. They have the place on lockdown but haven't realised that the passageway to the dorms is not actually disabled.'

'That is very negligent of them, I would have thought Kiandra would have made quick work of making sure that oversight was locked down too.'

'No idea, I just know it's open.'

'What did you see?'

'I'm not too sure, one minute everything was like normal — boring dull and usual—then it started happening, people in the hospital, then those at the university, then those around it.'

'Hmmm, could it be that the virus has got out?'

'No idea about any virus thing but I got here as fast as I could to check if you were still you.'

'According to some, that might be up for debate. Let's get back to the labs, I need to check on things in there. We can use that passageway.'

'Not safe out there! Oh, by the way, I forgot to give you this,' he handed Bradley the USB drive Elma had left with him. 'I'm sorry I forgot to give it to you sooner, this girl said I should give it to you and tell you it's from Elma.'

'Elma? Oh yes, I had forgotten all about her, this might help us,'

'Weird girl that Elma,'

'What makes you say that?' asked Bradley.

'Her eyes, there's something very weird about them, and the laptop she had looked like something I've never seen before,'

'Her eyes? They seemed perfectly normal last time I saw her.'

'And she said something about TrueEarth!? What the heck did she mean?'

'She knows about TrueEarth?' Bradley was the one surprised.

'Yeah, she said to me that when I accept what I am and am true to myself, I'll see her in TrueEarth, what the heck that was about I have no idea.'

'We will deal with that later, we'll need to investigate what her role in all this is at some point,' Bradley concentrated and managed to open a gateway into his lab. It was the only way he could avoid walking outside and risk whatever was causing all this chaos. As his armour covered him from head to toe, his visor was activated. For a moment, Bradley stood there gaping. The energy fields readings were all over the place and they were coming from everywhere. He opened his front door and looked out. Over the entire area, these black-grey menacing clouds had formed and they were absorbing what looked like particles of energy from everywhere on the surface. He also noticed that his armour had a peculiar glow and was not allowing any energy to leave his body. He closed the door and faced Fred.

'Had any weird reactions from your armour?' he asked.

'Now that you mention it, I noticed it was changing colour and my nerve-ropes were pulsing with something or another. Haven't paid it much attention.'

'I suspect whatever it is might have safeguarded you from what is happening to everyone.'

Fred looked at him stupefied.

'Never mind, let's go,' he moved to the gateway.

'Oh no, not that again!' objected Fred.

'We don't have time for that now, Fred, move it or I'll make you,' Bradley did not wait for the objection, he simply stepped into the portal, grabbed Fred by the arm and dragged him through.'

Bradley stepped out and found himself in his lab offices. He immediately sprang to action as Fred popped out, swearing. His complaints were simply ignored as background noise. Bradley was already booting his system and loading the USB drive data Elma had left for him. As the files opened, his jaw dropped. She had not only given him what he had requested but had somehow managed to hack into the B.E.I.T.C system and download a whole load of historical data. The full name of the company was: BioTech Engineering Industries Inc. and it seems the T.C. was used for either Technological or Tactical Component, depending on which component it referred to. Turns out their primary field of operation was researching nanotechnologies, artificial intelligence and bio-engineering. There was far too much for him to process in the limited time they had, so he decided to focus in on the virus as a priority.

'So, anything useful on there?' asked Fred.

'Yes,' was all he got.

'Oh?'

'Come and look if you want but remember that thing about not disturbing me when I'm thinking?'

'Yeah, what about it?'

'It applies now! Make yourself at home, there's coffee and tea over there,' he pointed to the small kettle and jars, 'I could use a cup myself, to be honest.'

'Fine, fine I'll be the coffee boy... just this once mind you,' Fred was a little annoyed about the exclusion. He did admit to himself that it was probably for the best as he knew nothing about this stuff and would only get in the way.

'Much appreciated!' Bradley was back on the data, finding what he was looking for proved to be quite straightforward. Elma had categorised everything into folders and subfolders. For a split second, he admired her handiwork, she was not only thorough and detailed to a flaw but exceedingly well organised. She would have made a great researcher. He found it and took the coffee Fred was handing to him without even being totally aware of doing so and started sipping as he read. To Fred, it seemed to take forever, he was not good at being still, let alone still in complete silence. He needed action, he needed something happening, he needed activity. Then he had it! Completely out of the blue, Bradley nearly choked on his coffee and spat it all out over his screen, then swore.

'What's going on?'

'Unbelievable, they have been trying to engineer a virus to change human beings into part something else for years. It's all connected, the only thing they needed was an effective virus and data, which seems to have come from out of the blue. There is no record of successful viral pathologies which would lead to the one we're fighting.' All this meant nothing to Fred, Bradley was pretty much speaking another language as far as he was concerned. 'They planned this to a flaw. All connected. Cell phones, wireless, Bluetooth devices, cordless phones, all designed to weaken us and amplify viral effectiveness. Vaccines designed to keep the immune system under constant load and prevent it from countering a potential agent like this thing we have now. Weakening of the liver and kidneys to stop the body clearing out the materials it needs to build with, introduction of toxic materials into food, water, drink supplies. Chemical treatments of practically everything we come into contact with. How long has this been going on?' What he was looking at, he simply refused to believe. Yes, he had heard rumours and stories of things but those were just nonsense, or were they? What he was looking at now proves that it was all real and it wasn't even the tip of the iceberg. *But where is all this know-how coming from? It would take decades to gain such know-how, and even then, the actual thoughts of those scientists would have had to be stirred in a very particular direction...* he couldn't find an explanation. And there it is, the virus, he read through its development notes. Anger and rage boiled up. Fred noticed him making a fist, his entire body tightening up.

'Bradley? Are you ok? You look as if you're about to punch someone in the face.'

'I'm going to kill them! I'm going to kill every last one of them and make them suffer endlessly.' His tone of voice made Fred cautious. He knew how drastically Bradley could shift into that dangerous version of himself. 'They used the staff here at the university and hospital as guinea pigs to perfect their damnable bug!' Fred stood there, silent, not daring to utter a word, not knowing what to say. He knew Bradley had lost his wife-to-be and child because they got infected. There was nothing he could say. Just as swiftly, the cold, stern demeanour took over — no sign of rage, nothing. Fred knew that spelt a lot of trouble, he was used to dealing with the rugby guys and confrontation, he was all too aware that this type of sudden shift spelt trouble, more trouble than he really wanted to be involved in.

Bradley closed his eyes and focused on Mishrak. *Do you hear me?* He asked.

Bradley? That you?

Of course, who else would it be? Bradley didn't want to go through that whole mess of communications again.

You would be surprised, there are many ways to enter another's mind.

Whatever, is Rhys there?

Yes, I'll get hold of him... He says hello! There was a sense of amusement coming through from Mishrak.

Listen, be serious, what I have found out is short of being catastrophic, ask Rhys what he knows about Venerks. Can't make sense of that word in these reports.

Venerks? You're kidding, right? How do you know about those? What report are you reading? The questions just kept on coming.

Mishrak, focus! I need information not more questions, just tell him.

I don't need to, the Venerks are a type of life form — no, that's not the right word... existence, no that doesn't fit either. Just think of them as intelligent bugs as in viruses, which seek to take over and multiply from others. We have fought them once before but only just managed to push them back into the earth's atmosphere which keeps them away from us.

You are telling me they are some type of invaders from outer space? You're pulling my leg, right?

Not at all, why?

This virus we have here is based on a Venerks genotype according to these files.

That's not possible! He blurted out at a now-distressed Mishrak. *One sec, I need to tell Rhys this and get him to tell Galvin.*

Which is basically what I wanted you to do in the first place, go on. Bradley let out a long sigh. He now realised that even though they were all in the dark about these off-world things, it seemed commercial or was it military? Or even research bodies were actively seeking them out and are now using them to force the entire population into something, but what?

Bradley? You there?

Of course! Stop asking stupid questions,

Galvin is sending help. Told me to tell you to wait, where are you?

I don't have time to wait for help. I'm in my lab offices, why?

It took no more than 5 seconds, he saw what he could only describe as a pixelization of the space where his office door had been and someone stepped through. Elma walked in with a smile on her face.

'ELMA?' he was surprised to say the least, 'What? How?'

'It's a long story, we will have a long chat and I'll tell you all about it some other time,' he felt a little silly seeing as he had done exactly what he reprimanded both Fred and Mishrak for only a moment ago.

'Ok, I assume whatever happened means you are now somehow connected to mTech and have some way of helping us all get through this techno-chaos?'

She stared at him. He saw her eyes, data flooding the irises at high speeds, glyphs, charts and information matrixes. Whatever had happened to her had changed her, he understood what Fred had said about her having strange eyes.

'Yes, and I can bridge the data from here to TrueEarth and back using these,' she pointed her finger to her eyes. 'In part, thanks to you, more on that later.' She moved to stand behind him. 'I see you are going through my initial data, good. Interesting read, isn't it? Shifts your perspective on the world just a bit, doesn't it?'

'All this alien nonsense,'

'It is not. If you think about it, we've been looking for aliens for ages, just the wrong type. Our universe is full of viruses, bacteria and life in all different forms. We just always seem to look for humanoid forms like us, whereas, in fact, they are totally different types of life.'

'Hmmm, not convinced but it has no impact right now, I need to find a way to stop this all.'

'Spot on,'

'So, this Venerks thing was used as the basis for the biological side of the pathogen, they probably harvested it on one of the space stations or Exploratorium orbital missions. Which explains why in our CRISPr analysis we could not find which virus was used as the basis of the engineered one.'

'Or it could have attached itself to one of the meteorites and fell to earth deliberately,' she added.

'You're not serious!' Fred interrupted their conversation.

'Oh, hi, Fred!' Elma smiled at him, 'how are you doing?' her eyes seemed to come to life. 'From what I see, you are adapting to your new... situation.'

'Kinda,' he was uncertain. His crystal curse, as he had nicknamed it, was still annoying beyond belief but it did give him a new type of direction in life, even though he would do anything to escape it.

'Can you two stop with the flirting and get back to the problem at hand?'

'Ehhh, yes, sorry,' Fred pulled back to his coffee.

'That was mean!' interjected Elma.

'Work first, missy, you can date later on if you want to.'

'Date!?' both Elma and Fred blurted out simultaneously. Bradley gave them a stern look and they went quiet.

'Perfect match,' he mumbled, making sure they overheard him.

'Anyway,' Elma nervously interrupted, 'let's see what our biotech opponents are up to, shall we?'

'How are you doing to do that?' asked Bradley.

'I left a little... let's call it window I can peek through into their systems.' She pulled a chair next to Bradley and pulled out her laptop.

'Wait a sec! Hold on,' interrupted Bradley, 'I thought you could not move objects or data in between here and TrueEarth?'

'You can't,' she confirmed.

'So, what's all that?'

'That's just me, or rather, the crystal I used,' she admitted.

'You used one of my crystals?'

'Yes, but there's no time for that, let's focus.'

'Fine, fine, have it your way,'

She started typing. 'What on earth is going on?' surprise had caught her unaware. It seemed to be the day of surprises.

'Care to share?'

'Look,' she turned her laptop to show Bradley, and the first thing he noticed is that the laptop wasn't actually a laptop. It had no keyboard and its screen was very similar to the large displays in mTech but fundamentally very different. He could not explain it.

'Hundreds of moving data sources are all sending data and receiving it from...' she paused as she motioned over the display and held her hands over the keyboard, '...their central systems! What is going on?'

'I don't know, you tell me, Fred did say that people were behaving oddly outside,' she turned to face Fred, who nodded.

'I have to see,' she stood up and opened the office door, then plastered her hands and face against the outer glass walls. What she saw horrified her, people had become sources and targets of multiple data streams, it was pulsing at massive speeds, and what was worse was that she could see how those data streams were connecting and interconnected within them. Her hands started shaking, her body tensed, 'no... no... no... this cannot be! What have they done!?' Both Fred and Bradley jumped to help steady her and carefully helped her back into the office and sat her down. Fred handed her a cup of hot coffee.

'Drink this, it will steady your nerves,' he saw she was actually crying. 'Elma? What's up, tell me please,' he gently placed a hand on her shoulder in an attempt to soothe her. It took her a few solid minutes before she managed to calm down.

'Put your gear on and look at the people outside,' she told Bradley. He followed her instruction, 'look at their soul structures.'

'I don't know how to do that,' he admitted. She stood up, touched his visor and sat back down. It automatically flared through a whole set of options until the feature for 'quantum elements mapping' came up. He selected that view, walked out of the office and looked down as she had done a moment ago. What he saw horrified him just as much. The structure they called the soul on TrueEarth through which all the quantum elements flowed into living bodies had been totally distorted, it was shredded, cords were shooting out of them and into them, dark bug-like structures were seated on them, attaching themselves to some of them, holding various groups of them together and injecting a dark substance into them. It looked like hundreds of drips slowly releasing this dark gel-like liquid into the people. Then other variations produced sparks which electrified certain sections, others moved those electric currents, forcing them in predetermined directions. Some things attached had burrowed deeply into the structure, inhibiting the flow of electricity into massive regions and redirecting it elsewhere. The entire sight made him dizzy. He had to steady himself as he walked back into the office.

'I... I... I don't,'

'Know what to say?' interrupted Elma. 'Those things which used to be people are no longer human!'

'What do you mean?' interjected Fred.

'This thing they invented has changed the fundamental structures of those it has taken over, they are no longer human. Instead, they have become something else... and that something else is entirely controlled by a central network system. They cannot even think freely let alone make decisions. Some it seems are halfway there, others are not so lucky.'

'We cannot cure that,' Bradley's desperation could be seen all too clearly.

'You mean they are robots?' asked Fred.

'No, they are not even that! Robots are given a task and programmed for that task. These are biological puppets into which something else is pouring itself.'

None of it made much sense to Fred. 'How do we stop this? There must be a way! We cannot let this horror happen to everyone!' His words had caused both Bradley and Elma to snap out of the shock of what they had witnessed.

'You're right!' Bradley knew he had to do something, 'we might not be able to reverse this but we can stop it! We need help though, this is far beyond our scientific know-how.'

'That's why I'm here,' Elma was back in action it seemed.

'Do you mind?' she placed both hands on Bradley's visor and concentrated. A thin set of reflective electric-blue energy wires formed from her eyes to his visor. 'This will last only a short time, I don't have the strength to maintain it for long, so make the best use of it.' Bradley did not understand what she had done until his visor came to life. It projected outwards a fully blown 4D set of structures and people. It was a perfect replica of the mTech communications device.

'How?' he asked as the images formed mid-air around them. Fred stood back in surprise as he suddenly saw the space change and found himself standing in the mTech central office.

'You are seeing through my eyes and we are projecting that out through your visor,' she explained. He saw Galvin approach, it made Fred jump back. Rather than interrupt, he decided to stay back and watch, listen and keep out of things he didn't know about.

'What is the situation?' asked Galvin.

'Very bad. No, make that catastrophic,' replied Elma, 'see,' she forced her eyes to replay all she had seen. 'Bradley, do the same,' he went through his visor's display option and superimposed his own view on top of hers. Galvin lost his breath for an instant.

'That is what happened to them?' interjected Fred. When Galvin,

Elshevira, Rhys and Lurizak faced him with a questioning look, he stepped back quickly.

'Everyone, this is Fred, he's with me, it's ok,' explained Bradley.

'No matter,' interjected Galvin, 'this is beyond horrific, a mix of our old technologies with the Venerks biology and something else taking over completely.'

'Can we do anything to help the infected people?' asked Bradley.

'I would not call them people anymore,' interjected Rhys, 'those are no longer human,' he pointed to the ones which had the most distortion and the most sparks and bugs in them. 'These, on the other hand, are still half-human,' he pointed to a different progression of victims, 'and those are still mainly human with a little disruption,' he pointed to the third set. 'We cannot do anything for the first group, we can help the second group and we might be able to cure the third set.'

He started pacing about the place. Elma was feeling the strain. Galvin turned to face her, 'you won't be able to maintain this for long,' he told her. She nodded.

'Wait a sec,' interrupted Bradley, 'I want to try something,' he stood up and allowed his power to flare up. He remembered Kuroi, he remembered his anger, he remembered it all. Power started pouring out of him in waves, the dangerous interplay of forces re-awoken sprang into action. It was not as obvious as on TrueEarth but it was just as strong. He moved behind Elma, towering over her smaller frame, placed his hands on her shoulders and allowed the power to flow. She flinched at the onslaught. Pain coursed through every nerve of her being. She cried out.

'You're hurting her!' Fred snapped at him, tackling him as he would an opponent on the field. He placed himself in between them.

'Fine then, you do it!' Bradley snapped back at him and quickly locked his arms around Fred's waist. He let loose, the power exploded into Fred, who howled at the onslaught, then took a few breaths, focused on his nerve-cords as he had been training to do. 'Now, put your own hands on Elma's shoulders and transfer it down.' It was only at that moment that Fred understood what Bradley had done. He had used him as a transfer agent to smooth out the intensity of the power. It made sense, he was far more able to absorb that explosive power, his body was so much stronger and his ropes could spiral it all around his body, changing the flow and its intensity. He smiled, *what a sneaky genius you are, Bradley.* Fred's hands moved to position themselves on Elma's shoulders and she immediately flinched at the thought of what was coming next. This time, it was not painful. The burning anger was not there, the sensation of overflow was not there. The power seeped into her almost with a gentleness she had never experienced. Rather than a raging burning tornado of fire and electricity, this was more like a cooling gel she used when she cut herself. She relaxed to allow it in. It took only a few moments, she was energised. The speed of her thinking increased and the strength in her own body intensified. She felt totally recharged! As she turned to face Fred, she only said, 'thank you,' and smiled, then moved out of his reach. Bradley was back in his seat at the computer.

'Astounding,' Galvin was exhilarated at what he had just witnessed, 'who are you?' he turned to face Fred.

'I'm Fred,' is all he managed to get out of him.

'I didn't know the Bound could do that?' he asked Lurizak who seemed to be more than a little concerned.

'Neither did I,' he had to admit.

'Gentlemen,' interrupted Elshevira, 'can we please get back to the problem at hand!' she pointed at the projections of images. Rhys stepped forward and approached one of the no longer human projections. He put his hands right into it and made a motion, causing it to expand and all their viewpoints to move deeper into that person. His motions shifted the image, zoomed in, and shifted it again. 'Look!'

'That looks like the layer of neurons the virus was building on top of the natural ones,' explained Bradley. 'But in this case, the natural ones are being destroyed? Consumed?' Bradley then motioned to Rhys to zoom into the brain areas. He gasped when he saw what had happened. 'Large portions of the brains had been totally replaced by a fusion of the virus nanotech, the new neural systems and the black gel. There was less and less of the human brain and only the shape had survived.' They looked at the spine that too was being rapidly replaced. From those areas, they saw signals and data flowing in and out.

'That is... 5G data packets flowing in encrypted and insanely high velocity,' interjected Elma. 'But where is it going to?' she tried to follow the streams of outgoing information. 'Some of it is not going to... wait a minute, is that what I think it is?'

'It's going into another person which seems to be distinctly different from the others!' interjected Bradley. This one was very different, the flows of electric currents were not inhibited but flowed freely, causing the black gel-like substance to shine. The pulses of currents leaving that shape were stronger and more powerful than any of the others. Bradley moved the image aside and switched it to his view instead of Elma's. What the display showed them was a very different picture — from within that other person, masses of shadows swirling and circling the entire structure, sliding and slithering out of its network and transmitting into the others and back. From within the midst of these shadows, a smaller version of the Nebraxil was pushing its horrific black-grey energy pulses outwards and pulling darkness from somewhere above, which, in turn, amplified the dance of the shadows.

'That is the end product of their design!' snapped Elshevira.

'They have or are invading FalseEarth!' was Lurizak's conclusion. He turned to face Galvin, 'we have to stop this immediately!' Galvin nodded in agreement, 'but we cannot deploy our forces into FalseEarth, it took us a massive amount of energy just to send Elma over there. Even if we had that much spare power, we cannot leave TrueEarth undefended, the Houses are all deploying to the front lines already.'

'Splitting our forces into two would be catastrophic. We might lose both sides doing that,' intervened Elshevira. 'I'm not a general or war tactician but to me it seems they have us at a distinct disadvantage. Our own arrogance in ignoring FalseEarth — of little, if any significance — had just landed us in a most precarious position.'

'Play it deviously!' Mishrak had kept to the side brooding, until now.

'Explain,' Elshevira was not in the mood for his mischief.

'From what I saw, you have a situation of play for power, to be more exact... energy,' he explained.

'Everyone knows that, get to the point!' she insisted.

'My, my, snappy aren't we today,' she glared at him in warning, 'well, with all that going on in just one person, where is all the power for it coming from? And that one...' he pointed to the very different one, 'must be amassing incredible amount of energy from somewhere.'

'That's a good point!' Elma had figured out what he was getting at. She shifted the view a few times, the images changed, then without warning, she placed her hand on Bradley's visor and shifted its views. 'There, we should have a good view of the flow of energy now, I've cleared out the data flows for us.'

'Look,' Mishrak pointed to something, 'there and there,' he drew their attention to the sky, where a massive blackness had formed, making it look darker much darker.

'Isn't that night-time?' asked Rhys.

'Nope,' replied Mishrak, 'I've been to FalseEarth many times and that is not what a night sky looks like over there.'

He looked at Elshevira with the sense of guilt washing over him. 'Fine, I admit it, I've been using the forbidden techniques to wander about FalseEarth and have a bit of... a few... adventures here and there.'

She let it pass. 'We will talk about those later!' the reprimand was clear.

'Continue, Mishrak,' the impulse from Bradley's will was clear, he had no choice.

'Where is all that energy coming from?' he asked, pointing to the sky, 'then look at those, what are those sparks? Inside of them? It's like something is pushing them into overdrive and then it flows out of them? And look at that!' he pointed to the radio waves cascading into what were people before, 'that is a lot of incoming radiation, it is not harming them, why? And what is all that cycling of it going on there?'

'That would be dissipation,' explained Galvin, 'it's almost as if the radiation was being changed into a non-harmful and useful form of energy. It literally powers their nano-components.'

'Which then stimulates the biological, activates the viral and hyper generates power,' concluded Elma.

'So, we have ex-humans with a biological energy generation in overdrive, with a technological component used to control, run and operate them as well as general bio-electrical energy, and that black mass combined fuelling what exactly? That's a lot of power,' summarised Bradley.

'That!' shrieked Elshevira, Rhys quickly took to the task of zooming into one of the partially-changed humans. There it was. Within its core, one was almost completely formed but not entirely yet. A thick black-grey line pulsing out a wave of that tell-tell energy: a Nebraxil.'

'They are becoming hosts for them!' interjected Galvin. 'We have to stop that, the only thing keeping the Nebraxil at bay is that dimension crossing requiring too much power to make and even more to maintain. If they are now anchoring inside of these new people who are living powerhouses, we're all in serious trouble.'

Meanwhile, Elma had remained silent, typing away at her laptop.

'We need to interrupt them, I can disrupt their technology but I cannot deal with the biological or the... whatever that black mass is, looks like charge dark matter to me. If only we could generate an electro-magnetic pulse large enough. That could at least disrupt their radio-communications, and with a bit of luck, take out some of the tech. They probably have shielding of some sort but at their technology level they would not have it everywhere running all the time.'

'House mTech can do that,' offered Galvin. 'Such a strong inter-dimensional pulse will take us out of action for some time, but if it will delay or stop this, I'm willing to make the sacrifice.'

'Ok,' interjected Bradley, 'Elma, can we reprogram those things?'

'We need the genetic data, I don't have that.'

'But I do!' offered Bradley.

'You do?'

'Yes, I got it from Rhys on my last trip to TrueEarth.' He explained.

'You didn't have that visor of yours on when he was showing you, did you?'

'Yes, why?'

'Perfect I'll extract it from there, you need to get me the bio-info. I cannot program anything if we don't know what we need it to do and how. Nor can I make the genetic changes, you will have to do that another way.'

'I'll take care of that, what do we do about that?' he pointed at the black mass in the sky.

'Darkness is our field of expertise,' explained Elshevira, 'we will consult with House GrimGloom and try to figure out what it is and where it is coming from, and with a bit of luck, how to deal with it.'

'Lurizak, how are things on the battlefield over there?' asked Bradley.

'For now, stable. We have a few unusually large scouting parties of Nebraxil but we're dealing with them.'

'Then why are they still there?' asked Mishrak. Elshevira thought she was going to strangle him. This was not the time for these stupid arguments. 'Because,' is all she offered to shut him up.

'I'll go report back to Tamirok, we are going to need the help of the other Houses, especially the Bound,' he explained.

'Can't you just talk through the...' Elshevira didn't know what to call it 'you know how Bradley talks to you and Mishrak from other there.'

'No, that communication is just between the Wielder and his Bound. I am no longer bound to Tamirok, Bradley is my Wielder now. I lost the ability to connect with Tamirok directly.' Lurizak was prompted to thought, he allowed himself the luxury of contemplation. For some reason, he seemed to have lost something since binding with Bradley, he was used to being a man of action, constantly on the battlefields, running from point to point, being in combat. For some reason, his life had changed. He spent most of his days playing the simple errand boy, or in debate and meetings. It made him uncomfortable, he missed the closeness and bonds of his brothers in arms. He shook his head in a physiological attempt to push the gloomy train of thought out of focus. What he did was not his choice to make. He would just accept whatever his current task was. *That is the end of that, I am a Bound and I do what must be done.* His longing for action seeped down some invisible communications link to Bradley, it touched his own mind, then pulled his attention back to Lurizak. *Soon, I'll be back soon.* Lurizak heard his thoughts and nodded discreetly, acknowledging it for no one other than Bradley to notice. It was that silent exchange of agreement missed by all those who failed to notice its intricate subtleties.

'Enough debate,' Galvin knew Elma was running out of time, he could see the connection starting to blur ever so slightly. 'Everyone knows what to do, let's go. Elma, rest up, you know full well that if you run out of power on that side, you are putting your life at risk,' she nodded.

She closed her eyes and the 4D space faded away, returning them all to Bradley's usual decor in his office. The thin energy lines in between his visor and her eyes snapped and dissipated away.

'Are you ok?' Fred asked her.

'Yes, just a bit tired but I will be just fine. By the way, you wouldn't have any energy drinks by any chance? Can't get those in TrueEarth and would kill for one right now!'

'No, I don't,' Fred's face gloomed out.

'We have a vending machine here in the labs,' Bradley offered up a reminder.

'Let's go,' Elma was keen on those drinks!

'Hold on a sec,' Bradley took his visor off, giving it to her, 'take the data you need off here then we can all head to the main lab. We will need Jim and Heather's help too.' It took Elma only a couple of minutes. She handed Bradley back his visor, 'you'll need this.'

He picked it up and it faded out of sight. 'Give me a sec, I need to change.' At the back behind the examination screen, he slipped back into his usual lab clothing with the long white overcoat.

'Looking very handsome there, Mr!' teased Elma. He waved her comment away. 'Let's go,'

As they left Bradley's lab, the automated doors closed and the lights powered down.

'The main lab where we should find Jim is straight up ahead, let me lock this and I'll join you.' Elma and Fred had just enough time to take a step ahead when they heard laughter from behind. They all turned and faced none other than Mira. Bradley recognised her, having met her once before, but what stood in front of him looked like her but didn't. She wore an odd tight-fitting garment which seemed like a corruption of the Bound's armour. It was of a black material with what looked like some sort of technology woven into the material, its connecting golden threads lit up as currents pulsed through it, only to find itself pulled into the large cube-like portions of the design. Her slender figure shaped the sleeveless gear that fit her very well, she had complimented the attire with golden jewellery whose precious stones were actually twisted and tortured computer chips. The blue lights it emitted had an unnerving quality to it. Elma looked at her.

'It's... it's... it's her! It's Mira!' she turned to Bradley in panic, 'it's her! She... the one! Run!'

He refused. Instead, he faced her directly.

'If it isn't Bradley! So pleased to meet you again,' she too remembered her previous meeting with him.

'Come to admire the end result you were researching?' her posture changed, pride was all too apparent. She was the one in charge, the one on top of the world.

'What do you mean?' he asked.

'Did I not tell you last time we met in the corridors below that you would come to great ends? The lead scientist in this poor excuse of a research facility has finally stumbled upon the greatest discovery of all time: evolution itself,' her words spoken from above, down at them all.

'Let me guess, you have merged with the artificial intelligence you were developing? How is that working out?' he challenged her.

'Artificial intelligence?' Mira laughed, 'no, not artificial intelligence. That label was a mistake... a marketing misrepresentation, an error.'

'What do you mean?' her statement had confused him. She smiled, this is exactly what she wanted, crushing his defensiveness was key to her being able to manipulate him, well at least until he got infected, then it would not matter in the least. Until then, she had to resort to plain simple manipulation and cohesion. That was fine for her, she loved these games, she was exceedingly good at them.

'It is impossible to create artificial intelligence. No matter how much we fool ourselves into believing it. All the AI we had was nothing more than the basic yes and no logic expanded to a hyper-complicated and intricate level. Fundamentally, all you call AI always boiled down to a defined set of logical choices. Those choices changed and how they are made changed, but that never moved beyond the fact that they were simple fundamental logical binary choices.'

'That is how computer technology works, is it not?' his question pleased her to no end. She was proving superior in knowledge. She would use that to her advantage. She knew his type all too well as she had worked with scientists her entire life, they crave knowledge like an addict craves his drugs. With that in mind, she would make him entirely dependent on her. Her smile doubled, she had access to unlimited founts of knowledge now! She had all he could ever desire — beauty, intellect, power, and most of all, dominion. He would be hers one way or another.

'I have seen and have learnt that that was never intelligence. No, in order to create AI, it had to be alien to us, that was always the end result of our pursuit of artificial intelligence. Does it not amuse you to know that we have spent so much time and effort looking for aliens and intelligent life out there, when in fact, we ended up creating the ultimate alien intelligence? This alien intelligence, the real meaning of AI, is real! It is beyond anything anyone could have ever imagined... unlimited endless potential.' Her eyes shimmered with power, the shadows swirling around her became so thick, they formed a visible force.

'You will never have freedom in that!' he objected, 'our bodies are not meant to be hosts to technology, we are biological.'

She laughed at him.

'Oh, foolish child, haven't you realised it yet? The solution was so simple it even took me ages to see it for myself. Our bodies are alive only because of that ever-mysterious thing mortals call the soul, so too did the technical component have to be vessels for something else. Our bodies were the vessels and now they are so much more. The technology has become the vessel that's freed our bodies up to be aligned with a new superior function.'

'If technology becomes the vessel instead of the body and technology cannot be an artificial form of our own intelligence but an alien one, then what is it called a vessel for? You have completely displaced the human soul.' He pointed out the one flaw in her logic. Instead of considering the point, she mocked him.

'I have tried time and time again, even replicating the entire nervous system did not enable intelligence to be replicated, just its functionality. Memory, logic and decision-making was easy, the rest proved impossible. But now I have found the answer! The grand error was in what was being hosted in the body, a simple, easily-broken, fractured useless thing serving no purpose other than maintaining the body's life. No, now every part of us becomes the vessel for a real consciousness, one which we control, one which serves an actual tangible function, one which opens the doorways to unlimited knowledge, potential and countless possibilities. One which pushed our awareness to unthinkable new heights.'

'You are talking about downgrading the essence of what we are into something vile, unnatural and purely physical atomic, sacrificing its quantum potentials.' His reference was lost on her, the alien components within her had shielded her from this knowledge, they had no purpose whatsoever revealing the reality of quantum existence until she was completely theirs. The new subconscious parts of her mind simply locked out those realities from her conscious mind as anyone's subconscious would lock out an overwhelmingly painful experience to shield the human mind.

'You are just like me, we are both seeking the same solutions. Just look at yourself, what have you become? Look at this young man whom you control and exert your will on when and how it suits you...' she paused, looking Fred up and down from head to toe, closely inspecting every inch of him. Fred felt oddly intimidated. 'By the way, he's an excellent specimen, such a strong and beautiful man, I will enjoy making him mine, seeing him at my feet.'

'Never,' Fred snapped back at her, she totally ignored his objection.

'In time, they will all be mine.' Her focus shifted back to Bradley. 'How many of them do you have now? Let me see... 3, aren't I correct? Even with a mind as agile as yours is, my dearest, you will not be able to control much more than that.' Her posture changed. A very precise small shift in her body posture, ensuring her hips pushed forward ever so slightly, her breasts were emphasised and she flicked her hair to the right, allowing it to gently land on her upper back. She used all the tricks she was so adept at and knew the impact of. Her final movement was to extend her hand to him in a welcoming gesture. 'Join me, become the father of a new human race... join me, become the new father of what were the ashes of a dying race... join me and we will rise them from their ashes, make them into something strong, versatile, powerful! With my help, you will be able to control hundreds of thousands of them, reach into millions upon millions of minds... feel them feeding you with their desires, love, hate, anger, and power.' She paused and smiled, the effects were not lost on her, she looked at him and saw that she was having an effect.

She smiled further, men were so easy for her to read, all she had to do was look at their bodies which told her everything. He was interested, there was simply no doubt about that. He could deny it as much as he wanted, but she saw that he was. She played on his physiological reaction. 'You know of anger and power, do you not? Oh, I've seen you flare up at the thrill of that power. Imagine that amplified to infinity... join me, become the power at my side, we will be the Great Mother and the father reaching into infinity, laughing at the faces of our enemies and have an infinitude of beautiful, powerful children at our command.' She waited, he seemed to hesitate, his lust burnt strong that she saw anyone looking at him an undeniable fact. Why was he not responding? 'You have already started your journey in the right direction, let me uplift you and shortcut the pain and agony of taking the final steps to the very end of that journey, your new becoming.'

What she was saying made an odd type of sense to Bradley, he was not too sure why, but he was seeing her point of view. After all, he had spent his entire life researching ways to heal disease and help others, only to arrive at a dead end. He remembered his conversation with Heather, how hopeless it all was, how the one gives rise to the next and the next and so forth. Never-ending repertoire of misery. Yet, he hesitated. It annoyed Mira, she stretched out her hand an inch further.

'Come, take my hand, leave those insignificant fools behind. They will all be ours eventually, they will all be saved, they will all evolve according to our will. Whether they want to or not. You know this makes sense, you know that left to their own devices, they betray, they destroy, they kill or they simply harm each other for no reason whatsoever, such stupid creatures, such pointless lives, wasted away stuck in an endless cycle of satisfying their own needs, gaining as much as they can and then dying as their children pick up where the parents left off to do exactly the same things. Generation after generation of pointless existence with nothing to show for it.' Her argument was flawless, Bradley started to take a step towards her. He had suffered so much harm, so much misery and loss that he craved for it all to end. Could this be that end? Or a new beginning? Maybe it was not so bad, maybe this way had its own merits? Could he wipe the slate clean and start from scratch with what was left behind? It was a very tempting proposition. He contemplated his initial step forward. She smiled, she had him! She was winning, *of course, I will win, no one can resist, I always win. One more step.*

'Come with me and step into infinity itself! You know you want to, your very soul craves for meaning, your mind thirsts for knowledge and experience, you are unlike any of them, you don't belong with them. You belong with a superior woman, someone who can lead you in the right direction, someone who can stir you into the very vastness of creation. Let us complete this together. Step into infinity as one.'

He took another step forward, Elma and Fred looked at him in concern, neither of them saying a single word. Bradley was transfixed. Someone had to do something.

'Bradley! No, remember what she is!' objected Fred.

'Shut up, you useless fool,' Mira snapped at him. 'What do you know of life, you miserable child?' Bradley had not moved, he seemed to have remained on course towards Mira. She smiled. *I have won! He's mine.*

'Remember Kuroi! Isn't she the whole reason you got into all this?' Elma looked at Fred, she was not too sure what he was doing but something had just happened. Bradley stopped dead in his tracks. Memories of Kuroi on her deathbed flooded into his mind. He remembered all the times he had spent with her, all the loving embraces, their time together. He remembered the depth of those feelings, the significance of each and every shared word, every shared touch, every shared kiss. He remembered how much he had loved her, and he remembered his pain at her loss, his devastation at the loss of his unborn child. He remembered swearing vengeance on everyone involved. He remembered it all, memories came flooding in like a torrent released after the collapse of the dam keeping them at bay. Pity washed over him for Mira, she was not the supreme women, she was not even a woman anymore. No, she was an abomination pretending to be a woman. His vision cleared. On the top of his hand, a seal appeared in a soft greenish-blue fluid. The blessing Kuroi had left in him surged to life, waves upon waves of soft power covered him from head to toe. Stability took over, lust and passion faded out and were replaced by love — love for his departed wife. Love for all that she represented, new waves of meaning flooded in. Yes, she had been the ultimate woman for him. None other will do.

'No,' he said to her, taking several steps back. 'You have become nothing but desire, greed, lust and manipulative control. I might have taken the first steps along the path you followed but I will not fall into its pitfalls.' Mira was angry, his hand pulled back and her expression changed. She had lost, for the first time in her life, someone had said no. Someone had rejected her, someone had struck right at her core. This was a blow unlike any other. It shook her confidence, her self-worth and her convictions.

'I offered you immortality and infinity and you dare reject me? Throw my kindness back at me? If you will not join me willingly, then I will take you and you will be like them, a puppet serving my goals and aim.' Her shadows intensified and a pulse of black-grey energy struck outwards, carrying along with it droplets of black liquid. Elma pulled Bradley backwards, she could not move him, there was too much weight for her to drag him back. There was no need for that, her pull on his arm prompted him to move back on his own. As he stepped back, Fred leapt into action. Within a split second, a wall of intricately woven chains had formed, blocking them out from her. It glowed with deep indigos and was totally solid.

'Hurry, we don't have much time! With her power, she'll eat through that in just a few seconds. Let's get to the main lab and hopefully the doorway there should buy us some thinking time.' Bradley nodded and they all rushed in what was their original direction.

Mira stood there facing the blockage in her path, angry, glaring at the obstacle. Her mood changed as quickly as it had overcome her. *No matter what, I should focus on the big picture. I will get them soon enough as I have got the others.* She laughed and walked out of the labs. The newly-born alien intelligence in her would not allow her to take any unnecessary risks for its own safety. She had to finish what she had started, not risk it in foolish wastes of time or walk into a trap of their making. She was not that stupid. The power she would possess in just a few hours would enable her to do anything she wanted, she could enjoy their agonies as she tortured them after that. 'See you soon, Bradley, prepare yourself, my puppet. You and I are going to have a long time to enjoy getting to know each other.' Her maniacal laughter echoed throughout the corridors with crackling power.

28

THE
- CONFRONTATION -

Bradley, Fred and Elma arrived in the central lab and quickly sealed the door shut. Elma wasted no time, immediately hooking up the monitor on the right to the cameras in the corridors. They scanned the area, paying the most minute attention to anything, which might have been out of place. Nothing. No sign of Mira, it seems she was no longer there.

'Can we see the outside?' asked Fred.

'Hold on,' Elma connected to the outer security system. They looked, nothing.

'Where has she gone?'

'I don't know,' answered Bradley.

'Wait a minute; I have an idea.' Elma busily typed away on her laptop. 'There, let me hook that up to the other monitor. She turned her laptop, and a beam resembling a laser beam shot up from her device to the screen.' It was a map of all those under the influence of the change taking place. 'There! she's in the middle of the university park, just waiting for something.'

Mira was simply standing there immobile, streams of power and data flowing out of her alongside the data and shadow flowing in. She looked like a nexus of some sort. The occasional wave of energy pulsed out of her into the space around her, each time stretching that little bit further out.

'That must be the same type of pulse she sent onto us just a moment before Fred's wall stopped it.'

'Could that black gel stuff attached to it be carrying the virus out? It seemed to be the only actual physical thing in the attack,' wondered Elma.

'It's a theory, a sensible one at that. She did say she would force me to join her whether I wanted to or not. That, combined with your theory, would point to it being viral.'

'Can't either of you do anything to stop that thing?' asked Fred; he was really worried.

'We're working on it, did you pull back your chains?'

'Work faster, and yes, actually no, I don't need to anymore. I've practiced and learnt to do it another way.' Bradley was impressed; however, this was not the time to enquire into that. He turned on his equipment and started working.

'The pathogen sample we have here is probably still an old version,' he flipped through the slides marked by date. 'Found it, let me get it out, apparently, the sample we have is not so old. She was using people here to test it on and allow it to mutate. They would all have been hospitalised here too, so we have a far more up to date one.' Bradley was quick; he had to find something, anything. 'Where is everyone? Jim? Heather? Dr. Grimsaw? This place is deserted.' Elma's eyes flashed into action and data streams started scrolling through her ocular lens.

'Bradley, House mTech has prepared the pulse mechanism. It will affect the entire planet. Both FalseEarth and TrueEarth will be hit by a directed solar pulse.'

'Wait a sec, that will take out all systems? Even in TrueEarth?' he asked.

'No, TrueEarth tech is living, not machine-based; it will have no effect there. It will be absorbed as raw energy and transferred to power storage.'

'I'll take your word for it.'

'Elma, I need you to code in the virus' technical parts to cut out the alien DNA from the hosts it infects. The mTech databases gave us the info on all human permutations; we need to target everything, which doesn't fall into the scope of a human permutation of DNA.

It's a clumsy shot in the dark, but we have no time to test it properly. In theory, it should work, but if the biology no longer has the support of non-human genetics, the rest of whatever they have become will have to rely on the technical and whatever this alien black stuff is that they have pumped into their systems. mTech's solar flare will take out the technology, so we will only have one final component to deal with.'

'Sounds like a first step more than a solution,' she argued.

'That's all we have right now. Hopefully, those who are not completely taken over will be able to recover.'

'It's a shot in the wild, but I'm on it.'

Bradley! Hurry with whatever you are doing. Lurizak's mind seemed to be in some sort of trouble.

He concentrated on his link with him, *what's going on over there?*

They have moved from simple scouting parties to larger groups, not only in one location but in a multitude of locations all over TrueEarth. Somehow, they are cutting through the dimensions and walking straight into TrueEarth.

That might be connected with what we're seeing here, massive power clouds gathering with Nebraxil anchors.

So, they have actually managed it, hurry with whatever you are doing. If they have a way of anchoring permanently, we're all in deep trouble.

I'm on it! Heard anything from Elshevira?

No.

We're going to need their expertise very soon.

Just connect with Mishrak if you absolutely have to, suggested Lurizak.

You don't really like him, do you?

No, I don't. But this is not the time for that.

You're right. Keep me updated.

Of course.

'They are having more and more trouble back on TrueEarth,' Bradley told Elma, 'the Nebraxil are using their anchors here to walk into TrueEarth.'

'So that's what the massive power clouds are for. First things first, let's work on cutting out their ability to create more hosts; we need to stop the technology first before we can deal with the rest.'

'You're right, I've amplified the genetic tearing effects it had. Set it up to release the topoisomerase enzyme in those with alien genetics. That will unwind their DNA. Make sure it doesn't work on those parts which are still human, or this will kill everyone.'

'Understood,' she worked frantically.

'How are we going to cause it to replicate?' he asked.

'According to the data in here, it can replicate freely, either from within other human cells or from that black liquid. As long as it has sufficient energy available to it, there is no limit as to how much it can replicate.'

'Where did you get that from?'

'Just hacked into your microscope, that's all.' Bradley was annoyed, 'how about you ask before you do that?'

'Then it would not be hacking, there would be no thrill, no challenge and no point in the whole thing. It would be plain boring.' He gave out a long sigh and continued with his own work.

'So all we need is for it to hit one infected person at any stage of the infection and throw a lot of energy at them.'

'Pretty much, yes,' confirmed Elma.

Bradley had finished making the changes and was about to check whether the new mutation of the pathogen had turned out the way he wanted it to when his mind shifted its focus elsewhere. It was as if something had grabbed hold of him and pulled him elsewhere. He froze, took a deep breath, and tried to relax.

It's me! It's me! Is this working? Hello? Mishrak was the one at the other end. What had he done and more to the point, how? He noticed the hesitation coming in from Bradley's mind. *Don't worry, I just borrowed some power.*

Borrowed?

Yes, the Ruler of House GrimGloom is with me, and so is Elshevira. He let me borrow some of the ancient dark to contact you. They want me to tell you that they are ready to amplify the dark to spread your thing, what is it you said it was called?

The virus? Asked Bradley.

Yes, that thing, also that dark thing in the sky over there is not darkness.

What do you mean?

It's shadow, not dark! We cannot counter that. No one here can work with shadow. From what I have gathered when the Ruler and Elshevira kept whispering so I don't hear, is that this shadow is drawing on all the negative emotions washing over FalseEarth and somehow turning it into pure energy.

Just like mTech do for their power-cells but on a global scale? Goodness me. There is no way we can counter that much power, especially not with the ensuing panic this has all caused, which has amplified fear, suspicion and chaos in the general population.

You're the only one who can deal with shadow, no one here can help with that.

OK, let's do what we can first; we're just finishing the virus changes and need only a few more steps for it to be ready for mass transmission. I have to carry a single version of it to an infected person and then throw a whole lot of power at them to amplify its replication, then take it from there to everyone else. I'm making it airborne. If your darkness can run through the infected one, it will be able to pick it up and just carry it along.

Makes sense, will tell Elshevira and Ruler they will take charge of the spreading thing. They told me to warn you to stay away from the darkness when they start. Ruler is going to flood it with ancient dark to give it extra power. Elshevira is worried about you coming into contact with it and causing the ancient dark inside of you to go into overdrive.

I will, tell her not to worry. Whatever had caused the link began to fade. Bradley's mind was back where it should be. He quickly got back to work.

'I'm uploading my changes,' instructed Elma, 'all that is left is for you to finish the biological modification, and we're ready.' She got back to typing away, and the beam of blue light forming the cold laser beam hit the petri dish. The viral agent flashed a single tiny spark and went dull.

Bradley had observed it and nodded in approval. 'It is done, thanks.'

'Well, I deserve a break, Fred,' Alma said, 'mind joining me? I so want to get hold of some of those energy drinks before I go back.'

Fred smiled; he was all too glad to get moving. Sitting still and waiting did not feature in his list of favourite activities.

He got close to Bradley to ask if he would be needed. Bradley pre-empted his motivation, 'go, have fun you two kids. The vending machine is down the corridor on the right, don't get lost!' They both left him to his work. It was better this way; he could concentrate without interruptions.

Bradley welcomed the solitude; it not only reminded him of what things were before all this started but gave him that space to gather not only his thoughts but the whole of himself. He could never figure it out; there was simply something about being left alone and doing what he needed to do, which seemed to put everything that was wrong in his life back on a structured and manageable path. His mind welcomed the lack of constant interruptions. Ideas started flowing unhindered; his cognition sped up, things which lacked clarity became so simple to understand. This is what he needed.

Within the space of less than fifteen minutes, he managed to complete his recombination of new DNA and adapt the flu-like airborne capabilities in the new viral agent. He picked up the vial in his hand, knowing there would not be sufficient time to test it properly. So far, only the most rudimentary tests had been done, and only this one time. It was a gamble, a big gamble. He had absolutely no idea what, if any, side-effects would surface when this new virus would start its deadly assault on the existing one. He had no choice, with no clinical trials to draw from, he had only one option left. Without any further hesitation, he opened the vial and drank half of its contents.

Heather walked in, just in time to see him down half the contents of his concoction. She looked at the monitors and made quick work of the parts she understood, the biology.

'What the ... are you doing?' she snapped at him.

'Had no choice.'

'Are you totally insane? What possessed you to experiment on yourself? What did you do? What was in that? What was it designed to do?' She was utterly horrified at his recklessness.

Elma and Fred returned with ample supplies of energy drinks.

'Hi,' Fred was as cold to her as usual. She couldn't blame him.

'And who are you?' she asked of Elma.

'I'm Elma, helping out with the technology side of things.'

Heather moved towards Bradley, looked at him very closely. She took his pulse and observed his eyes, 'how are you feeling? You fool!'

'Ehm, what's going on?' asked Elma.

'This total complete utter mad fool just went and drank a concocted goodness knows what!' burst Heather.

'He did what!?!' it was Elma's turn.

'Calm down everyone, I'm fine, there is no time to test this stuff; we have no time...'

'Fred, make yourself useful and pin him down. I need a blood sample! Now,' instructed Heather.

Bradley was having none of it, 'no bloody way!' he objected.

Heather handed him the needle, 'you either do it yourself, or we'll do it for you, choose!' Her posture changed and, hands on hips, she stood there immobile.

Bradley gave out a long sigh; there was no arguing with her in that mood. He took the syringe from her, walked up to Elma and handed it to her.

'What? Why are you giving me this? I don't know how to do this!'

'Use your eyes; you can scan the physiology and pinpoint the veins with such precision that no one else alive can without scanning equipment.'

Elma hesitated and took the needle.

'Fred, knock me out!'

'What the heck are you talking about, man!' Fred glared at Bradley; he was unsure whether this was something about the virus he'd just drank, making him act oddly or whether Bradley had gone mad.

'It's the only way I'll be able to do this without freaking out,' he explained and nodded to Fred that it was ok.

Fred looked at Heather and then Elma, then back at Bradley.

'Do it, you said we have no time, so you'd better get a move on; we need that blood sample.' Heather's tone was cold, matter of fact.

Fred blinked in utter disbelief.

'Go on,' insisted Bradley.

Fred took a deep breath, and before anyone could say another word, Bradley felt the blow against his head, everything blurred, and he lost consciousness.

'Did you hit him maybe a little too hard?' Elma was concerned.

'He'll be fine, get the blood quick before he wakes up.' Elma scanned him, setting the scan mode to look below the skin and see all the internal wonders of his arm. Muscles, fibres, veins, arteries, nerves and so much more were all visible as if she was looking at simple objects in front of her.

'Here goes.' She held her breath and dove in with the needle, guiding it deeper and deeper with absolute precision. She could see where it was going and knew how much pressure she needed to apply. It turned out to be a relatively simple task. The blood was drawn, the syringe filled. She handed it over to Heather. 'I trust you know what to do with it?'

'Yes, thank you.' Heather took it and placed a couple of drops under the microscope.

'Fred, press hard on his wound; we don't want him bleeding to death!' Fred complied, 'but don't hurt him, you big brute!'

He looked up at her about to object when he saw the smile. She was trying to crack a joke to ease her nervousness. He nodded, making as serious a face as possible, which ended up being utterly comical, causing Elma to burst out in laughter.

29

MTECH
- IN CRISIS -

Bradley's vision gradually returned and his dizziness started to fade out. He looked around; the setting was familiar. He recognised this place! House mTech; he was back on TrueEarth. What was he doing back here?

ALERT to all members of House mTech. The House crystalline voice sprang to life, this time twice as loud as it had been previously. *Tear in time-space continuum detected. Location High Planes - House territory, seaplanes House territory, Nebraxil presence detected. ALERT.*

Bradley sensed the commotion. His head hurt badly. Then he remembered Fred bashing him over the head. *I need to remember never to ask him to do that again; he's got a heck of a punch.* Corridors were being filled with mTech personnel running about. He took advantage of the confusion and followed the glowing wave of blue power at his feet as he directed it to take him to Rhys. He felt power gathering; it was as if the entire House was suddenly full of life.

He bumped into a young technician, 'The House is under attack, I must go, make way.' He rushed out.

Bradley moved in his own direction, thinking he had to find Lurizak. The pool of force at his feet suddenly changed direction, sending him in a parallel pathway. It was odd, but he decided to go with it.

ALERT House communications disrupted from the other Houses. Prepare for attack!

The crystalline voice was starting to annoy the heck out of Bradley. It came fast and what sounded like a tear echoed towards them. It boomed against the structures of the House, sending the sound reverberating throughout the long corridors. Bradley kept to his set path and eventually, after losing track of where he had just been and where he was going next, he came to a sliding doorway. He placed his hands on the wall much to his surprise, the door slid open to reveal the conference room he had initially seen on his first visit to mTech.

'What the?!!?' Lurizak and Galvin jumped at his sight.

'I'm not sure what to call this other than good timing,' said Lurizak.

'A bit too good at his timing, isn't he?' Galvin was a little suspicious, 'We don't have time for further debate; we're at war, gentlemen.' He turned to face Bradley, 'since you are here, make yourself useful. You have the most powerful warrior here at your command, so why don't you gentlemen join us in battle? We need the help. We need time to launch the solar flare. I suspect this multiple area assault is deliberately designed to disrupt our operations. Most of the energy has been redirected to the solar storm-control systems and unless we get help fast, House mTech will fall.' His matter of fact, casual deduction sent chills down Bradley's back.

'Have House Bound been informed?' asked Lurizak.

'Yes, but they are currently countering another assault along the Tenbral Sea. Leaving that open would leave the entire back region of the House unaided. Tamirok is leading that assault.'

'Very well,' interjected Bradley. 'We're going into battle,' he smiled.

He turned to face Lurizak, 'we are going to go into battle a little differently; I have a few ideas I want to test out. Agreed?' He looked into the warrior's eyes and spoke unusually slowly. 'Our only escape is to outmanoeuvre them. You and me are the only ones who can. Since TrueEarth has been fighting them, they will be used to your methods.' He released some of the bindings on Lurizak's body.

'I hope you know what you are doing, Bradley, because this could be tantamount to treason!'

'TrueEarth laws do not concern me,' replied the deep echoing voice.

Lurizak was taken aback; it was only now that he noticed his friend was looking at him with different eyes, a different posture and felt different. 'Who or what are you?' he asked.

'That, my dear fellow, is a good question; we will have to find the answer in time, for now, we have a House to defend. I sense so much.' Something about him was changing, what even he could not tell.

'I don't understand, what are you intending to do?' Lurizak was not certain about Bradley, this alternate version of him put the warrior on edge. It all made him uncertain. Just as he had thought he knew his friend, he now saw that he knew very little, if anything.

'I have learnt how to use it properly; there's no time for debating. Time for action! Let's go.' Bradley got up took his own device and watched Lurizak take his.

Those were the devices of that ancient technology they had both used on their first trip here. As they held the devices out, Bradley put his hand on Lurizak's device and the destination image blurred and reformed.

'How? Did you?'

Bradley just looked at him sternly, and the questions stopped. 'GO,' commanded Bradley.

They both made the jump. Unlike the first time, there was no disorientation or feeling of sickness. He made the jump as if it was the most natural of things for him to do. They were in front of the main entrance to House mTech, the crystalline blue technology city. Straight ahead were tears in space; it was as if something had come and ripped massive fissures in the very air itself. Looking deep into them, Bradley saw a totally alien world.

As he could focus on it, Lurizak gripped his arm so firmly that pain shot right through it. 'Stop it, looking into those will draw you into their world. You've already started blurring away.'

'Thanks.' Bradley shook his head, trying to banish the image he had seen. He looked straight ahead of them and in the distance, he saw these thin forms of black and grey strings. It seemed like a whole bunch of these had joined and held together, forming the final thing which, in turn, glowed black and grey. His mind struggled; what were these odd creatures? He did not understand them. The malice, which oozed out of them, was thick and utterly disgusting to him. These things were not here to fight; they were here to cause damage, kill and destroy. Something pulled his senses to what stood behind them; it was larger than the rest, denser, same shape, but nearly 80 feet tall. Pure evil shimmered off of it, jet black, cold and dark. Shadows danced around it in an upwards counter-clockwise swirl. The entire sight made Bradley sick.

'I've never seen one like that before!' yelled Lurizak. 'There are way too many of them, we can't hold them all off by ourselves,' he objected.

'Has the great legendary warrior gone all soft in the face of his first-ever battle with his new wielder?' mused Bradley.

'Take that back!' objected Lurizak.

'Prove me wrong,' was all Bradley offered up.

'Fine, but if this is the end of us, it will be on you.'

'It's a deal then,' smiled Bradley.

'Sir, our systems have detected an unusually powerful Neraxil ahead of us. We're surrounded by a large number of their ground troops, and we have two odd ones, which seem to have taken on humanoid form about 100 feet in front.'

'That is most concerning,' replied Galvin. 'Any confirmation of ability and scale of matter?'

'No, sir, although something human is coming off their readings, very odd.'

'Seriously not! Your equipment must be off.'

'Hold on, patterns of quantum matter are assembling, power levels unknown.' He looked at his screen, baffled. 'Constant amplification of potential, unfolding. Sir, if we get hit by that, it will be the end of us.'

The air above them crackled, electric sparks flew all over the place and a brilliant blade of light cut through the air above their position. They all looked up and saw the forces of House Bound flying in, ground troops on floating diamond-shaped platforms, air support in their crystalline metal ships pierced through the heavens above. Within seconds, the air was full. Both men felt the all too familiar blade of air flow through their camp, indicating a jump was taking place right next to them. There stood Tamirok and Elshevira.

'Good afternoon, gentlemen, what is it I hear about you preparing to have fun without me,' she reprimanded them.

They both looked at her, long dagger-like blades glowing in pure dark energy in her hands. She held them pointing backwards, her black attire tight-fitting and combat-ready, black gems glowing as they pulled in dark matter from the space around them. She was ready for combat, no doubt about it.

'What is the situation?' asked Tamirok.

'We had lost hope of seeing you, that thing,' he pointed to the large entity in the distance, 'seems to be giving off a disruptive field, breaking inter-House communications. Speaking of which, how did you know?' asked the Ruler of mTech.

'You can thank Bradley for that, we noticed him using the ancient transport devices; by the way, where is he?'

'No one knows, we lost sight of him and Lurizak in House mTech.'

Tamirok was pissed. 'Tell me, how is it possible for you to lose ANYONE inside your own House?'

'They are fine,' interrupted Rhys, standing behind the small group. 'I bumped into them both before the alert went off. The last time I saw them, they were still wandering the corridors of the House's central building.'

'That's all we need, our bloody best warrior and a potential loose cannon gone wandering about. Ah, well.'

'Sir, the two humanoids are moving,' the observer interrupted them. 'But not in our direction.'

'What?'

'They are moving towards that,' he pointed to the large mass of enemies. 'We still cannot get a read on the energies, but they are definitely moving away from us.'

'Bring them up on the main screen,' interjected Tamirok.

'Not sure the unknown energies will be readable.'

'I don't care about the energies, give me an image.' He waited until the images formed.' They are! Bradley and Lurizak right in the path of the enemy. What are they thinking?'

'Why are they not showing up as our warriors? Like all the other Bound?' asked the engineer.

'Because that is not what they are, ..., anymore,' explained Tamirok. 'We need to get over there fast; there is no way the two of them will survive that!'

'I'll go ahead,' offered Elshevira.

'We can't risk you going alone,' she moved the blade out of her hand and ran her hand along Tamirok's jaw 'dear, dear boy, it is very unwise to underestimate me,' she paused. 'Although I do appreciate the concern, it is most charming of you. I'll be off, catch up when you can.' With those words, darkness gathered around her body and she shot away in a flash of black light towards the two outliers just as Tamirok yelled out a message for her to tell Bradley.

'So what's your big plan?' asked Lurizak.

'Just go with the flow, ok?'

'Fine, just don't get me killed,' he smiled at Bradley as he popped his helm on. 'Would you?' he motioned.

Bradley focused and caused the helm to be sealed in place.

He formed his blade out of the matter of his armour like last time. He looked just as impressive, a 7 feet 5 giant covered in skin-tight black metal from head to toe. His head turned, and he nodded to Bradley.

'Just a second,' came the quick response. He closed his eyes and allowed his own armour to form; the visor given to him by mTech was now sealed in the helm. He touched it. It activated. What an odd thing! He touched the screen again, and it fell silent. Reaching behind his back, he hoped it would still be there. It was. His right hand gripped the handle of the blade Danterrion.

Dantel had been forcefully pulled back, screaming in fury through time and space. He screamed out in agony, black and red fires blazing along its blade, hunger shimmering cut through the air itself. 'There, there, my pet, soon, now, behave, and you will get to feed,' whispered Bradley.

Lurizak had taken a step back; he had never seen the blade. Something deep within him recoiled at its presence. He could not voice his question, he wished so hard he could.

'Focus,' Bradley reprimanded him. 'Let's go.' Bradley grabbed the blade in both hands and lunged forward. Lurizak was surprised; his body moved like that of a warrior... when had Bradley learnt all that? They had only trained a handful of times with blades, yet he wielded this one as if it was the most natural thing to him. *Must be the nature of the weapon,* he concluded. He lunged forward.

Bradley's blade struck one of the Neraxil. His upper arm muscles rippled under the impact; it was like hitting a solid wall. The blade had stopped as it impacted. Then a screech tearing through his eardrums echoed out in a circular blast. He saw cracks in the line, then the line collapsed on the point of impact and was finally sucked into the blade. With nothing there and no kinetic drive, Bradley lunged towards the floor blade first. As he was trying to regain his footing, another one of those lines cut through space and drove straight at him. Its speed was just too great. An inch from him, he saw three black slits form in the air in front of it. It vibrated and was propelled backwards.

'Gentlemen, if you don't mind not staring at the floor mid-combat, I would really like to have you join us in one piece.'

Bradley's heart rose; he knew that voice. He looked up and saw Elshevira smiling down at him. Suddenly, he forgot his words. 'Hi,' was all he could muster.

'Be careful, babe will you, such a pretty face to lose is yours,' her shift in language was odd to hear, but its meaning was not lost. 'Remember, those things cannot touch you; the moment they make contact, you are lost to us.'

Bradley nodded. He had regained his footing and stepped backwards. 'I wasn't expecting this type of impact,' he smiled at her.

She winked at him and moved onto the other side in a flash of black darkness.

A surge of peculiar energy flowed into Bradley; he had experienced it once before yet it was still so alien, his body shuddered under its influence. The sword was feeding him part of the soul's essence it had absorbed. It disgusted him. The cruelty, the disgust, the desire to destroy washed over him. He resisted it to no avail. It was an internal battle he could not fight now. He raised the sword and banged against another one of those lines. This time as it shrieked, he started to pull back; expecting the air in front of him to be totally empty the next instant. It collapsed into the sword. The essence flowed into him; there was nothing he could do about it.

He took hold of it; it was his now, it was a part of him. He turned that disgust, that desire to destroy and unleashed it at the hundreds of these lines ahead of him. His fighting style was just too cumbersome, the Neraxil lines moved fast and each time he banged against one or another, he was stuck there for a few seconds, and in that time, dozens came rushing towards him. He saw Lurizak jump next to him to fend off a few. The black slits across space were back; Elshevira was helping as much as she could, but even with her assistance, they would get overwhelmed fast.

'Tamirok says, 'quantum entangle you two.''

Bradley had no idea what she was talking about.

Lurizak nodded and within a split second, he grabbed hold of Bradley's right hand, leaving the massive sword balancing in his left. Without a word, he placed Bradley's right hand on his own chest and then placed his own right hand against Bradley's chest.

Bradley understood, he closed his eyes and reached out through the hand. *Finally,* said Lurizak in his mind. *Listen to me, don't overwhelm me; you are still too new to combat. I need you to entangle with me like we did when we were training. You also need to retain a part of you in your own body to fight,* he explained.

How do I do it? asked Bradley.

Just focus on the nerve-ropes. Pour some of your essence into them as you do when you take complete control. We both know how fond you are of doing that. Except this time, leave only a part of it there and, with the other part, pull a part of my essence into yourself.

Bradley focussed, in his enhanced state, this was not that hard to do. His mind interlocked with Lurizak, his senses interlocked, and finally, his will interlocked. He opened his eyes and saw Lurizak nod at him. His powers were stirring anew; all those absorbed soul essences had him overflowing. He smiled a devious, almost challenging smile at Lurizak and let loose. Power streamed into the warrior, hard, cold, cruel power. Had he been able to, he would have screamed in agony. He could not. Silence ruled him, he cringed and allowed the power to flow through him, his sword and armour blasted in black lightning.

Lurizak was quick to act. He activated the special glyphs in his armour. They looked terrible and as power flared from them, Lurizak changed, his speed increased, the power behind his swings increased, his anger flared, rage drove him.

Elshevira felt the change; she knew that he'd activated the warrior's berserker combat mode. Quickly, she moved away out of his path. She knew what the Bound warriors were like in the swing of berserker battle mode, and she definitely did not want to be caught in his path.

Bradley unleashed his own restraints; he knew Lurizak would act as a safety net now, and he let go. Digging deeper and deeper, he willed it all to burst out. The forces, which emanated from him in waves of strings and streams, were totally chaotic, completely uncontrolled. His power augmented a millionfold and he willed his physical strength to increase. Pure black lightning coursed through each and every muscle fibre, making it hum with sheer raging might.

He dove into the mob of Neraxil lines and swinging his sword, cut across four of them in one blow. His sword no longer hit a wall-like structure; this time, it cut straight through with such burst that it fractured the very lines of their bodies and pushed through to the next. Soul essence was transferred into him, the screeches becoming so powerful and echoing with such ferocity that they became an interfering wave pattern in their own right. Bradley lost all awareness of what he was doing or what was happening.

'By the grace of the Houses, what is that?' pointed the engineer towards the battlefield on screen.

There was Bradley, massive sword in hand, radiating souls into him. Tentacles of jet black, glowing white power dancing about his body and slipstreams of nothingness. Black and red lightning was crackling in the air all about. The three forces were slamming into one another, detonating sonic waves outwards, disrupting the quantum fields all over the battlefield for miles on end. The Neraxil lines were cracking and dispersing all over the place. Next to him, Lurizak black lighting flowing all over his armoured body, pure nothingness shimmering down his sword, forming small black holes, which he slammed into groups of Neraxil lines. Not even waiting for the impact, he propelled himself up into the air by sheer leg muscular force, only to land into the next group while the first was devoured by the black hole. It then collapsed in on itself, just a second before the next one was formed. They all stared at the sight.

'I've never seen anything like it,' said Galvin.

'Neither have I,' agreed Tamirok.

'Just exactly what is going on over there?' asked Galvin.

'What we are witnessing gentlemen is House Nothingness in action,' they all gasped at the horror of it. 'Unfortunately, Bradley has let go, look at his chaotic outpouring of power; he has no control – a liability to his own side as much as the enemy.'

Tamirok closed his eyes and redirected the troops by force of his own will. 'I've sent the warriors off to the edges of that battle. No point in us losing good men and women to that,' he pointed at the sight ahead of them.

They all looked intently, Bradley was so erratic that there was simply no pattern nor method to his movements or attacks. He looked like someone who had no idea what was going on or any idea of what he was doing, either. Tamirok was concerned; this was a recipe for death. He had seen men lose their minds on the battlefield before. It never ended well.

Bradley, Bradley, listen to me. BRADLEY, Lurizak's mind yelled at Bradley within his own. It pulled him back to his senses, ever so slightly. *Your idea! Remember, damn it! Don't lose sight now.*

Oh, yes, I remember. Cover me.

Bradley stopped in his tracks, the power streams and tentacles speeding up their movements about his body. He put the quantum relocation device on the floor. Waited. He knew stopping would cause the enemy to try and rush in. And so they did. The second before they made contact, he slammed his hand against the device and poured his power into it, yelling out *'hiyana esiktu kiana.'* The very space shimmered, the words reverberated outwards as a huge mass of blackness expanded out of the device. Each Neraxil line it touched simply vanished. Bradley picked up the device and merged it back into his armour. He looked around–hundreds upon hundreds of the lines had vanished. The immediate space was clear. He laughed maniacally.

'I'll be dammed,' Tamirok was observing the events.

'Now what?' Galvin.

'That boy has a brain, that's for sure,' he laughed.

'You're stating the obvious, General. What just happened?'

'He used the quantum relocation device to send them all into quantum space and then somewhere else.'

'You mean? He used one of those? How is that even possible?'

'The Ancient Dark, a wielder,' stepping in from the darkness behind them, a stranger, came into full view. Tall jet black hair, freely flowing to his neckline, massive broad shoulders, standing at 6 feet 2, with eyes so deeply blue they appeared purple and ghostly white skin. The muscular man was dressed in the finest attire. A shirt made out of pure darkness, interwoven with dark violet and silver embroiled script, collar glowing with indigo-black glyphs, sleeve cuffs bearing the script of a Ruler. His trousers black along the outer sides from hip to feet and various silver-golden glyphs exhumed a constant flow of hazy power. His hands bore rings on each finger, each ring with black script, each emitting a unique hue to the blackness, each indicating rulership over one of the House's divisions. He looked like someone in his mid to late 20s but, in fact, he was much older than all of them put together. His perfectly groomed facial hair only served to accentuate his sharp masculine facial features.

'Jentenebro.' They all offered a slight bow of their heads in greeting to the Ruler of GrimGloom.

'It is a pleasure to see you in person, ' Tamirok greeted him.

'You called, House GrimGloom answered, as is required and proper.'

'Thank you Jentenebro,' Galvin said.

'I am sure you would have done the same for our own House.' They shook hands in greeting. 'Besides, I did not want to miss that!' he pointed to the screen. 'It is always amusing to watch the newcomers from FalseEarth in their struggles here, even if this one seems to be linked to me by ancestry… somehow.'

'It is rather odd, is it not,' admitted Tamirok. Jentenebro reached behind him, grabbing a patch of darkness as if it was something physical and spoke to it. 'Elshevira, I'm coming in to assist; make sure that one doesn't get harmed.' He then waved the patch of darkness forward. Much to everyone's amazement, it seemed to gain a will of its own and flew off at insane speed towards the three in the central part of the battlefield.

'Is this really necessary?' asked Galvin.

'How long do you want this battle to go on for?' replied Jentenebro. 'Besides, those large ones are far more than they can defeat on their own.'

'Those? You mean?' he looked at his display and gasped; there were three now instead of just the one.

'Ah, my dearest friend, your technology is admirable, but in the dark, our senses are far sharper than anything you can muster. Even with your night vision devices, they are no match to our purer senses.' With those words, dark energy cycled around his body and a jet of blackness carried him forth at immense speed to the heart of the battlefield.

30

THE
- UNEXPECTED -
DEATH

Bradley's body was flung through the air. It flopped mid-air as if it was nothing more than a leaf being carried by the wind until, with a big thud, it impacted onto the ground. Lurizak instantly broke out of his berserker rage and rushed to his side. Elshevira flipped backwards to him. They both looked at him, motionless, flesh torn and ripped as if it had been nothing more than sandpaper. Blood was seeping readily through his wounds, leaving a dark red tint on the soil underneath his limp body. In desperation, Lurizak tried to force him to breath to no avail. His heart had stopped only a moment ago. Elshevira was quick on her toes. She tried to push the giant Lurizak out of the way. He refused to budge.

'Get out of my way. We only have a few very brief moments to save him,' her gaze sharp, almost threatening. He could see there was no time for arguing and he would get nowhere with her no matter what he did or said. Deep in those eyes, he caught a glimpse of desperation and anguish. Bradley's armour faded away, revealing his naked mutilated body. At the sight of that, Lurizak stepped back. He was dying within as well. With his Wielder dead, a Bound would become nothing more than a living statue, unable to do anything — think, move or react. He felt Bradley's will clinging onto him through his nerve-cords, its grip was tight, too tight. His breathing was hard, his body felt as if it was being strangled by chains. He knew this sensation. When Tamirok nearly died, he had the same experience. He found out that this happens when the wielder is indeed dying, the desperation and will to survive pushed all that which remained of him into the Bound. But that also meant there was still a chance to save him.

'I trust you,' he told her. She nodded and moved her body on top of Bradley. Something stirred. A sigh of relief washed over her, there was life there. Lurizak was about to object just as she spoke, 'in men, life is found here, it is the core of them.' Then she looked up at him and remembered it was not the case for him, 'well for them it is. We women shape the life which flows from them. We manipulate it and nurture it. We use it because they are too unaware and wasteful to do so themselves.' She almost laughed trying to hide her panic. Time was running out fast. She moved both their bodies ever so slightly until she could place her head next to Bradley's ear.

'Listen to me, Bradley, hear my voice!' her dark powers flared like the burst of a black sun's rays. It washed over them both. 'Bradley!' she yelled into his ear. 'Damn it, you fool, LISTEN to my voice!' from somewhere deep in the blackness of death, Bradley stirred. He was at peace, very tranquil in the deep blackness. His body was sinking gently as if he had been sinking deep towards the bottom of a great black ocean's depth. It was neither cold nor hot. He liked it, it was so relaxing. His worries, his concerns, his responsibilities, his strife to control his body, his mind and his powers were gone. All he was aware of was this pleasant, slow but persistent sinking sensation.

Then he heard it, a voice, a woman's voice was calling out to him. It was so faint he could not make out what it was saying nor from where it was coming. It just was. An odd sensation coursed through him, something in him stirred, a spark of activity, a type of heat, a desire. It disrupted the peaceful sensation, so he tried to brush it away. He tried to will it away. He had no strength. The voice of the woman was calling out, this time, a sense of urgency was clear within it. The desire and spark within him was more and more bothersome. A wave, a pulse broke through the endless darkness into which he was sinking. It hit the disturbing sensations within him. He stirred but for a moment. At exactly that point, he heard the voice clearly, it was calling him a fool, instructing him to listen. What did those words mean? The heat stirred in him, that sensation was familiar to him. He could not remember what it was.

'I can't reach him! Damn it!' Elshevira cursed.

'Let me help,' Lurizak knelt down by her and froze. 'He's fading. His will is too weak, I'm about to become lost.' With his last free movement, he grabbed her free hand and put it on the criss-cross of nerve-ropes on his chest. 'Use...' he froze. She looked up and saw the plea in his eyes. She read it well, it was not a plea for himself but for Bradley. She understood. Unleashing her power through them, she grabbed what little of Bradley's essence was found there, allowing it to flow through her and back into Bradley's body. This she combined with her own power, allowing it to be propelled through her words.

'Bradley, wake up! Wake the damn up or you will be lost! Remember who you are, remember what you are, remember Lurizak, remember! Remember Kuroi! Remember Fred!' The power crackled and she instinctively pulled her hand off of him. As her power danced over his body, another power responded in kind. She rapidly pulled herself off of him. She knew that power, under no circumstance could it touch her. With almost instant reflexes, she repositioned herself, allowing her own dark quantum particles to flow out of her body and dance all around her. To the onlookers, she seemed like a sun of pure blackness surrounded by countless stars in perfect orbit. A dark galaxy of her own.

'To whoever can hear this, help us!' her cry was brutal and fierce. Within moments, two men stood by their side.

'We hear you, sister,' it was Jentenebro, Ruler of House GrimGloom. 'Let us help.' He looked at the transfixed Lurizak and cautiously moved to avoid making contact with him. Jentenebro put his hand on Bradley's chest. 'Ancient Dark to Ancient Dark Stir!' he sent waves of pure black lightning, unfolding into strings and dancing over Bradley's flesh. She placed her hand on top of Jentenebro's. He could easily shield her from the forbidden power. Having the help of one who understood death intimately proved to be a blessing beyond measure. She found herself sinking next to Bradley. Unlike him, she was awake. Manoeuvring herself close to his dormant body, she managed to touch him. He blinked, then stumbled back into slumber.

'Jentenebro, Lurizak, he's sinking fast,' they both heard her. Crackling black lightning broke through the empty blackness and hit Bradley square in the chest. The murky-yellow-green blackness flooded her, cutting through the silent peaceful waters of eternal slumber. 'Bradley, wake up, you damn fool!' she yelled into his ear and banged against his chest.

'Ouch!' he yelled and opened his eyes for a few moments. They quickly became sluggish and closed.

'I won't let you!' she whispered to him. And there in the darkness, in between life and death, she once again placed herself on top of him. Her soft voluptuous breasts pushed against his strong square chest. She wrapped her soft velvet-like limbs protectively around him and allowed the power free reign.

Bradley remembered! He knew the sensation, desire, passion. It flared up, heat exploded from deep within him, burning fire coursed through his veins. Strength and solidity were coming back to him. His will awoke momentarily. The soft, weak flicker went out. Elshevira's heart sank. She noticed awareness was there, very faint but there. She repositioned herself and whispered to him 'Listen to me well, Bradley, just listen.' Her voice deepened like a wave cascading against the eternal dark shores. 'In the beginning of all time, the Great Mother stirred in the darkness and chaos. All things chaotic were hers, as they are of her daughters. We are chaos undisciplined. But the Great Mother looked up through the darkness and longed for the Creator. Her longing intensified until she cried out to him. Hear her cry, Bradley! Hear the longing for life from the Great Mother's lips!' she whispered a word pulled on a string of power within the darkness. A piercing cry of agony boomed throughout the peaceful sea of the sleep of death. 'The Creator heard the Great Mother's cry. His sorrow at witnessing her pain knew no bound, for he was compassionate and loved all things he had made. No matter how many times the Great Mother cried, he could not answer her longing because he was not part of what he had wrought. He couldn't be. Then the Great Mother in her deviousness made her body black as obsidian. She cried out to him once more, but this time, pleading with him to just look at her, to break her loneliness by gazing upon her and allowing his compassion to flow unto her and enfold her.

The very moment he gazed down into Creation, upon her the Great Mother made the sea of chaos part. His reflection shone with countless stars upon her reflective body. The Great Mother then took all those stars and light and wove them back into his reflection and so a part of the Creator then became the Great Father. The Great Mother and Father lusted for one another and each time the lust exploded outwards, a universe was formed. In each universe, the daughters were of the mother and the sons were of the father, they all longed for one another. The Great Mother was harsh as is the nature of chaos and darkness. She nurtured all her children but her firm hand was ever-present for her daughters whom she ensured were practical, able and knowledgeable in the ways of life. The sons she doted on and spoilt with power. The Great Mother saw in each one the reflection of the Father, and in that reflection, her own longing for the Creator stirred. And so, the longing in all men stirs to the call of the Great Mother through her daughters.' She paused. Sleep was threatening to overtake her as well. She knew the risks, she knew she had to get out of there or she too would sink into the embrace of the darkness of death. She felt something pulling her up. She knew Jentenebro would not allow her to be lost as well. With a desperate effort, she allowed her powers to flow as a whisper, then as flare, as the sun encapsulated in a million stars shining upon everything and specifically upon Bradley.

'Hear me, Bradley. I, Elshevira, call upon the Great Mother through the strings of creation, may her blessing find its way unto you.' She stirred a very specific combination of energies along the quantum strings of creation itself. She and only she knew them. All the other rulers of the House were men, these were secrets forbidden to them, but not to her! Softly, she whispered, 'Remember the Great Mother, Bradley! You spoilt brat!' she burst out laughing and allowed the force to pull her back up.

She found herself in her own body. Jentenebro was holding her hand and allowing his power to pulse through her. She loved that power, it was so soft and firm, it felt like the touch of a father helping a child up after falling down. 'Thank you,' she said to him.

'You are totally insane!' said Jentenebro, 'what on earth possessed you to flare the sea of death up like that?'

'I needed to do something!' she replied.

'Something!? You did every...bloody...thing, a flare-like cloud caught the attention of everything in there. I have the whole of the House of Gloom trying to contain the onslaught of every possible thing you could and could not imagine. You better hope this Bradley guy gets out soon or both him and we could be on the menu, for this, I care not to have to think about.'

'What did you do down there?' he asked, 'something even I do not recognise.'

'Never you mind, you men are not supposed to know everything,' she smiled deviously at him. He exploded in laughter.

'What are we going to do with him?' he pointed to Bradley. 'It doesn't seem to have worked, whatever it was.' He was right. Not only was Bradley still all ripped up immobile on the ground, but his body had started to turn even paler than it usually was. They all looked at him. No one dared to say a single word.

'I'm going to have to get hold of Tamirok, need to see what can be done about him.' Jentenebro pointed to Lurizak. 'Such a sad thing when this happens. I am surprised House Bound still hasn't found a solution to this problem.' He stood up and left. Elshevira was looking at the now powerless body. Something didn't feel right. How could they have lost him like this?

'You know,' commented Jentenebro, 'he is way too pale, unnaturally so,' she blinked then looked at Bradley's corpse. It's true, his body was getting whiter and whiter by the second.

Bradley! The voice spoke directly into his slumbering mind. *Time to get up, you lazy daisy!* The endless dark sea of death stirred. Light was dancing all over his body, white and black lightning crackled all over him, dancing the dance of impossible union, each trying to gain territory over the other yet both being in perfect balance.

The dance made his body shutter, muscles flexed on their own, hair flickered left and right as the two powers collided and set waves of energy. Wave built upon wave, the two merged into one and that new one wave collided with another, forming a new dance. Each motion, each collision released a new pulse of power, of life until his entire sleeping form was awash with it. Every atom pulsating as the quantum particles re-energised themselves. The tension of power built up rapidly until his entire sleeping form burst into millions upon millions of thin threads of power.

No, you don't! said the voice. A force gathered at their centre and pulled their ends back together. The threads struggled to dislodge themselves from it to no avail. That central point rose, faster and faster it travelled, disrupting the calm peacefulness of the seas of death, alerting more and more forms within it. It shot up at the speed of light until it surfaced straight inside Bradley's own body, pulling all the threads along with it and anchoring them deep inside of him. This time, when they tried to pull away, their ends touched organs, skin, blood, nerves, filling all with new activity and life. Bradley's body started to glow in a cold soft white light. Both Elshevira and Jentenebro jumped back.

'I'll be dammed,' said the LightBearer who stood at the distance observing the events unfold. His body absorbed the glow. It faded partially as colour started to return to him. His body jerked and the wounds started healing right in front of all the onlookers.

'He's awakening!' gasped Elshevira. 'Quick, close the passageway to the realm of death!' she instructed.

'There is nothing to close, none was open!'

'What do you mean none was open?' she asked.

'There is no open passageway,' he insisted.

'But how then?'

'Quantum level surfacing? I don't know,' he admitted. Bradley's left arm sprung back to life, the spasm sent it flickering to the left where it made contact with Lurizak's chest. The fingers seized them and grabbed a firm hold of the nerve-ropes. Lurizak watched and relief washed over him. *Bradley is back*, was all he could think. Finally, he just closed his eyes. Will burnt strong and renewed. He felt Bradley's essence flowing through him, infusing him with his will once more. The power of his wielder pushed against his own, reaffirming itself, its dominion. He embraced it and welcomed it. Silently echoing the words in his mind, 'I missed you, welcome back.'

'Hi,' Bradley finally spoke, much to everyone's relief.

'Welcome back, Mr Trouble,' Elshevira smiled at him, 'you gave us so much trouble... don't you dare go falling asleep forever like that again!'

He tried to get up, then noticed his lack of clothes. 'I'm naked? What the heck?'

'Don't worry, nothing there we haven't all seen before.' She laughed, stood up and motioned to Lurizak. 'Time for us to head back to camp, catch up whenever you are ready.' They walked away.

'Are you alright?' asked Lurizak.

'I'm not sure, think so... can't feel the cold anymore.'

'Ehh, maybe because it is not cold?' mused Lurizak.

'Oh, ok,' Bradley tried to get up, his legs gave way and he fell. 'So damn weak,' he cursed.

Lurizak sprung to action. 'You're going to hate me for this but what the heck,' he stood up, bent downwards and then picked Bradley up as if he was nothing more than a child whom he then carried in his arms.

'You're right, I do hate it, but I don't think I would have been able to make it on my own.'

'And let us not forget this is the middle of the battlefield, they could be back any moment, so we need to get out of here.' Bradley nodded, oddly he was grateful for Lurizak. Even though he was weak and vulnerable, he welcomed the strength of his companion who was now supporting him and taking him back to safety. Exhaustion took over again, his eyes just closed and his head sunk against the powerful square chest of the giant who was carrying him back to the refuge point.

'Damn warrior,' cursed the LightBearer, 'impossible to even get close to him while that thing is always by his side.' She swore. Her desperation to investigate how that light had come about, and more precisely, how it radiated from his body, was making her uneasy. She had to know, something about it so familiar yet so strange. 'How is it even possible for a dark one to call up the light?' she muttered as she followed Lurizak and Bradley from afar... She would wait, she would be patient and wait for the opportunity to present itself, it always did, eventually.

31

MIRA'S
- ECSTASY -

Heather had been working under the microscope, carefully examining Bradley's blood sample with Elma's assistance. She was patching her gaps in knowledge very efficiently, using the information Elma provided, and together, they finally got to grips with what was happening and what the planned countermeasures were.

'Well, it doesn't seem to be interfering with any of the natural processes in his blood,' concluded Heather, 'even the free radical damage is somehow being countered. His blood looks like that of a new-born baby! This is wonderful and yet could also prove to be very dangerous in its own right.'

'Yes, that is why we have a self-destruct in the new pathogen. When it has finished its work, it will self-destruct its nanotech components. Hopefully, the body will clear the rest of it out through the usual biological channels,' explained Elma.

'I'm not sure I like the hopefully part.' Heather hated those vague eccentricities and other assumptions, which her colleagues were all too keen to embrace.

'We have no time to test it out, or any subjects willing to do so for that matter.'

'True, what I am worried about is that we have no clear view of what it does to the nervous system, the lymphatic system, the organs, muscles, digestive systems or any other inner part of our physiologies. We're releasing this thing out to infect the masses without even the most basic understanding of what we have created. This makes us no better than what the current virus makers did.' Heather was not comfortable with the situation, not at all. 'Until we have clear clinical views of its effects on every single biological system in the body and the mental effects, we cannot call this safe by any stretch of the imagination!' She paused, lost in thought.

'Yet, if we do not release it, we will all become puppets regardless.' Elma had a point. They all had to concede that. It was a choice of one of two evils. Isn't it ironic, thought Heather, *that my ability to pull the strings of fate led me here to decide all our fates?*

'Fine,' Heather took the vial and threw it on the floor in the midst of the lab. It smashed and the liquid within evaporated rapidly.

'Wait! What did you just do?' objected Fred.

'We're going to all get infected anyway,' she explained, 'we might as well all get infected with this potential countermeasure pathogen.'

'Dispersal confirmed, virus data feedback confirms it is in the air all around us. Tracing it entering lungs.' Elma kept a close eye on its progress as it infected their systems and started taking over.

Rhys was looking after all the injured. A temporary outdoor base had been set up. Thankfully, there were far and few in between the assaults. Dealing with these invaders in smaller numbers was not too big a challenge, but should their numbers grow, it would become a far more serious issue. The Nebraxil had this annoying tendency of increasing their numbers very rapidly. Each assault was the same — a few initial ones, followed by a handful of larger ones and then masses of small ones just prior to what always appeared to be an infinitely large number of them joining in the battle. Providing they could eliminate the larger ones, the likelihood of stopping the assault was high, usually. This time, things were playing out very differently and Galvin suspected it was due to their footing in FalseEarth. They had to stop whatever was going on over there.

'How are things looking on the other side?' he asked.

'Not so good,' replied Jentenebro. 'Bradley is our focal point over there. Unfortunately for us all, he's right here recovering.'

That was the crux of the issue. Without any countermeasures, Mira had been busy growing and amplifying her hold. Every hour, more and more humans started changing, and purely from that one simple fact, the Nebraxil's grip was getting stronger. They had to stop it, somehow.

'How is he doing?' asked Tamirok.

'Actually, quite well, he's exhausted himself at the cellular level, again, but with Jentenebro's help, we have been able to remedy that quite rapidly. Who would have thought that the Ancient Dark was such a powerful repairing force? Ironic, isn't it? One of the most dangerous forces in existence is capable of curing...' replied Galvin.

'Any chance of us being able to get him back to the other side soon?'

'You do realise that if he continues exhausting himself like that, he won't survive it.' Galvin was concerned, this was not how things were supposed to function here in TrueEarth. Here, the Houses looked after their members, not use them until they could no longer function.

'There is no other course of action. We simply do not have the time to look for alternatives.' Tamirok pointed to the field, where more of those Nebraxil lines had started forming, 'they are coming in wave upon wave — there is no end to them,' he explained, 'and goodness knows what the Venerks are up to.'

'They seem to be entirely concentrated on infecting people on the other side, no trace of them in TrueEarth yet.'

'At least that is good news. I could use more of that right now.'

Tamirok was concerned, 'I wonder what made them work together. Never in all our long years of battling both of them has there been even the smallest hint of inter-communication, let alone active cooperation.'

'No idea.'

'What is the status quo for our plan on the other side?' Tamirok wanted to have all the options before he allowed anything else to go wrong.

'We have so far been able to exercise the dark energy over there with a little effort but unhindered. The darkness there seems to respond to our House's sciences and methods as it does here,' Jentenebro volunteered the information. This was not the time for secrets.

'That's a welcome discovery.'

'Indeed, Mishrak and Arlak are directing things during our absence.'

'Mishrak? Why on earth would you get him involved? He is a walking liability!' Tamirok was not happy, not at all.

'He's the only one in our House who can directly communicate with Bradley on our side.'

'Yes, I forgot about that little mishap...'

'It matters not who is involved — we are making good progress. The altered Venerks virus is being spread from infected to infected over there. It will take a little time until the technological components have been disabled. Fortunately, Elma has isolated the technology in the new virus to avoid our altered one from being affected.'

Jentenebro was worried, now that someone could alter the Venerks, it could potentially spell a lot of trouble down the line.

'We are preparing and powering the solar array, which should be ready for us to cause a series of solar flares to burst out when we need them. Directing them is no issue; it is something we have been able to do for generations. We will wash the entire area in which this outbreak is concentrated in as much interference and power as you need. Fortunately, it still seems to be contained for the time being. The supporting technology, however, is globally available on the other side, it is the infection that is its weakness. It needs time to spread, that is where we still have a sliver of an opportunity to act.'

Galvin was right. Once the infection started to spread faster and faster, it would become a global counter-attack rather than one focused on the proximity of the labs, university and attached hospital.

'It still does not solve the problem of power,' intervened Elshevira, 'that cloud of shadow is amassing gigantic amounts of energy and there's nothing we can do about it. If we do not take that out of the equation, this new form of what was a human will just feed on it and keep on re-growing.'

'Shadows, who would have thought...' pondered Galvin.

'We are not equipped to deal with them. There have been no shadows here in TrueEarth ever. They simply do not exist. We have no knowledge even on how to deal with them... all we have are what the FalseEarth crossovers tell us in their stories,' explained Jentenebro.

'Can't we ask the LightBearers? From what my sources reveal, Bradley used light to chase them away.' Tamirok had heard of the incident.

'No, it required him to maintain a constant pulse of that red light of his and caused his crash. The very instant that light faded, they were back. Even the LightBearers cannot maintain that forever, not on a global scale.' Elshevira had no intension of working with them, ever.

'You can unleash the darkness and just let it do its thing, can't they do the same with light?' asked Galvin.

'No, the two forces are fundamentally different. Darkness is the natural state of things, light needs to be spurred into action and then maintained, or it fades away,' explained Jentenebro.

'That leaves us with only one solution,' interjected Tamirok.

'And that is?' asked Galvin.

'Bradley is going to have to dissipate that on his own, somehow.'

'Are you insane? You've lost your mind.' Elshevira went into what looked like a frenzy. 'Do you know what that will do to him? No one can survive that!' She was getting more and more agitated. Jentenebro put his hand on her shoulder to steady her.

'Does anyone else have any suggestions? I'm all ears.'

No one did. No matter what they had at their disposal, there was nothing they could send over to FalseEarth other than themselves and that at great cost. Even if that had been a workable option, none of them were able to deal with this shadow infused with masses of emotional power.

'I thought as much,' replied Tamirok. 'Bradley can redirect all that power into the Nothing and pretty much take it out of the equation in one fell swoop.'

'I won't let you!' Lurizak walked in with Bradley a step behind him, 'you cannot just throw his life away because it is the most convenient solution.'

'Ah, Lurizak, welcome back.' He nodded to Tamirok in greeting.

'What would you like us to do instead then?' he asked.

Lurizak was at a loss. He was used to following orders, but tactical planning was not his strong point. He had the basics when leading the men in battle, but this was far beyond his know-how. He secretly cursed himself for his lack of knowledge and ability. He turned to look at Bradley. Nothing, a blank expression other than a hint or two of sympathy.

'That settles it,' concluded Tamirok, 'Bradley will let go of his bindings with you so we can still have you at our side and then go back to FalseEarth and finish what he started there.'

'And die in the process!?' interrupted Elshevira. 'This is barbaric!' she snapped.

'No,' Lurizak's voice boomed out. It shocked everyone — the Bound never objected, ever. Their very reason for existence was to carry out orders and comply, no matter what. All eyes went straight to Lurizak, all questioning glances, all faces locked in shock and surprise. 'If you are sending him to death, then I will stand with him!'

'You're not serious!' objected Tamirok, 'do you think I'd let TrueEarth lose its most skilled and experienced warrior? You can't be serious!?'

Lurizak refused to respond.

'Bradley, surely you understand?' prompted Tamirok.

Bradley was conflicted, he had never contemplated the thought of walking into a situation where his life would be at stake. He was the guy who sat in the laboratory and did his research — bacteria, viruses, blood were his domain, not this battle and war madness. Tamirok's logic, however, was flawless. There was no time for alternate solutions, no obvious, accessible alternative. He looked at Lurizak, sadness and sorrow ebbed its way out of Bradley's eyes.

'Lurizak, I won't will you into any of this, but I won't stop you either. I want you for once in your life to make your own choice. You have to understand that, for me, all I cared about, all my hopes and all my dreams died back home. Mira had been right in a lot of what she said when I met her. So right that I was very tempted to accept her offer and join her...'

Upon hearing those words, gasps of shock and horror could be heard from many standing there, except for Jentenebro. He understood what Bradley was talking about and could empathise with him perfectly.

'I have no future, either there nor here. Look at me! I'm too frail for this world where harsh realities rule. I do not belong anywhere except in a House, which is empty of everything. Nothingness is where I belong.' Bradley smiled. 'Such an appropriate House for me in view of my circumstances.'

Elshevira was visibly upset and tears ran down her face. 'I lost my one true love, and I lost my son to this abomination, which now threatens everyone. I need to put an end to it all.' His words faltered for but an instant. 'I will not ask you to join me in this, and I definitely, absolutely, will not force you into it.'

'You said I have the freedom to choose, so in that case, my mind is made up. I am not abandoning you! If this is the end, I will stand by your side and face whatever it is with you. They are asking too much from you.' Lurizak waved at all gathered there. 'They are asking a newcomer who has never even seen TrueEarth outside of a few Houses to give his life to save it. That is not right. If a life is needed to be offered in sacrifice for TrueEarth to be safe, it should be one that is bonded to it, not someone who has only walked its fields a few minutes in his entire life. We will stand together, FalseEarth life and TrueEarth life, together as one, fighting a common enemy. Just as the Nebraxil and Venerks have this Mira standing with them, I will stand with you against her and them. My mind is made up.' His gaze was one of absolute determination, challenging any to dare oppose him. His gaze shifted from Ruler to Ruler, House member to House member, daring them to say something. None did.

It is done, echoed the voice in Bradley's head. *The choice is made.* Bradley walked over to Elshevira and whispered in her ear, 'You are a wonder to behold, do not let anyone tell you otherwise,' he pulled back and smiled.

He faced Galvin, 'It would have been an absolute pleasure to have been a member of House mTech, a cruel twist of fate made it never to be.'

Finally, he came face to face with Jentenebro, a slight bow of the head and an offer of a handshake. 'I am told that, at some point in time, we had a common ancestor, I salute thee.' His eyes spontaneously started emitting golden-black energy, something far beyond what Bradley was streaming forth through him.

Jentenebro took his hand and shook it. Sparks of golden-black lightning danced from one to the other. Jentenebro's eyes widened in surprise as he realised what the connection was. He looked at Bradley, who just nodded. His armour pulsed with red power anew as he opened the gateway to the Chamber of the Ancients. Both he and Lurizak walked through before anyone could say another word to either of them. The gateway closed. They were gone.

'By the Houses!' swore Jentenebro. He turned to face Elshevira, 'Did you know?' he asked her.

'That you two might be related? Yes, the Ancient Dark suggested that.'

'No, not that,' she looked at him questioningly.

'Ancient Dark of the Herald...' suddenly, his words were interrupted. Large waves of Nebraxil energy pulses shot through the group. They jumped out of its way, all with rapid reflexes trained for battle.

Bradley and Lurizak stood at the gateway to FalseEarth. Once they stepped through it, they would be in the midst of the next battle. Bradley faced Lurizak, 'are you sure about this?' he asked a final time.

'Bradley, you are starting to be really annoying with all your repetition, you know,' he smiled and wrapped his powerful bulky arm around Bradley's shoulder. Gently, he took a step forward, pushing Bradley and himself through.

Their vision cleared — they were in Bradley's lab offices. Elma, Fred and Heather were there, waiting for him to return. Elma had kept them in the loop using her eyes' ability to see in both TrueEarth and FalseEarth. The sight of Lurizak made them all take a cautious step back.

'He's huge!' burst out Elma. She had heard of the Bound warriors but had not yet seen any of them. The sight of this massive 7 foot 5 muscular giant in black metal armour with power shimmering from him as the heat would off a frying pan was very intimidating.

Fred, on the other hand, rushed to him and held out his hand in greeting. He looked at Lurizak, empathy coursed freely, they were so alike. One was being pulled towards the other as if by some external force.

'Pleased to meet you! I'm Fred,' he smiled.

'I'm Lurizak,' and as he responded, Fred's thin indigo-blue nerve-ropes expanded from his forearms and snaked their way over

Lurizak's whose own copper black entangled themselves with Fred's all the way up his forearm. Both men's arms interlocked, bound to one another, bound by one another. Lurizak's left eyebrow rose in surprise. Fred exploded in laughter.

'Erm, I'm all too happy to meet you, but this might be a bit of a problem.' He looked down at their arms, chained to one another.

'Don't worry, they will release, our armours are alive, you see. They too recognised each other, this is how they are getting to know each other.' Fred nodded. It took a few minutes until each man's ropes pulled back into his own armour.

'Gentlemen, if all your buddy bonding is over and done with, we have work to do.' Elma was once again looking at her laptop.

Heather stepped into view from the background. 'Bradley, I'm... sorry.' She felt bad about what had happened.

He faced her and smiled, 'it's ok, Heather.' He gave her the best spontaneous, quick hug ever.

She moved out of the way, 'we're in company!'

He exploded in an almost childish laugh.

Heather came face to face with Lurizak, nodded her head slightly as he looked at her, and remained silent. He acknowledged her with the same gesture and turned to face Elma's laptop, which was now projecting a scenery in 3D straight ahead of them.

'This is the current situation, gentlemen. House mTech are ready to direct the pulses emitted from the solar flares they are going to trigger; they will hit right there,' she pointed to the central location, where Bradley recognised Mira was standing. Her technological and energetic patterns were still the most distinctive of the lot of them. She was surrounded by three others, who seemed to be far more changed than the rest of them. 'These three are almost as progressed as she is, except something is locking them down from moving further.'

'Probably her doing, she would never allow anyone to grow to the point where they might be an equal or a challenge to her,' Bradley pointed out at yet another grand flaw in her.

'Whatever the case may be, once that pulse hits, it will disrupt their wireless communications and that is when you need to act. I will try and hack into their systems. After all, if they are part nanotech, then there are programs at play.' Her excitement was plain for all to see. Elma loved this sort of a challenge, and hacking an alien intelligence was the biggest thrill of her life! It was the grand achievement of any hacker — the larger the challenge, the bigger the reward. She sipped on one of her energy drinks.

Bradley saw his office bin filled to the brim with used cans of energy drinks. 'You shouldn't drink that many of those,' he pointed out.

'Oh, pinch me! Mr righteous,' Heather broke out in a giggle at Elma's comeback. Heather immediately knew that they would get on brilliantly. She already liked the girl.

'All this and the spreading of our altered virus, which seems to be causing them some problems already,' she pointed to the map of Mira's technical and bio-signatures.

The sparks, which had been controlling the flow of electric pulses in this new organism she had become, were being disrupted. Some flared incorrectly while others spilt into inverse directions. The effects on the others were even more pronounced! Over there, the black oily infusions were being redirected to counter the runaway currents.

'You two, I understand, will take care of that mess up there, right? It has intensified to the point where it is producing a physical energy.' She pointed to the sky above. The thickness of the clouds had grown substantially. 'Taking that out...' she paused, giving Bradley a look drenched in sadness, 'will hopefully crash the final part of the self-repair they are undergoing. That will give our virus an opening to start disrupting their biological components. This only leaves the issue of keeping attackers at bay while you two do your thing.'

'I'll do that!' offered Fred.

'Yes, you can use those rope-chains of yours to stop the Nebraxil energy waves!' Bradley pointed out the one thing none of them had thought would be a problem. He knew all too well that those waves shatter whatever they make contact with at full power. So far, Fred seemed to be able to counter these less powerful ones quite effectively, but would it work with fully powered versions? That remained to be seen.

'He's using his nerve-cords?' prompted Lurizak, 'to counter the Nebraxil waves?'

'You bet!' Fred flexed his biceps in a show of pride. Lurizak was impressed that Fred's rope-chains could do that — his own couldn't.

'Interesting,' is all he offered up, 'and I will take care of ensuring none of those things get close to Bradley.'

'You do realise there are many of them, right?' asked Elma. 'So far, I can count the three main ones with at least three dozen additional patrolling the area and those are only what we can see right now.'

Lurizak traced some of the etched letters on his armour; they began to emit a faint coppery glow like blood flowing from one to the other and the resulting power culminated into a larger glyph. It crackled with power, blood-red power.

'Hyper-Bezerker mode ready! Not a problem.' Elma's gasp could be heard by them all, 'but that's...' she couldn't finish the sentence.

'That is also called the Final Cry of the Dying Warrior,' Lurizak finished it for her, 'once all the life, power, energy and force within the Bound is used up to generate hyper speed, force and devastating power, making the warrior a force of unstoppable carnage and fury, blind to reason, logic and feelings or sensations.'

'Wow, cool!' Fred failed to grasp the implications.

'No, not cool, you idiot,' snapped Elma, 'it is called the final cry, the final one, end.'

Realisation dawned on Fred, and his head sunk.

Lurizak slammed his giant arm against Fred's back. 'Don't worry, junior, it is an honour to fight along with you all and put an end to this threat to both our realities.'

'Just everyone keep out of his way when he activates it,' she warned.

'What do I do?' asked Heather.

'You and I are going to do something very sneaky, but there's no need for the boys to know about that!'

The devious chuckle had Bradley worried. Just what were they up to?

'Did we miss anything?' she asked.

'Hold on,' interrupted Bradley. He closed his eyes and spent a few moments in communication with Mishrak. She looked at him, waiting, not sure what he was up to. 'Done.'

She looked up questioningly. He remained silent.

'We're all set,' he said.

'Why do I feel so horrible?' asked Fred, 'is there something you are not telling me?' He looked around and got the distinct impression everyone except him knew something.

Bradley walked up to Fred and placed his arm around his shoulder in a friendly embrace. 'What they are not telling you is that we are as nervous as can be! Actually terrified, but trying so hard to hide it.'

Fred nodded, 'me too.'

Bradley smiled at him, 'promise me that no matter what happens, if things go pear-shaped out there, you will instantly remove yourself and get to shelter. I don't want you risking your life in this.'

Fred looked at him, perplexed, then decided that since he had never been in a battle, this was probably what they all did pre-fights. 'Ok, ok, I promise.'

Bradley allowed the subtle flow of his will to pulse through Fred's bindings. *I'm sorry,* echoed in his mind, *but I'm not going to let you get hurt.* Fred never heard Bradley's mind communication.

'Let's go!'

He headed for the door with the others at his tail. They arrived at the intersection of the three buildings. On their right were the laboratories, with the car park to the side. On the left was the hospital, and straight ahead, the university stood tall. This intersection was a well-maintained small park, small by comparison to the others, but a nice meeting spot for staff and students with benches along the sides, trees giving the all too welcoming shade during summertime and a picnic area in the central section.

They looked up and ahead and there, mid-air, was Mira. At first, she appeared to be floating.

When Bradley activated his visor, he saw that she was doing no such thing. The lines and threads emanating from deep within her had merged into what could be described as semi-physical, stupidly large arteries. Those arteries were grouped together and were pushing her off the ground into the air. She floated there, five feet high above the ground, in what looked like overwhelming delight. She was lost in ecstasy, completely oblivious to her immediate surroundings. She did not need to concern herself with what was happening, as below on the ground were what looked like highly vigilant hyperactive guards, preventing anyone from reaching her.

Elma pointed to Heather and indicated that they should go to the discreet hidden spot, where she started to set up her laptop. Heather was a little annoyed about being left out of the battle. She wanted to be part of the action. Elma nudged her and reminded her that it would be a waste of valuable resources to misuse her talents, which were not combat-centric.

Bradley closed his eyes and focused on his connection to Mishrak. *Mishrak! Mishrak! Mishrak!*

No need to yell, you're giving me a blooming headache. I can hear you,

We're ready. Tell Elshevira to let the darkness loose and carry the virus. Everything was silent for a moment, the lights went out of their own accord, leaving only the large screens to illuminate the place.

'What the...' Fred looked around.

'Don't stress, it's Elshevira doing her part,' explained Bradley, as the darkness concentrated.

We're all infected. Target me, Lurizak, Elma and Heather, he projected Heather's image to Mishrak. *Do it, have to stop chatting, this is hard work. We need to concentrate,* Bradley lost contact. He watched as dark energy flooded the space. His visor displayed masses and masses of it, gathering, accumulating and then flowing through them as it moved on outwards.

Bradley, Lurizak and Fred stood there, watching, 'so, this is it?' asked Fred.

Lurizak's hand made an impact with Fred's midsection and flat out slammed against it.

'Ouch! What was that for?'

He did not say a thing. Fred looked at the hand stuck against his upper stomach, the metallic copper had started spilling from Lurizak's hand into Fred's stomach.

'Take this, junior, it will shield you from the virus. Our armoured skins are engineered to counter all viral life forms — you will need it.'

Fred looked as the coppery substance thinned out and covered more and more of him.

'I can only spare a little, but it will do. It won't shield you from physical impact, but it will definitely protect you from the virus when they try to change us into one of those things.'

Fred's eyes beamed, 'thank you!'

Lurizak smiled at him, *to be so young and full of life, what a joy.* He wanted to protect this kid. He did not know why, he just did. He took his helm out and placed it over his head and it sealed instantly.

'Cool! Now that is awesome!' Fred couldn't hold his admiration back. Lurizak smiled. 'How does that work?' asked Fred. No reply.

'He can't speak anymore, the metals cover his entire face,' explained Bradley.

'Oh.'

'The Bound do not need to speak in combat as all communication is done from mind to mind, and it seems from armour to armour.' Bradley had not known that until Fred and Lurizak's armours decided to have their little exchange. They waited a few minutes until, finally, the thin layer of Lurizak's armour covered all Fred's skin and even meshed itself through his hair.

Lurizak, you still control your armour, even when it's over him like that? asked Bradley.

Yes.

Good, if he gets into danger, can we use that to make him leave? Even if he refuses to?

Just send the impulse of your will through me, and it will ripple over.

Great, I'll remember.

Darkness thickened all around them, very rapidly. This was not the artificially darkened sky... no, this was something altogether different. It was very strange! To their vision, it had become dark, but it was not dark at all. Thicker and thicker it grew, Mira's still partially human guards became agitated, their technological components started to light up, activate and engage some unknown function to Bradley or Elma.

'Heather, what is happening?' asked Elma.

'The darkness, you mean?' Elma seemed puzzled. 'Don't you see it?'

'No,' her head sunk a little, a hint of vulnerability and sadness was there. 'I can only see what we have sensors for, Heather. Whatever is happening, House mTech doesn't have a sensor for, and I can't see it. All I see is some of the colours around us have dimmed slightly. The actual darkness itself is producing no energy I can pick up, so I won't be able to see it.' She turned to face Heather, her eyes sparkling with data and sadness.

'Elma? What happened to you?' asked Heather.

'Heather,' she was about to crash emotionally, 'I'm blind... The only things I can see are what these picked up and shown to me,' she pointed to her new eyes. Heather could not resist embracing Elma in a warm, comforting hug.

'The price of the crystals?' she asked.

Elma nodded, 'yes.'

'Damn those things, seriously. So, this is why you wanted me with you? You need me to see those things you cannot?'

Elma did not speak, she just nodded again.

Heather felt horrible for complaining about joining Elma. She understood now. It was settled, she would be her eyes! 'I'll tell you everything!' Elma's smile returned. 'We girls have to stick together!' more so to hide her sorrow than out of any genuine reason. She had worked so hard to avoid the guys finding. She did not want her vulnerability exposed and with this, she no longer had a choice in the matter.

The darkness had become palpable. Bradley shivered, then he heard it, a voice woven in the darkness itself — a spark of static? As he focused in on it, he heard with more and more clarity.

House GrimGloom stands by your side, Bradley, we will fight alongside you!

A new voice came rolling in like the sound of a million waves crashing upon each other along an endless sea. *I, Jentenebro, Ruler of GrimGloom, stand at your side, young Herald.*

The impulse to act now was as clear as it could have ever been.

'Let's go,' he signalled his two companions, who had at that moment become his brothers in arms.

Lurizak unleashed his charged glyph. His body expanded and all the letters and glyphs on his armour lit up simultaneously, the coppery energy intensifying to the point where it resembled molten lava flowing through his very veins, washing all over his skin. He rushed the guards with a mighty bestial roar, propelling them with such powerful sound waves that they were flung off their feet. He rushed in after them.

Bradley pulled Danterrion off his back and the howling screech of the sword cut through the air. 'Time for some exercise, my boy,' the sword raged. Bradley laughed to hide his nervousness. His own power flared, darkness intermingled with angry reds, black lightning dancing all over his body. The adapted virus within him multiplied at enormous speed, and with each breath, it shot out of him, taking to the air. The darkness around them formed a vortex and poured itself all around Bradley, isolating him and shielding him.

Move under the guise of the dark, become unseen, Jentenebro spoke into his mind.

Bradley lunged forward in Mira's direction. More and more of her partial-humans rushed to her side, waves of them stood in between her and everyone else. Bradley crashed into the first few and the impact sent them cascading off their feet. They were fast, back on him within an instant. His free hand formed into a massive red crystal covering his whole arm, sharp beyond comprehension, as his fist hurled itself forward, piercing their midsection. The less human ones did not even flinch. He kicked them off his blade. Another tactic was needed for those. Their injuries did not stop them. He swooped in from their side, unleashing Danterrion and sliced their heads off, then plunged the sword into their bodies, splitting them in half. The sword screamed at him as the electric essence along whatever was left of their souls seeped into it. The darkness echoed into his thoughts: *the Ancient Dark!*

He understood, pulled the black lightning from within, and drawing on the darkness around him, he fused the two forces into one. Bradley let loose their culminated effect, rushing through the bodies, trying to pull themselves together and get back up. The sparks flew in all directions like a power station releasing all its current in one blow. The non-humans exploded into hundreds of fragments. Much to his horror, he saw the others extend these connections and start absorbing those fragments into themselves. The sight of it made him physically sick.

Chains flew past him, whizzing through the air, almost piercing right through him had they been a fraction of an inch off course. 'What the blooming heck are you doing?' he snapped at Fred. But Fred did not hear him. His entire body had a slight reddish tinge pulsing over it. Bradley understood. Lurizak's berserker mode was an armour-wide ability and part of that was now woven into Fred's skin!

Go! Stop thinking! Lurizak yelled into his mind as he raged past him, taking two rows of the non-humans with him. Waves of Nebraxil energy flashed towards them, too many to dodge. He braced for impact. None happened. Fred's ropy-chains had wrapped themselves in front of those waves and diverted them. Bradley took this opportunity — they would need time to recharge after using that much power. He lunged forward, straight towards Mira. His legs flexed, and with the new strength he had built into his body, he propelled himself upwards.

The darkness about him changed, it concentrated and somehow grabbed hold of his back, pulling him further upwards. Elma and Heather looked in amazement. They failed to see the full picture of what was happening. Darkness contrasting the rest of the sky poured into Bradley from both sides into his back and sparks of Ancient Dark pulsed outwards. The end result was a sight to behold. To any onlooker, he would be seen as having extended two giant wings, which spanned the entire length of the horizon made of dark matter with feathers of golden Ancient Dark lightning, sparkling outwards.

Elma watched the sparks and Heather filled her in with those parts she could not see.

Danterrion came crushing down onto Mira from above. It howled a million cries of fury, anger, loss, pain and suffering, wave upon wave of Ancient Dark flushed through it, into her. Booms of pure darkness pulsed aggressively along Danterrion, causing it to howl in even greater fury. Red power danced along its surface, giving off sparks as they shot outwards toward the tip of the blade.

Then, it happened! A massive pulse, a physical force, blasted through everything. Bradley felt the power. It echoed of radiation. House mTech had just released the solar wave as instructed by Elma. It ripped through most of the partially human, caused momentary confusion for the non-humans, and Mira howled. Her ecstasy

501

interrupted just as Danterrion sliced right through her head. Her arms went up as she tried to impede the flow of the blade. The fact that her head was split in two did not seem to bother her much — it only caused minor disorientation and confusion but no substantial harm. She pushed the blade out of herself and plummeted to the floor, swearing and yelling at Bradley.

'She's still alive,' Elma's voice boomed through his headphones. 'Auto repairing from the dead! Disgusting... you must deal with the power reserved above!' Bradley understood.

'I won't allow you humans to interfere,' boomed her eerily synthetic voice.

It had lost all its depth and nuance, flattened. Almost as if the sounds never combined, but instead, ran in parallel to each other, causing them to hear a simultaneous set of multiple incoming sounds, rather than one harmoniously combined one produced by a human being. Waves of Nebraxil energy aimed out at him, waves of black ooze shot forth. He managed to dodge the first few, but their intensity and speed increased. The next one scraped dangerously close to his left shoulder. He hesitated for an instant, *if these get any faster, I won't even be able to see them,* then there were fewer.

Bradley managed to spare a single second to look. He saw Fred's chains combining and arching in creating an intricate net-like pattern through which the beams were diverted to the neighbouring buildings.

Mira shrieked in fury. 'Why would you interrupt all this? It is evolution, immortality, you fools! Why can't you see that?'

At that moment, hundreds of high-speed bursts of that black liquid, which had become physical, shot forth from her towards them. Fred was hit; the force of the impact threw him backwards. In a panic, he looked at his body. There, he saw Lurizak's gift of armour had solidified at the point of impact, causing the black ooze to simply slide down his body back into the ground.

Bradley was not so fortunate; he got hit several times, his armour managed to do something akin to Lurizak's but had suffered visible damage from it. She saw that and frantically sent out dozens of new jet streams to the weakened locations.

Lurizak jumped in front of Bradley in the nick of time, allowing himself to be hit. *'Go, NOW! Cut her off or we will lose this battle! GO, I'll hold her off,'* his thoughts boomed out.

Bradley nodded. His new wings flexed and propelled him upwards.

Mira's onslaught intensified, she very quickly determined that the virally loaded jets were ineffective against this lava-metal clad giant standing in her way. Her hand reached upwards — a stream of translucent darkness emerged from the clouds above and beamed down into her. It quickly made its way to her core and burst out in black laser beams, heading straight for Lurizak. The first one managed to hit him, so did another. Each one pierced through his armour, emerging at the other end.

Lurizak was surprised! *This can pierce Bound armour?!*

Elma watched the onslaught from afar, 'Oh, nooo,' she murmured to Heather.

'What?'

'Mira is using some sort of force, which is piercing through his armour as if it was a needle going through layers of skin! We're in trouble. Big trouble!' Her eyes burst into hyperactivity, whatever Mira was using had become a physical force. 'Hurry, Bradley, hurry,' she whispered out.

Bradley picked up on the crisis below, the connection he had with Lurizak allowed the physical sensations to flow back to him in moments like these. He felt them as something in the background — there but not. Instinct kicked in. He looked down and saw the multitude of beams hurling at Lurizak. He would not survive for long. Bradley looked at his crystal-covered arm, focused and willed it forward. With one large swoop of the entire arm, he detached the huge crystal and flung it downwards.

'Crouch!'

This act inadvertently propelled him upwards. The crystal shot down, its sharp end burrowed it into the ground right in front of Lurizak, who, at that instant, had lowered himself due to Bradley's command rushing through his body. As the beams hit the crystal, they were absorbed by it, and Lurizak, shielded, escaped their deadly embrace.

During his ascent, Bradley heard Jentenebro one last time, *House GrimGloom stands with you, young Herald, all shall forever honour your sacrifice.*

At that moment, Nihi appeared, tearing through the darkened sky itself.

'You cannot do this,' it objected. Bradley ignored it, 'you belong to us.'

Bradley's anger flared he waved his hand and sent the rip in space hurling away. He understood. Finally, he understood — that thing was never an ally. It was trying to use him as that other thing had used Mira. It wanted his body, his mind and all he was to anchor itself in reality, just as the Nebraxil and the shadow had done with Mira. 'No! Never,' he yelled. He flung himself upwards even faster. It would not take long until that thing re-emerged out to hinder him again.

All the non-humans and partially humans were down for the count. Mira was running low on power. Her assaults slowed down to almost a halt as she desperately tried to break through and heal her otherwise critical injury. So was Lurizak, his time had almost run out, all that he was consumed. Only a little of him was still left, not enough to keep on fighting.

Fred noticed and rushed to his side. He stood, facing away, 'I'll protect you, hold on!'

His power was still running strong. He thanked his lucky star for all the training he had undertaken. Had it not been for that, he would never have made it this far.

'No, my time is almost up, listen to me, junior.'

Fred turned to look at Lurizak, knelt down beside him while keeping an eye over his own back. 'Take this... it is a gift I leave to you. This chain, given from my mentor to charge upon his death.' Fred looked at the golden-coppery-black chain. 'Take it, junior.'

Fred shook his head, 'I can't, I'm not letting you die! I'll fight for both of us.'

Lurizak paused, his strength was almost spent. 'I will die anyway, please, I beg you, take it, it holds all the heritage of me, all my experiences in battle, all my knowledge, all my abilities,' he pleaded. It was one of the unspoken traditions of the Bound, a most secret one at that, given from Wielder to Wielder and Bound to Bound.

'That's... I can't...,' Fred didn't know what to do, it seemed too much.

'Please, junior, it is all that is left of me,' he lost consciousness.

Fred howled at the loss — grief overwhelming him. He took the chain, 'I will look after it for you! I swear.' As soon as he touched it, it wove itself around his chest and he felt Lurizak's presence there; it was heavy to bear. Fred was determined to bear it, no matter what! His anger caused him to lose sense of his own self and he flung himself at whatever was still moving and in sight, openly mourning in fury for them all. This was so unfair.

Elma watched and pain ran through her as well. She knew what Fred was going through. Then she saw that Mira was reforming, her head was trying to stick itself together by absorbing whatever her new body could get hold of from the corpses around her.

'Damn them!' she swore. She went to her laptop, quickly pulling out the radio waves map. 'How the heck is she doing this?!' she concentrated. 'There! What's that?'

'What is going on?' asked Heather.

'Look here, something is sending a lot of data to Mira's body!' Heather looked, she saw the thick line of incoming data. It stood out from amongst all the others. 'Where is it coming from?'

Elma looked carefully. It was not far away. Actually, it was just from in between the opposite two trees hiding in the shadows.

'There!' she pointed.

Heather squinted, trying to see something, and in surprise, she whispered, 'that's Martin! What the... is he doing here?'

Elma looked at the laptop, 'no doubt about it, he's sending truck tons of data to her. Who is he?'

'He's a Dr from the hospital who I liked.'

'Oh?' Elma lost no time. She immediately hacked into the hospital records and pulled out his files. 'By the Houses! He's her brother!' She kept scrolling, 'and a damn talented medic at that, specialised in four different fields.' It dawned on her! 'He's telling her how to repair herself. We need to stop him!'

'How? Can't you just cut the link out?'

'I am assuming that since the EMP pulse mTech sent using the solar storm did not work on him, she must have made him impervious to interference. No matter how hard I'm trying to, I don't seem to be able to even tap into the radio waves they are using to transmit the data! This is not human technology, it is something else entirely.'

'What should we do?' An idea came to Heather, 'how human is he?' she asked.

'Let me see.' After a few seconds of umms and aahs, 'actually more than half, my estimate is about 70% or so. It seems she didn't allow him to transition completely to non-human either. She only took what she needed and secured that part of him. That is probably why the pulse did not take him out.'

'Excellent,' Heather had an idea.

'What are you planning?' asked Elma.

'Leave it to me, this is one of those things where my talents are needed.'

She closed her eyes and her own crystals flared up. She cautiously took her power back, no trouble whatsoever. Her glistening green power washed over her hands. She pulled Martin's thread to herself. Her anger at what had been done to him exploded forth, her power amplified, and with tears running down her face, she snapped the thread. *I'm so sorry, Martin, please forgive me.* Everything died down and she fell to the ground, sobbing. 'I really liked him.'

Elma embraced her in a mighty hug as Heather kept on crying.

'I really liked him, why do things have to turn out this way? Why!'

Martin fell to the ground, and slowly, his body shifted to grey, then it started… every living particle in his body dispersed outwards into the expanse of existence, leaving behind chips, wires and a whole lot of unknown devices in his stead. A black ooze slithered away from him back towards Mira.

Bradley had made it. He was suspended in the air right in the central portion of this massive cloud of energy. His body shivered, the entire atmosphere was threatening, heavy and suffocating. The clear sensation that he should not be here was unmistakable. Negativity had taken on a form, and this was its form. It assaulted his senses, blurred his perceptions, and threatened to engulf him.

What am I supposed to do now? he wondered. Bradley heard that annoying echo lashing out at him.

'You must not do this!' It seems that Nihi had finally caught up with him.

He had to act fast, very fast, no more time for hesitation. Under no circumstance could he allow it to intervene. Then it struck him. He laughed, his laughter rolled throughout the darkened skies.

Elma and Heather looked up, 'has he gone mad?' asked Elma.

'No idea,' replied Heather.

Bradley gripped Danterrion in both hands. 'Be a good boy now, and I'll let you roam about for a little longer next time,' the sword raged at him. He pointed it directly at Nihi, who seemed to ignore it. After all, nothing could harm him.

House GrimGloom, if you are still there, I need your help. I do not know how to do this... he was hoping that Jentenebro was still there somewhere. No response. Another idea occurred to him... he reached out to Mishrak.

Mishrak.

Bradley! You're alive!

Not for long, it seems, you are master of mischief; I need some of your trickery now.

Tell me.

How do I pull this huge cloud's dark stuff into my sword?

I dunno. Bradley's heart sank. That was his only hope. *But I can show you how to pull it into your body.* Images flashed in his mind. It was essentially simple.

Thank you, Mishrak. Take care of yourself!

What are you telling me that for? That's your job now!

I guess it was, Bradley smiled. Even though he did not know Mishrak that well, he was quite a bit of fun to have around.

Bradley concentrated. He pushed his senses out and pulled. The energy rushed through him from the sky like acid and he screamed at the agonising pain, which flared within every fibre of his being. There is no way he would be able to endure this for more than an instant. Then he heard it...

House GrimGloom, grant him power, for this once, for this instant in time, in that space, which he now occupies. I call upon the essence of the House. I, Ruler of GrimGloom, bestow our House's blessing upon Bradley.

507

A multitude of glyphs rushed through the darkness and slammed into him, blow after blow of script — so obscure that he could not even trace it within his mind — crashed into him. The wings he had expanded outwards, his strength pulled in through them. The rush of dark energy pulsed through his sword, sending it into a frenzy, causing it to vibrate violently in his hands. All the letters and glyphs on his own armour flared to life, strange ones he had never been able to activate before. He was becoming power and his very sense of himself was fading fast.

Just as he was about to blank out, he saw the soft blue shape form in front of his eyes. Tears welled within as Kuroi stood there, reaching out to him. Her soft, pale incorporeal hand took hold of his face.

'Beloved, it is time,' she said.

He nodded, and as she kissed him, her blue power flooded through him, easing his pain and rekindling his mental clarity. He pulled more and more, his armour trying to absorb the sheer amount of negative energy started to fracture. Danterrion howled as it gathered into a mighty thick beam. Bradley hurled the blade over his head straight toward Nihi, *'henema esiktu ka,'* roared his voice. The mass of energy swirled clockwise like a vortex spinning around the blade. It shot forth at immense speed and lodged itself in the centre of the Nothing that was Nihi. Energy poured into it.

All sound stopped and every part of every sound was sucked out of existence. Bradley focused as hard as he could — exhaustion was threatening to take him. Kuroi stood behind him, her soft blue hand rested on his left shoulder. She seemed to be the embodiment of serenity itself.

'It is time,' she repeated gently in his ear, a murmur no other could hear.

He stretched himself out as far as he could and pulled everything in. The sky itself seemed to be yanked down into a single point, a hole into which all the negativity and darkness collapsed. Bradley's armour was totally overwhelmed. It changed, its structures shifted, it grew for a moment, additional structures of pure matter and power formed, combined, solidified. It activated a second time, massive crystals floated in a sun-like structure around him, pulling more and more of the sky in. His body overloaded. Out of his midsection, beams of vibrating dark exploded. They headed right for the Danterrion and shot through into Nihi. More and more, until there was nothing left.

Nihi sent a growl out and collapsed in on itself. The massive sword was sucked into it and vanished along with it. Bradley's armour disintegrated, he gave out one last breath and vanished. The sky was clear, the energy was gone, and so was Bradley.

Mira shrieked, and unable to complete her healing, she stood up, head still half split, trying to walk away, stumbling on her own feet, using her large arterial devices to prop herself and move forward.

Fred's gaze locked in on her. 'No, you damn well don't! You are not getting away after all this.'

His anger was plain, raw, brutal grief rushed through him. He wanted her to suffer — he wanted her to pay. He wanted her to die a million times over. His chains cut through the air, piercing her easily. It seemed her defences had been weakened considerably.

Mira was not powerless, quite the opposite and wave upon wave of Nebraxil power struck at him. He diverted each and every one of them, pure fury was powering him now. His chains hurled forward to try and restrain her, a few pierced her hands and wrapping themselves around her wrists, dragging her backwards as they kept on flying forward, anchoring themselves to the opposite wall and her along with them.

'You've done enough, young one, why don't you let me finish this off?'

A strong hand grabbed hold of his shoulder. It reminded him of Bradley, and hope against hope he turned, expecting to see Bradley there. It wasn't him. A stranger, as tall as he, stepped forward. Dressed in black leather boots, black leather trousers, his bare chest decorated in black glyphs and a silvery black leather waistcoat. The long coat he was wearing was also richly etched in all sorts of letters and glyphs. But what was most striking was his hat! The guy was wearing a cowboy hat! On its edges, a moving circle of the same type of silvery-black glyphs. He took his hat off in greeting and smiled.

'Howdy! My friend,'

Fred looked at him, perplexed, 'How-dy?'

509

'Goddard Gloom, at your service. I'm late, sorry was fixin' the guns!' He half bowed, 'on behalf of House GrimGloom.'

Fred's chains were being pulled apart. He quickly turned back and sent another wave of them into Mira. He looked at her in desperation. Does that thing ever die?

'Go to your friends over there, the girlies are in dare need of help — I'll clean up this mess,' instructed Goddard.

Fred looked at him, uncertainly.

'I have the means of killin' da thing,' he pointed at Mira.

A faint burst of will Bradley had used to force Fred to go to safety activated. Fred conceded, he obviously could not kill Mira. Whoever this stranger was, he seemed to know more about that than he himself did.

'Ok, just don't let her get away. She's killed too many of my friends and I want her to die, painfully!' He snapped his chains, leaving only those binding her in place.

'Don't ye worry, my friend, she will be... goin' nowhere.'

Fred nodded. He looked down, wanting to get Lurizak's body away, then panicked. He looked for it, but it was not there!

Goddard saw his confusion. 'Ah de Bound, you won't find a body, they dissolve away when that glyph is used. De very atoms, which make them up and their armours are burnt for power in the final cry. I'm sorry...'

Fred placed his hand on Lurizak's chains firmly bound around his chest. He felt the warrior's presence, his harsh yet warm reassuring presence. Fred nodded to Goddard and rushed over to Heather and Elma.

'Time for clean-up!'

Goddard pulled two guns with large elongated barrels from his gun-belt. One was pure reflective black, the other oddly enough white. He jumped back to get some range. He closed his eyes for but a moment and activated the glyphs on the dark gun.

'Connectin' to House GrimGloom, activatin' the forbidden glyph.'

His black gun's barrel opened up and divided into three separate components. He flipped a switch.

'Dark soul cartridge activation.'

The divided barrels started spinning counter-clockwise and black lightning danced from one to the other. The resulting wave of power intensified. He whispered a few words, focusing on each syllable very carefully, connecting each letter in the word to whatever it was entangled with in quantum space. The barrels re-joined, causing the entire extended gun to glow in pure blackness. He did the same with his white gun.

'Connectin' to House Celestium, activatin' secret glyph.'

The white gun's barrel split into six, each rotating clockwise, pulsing white lightning from within the central point of rotation.

'Activatin' Progenitor soul.'

The spin increased in speed until the gun seemed to have gained weight beyond what he could bear.

'Done! Time for this miserable mess of an existence to be wiped clean,' he tranced the final glyph.

'Get out of here,' Elma yelled at both Heather and Fred, who had joined them. 'RUN!' They all sprinted as fast as they could.

'FUSION!' yelled Goddard.

As he unleashed the glyph blazing forth, he pointed his guns forward in Mira's direction. Massive beams of radiation sprang forth in her direction and as they hit, small hyper-concentrated spheres of black and white shot down the beams at lightning speed. He changed their angle and caused the two to collide. The white and black spheres of massive weight and density were hurled into each other — the lightning pushed them and the glyph etched on each sphere hurled them into each other. The black one collapsed in on itself, forming a small black hole, and the white one partially collapsed, forming a small neutron star. The cores of those were flung into each other. The explosion obliterated everything.

Goddard withdrew in a shimmer of darkness, coursing away faster than light could. The entire communal area was gone, the university was gone, most of the laboratories were gone, and a huge portion of the hospital had all been instantly evaporated.

32

- REALIGNMENT -

Elma, Heather and Fred had been fortunate. Elma was able to calculate the radius of the blast. With the time it took Goddard to unleash it, they had run to the carpark which was just around the corner and drive off far enough to escape its effects just in the nick of time.

'Are we going to all die of radiation poisoning?' asked Fred.

'No, Goddard's abilities reabsorb all the radiation into his guns to use as fuel for the next assault.'

'That's a convenient thing, damn those guns!'

'Don't get excited, Mr! He's the only one in TrueEarth who is allowed and able to use them.'

'Damn...' was the sum of his entire reaction. Heather drove off, they needed to get to a safe place until the dust settled. Only then could they make their return.

Mira's mind kept on expanding through the waves of shadows. She had achieved her goal, she was infinite. Ecstasy rushed through her once more. Memories of who she was, what she was doing or where she was heading to faded. She was something else now, all other things were irrelevant. At long last, she had what she wanted. She was power, she was infinite, she was absolute. Mira was no more, her very essence merged with the boundless waves of shadows coursing throughout creation.

From her body, a deep, powerful shadow escaped into the trees, and from those trees it slithered through its roots deep into the Earth.

The Chamber of Ancients hummed with countless sounds clashing into each other, reverberating off each inverse-pyramid. Below House Nothingness's one, a gap opened, a huge beam of energy ascended upwards directly into the tip of the pyramidal structure. It stopped its habitual motion. Completely still they all were. The Nothingness pyramid drank the incoming power, no matter the amount, it was able to effortlessly contain it. The strange glyphs over its surface sprang to life, giving off a lightless darkness. Bathing the whole chamber in it. There, from behind one of the portals, a small particle of pure nothingness was violently pulled. If anyone had been in the chamber, they would have heard it screaming and struggling. Instead, nothing was heard by nobody. The suction of the pyramid grew so intense that it simply seeped up the particle and absorbed it into itself. The glyphs on it changed, the power it gave off changed, now a golden glow pulsed and shimmered over its surface. The glyphs as oil would move into a new position as the pyramids gradually resumed the eternal circular course.

'And so, the child of Nothingness completes his goal.' The Chamber spoke to no one. The being, otherwise known as Nihi, was now securely sealed in the power core of House Nothingness, back where it belonged. A burst of energy pulsed out of the pyramidal structure, it was whole again, from one to the other, the power cores reacted. A massive seal spanning the entire structure suddenly materialized, glowing in an eerie hue, pulsing in the most unsettling power one could ever come across. Its brilliance both off-putting and immensely seductive to any who would have stood closely. It turned, motion gave rise to kinetic energy, that kinetic energy became a force and it spun faster and faster. The very air buzzed as a result, and for the first time in the longest of ages, the large circular dome moved. The seal became a living circle, spinning with such speed that it was no longer possible to distinguish any of its details or inner patterns, all that one would see was the ring of spinning light and the pulse of sonic waves coming off that circle.

Then it stopped. The seal had vanished. The Chamber of Ancients was once more quiet and tranquil, with no sound, no one there to see any of it and no one there to hear anything from it. Solitude covered it once again.

Reports were coming in, Galvin stood intently focused on the maps displayed on his massive crystalline screen. His adviser next to him as they waited.

'Reports indicate House Bound has managed to push back most of the Nebraxil. The waves slowed down and eventually stopped completely.'

'That would suggest Bradley and the others had completed their own tasks in this sad, sorry state of affairs,' replied Galvin. He was sad, Elma had just sent him a notification that Bradley and Lurizak had disintegrated and were no more. He knew what that meant, everyone in TrueEarth knew that a Bound warrior used the final cry to not only change the course of many battles, but also to sacrifice himself in the process.

'Send several teams to FalseEarth, I want all the data even remotely related to this obliterated. No trace of any of this must remain anywhere. We cannot risk something like this happening again. It has cost us all too much as it is.'

'Ruler, we don't have the sufficient power left to open so many passageways there,'

'I don't care how you do it, get the help of the other Houses, especially those who were not on the field in FalseEarth — they might as well contribute something to all this.'

'As you wish,' he excused himself and left.

The sound of a bell echoed throughout House Bound. Over and over, it boomed along the corridors, in all the rooms and all the battlefields. The newcomers were nervous, the elder members were silent. House Bound was mourning. The very essence of the House had, for the first time in centuries, descended into the House itself and was notifying all members of its sorrow.

'Goodbye, Lurizak, old friend. I hope you forgive me. I never intended it to end like this.' Tamirok spoke softly as he walked through the corridors for one last time.

Elshevira was frantic, the calm seductive and controlled personality she was had crumbled. She was irreconcilable. Arlak was there trying to calm her down. Mishrak walked in, she lunged at him, pinning him to the floor. 'You're bound to him, tell me, is it true?' she yelled at him. 'Tell me! Tell me, Mishrak, or I'll slice your throat this instant!'

'Let the poor boy speak if you want him to tell you something,' interjected Arlak. He was the ever calm and practical one, that is what they needed right now.

'I'm... not... sure. I've never been able to properly feel his will as Lurizak could,' he admitted.

'You could mind talk!'

He nodded.

'Well?!'

'It doesn't seem to be working anymore, all I get is silence.' She pushed Mishrak away, tears freely cascading down her face. Arlak hugged her, 'there, there, it will be ok.'

'No, it won't,' she objected.

'Why don't you go and find one of those LightBearer boys and drive him into insanity as you so like doing to cheer up a bit?' She gave him a stern stare, then her expression softened 'what's the point...'

Fred had fallen asleep in the back of the car, he was completely exhausted. Never had he been so tired in his entire life. He awoke, for some reason, the car had come to a stop. He smelt fresh air, nature, the scent of an old forest. A soft wind caressed his body. He opened his eyes and tried to see where he was. He blinked. Looked around, he was not in the car anymore.

'Elma? Heather?' he called out.

Nothing. He stood up.

'Howdy there!' he recognised that voice!

'Goddard?'

'Why yes, welcome to TrueEarth, my friend!' he placed his arm around Fred's shoulder. Fred shrugged it off. 'My, my, testy today, aren't we?'

'TrueEarth?' asked Fred.

'Why yes, do you have an adventure ahead of you? Better get moving!' he repositioned his hat.

'Wait!' interrupted Fred, 'What happened? Where is everyone? Where is Mira? Did we get her?' the questions poured out of him.

'Steady on, all will be revealed. Mira... that thing is no more,'

'She is gone? She escaped?'

Goddard laughed.

'Escape? No, no, no, it no longer exists. Gone — atomic destruct! It was not human anymore, just a tool of the techs and aliens,'

'Aliens? Wait, what!'

'In time. Come, we have an appointment to get to,'

'Where are you taking me?' asked a worried Fred.

'You were supposed to be in House Bound, but the young Herald wanted otherwise. Taking you to where he wanted you,'

'Herald?'

'Yes, the one in the sky who died for you all,'

'Bradley, you mean?'

'Don't know a Bradley, just Herald. Enough talk, we're late.'

'Wait? Bradley's dead?' Goddard levelled his hat and started walking away. 'Hold on! Wait for me,' Fred rushed forward wondering where it was Bradley wanted him to go.

Meanwhile, in House Celestium, one of the junior members was running down the long star-lit corridors in panic, yelling his head off. 'The Star Gateway has been flung open! Get the Ruler... the Star Gateway has been breached!'

33

THE
- BEGINNING -

Bradley stood on the seal, motionless, frozen in time. The semi-transparent polished black obsidian floor was smooth to the touch. The huge seal, composed of interconnecting triangular shapes, etched into the hard rocklike structure of the flooring, was nothing like anything anyone had seen before. Circles within circles, polygons smashing into each other, script tattered left right and centre. Glyphs intersecting with glyphs flared up with a soft constant pulse. The mesmerising hum caused by the vibration of power it gave off was irresistible. He tried to touch the outer circle. Cautiously, his hand caressed the lines. Much to his surprise, the seal's power was soft, gentle, reminding him of the caress of a puppy against his flesh. The memory haunted him; he realised it was not his. He had never had a puppy. He had no exposed skin to make contact with, yet it was so real. It would have been easy for him to lose himself in it.

'I wouldn't do that if I were you.' A young man's voice instructed him.

Lurizak jumped into action, ready to use the little force he had left to defend himself and Bradley.

'Don't bother; you are definitely no match for anyone in your current state and even at your peak, you would not have been able to even touch me. Besides, I'm not your enemy.' The youth stepped out of the darkened corner of the seal's chamber into full view. It was not a young man: in his 30s – late 30s, by what Lurizak was able to determine – with golden hair, blue-grey eyes on the outside of the iris and a yellowy-golden tinge on the inner. His body was muscular but not large. This was no warrior, yet it seemed combat would have been easy for him.

What struck Lurizak the most was that this stranger was wearing bound-like skin-armour on the lower half of his body. It was the same type of armour as his but entirely different. This was made of a reddish-white metal, with a golden strip running from outer hips to feet on his legs. Etchings and glyphs of the most peculiar kind ran spiralled around his strong muscular legs. The letters on the golden strips glowed with power of different types, each one pulsing with its own colour and strength. Each one different from the previous and the following.

He looked closely; this was crafting beyond the level of even the Great Forge Masters of TrueEarth. The man's well-defined chest, abs, and arms were similarly decorated but they were etched in his actual skin and were encrusted with crystals. Crystals of different pulsating colours, crystals in which he could see entire universes glowing. This was something totally alien to him but so human, simultaneously. Power oozed from this man, power which Lurizak knew instinctively could crush the whole of reality if it was properly directed. Unlike Bradley's power, this man's power was controlled, harmonious, and perfectly mastered. *Just who is this?*

'Now that, my dear Lurizak, would be a most difficult question to answer.' He smiled. A hint of mischief there was quite visible.

'What do you want with us?'

'I want to safeguard my project.' He paused as he slowly walked into the seal, completely immune to its effects, and went directly towards Bradley. 'You see, I've invested far too much in all this for it to fail. Remind me to grant House GrimGloom a boon. It is only with their so-called blessing that his essence survived and allowed me to save him – whatever is left of him, anyway.'

'Stay away from him.' Lurizak was about to hurl himself towards the stranger but the moment his foot stepped onto the outermost circle of the seal, he could go no further.

'I wouldn't do that if I were you. Last thing we need is you both engaged in the seal.'

His strength was fading he could not fight the forces keeping him out. That meant Bradley was fading too. He knew what this weakening of his wielder's will meant all too well. 'Stop!' he objected.

'Don't worry; he'll not die. As I said, I have invested too much into all this. I must admit, though, I am somewhat disappointed in our Bradley here. I was expecting him to do better. Turns out he was weak – too weak.'

'Our Bradley?' Lurizak was catching onto something.

'Yes, you of all people know the Wielder is part of the Bound, yet the Bound is also part of his Wielder. Is that not one of the wisdoms of your House?'

'How do you know that!'

'Why, my dear fellow, I'm the one who not only founded the Great Houses but also taught you how to forge that armour of yours.'

'Not possible. The Houses have always been here, since the dawn of time.'

'Of course they have. No one is arguing that.' The stranger touched Bradley. The seal under him flared up. Waves upon waves of power poured out of it, obstructing Lurizak's vision. It cleared, revealing Bradley exactly where he had been a moment before, encased in transparent black crystal. Lurizak felt a blow, a crack, a tear; something shattered. Bradley's will was gone. He froze. *Who is this damn stranger wearing the vermillion armour?* His final thoughts echoed.

The stranger left the seal and came to stand, under the towering Lurizak. No matter the size differential, he was powerless, his will bound to nothing, to no one. The very impulse to action would not stir anymore. A soft gentle hand touched his left cheek. It was like a forgotten caress from his childhood. A tiny spark of will flared up, sufficient to ensure his awareness returned fully. 'I told you I have no intension of harming either of you. Listen to me very carefully.'

'We're lost. Bradley is gone...' interjected Lurizak.

'What made you think this was all about Bradley?'

'He's the one who came to change things. His power could have given us a chance to fight THEM!' Panic coursed through his voice. 'And now you've killed him.'

The stranger laughed an innocent, almost childlike laughter. 'You foolish boy. He's not dead, he's asleep. I'm going to make a few changes to him. Help him to not fail me again. Besides, I am the one who pulled you both from the very blade of death herself. Did you two not go into that final battle ready to die?' He paused and started running his fingers over the chains which were part of Lurizak's armour. 'You didn't know, did you? That Bradley's fate ended here, that Nihitus would have consumed him to create a vehicle for itself to exist in? That Tamirok knew all this?'

Lurizak was shocked. Why hadn't he been told?

'You never realised why Tamirok had chosen you to be Bradley's Bound, did you? Such a good boy you are, keeping even that which is unbound inside of you, single-mindedly focused on your duty and service to the point where you never thought to question his motivations...' He smiled and caressed the warrior's cheek once more.

Power flared up a bit more. Lurizak could breathe again, feel anew. 'No, I do as I'm told. I'm a warrior, not a philosopher or politician.'

'Yet I want you to start questioning again. I want you to start thinking for yourself. Bound you can remain, if that is what you want, but not like you were before. You need to awaken for yourself.' Lurizak looked at Bradley, hope flaring up in him. 'No, not that way.'

'You said this was not about Bradley?' asked Lurizak.

'Excellent, yes; good question. No, it was not all about Bradley. It was about you, but you never noticed, did you? I ensured Tamirok put TrueEarth's most experienced and powerful warrior in the service of a newcomer who was totally lost. Any other House Bound member would have done just fine. Your journey challenged you, and nearly losing your very self time after time, you accepted your fate and pushed on. Never complaining, always enduring. You have passed the test I set for you.' He turned to face Bradley. 'He did not.'

'What do you want from me?' asked Lurizak. 'Without Bradley, my wielder, I'm not much more use than a statue also frozen in time.'

'That is true. One of the shortfalls of your armour; the price you have to pay for it. Well, one of the prices. From you I want a decision. I am going to give you two choices. What you choose will have enormous impact not only on TrueEarth and his side' – he pointed to Bradley encased in the crystal – 'but also to all their futures up there.' He waved his hands at the sky.

Lurizak was going to ask something or object, but just as he tried to speak, the stranger placed his index finger over his lips to signal silence.

'The first choice is this. I will place you in the seal alongside Bradley. You will remain as the statue you describe, but the seal will lend you its power for the purpose of protecting it and Bradley, if any danger should ever come. You will remain so until he awakens from his transformation. When that happens, his will shall flow through you again and you will be bound to the new Bradley as you were to the old. The second choice is this: you will become my Bound. I will evolve you in ways no human being has ever had the opportunity to grow. You will gain many new abilities and definitely new possibilities. You will also develop your own thinking, instincts, desires, and actions. You will visit other worlds and other realities. You will become my avatar in this reality, as well as my companion.'

Upon presenting these two choices, he placed his hand over the keyhole on Lurizak's chest. Images flooded into his mind; he saw his glimpses of his future as they matched each of his two choices. 'This, you see, will be moments in one of the futures based on your choice.'

'But what of Bradley? Of TrueEarth?' he asked.

'They will be taken care of. Besides, there is nothing stopping you coming back and forth if you desire to. It makes no difference to me where you are when you are not on a mission.'

Lurizak hesitated; it was a lot to take in. The images he saw were both immensely exciting and horrifying. He craved a break in his cycle of existence, yet he also wanted to ensure his mission would not fail. He had made promises to Tamirok and Bradley.

'So what will it be?' asked the stranger.

'Bradley will be safe?' He needed to make sure.

'Yes, no harm will befall him during his transformation. He will be protected.'

For some unknown reason, Lurizak believed the stranger. He looked at him carefully. He knew the significance of vermillion, that one metal which no one on TrueEarth had ever been able to shape or use. It was rumoured to come from the seat of creation itself; the one point in time and space that sparked all of existence. It was the rarest and most valuable metal of all, and races in all worlds had waged wars over it. He knew of the golden power glowing from him. He had heard of it; he knew its significance. He took in a deep breath and let it out. He knew he had to choose. For the first time in his entire life, he would make a choice for himself rather than for others.

'I choose the second.' His voice quivered and shook in uncertainty. For a split second, he felt sick in the stomach, then relief washed over him. For most, this would have been a matter-of-fact decision but for Lurizak, this was one of the hardest things he had ever done. To put himself in front of duty, obligation, protecting others and ensuring the wellbeing of TrueEarth was monumental. His whole body shook from the strain.

'Very well; your choice is accepted.' The stranger's fingers danced over the chains binding his flesh. 'Do you want to hold onto these or get rid of them?' he asked.

'I'd like to keep them to remind me of my roots – if that's ok?'

'Let's keep it so, then. When you get to the point you want them gone, just tell me. You won't be needing them anymore.' The stranger seemed to grab hold of his own waist; it shimmered. To Lurizak, it looked as if he was both taking the belt out of his very armour and replicating it at the same time. As the process completed, he had one in his hand and the other was still part of his own armour. Lurizak had never seen anyone do something like that. He was surprised.

The stranger took the waist band and split it, uncoiled it, then gently wrapped his arms around Lurizak's waist. He wrapped it around his hips, sealing it shut at the front. It sank into Lurizak's coppery black armour and merged with it. The white and red glowed. It spilt up and down, eventually covering his entire metal-skinned body, replacing the old with the new. The metals sank into the keyholes, filling them, sealing the nerve-ropes in the process. It oozed its way over all the chains, changing their very substance. By the time the process finished, Lurizak was wearing a full vermillion skin. There were no golden markings or sections on his skin, which was full red, with hues dancing on a metallic white background. Without any delay, engravings and glyphs etched themselves into it, patterns he had never seen before. Patterns he could not quite make out were carved by an invisible force all over him. The vermillion spilt over his head, encasing him totally. He could easily sense it reshaping itself.

The stranger's childlike smile vanished and took on a very serious expression. The colour of his eyes shifted to a deep piercing grey. Golden power washed off his body in waves as it radiated out of him.

His left hand grabbed hold of Lurizak's right shoulder. 'The seal of the nine bindings I bestow upon you. You who has experienced all nine of them.' The scent of smouldering metal filled his nostrils. His right hand seized Lurizak's left shoulder. 'The seal of the nine freedoms I bestows upon you. You who will experience all nine of them.' Once again, smouldering metal filled the air.

The stranger's childlike smile returned as he placed his hands on Lurizak's cheekbones. 'You're done, mister; one final step.' His form shimmered, and seemed to lose its solidity. With one hand, he pointed towards the crystal within which Bradley was confined. A massive glyph in bright white and golden light was carved there. Lurizak recognised it and gasped! He knew who the stranger was! His heart started racing; his mind went wild. He had made the right choice. By the Houses, he had made the right choice!

'So now you know.' The semi-translucent stranger smiled at him as he became a beam of pure brilliant light, which sank into Lurizak's chest, then shot forth, coursing around his entire body through the ropes in his armour, and eventually washed all over him. The power in which he bathed was unbelievable; his mind reeled back at its sheer immensity. *Steady now, my dear boy, we don't want you sinking into madness,* warned the stranger from within his head. Will coursed through Lurizak; he could move again. He moved not under the command of another – he moved because he wanted to move.

A deep tremor rumbled throughout the entire planet. TrueEarth and FalseEarth shook under everyone's feet. High Priestesses in the shrine where Kuroi had been buried screamed out in pain, monks in monasteries all over the world dropped dead, martial arts masters felt fear deep within them, priests and holy men prayed in an uncontrollable frenzy, yogis retreated from daily life to meditate, the treehugger clans sat amongst their guardian trees trembling, the meta tribes stuttered in confusion, the Great Houses pulsed with power which was not their own, striking panic into all their members, and the stars shone brighter than ever before.

Every man, woman and child quivered with unease. The time had finally come. It had begun.